Nothing Left To Lose

By Kirsty Moseley

ISBN -10: 1492787701
ISBN-13: 978-1492787709

Acknowledgements

Special thanks go to Mollie Wilson for making the gorgeous cover that fits the story so well.

Another thanks must go to Emily Ruston and Dani Ellenby, for their incredible job editing and, of course, pointing out things that I hadn't even considered! x

To my beta readers: You girls (and let's not forget Darrell!) amaze me. Thanks so much for your input, speedy response and encouragement. You are all my superstars.

This book is for Lee – my real life Ashton (just without the SWAT uniform). Love you, forever and always. xx

Chapter One

Sweet sixteen is a day that every girl should remember as special in their lives. In some cultures, it's even considered to be the start of passage into womanhood. My sixteenth was anything but sweet; it was more like the passage into hell on earth. March 12 was the day my dreams died and my life was sent into a downward spiral of pain, grief and terror. My sixteenth birthday left an irrevocable scar on me, and was the beginning of events that I would see repeatedly in my nightmares.

Right now I was standing in the cold of the night, queuing for admittance outside club Ozone – unknowingly waiting for my traumatic ordeal to begin. The balls of my feet were already aching, a product of the ridiculously high heels that I wore. The cool wind whipped around me, making the little black dress that I was wearing billow around my thighs. My perfect boyfriend, Jack Roberts, was rubbing my arms, trying to warm me up. We'd been standing in line for the club for almost an hour, and finally were quite near the front.

"Jack, I'm not sure this is gonna work. Maybe we should just go watch a movie or something?" I whispered, eyeing the doorman, who was looking at the line suspiciously.

"Anna, it'll work. You asked me to take you to a club for your birthday, so I'm doing exactly that," he replied, cupping his chilly hands around my face.

I looked at him and my heart stuttered. I loved this boy with everything I had in me. He was kind, loving, caring, generous, thoughtful, and not to mention handsome. With his short blond hair and sparkling blue eyes, he was every girl's dream. Literally. Every girl I knew was in love with my boyfriend, but he had only ever had eyes for me. We'd met when we were five years old. He'd asked me to be his girlfriend the first time I saw him, and we'd been together ever since. He was my everything, and we would be together forever. We already had everything planned – finish school, then college, then Jack would become a doctor like he'd always wanted to be, and I would become an artist. Eventually, we would get married and have kids. Perfect.

Three months ago, Jack had asked me what I wanted to do to celebrate my birthday; he said that I could choose anything in the world and we would do it. So I decided to go out to a club, and then I wanted to stay at a hotel, where we would have sex for the first time. After three months of planning and scheming, we had finally convinced our parents to let us stay out. Jack had gotten us both a fake ID card, and I was so excited that I could barely contain myself.

Now that we were here though, in the cold, surrounded by half-drunken people, all I wanted to do was go back to the hotel and have him run his hands all over my body to warm me up, and then we would finally be together physically.

I smiled up at him, my stomach clenching in anticipation. He smiled back and bent his head to kiss me. I melted against him. When Jack kissed me, I felt amazing, like my heart was flying, and like I was the luckiest girl in the world. His hands slipped down to my ass, squeezing gently, causing a small smile to tug at the corners of my mouth.

When he broke the kiss, he pulled back, grinning at me. His eyes sparkled in the dim street lights. "I love you, Anna."

My heart throbbed again as my whole body broke out in goosebumps. I loved the sound of those three words coming out of his mouth; I still wasn't used to hearing them even after all these years.

"I love you too," I replied, and I did. I loved him more than anything. He kissed me again, pulling my body closer to his.

A gentle tap on my shoulder made me jump and break the kiss.

"Hi," a male voice said from behind me.

I turned around to see a man who was probably in his mid-twenties. He wasn't in the line of people waiting to enter the club; he stood the other side of the ropes. He was quite good-looking, with nicely styled, dark brown hair and brown eyes. A sleek, black, button down shirt covered his broad shoulders, and he'd paired it with black pants and extremely expensive-looking shoes. He was looking me over slowly.

"Er, hi," I replied, smiling sweetly, trying to be friendly in case he worked here. He wasn't on his own; two other guys stood behind him.

"I'm Carter," the brown haired guy said, holding out his hand for me to shake.

"Anna." I put my hand in his, shaking it politely. He didn't let go, instead he pulled me towards him, away from Jack.

"I can get you in if you want, saves you waiting in the cold," he offered, smiling. My insides bubbled with excitement at the thought of getting into the club. I looked back at Jack, who was frowning angrily and glaring at my hand that the guy still held.

"Yeah? That'd be great! It's freezing out here," I chirped happily, trying not to jump up and down on the spot from excitement.

Carter laughed. "Come on then, Anna." He nodded to one of the people that he was with, and they immediately unclipped the rope so I could step out of the line.

I reached back and grabbed Jack's hand, grinning ecstatically.

"Er, Princess, your boy's not invited," Carter said, sneering at Jack as if he was something he'd just stepped in.

Confusion settled over me. "What? I thought you said you could get us in."

He finally let go of my hand and stepped back. "I said I could get *you* in. We don't need any spectators." He jerked his chin towards Jack as his eyebrows furrowed in annoyance.

I frowned angrily. *What a jerk!* He'd interrupted me and Jack making out, but thought I'd go into the club with him and leave Jack outside? "Right, well no thanks, I'm with my boyfriend. I thought you meant both of us. Sorry." I took the rope back out of the other guy's hand and clipped it back to the ring, then wrapped my arms around the love of my life, glaring at Carter.

Carter shrugged. "Suit yourself. Maybe you'll save me a dance." He smirked at me before he turned and walked straight into the club.

"What a jackass!" I growled, watching his disappearing back. Jack laughed, and all my anger melted away instantly at the sound. "What's so funny?" I asked, smiling at him.

"You just can't help yourself, can you? You make guys fall for you without even trying." He grinned as he wrapped his arms around me, pulling me closer to his body.

"I know, it must be my irresistible charm," I joked, fluttering my eyelashes.

"Either that or your incredible legs," he teased, hesitantly rubbing his hands over my thighs. I slapped his chest playfully and pulled him down to kiss me again.

After about another half an hour, we were finally ushered through into the club with no problems. The doorman barely even glanced at our IDs. Once we were through the door, I jumped up and down, squealing excitedly. "This is awesome!" I cried, grabbing his hand and immediately pulling him to the dance floor. The music was so loud you could almost feel the vibrations through the floor.

"Let's get a drink," he shouted in my ear after a couple of songs. I nodded and he took my hand, leading me towards the bar. We had a quick drink and then went straight back to dancing, losing ourselves in the rhythm of the loud music. He had one hand on my backside the whole time,

3

making me feel hot and bothered. When he bent his head and kissed me, I tangled my hands in his hair, kissing him back with everything I had. We'd only been inside for an hour, but I was ready to leave. The club was fantastic but what I really wanted was what we planned for after – my night with him.

"Jack, want to go?" I asked, running my hands down his chest. He grinned at me and nodded eagerly. He had been ready to take our relationship to the next level for the last six months but we'd wanted to wait until we were both sixteen.

He took my hand and we made our way out of the club, weaving through the crowd of drunken people that were milling around enjoying their night. As we got near the stairs that led down to the front lobby, the guy that I spoke to in the line outside, Carter, stepped out and held his hand in front of us to stop.

"Hi, Princess. How about that dance?" he asked, looking me over slowly.

"No thanks, we're leaving," I declined confidently.

"Oh, I don't think so." He smiled and took my hand, yanking me forwards, away from Jack. My mouth popped open in shock.

"Get your fucking hands off her!" Jack growled menacingly, stepping forward. I looked back at him with wide eyes, wondering if there was going to be some kind of fight. Before I could even comprehend what had happened, someone grabbed him from behind, holding his arms behind his back securely.

I struggled to get out of Carter's hold, ripping my hand from his. "Get the hell off me! Let him go! I don't want to dance with you; I'm leaving with my boyfriend!" I cried angrily.

Carter smiled wickedly, not seeming bothered by this confrontation in the slightest. "One dance is all I ask, and then you can go," he offered, waving his hand dismissively. Jack made a furious snorting sound so the guy that was holding him shoved him roughly against the wall, holding him there. I screamed and looked around wildly for some help.

"For fuck's sake! You touch her and I'll kill you!" Jack growled.

"No one speaks to me like that!" Carter shouted angrily.

He stepped forward and punched Jack in the face, splitting his lip. Almost instantly, blood poured down his face. Carter pulled his arm back, obviously about to deliver a second blow. He looked murderously angry; his whole face was contorted in rage. Panic rushed through my system at the thought of this guy hurting Jack. I couldn't let that happen. I wouldn't.

"No! Okay, okay, I'll dance! One dance, just please don't hurt him, please," I begged, with tears rolling down my cheeks.

"No, Anna!" Jack shouted, spitting blood onto the floor. I looked at him and felt my chin quiver at the sight of his bleeding face. My heart was beating so fast that I thought I would pass out.

"It's alright. One dance, I don't mind," I lied, forcing a small smile.

4

Carter laughed and grabbed my hand, pulling me towards the dance floor. He pulled me into his chest, wrapping his arms around me tightly, his face inches from mine. I felt sick; my skin was crawling. I turned my face away, refusing to look at him as he ground his crotch into my hip. Bile rose in my throat, so I quickly swallowed it down. One of his hands slipped down to my ass, the other onto my thigh. I closed my eyes and willed the song to be over; my body was shaking in anger and fear. I just prayed they weren't hurting Jack while I wasn't there.

Finally, after what seemed like forever, the song finished. I put my hands on his chest and pushed as hard as I could, but he didn't let go, he just held me tighter, laughing.

"You know, you're so beautiful, Princess," he breathed in my ear.

"Please, you said one dance, please," I begged, trying to squirm out of his hold.

"I've changed my mind. One's not enough," he purred, kissing my neck.

I gasped and pushed him again, panic washing over me as I squirmed, trying to get some distance between us. This time he dug his fingers into my sides roughly. Pain shot through me, making me cry out, but no one could hear because the music was still thumping around us.

"Please! Why are you doing this?" I cried, tears falling down my face.

He ran his tongue up my face, licking my tears away. "Mmm," he breathed; it was almost a moan of appreciation. He slipped his hand under my dress and rubbed his fingers against my panties.

Immediately I clamped my legs together to try and stop his touch. "No! Please let me go. Jack!" I screamed, thrashing, trying desperately to get out of his hold. No one even batted an eyelid at us.

"Fine, let's go find your precious Jack," he sneered, pushing me roughly towards the stairs. I stumbled up the stairs as fast as my legs would carry me. My heart was in my throat the whole time. When I got to the top, my eyes settled on Jack; he was still being held against the wall by the same blond guy. As soon as he saw me, he started to struggle against the restraining hands.

"Let him go, please," I begged, trying to get to him. I saw Carter nod his head and instantly the other guy let go. As soon as he was free, Jack grabbed me and pushed me behind him protectively.

"Whoa, easy there boy, no harm done," Carter mused, sneering distastefully. "Although your girlfriend there is sexy as hell." He looked me over slowly, licking his lips.

I cringed into Jack's back, my skin crawling because of the way he was looking at me. Suddenly Jack launched himself at him, his fist connecting with Carter's stomach. Carter doubled over with a groan and the two men he was with grabbed Jack again as he fought and struggled against their hands. I looked around for help, but no one was coming. Why was no one helping us? People weren't paying even the slightest bit of attention to us as they drank, laughed and danced around us, not even looking in our direction as the music thumped and vibrated off the walls. My hands were shaking; my heart was beating way too fast. I already knew they were going to hurt him. All I could think was that he'd said we could leave, Carter had said we could go, so why did Jack have to do that?

"Please, please!" I screamed as one man held him and the other punched him over and over in the stomach. I grabbed at the one hitting him, trying to pull him away but Carter's arms wrapped around me, lifting me off my feet and pulling me back a couple of paces.

"Door," Carter barked angrily.

The blond guy nodded, and suddenly they were dragging Jack away. I jerked out of Carter's grasp and ran after them, still crying and screaming hysterically. They dragged him through a fire door. As I reached to try and help him again, Carter grabbed hold of my arm roughly and slammed the door behind him so we were outside on some sort of fire escape. He threw me backwards, making me lose my footing and stumble into the wall. The side of my head connected with the rough bricks; the pain and shock of it made my vision cloudy. I could feel the slight trickle of blood down the side of my face. I squeezed my eyes closed, fighting against the pain that was making my legs weak.

I could hear Jack grunting and groaning, so I forced my eyes open against the blackness that was trying to engulf me. He was on the floor and they were taking turns kicking him; his face was covered in blood, his eyes desperate and scared.

I couldn't breathe. This was like something out of a nightmare, a nightmare that I couldn't escape from.

I needed to stop this – now. "What do you want? I've got money, I can get you money! Please?" I screamed. One of the guys pulled out a metal-looking thing like the police have; he snapped it out and started beating my already broken boyfriend with it. I heard the bones crack in his arm. "PLEASE STOP! I'll do anything. PLEASE?" I screamed, gasping for breath. I crawled over to Jack and wrapped my arms around his broken body.

"Run," he croaked, his voice barely above a whisper. He squeezed his eyes shut, his jaw clenching tightly as he groaned.

"Jack, please. You're okay, it's okay. I love you. Please," I begged, sobbing against his bleeding face.

He winced and put his arm around me, digging his fingers into my back. "Run, Anna. Get away, please!"

Carter's hands clamped around my upper arms, pulling me to my feet and away from Jack. The other two guys both bent and gripped Jack's arms, pulling him up too. He screamed as they touched him. The sound of his pain made my legs feel weak. Carter wrapped his arms around me from behind and kissed my neck while Jack watched with a horrified expression on his face as he gasped for breath. Carter's hand snaked up my side

6

coming to rest on my breast, squeezing roughly. Before I knew it was going to happen, I bent over and was violently sick.

He laughed wickedly and pulled me back to him roughly, his chest pressing against my back. "I'm going to enjoy fucking your girlfriend and hearing her scream for you," he said to Jack. Jack's head snapped up, his eyes filled with hate and rage as he started struggling again even though he was probably in indescribable amounts of pain. The three guys laughed at him as he continued his futile struggle, shouting a string of expletives. "You have anything you want to say to your boyfriend?" Carter whispered in my ear.

Anything I want to say… *Please let this be over, please just leave us so I can get some help.* "I love you," I croaked through my sobs.

"I love you too," Jack whispered.

Carter nodded at his guys, and they lifted Jack off of his feet as if he weighed nothing at all. I tried to jerk forward but Carter had me pinned in place against him. I didn't even get time to think about what was about to happen next, it all happened so fast that I could barely even comprehend it. The two guys carried Jack back a couple of feet and then threw him off the fire escape.

My heart stopped. *Did they just throw him off the… No. No way.* This had to be a dream; the worst dream I'd ever had in my life. I needed to wake up, I couldn't take this. My ears registered his scream as it sounded for a couple of seconds during his fall. I heard a muffled thump and then all that was left was the echo of the music coming from the club behind me.

I couldn't breathe. My heart was breaking into a million pieces as I replayed the last couple of seconds in my head. In my mind's eye, I saw Jack's face as the two guys' hands left his body and he started falling. I'd never seen anyone look more terrified or helpless.

I threw off Carter's hold and ran towards the railing, praying that he was somehow okay, praying that this was some kind of joke or dream and that I wasn't going to see the love of my life when I looked down. I wasn't that lucky though. As I leant over the railing and squinted through my tears, I saw the worst image I had ever seen in my life. Jack was sprawled out on the floor with a pool of blood seeping out underneath him. His arms and legs were at impossible angles; he wasn't moving.

The pain in my heart doubled as my whole body seemed to go cold. We were three flights up; he wouldn't have survived that after the beating he'd just sustained. The way he was lying there, motionless, I could tell there was no hope. He was gone.

I turned away quickly and was sick again. I was hyperventilating, struggling to draw breath as the image refused to leave my mind. My legs wouldn't support me anymore, so I slumped into the pool of my own vomit. Silent tears fell down my face as my heart shattered into a million pieces.

The love of my life was dead. All our plans that we'd made would never happen. He'd died because of me. I'd wanted to come to this stupid club, and now he was dead. I hadn't even had the chance to make love to him.

Black spots started to appear in my vision as I heard the rush of my blood pounding through my ears. I was going to pass out; I could feel the nothingness building inside me as my fingers and face started to tingle.

Jack was dead. He'd left me. I didn't want to live – not without him. I couldn't. The grief was crushing me.

I grabbed the railing and used the last of my strength to pull myself up onto my feet. I didn't look down; I couldn't see him like that again. I kept my eyes straight ahead as I swung my leg over the railing. *Please let this kill me,* I begged silently. Closing my eyes, I prepared to jump. My ears were ringing. I was numb. I let go of the railing and smiled because I wouldn't have to feel this heartache any longer.

Just as the air stirred around me and I stepped into the nothingness, I felt something grab my waist.

"Whoa there, Princess. Now that's just a waste." I heard just before I passed out.

Chapter Two

~ Ashton Taylor ~

Sweat was running down my back as I stood there, straight as a poker, eyes front, hands down by my sides like I'd been taught. The blistering midday sun was beating down on me while I was decked out in full S.W.A.T uniform, including black, army style pants that have over a dozen pockets, black T-shirt, black tactical vest and jacket. They liked us to look good for these things.

"How long are they gonna make us stand here? I'm fucking dying!" Nate, my partner, hissed at me through his teeth.

"Not long now; Weston's started to get hungry. See how he's shifting in his seat? He'll wrap this up soon and head straight for the buffet," I whispered back jokingly. Nate grinned and glanced over at our commanding officer. As if on cue, Officer Weston rose to his feet. "Buffet table here we come," I mumbled. Nate laughed next to me, quickly turning it into a cough when Officer Weston raised one eyebrow in warning.

"Attention, graduates. Training teams are going to be announced. For those of you that graduated top two in the class," Officer Weston said, glancing at me and Nate proudly, "you will remain behind because you've already been assigned to departments."

I smiled at those words. Nate and I had graduated top two of our year, with me in first place and it was an honour to be assigned to a department straight from graduation. It didn't happen particularly often, and you were only offered it if your reputation was known of in high places. The two of us were a wicked partnership, and apparently I had been headhunted for a special mission of 'utmost importance', or so Weston had informed me this morning.

My insides squirmed in anticipation. I was hoping for SWAT Front Line; they were the guys who were always first on site, who always saw action, but I knew it wouldn't be that. No one had ever gone into that team without at least ten years' field experience. They were the best of the best, and usually they only had an opening if someone died or requested a transfer. I knew that neither had happened recently, but I still couldn't help but hope.

Officer Weston finally finished his speech, and the guys all trailed off towards the hall, where they had laid on a buffet of stale sandwiches and potato chips. No expense spared. No one minded though because my entire graduating year was hitting a bar tonight in celebration, and I was planning on getting wasted.

Nate and I waited behind as requested. "Taylor, Peters, follow me," Officer Weston ordered, walking into his shabby office. He sat down behind his desk and motioned for us to sit. I couldn't keep the smile off my face. "Right, Peters, your presence has been requested at Division Six," he said proudly. I grinned happily and slapped Nate a high-five.

"Oh shit yeah! That's what I'm talking about!" Nate shouted, jumping out of his chair and pumping the air with his fist.

"Sit down, Nate," Weston laughed, shaking his head in amusement.

Division Six was a fantastic opportunity; he would get direct field experience, and they also had specialised areas which they could train you in. Nate wanted to be a sharp shooter and was incredible with long-range shooting.

"Okay, so they want you from Monday. You'll report to Officer Tate at 9 a.m. sharp. Don't be late. Here's your file, make sure you read it," Weston stated, handing Nate a brown envelope.

"Yes, sir, and thank you, sir," Nate answered, saluting respectfully, yet grinning moronically.

"Okay, Nate, you go enjoy the food. I need to speak to Ashton in private," Weston instructed, nodding for him to leave. I slapped Nate another high-five on his way past, silently praying that I got something as good as his. Officer Weston waited until the door closed before he spoke. "Ashton, you've been requested for something important. You're not going to like this," he winced, shaking his head.

My heart sank at the look on his face. This obviously wasn't something good. "Okay, sir, I'm listening," I said confidently. I was up for any challenge they could throw at me. I worked hard and it paid off. I had graduated first in every assessment, apart from long-range shooting, in which I came a close second to Nate. I held five different department records, including hand-to-hand combat, tactical planning, and hostage management. No one had ever graduated with the honours I had.

He sighed and held a brown envelope towards me. Frowning, I took it and tore it open eagerly, finding a police file inside for an Annabelle Spencer. I flicked it open curiously, not having a clue what this was about.

On the first page, there was a photo of her. She was incredibly beautiful. According to this, she was nineteen and a college student.

I glanced up at Weston. "Who's this?" I asked, confused as to why he had given me this girl's file.

"That is the daughter of an extremely important man. She's Annabelle Spencer, daughter of Senator Tom Spencer," he said respectfully.

My interest was instantly piqued. Tom Spencer was a Presidential candidate who was expected to take over the oval office come the election later this year; he was highly respected and, from what I'd heard, was supposed to be a great man.

"Okay, so why do I have her file?" I questioned, flicking through it and scanning the pages. She was recently expelled from Stanford. She had attended four other colleges in the last year and a half, and had been expelled from every one for violence or damage to property.

"When she was sixteen, she was abducted by Carter Thomas. He killed her boyfriend in a club and then held her against her will for almost a year. The only reason she was found was because the police raided his home for drugs and discovered her there. You do know who Carter Thomas is, don't you?" he asked, raising his eyebrows at me.

I nodded quickly. Everyone knew who Carter Thomas was; he was the head of a crime syndicate and responsible for the deaths of almost a thousand people when he'd set bombs off in the middle of rush hour in four different subways simultaneously. Everyone knew it was him, but it could never be directly proven, and key witnesses or evidence had a strange habit of going missing just in the nick of time. He regularly ran drugs and was heavily involved in human trafficking from Romania.

"He's currently serving a life sentence for the murder of Miss Spencer's boyfriend, Jackson Roberts. She was a witness for the prosecution, and there was also evidence that has linked him directly to the murder. Everyone knows who he is and what he does, but he's always slipped through our fingers. The murder of Jackson Roberts is the only thing that's ever gotten as far as a trial. Him being convicted was one of the best things for our country," Weston said, his expression hard.

"Okay, sir, so what does this have to do with me?" I asked, still not understanding why I was being told about this in the first place.

Weston sat back in his chair. "Well, Carter Thomas has an appeal coming up later this year. Apparently, some evidence may have been incorrectly collected or something. Miss Spencer was the only witness that made it to the trial the first time; there's a good chance she may be called to give evidence again. There have been death threats made against her, most of them because of who her father is, but lately her family have been receiving threats which they believe are coming from Carter's organisation."

He seemed to be watching me, waiting for my reaction. I still didn't get it. I'd been selected for a special assignment, yet he was telling me about some girl. What did this have to do with me? This wasn't SWAT business.

11

He took a deep breath. "Okay, I'm just gonna say it; she goes through bodyguards like you do cold beers. She gets assigned a new one, and within a week she makes them quit. They refuse to work with her. She's a real livewire from what I understand, a real hard-ass bitch. But this girl is extremely important, not only because she may be required to give evidence against Thomas, but also as the probable future President's daughter. Her father has requested someone who will be able to deal with her on a day-to-day basis. There's a specific age bracket because they'll be required to attend college with her and essentially be her shadow until the end of the court case."

It suddenly dawned on me where this meeting was going. I stared at him in disbelief, shaking my head and throwing the file onto his desk. "That's complete bullshit! I'm SWAT; I'm not some fucking babysitter!" I shouted, pointing at the file distastefully.

"This isn't up for debate. They wanted the best agent within an eight year age bracket, they picked the best agents across every department, sending the top ten to Senator Spencer, and he picked you specifically! You were the only graduate to be considered. You should consider this a great honour," Weston said persuasively.

I growled in frustration. "Why are we even getting involved? If she's the daughter of a Senator then this should be secret service, not us," I countered.

He sighed. "She's been through most of the guys there, Taylor. Plus, there aren't that many agents there within the age bracket; most people go into secret service a little further down the line in their careers," he explained, shrugging. He cocked his head to the side, his eyes boring into mine. "Ashton, it's just until the end of the court case. Eight months, that's all. Senator Spencer has guaranteed you your choice of posts after that time. Anything you want, even Front Line."

My head snapped up at those words. "Seriously?"

He smiled and nodded. "I knew that would get your attention, but I need you to understand that this is a very important job. It may not sound it, but if she dies and the case falls apart, then Carter Thomas will be released and hundreds, if not thousands, of people could be killed over the coming years," he said gravely.

Right, okay, I get it. Do a good job babysitting for eight months, get dream job. Done! "Okay, I understand, sir." I was smiling now.

"You can't tell anyone about this. You'll need to say you've been assigned somewhere out of state. You'll be undercover with her." He picked up the file that I'd tossed onto his desk and handed it to me.

I flicked it open again and looked at the picture of the girl. *Fuck, I sure hope I get undercover with her!* I mused. She was just my type, dark hair and dark eyes, and she was the prettiest damn thing I'd ever seen. I couldn't tell what her body was like because she was wearing baggy jeans and a hoodie, but her face was so beautiful that she could be a supermodel.

"Okay, make sure you read the briefing file. There's a DVD in there too, which is the security footage of her old school and the reason she got expelled. Like I said, she's kind of a badass; the reasons for it are in the file, which doesn't make for good bedtime reading." He grimaced and rubbed the back of his neck as he said it. I looked down at the file nervously, wondering what could be so bad that Weston was all jittery and uncomfortable about it. "Right, well I guess that's all. I've mocked up a fake assignment for you in case people ask. A flight has been booked for you for tomorrow morning and your tickets are in the back of the file. Pack casual; they'll have stuff waiting there for you too, so don't go too overboard with the clothes. Only a few people are in the loop on this due to the sensitivity of it; they're not sure if there's a leak in one of the departments, so if you need anything, you call either me or Commander Erikson. His details are in the back of the file. Good luck, Ashton," he said finally.

He stood up, holding out his hand to me; I shook it then saluted him respectfully, before walking out the door. Heading around the corner, I pulled out the mock assignment, memorising all of the details before I went to join the party with the other graduates.

I didn't stay out long with the other boys; my flight was due to leave at eight thirty the next morning, so I had to pack and make sure I was ready to leave. Once in the solitude of my bedroom, I grabbed the file and stretched out on my bed to read it. As I was expecting, it was pretty harrowing.

Annabelle had been held by Carter Thomas for just over ten months. He had thought of her as his girlfriend, even though he was nine years older than her. She hadn't been allowed to leave his house and he would beat her and mentally torture her. She had tried to kill herself by slitting her wrists when she was first taken and had been found locked in a cupboard – bruised, broken and almost catatonic. She had refused to speak to anyone for two weeks after this, and then her first words were to a police officer, begging him to kill her.

I gulped and flipped to the next page, which showed photos of her the day she was found, and her injuries for the police file. They weren't nice to look at. Bile rose in my throat at the sight of her swollen and bruised face and arms. The medical report showed she had a freshly broken rib and finger, and old, healed fractures of her ribs, wrist and collarbone.

My heart was beating out of my chest, grieving for the sixteen year old girl who witnessed her boyfriend's murder and then was abused physically, mentally, and sexually for over ten months.

Three and a half years on, the nice, young girl that everyone loved had turned into a bitter, nasty bitch. She was socially alienated, shying away from all relationships, and emotionally cutting herself off from her friends and family. I wasn't allowed 'under any circumstances' to touch her, unless the need arose in a combat situation. She had attempted suicide on two other occasions, both times by swallowing pills, but someone had found her

13

in time. Both attempts had been on her birthday. I glanced at her date of birth and saw that her next birthday was in six months' time. I made a mental note to be extra vigilant.

It appeared that Annabelle got into trouble a lot. I pushed the DVD into the player and sat on the floor to watch it, eager to see the reason she was excluded from her last school.

The footage came on, and a classroom came into focus. People were sitting around on desks, talking, obviously waiting for their lessons to start. I spotted her immediately; she was wearing baggy jeans and a baggy sweatshirt. As she walked past a guy who was laughing with his friends, he slapped her ass.

She practically jumped a mile into the air before rounding on him. "Don't touch me," she spat harshly.

"Sorry, princess," he laughed, holding his hands up innocently.

She flinched as if he'd hit her. "Don't ever call me that again," she said quietly, looking both scared and angry at the same time.

"Call you what… princess?" he mocked.

She flinched again before her expression turned hard. "If you call me that again, I'm gonna break your nose and your balls," she retorted.

The guy and his friends just laughed at her threat. She smiled sweetly as he bent his face close to hers. "Okay, princess," he said sarcastically.

Before he could even flinch, she punched him in the stomach then kneed him in the groin. As he bent over in pain, she grabbed the back of his hair and smashed his face into her knee, breaking his nose easily. He slumped down to the floor, crying in agony.

She patted him on the head, still smiling sweetly. "Told ya," she chirped, before grabbing her bag and storming out of the room with everyone watching her in shock.

I burst out laughing. She definitely was a badass.

I flicked through the rest of the file. Apparently, she didn't have friends anymore, didn't date, and didn't go to parties. The notes said that she didn't trust anyone and was extremely suspicious. She was bordering on depression and suffered from recurring night terrors. In the last three years, she had become totally focussed on martial arts and was well trained in self-defence, karate and kickboxing.

On the last page was my brief. I was to be posing as her boyfriend. I groaned out loud when I read the B word. I was to amend my age from my actual twenty-one to nineteen – the same as her. We would be doing the same college classes, which were Art and Graphic Design. I sighed deeply and carried on reading. I was to live with her on the college campus in a two bed apartment. I wasn't allowed time off apart from the scheduled college breaks, at which time she would go back to the family home, and I would be allowed to do as I pleased because she would be protected by other agents.

There would be one other bodyguard in full uniform, which was the standard secret service bodyguard that they assigned to close family members of the Senator. The guy's name was Dean Michaels. Apparently, they would assign a night guard to watch the building while we slept. I was to remain undercover at all times, which meant no dating and no sex for eight months. I groaned at that. *This is going to be the longest eight months of my life.*

Upon my arrival at the airport, I was to be collected by helicopter and taken to the Senator's summer residence, where we would stay for almost a week, getting to know each other, before moving to the apartment for college. According to the file, Annabelle didn't know about the death threats against her; she was just told that they were beefing up her security due to the upcoming election.

I stored the numbers of Officer Weston and Commander Erikson into my cell phone, and then started packing casual clothes for college. Afterwards, I crawled over to my bed in my crappy, little apartment that Nate and I rented together and climbed under the sheets. I'd said goodbye to the guys already. I was really going to miss Nate; we had become great friends during the last four years' training. He was more like a brother to me in some ways.

I didn't have anyone else to say goodbye to. I had no family; my parents had died in a car accident when I was ten, and I had bounced around from foster home to foster home until I was seventeen, when I had finally gotten a place of my own. I closed my eyes and willed myself to fall asleep quickly because tomorrow was going to be a long day.

The flight was good. It was only for two hours but they still put me in first class and I dozed off for almost the entire trip. I hadn't slept well the night before. Every time I'd shut my eyes, I had seen Annabelle looking at me with her cold hard eyes, begging me to help her. Then I would pull open a cupboard to see her beaten and broken on the floor and I would jerk awake in a cold sweat. I had a feeling that this was going to be a harder assignment than I had first thought. I hadn't even met her yet and already I wanted to protect her.

When the plane finally landed, I was ushered through the checkpoints to a private helipad on the other side of the airport. A tall guy in a black suit held his hand out to me; he was probably in his mid-thirties, with sandy hair and brown eyes.

"Hi, I'm Dean Michaels, Miss Spencer's far guard," he greeted me as I shook his hand.

I smiled politely. "Ashton Taylor. Nice to meet you."

He showed me to the helicopter and we put on our headphones. "The trip's about thirty minutes. You'll like the summer house; it's nice, and right on the lake," he said, smiling.

"Right, sounds good. So, what can you tell me about Annabelle?" I asked, watching his face closely for his reaction.

He frowned before speaking and seemed to be choosing his words carefully. "Miss Spencer is very… difficult. You need to watch her all the time; she can get in trouble easily. She's had twenty-three near guards in the last three years; the longest one lasted just over three months. I've worked as her far guard for a year and a half, and the only reason I've managed to last so long is because I don't have regular contact with her." He shook his head seeming a little annoyed.

"The near guards get fired within three months?" I asked, slightly panicky. If I couldn't last the full eight months, I wouldn't get my choice of assignments.

"No, man, they quit! She makes it her personal mission to make them leave. I think she sees it as some sort of challenge. Her record so far is four days," he laughed.

A lump formed in my throat, so I quickly swallowed it. "So, she doesn't want a near guard, or what?" I asked. *What is it with this girl? Maybe she needs to know about the threats against her so that she'll be easier to protect, because there is no way I'm quitting.*

"Nope, she doesn't want any guards at all. I think she tolerates me because I stay out of her way and keep a distance. She doesn't like company; she'd rather be on her own. She's been through a lot, and it's changed her," he replied casually.

"Does she know I'm coming?" I asked, looking out over the fields that we were flying over.

He laughed quietly. "Yeah."

I looked back at his face; he shook his head and laughed again. I smiled in understanding. She didn't want me there – that much was obvious from his reaction.

"Senator Spencer gave me your file. How the hell did a guy like you, who's top of your class and the academy's new golden boy, end up with a shitty assignment like this?" he asked, looking genuinely curious.

I closed my eyes and rested my head on the seat back. "I have no idea," I mumbled. I was still asking myself the same question. I could see the importance of it, but surely there could have been someone else for the job that came from a protection background. I stayed quiet for the rest of the trip.

After what seemed like forever, we landed outside an expansive house that was right on the lake. I followed Dean into the house, trying not to react to the sheer size of it. I trudged behind him, looking around in awe at the real wooden floors, the heavy drapes, the framed artwork on the walls. It was like something out of a magazine. Dean stopped outside a door and chatted to a lady sitting at the desk; she was probably in her mid-fifties and she glanced over at me with a friendly smile.

I cleared my throat and put out my hand in greeting. "Hello, ma'am. Ashton Taylor, it's nice to meet you."

Her eyes widened as her gaze flicked over me before placing her hand in mine. "It's nice to meet you too. My name's Maddy Richards and I'm Senator Spencer's Personal Assistant. I'll just let him know you're here, he'd like to speak to you," she said in a business-like tone. She picked up the phone and spoke briefly. "Okay he's free right now, you can go in." She nodded towards a door on my right.

A wave of nerves suddenly hit me as I realised that I was about to meet the probable next President of the United States. I swallowed my nerves and went in as instructed. He was sat behind a large, wooden desk, and there was a lady sitting on the couch, drinking tea. She was very pretty and had dark brown hair, which she had pulled into a bun, and brown eyes. She looked somewhat familiar; maybe I'd seen her on TV or something.

Senator Spencer stood up, smiling at me, and walked over, holding out his hand. He was a very imposing man on television, but it was even more apparent in person. He oozed confidence and ability, and had an air about him that certainly explained why he was tipped to win the upcoming election.

I shook his hand confidently. "It's very nice to meet you, sir."

"You too, Agent Taylor. This is my wife, Melissa." He gestured to the lady on the couch. I turned and smiled as it clicked into place why she'd looked so familiar when I stepped into the room. She looked like Annabelle, but Annabelle had a radiant beauty that far surpassed her mother's.

"It's nice to meet you, ma'am," I nodded.

"You too. Hopefully you'll last longer than the other near guards; Annabelle needs some stability," she said sadly.

Senator Spencer cleared his throat. "So, Agent Taylor, I've read your file, and I must say it's mighty impressive. Your reputation is incredible at the agency. They have exceptionally high hopes for you." He gestured to the couch for me to sit. "You've read your brief, I assume?" I nodded in confirmation and sat as instructed. "Do you have any questions before you meet Annabelle?"

I nodded. "Only one, sir. I was wondering why you don't just tell Miss Spencer about the threats so that she would be more cooperative with her guards. It would be a lot easier to protect her, and ultimately make her safer, if she were more accommodating."

Mrs Spencer gasped and the Senator shook his head fiercely. "Annabelle is very fragile. She doesn't like to show it, but she's still grieving for Jack, and what that animal did to her." His hand clenched into a fist before he took a deep breath and composed himself. I liked this guy already. "She can't be told. She barely copes as it is, she doesn't need anything else to worry about on top." He stood up and walked to his desk,

17

picking up his phone. "Maddy, could you have Annabelle come in here now, please?"

His face still looked sad with deep pain across it. This man had worries about his daughter that no father should ever have to go through. I hadn't thought about them when I read her file. Thinking about it now though, I realised that they had been through hell too. Their sixteen year old daughter goes missing, presumed dead, then months later she's found broken, abused, and totally a changed person. They had to watch her sink into depression and attempt suicide and turn into a cold, heartless person, and now they couldn't even hug her or hold her hand.

The phone on the desk buzzed, and Maddy's voice came through the intercom. "Senator, Annabelle's here," she announced.

"Okay, Maddy, send her in," the Senator answered, glancing at me, his expression almost apologetic.

A few seconds later she walked into the room. As soon as I laid eyes on her, I knew I was in trouble. She looked so incredibly vulnerable. Her eyes were cold and distant and held a pain that I couldn't bear to think about. She had seen things that no one should ever see. Carter had broken not only her body, but her spirit too.

Her eyes only flicked to me for a split second and held no reaction whatsoever before she turned to her father. My heart skipped a beat and my stomach tied in a knot. I wanted to run to her, wrap my arms around her, and tell her everything would be okay. I wanted to make her smile and hear her laugh.

Oh fuck it; I really am in deep shit!

Chapter Three

~ Anna ~

When my cell phone vibrated on the side, I was laying on my bed with my arm covering my eyes, trying to block out the midmorning sun that was streaming through my window. I groaned and rolled to the side, stretching my arm out to reach for it. Every single one of my muscles protested from the slight movement. My whole body hurt from the run that I'd taken earlier in the morning. I'd pushed it too far today. After speaking to my father first thing and learning that I was going to be getting a new near guard today, and the bombshell that he'd dropped on me about the guy posing as my boyfriend, I'd taken my frustrations out in the gym, running on the treadmill until I'd vomited and almost passed out.

Finally catching my phone with my fingertips, I pressed it to my ear and stared up at the ceiling. "Yeah, what?" I muttered into the phone, already knowing what this would be about. My father had told me that I'd get a call when the new guard arrived, and I would have to show him around the house and get to know him ready for next week when we both went to the new school.

Maddy's overly cheerful voice greeted me. "Hi, Annabelle. Could you come down to your father's office, please? Agent Taylor is here, and he'd like to meet you."

I sighed and closed my eyes in defeat. "Fine, I'll be there in a minute." I disconnected the call before she could answer, and then headed out of my room on my wobbly legs. As I trudged through the house, I kept my eyes on the ground so that no one would try to speak to me. Not that they tried often anymore; I'd made it clear to people that I didn't want to interact.

As I let myself into Maddy's office, she looked up and smiled, but it was tight and wary. It seemed as if everyone had a problem with how to behave around me now. "You'll like this one, Annabelle, he's so handsome!" she gushed, raising one eyebrow excitedly.

I frowned and folded my arms across my chest as I made a distasteful, scoffing sound in the back of my throat. Her comment was both inappropriate and unwelcome. It didn't matter what he looked like, all that mattered was the fact that I didn't want another guard. All they ever did was come in, disrupt my life, and then leave me after a couple of months when they realised that I wasn't even worth protecting.

When she waved her hand at my father's office door, signalling for me to go in, I shoved it open and stepped inside. The room went quiet instantly, and my gaze flicked to the stranger standing in the middle of the room.

I felt my eyes widen from shock. Maddy was right, he certainly was handsome. His black hair was shorter around the sides, but fell across his forehead messily, and he had the most beautiful dark green eyes that I had ever seen. His face was perfect, just like an angel's. His body would be incredible too – I could see that even though it was covered by a plain, white T-shirt and ripped jeans. He actually looked like he'd just stepped out of a magazine shoot and was easily the most beautiful boy I'd ever seen.

I took all this in within a second before my eyes went back to his. His gaze was raking over me slowly, his mouth slightly open as he took in every inch of me, making me want to squirm on the spot or run away as fast as my legs would carry me. Lust was written plain across his angelic features, and it made my stomach ache.

I kept my expression neutral and quickly looked away to my father, who was watching me with tight eyes. Clearly he was uncomfortable after our little spat that had taken place in my bedroom this morning when he'd told me about this new guarding arrangement.

"So, this is him then? The new near guard *boyfriend*," I asked, saying the last word angrily.

He nodded. "Yes, Annabelle. This is Agent Taylor. Agent Taylor, this is my daughter, Annabelle Spencer," my dad answered, looking between the two of us warily.

The beautiful stranger extended his right hand towards me. "Hi, Miss Spencer, I'm Ashton. It's nice to meet you."

I recoiled slightly, but tried not to show my nerves. I didn't like to show people that I was afraid. My eyes flicked down to his extended hand and my heart started to race at the thought of him touching me. Physical attention, especially from men I didn't know, made my lungs constrict and my body go cold. It had done ever since Carter. I glanced back up at the agent's face. He was smiling at me; his eyes warm and friendly. I swallowed the fear away and raised my hand to his, trying to be confident, but I could see that I was shaking as I shook his hand briefly. His eyes never left mine, making me feel slightly relaxed, despite the fact that a man I didn't know was touching me. As I dropped his hand, I stepped back and folded my arms over my chest; my mother was watching me with wide eyes as if waiting to see what I would do.

I raised my chin as I faked a confident smile, dragging my eyes over him from his head down to his toes. "Well, Ashton, you don't look like the normal guys I get assigned. I'm gonna be generous and say that you'll last a week, maybe even ten days, before you request a reassignment," I teased cockily.

One side of his full lips pulled up as he shook his head. "Actually, Miss Spencer, I'm here for eight months, and I don't quit," he replied confidently, folding his arms across his chest too, mirroring me.

The arrogance he was exuding made one of my eyebrows rise, but I fought desperately to hold back any reaction to him. "You can call me Anna." I waved my hand dismissively, ignoring his attitude.

"Anna it is then." His answering smile was gorgeous and seemed to light his whole face.

My mother cleared her throat obviously. "Why don't you show Agent Taylor to his room, Annabelle? Maybe you could give him a tour of the house and grounds too. Show him where the lake is."

I frowned at that. They always expected me to play nicely with these agents. I had no idea why though, because they never lasted long and then the whole routine would start all over again. "I'll show him to his room, but he's a big boy, I'm sure he can find the lake himself. I mean, you can't miss the damn thing, it's right there." I turned and stalked out of the room, ignoring Ashton exchanging pleasantries with my parents behind me.

As I stalked up the hallway, fast footsteps sounded as he ran to catch me up. "Thanks for waiting," he muttered sarcastically.

I scowled over at him. In all honesty, I was a little surprised at his attitude. Usually the guards were all *'Yes, Miss Spencer. No, Miss Spencer'*. Clearly this guy had some balls. "Whatever, pretty boy. You want me to show you to your room or not?" I snapped. My body still hurt and I wanted to take a nap before dinner.

"Sure, that'd be great." His arm slipped around my shoulder. My heart seemed to stop before my body reacted immediately. I ducked under his arm and put both hands on his chest, shoving him as hard as I could. Because I'd caught him off guard, he stumbled back a step and looked at me with wide, horrified eyes. My teeth clenched together as I pulled back my right arm, throwing a punch in the general direction of his face. But he was too fast for me and threw his arm up to block my hit before holding both hands up innocently.

"I'm sorry! I shouldn't have done that, I'm sorry," he apologised quickly, shaking his head.

Tears welled in my eyes as my body shook from the shock of it. Male attention wasn't something I could deal with anymore. It brought back too many memories that I could barely even cope with.

"That's it, you're gone," I growled, spinning on my heel, about to march back to my father's office and demand that he be transferred.

"Oh shit, come on, no, please? I promise that won't ever happen again, I just forgot myself, that's all. Please? I need this job," he begged, as I marched down the hallway.

The pleading tone to his voice seemed to strike a chord inside me and I stopped, gritting my teeth, considering. I swallowed the lump that formed in my throat and turned to face him. I could see how sorry he was just by his slumped shoulders.

"You're an asshole," I spat venomously. These men had no idea of the power they held over me and how much even just a casual touch could affect me for days afterwards.

He nodded, holding up his hands innocently.

"Don't ever touch me again. You're already hanging by a thread," I muttered, shaking my head angrily. I had no idea why I was giving him another chance. Usually I would have strutted into my father's office and demanded they send him away, but the sorrow in his eyes was evident, so I knew it was just an innocent move that wouldn't occur again anytime soon.

He nodded in agreement, so I resumed the tour. As we walked past doors in the hallway, I said the names of the rooms but didn't give him a chance to look in them. He could find his own way around; I didn't owe him anything.

"Kitchen. Dining room. Games room. Lounge. Den. The gym's down there," I said, pointing to my favourite part of the whole house.

"Wait, you have your own gym? Can I see it?" he asked excitedly. I risked a sideways glance at him. He was grinning happily; he obviously liked to exercise, which was actually pretty apparent by his toned physique.

"Sure, go ahead." I smiled and waved him into the gym. As soon as he was out of sight, I abandoned my tour and walked up to my room, slamming the door behind me. I threw myself down on the bed, sighing deeply. Eight months I'd been told he was here for. He definitely wouldn't last more than a month, tops.

After about half an hour, there was a knock on my bedroom door. I groaned at the interruption, shoving my sketch pad under my pillow. "What do you want?" I called, not in the mood to socialise any more today.

"Can I come in?" Ashton retorted. I pushed myself up from the bed, chuckling wickedly because he was clearly annoyed with me for running off and leaving him. As I pulled open the door, his annoyed face greeted me. "Yeah, that was funny," he said sarcastically. I full on laughed and cocked my head to the side, not caring that he was annoyed with me. His frown deepened. "I need to come in and pace your room."

My grip on my door handle tightened as I pulled it close to my side, blocking his entry. "What? Go pace in your own room, it's right next door," I scoffed, nodding towards the door next to mine.

"Yeah I know, someone showed me after you ditched me," he muttered sarcastically. "I didn't mean I wanted to pace *in* your room though. I need to pace your room out so I know where everything is."

I frowned, not liking the idea of having someone in my private space. I didn't usually allow agents in my room, but his stern expression told me that he wasn't going away until he'd done whatever it was that he wanted. I sighed deeply and shoved open my door, gesturing for him to come in. "You're freaking weird! No one else has paced my room before."

As he walked in, his eyes flitted around. My bedroom was plain apart from my sketches that were stuck all over one wall; they were all to do with the same thing – Jack. No one knew that though, everyone just thought they were different things – a pair of blue eyes here, a dandelion there, a football stadium with a player celebrating, a smudge that was the exact shape of his birthmark he had on the edge of his hairline. I had drawn them all last year. I didn't draw Jack anymore; I tried to, but it just hurt too much. Last year was when I decided to stop feeling anything, and drawing Jack just made the pain come back in droves. The things I drew now I didn't show anyone, they were too dark. I didn't put them on my wall; I hid them or destroyed them before anyone saw and demanded that I seek help again. I refused to go back to the hospital.

"These are really great," Ashton complimented, looking at my wall of sketches.

I sat on my bed and pulled my knees up to my chest. "Thanks," I mumbled, watching him look at each one individually.

"What's this one?" he asked, pointing to one of Jack's birthmark.

I sighed, shrugging. "What does it look like to you? It's one of those inkblot tests. It's whatever you think it is."

He turned back to it, cocking his head to the side, staring at it intently for a few seconds before he spoke. "Huh, well then maybe I'm hungry because this looks like a cheeseburger and fries, heavy on the ketchup." Not expecting such a witty response, his comment caught me off guard and, uncharacteristically, I burst out laughing. He turned back to me and smiled, seeming almost proud of himself. "So I'd better get pacing, it may take a while." He smiled at me apologetically.

I sat back against the headboard and watched him walking around my room. Starting at the door, he would pace to the bed, then the door to the closet, the door to the window, bed to the window, bed to the closet. He went on and on for about twenty minutes. I watched him silently the whole time, just resting my chin on my knees. He was very methodical, but I had no idea why he was doing it.

"Okay, I'm done. I just need to ask you a few questions, then I'll let you get back to hating me or whatever you were doing before I came in," he said, smiling.

I rolled my eyes. "Fine, Pretty Boy, what do you want to know?"

"What side of the bed do you sleep on?"

"What the hell does that have to do with anything?" My temper was rising again, I could feel it.

He shrugged innocently. "I need to know so that if I have to come in and get you, I'll know where you'll be."

"Oh for goodness' sake! None of the other guards have done anything like this or asked stupid questions! No one can get in the house. We have security, dumbass," I spat acidly.

A smile tugged at one corner of his mouth. "Just humour me, please. I need all the information so I can keep you safe. I don't care what other guards have done; I'm here to stay, so at least you'll only have to go through this once."

I laughed humourlessly. "You'll quit, Pretty Boy, trust me, they all do. Everyone leaves me eventually," I stated confidently.

His cocky smile fell from his face immediately at my words. "Please just answer the questions so I can keep you safe." He pouted, looking like a lost puppy.

I gulped as I realised that he'd just used the cute puppy dog face on me, Jack used to pull that trick all the time. "Ugh fine, I tend to sleep in the middle of the bed."

"Okay. Do you have any weapons in your room?" he asked, looking round as if he could see anything. I shook my head in response. He nodded. "Can you shoot a gun?"

I recoiled at the word. I hated guns, I'd seen too many of them in my lifetime already. "No," I croaked, my mouth suddenly dry.

He pursed his lips before nodding. "I'll teach you to shoot. Just in case. You can never be too prepared for anything."

Needing this conversation to be over and for him to leave the only place I considered a sanctuary, I shrugged in agreement. "Are you done now?" I asked, nodding towards the door, signalling for him to leave.

"Er… I just have one more thing, but I don't want to upset you or anything," he said quietly. I took a deep breath and waited for him to continue. "I'm supposed to be your boyfriend. For people to believe that lie, I'm going to have to touch you from time to time."

Instantly, my heart slammed in my chest and a wave of nausea rolled over me. He scooted closer to me on the bed. I flinched at his closeness and jumped up quickly, holding my hands in front of me in protest. "Don't, just don't," I muttered, looking at him pleadingly. My lunch was threatening to come back up.

"I'm not going to touch you. I just… Anna, to pull this off I'm going to have to be able to touch you in public. Maybe just hold your hand," he suggested, standing too but making no moves to come near me.

"Why don't we just say we're friends?" I offered.

He shook his head. "No. The reason they want me as your boyfriend is to keep the guys away from you. Apparently it's always the guys that get you kicked out," he countered, chuckling at something.

"No, actually it's always my temper that gets me kicked out," I corrected, smiling weakly as I backed up another step. "Hey, we could say I'm a lesbian," I bargained, praying he'd agree.

He chuckled, watching me as I backed up again. "Let's just stick to the brief. I just need you to know that I'm here to protect you. I would never hurt you, ever." His eyes locked onto mine as he stepped forwards.

I held my breath, wondering if he too could hear my heart racing. He stopped in front of me and held out his hand, smiling reassuringly. My eyes dropped to it, and I shook my head. I couldn't do it. It would bring back memories of *him*, and I couldn't think about him.

"Please, I can't," I begged, swallowing the lump that was stuck in my throat.

"I will never hurt you. I want to protect you," he whispered.

Oh come on, Anna, get a grip of yourself! He's an agent here to protect you, you're in a house full of people, he's not going to attack you! Just move your hand and stop being such a damn wimp! My mental chastising had a positive impact on my confidence, so I raised a trembling hand and put it in his. His fingers threaded through mine, and he squeezed gently. I looked at my hand, shocked. It didn't actually feel too bad, it was quite pleasant actually, warm and soft. Some of my stress evaporated, and I glanced up at his handsome face; a small satisfied smile graced his lips.

"That's great, Anna. Maybe if we tried to hold hands for a little a bit every day, then you'd get used to it before we start college next week," he suggested.

"You won't be here next week, Pretty Boy," I answered confidently.

He laughed incredulously. "Anna, I don't quit, I never quit, so you'd better get used to me. I'm going to be around for a while, whether you like it or not," he replied arrogantly.

I yanked my hand out of his and folded my arms across my chest. "I don't need a fucking babysitter! I can take care of myself," I stated, annoyed again.

He raised one eyebrow and smiled wickedly. "Really? You can take care of yourself? So if I wanted to throw you down on the bed, I couldn't do that?"

Oh God! My heart took off in double time. "Ashton, if you touch me, I'm gonna break your pretty face," I warned.

A confident smile crept onto his lips. "You couldn't land one punch before I pin you to the bed."

25

He took a step forward and I didn't give him the opportunity to touch me. I shot my hand out to punch him in the stomach, but he knocked my hand away easily before it got anywhere near him. My stomach clenched with fear because that small move showed me that he was faster than me. Panic made my blood go cold, but I wasn't willing to concede yet. I'd never give up without a fight again. He took another step towards me and I sent a kick towards him as hard as I could. He sidestepped it easily, caught my leg and closed the distance between us so fast that I didn't have time to react. His free arm wrapped around my waist, and he threw us both onto the bed.

As he landed on top of me, I felt the scream ripping its way up my throat as the panic took over. He put one hand over my mouth and grabbed my hands with the other, pinning them above my head, his body pressing me into the bed. I screamed and thrashed, trying to throw him off me as I squeezed my eyes shut, trying to think of anything other than Carter, but I couldn't stop myself from returning to those memories again. In my head, I saw his brown eyes sparkling with excitement as he prepared to rape me. I heaved and turned my head to the side in defeat, letting the tears fall as I just stopped struggling. There was no point, he was too strong for me.

I waited for the pain, but it never came. I opened my eyes slowly and looked up. Ashton was still holding me down on the bed, but somehow he wasn't heavy, as if he was holding his weight off me.

"I won't hurt you, I promise. Trust me," he whispered as he took his hand off of my mouth. My tears were still falling so he wiped them away gently. "I just wanted to show you that you need me. I want to protect you. You need me, so please don't keep making this difficult. I won't leave you like the others," he said softly.

I looked up into his deep green eyes, and I could see the sincerity there; they were kind, caring, and gentle eyes. They were the complete opposite of the brown eyes I'd been envisioning a few seconds before. I believed him. Ashton wouldn't quit after a week, and he wasn't going to hurt me.

"Okay, but please get off me," I begged, my voice trembling as I spoke.

"I will, but I think this is good for you. You can't go through life on your own, afraid to let people touch you, afraid to let people in, in case they leave you. What happened to you won't happen again, I promise," he said, looking pained.

I closed my eyes and let the tears fall. The grief, pain and disgust returned in droves. I'd been able to push the pain away for months now, refusing to acknowledge that I was forever broken, just walking around like an emotionless zombie; the only thing I allowed myself to feel was anger.

"Do you need me to get off, or can you cope for a couple of minutes?" he asked quietly.

26

I took in a shaky breath. "Please don't hurt me," I whispered, turning my head to the side again.

"I won't." He let go of my hands, but I couldn't move; it was like my body was frozen in place.

I still felt sick, but for some reason I trusted him. I didn't want to, I genuinely didn't, but I couldn't help myself. He didn't move at all, didn't even shift his weight. I kept my eyes squeezed closed. I knew he was looking at me but I wanted to stay in control, and the only thing that was keeping me in control of myself was counting his heartbeats that I could feel against my chest.

After a couple of minutes, he pushed himself off me and stood up. "See, you did great. I just need you to trust me," he congratulated, offering his hand to help me up. I rolled on to my side and pulled my knees up to my chest in the foetal position as my body suddenly racked with sobs. "Oh shit! I'm sorry, Anna! Why didn't you say? I would've gotten off, I swear!" he gasped, sounding horrified, making no moves to come near me again.

"Just leave, I just want to be on my own," I begged. I didn't want him here; he was making everything worse with his stupid, nice guy attitude and cocky, good looks.

Silence filled the room for a few seconds before he finally agreed. "I'll just be next door then. I'm really sorry."

I didn't open my eyes until I heard the click of the door. Weakly, I crawled up the bed, pulled the soft pillow over my face, and then screamed until I lost my breath. Thoughts were rushing through my brain too fast for me to comprehend: Why did I not mind him being on top of me? Why did I let him do that to me? And most importantly, why did it upset me when he moved away?

Guilt. It was eating me up inside because I'd just enjoyed another man's touch. I felt so guilty that I wanted to vomit. *Oh God, Jack, I'm so sorry! I won't let that happen again, I promise,* I mentally chanted in my head.

I rolled over and picked up the photo that I had by the side of my bed. Jack's handsome face greeted me, making me feel even worse for letting Ashton touch me. We were just fifteen when the photo was taken, merely a year before everything turned upside-down. We were at the beach. He was smiling his beautiful smile and had his arms wrapped tightly around my waist. I was laughing at something goofy he'd whispered in my ear just as the photo was taken. Everyday I wished I could remember what it was that he'd said. I rubbed my thumb across his face. I missed him so much; it was like a knife in the heart everyday.

That night I cried myself to sleep – something I hadn't done for months.

I woke up screaming. I'd been dreaming about Carter again as usual. My heart was pounding in my ears as I sat up, panting, trying to get my breath back the same as I did every night. I raised my knees up and put my head between them.

Suddenly my door burst open and the lights flicked on, almost blinding me. I whimpered in surprise but looked up to see Ashton in just his boxer shorts. His eyes were darting around my room. He held a gun in one hand, pointing straight out in front of him; his other arm was across his body, and he had a wicked-looking knife in his hand. His expression was totally focussed and murderously angry. He looked like a mean SWAT agent now, not a pretty boy model.

He crossed the room in a split second. "Get up and get behind me. Now!" he ordered. I instantly jumped out of the bed, wondering what was going on. Was someone in the house?

As soon as I was behind him, he started backing up, making me move with him. I almost stumbled and gripped my hands on his hips to steady myself. We backed up until I bumped into the wall behind me, making me whimper. He pressed his back against my chest, shielding me with his body as he continued to scan my room.

"Shh!" he hissed. I whimpered again and clamped my hand over my mouth, pressing my face hard into his bare back to silence myself. "Where?" he whispered fiercely. "Where are they?"

I pulled back so I could take my hand off my mouth. "Where's who? I don't know," I whispered back, pressing into his body, trying to melt into him.

"Who was in your room? Why were you screaming?" he questioned, clearly confused now too.

Realisation washed over me. "Oh shit! You came in here because I was screaming?" I breathed a sigh of relief as the shock slowly faded from my stressed body.

"Yeah… what?" He shook his head, still scanning my room for danger.

"Nothing, it's nothing. I was dreaming. I'm sorry." I felt like a complete loser in that second. Everyone had moved bedrooms so that I was the only one down this end of the hall because I woke up screaming every night. I hadn't even thought about waking Ashton up. Everyone else just ignored me now.

He turned around to face me, looking concerned, still standing close to me, his chest almost pressing into mine. "You were dreaming?" he asked quietly. I nodded in response. He blew out a large breath and swapped his knife into his gun hand so he could drag his hand through his messy bed hair. "Holy fuck. You were screaming as if you were being murdered," he said, looking at me, wide eyed.

"Maybe I was," I murmured.

He raised his hand and brushed some hair over my shoulder before taking hold of my hand. "It's because of what I did earlier, wasn't it?" he muttered. His voice was full of remorse.

I shook my head fiercely. "No, it wasn't," I assured him. "I have nightmares every night, it had nothing to do with you," I promised. He squeezed my hand gently, sending little tingles up my arm. I frowned, noticing how I didn't hate that he was touching me. Maybe it was just practice, like he'd suggested. "Maybe you should change rooms. There's another room upstairs, you won't hear me then." My eyes dropped to my feet as heat flooded my face from embarrassment.

"Do you dream like that every night?" he asked, bending his head to look into my eyes.

"Yeah," I nodded. "But I don't want to talk about it, so please don't ask. I'm sorry I woke you up."

His green eyes locked on mine. They were strangely calming. "I don't mind that you woke me up. I just wish you'd let me try and help you."

Help me? No one could help me; it was too late for that. The only person that could help me had died.

"You can't." I put my hand on his chest and pushed him away from me. He was standing so close and I was getting hot, trapped in the corner. I needed some air.

"I can, you just need to let me in," he said, catching my hand again.

I groaned in frustration. "Ashton, please just leave. I just need some air or something. I'm sorry I woke you, I won't go back to sleep again so you can get some sleep." I stepped away from him, needing a little personal space.

He shook his head adamantly. "You can go back to sleep. I'll watch over you. That way you might not have any more nightmares," he suggested, gripping the back of my dresser chair and pulling it to the side of the bed.

I laughed incredulously. "And that's part of your new job description?" I shot back sarcastically.

He shook his head, turning on my bedside lamp before walking over to switch the ceiling lights off. "Nope. But I want you to feel safe with me so I'll do whatever it takes."

I scoffed, watching as plopped himself down in the chair. "So you're going to watch me sleep?"

"Yeah," he confirmed, setting his gun and knife on the floor at the side of the chair.

I gulped at his stern expression. "Ashton, seriously, please just go to bed. I won't wake you again." I reached over and picked up a book from the side and got comfy on my bed to read it.

He sighed deeply. "Look, when you get to know me, you'll know that once I've made my mind up about something, there's not much that can change it. Now I'm either gonna sit here and watch you sleep, or I'm gonna sit here and watch you read," he stated, smiling at me cockily.

I frowned as I read his expression. It was deadly serious; he wasn't going back to sleep either way. We glared at each other for a couple of minutes, neither of us wanting to back down. Finally, I sighed deeply, knowing I'd lost. What he didn't know was that I would still have nightmares with him sitting there anyway, so this little thing was pointless. My father had already tried sitting in the room while I slept; nothing helped. I'd tried everything, drugs, hypnotists, yoga; nothing had any effect on them. Maybe Ashton needed to find that out the hard way and lose a night of sleep before he'd give up trying to help me.

I sighed and tossed my book in his direction. "Fine. Wanna read that?" I asked as he caught it.

He grinned and looked at the cover. "You like vampires?" he asked, holding up my battered and abused copy of Twilight.

I smiled back. "I like that one," I admitted, settling back into the bed and just watching him flick through to the first page. "Good night."

"Night, Anna." Sitting there reading, in just a pair of black boxers, I saw no sign of the badass from minutes before, he was back to male model again now.

I closed my eyes and willed myself to sleep, knowing that it wouldn't come easy. It never did.

Chapter Four

I woke in the morning after having one of the best night's sleep I'd had in years. I had laid awake for ages with my back to him, listening to him flipping the pages of the book. But the thing that I remembered most about last night was the moment I realised he'd fallen asleep. Ashton Taylor, easily the most handsome man I had seen in a long time, snored. And not just a little, quiet snore either; it was a loud chainsaw-type sound. For a long time I'd laid there, giggling to myself, as I watched him with his head propped against his hand, his legs folded under him and the book abandoned on his lap. It was actually a cute sight. I'd eventually fallen asleep too, still hearing the sound of his snores even in my dreams. It was nice actually because it was like they'd stopped me from going into a deep sleep. I hadn't had any more nightmares last night, just like he'd hoped.

I sighed contentedly and looked over at him still slumped in the same position. He would probably suffer for the awkward position all day long. I smiled weakly and pulled the sheets up around my shoulders as he stirred too, wincing as he moved and blinked a couple of times.

"Hi," I greeted, unsure what I was supposed to say. This was a first for me.

"Morning," he yawned, sitting forward and arching his back, letting out a little groan. "You sleep okay?"

I smiled and nodded, wondering if I should tease him for snoring so loud. I decided against it, after all, he *had* attempted to stay awake all night so I could sleep. It wasn't my place to make fun of him after he'd forgone his bed for me. "Actually, yeah I did. Thanks," I answered sheepishly.

He grinned triumphantly, swinging his legs off the chair and standing up, stretching. Without my permission, my eyes instantly raked down his body, taking in every inch of his perfection from his tanned skin, his chiselled abs and the little V-line that disappeared down into his underwear. I gulped and closed my eyes quickly before he caught me watching him.

31

"You think I could maybe borrow this so I can read the end?" he asked.

I opened my eyes to see him awkwardly holding up my book. I smiled and nodded, noting his obvious embarrassment that he was enjoying a book aimed predominantly at teenage girls. "No need to be embarrassed, you can't beat a good vampire novel. I've got the other three as well if you want them."

He laughed and shrugged. "I'm not embarrassed; I'm just waiting for the teasing to start because I read a chick book."

"Chick book," I laughed at his derogatory choice of words, sitting up and shaking my head.

He smiled and nodded back towards the door. "I'm gonna go grab a shower." When he bent down to retrieve his gun and knife from the floor, my eyes sneakily dropped down to his behind. I arched one eyebrow in appreciation. The back view was actually just as good as the front. After collecting his weapons, he strutted across the room, pulling open the door. Before he could leave I called his name, making him turn to look at me expectantly.

"Thank you for last night. That was nice of you," I admitted. The words were hard to say. I wasn't used to being nice to people lately so I was kind of unsure how to do it.

His lips curved into a beautiful smile. "Anytime."

As he closed the door behind him, I pushed myself out of the bed, deciding that I would take a shower too.

After, I didn't bother drying my hair or putting on make-up – I never did. I threw on a pair of loose combat-style jeans and a black tank top with a black, baggy sweatshirt over the top, and then headed downstairs for breakfast.

As I walked into the kitchen, I saw Ashton sitting at the breakfast bar with a huge stack of pancakes in front of him. The kitchen staff were falling all over him. Sarah, the waitress, was flirting with him shamelessly, her cleavage almost popping out of her shirt that was never normally undone like that.

My stomach was already full of anguish over what was going to happen this morning, so instead of eating a proper breakfast, I just grabbed a banana, ignoring how Mary, the chef, frowned disapprovingly.

Ashton turned and smiled at me. This earned me a nasty look from Sarah because she'd lost his attention. While I poured a glass of orange juice, she stepped closer to him, pulling her shoulders back to make her breasts look like they were about to pop out of her shirt. "So, Ashton, I have a few hours off today, would you like to do something?" she asked, raising one eyebrow in a silent offer of nakedness, I assumed.

A frown lined his forehead as he shook his head. "Actually I was hoping that Anna would want to hang out with me today," he replied, turning to me.

The banana seemed to get stuck in my throat. "I'm busy today." I had things I needed to do.

One of his eyebrows rose in question. "Oh really, what are you doing?"

I swallowed loudly. This was why I didn't like having guards; they were always trying to get into things that had nothing to do with them. "I've got things to do. It's not really any of your business," I replied rudely, downing the last of my juice before tossing the banana skin into the trash can and storming out of the room before he could question me further.

Pulling my keys out of my pocket, I strutted out of the front door and over to my car. Just as I opened the door and slid in, I heard him shout, "Hey! Where the hell are you going?"

I winced as I saw Ashton jog out of the house, frowning angrily in my direction. Annoyance bubbled in my stomach because I didn't want him with me. Deciding to leave before he could insist I let him come, I threw the car into drive and shoved my foot down on the gas. Instead of watching me leave like I'd assumed he would, he jumped into the path of the car. My eyes widened in horror as I slammed my foot down on the brake and held my breath, waiting for the thud of his body to hit the car. It didn't, instead almost as soon as the car stopped, the passenger door opened and he climbed in, still glaring at me.

"No! Get the fuck out of my car!"

"You were going to leave the estate?" he snapped incredulously.

"Yes! I've got things to do, and you can't come," I ranted, giving him my best warning glare and slamming my hand down on the steering wheel in frustration.

"Anna, you can't just leave without me! I mean, have you even told Dean you were leaving?" he asked, running his hand through his hair.

"No. I'll only be an hour or so. Just get out, Agent Taylor," I spat nastily.

"No. For Christ's sake, you can't just leave without me!" he growled, shaking his head fiercely.

I closed my eyes and tried to calm myself as I realised I wasn't going to win this argument. "Fine."

I put the car back into drive and sped out of the driveway. I smirked as he quickly snapped on his seatbelt and gripped the door handle so tightly that his knuckles went white. I sped down the narrow lanes that I knew like the back of my hand until I got to the small row of shops that constituted Main Street. Taking the last space available, I turned to look at Ashton. I smiled wickedly at his tense jaw and straight back. *That'll teach you for not getting out of my car!*

"I'm just going to jump out, why don't you wait here for me?" I teased, knowing he'd follow me regardless of what I'd said. I leant into the back and snagged my purse before climbing out of the car and heading into the florist. While I purchased a bunch of daisies, Ashton hovered behind me, silently looking around the empty store as if some knife-wielding madman was going to jump out and butcher me.

When we finally made our way back to the car, he winced. "Can I drive?" The hopefulness to his voice was unmistakable.

I raised one eyebrow and shook my head in answer, smirking at him. *Maybe next time you'll learn and just stay at home.* He groaned, and I noticed with some measure of satisfaction that he fastened his seatbelt as soon as he was in his seat before gripping the door handle tightly again.

A small smile graced my lips as my foot pressed down onto the accelerator and the car lurched along the road. Dodging and overtaking cars that were in my way, I finally arrived at my destination. Ashton glanced at me quickly as I pulled into the parking lot of the cemetery. Understanding and sorrow crossed his face, and I tightened my hands around the steering wheel until my skin pinched and started to burn.

"Is there anything I can say or do to make you wait here for me?" I asked quietly. I didn't want him here. I needed privacy for this.

He cleared his throat awkwardly. "I'm sorry, Anna, but I can't."

My heart sank. I took a shaky breath to try and calm myself and then nodded, grabbed the flowers from the backseat and walked off without waiting for him. I could hear him a few steps behind, but he didn't try to catch up with me. As I walked the familiar path to Jack's grave, I stopped to collect any dandelions that I saw on the way. Finally, I reached it.

JACKSON IAN ROBERTS
January 19, 1992 - March 12, 2008
Beloved son, brother, and friend
Taken from us too soon. We will miss you
Sleep tight.

I ran my fingers over the letters of his name before collecting the wilted flowers and sweeping the fallen leaves from his grave. I put the daisies on the grass and sprinkled the dandelions over the top of the marble headstone before sitting down.

I swallowed the lump in my throat. "Hey, Jack. I just wanted to come and say hi and to let you know that I miss you, even though you probably know that already." I smiled weakly and ran my hand over the grass. "Not much new to tell you really…" I paused, trying to think of what had happened since I was here last. "I got my car fixed, so it's not making that humming noise anymore. Oh, and I finally threw out my old sneakers, you know the yellow ones that you hated? Well they finally ripped and the sole came totally off, so that should make you happy," I sighed deeply. "I got a new near guard because Agent Jenks quit last week. I told you he couldn't handle it. He only lasted a month, the lightweight." I chuckled wickedly. I'd known that guy wouldn't last very long; I had seen it in his eyes.

"Er… I got a text from your mom asking me to come over for dinner sometime this week but, to be honest, I don't think I'll go. I hope you don't mind, but I just can't stand going to your house; it's just too hard and I can't do it anymore. I know you understand." My teeth sank into my bottom lip as I tried not to let the sadness take over. I picked a few strands of grass to distract myself.

"Your brother's doing well. From what I've heard he's a real star on the football field, so maybe those games you two played as kids, paid off. Apparently, he's a bit of a ladies' man too; he's getting himself quite the reputation for being a player."

I looked up at the sky; it was a beautiful day, perfect, not a cloud in sight. "I got kicked out of school again," I said quietly, a little embarrassed. "I know, I know, it's the second one this school year and the semester only started like a month and a half ago. You're probably up there laughing your ass off at me, but hey, whatever, right? Look to the future, that's what you always used to say. But it's so hard, Jack, so hard." A tear finally escaped down my cheek. I fought hard to keep them at bay; I didn't like to cry here, I didn't like the thought of crying in front of him in case I made him sad.

I pinched the skin on the inside of my elbow to distract myself from the pain that was building up inside me. "So anyway, as of next week, I'm going to ASU." That was the latest college my dad could bribe me into. "I'm really going to try there because this is the last time I can start over. If I can't do it, then I'm just going to drop out and give up. I know we promised that we'd never give up on our dreams, but it's just too hard for me to keep starting over and over." I wiped my face and took a few deep breaths, pushing away the grief that was trying to pull me under. "I won't be able to come here as much to see you because it's a few hours away, but that doesn't mean I'm not thinking of you and missing you because I do that whether I'm here or not, and I know that you know that." I smiled through my heartbreak. He had to know how much I missed him, I told him every day.

I sat in silence for a few minutes, listening to the birds singing in the tree nearby. "I guess I'd better go," I conceded, standing up. I kissed my fingertips and traced his name one more time. "I'm so sorry. Please forgive me. I love you, Jack, and I always will," I vowed, wiping another tear that escaped. I needed to go before I broke down; I didn't want him to see that. "Bye, baby." I turned on my heel and walked away.

Ashton was leaning against a tree about ten feet away from Jack's grave. He was close enough to have heard everything that I said, I was sure of it. His face was the mask of sympathy, but he didn't say anything; he just walked alongside me silently.

When we got to the car, he opened the driver's door for me. "Will you drive?" I asked quietly, holding out the keys to him.

"Sure thing," he answered, following me around to the passenger side and opening the door for me before going back to get in his side. After a few minutes of driving in silence, he looked over at me. "You okay?"

"Yep," I lied, trying to pretend that my heart wasn't breaking all over again the same as it did every time I left Jack's grave.

"I'm sorry I couldn't give you more privacy."

I nodded, not wanting to talk about it. "It's fine," I mumbled, looking out of my window, swallowing the sobs that were fighting to break free.

His hand closed over mine in silent support. It was a small gesture and one that normally would have had me freaking out and my body in a nervous state, but actually it felt nice, comforting, reassuring, and it made me feel safe. I squeezed his hand a little as a 'thank you' and carried on staring out of my window at the fields and trees that whizzed past.

As soon as we pulled into the drive, I saw Dean leaning up against the porch, his arms folded over his chest and a scowl on his face. Ashton groaned. "That's just perfect! Well, it was nice working with you, Anna," he mumbled, shaking his head.

I scoffed. "Yeah right, you think you'll get in trouble? Dean won't say anything, you don't need to worry," I assured him, climbing out of the car.

I forced a polite smile as Dean pushed himself away from the wall, glaring at me. "Where the fuck have you been, Annabelle?" he spat.

I raised one eyebrow. "Wow, language, Agent Michaels, there are ladies present," I joked, nodding in Ashton's direction.

My far guard didn't laugh. "Annabelle, how many times do I have to tell you? You can't just leave without me. Where the hell have you been anyway?" His eyes darted around the long driveway, probably checking to see if anyone saw us.

I rolled my eyes. "Oh, just chill! I came back, didn't I? You're just pissed because you had to cover for me again."

His murderous glare turned in Ashton's direction. "Why didn't you tell me you were going? Shit, Taylor, I know you're new to all this but I'll give you a clue, you're near guard, I'm far guard, we *both* need to guard!"

I laughed at his annoyance. Technically he should have been used to this happening by now; I snuck out at least twice a week when I was here at the lake house. "Aww, Dean, are you jealous I took him with me and not you? Are you feeling a little left out?" I teased in a singsong voice.

Ashton didn't look amused; his eyes narrowed in a clear 'shut the hell up' warning. "Dean, I didn't know we were going, I barely got in the car before she drove off," he interjected innocently.

My far guard turned back to me. "Where did you go?"

"That's none of your fucking business, Agent," I retorted, now just as annoyed as he was.

"Taylor?" he prompted, looking back Ashton. I looked at my new guard pleadingly, silently begging him not to say anything. Once the guards knew I went there when I snuck out, I'd never get peace there again.

Ashton sighed. "Look, Anna would rather I not say," he answered, sidestepping Dean and wrapping his hand around my upper arm. "We're back now. I apologise, she apologises, let's leave it at that. It won't happen again," he said sternly, giving me a gentle push in the direction of the house.

As soon as we were inside the house, I pulled my arm out of his grasp. "I didn't apologise," I stated sarcastically.

He laughed and nodded. "I noticed," he replied, smiling. "So, considering as I just took one for you and kept your secret, how about you show me this lake?"

I rolled my eyes. "You haven't seen the lake yet?" He shook his head in response. "Come with me." I turned and stalked towards my bedroom, listening to him trudge along behind me. When I got to my room I gestured towards my window and the beautiful view of the lake that I had. "There it is, Pretty Boy."

He laughed and rolled his eyes. "Right, well thanks, but I was thinking we could get a boat or something, maybe go for a swim? We need to get to know each other ready for next week. I know nothing about you other than what I've read in your file."

My heart sank. *A file? I have a file?* "What kind of file?" I asked, not really wanting to know the answer.

His face fell, and he shifted on his feet uncomfortably. "Er, well, you have a file that gave me all the information I need for my job. You know, like your schools, your routine. A brief overview of your character. It had some stuff about Jackson."

I stiffened. "Jack. He liked Jack, not Jackson. He hated being called Jackson." I frowned down at my feet.

"Right, okay. There wasn't really that much in there about you and what you like and don't like. If I'm gonna pretend to be your boyfriend, I figure I should at least know some stuff about you." He bent his head, trying to catch my eye.

I gulped. He hadn't said anything about Carter, did he know about Carter? "Did it say anything about Carter in my file?" I asked, my voice breaking when I said his name. Bile rose in my throat. I hated to talk about him, my therapist made me talk about him which wasn't good for my whole staying emotionless plan.

He nodded. "Yeah it did," was all he said.

The frustrated anger came out of nowhere. "Right, of course it did. I should have known, I forgot that I'm not entitled to privacy anymore," I snapped. A tear fell down my cheek, so I swiped it away angrily. I hated the fact that everyone knew; it was no one else's business.

"I'm sorry, Anna, I needed the information to help keep you safe." Ashton took hold of my hand, squeezing it gently.

I snorted, wrenching my hand out of grasp. "How the hell would knowing that stuff keep me safe? That's private stuff, no one should know about it! I don't want anyone to know!" I shouted, making him flinch. My blood felt like it was boiling in my veins. Everyone always thought they knew what was best for me, but in reality, they all just made it ten times worse. I didn't need their pity.

"It didn't go into details. Just an overview," he countered, frowning, looking a little concerned I was going to break or something.

"Oh, it didn't go into details? You want the details, Ashton? You want me to tell you why I wake up screaming every night? Want me to tell you how I tried to kill myself by slitting my wrists and the fucker saved me just so he could live in some little, sick fantasy where we played house? You want to know that apparently he was in love with me, love at first sight he said? That's why he killed Jack right in front of me, because he wanted me to himself! He had Jack beaten so badly that I can still hear the sounds of his bones snapping, I can still see the terrified look in his eyes just before they threw him over the fire escape," I ranted, taking a shaky breath.

Ashton had gone pale.

"You want to know that exactly a week after my sixteenth birthday, he raped me and took my virginity? And then he raped me every day after that? You want to know that he got me pregnant and was so angry about it that he threw me down the stairs and then kicked me in the stomach repeatedly until I had a miscarriage? Huh, you want to know that? Shall I carry on?" I shouted. He flinched and shook his head; his eyes alight with both concern and horror.

I couldn't stop, it was pouring out of me now. "Did it say in my file that I didn't leave his house the whole time I was there? That I wasn't allowed to eat every day, that if I said something he didn't like or didn't do as I was asked, that he would beat me until I blacked out?" My chin wobbled at the memories. "Did it say in the file that he tried to be the perfect boyfriend? Or that he gave me everything a girl could ask for – designer clothes, shoes, purses, flowers, chocolates? I had laptops that couldn't go on the internet. I had the latest cell phone that could only dial his number. He even got me a puppy which he let me keep just long enough for me to fall in love with it before he drowned it in the pool for peeing on the carpet. Every night in my dreams I see him kill Jack. He was murdered because of me. Did it say any of that in my file?" I asked venomously. "Do you want to know what hurts me the most everyday? The fact that I would have gone with him willingly if he would have just let Jack go. I would go through that for the rest of my life if it meant Jack could have lived. He didn't deserve to die, especially not because of me," I whispered, unable to keep the tears away any longer.

"Anna, I'm so sorry," Ashton croaked, stepping forward and wrapping his arms around me.

I sobbed uncontrollably against his chest as his arms tightened around me. I'd never told anyone that; I'd refused to give the police any details, just the basic facts. I didn't want to press charges against him because I couldn't talk about it; I couldn't tell anyone what he'd done to me. And that was the first time I'd ever mentioned the fact that I'd had a miscarriage.

When I finally managed to calm myself, he pulled away and looked at me tenderly; his eyes were soft and warm and filled with compassion. "I'm sorry this happened to you, but I promise he won't ever hurt you again," he said fiercely, his jaw becoming tight.

I shook my head at his words. "Don't worry, Ashton, he can't hurt me anymore, no one can. I have nothing left to lose," I said honestly.

This seemed to upset him, and a pained look crossed his face. "Don't say that, I can't hear that," he whispered, looking at me pleadingly. I pushed him away and stalked to the bathroom, locking myself in and taking another shower to try and rid myself of the dirty feeling that always crept over me when I thought about Carter.

Chapter Five

When I got out of the shower, I felt much better. It actually felt good to have said all of that out loud, for someone to finally know some of what I went through. I never thought it would, but saying the words out loud took some of the anger away that was always boiling just under the surface.

I sat on my bed wrapped in my towel. So far, Ashton had been nothing but nice to me, and I'd repaid him by blurting out all of that horrible stuff and being a bitch to him. My gaze fell on my drawer that housed my swimwear. I chewed on my lip. I somehow felt like I owed him something – and he wanted to see the lake. Maybe, just for today, I could cut him some slack. It would be nice to take in some sunshine, and I loved the lake too.

I sighed as I made up my mind. Gripping my hair, I scraped it back into a messy bun before heading over to my drawers and pulling out my black, all in one swimsuit. After slipping it on, I covered it with a pair of baggy jeans and a long tee.

When I knocked on Ashton's bedroom door I heard bedsprings creak from inside before he opened it, seeming surprised to see me.

I smiled awkwardly. "Hi."

"Hi," he replied softly. He still looked upset.

I took a deep breath. "So, I'm sorry I went off on one at you. I shouldn't have said all those things to you, that wasn't fair of me, so I apologise."

He smiled weakly. "You don't have to apologise, Anna. I want you to be able to tell me things and trust me with it. I promise I won't say anything to anyone if you don't want me to."

I nodded. "Thanks. Well, I was wondering if you still wanted to go for that swim." I winced, waiting for him to tell me to take a hike or something for being such a bitch to him. Instead, he grinned and his whole face lit up.

"Yeah, I do," he said cheerfully.

"Okay, well I've asked Sarah to take you," I teased, laughing.

"Ha ha, you're hilarious," he muttered sarcastically, reaching for my hand and giving me a tug into his bedroom.

I glanced at the bed; the pillows were propped up against the headboard, and my book was face down on the middle of the bed. I grinned and pointed to it. "So, where you up to?"

"Edward and Bella have just arrived at the baseball field," he replied, going to his drawers and grabbing a pair of black shorts. "I'm just gonna go put these on. You need to get a swimsuit on or something?" he asked, heading towards his bathroom.

"No, I've already got mine on," I answered, shrugging.

"Oh yeah? What would have happened if I'd said I didn't want to go?" he asked, raising his eyebrows.

I shrugged easily. "I would've taken Dean. He was obviously feeling left out earlier. He wouldn't turn me down," I joked, smiling at him.

He laughed and shook his head. "I wouldn't turn you down either." He smiled and then disappeared into the bathroom.

I sat on his bed and grabbed the book just for something to do. He had his page marked so I flicked it open and a photo fell out that he was using as a bookmark. I turned it over to look at it. It was of him and four other guys. He had his arm around a blond guy next to him; they were all grinning and laughing, but that wasn't the reason why I couldn't look away from it.

All five of them were dressed in black SWAT uniforms. Ashton had a huge gun hanging off his shoulder and another smaller gun strapped to this side. He looked so sexy that my mouth actually started to water and my body started to get hot all over. I couldn't drag my eyes away from his smiling face in the photo, he looked so happy. I silently wondered who the other guys were and if they were close. The uniform was the hottest thing I'd ever seen.

"Hey, don't lose my page."

I jumped a mile, shoving the photo back into the book and snapping it shut. I hadn't even heard him come back into the room because I was too busy perving on his photo. "Er yeah right, I won't." I dropped the book quickly, praying I wasn't blushing.

"You ready to go then?" he asked, folding two towels and putting them under his arm.

"Yep. Did you want to take a row boat over to the floating dock?" I asked as we walked through the house.

"Sounds good. Let's stop and get snacks first," he suggested, rubbing his flat stomach in a small circle. His hand closed around mine as we walked and I looked down at it, unsure what to think or feel. His plan was to hold hands a little each day so that I'd get used to it before we went to school, but I hadn't expected it to actually work. But with his warm hand wrapped around mine, I realised that I actually quite liked the feel of it.

After a quick stop in the kitchen to grab several packs of cookies and chips, some fruit and a couple of bottles of water, I led him through the vast grounds and over to the little jetty around the back of my parents' property.

"Which one do you want to take?" I questioned, nodding at the row boats that were tied there. They were all the same, just painted different colours.

"How about blue, that's my favourite colour," he said and I smiled as he climbed into the boat, setting down the bag of food he'd insisted on carrying.

When he turned back to help me, I scoffed and knocked his hand away. "I'm not some damsel that needs everything doing for her," I muttered, shaking my head as I jumped lightly into the boat.

He sighed dramatically and sat down. "Right I forgot, Little Miss Independent." He rolled his eyes, smiling at me.

I grinned and grabbed the oars, starting to row in the general direction of the floating dock. "You can row back," I offered, chuckling at his disgruntled expression.

"You're not letting me be very romantic," he grumbled, crossing his arms in mock annoyance.

"Why the hell would you want to be romantic?" I asked, laughing.

"Well, I'm not making a very good impression on our first date, am I?" he replied, pouting.

Oh my God, date? He doesn't think this is an actual date, does he? "This isn't a date," I said quietly.

He laughed. "Yeah, it kinda is. You are my girlfriend after all," he countered, shrugging.

I stiffened at the word 'girlfriend'. "No I'm not. My boyfriend died. You're just doing your job," I retorted, glaring at him angrily.

His face dropped and his eyes tightened. "Anna, I was just kidding. I meant if people ask, we can say this was our first date. I mean, we've gotta have stories and stuff, right?" he continued cautiously.

I sighed and ignored him, rowing harder until we reached the floating dock that was almost in the middle of the lake. When the boat bumped against the edge of the dock, he jumped out, tying it securely before holding his hand down to help me up.

"I don't need your help," I protested, annoyed again.

He sighed deeply. "Listen, Anna, this is what guys do for their girls. We need to start acting like a couple now so that it'll be easier next week. It's not a big deal; I just want to help you out of the boat. Please stop being difficult," he countered, grabbing my hand and helping me onto the deck. "Jeez, you're stubborn." He shook his head, laughing. "Most girls would've fallen for my charm by now," he boasted, smiling at me.

I snorted at his cocky attitude. "If you're expecting me to fall for you, then you're going to be very disappointed," I said seriously.

He chuckled. "I know, I can tell," he answered, grinning. I rolled my eyes at him and took my jeans off, plopping down on the dock in just my long, baggy T-shirt. I grabbed an apple out of the bag, nibbling on it absentmindedly.

When he stripped down to his shorts, exposing that incredible toned and tanned body that looked like something out of a celebrity magazine, I slipped on my shades so that he wouldn't see my eyes wander in his direction. I forced my gaze away from him and focussed on my apple. I actually felt immensely guilty for looking at him in that way. I had never looked at a man the way I kept looking at Ashton, not since Jack. No one ever caught my interest, and I felt like I was being unfaithful to Jack's memory by looking at my new guard.

Ashton sat down next to me, stretching out his long legs. "Let's start with the getting to know each other. What's your favourite colour?" he asked casually.

"Green," I answered, closing my eyes and lying back on the wooden dock. I loved it out here; the way the dock rocked slightly on the water was soothing. I often came out here and just lay in the peace and quiet.

"Favourite flower?"

"Dandelion," I replied, then bit my lip. "I mean roses, white roses," I amended, frowning.

"Dandelions? You like weeds? Why?" he asked, eyeing me curiously.

Oh for goodness' sake! Why does this guy want to know everything about me and always see through my lies? I sighed. "Jack gave me a big bunch of dandelions when he asked me out when we were five," I admitted, smiling at the memory.

He laughed. "That's sweet. He sounds like he was a nice guy." I nodded, and he smiled at me. "Maybe he was a bit cheap though," he added jokingly.

I smiled and looked at him. "He was a great guy, you'd have liked him, everyone liked him." I rolled onto my front, putting my arms under my chin, watching the water ripple around the dock.

There was an uncomfortable silence for a few minutes before he spoke again. "Favourite food? Mine's a tuna melt baked potato because that's about the only thing I can cook," he laughed.

"Seriously, you can't cook? Do you still live with your parents? Does your mommy do everything for you? I bet she still washes your clothes," I teased, grinning at him.

A sad smile crossed his face. "My parents died when I was ten, I grew up in foster homes," he replied. "And no, I can't cook. I'm pretty good at burning stuff though."

I winced and looked at him apologetically because of my insensitive joke about his mom. "I'm sorry, I didn't know. I shouldn't have said that."

He smiled and shook his head, shrugging casually. "It's fine; it was a long time ago. Favourite food?"

"Er, chocolate fudge cake? I'm a dessert girl," I admitted, smiling, grateful for the change of subject.

He laughed. "Right, I should have guessed by the size of you," he joked, poking me in the ribs.

"Hey, don't make fun of a girl's weight!" I scolded, trying to look stern. I knew he was joking though; I worked out a lot, so my figure was toned, I just hid it under baggy clothes so no one could see.

"Whoa there, sorry, ma'am," he replied, holding up his hands in an 'I surrender' fashion. My stomach fluttered when he called me 'ma'am'. From his mouth, it actually sounded incredibly sexy.

The questioning continued for about another hour and in that time I learnt a lot about him. He'd graduated two days ago – this was his first proper assignment. He'd never been undercover before. He was originally from Boston but moved around a lot because of the foster homes. He had no other family or siblings. His best friend from the academy was called Nate, and he was like a brother to him. They shared an apartment in LA. Apparently, he *did* know how to wash his own clothes. His dream job was SWAT Front Line.

He was really easy to talk to and was actually a funny guy. We ate while we talked, and boy he can eat a lot! I'd never seen anyone pack away as much food as he did, not without feeling sick anyway.

"How long shall we say we've been together?" he asked cautiously as he polished off the last pack of chips.

I shrugged. "I don't care." It honestly didn't matter how long we said we'd been together. It wasn't like a load of people were going to be hanging around and chatting to us about our relationship.

"I think we should go for a year. That way we won't have to be too touchy-feely. People are usually over that first passion thing by a year, aren't they?" he asked thoughtfully. I glanced at him and laughed as I realised why he seemed so unsure. "What?" he asked, grinning.

"Have you never had a relationship before?" I asked curiously. It seemed impossible that a gorgeous guy like him was without a girlfriend.

"Nope, not really. I mean, I've been out with girls but never seriously. You'll be my first," he joked, winking at me.

I raised one eyebrow knowingly. "And by never seriously, you mean you screw girls for fun before you screw them over," I retorted.

He frowned, looking a little hurt. "I don't screw girls over! I just never really met anyone I wanted to be with properly before, and even if I had met the right girl, I wouldn't have had time, my training took up a lot of my time," he protested, shrugging.

"You're a player."

"I am not!" he protested adamantly.

I nodded, giving him a sarcastic expression and laughed. "Whatever! Wanna swim?" I stood up, throwing my shades down onto his pile of clothes.

"Sure. Is the water warm?" he asked, sticking his foot in. He immediately gasped and jerked his foot out. "Holy shit! That's freezing. We can't swim in that," he mumbled, shaking his foot to dry it.

"Oh quit being a baby, I thought you were a tough guy," I teased.

"Yeah, I can fight and shoot bullets, but man, that is cold!" he whined like a little girl.

I pulled my T-shirt off over my head. When I looked back at him, he was staring at me, his mouth was slightly open, and his eyes were wide and raking over my body slowly. My stomach tightened into a knot when I realised he was checking me out. I wanted to pull the shirt back on and run, but there was something in his eyes that made me want to trust him; I knew he wouldn't hurt me. So instead of putting the shirt back on, I folded it up deliberately slowly before dropping it on top of my jeans.

He hadn't moved. It was like he was stuck on the spot, just staring at me. Taking advantage of his distraction, I stalked over to his side, smiling sweetly. When I got closer to him, my heart started to speed up fractionally, but it wasn't from fear. When I was close enough, I raised my hands, putting them on his chest, making his full lips part and his eyes tighten. I grinned wickedly and shoved on his chest as hard as I could. Distracted, he lost his footing and stumbled backwards into the lake.

I burst out laughing as he broke the surface again, gasping and immediately swimming for the ladder. "Holy shit, that's cold!" he rasped. I quickly moved to the ladder, sitting down and dangling my legs into the cold water so that he couldn't get out. "Come on, let me out, it's freezing!" he whined, half climbing out of the water so that we were at the same level.

"No way. You're in now, you'll get used to it in a minute or two," I said confidently.

A wicked smile slipped onto his face as his arm snaked around my waist. I gasped, knowing too late what was happening. His body twisted and he threw me into the water. The cold shocked my body and made me stiffen automatically; I kicked for the top and gasped when my head broke the surface.

"Oh shit," I groaned, squeezing my eyes shut, kicking my legs to stay afloat as the cold water attacked my system.

"Bet you want to get out now, huh?" he asked from behind me. I looked back at him; he was standing on the dock, his hair dripping. The sunlight kissed his wet skin, making him look sexy as hell.

"Oh come on, Pretty Boy, you afraid of a little cold water?" I jeered, swimming off.

I heard a splash and knew that he had dived back in; seconds later he grabbed my ankle. I laughed as I tried to carry on swimming, but he just pulled me back to him. I turned around and splashed him in the face, which just started a splashing war. It was fun and I hadn't had fun for years. His easy smile and the beautiful surroundings made me feel more relaxed and unlike the uptight, frightened girl I had become. I felt younger somehow.

After a while, my teeth started to chatter noisily and my body was shivering uncontrollably. "Come on, let's get back to the dock and get dried off before we get hypothermia," he suggested, turning his back to me.

I quickly grabbed around his neck and wrapped my legs around his waist so I was on his back. "I'm too cold, you'll have to carry me, tough guy," I joked through my chattering teeth.

He laughed quietly but didn't protest. As he swam for the dock I could feel his warmth seeping into my skin from everywhere our bodies touched. When we got to the dock, I climbed off his back and forced my shaking legs to climb the ladder. Picking up the two fluffy towels, I wrapped one around my body and turned, holding the other out towards him.

When I laid eyes on him, my stomach dropped into my toes. He was just pulling himself out of the lake. The water was running down his goosebump-covered body, and I secretly envisioned rubbing the towel all over him. *Actually, screw the towel; I want to rub my hands all over him…*

"Great idea, Anna, swimming in the lake. Next time let's go to a pool," he suggested, roughly rubbing his hand in his hair, flicking droplets of water everywhere.

I laughed awkwardly at the thoughts that were playing out inside my head. All of them involved me being about three feet closer to him. "You were the one who chose the lake. We do have a heated indoor swimming pool and a Jacuzzi. If you wanted that then you should have said," I countered, grinning.

His mouth popped open in shock. "Damn it! You have a heated pool yet you've just made me swim in icy water?"

"Oh yeah, but where's the romance in a heated pool, huh?" I joked.

He closed the distance between us and took his towel from my hand. A sexy smile tugged at the corners of his mouth as he twisted it in his hands before looping it around the back of my neck, pulling me closer to him. I gasped and stiffened, shocked by the close proximity. My heart was beating way too fast as he leant in even closer, my stomach was clenching. It was one thing for my mind to play out a little fantasy of our bodies pressing together, but now that it was real and I wasn't in control, I started to panic.

As his mouth inched towards mine and his breath blew across my lips, I jerked my knee up towards his groin. Obviously predicting my strike, he jumped backwards, laughing to himself as he avoided my blow.

"You're right, a freezing cold lake is much more romantic," he agreed, still chuckling to himself. My breathing started to slow down, my heart rate returned to normal now that he was further away from me.

"You're an idiot," I muttered, taking his towel off my shoulders and throwing it at him. He grinned and caught it effortlessly, rubbing his hair with it, making it stick out at all angles while I pulled on my clothes over the top of my damp swimsuit.

"You ready to go?" he asked finally, picking up his folded clothes and the bag containing empty wrappers from all of the food he'd consumed.

"Yep," I confirmed, climbing into the boat.

He rowed on the way back and I closed my eyes, leaning my head back, enjoying the last of the sunshine. I'd had a nice day. I hadn't thought that for a long time.

Chapter Six

As we stepped in through the front door, Sarah looked up from her dusting task, and a large, predatory smile crept onto her face. Ashton sighed next to me but smiled back. When she set down her duster and sauntered towards him, swaying her hips, something settled in the pit of my stomach, something unfamiliar and unwelcome. My eyebrows knitted together when I realised that it was actually a slightly jealous feeling. The feeling actually scared me because in spending the day with him and getting to know him a little, I realised that I actually enjoyed his company. That was the worst thing that could happen to me. I didn't want to spend time with people, grow to like them and let them into my life, only to have them march right out again and leave me. For the last few years, since Jack had died, I'd deliberately alienated myself so that wouldn't happen. I couldn't get hurt again, so this was like a pre-emptive strike before they abandoned me.

Clenching my jaw, I shook my head at myself and forced the jealous feeling away. There was no way in hell I was letting myself get jealous over a bodyguard; Sarah was welcome to him.

Needing to distract myself from the fact that I'd almost done the unthinkable and made a friend, I decided to go to the gym for a while. "See you later," I muttered, stalking off to my bedroom as Sarah twirled a lock of her hair around her finger and looked at Ashton through her eyelashes. After changing into workout clothes, I marched downstairs and into the gym. Not bothering to stretch beforehand, I stepped onto the treadmill and turned it on slowly while I put on my iPod and cranked it up as high as I could stand.

My run started out at a gentle jog but, as usual, quickly changed into something else entirely. Running was my thing. Running made my body ache and gave me something to focus on when I was struggling to keep myself sane everyday. I gritted my teeth as my legs burned from the effort of running at a flat out sprint for over twenty minutes. I was going to have to stop soon.

Wanting to enjoy thinking about nothing other than the physical pain for a few minutes more, I cranked up the speed even faster. I was running so fast that I could barely keep up. I could only run for another couple of minutes before I started to get a little light-headed and my hands started to tingle, so I slowed it down until I could stop.

As soon as I stopped, my legs refused to support me any longer. I slumped to the floor gasping for breath as I put my head between my knees, listening to the lyrics of the Usher song I had blasting through my iPod. When the tingles had subsided from my fingers and I no longer wanted to vomit, I flopped back onto my back and closed my eyes.

Suddenly my earphones were pulled from my ears. Shocked because I hadn't realised someone else was here, I opened my eyes to see Ashton standing over me, frowning. "Why do you do that to yourself? Shit, Anna, I watched you run as fast as you could for fifteen minutes and you were already sprinting when I came in!" he cried incredulously.

I gritted my teeth, ignoring his obvious agitation, and pushed myself up to sitting. "Whatever," I dismissed. "Want to show me how you keep blocking my hits all the time?"

"You want me to fight you?" he asked, raising one eyebrow in disbelief.

"I don't want you to hit me if that's what you're thinking, but I actually thought I was pretty good at self-defence until I met you," I admitted.

He shook his head. "Anna, I think you need to rest, surely you've done enough for today," he countered, his expression turning hard.

I stood up; my legs wobbled and threatened to give out on me. "Ashton, this is my routine, usually it's a morning routine but I had somewhere to be this morning, so I'm doing it now instead. I always run then have a few minutes with the punch bag. If you want to help me then great, if you don't then just get out and stop interrupting me before I cool down," I growled as I pushed past him, grabbing the training gloves from the side and putting them on. I then proceeded to punch and kick the stuffing out of the punch bag.

He sighed. "I'll show you a few things if you want. But you need to stop this. This isn't good for you, you shouldn't train like this. It's crazy," he replied sharply.

I huffed and turned around to face him. He wasn't dressed for training; he was still wearing the jeans and T-shirt he'd worn to the lake. He took off his shoes and socks, and then his T-shirt and belt so he was just wearing his jeans.

He looked at me cockily. "Take your shoes off then, we're only practicing, I don't wanna get hurt."

I smiled, knowing that he didn't think I was going to be able to hit him. To be honest, I probably wouldn't. I'd tried three times already and hadn't gotten anywhere near him. I slipped off my shoes and walked over to the training mats.

I turned back to Ashton, who was standing there looking like a cocky, arrogant Greek God. "I'm gonna attack you and I want you to fight me off. You can really hit me, it's fine. After, I'll tell you where you can improve, okay?" he instructed, looking like he genuinely didn't want to do this.

I nodded and waited for him to approach. When he moved towards me, I quickly ducked out of the way, kicking my leg out towards his stomach. His hand wrapped around my ankle, holding it still as he swept my other leg out from under me. I slammed back into the padded mat with him on top of me.

"Holy shit!" I gasped, trying to get the air back into my lungs. *That was freaking awesome!*

"You okay?" he asked, looking a bit concerned as he hovered above me.

I nodded. "Again," I instructed, pushing him up. He shook his head, frowning, but helped me to my feet regardless of his noticeable unwillingness to do this.

Within a minute I was on the floor again. I groaned as I rolled onto my side and pushed myself to my feet. My whole body was aching from my run, but I refused to quit. I faced him, watching as he winced. "Again," I barked, bringing my arms up to protect my face. He sighed heavily and moved to attack me.

After the fifth time of landing flat on my back, he pinned me to the floor, his body pressing into mine. "Enough now," he said sternly. He wasn't even slightly out of breath, whereas I was panting and sweating like a pig.

"No, not yet," I whined, struggling to talk through my wheezy breath.

"That's enough for today, Anna. I can't do this. Look at you! If you want, I'll teach you, but you need to slow down, you can't keep doing this to yourself," he protested.

"Just one more time. Please?" I begged, trying to wriggle my arms free.

"Okay, one more, if you'll tell me why you do this to your body. Why do you train so hard?" he bargained, frowning.

I gulped, knowing I needed to tell the truth if I wanted him to train me. "I want to be able to defend myself, and if the time comes and I ever see him again, I want to be able to kill him," I confided.

He blinked. "It looks to me like you're trying to kill yourself too," he observed, concern clear across his face.

I shrugged at his comment. "Whatever. Him, me, what's the difference? Either way it doesn't matter," I retorted, turning my head away from his intense gaze.

He sucked in a shaky breath and his grip loosened on my wrists before he pushed himself up, pulling me to my feet. A pained looked was etched on his face as he spoke, "One more then like I promised, and then that's it for today. Agreed?"

"Agreed." I shifted into a slight crouch, preparing for him to attack me again.

He moved and came at me from the side. I quickly whipped around and landed a punch to his side, but he barely seemed to notice. Grabbing my shoulders, he knocked my feet out and we both landed on the floor within about five seconds.

A defeated tear fell down my face and he quickly wiped it away. "Did I hurt you? Are you okay?" he asked urgently.

I shook my head. I wasn't in pain; I just couldn't believe that all this time I thought I was getting somewhere, that I would be able to inflict some real damage to Carter if I ever saw him again, and now nothing. I couldn't even land a decent enough hit to cause any pain. My world was shattering around me; everything I'd worked for over the last three years, the hours of training I'd put in, they weren't worth shit.

"I'm fine. Not hurt," I croaked, willing myself not to break down.

"Then why are you crying?" he asked, wiping my tears away again.

"I just thought I'd be able to at least defend myself, but I can't even do that!" I croaked, squeezing my eyes shut, trying to gain control of my emotions.

"Hey, you can defend yourself. You can. Anna, I've been trained extensively; I was the best in hand-to-hand combat in my year. I'm SWAT, Anna, you wouldn't be able to beat me, but I'll help you, I will. If you were fighting a normal guy, you could kick his ass, I swear," he assured me, wiping the sweat from my forehead.

I groaned and closed my eyes. I didn't even realise he was still on top of me until he put his head down in the crook of my neck and planted a soft kiss on my shoulder.

Shockwaves radiated through my whole body. I stiffened. "Get off, get off me, now!" I almost screamed. He jumped up and backed away quickly, his hands up, obviously trying not to scare me. I rolled to my side and pushed myself up. My whole body was shaking violently; I scooted to the wall and sat there watching him.

He slumped to the floor on the opposite side of the gym and put his head in his hands. "I'm sorry; I don't know why I did that. Are you okay?" he asked quietly.

I nodded. I was okay, my body was shaking from the shock, but I was okay. "Don't do that again," I croaked around the lump in my throat. He shook his head quickly, watching me with caution.

My chin trembled as I pushed myself up to standing. Immediately, my weary body protested from the movement. I'd really overdone it this time. My legs were wobbly as I made my way out of the gym and up to my bedroom so I could take a bath. I focussed on the pain in my body so that I wouldn't think about what had just happened. It worked, somewhat.

At seven thirty, I knew my presence was required downstairs, as usual. Dinner with the parents. "Hi, honey," my mom chirped, as I walked into the formal dining room.

"Hey," I grunted, plopping myself down at the table.

"Sweetheart, we invited Agent Taylor to dine with us tonight. He'll be down in a minute," my dad said, smiling awkwardly.

"Why? Why would you do that? You've never invited a guard to eat with us before," I asked, a little annoyed.

"Well, he's not like the normal guards, honey; he'll be a lot more involved. He's posing as your boyfriend so you two need to get to know each other ready for next week," my mom replied, smiling cheerfully.

I frowned, trying to work out her apparent excitement. Just then he walked in and all eyes snapped to him. He was wearing black dress pants and a light grey button-down shirt. Obviously dressed to impress my father.

I sighed and averted my eyes, watching my mother who was grinning happily. "Good evening, Agent Taylor," she smiled, nodding at him.

"Good evening, ma'am," he greeted. My father stood and shook his hand. "It's nice to see you again, sir," Ashton said politely.

"You too, son. Have a seat there next to Annabelle," my dad replied, pointing to the chair next to mine. I played with my napkin as Ashton sat down. I could feel his eyes on me, but I refused to look at him.

"Hi, Anna," he said softly.

"Hi," I replied, nodding in acknowledgement, still not looking at him.

"Are you okay? You know, after earlier?" he asked.

I forced a smile and looked over at him. His eyes were showing remorse, he was really feeling guilty; he was almost in pain by the look of it. "I'm fine, honestly." I smiled reassuringly. He looked like he visibly relaxed and smiled back; he was probably relieved I hadn't said anything to my father and ordered his transfer. "So, what's for dinner tonight?" I asked, looking away from his beautiful green eyes and trying to change the subject.

"Er, well I think it's steak," my mom answered, sounding unsure.

I laughed. "Oh, Ashton only eats baked potatoes and cheeseburgers," I joked.

He laughed too, shaking his head. "No, I said I only *cooked* baked potatoes. I eat anything," he corrected, grinning.

I smiled and looked back seeing that my mother was watching me with wide, hopeful eyes. My easy smile faded because she was acting weird.

"Why do you keep looking at me like that?" There was definitely something going on.

"I just… I haven't seen you laugh since before Jack…" she trailed off, her face falling as she probably realised what she was about to say.

I closed my eyes as understanding washed over me. "Right, since Jack died. Now I get it. That's why Ashton's been invited to dinner. You think that suddenly I'm gonna forget Jack and fall all over the hot new guard? Is that your plan?" I asked angrily, glaring at her.

She shook her head in response, wincing. "No, it's just that we've been hearing stories all day, people have seen you making jokes, laughing and smiling. A couple of the staff said that they saw you two holding hands. Everyone's just wondering, that's all."

I turned to my father. "And are you wondering, Dad? Planning on getting to know him better, check and see if he's good enough for your fucked up daughter? What do you think? Does he get your approval?"

"Annabelle, that's enough! You must be able to see our side, the first time you met him you shook his hand, for goodness' sake. Do you know what I would give to be able to do that? To hold your hand, or kiss you goodnight? It's strange for us to witness. We were just wondering if there was something going on, that's all," my dad countered, frowning guiltily.

I snorted, pushing my chair back making a loud scrape on the wooden floor as I stood up. "Yeah, there's something going on," I lied. "He's a really good fuck; he made me scream good and proper. Is that what you wanted to hear? One great screw and I'm over Jack, all my problems just, poof, up into thin air. Are you fucking crazy?" I growled. I glanced down at Ashton, who looked so uncomfortable he was probably thinking about hiding under the table.

"Language, Annabelle! We raised you better than that," my father chastised.

"Right, I forgot. I *was* raised better than that, but you know what? That daughter of yours died the day her boyfriend was murdered! The day everything went to shit, the day my whole fucking perfect life got turned upside down. I'm sorry that I'm not that person anymore, but I'm not going to suddenly get better just because I talked to a guy." I took a deep breath before I continued my angry rant. "That girl you knew, she's gone, and she's not coming back. I wish you'd all get used to it and stop reading something out of nothing. This guy," I pointed at Ashton, "he'll be gone soon, just like all the others, and then you'll be wondering what all the fucking fuss was about," I growled, turning on my heel and walking out, leaving them all sitting there, staring after me with open mouths.

I stormed off to my bedroom, slamming the door behind me and making it rattle on its hinges. Throwing myself down on the bed, I buried my face into a pillow and screamed until my throat was hoarse. I hated that they assumed things that I could never give. I hated that they still expected me to suddenly get over it and move on. I couldn't move on, and I didn't even want to try.

After a little while my stomach growled angrily, obviously chastising me for not waiting until after dinner before making my scene. I sighed and shook my head before getting up and searching out my sketchpad and charcoal before settling on the floor.

Sometime later, there was a knock at my door. "Go away!" I shouted.

Without permission, the door opened and Ashton walked in, smiling sheepishly. "Hey, I know you said go away but I've got something for you."

I scowled at the intrusion. "Unless it's a bottle of vodka, I don't want it."

"It's better than a bottle of vodka," he replied.

My interest was now piqued. "Really, what is it?"

He smiled and sat down next to me, crossing his long legs. He brought his arm out from behind his back and plopped a plate down in front of me. I gasped when I saw what it was, my mouth already filling with saliva at the thought of it. Chocolate fudge cake.

"You should've stuck around, the food was good," he teased, smiling at me.

I burst into a fit of embarrassed giggles. "I'm really sorry about that, I can't believe they did that, and then I said – well, you heard what I said. I'm sorry," I apologised, grimacing.

He shrugged easily. "Hey, it could have been worse; at least you said I was a good fuck."

Another round of giggles escaped as my face flamed with heat. "Sorry," I muttered when I regained control of myself.

"No probs. I thought your dad was gonna kill me though. The look on his face!" he winced, shaking his head but looking amused at the same time.

"What did they say about me when I left?" I asked, cutting a chunk off the cake he'd brought.

"Not much, it was a little awkward. They mostly apologised for jumping to conclusions. They mean well; they're just worried about you. I think they're hoping that you're going to get better, that there's some magical cure out there and that one day you're going to wake up and be their little girl again."

"I'm not that girl anymore," I muttered, eating the last mouthful of cake.

"I know that. I think they got their hopes up though."

I nodded. I knew they wanted a quick fix, but I needed them to understand that I was broken and that no amount of fixing would ever make me right. There was always going to be a piece missing. Ashton cleared his throat.

"Listen, I'm sorry about earlier. What I did in the gym, I shouldn't have done that, and I promise I'll never do it again. It's just that you were upset and I wanted to comfort you. It just happened, that's all. I didn't mean anything by it," he said uncomfortably.

"Let's just forget it, okay?" I suggested, shrugging it off.

He smiled gratefully. "Thanks." He looked down and gasped. "Holy crap, that's awesome!" he cried suddenly, picking up my sketchpad.

I looked down too; I had no idea what I had drawn because I wasn't really paying attention. I looked at the page. It was the deck on the lake with the little row boat tied to the side of it; Ashton was standing on the deck running a hand through his hair. I gulped, embarrassed that I'd drawn a picture of him, half naked, and he'd seen it.

"This is incredible. You're really talented, Anna. You want to be an artist or something?" he asked with wide eyes.

I nodded. "Yeah I guess."

He was staring at the picture in apparent awe. "I've never had anyone draw me before."

"You can have it if you want," I offered, shrugging.

"Seriously?"

"Yeah sure, why not," I said dismissively, taking the sketchpad and tearing it out.

He took it, smiling gratefully. "How come you're not in it?" he asked, looking down at it again.

I shrugged. "How could I be in it? That's my point of view, I can't see myself."

He smiled. "Right yeah, didn't think of that. I wish you were in it though, that'd make the picture better."

"Of course it would because I'm *so* beautiful," I joked, shaking my head in amusement.

"Yeah, that's right. Anyway, I'd better get going to bed, it's getting pretty late." He pushed himself up and was almost at the door when I remembered the photo that he was using as a bookmark.

"Oh, Ashton, wait, I've got something for you." I crawled over to my desk drawer and pulled out the photo frame and bookmark that I sorted out for him earlier so that he wouldn't have to ruin his photo. "Here." I plopped the two items into his hands.

He looked down at them for a long time but didn't speak.

I winced. *He doesn't like the frame.* "Sorry it's a bit girly. You don't have to use it, I just thought it'd keep your photo safe, it obviously means a lot to you for you to bring it with you, so…" I trailed off, wishing I hadn't given it to him in the first place.

His green eyes met mine, seeming like he was struggling to understand something. "This is great. Really thoughtful. Thank you, I love it."

"No problem," I replied uncomfortably, looking away from his intense gaze.

"Well, I'll see you in the morning," he mumbled as he walked out of the door.

"Yeah, good night, and thanks for the cake," I called, smiling gratefully. After changing into pyjama shorts and tank top, I climbed into bed, exhausted.

I'm sitting by the side of the pool. My arm aches. I look down at the enormous bruise that spreads across the top of my arm and covers my shoulder.

"There you are, Princess," Carter says. My insides squirm as he sits down behind me on the lounge chair I'm stretched out on. "Mmm, you look good today," he purrs, slipping his hand inside my bikini top to cup one of my breasts.

"Carter, please, my shoulder's sore."

He sighs dejectedly and pulls me back so I'm leaning against his chest. His other arm wraps around me, pinning me to him. "I love you, Princess," he whispers in my ear.

Disgust washes over me and I struggle not to show it. "Love you too," I choke out. I hate saying the words; each one feels like it rips my heart out. His arm tightens on me as he lets out a contented sigh and lies back to soak up the Miami sunshine. I take a deep breath, knowing this probably won't end well, but I have to ask. "Carter, can I call my mom? It's her birthday today. Please, baby?" I beg, closing my eyes.

His body stiffens and he pulls his hand out of my bikini top quickly. "Princess, for fuck's sake, why do you have to ruin a perfectly good moment by talking about them? I'm your family now, they're nothing to you! Why can't you just be happy? I make you happy, don't I? I give you everything, but you're so fucking ungrateful!" he shouts, pushing me away from him and climbing off the sun lounger. His angry eyes latch onto mine and I try not to flinch.

I nod quickly. "You make me happy, of course. I just thought I could say happy birthday," I reply quietly. Why, why did I do that? Why did I have to bring them up again? So stupid, Anna!

His face softens as he sighs and pushes me down on the sun lounger, climbing on top of me. "Tell me you love me again," he purrs, dipping his head and kissing my neck.

"I love you," I lie quickly, not missing a beat.

One of his hands pushes down inside my bikini bottoms, and I bite the inside of my cheek. "You're so hot, Princess," he moans appreciatively. I close my eyes and turn my face away from his, not wanting to see him enjoy himself. "Tell me you've only ever loved me," he instructs, tracing his tongue across the bruise on my shoulder.

My heart sinks as my blood seems to turn into ice in my veins. He is testing me again. "No," I whisper. I won't do that; I can't do that to Jack.

His head snaps up, his eyes fill with rage. He looks so angry that I flinch. "Tell me you never loved him, Princess," he growls through his teeth.

I shake my head sadly. "I can't say that, Carter. I won't," I respond, knowing that he will beat me for it; he always does when I fail the test, but I can't betray Jack like that. I hold my breath as he pulls his arm back and punches me full in the face.

I bolted upright, screaming. My breath was coming out in pants as I quickly put my head between my knees. *Oh God, it was a dream! Just a dream. It's over,* I repeated over in my head.

My door slammed open and Ashton ran in with his gun and knife in his hands again, looking around my room. "You dreaming?" he asked, pointing his gun around my room. I nodded, and he visibly relaxed. "Shit! You need to stop doing this to yourself, I won't let anyone hurt you, you have nothing to worry about," he said fiercely.

He knelt down by the side of my bed, looking at me intently, taking my hand and rubbing his thumb across the back of it soothingly while I struggled to catch my breath.

When I calmed down, I looked at him apologetically. He looked so worried and concerned that I started to feel awful. "I'm sorry. I think you should change rooms," I suggested weakly.

He stood up and walked quickly to the door. "I'll be right back, okay?" he said as he walked out.

He came back less than a minute later with my book in his hand, wearing a pair of faded jeans and a white T-shirt. I frowned, silently wondering where he was going. Wordlessly, he gripped the back of my dresser chair and dragged it to the side of the bed, plopping himself down in it.

My eyes widened as I realised what he was doing. "No! No way, not again! Go to bed, Ashton, you're not sitting in the chair all night again!" I protested, shaking my head adamantly. It was incredibly sweet of him, but he'd end up with a bad back if he sat up again all night.

He shrugged casually. "It's fine, I'll just sleep in the morning. We could make this work; I could go to sleep when we get in from school and then be up while you go to sleep in the night. It'll work out fine," he assured me, smiling.

I almost choked on air. He was offering to change his sleeping pattern because he thought it would help me? Clearly I'd underestimated what a nice guy he was. "No, just go to bed. This is my problem, not yours," I retorted, angry at myself for disrupting his sleep.

He chuckled and shook his head. "It's not up for debate. Now can you shush? I want to see if James kills Bella," he scolded, glaring at me jokingly. I couldn't help but laugh. He smiled. "Go to sleep, we'll talk about it in the morning, okay?"

I sighed and flopped back into the bed, untangling myself from the sheets that had wrapped around me while I'd had my nightmare. I was disgusted with myself for being so screwed up that I was keeping someone else awake all night. I glanced over at him; he was reading with a small smile on his handsome face. It was hard to believe that real people actually looked like him.

After about ten minutes of trying, I couldn't make myself fall asleep. I couldn't let him do this, it wasn't fair on him. It was my fault, yet he was paying for it. He'd probably end up falling asleep awkwardly again, and his back would ache all day tomorrow. The only solution I could see that might work was if I just let him sleep in here with me, maybe that would stop the dreams and then he'd be able to sleep too. The thought of him in my bed scared the life out of me. The only guy I had ever slept in a bed with was Carter; I shuddered and pushed the thoughts of him away quickly.

I took a deep breath and sat up, scooting to the far side of the bed so I wouldn't be near him. "Ashton, just get in the bed," I instructed.

One of his dark eyebrows rose in question. "Huh?"

I sighed deeply, trying to keep my nerves under control. "Look, just get in the bed, okay? I'm not letting you sit awake all night because I'm some kind of freaking psycho. If you want to stay in here so I don't dream about him, then fine, but you're not sitting in the chair all night," I said sternly. He looked completely unsure; his wary expression told me that he thought I'd lost my mind. "Let's just give it a try, okay? If I can't handle it then I'll let you know, but this just seems to be a good solution – one that involves us both getting some sleep," I encouraged, patting the empty side for him to get in.

"But I really wanted to know if Bella gets killed," he whined jokingly.

I rolled my eyes. "She's in the next three books if that gives you a clue," I retorted, laughing.

He gasped and looked at me with mock horror. "I can't believe you just ruined the end for me!" He moved and sat on the bed slowly, still watching my face.

I laughed. "Right, sorry about that, Pretty Boy." I settled myself on the edge of the bed, as far away from him as I could get without falling out.

He lay down on top of the sheets cautiously, watching my face the whole time. "You sure this is okay? I mean, I don't mind staying awake," he offered.

"Just stop would you? It's fine."

He grinned and reached over, turning off my bedside light so that darkness cloaked my room. I gritted my teeth and tried to stay in control of myself. It was weird being in a bed with him. He didn't move. In fact, he lay so still that I could barely tell he was there, apart from hearing his breathing. The sound was comforting somehow. He was lying as far away from me as he could get, on top of the sheets so that I was pinned underneath. I had the distinct impression that he was trying not to move in case he scared me. After a while, I rolled onto my side trying to see if he was awake or asleep, but it was too dark.

"You okay?" he whispered, making me jump.

Okay, well he's awake, that answers that question! "I'm fine, Pretty Boy," I promised. The mattress moved slightly, and the outline of his figure shifted as he rolled to his side too. My body started to react to him being so close to me – but not in the way I was expecting it to. My stomach got a little fluttery and I started to feel nervous. I wondered if he was going to touch me. A small part of me actually pondered what it would feel like if he did.

"Why do you call me pretty boy?" he asked quietly. I gulped as his fingers touched the back of my hand that was gripped on the edge of the sheets. For some reason though, I didn't flinch away from him. This must have encouraged him as his hand closed over mine, loosening my fist from the sheets and weaving his fingers through mine.

I smiled weakly into the darkness. "You don't really look like a tough guy, you're more of a pretty boy," I answered.

A soft chuckle came from his direction. "You don't think I'm a tough guy?"

I chuckled too. "Well, when I first met you I would have said no, but after last night when you came in with your gun, I'd say you were definitely badass," I admitted.

"So I'm only badass with a gun?" he replied sarcastically.

"Yeah, you're more like a male model, slash, badass," I joked, squeezing his hand gently to show I was just joking.

He chuckled and pulled on my hand, making my body move closer to his. I swallowed my nervousness, but there was still a large gap between us, I just wasn't on the edge of the bed anymore. "There, that's better, you said you like to sleep in the middle of the bed," he said, sounding satisfied. His thumb traced along the jagged scar that lined the inside of my wrist where I'd run the razor across when I'd woken up at Carter's house the day after my sixteenth birthday. The scar was mirrored on my other arm too. Unfortunately for me, my attempt was thwarted back then so I'd had to endure my time with Carter, and everyday without Jack after.

"Goodnight, Anna."

"Night."

He didn't move again after that. I laid there, straining my eyes in the darkness to try and make him out, but to no avail. Half an hour later, the snoring started. I giggled, chewing on my lip, listening to the sound rumble through his chest. I closed my eyes, feeling something that I hadn't felt since my sixteenth birthday. I felt safe. The sound of his snoring followed me into a peaceful sleep.

Chapter Seven

When I woke in the morning, I was pinned down onto the mattress. Panic surged through me until I heard the soft snore and realised it was Ashton. I was on my back, and he was lying half on his side with his other half on me, his arm and leg slung casually over me and his face buried in the crook of my neck.

A quick glance at the alarm clock told me it was almost eleven thirty in the morning. I'd never slept in this late in my life, well, not without a substantial hangover anyway. Ashton moved slightly, his hand cupped the side of my head as his face nuzzled into my neck, making a sleepy moaning sound. I smiled and poked him in the ribs roughly.

He grunted and jerked up, frowning at me through sleepy, half open eyes. His nose scrunched up as he regarded me with clear confusion for a split second before his eyes widened. He gasped and jumped out of the bed so fast that he almost fell on his butt.

"Whoa, shit! I'm sorry! You okay?" he asked, his voice panicked, holding up his hands innocently. I nodded and smiled at him, trying not to laugh. He looked so funny; I'd never seen anyone move so fast. He blew out a big breath and his shoulders relaxed as he raked a hand through his messy black hair.

"I'm fine, calm down." I sat up, stretching my arms above my head. I groaned as my joints cracked and protested to the movement. My body ached all over; my muscles were tight and uncomfortable from my feeble attempts at fighting him the day before.

"Jeez, Anna, I'm really sorry. I didn't realise I was asleep on you like that. You should have pushed me off or something." He winced apologetically. I smiled as I noticed how cute he looked when he'd just woken up. His eyes were still sleepy; he had the line of my tank top imprinted across the bottom of his jaw where he'd been asleep on me, and his hair was sticking up everywhere.

"Don't worry about it, the lying on me was fine, it was the snoring I almost smothered you for," I joked, climbing out of the bed and grabbing my bath robe.

"I don't snore!" he protested, and then he frowned, looking at me curiously. "Do I?"

I burst out laughing, raising one eyebrow incredulously. "You don't know whether you snore or not? Haven't girls ever told you?" I scoffed. *How could any girl not tease the life out of him for it? He was so loud, I'm surprised he didn't wake himself up.*

He sat on the edge of the bed and shrugged. "I've never stayed the night with a girl before."

I glanced over my shoulder to see if he was joking. Nope, no signs of humour there. "Really? How come?" I asked, plopping down on the bed next to him and crossing my legs.

"I told you, I've never really had a girlfriend, so…" he trailed off, shrugging casually.

"Wow, you really are a player! So you fuck the girls then it's just like what, *'Thanks, ma'am'*, and you leave?" I guessed, laughing.

He rolled his eyes. "I'm not a player! I told you, I've just never met anyone who I wanted to spend the night with," he explained.

I smiled. "Until now."

He nodded. "Yeah, until now. But I've never once said 'thanks ma'am'!" he said, grinning.

Before I could protest, his arm shot across my shoulders and he pushed me so that I fell back on to the bed. He lay down next to me, pressing his body to my side. My heart started to race, but I wasn't scared because I could see he was joking. He was watching me intently, probably to make sure he was alright doing this.

"Well, thanks for letting me spend the night, ma'am" he whispered sexily. My breath caught in my throat at the husky sound of his voice.

"You're welcome, Agent," I answered. "And thanks for staying the night, I slept really well." I could feel the blush heating my cheeks because I'd spent the night in a bed with him and I'd had his body wrapped around mine when I woke.

"Me too." He rolled off me and walked to the door as if nothing had happened. "Want to meet me for breakfast?" he asked, stopping at the door.

"Um, it's a bit late for breakfast, but I'll eat lunch with you." I nodded at my alarm clock, showing him the time.

He looked at the clock and shook his head, looking a little bemused. "Right, okay, lunch then," he corrected, his eyes twinkling with amusement. "Come get me when you're ready." He closed the door firmly behind him and I walked over to my closet, picking out clothes for the day. After running a brush through my wild hair a couple of times, it became apparent that there was no salvaging it. Instead, I pulled it up into a ponytail and clipped my bangs to the side. I looked in the mirror and frowned. I looked the same as I did every other day: baggy and loose. I longed to wear normal clothes, but it was easier this way to go unnoticed; it actually scared me when guys started to look at me with lust in their eyes.

I knew every man wasn't like Carter, but just in case, I couldn't bring myself to show any skin or curves. It was funny how that was different with Ashton. I hadn't thought twice about wearing my swimsuit in front of him yesterday. There was something about him that just made me trust him, giving me more confidence around him.

When I was done, I made my way out to Ashton's room. "Hey," he greeted cheerfully as he opened his door.

"Hey."

"So, what do you want to do today? Is there anything good to do around here?" he asked as we walked down to the kitchen for lunch.

"Not really. There's a small shopping mall about half an hour away. Want to go there? I could buy some new art supplies, ready for school," I offered, shrugging.

"Sure okay, sounds good," he agreed, smiling happily.

"Wow, you're easy to please," I teased, elbowing him in the ribs playfully.

He smiled. "I guess. I just don't get much time off from training, so I don't get to do normal things like that often."

"Well, that sucks," I said frowning.

"It doesn't suck! I love my job; it's all I've ever wanted to do. The training's finished now so things should calm down," he explained, shrugging.

"Well not really, I mean, you got stuck on some crappy assignment to babysit me. My dad said that you won't even get time off apart from scheduled school breaks. You must suck at being SWAT if they stuck you here," I joked, smirking at him. *Bless him; I bet he barely passed his training!*

"Actually, I graduated top of my class with honours. I hold five new records at the academy, which I was the only one to break in twenty years," he replied dismissively like it was no big deal.

I recoiled, shocked at the revelations. "Seriously? Then why did you get shipped off here with me? I mean, if you're some awesome badass, why waste you here body guarding me? It's not even a SWAT job, it's the secret service's responsibility to guard a Senator and his family." I looked at him, confused. It just seemed like a waste of talent to me.

He looked a little uncomfortable. "I don't know. I just go wherever they assign me. Anyway, I'm glad I got 'shipped off here' as you put it, otherwise we wouldn't have met," he flirted, smiling at me cockily.

"Yeah, because otherwise you'd still be holding that claim of never spending the night with a girl, like the badass player that you are." I pushed him sideways playfully so I could step through the door into the inner hallway first. He didn't reply. He just grabbed my waist, lifting me off my feet and threw me easily over his shoulder as he carried on walking in the direction of the kitchen. I gasped as everything turned upside down. "Whoa, holy crap! Put me down, right now!" I shouted, but the order lost some of its authority when I started laughing.

"Nope, not until you apologise for calling me a player," he refused playfully.

"Ashton, put me down!" I instructed, struggling to get off him.

"I didn't hear you apologise."

"Agent Taylor, you put me down right now. I know people, I could have you assassinated!" I joked.

He burst out laughing. "Right, and who do you know that could assassinate me?" he asked, still chuckling.

"Dean."

"Dean Michaels? That guy likes me more than he does you, and I've only met him twice, it would be easier to get him to assassinate you!" he countered, laughing wickedly.

"Put me down! All the blood's rushing to my head," I whined, giving up on my struggling because I could barely move an inch from the hold he had on me.

"Wow, you whine like a baby, Anna. Where's the fighting spirit? You could have wrapped your arms around my waist to give yourself more stability and kneed me in the face, you know. I thought you were big on the self-defence," he teased. He tugged on my legs, making me slide down into his arms before he sat me on the kitchen counter. He was grinning from ear to ear.

"No way! I could barely move, I tried to get down," I protested, righting my clothes and trying to catch my breath from the experience of it.

"You have much to learn, young grasshopper," he said, patting me on the head like a child.

"Whatever. Just keep your hands off me in the future, player," I stated, grinning.

He sighed and rolled his eyes, grinning sexily. "Yes, ma'am."

Movement from my right suddenly made me aware that we weren't in the room alone. I flicked my eyes around quickly, taking in the shocked faces of my parents and half of the kitchen staff that were up the other end of the kitchen. I gasped and dropped my eyes to the floor, scooting forwards and jumping off the counter.

Ashton groaned and a subtle blush crept over his cheekbones. I couldn't help but notice how cute he looked with the pink on his cheeks; it was certainly a good look for him.

"Good afternoon, Annabelle. Agent Taylor," my father said after a second or two of uncomfortable silence.

"Hi," I mumbled, fighting to regain my composure and cool my own burning cheeks.

63

"Good afternoon, sir, ma'am," Ashton said, nodding politely, clearly uncomfortable because he hadn't known they were there either.

"Er, maybe we could get some lunch out instead, what do you think?" I asked Ashton, still blushing, just wanting to be out of here already.

"Whatever you want, Miss Spencer." He shrugged casually, a smirk on his lips, probably at my red face. He pulled out his cell phone, tapping away before shoving it back into his pocket.

I looked back up at my parents who were still watching me like a hawk. "I'll, er, see you guys later," I muttered. "And I'm sorry about last night. I shouldn't have said a lot of those things. I'm not saying they weren't true, but I shouldn't have said them anyway," I shrugged awkwardly, looking at them apologetically.

My mom smiled sadly. "That's okay, Annabelle. We shouldn't have jumped to conclusions like that, it wasn't fair, and I shouldn't have brought up Jack. I'm sorry."

"You can talk about him, that doesn't upset me. I just don't like you assuming that someone could ever replace him because they can't," I said confidently. I knew that for a fact – I would never love anyone like I loved Jack, and I hated people saying that I would get over him in time.

"Honey, I wasn't saying that at all, but I think you're under some misunderstanding that you can't be with anyone because Jack died. He wouldn't want you to be like this," my mom countered.

I laughed at her statement; I'd heard that so many times from so many different therapists – repetition still didn't make it true. "You're right, he wouldn't. I'm sure he wouldn't have wanted me to get stuck with Carter either, but what we want and what happens are two different things entirely," I said casually, making my parents flinch.

"And if the situation were reversed, you'd want Jack to be like this, would you? Unhappy and alone?" my mother asked quietly.

"Of course not!" I shot back angrily. I'd never want him to have to go through this, thankfully he didn't have to.

"Well then, maybe you should think about what Jack would want," she suggested.

"I think about what Jack would want every minute of every day, Mom," I said quietly.

"Oh, baby, I didn't mean it that way!" she gasped, looking upset. She jumped up from her chair and came forward to hug me; I shrank back unconsciously, not wanting to build bridges with her. I bumped into Ashton who was standing just behind me. He placed his hands on my waist, steadying me.

My mom's face dropped when I moved away, and the guilt washed through me because all I ever did was hurt them. In trying to make myself less vulnerable by shutting people out, I knew I was hurting them but I just couldn't help it.

I groaned and shook my head. "Look, let's just leave it at that," I said quietly. One of Ashton's hands was still placed on my waist, so I focussed on the heat of his skin that was emanating through the fabric of my shirt rather than my mom's sad expression. "I'll see you at dinner." I forced a fake smile before I turned and motioned for Ashton to leave.

Ashton nodded at my parents respectfully as we walked out of the room. "You okay?" he asked as we rounded the corner.

"Yeah, I'm just peachy," I lied, shooting him a 'shut up' face.

He smiled sarcastically. "Of course you are."

"Ashton, I don't want to talk about this, please can we leave it? I don't want any more lectures," I muttered.

"Okay, but if you need to talk to anyone about anything, then you can talk to me, I want you to know that," he said softly. I looked up at him, seeing that he was watching me intently, his sincerity shining from his eyes. I smiled gratefully, knowing that I wouldn't put that burden on someone else again. I'd already told him more than I'd told anyone else. I wouldn't make that mistake again. "This is the part where you say the same to me," he prompted, nudging my ribs with his elbow.

I chuckled. "Right, sorry. Well, if you ever need to talk about anything, I'll be here for you too," I replied, shaking my head amused. His hand took mine casually as we walked down the hallway. I didn't actually even think about holding his hand now, it just felt natural, which was weird, but at least it would make it easier for us next week with me being able to be so casual with him.

He raised one eyebrow. "Well actually there is something I would like to talk to you about."

Well, shit, that backfired! I swallowed my groan. "Well then I'm all ears, Pretty Boy," I said, smiling uncomfortably.

He cocked his head to the side, regarding me quizzically as we walked. "Well, I was wondering, why is it that you let me touch you and no one else?"

"You want the honest answer?" I asked just as we reached the front door.

"Of course," he said simply. He looked like he was trying to pull the answers straight from my eyes where he was watching me so intently.

"I honestly don't know," I shrugged. That was the truth, I didn't know what it was, but there was just something about him that made me want to trust him. I would trust this guy with my life yet I had known him for less than three days. It confused me, but it was true.

His frown grew more pronounced. "I watched you shy away from your own mother because you don't like to get close to people, yet you let me sleep in your bed and lie all over you. I don't get it. Don't get me wrong, I'm taking it as a compliment, even if it's not meant as one."

I sighed and chewed on my lip. "Take it however you want. I'm fed up with trying to explain the way my brain works sometimes." I smiled

65

sadly, digging in my pocket for my car keys as we approached the garage. When the automatic door rolled up, I led him to my 'other' car.

His eyes widened as his mouth popped open in wonder and awe. I smiled. *Yep, typical boy reaction to my car!* "Oh, nice!" he purred, touching the hood of my maroon Aston Martin Vanquish appreciatively. As I held up the keys, he flinched, and I chuckled wickedly. "What? Why are you laughing? You think I'm scared to admit that your driving frightens the crap out of me?" he asked, laughing.

"You'd rather drive, Pretty Boy?" I teased, smirking at him.

"Definitely." He held out his hands for the keys, but he looked like he wasn't actually expecting me to give them to him.

I sighed dramatically and threw him the keys. "Fine, but you take care of my baby."

He looked shocked for a few seconds then smiled sexily. "Don't worry, Anna, I'll take care of you and your baby," he stated, patting the roof of my car gently. I laughed and got in the passenger's side, watching him as he slid in behind the wheel with an awed expression etched on his face. "If you have this, then why did we take a Jeep out yesterday?" he asked, running his hands around the wheel lovingly.

I shrugged. "I don't like to drive this car."

"So why are we taking it?" he asked, frowning and looking confused.

"I thought you'd like to drive it. You look like a pretty car type of pretty boy," I replied, smirking and winking at him. He looked at me strangely, just like he did when I gave him the photo frame last night. "What is that look?" I asked before I could stop myself.

"What look?" he questioned, still doing it.

"That look on your face right now. What are you thinking? You had that same face last night when I gave you that photo frame," I said, biting my lip wishing I hadn't asked.

He turned, looking out of the windshield as he started the car. "I was just thinking that you're extremely thoughtful and that no one has ever really thought of me like that, that's all. I'm not used to getting gifts or having people think of me. It's weird; I don't quite know how to deal with it."

I swallowed the lump that formed in my throat. "Because you grew up in foster homes?"

He nodded stiffly. "Yeah, I never really had a family or anything from the age of ten, so I never got presents and stuff. I just got used to it, I guess," he explained, pulling out of the driveway.

"When's your birthday?" I asked curiously, after a couple of minutes of uncomfortable silence.

"November fifteenth."

"How old are you?" I asked, trying to commit the date to memory so I could get him a present.

"I'm twenty-one," he answered, smiling. He was obviously enjoying driving my car.

"You can put your foot down, I don't mind a bit of speed," I suggested, looking at the speedometer to see that he was just one under the speed limit.

"Yeah? And what if I get you killed?" he teased, grinning at me.

I shrugged and spoke before I could stop myself. "Then you'd be doing me a favour." He slammed on the breaks and pulled the car to a stop, looking at me shocked and actually a little horrified. "What?" I asked, looking around for some animal or something that we hit.

"Please don't ever think that again, Anna. That's not nice to hear," he said sadly. "You actually want to die?" he inquired, his face serious.

"Everyday," I confirmed, not looking away from his gaze.

He gulped. "Why?"

"Why not? What have I got to live for? A whole life on my own? Waking up every day with the knowledge that I got one of the nicest people in the world killed? Knowing that I'll never have that again, never feel loved, never feel whole, or clean, or pure? Why would I want to live?" I asked seriously.

He looked so sad, his eyes glazed over. "You don't have to be on your own. You might meet someone, fall in love again. As for feeling clean or pure, that may not ever change if you don't let it. That's a state of mind; you need to let it go because there's nothing else you can do about it. And you didn't get Jack killed, he was murdered by a sick asshole. It wasn't your fault," he said softly, reaching for my hand and squeezing gently.

I sighed deeply. "Ashton, I've heard all of that in every single one of my therapy sessions, and I'll tell you the same thing that I tell them. I don't care what anyone else says, I *know* it was my fault, so let's just drop it and change the subject," I suggested, tugging my hand from his and turning on the radio.

He sighed and gripped the wheel tightly. "Anna, you shouldn't-"

"You gonna drive, or shall we just go back to the house?" I interjected, putting my feet up on the dashboard.

"Anna, it wasn't your fault," he whispered, looking at me pleadingly.

"I know it wasn't," I lied easily. This was the other tactic I used on my therapist occasionally.

"You don't believe that," he stated, gripping my chin between his thumb and forefinger, turning my face so I had to look at him.

Frustration built up inside me. I didn't want to be having this conversation, not with him, not with anyone. "Oh for fuck's sake, Ashton! You don't want the truth, you don't want the lie! What the hell do you want me to say? What will make you drive us to the fucking mall?" I ranted, throwing my hands up dramatically.

He looked at me a little shocked before he laughed at my outburst. I felt the smile twitch the corner of my mouth and then I laughed too before he composed himself. "Right then, Miss Spencer, you want to see good driving?" he asked, waggling his eyebrows at me. I nodded, a little unsure if that was the right answer, and his eyes sparkled with excitement as he gunned the engine loudly. He pulled away with the tyres squealing. We sped down the winding road so fast that everything was just a blur. He was a kick-ass driver and my heart was beating so fast, I thought I would die of a heart attack. As we approached the populated area he slowed right down to normal, legal speed, glancing over at me and grinning his ass off.

"Enjoy yourself?" I asked, chuckling and still trying to calm my racing heart.

"Shit yeah, this car is awesome!" he gushed, rubbing the dashboard lovingly.

"Well, I'll tell you what, if you can last the full eight months, you can have it," I bargained, shrugging. He laughed and shook his head, obviously thinking I was kidding around.

Chapter Eight

The shopping was a pleasant change. It was good to get out of the house for a little while. The only trouble was that I felt like I was on my own for most of the time. Ashton was constantly distracted and checking everything out discreetly, so it was almost as if I was talking to myself half the time.

"Maybe you should have told Dean where we were going and then you could have actually relaxed and paid attention to what we're talking about," I snapped as we sat in the café, refuelling before we planned to shop some more. I glared at him as he watched a group of teenagers walk past near me, rather than answering the question I'd just directed at him.

"I told him, he's back there," he replied, motioning over his shoulder with his head.

A quick glance in that direction and I spotted Dean in plain clothes, lingering three stores away. I sighed and frowned, hating being followed around.

Just as I was finishing up my coffee, two familiar figures caught my eye through the window.

Oh God, it can't be! Jack!

My eyes widened at the sight of his blond, unruly hair and straight nose as he sauntered across the mall in his loose fit jeans and GAP T-shirt. I jerked in my seat, confused. My heart stopped and then took off in a sprint.

But as one side of his mouth pulled up into a smile, my happiness and hope that maybe the last three years had been a dream faded, and I came back to reality with a huge, painful bump. My heart broke with loss all over again as I realised that it wasn't my Jack after all, it was his younger brother, Michael.

Accompanying Michael was his mother, Pam… and now that they'd seen me, it appeared that they were heading straight for me. Pam smiled warmly, but my eyes just flicked back to Michael again. My whole body seemed to go cold. I hadn't seen him for over a year, and I had forgotten how much he looked like his brother. He wasn't built the same as Jack and was maybe an inch taller, but facially they could have been twins. And he was the age now that Jack had been when he'd died.

My hands started to shake uncontrollably, making my cup rattle against the little plate that it sat on. A little whimper left my lips because usually I had time to prepare for seeing them, usually it was on my terms and I had some warning. I'd never just run into them like this and I wasn't sure I could deal with it.

Ashton stood quickly, gripping my upper arm and hoisting me out of my seat, pushing me against the wall that was behind me. His body tensed as he span on the spot, pressing his back against my chest and shielding me with his body, like he had that first night he came into my room when I was screaming.

"What is it?" he asked fiercely, reaching into his jacket pocket, probably holding his gun or his knife.

I whimpered and pressed my face into his shoulder, closing my eyes. I couldn't speak. I could barely even breathe properly. Grief was overwhelming me, seeming to all come back at once so that I was drowning in it. I wanted to cry. I wanted to scream and shout and wail, but nothing was coming out. There was no escape for my sadness as it just built inside me, crushing me, filling me up.

I was dimly aware of Ashton's cell phone ringing and him answering it in short, terse sentences. When he turned back to me and cupped my face in his hands, I looked up into his green eyes and felt my chin tremble. I couldn't cope with it. The grief was fresh and raw again, like it had only just happened, like I'd only just lost Jack and watched him die.

"Breathe," Ashton whispered. "Anna, just breathe for me. Everything is going to be fine. I know you're panicking, but listen to my voice. Nothing will hurt you." My breathing continued to come out in small pants as I dug my fingers into his sides, completely lost in grief and guilt. "Can you hear your heart beating?" he asked as he brushed my hair over my shoulder. "If you can hear your heart, then count the beats and just try to breathe so you can calm down. I won't let anything hurt you."

My eyes flicked to Pam and Michael, who were standing there watching me with wide, horrified eyes. Pam was crying, covering her mouth with her hand. Michael frowned and shook his head, turning to his mother and saying something I couldn't hear.

I looked back to Ashton, swallowing my sadness. What I hated the most was the fact that I was upsetting Pam by being upset. She'd been through enough already – losing her son because of me. I needed to get a grip of myself. Doing as Ashton said, I tried to focus on my heartbeats that were drumming in my ears as he smiled and nodded in encouragement.

70

Slowly, my breathing returned to normal as I fought my way through the emotional storm that was trying to drown me.

"I'll ask them to leave," he suggested, pulling away from me when my breathing was stable and I could no longer hear my heart hammering in my ears.

I gulped and shook my head. "No, don't," I croaked, standing up straighter.

His eyebrows knitted together as he nodded and pulled back, setting his hand on the small of my back. I forced a smile as I turned to face the mother of the boy that I got killed, and his brother, who had inherited every single feature that I loved about my boyfriend.

"Hi," I greeted awkwardly.

Pam sniffed and smiled back, stepping closer to me. "Oh, Anna. I'm sorry we upset you," she said kindly, wiping her own tears away. "How are you? We've missed you."

I nodded. "I've missed you guys too." That wasn't the truth though. I didn't allow myself to think about them much because it brought back too many memories. It was easier for me to blank them out altogether and not ever let myself think about them or how welcome they always made me feel.

"Can I get a hug?" she asked hopefully.

I gritted my teeth so tightly that it made my jaw ache, but nodded in agreement, letting her envelop me in a hug that was so familiar that it was like I was ten years old again and I'd just gone to her with a scraped knee.

When she broke the embrace, Michael stepped forward, holding his arms open for a hug too. A small whimper escaped my lips as I smiled through my heartbreak. When his arms wrapped around me, I closed my eyes and hugged him just that bit too tight and for that bit too long. Part of me didn't ever want to let go.

He stepped back, running a hand through his hair just like Jack used to do. "Not seen you in ages. You should come around more," he stated.

Tears welled in my eyes because even his voice was similar to his brother's. He looked so much like Jack that I could barely stand to look at him, yet at the same time, I couldn't look away. My grief was threatening to crush me. I wasn't sure how much longer I could look at him without either throwing myself at him and begging him to hold me, or sobbing until I couldn't breathe.

Pam set her hand on my arm. "Anna, did you get my text? We'd love to have you over for dinner or something before you go back to school. We miss you at the house," she cooed, squeezing my arm gently.

I swallowed a couple of times, scrambling to come up with an answer to that. "Um… I'm not sure if I'm going to get time. We're leaving in a couple of days, and there's a lot to do before college." I turned and motioned to Ashton. "This is Ashton. Ashton, this is Pamela and Michael

Roberts," I introduced weakly, praying that no one noticed that my hands were shaking.

Ashton shook hands with them both and exchanged pleasantries when suddenly his cell phone rang again in his pocket. "Sorry. Excuse me," he apologised, turning to answer it. He turned back a few seconds later. "I'm really sorry, Anna, but we have to get going. There are some things I need to pick up on our way back to the house," he instructed.

I'd never been more grateful for a phone call in my life. I couldn't hold myself together much longer. I was struggling to keep the panic and horror from seeping into my voice as I talked to them. Soon I would break down, and I didn't want Pam to have to witness it.

After exchanging goodbyes and promising that I'd try to make time to visit them before going to school the following week, I let Ashton lead me along and out of the emergency exit of the mall.

I gulped in the fresh air greedily as the tears finally made their appearance. Ashton's face was a mask of worry and sympathy as he gripped my hand and tugged me across the parking lot towards where we'd parked.

By the time we were almost at the car, I couldn't walk any further and my legs gave out on me. I slumped down to the floor, sobbing against the asphalt. Ashton's arms slipped under me, lifting me and carrying me the rest of the way. He climbed in the car, still holding me against his chest as he set me in his lap.

Feeling needy and almost desperate for comfort, I wrapped my arms around his neck and sobbed on his shoulder until I was almost sick. The whole time he just stroked my back and rocked me gently.

After about ten minutes, my tears had dried up so all I was left with was the hitched breathing and the blocked nose. I swiped angrily at my face, wiping the last of my tears. "I'm sorry," I mumbled, my voice hoarse from all the crying.

"He looked like him, didn't he?" he replied sadly. I nodded, biting my bottom lip hard enough to draw blood. "Whoa! Careful," he scolded, grabbing a Kleenex and dabbing it on my lip gently.

I pushed his hand away. "We'd better get going if we have some stuff to pick up," I said quietly, my voice still hitching from the last spasms of my sobs.

"We don't have anything to pick up; I just said that so we could leave. You looked like you didn't have much longer in you, and we made it just in time," he explained, grimacing.

"Well, who called you?" I asked, confused.

"No one. I used the self-ringer," he replied, smiling grimly.

Oh God, he did that to get me out of there before I broke down in front of everyone? I wrapped my arms around his neck again and hugged him gratefully. "Thank you," I whispered. It meant a lot to me that he would do that; I would have hated myself if I'd broken down in front of Jack's mom like I had in front of Ashton. He smelled so good that I didn't want to let

72

go yet, so I buried my face into the side of his neck and closed my eyes, enjoying being close to someone for the first time in over three years.

"It's my job to take care of you, isn't it?" he replied softly, hugging me back.

"Yeah, for as long as you're here," I croaked. Now he'd seen the real me, the crying, weak and hysterical girl, he'd be requesting that transfer any day now.

He sighed, tightening his arms on my waist. "Anna, I won't leave you like the others, I promise. Even after my assignment's done, I'll still be there if you need me."

"Yeah, okay," I replied sarcastically. Everybody left eventually; I'd just hardened myself so that it didn't matter anymore.

I lifted my head off his shoulder so I could look at him, but I didn't move from his lap. I just sat there, soaking up the comfort and support that he provided, loving being close to someone again and having something else to think about, other than the gaping hole that was where my heart used to be. He smiled, and I just looked into his beautiful, green eyes. They were like an emerald green colour, flecked with both a lighter green and a hazel brown. They were easily the most beautiful eyes I had ever seen in my life. I dragged my gaze over his face, taking in every perfect inch of it – the line of his jaw, and the curve of his lip. His breath was blowing across my face and the hair on the nape of my neck prickled. The car seemed to be getting hotter, the air growing thicker somehow. I could feel the heat and desire coursing up through my veins and I gulped as my body started to tingle in places that hadn't wanted anyone since Jack. I was longing for him to lean in and press those soft-looking lips against mine.

Suddenly my thoughts actually caught up with me and I realised just what it was that I was starting to fantasise about. Hatred and self-loathing hit me like a bucket of cold water. I hated the fact that I had looked at him like that and that I'd been untrue to Jack because, like it or not, I was actually attracted to Ashton.

I looked away, closing my eyes as I pushed myself up off his lap and climbed into the passenger seat. "Can we go home?" I whispered, not able to look at him again. I had no idea what was happening to me, or why he was suddenly making me feel like this. For three years, I'd felt nothing but rage, pain and grief inside me, but now I felt a little something else inside – and I didn't like it one bit.

He nodded and started the car while I clipped on my seatbelt. The drive home was silent. I had no idea what to say or do, so I said and did nothing other than watch the trees whizz past. As we pulled into the driveway of my house, I gripped the hood of my sweater and pulled it up, partially covering my face. I didn't want anyone to know I'd been crying. Ashton followed me silently through the house, with his hand on the small of my back the whole time. I knew he was only trying to be supportive, but

I started to resent the fact that he kept touching me all the time, and that I allowed him to.

As I stopped outside my bedroom, I turned and shrugged. "I'm just gonna draw for a bit then catch an early night."

He nodded and opened his mouth to reply, but I didn't give him the chance before I slipped into my room and closed the door in his face. I needed privacy; the sadness was still churning in the pit of my stomach and I wanted to be alone so I could try and deal with it.

I didn't get much drawing done though. Instead, I'd sat there for almost an hour, scratching, pinching and picking at the skin on the inside of my left elbow until my nails were covered in blood and my skin was red raw and sore-looking. I'd taken to self-harming not long after I was found at Carter's house. Sometimes it helped me to release my emotions, sometimes, like today, it did nothing other than make me bleed.

Later that night, I fell into a horror-filled sleep, where I saw my boyfriend murdered over and over again by the man that haunted my every waking moment.

When Ashton burst into my room again, for the third night running, I just apologised and closed my eyes before turning my back on him, not wanting to see his pitying expression. Without asking, he climbed onto my bed with me and scooted close to my back, wrapping his arm over my stomach.

"You seem to sleep better with me in here," he whispered. I didn't answer. There was no answer for that. I did, there was no denying it. And to be honest, if his snoring stopped me from seeing Jack's broken face again for the night, then I welcomed the distraction.

Chapter Nine

I woke in the morning with him still spooning me from behind. His arms were wrapped around me securely as his breath blew into my hair. I smiled to myself. *For someone who has never spent the night with a girl, he sure is cuddly!*

I closed my eyes and enjoyed the closeness of him. It felt nice having someone hold me who wasn't after anything; if Carter had held me like this, it usually meant he wanted sex. I moved slightly to get more comfortable and his arms tightened around me. He sighed, and his leg tangled in with mine as his hand brushed against my thigh. My breath caught in my throat.

I gulped as unfamiliar feelings started creeping up on me, the same feelings that had started building yesterday in the car. My skin was prickling with sensation as my stomach fluttered. An unsatisfied ache, a longing for something unknown, filled my body. I'd never felt this kind of thing before, not of this magnitude anyway. The lust I felt inside was all consuming. I wondered what would happen if I turned around and kissed him, or if I ran my hand down his sculpted chest. Would he freak out and ask me what the heck I was doing?

Swallowing loudly, I rolled over to face him. The feelings of longing and need grew even more when I laid eyes on his beautiful, sleeping face. His body was so close, pressed against mine, and hard, toned and mouth-wateringly perfect. Before I even knew what I was doing, I'd bent forward and brushed my lips against his, just once, just needing to know what it would feel like. As soon as his lips touched mine, desire pulsed through my body. I laid my head back down and licked my lips, fighting the urge to kiss him again.

His eyes fluttered open, and a confused, shocked expression flitted across his face.

No! No, no, no, no! Oh my goodness, why did I do that? I gasped in horror because of what I'd just done – and the fact that I'd been caught doing it. My face flushed with embarrassment as I squirmed, trying to come up with words to explain my behaviour. I needed to apologise quickly because I'd just overstepped a line that should never be crossed.

"I-I'm really sorry! Oh God, I can't believe I did that! I'm so sorry, Ashton." I blushed like crazy and my voice wavered as I spoke.

Instead of answering, he bent his head and pressed his lips to mine again for a split second, before pulling back and looking at me cautiously. His expression was worried, nervous, scared even. It was almost as if he was waiting for me to freak out and punch him in the face.

My eyes widened in shock. I literally had no idea what to do or think. The only thing that registered in my mind was how nice it felt and how soft his lips were. My whole body was tingling with desire, my lips burning. I wanted more. Without my conscious consent, my hand moved to the back of his head, threading through his soft hair as I guided his mouth back down to mine, needing him like I needed the air in my lungs.

As his lips pressed against mine, he made a soft moan in the back of his throat as he pressed his body to mine. My mind was whirling, spinning, not making any sense as the sensations and passion took over, making my body ache for something that I'd not dared to think about since Jack was alive. When his tongue grazed my lip, the kiss deepened and changed to something even more desperate and fulfilling. His taste and the way his body pressed against mine made me forget who I was. It was glorious.

He cupped my face as he guided me onto my back and hovered above me, pressing me down into the soft mattress. I whimpered as the desire built. My fingers dug into his back, clutching him closer to me as one of his hands slowly trailed down my neck, across my side until finally, his fingertips brushed against the skin of my stomach. He was doing everything slowly, as if waiting for me to stop him. His hesitancy caught me off-guard and made me doubt that this was a good idea. After all, I didn't really want to be doing this with my new bodyguard, did I? My body answered for me. Yes, yes I did. As his hand pushed up under my pyjama top and headed up to cup my breasts, I let out a little moan and arched into him, needing to get him closer to me, to be consumed by him, to be one with him.

As the kiss finally broke and he trailed his tongue down my neck, I was panting for breath and my body was on high alert. I closed my eyes as he inched my pyjama top up slowly. He was moving and doing everything so slowly, as if he thought I was going to freak out at any second.

"You can stop treating me like glass, Ashton, I'm not gonna break," I whispered, wriggling under him, trying to feel as much of his body on mine as I could. He paused, pulling back from me gently before he nodded in acknowledgement, gripped my shirt and pulled it over my head in one swift motion.

I gasped, shocked how quickly it had happened. My face filled with heat because I was now half-naked in front of him. Insecurity and nervousness made me wince as I looked up at him. Only one man had ever seen me topless, and that wasn't my choice. But my concern that he wasn't going to like what he saw was immediately diminished when his eyes narrowed and his bottom lip rolled up into his mouth. The little moan of appreciation that he made set what felt like a hundred butterflies loose in my stomach.

"So beautiful," he croaked, dropping my shirt over the side of the bed and hovering above me again, looking straight into my eyes. "So, so beautiful."

His lips pressed against mine as he settled himself on top of me. I smiled against his mouth, looping my arms around his neck. It was like a dream, a nice one, one that I didn't ever want to wake up from. The attention from him made me feel special, attractive and desired.

As his hands lavished attention on my body, I took the opportunity to touch him too. My fingertips glided over his chest, feeling the little bumps of his muscles, tracing the lines of them. He shivered, pulling his mouth from mine, heading down and closing his mouth over one of my nipples. I gasped at the sensation, unaware that anything could actually feel this good with a man. The passion and need for him was incredible and all-consuming. My whole body was screaming for more.

His mouth headed lower. His hot tongue drew a circular pattern around my belly button before his teeth nipped gently at my overheated skin. When I felt the waistband of my shorts move, I raised my hips from the mattress in silent encouragement. This was all taking too long. I needed more, I couldn't wait. I'd never wanted anyone like I wanted him, not even Jack. To be fair, Jack and I were so young that I hadn't even known that this level of desire actually existed. Cool air hit my thighs as he eased my shorts down.

I was lost. Lost in the bliss of Ashton Taylor and the sensations and feelings he was causing within me. His hands and mouth on my body made me feel both hot and cold at the same time. My mind was whirling, unable to form any coherent thoughts other than one: *please don't stop.*

When his mouth found mine again, he let out a little moan as one of his hands fisted into my hair. His excitement was evident as he ground his hips against mine. A shiver of desire made my eyes flutter shut as my whole body started to ache. My hands slid down his back, catching hold of the top of his boxers and pushing them down, trailing my nails across his pert, little behind as I did so. When the material was at his knees he kicked them off quickly, and one of his hands slid between our bodies as his mouth claimed mine in a kiss that was full of fire and passion.

My body jerked as his hand moved to the apex of my legs, brushing against my overheated skin. Little ripples of pleasure burst from within me, and he groaned. "So wet. Fuck, Anna," he mumbled, pushing his hand down further. I gasped as his fingers pushed inside me gently. More of those little, pleasurable ripples erupted and I arched my back, gripping his shoulders for support.

He sucked on the spot just below my ear as his fingers started moving inside me slowly. My teeth sank into my bottom lip as my heart started to race. Not able to endure any more waiting, I shook my head, guiding his mouth back to mine again. "I've had enough foreplay, Ashton," I mumbled against his lips, wriggling as my whole body seemed to get hotter and hotter by the second. Something was building inside me, some sort of frenzy.

Ashton pulled away fractionally. A pained, disappointed frown lined his forehead. "I don't have a condom. Do you have one?" he asked, still working his fingers inside me.

I couldn't answer. The ripples of desire had turned into waves – giant, intense waves that crashed over me. He was pushing me towards something, and I knew it would be good whatever it was. My blood seemed to whoosh in my ears as my insides throbbed and twitched. My back arched off the mattress as I gripped his shoulders tightly, crying out his name. For a few blissful seconds, it felt as if I was flying, as the sensations drove me higher and higher, until my body sagged and a contented sigh left my lips and all that was left was the residual ebb of pleasure and the flutter of my inner muscles.

I swallowed, still panting for breath as I looked up at him a little confused. I'd never felt anything like that before. I'd never even dreamt that my body could feel like that. The only feelings that I'd ever had during sex were pain, disgust and shame. But at the moment, I felt incredible.

Ashton smiled down at me, his green eyes glittering with what looked like pride as he bent to kiss me again. "Do you have a condom, Anna?" he repeated, peppering little kisses across my cheek.

"No."

He groaned quietly and pressed his face into the side of my neck, his shoulders slumping in defeat. Shifting one leg out from under him, I wrapped it around his waist, clamping him to me as I wriggled. At this point, I was past caring if I got pregnant. I wanted that flying, weightless, carefree feeling again. But this time I wanted to take him along with me. Gripping my hand in the back of his hair, I pulled his mouth to mine, kissing him almost desperately as I raised my hips in silent invitation, desperately needing more from him because I didn't ever want this experience to end.

He groaned and shook his head, breaking the kiss. "We can't. I want to, so bad, but we can't," he whined. His voice was pained. He almost looked as disappointed as I felt, almost, but not quite.

My heart sank as I pressed my face into his chest and let his delicious smell fill my lungs. "Please?" I begged, clutching him closer.

He dragged in a breath through his teeth as his shoulders stiffened under my hands. "I could pull out before I finish," he suggested. I moved back to look at him, my pulse quickening at his words. "If you want I could do that," he offered, looking at me curiously, his expression torn.

Oh hell yeah! I nodded eagerly as my body rejoiced. My leg unconsciously tightened around his waist as he shifted on top of me. He gulped and cupped my face in his hands, looking me right in the eyes.

"You really want this, Anna? You're sure?" he asked, watching my face.

I wasn't even sure I had the words to describe how much I wanted it. In fact, it wasn't a want, it was a need. I *needed* it to happen. "Yeah," I confirmed, begging him with my eyes. "Please, Ashton?"

He grinned and his hand slid down, gripping my thigh as he pushed his hips forward. My breath came out in one big burst as he slid home inside me and his hips met mine, filling me completely. He gasped, and his eyes widened as his fingers dug into my leg. "Fuck. So tight," he grunted. "You okay?"

I bit my lip to stop myself from moaning too loudly at the pleasure of having him inside me. "Oh hell yeah," I confirmed, tightening my leg around his waist like a death grip in case he changed his mind and tried to get away. He grinned – probably at my over-the-top enthusiasm. His mouth claimed mine in a scorching hot kiss that seemed to wake up every part of my body, parts that I thought were long since dead.

He built up a slow, steady rhythm. Every time he moved, my body tingled and throbbed. I was aching for something else, something more, but I didn't even know what it was that I wanted. I actually had no idea what I was doing. Trying to match his movements, I raised my hips to meet his. My moans were bordering on obscene as I leant forward and bit his shoulder gently, moaning against his skin, muffling the sound. Every move he made was gentle and caring; his hands worshipped my body and his mouth never once seemed to leave my skin.

As perspiration glistened on his forehead and his back started to get slightly slick under my fingers, my body was screaming at me for something. Seeming to sense it too, he gripped my other leg and guided that around his waist too before his hand slid to the small of my back, lifting my behind off the mattress a little as he continued to thrust into me. The new angle changed the feel of it completely, seeming to allow him deeper inside me. I gasped, bending my head and kissing his chest gratefully.

"Okay?" he asked breathlessly, as he thrust a little harder this time.

I nodded, squeezing my eyes shut as every nerve in my body seemed to spark and flicker. "Please don't stop," I begged, tightening my legs on him.

He chuckled, slamming home again. "I won't," he whispered, as I ran my fingers through his already messy hair. "Fuck. So good," he moaned, looking down at me through heavily-lidded, clearly awed eyes.

The same sensation was building like an inferno inside me. My eyes narrowed as I pressed my mouth against his, ravishing his mouth with my tongue. As if he knew I was close to my end too, his fingers bit into my butt as he sped up. The friction he was creating inside me was almost too much to bear. In an attempt to get him impossibly closer, I raised my quivering legs even higher, lifting most of my body off the bed. He grunted and seemed to lose control of himself as he slammed into me harder and harder, moaning my name.

My orgasm hit me like a train, even more powerful than the last time. My whole body seemed to convulse and shake as I squeezed my eyes shut. He groaned my name as my inner muscles tightened around him, trying to force him to climax.

He pulled out of me quickly and his body tensed too, coming onto my stomach. I watched the way his eyes squeezed shut and his jaw tightened, listening to the sexy, little moan of pleasure he made as he finished too. He slumped down on top of me, pinning me down on the mattress with his weight, but it was a pleasant weight, it felt comforting somehow.

I closed my eyes and smiled as he peppered little kisses around the base of my throat. My whole body was spent. My muscles felt like jelly as I struggled to catch my breath. He sighed contentedly, lifting his weight off me, only to plop down at my side and throw a heavy arm across my torso. As he moved and our bodies brushed together, I could feel the evidence of his climax on my stomach.

I rolled to my side so I was facing him. He was watching me with a contented smile on his face. A soft giggle escaped my lips because of his awed expression. The way he was looking at me made my tummy flutter due to the intensity of it. I smiled and reached up, pushing his hair off his sweaty forehead, guiding it to stand up on end. I chuckled wickedly as it stayed in that position. Messy sex hair certainly suited him.

"Well, I'd say you just added a whole new chapter to the '*how to be a bodyguard*' book. I don't think I've ever had a person guard my body that closely before," I teased, blushing as I said it.

He laughed and tightened his arm across my body, clamping me to his side. "Mmm, I think I'm gonna be good at this body guarding job. I take my job incredibly seriously," he purred, trailing his fingers down my spine, making me shiver.

"Ashton, do you mind if I count that as my first time? I mean, my real first time wasn't something I want to remember." The words tumbled from my mouth before I could even contemplate how embarrassing they would be. I winced, horrified.

"I would be honoured, Miss Spencer," he replied, dipping his head and kissing me softly.

I smiled against his mouth, slipping one arm around his neck. When his arm tightened on me and he rolled onto his back, I squeaked, giggling as I was dragged on top of him. His hand slipped down to cup my ass as the kiss deepened, growing in intensity again. When the kiss finally broke, I dragged in a ragged breath. The room seemed to be too hot and stuffy. I needed a little air. Gulping nervously, I sat up, straddling him. He smiled up at me, folding one arm under his head as his other hand drew a lazy pattern on my thigh.

The way he was looking at me made a blush creep up my neck and spread across my face. Neither of us spoke. Suddenly, my cell phone started vibrating on my bedside cabinet, cutting through the silence and making us both jump. Leaning over and snagging the phone from the side, I frowned down at the number that belonged to my father.

"Dad?" I answered, suddenly now very aware that I was naked with my near guard laid out between my thighs.

Ashton's body jerked as his eyes widened.

"Hi, Annabelle. I wanted to speak to Agent Taylor, but he's not answering his cell. I wondered if he was with you?" my dad quizzed.

My mouth popped open in shock as I tried to come up with some lie that would placate him. "Um, no Ashton's not with me." I winced, looking at him for help. "I think he said he was going for… er…" Ashton suddenly used his hand to mime his fingers dancing across the palm of his hand. I raised one eyebrow. "A dance class?" I guessed. Ashton chuckled quietly, shaking his head and slapping his forehead with the palm of his hand.

"A dance class?" my father repeated incredulously.

I closed my eyes as I suddenly realised what Ashton was actually miming. Someone running. *Hmm, that would have been a better excuse.* I sighed. "Dad, look, I don't know where he is, alright? For all I know he could be at a dance class. He's probably gone for a run or something," I snapped, covering the mouthpiece of my phone as Ashton's chuckle turned into an outright laugh.

"Right, okay, well if you see him, could you ask him to come and speak to me about some arrangements for next week?" my dad requested.

"Sure thing," I answered, pressing the end button and dropping my phone down onto the bed.

"Dance class?" Ashton teased, shaking his head at me.

I sighed and flopped down onto the bed. "He wants to see you to talk about some arrangements for next week," I stated, wanting to change the subject.

He frowned but nodded; clearly now wondering what my father wanted to see him about. Settling himself down against my side, he ran his fingers through my hair. "You're so beautiful," he whispered, leaning in and planting a soft kiss on the tip of my nose. I smiled as his eyes latched onto mine and I became trapped in the beautiful green of them. After a couple of minutes of silence, he groaned. "I'd better go speak to your father." He pushed himself up onto all fours, leaning over me, kissing me fiercely. "I'll see you in a bit. Maybe we could go for a walk or something?"

"Yeah okay, sure," I agreed, shrugging.

He kissed down the side of my neck and across my body, lingering on my breasts, then climbed out of the bed, frowning and not looking too happy about having to leave. I watched his pert, little behind as he pulled on his boxer shorts, picked up his weapons from the night before, and then strutted confidently to the door.

Just before he stepped out of my room, he turned back to me and a cocky smile slipped onto his face. "I knew you'd fall for me sooner or later. And thanks very much, ma'am," he stated, winking before stepping out and closing the door firmly behind him.

My heart dropped down into my stomach. *Fall for him? I haven't fallen for him, I love Jack. Oh my God… Jack!* My eyes widened in horror as my head whipped to the side, seeing the photo on my sideboard. He was smiling at me as usual. I started to feel nauseous; I ran to the bathroom and was sick violently until nothing else would come out.

Turning the shower to as hot as it would go, I climbed in, sobbing under the spray. My tears mingled with the water jets, circling down the drain as I scrubbed the sex smell from my skin.

When I got out, I still didn't feel better. It wasn't the dirty feeling that sometimes overcame me when I thought about Carter, no, this was worse in some ways. I literally repulsed myself from the inside out. I'd just done that with Ashton, and hadn't even spared Jack a single thought until it was too late.

I dressed as quickly as possible, not even bothering to brush my sopping wet, tangled hair before I stalked over to the bed and ripped the sheets and covers from it, tossing them into the laundry basket.

Once I'd opened the windows, I ran out of my room as fast as my legs would carry me. As soon as I was in my car, I threw it into drive and sped out of the drive with the tyres squealing. I knew where I was going, I needed to see Jack and beg him to forgive me.

Chapter Ten

~ Ashton ~

As I walked out of her room, I couldn't keep the triumphant smile off of my face. I headed into my room and flopped onto the bed, thinking about what had just happened. I'd wanted her since that first moment I'd laid my eyes on her. Anna was an incredible person, so vulnerable, hurt, and beautiful. Sure she was damaged, but maybe I could fix her. I could help her heal if she'd let me. Clearly she tried to play the bitch because she didn't want people close to her, but I could see through her act easy enough. She literally blew my mind, and I'd never met anyone like her.

Even though I was attracted to her, I never would have made a move on her because of what she'd been through. Just now though, *she* was the one that had instigated things between us and took the first step to move on. I loved that. I was so physically attracted to her that it was unreal, I wanted her so much, but more importantly, I wanted something I'd never wanted before, I wanted to *be* with her. The sex wasn't important – not that I hadn't wanted to make love to her, of course, because I'd actually wanted that so badly I could have died from the need – but the thing I wanted most in the world was to see her happy. These feelings I had for her scared the life out of me. I'd never even had a girlfriend before, yet I was already crazy about her and I'd only known her for three days.

A soft sigh escaped my lips as I thought about her face as it had looked just now. She'd looked so happy that I couldn't help but feel proud of myself. Usually her eyes were hard, closed off and sad, but just now they'd sparkled with a happiness that made my heart fly. She truly was the most beautiful thing I had ever seen in my life, even with the messed up bed hair, she had still taken my breath away.

My mind wandered to her naked, writhing under me as she moaned my name. I wouldn't be forgetting that in a long time, that was for sure. I could actually die right now and be a happy man. The sex had been incredible; better than anything I had ever felt in my life. It had felt different to the usual flings I had; it was more intimate and special.

We hadn't used protection which was a little worrying, but I knew that if the worst did happen and she did get pregnant, I'd be there for her. The chances of that happening were slim, but we'd cross that bridge if we needed to. A small smile tugged at the corner of my mouth as a cute image formed in my mind – a baby with her brown eyes and cute, little button nose. Although I'd never imagined having kids before, that would be one gorgeous baby if it looked like its momma.

I sighed contentedly and rubbed a hand over my face. I genuinely wasn't expecting anything like this to happen when I took this assignment. I'd never felt anything for a girl before, it all happened so suddenly too. She'd stolen my heart in three days, well, she'd actually had it in about three seconds. As soon as she'd walked into her father's office, I knew I was done for.

I pushed myself up off the bed, stretching my arms above my head and feeling the familiar burn of after sex muscle tightening. I grinned and grabbed some jeans and a button down shirt, deciding I should probably go and speak to the senator and see what he wanted. Once I was dressed, I shoved my gun into its ankle holster and headed out. I stopped outside her door, wondering if it would be a little too forward if I knocked just so I could see her again, kiss her again and pull her close to me. I wanted her so close that she'd melt into me. It was probably a little fast for her, after all, I'd only met her three days ago and I'd already slept with her. That certainly wasn't something I was expecting, even with my reputation for a quick score.

I traced my hand across the wood of her door. My eyes closed, and I laughed quietly as I realised something – I was turning into some sort of weirdo stalker. I was standing outside her door, thinking about her; normally I'd arrest guys that did that. I forced myself to walk away from the door. I needed to speak to her father, and then maybe I'd take her for a picnic or something, show her what a good boyfriend I could be.

As I was walking through the house, I decided that my new favourite place in the world was here with Anna; it used to be the shooting range at the training academy, but she had that beat easily. I was certainly going to be guarding her body extremely closely from now on. I grinned at the thought of that happening again, and again, and again. *Man, I love this job!* And pretty soon I had a feeling I was going to love her too – I was already half way there and I had only known her for three days. I'd never believed in love at first sight until I met Anna.

When I got to his outer office, his PA buzzed me straight through. Senator Spencer was sitting behind his desk with a grim expression on his face. He stood as I entered. "Agent Taylor, I need to speak to you," he said, smiling sadly, nodding towards the chair opposite him. I sat quickly and waited for him to speak. "Agent Taylor, we've received another letter from him, I just needed to make you aware," he stated, sliding a piece of paper across his desk.

I stiffened, and my heart took off in a sprint. Another letter from Carter. I wanted to run from the room and wrap her in my arms, never letting go. I would die before I let him hurt her again and if I ever saw him, I wasn't sure I'd be able to restrain myself from killing him.

I took the note and read it over quickly; it was addressed, 'Dear Princess'. Realisation hit me: that guy on the CCTV footage had called her princess too, that's why she'd gotten kicked out of school. It was essentially a love letter expressing how much he missed her, how he couldn't wait for them to be together again, and how he was expecting her cooperation at the appeal, should she be called upon to give evidence against him again. He wanted to take her away and treat her like the princess that she was. He went into a lot of crude detail about all of the things he wanted to do to her. I felt the bile rise in my throat, so I quickly swallowed it down, trying not to picture the images that were trying to force their way into my head.

I was so angry that my hands were shaking. I looked up at the senator; he looked extremely sad and tired. "This came this morning, sir?" I asked, folding the note and handing it back to him.

He nodded. "I have the others if you want to read them," he offered, rifling through his desk drawers.

"Er... No thanks, sir. Unless there's anything in there I need to see," I said uncomfortably. I wasn't sure I could read another one of those.

He waved his hand at it, a look of disgust on his face. "No, they're basically the same as this one."

"How many have there been, sir?" I asked curiously. That information wasn't in the file.

He sighed. "He sends one a week, every week for the last three years. Always the same thing," he answered. I gasped at the revelation. *One a freaking week for three years and they haven't told her?* I'd assumed that it was only since the retrial was ordered. "We get one of those love letters from him, and a death threat from somewhere within his organisation," he added grimly.

"Sir, you're sure we can't tell Miss Spencer? I really think she would be better off knowing. It would help her guards if she was more cooperative with us." My mind shot to her naked in the bed, where she'd seemed very cooperative indeed.

"No, Agent Taylor. It's my decision, and I feel that she's too fragile," he refused, shaking his head fiercely. I nodded in agreement. I knew she was fragile; I'd seen her sobbing her heart out, shaking. Fragile didn't even seem the right word to describe Anna's state of mind. "I think she's gotten much stronger since you came. She seems to like you. I've never seen her like that with anyone since it happened. I mean, she smiles for goodness' sake, and the contact you have with her boggles my mind," he said, shaking his head in disbelief.

Oh yeah, it boggles my mind too alright! I bit my lip to suppress the smile that was trying to escape at the thought of the contact I just had with her, and hopefully would have with her again in a little while.

Suddenly my cell phone rang; I looked at Senator Spencer apologetically and reached to reject the call, but then saw it was from Dean, Anna's far guard. "I'm sorry, sir, I need to take this." He nodded, so I answered it quickly. "Dean, what is it?"

"Where the hell are you? For fuck's sake, you can't just keep taking off and leaving me! If the senator finds out I'm not with you, he's gonna have my balls!" he shouted angrily.

Where am I? What the heck is that about? "I'm with the senator right now. What's the problem?" I asked, confused.

He gasped. "Well, fuck it! She went on her own then!"

I jumped out of the chair as my heart started crashing in my chest. "Anna? What? She left?" I cried, annoyed. *Damn that girl!* The senator jumped up too, looking at me curiously. "Did she take a car? When did she leave?" I asked quickly, double checking to make sure I had my gun in my ankle holster.

"She sped out of here about ten minutes ago. I thought you were with her," he growled. She obviously did this little disappearing act a lot.

I took a deep breath and closed my eyes, my mind whirling. Where would she go? I thought about what I knew about her, and all my thoughts led me to just one place. Jack. She'd be at the cemetery.

"Get a car, I know where she is," I ordered, disconnecting the call and pushing the phone into my pocket. I turned back to the senator. "Sir, Miss Spencer's left without guards; I think I know where she is. I'll come and speak to you later."

"Where do you think she is, son?" he asked, looking at me desperately.

"At the cemetery with Jack." I turned and rushed out of the door, running as fast as I could to the carport. "I'll drive." I snatched the keys out of Dean's hand and jumped in the driver's side. I waited impatiently for him to run to the passenger seat, and took off while he was still doing his seat belt. "Why the hell weren't you watching her?" I snapped accusingly.

He glared at me. "As if that girl could be watched! She does what she wants! She doesn't want guards. She's always running off like this, it annoys the hell out of me," he growled, folding his arms over his chest.

As I pulled into the cemetery parking lot and stopped next to her car, Dean looked at me curiously. My muscles loosened now that I'd found her. "Just wait here. She won't want to come away, so I'll have to give her some time there," I instructed, jumping out of the car without waiting for an answer.

I ran up the path that we had walked the other day and stopped at the top of the hill, looking down. She was sitting there at his grave, cross-legged, trailing her fingers along the letters of his headstone. She was sobbing uncontrollably. My heart broke at the sight of her, she looked so terribly sad.

I stood there, just watching her for a few minutes. I couldn't think of anything that had made her act like this. When I'd left her earlier she was fine. Then I wondered if maybe *I* was the problem. She was probably conflicted with what happened. Her fleeing to his grave was a clear indication that she felt guilty or something. I frowned, hoping I was wrong there. I didn't want her to feel guilty. Maybe she felt like I was trying to replace him and what they had. I wasn't trying to take his place in her heart though; I actually wanted my own place.

When I could stand it no longer, I headed down there. She jumped, startled, when my shadow fell over her. Her eyes met mine and I fought back my urge to recoil. Her eyes were the cold, hard eyes of the broken girl. The heartless bitch was back.

She didn't speak; she just turned her head back to the gravestone. I read over it as I sat down behind her, putting my legs either side of her body and scooting forwards so that her back was pressed against my chest. The scent of her still damp hair was all around me, confusing my senses.

I wanted to wrap my arms around her and rock her soothingly, but I had a feeling that would just make matters worse. So instead, I just let her cry. I was dying to ask her to give me a chance, but I knew I needed to give her more time. She was obviously having trouble dealing with what happened this morning. I'd just have to wait and be here for her. When she was ready to try and move on from what happened, then I'd be there. I closed my eyes and waited for her to tell me she didn't want me.

~ Anna ~

After breaking the speed limit the whole way to the cemetery, I made my way up the familiar path to his grave, zigzagging amongst some of the gravestones to pick a few dandelions. When I got to his resting place I brushed the old dandelions away and sprinkled the new ones across the top of the headstone.

I plopped down on the grass and closed my eyes, hating myself. "I'm so sorry. I don't know what happened. I know I shouldn't have done it, I know, and I'm sorry. I'm so sorry. Please forgive me, baby, please?" I begged, unable to stop the tears this time.

My heart was breaking all over again, and I didn't know what to do. I was starting to like Ashton, I could feel it building, and I wanted his body so much that it was almost painful. I still wanted him now. But how could I have done that to Jack? Sweet, loving Jack, who never even looked at another girl? The love of my life died because of me, and how did I repay him? I slept with someone that I only met three days before, and not only that, but Jack hadn't even entered my head until Ashton left the room. It was like my new near guard had some kind of spell on me.

I traced my fingers along the lettering of Jack's name. I felt like a worthless piece of trash, a horrible person and a downright useless girlfriend.

Suddenly a shadow fell over me and I jumped, looking around quickly. Ashton smiled down at me sadly. I turned away, afraid to look into his beautiful green eyes in case I got stuck there. My heart was going crazy because of his presence. I felt him sit down behind me, setting his legs either side of my body as he scooted close to my back.

I closed my eyes, hating the comforting feeling of being close to him. I didn't deserve to be comforted. My body hitched with sobs again, but he didn't move to hold me or anything, he just sat close to me. His body heat was seeping into my back and made my skin tingle. I cried harder because the reactions he caused in me were both unconscious and unwelcome. I didn't want to feel anything for anyone else; in fact, I didn't want to feel anything at all. I liked being numb and emotionless. But lately, all of that seemed to go out of the window.

"Are you okay?" he whispered in my ear, a little while later. I couldn't speak, so I just shook my head. "Please tell me what's wrong," he begged. He sounded so upset that I wanted to turn and hold him. But I couldn't do that. Not to Jack. I wouldn't do it again, never ever again.

"Nothing. Just leave me alone," I croaked.

"Anna, talk to me, please? Is it what happened this morning?" he asked quietly.

Is it about this morning? Damn, that's just a stupid question! Of course it's about this morning! I danced all over my boyfriend's memory. And I enjoyed it so much that I wanted to do it again, and again, and again. But I won't.

"That won't happen again." I pushed myself away from his warm, safe body, taking one last look at Jack's grave.

"Anna?" he whispered. His pleading voice sent a little quiver down my spine that I refused to acknowledge. I shook my head and looked at him, positive that it would never happen again. If he kept pushing me then I'd have to get him transferred; I didn't want to do that, but I would if I needed to.

"No. It won't happen again. If you want to keep your job, Agent, then you'll stay the hell away from me," I spat nastily. I saw the look of hurt and pain cross his eyes, and I turned away quickly so I didn't see it again. Touching the smooth marble of Jack's headstone, I sniffed loudly. "Bye, baby," I muttered, swallowing another sob. I walked off quickly before I started to cry again, I refused to cry again today.

When I got to the parking lot, Dean jumped out of his car, slamming the door angrily. His hard eyes narrowed as he stalked towards me. "What the hell, Annabelle? For the last fucking time, you need to take us with you when you leave!"

He sounded so angry that my stomach clenched in fear. I frowned and carried on walking, trying to ignore him. "Screw you, Dean. Just get lost, okay?" I replied venomously when he continued to glare at me.

"You're a little bitch!" he spat, his face radiating anger. He grabbed my arm roughly and pulled me to stop. I flinched, thinking he was going to strike me. I held my breath, readying myself for the blow. Before anything happened, Ashton gripped his shoulders and yanked him away from me, slamming him against the car, making a huge crash echo in the empty parking lot. I whimpered and looked at the scene, shocked.

Ashton's jaw was tight as he stepped closer to Dean. "You don't ever touch her again! I don't care who you are, I will put you down if you even look at her harshly again. You got that, Agent Michaels?" Ashton's voice rang with authority and menace. Dean nodded quickly, his mouth popping open in shock. Ashton shoved him away, making Dean stumble and almost fall. "Go. I'll ride with Anna," Ashton ordered. He turned back and waved his hand for me to get into the car, but I couldn't move, my body was frozen on the spot. "Anna, get in the car," he said softly, taking the keys from my hand and opening the passenger door. That snapped me out of it and I climbed in quickly, looking down at my lap.

From the corner of my eye, I watched him walk to the driver's side; he looked like he was trying to calm himself. I needed to say something to him, what he just did was so sweet and protective. Dean wouldn't have hurt me, but Ashton hadn't hesitated for a second in protecting me.

I waited for him to climb in and buckle his seatbelt before I spoke. He didn't even glance at me as he started the engine. "Thank you," I mumbled, still not able to look at him. I needed to stay strong, and his eyes wouldn't let me do that.

"You don't need to thank me, it's my job," he replied sarcastically. I cringed at the tone of his voice; he was obviously annoyed that I'd suggested I'd get him fired. I felt like a first class bitch. He hadn't done anything wrong at all – it was *my* fault that I cheated on Jack, not his.

He put the car into drive and he didn't speak to me again. In fact, he didn't even glance in my direction, but I couldn't help stealing little glances at him from the corner of my eye as he drove. He looked so handsome in his blue shirt with the sleeves rolled up at the elbows; blue worked really nicely with his skin tone. I bit my lip and ripped my eyes away from him to watch the road, hating that I'd noticed.

We finally pulled up at the house after what seemed like a week of driving in an uncomfortable silence. I grabbed the door handle, but the ominous click of the lock told me I wasn't going anywhere until he'd said his piece. If anyone else had trapped me in a car with them, I would be totally freaking out, but deep down I knew he wouldn't physically hurt me. Mentally he would probably hurt me a lot when I agonised over what we'd done and how he'd somehow made me open myself up to him.

"Open the doors," I instructed, focusing my gaze on the house, wishing I could get inside and away from him.

"I just need to say something first, and I need you to look at me so you know I'm serious," he replied flatly.

I didn't want to look at him; I hated to see that hurt expression on his handsome face. I knew I had to do it though; he obviously wasn't going to let me go until I'd been reprimanded for sneaking off without guards. I willed myself to stay strong and turned to look at him, avoiding his eyes and looking at the spot just below his eyes instead.

"I know you were upset, but you *will not* leave without me again. If you don't take me, you take someone else, but you *do not* go out on your own again. Do you understand me, Miss Spencer?" he asked angrily.

I recoiled at the use of my name. Somehow, him using my title like that showed me how angry he was with me. I should have been glad. If I'd annoyed anyone else as much as I appeared to have annoyed him, I would think that a successful morning, but with Ashton it actually pained me to know that he was upset with me. Irrational anger was building in the pit of my stomach because I couldn't seem to treat him the way I treated everyone else.

"Is that understood?" His voice was hard and authoritative as he prompted me for an answer.

"Yes. Now open the door," I snapped.

His gaze held mine for another couple of seconds before he flicked the lock button, dismissing me. I frowned and pushed the door open, ignoring Dean watching me from the other car. I turned on my heel and ran into the house, needing to get away from everything and everyone. My thoughts turned to the gym. I didn't even bother changing into my workout clothes before heading in there to try and work out some of the frustration that was crushing me inside.

Needing to do more than run today, I put on the training gloves and went straight to work on the punch bag, hitting and kicking it until my fingers arched. Spent and exhausted, I stepped back, putting my hands on my knees as I caught my breath. Sweat trickled down my back, and I silently wished I'd stopped to get a bottle of water before coming in here.

"I wouldn't want to be on the other end of that anger."

I twisted on the spot, gasping because I hadn't heard anyone come in. Ashton was leaning casually against the wall, watching me. "What the hell do you want?" I asked, frowning. *Why can't he just leave me alone?*

"Want to go for that walk now?" he offered, raising one eyebrow.

90

Is he kidding me? I told him to stay away from me! "No thanks. Want to train me how to fight?" I countered, shrugging.

He sighed and nodded, kicking off his shoes and walking over to the mats. He pulled his shirt over his head and a wave of desire shot straight through my body. I bit back my moan of desire as memories of this morning flooded my brain. I kicked off my shoes and socks and followed him, pulling off the gloves and tossing them in the corner.

His eyes were cautious as he shifted his weight onto his back leg. "Same as yesterday then, I'll try to grab you and you fight me off, okay?"

I nodded in agreement, taking a deep breath and waiting for him to move. Anger was bubbling through me, I used it to help me focus. He came forward, so I punched him in the stomach, but he saw me move so he jumped back again to avoid it, my hand barely grazing his skin.

He came forward again, and this time I channelled all my hate and hurt into it. I punched him in the chest and slapped his hand away as he tried to grab me, bringing my leg to kick him in the thigh, but he blocked it with his arm, pushing my leg away, making me lose my balance. I regained control quickly and hit him a couple of more times, each one he blocked easily.

I got even angrier because fighting him made me feel so vulnerable. *How am I supposed to hurt Carter if I can't even land one hit?* As soon as I thought about him, Carter's smiling face swam in front of my eyes. Something seemed to snap inside me. I really went for it, punching and kicking at him, but he blocked me easily. I pretended to punch him in the stomach but quickly moved and elbowed him in the face. As he grunted in surprise, I took my opportunity and put my leg behind his, shoving him as hard as I could.

He fell backwards, grabbing me tightly and pulling me down with him. As soon as he hit the floor, he hooked his legs over mine and flipped me easily onto my back, pinning me to the mat with his weight.

"Calm down, Anna," he said soothingly. I couldn't calm down; I could barely breathe through my anger. I wanted to kill him; I wanted to rip his head off. I wanted to tear him apart. I thrashed, trying to get him off me, but he was just too heavy and strong. "Calm down, Anna," he repeated. I closed my eyes and willed myself to calm, but all I could see was Carter. I didn't realise I was crying until he wiped my tears away tenderly. "Shh, it's okay, Baby Girl," he whispered, sitting up and pulling me onto his lap, rocking me gently. I wrapped my arms around his neck and sobbed onto his shoulder. "You did great, Anna. That was really impressive, you definitely kicked ass," he said, rubbing my back.

When I was finally in control of my emotions, I sniffed loudly and pulled back to look at him. His eyes were sparkling with excitement as they locked onto mine. A flash of red caught my eye so I looked down at his mouth, seeing that his lip was bleeding a little.

I gasped, reaching out to touch it hesitantly. "Holy shit, Ashton. I'm so sorry," I mumbled weakly.

He shook his head dismissively. "It's fine. It was worth it to see you fight like that. You fight like an alley cat on speed," he replied, grinning at me proudly.

I burst out laughing at his randomness. "An alley cat on speed? Where the heck did that come from?" I pulled my T-shirt up and dabbed his bottom lip with it to stop it from bleeding. My face was inches from his and I could feel the desire building inside me. I pulled my T-shirt away from his mouth. The bleeding had stopped, but there was a small cut there. Wanting to somehow take the pain away, I bent my head and kissed it gently. He made a moaning sound in his throat that made my insides quiver as he kissed me back immediately. His arm tightened on me, holding me securely on his lap as his other hand tangled into my hair.

The way he kissed me made my whole body tingle; it was so passionate, yet so soft and tender at the same time. It was perfect.

His mouth left mine only to kiss my neck instead. Digging my fingers into his shoulders, I pressed myself to him, loving the heat that emanated from his skin. My heart was flying as the sensations were taking over. Something was pulling at the edges of my subconscious, a thought or feeling, but I was trying my best to ignore it and just enjoy his attention and the feel of his mouth on my skin. But something was most definitely telling me that this was wrong and that I shouldn't be doing this... Jack.

I gasped, jerking back out of his lap, pushing myself awkwardly to my feet as I shook my head, horrified with myself once again. I needed to leave, I needed to get away, this couldn't keep happening.

"Anna?"

I shook my head, turning on my heel to leave, but he jumped up and blocked my path to the door, holding up his hands in protest.

"No! Tell me what's wrong. Let me in, please? I swear I won't hurt you! I swear." He was giving me the puppy dog face, begging me with his eyes.

"I can't," I answered, shaking my head as my eyes overflowed with tears. "I'm sorry. I'm still in love with Jack, and I can't do this."

He stepped forward, catching my face between his hands, tilting my head up so I had to meet his eyes. "I know you still love him, and that's okay, but if you could let me in, maybe, in time, I could make you love me too."

I tried not to react to his pleading tone. I knew that if I let him in like he asked then he would break my heart; there was no doubt in my mind about that. And I just couldn't stand any more heartbreak. His mouth inched towards mine again, so I pulled my face out of his hands and gulped, trying to find the right words.

"Look, Ashton, you're really hot, and that's all there is to it. I just wanted your body, I don't want you. I don't want anyone apart from my Jack," I replied confidently, maybe even a little harshly.

His forehead creased with a frown. "Your Jack died, Anna. You can't have him."

I gasped at his insensitivity. "Don't you dare talk about him again! I'm serious. And if you ever touch me more than necessary for your job, Agent Taylor, I will have you transferred, and it won't be to the stupid front line either!" I spat.

"Bitchy doesn't suit your beauty, Anna," he said simply, looking hurt.

My anger started to deteriorate instantly but I fought to hold on to it. I couldn't keep letting this guy change the way I lived my life; I was doing fine before he came along. "Stop being such a nice guy all the time! You're making my life hard, Ashton. I can't cope with any more, please, please just stop this. This isn't a game for me," I begged weakly, dropping my eyes to the floor.

He stepped forward and hooked his finger under my chin, lifting my head. "It's not a game for me either. I'll stop if that's what you need, but whenever you decide you're ready, if at all, I'll be here," he whispered, bending forward and planting a soft kiss on my cheek. Then, without another word, he was gone and the gym door swung closed behind him.

I stared at the door for a full five minutes, not knowing what to think. I knew only one thing for sure – next week we were going to be pretending to be boyfriend and girlfriend, so we were going to have to get this little sexual tension speed bump out of the way before then.

Deep down, I knew he wouldn't quit his job before the allotted time was up, which meant I had eight months of his presence to cope with before he would poof into a puff of smoke and the problem would be solved. We needed to set some ground rules if this was going to work and then maybe, just maybe, I could get through the eight months unscathed.

Chapter Eleven

I sloped off to my room and showered, scrubbing all the sweat off me from the workout. When I was out and dry, I pulled on baggy combat pants, a V-neck top and a pair of Converse. Scraping my wet hair back into a messy bun, I took deep breaths, struggling to find the courage to talk to Ashton again. With shaky legs, I made the five steps from my bedroom door to his, hesitating outside before knocking. As I waited for him to answer, every instinct in my body was telling me to turn and run as far away from this guy as possible, because he was the only one that seemed to be able to make me question my 'don't get close to people' plan.

He opened the door with a polite smile, but that quickly fell from his face when he spotted me. I gulped awkwardly. "Hi. I'm thinking that maybe we should talk," I muttered, picking at the skin on the side of my fingernail. "Want to go for that walk or something?"

His answering nod was a little stiff. "Yeah. Come in, let me just get some shoes on." He walked into his room, pushing the door open wider in invitation. I hugged myself, barely stepping over the threshold as I watched him push his feet into a pair of sneakers before tugging on the bottom of his jeans and clipping something black to his ankle.

I frowned at it. "What's that?" I asked curiously. Without answering, he pulled the material up, exposing an ankle holster and black handgun. The air rushed out of my lungs as I recoiled. "Holy shit, Ashton! You could shoot your foot off!" I cried, horrified.

He laughed humourlessly and shook his head. "I have the safety on," he replied, standing up straight again. "We really should arrange for you to have some shooting lessons so that you know how to handle a gun."

My eyes were trained on the bump at the bottom of his jeans. "I don't want shooting lessons."

He shrugged, picking his cell phone from the side and pushing it into his pocket. "I would've thought you'd want to know how to defend yourself," he countered.

"I don't like guns," I admitted, "and why would I need to learn how to shoot, anyway? I've got you and that idiot Dean for that." I smiled weakly, trying to alleviate some of the tension that was in the air.

He smiled in response and motioned towards the door. "So, why don't you like guns?" he asked, putting his hand on the small of my back as we walked through the house.

I winced. "Carter liked guns. I've seen a lot of people get shot." I immediately tried not to think of the other reason I didn't like guns, the thing that made me so terrified of guns that it would wake me up in the night. He groaned, and his hand closed over mine tightly. I shook my head, not needing to look at him to know that he felt sorry for me. "Don't worry about it; I just don't like the thought of guns, that's all. The noise scares me," I added, shuddering.

"Well then, I definitely think you should go for some lessons. You should get used to the sound so it doesn't scare you anymore," he suggested. I had a feeling that if he was there with me then I wouldn't be scared anyway, but I didn't want to tell him that.

We walked out of the house, and I immediately turned to the left. We had extensive grounds here at the lake house and a few minutes' walk away, there was an old play park that I grew up using. I could probably use some pleasant and familiar surroundings while we had this conversation.

As we left the house behind us and strolled across the grass, I took a deep breath, knowing I needed to start sooner or later. "So, I need to talk to you. Um... I don't really know what to say or how to say it, so I'll just go for the truth, okay?" I offered, looking at him from the corner of my eye. He nodded, watching me intently, his eyes a little apprehensive. "Okay well, I don't want anything from you. I can't be with you again like this morning. I just can't do that, so there's no point in you thinking any differently." I frowned because of how uncomfortable this conversation was. "I really enjoyed what happened this morning, I'm not gonna lie about it. That really was my first time in so many ways, so thank you. I just... I don't want that to happen again." I actually didn't believe a word of what I was saying. Physically, I *did* want it to happen again, but for the sake of my mental health, I needed to set the boundaries because I couldn't cope with the guilt of it afterwards.

He hadn't said a word since I'd started speaking. The silence hung in the air as I kept my gaze firmly on the ground. The swing set of the park came into view, so I headed over to it, plopping myself on the seat, knowing I needed to continue. I was only half done with my prepared speech.

Wordlessly, he stepped behind me, giving me a little push on the swing. I cleared my throat, grateful that he was behind me and unable to see me cringe as I set the rules. "As of next week, you're officially my boyfriend, so I think we need to set some rules and stuff," I stated, making the word boyfriend sound like a dirty word.

"Yeah, good idea," he agreed quietly. His tone was a little hurt and defeated, but I didn't know how to help that.

"Okay, well, hand holding is fine," I started, "and I don't mind if you put your arm around me or hug me. But I don't want you touching me in a sexual way."

"No sexual touching. Got it," he confirmed, his voice coloured with amusement. I laughed nervously, leaning back as my swing propelled forward again. Silence hung in the air for a minute and then he spoke again, "Alright, if you're done with your rules, there are a couple of things I need clarification on." He walked around to the front of the swings, his lips pursed in thought.

Is there something I hadn't thought of? "What's that?"

"Kissing?" He raised his eyebrows in question.

My eyes widened. "I don't-" I shook my head, not wanting that to happen again. Kissing was classed as sexual touching in my book; it was the start to something that really couldn't happen again.

He sighed and raked a hand through his hair. "Anna, we're gonna need to kiss in public occasionally. Couples kiss…"

I nodded in agreement. He was right there; if the boyfriend façade was going to hold, I was going to have to kiss him a couple of times, at least in the first few days. "Okay, yeah I guess."

"What about dating?" he asked.

Damn it, I didn't think about that either! "Yeah, of course, that's fine. We'll say we have an open relationship, and then that way you can still see other girls," I agreed, nodding. That way he could still live his life whilst stuck guarding mine.

He burst out laughing, shaking his head. "I didn't mean me dating other girls!" he choked out, chuckling wickedly.

For some reason my stomach unclenched when he said that. Although it shouldn't have, a small amount of jealousy had settled over me at the thought of him being with someone else. "What then?"

As my swing propelled towards him, he reached out, gripping my ankles and gently pulled me to a stop as he crouched down in front of me. I sucked in a breath through my teeth, knowing that I might have to rethink the rules we'd just made. Even that little action was sexy as hell, yet it wasn't sexual at all. I had a feeling it was just his hands on my body that kept sending me over the edge.

"I meant *us* dating," he clarified. "We're supposed to be a couple; couples go out together, don't they? Movies, dinner, dancing. Do you dance?"

"Yeah, I dance. Well, not really anymore, I mean, I don't go anywhere to dance so…" I trailed off, looking at the floor. I used to like to dance, but that was the old Anna that was confident in her body, the happy-go-lucky girl that liked to giggle and smile up at the sunshine and eat picnics with her friends.

"So maybe if we ever go out somewhere I might get to dance with you," he suggested, raising one eyebrow in question. I bit my lip and nodded. I wasn't anticipating going to parties, but I didn't want to explain that to him right now. All I was interested in was trying to make it through college without being kicked out again. A boyish grin crept onto his face. "So, I can take you out on dates and dance with you at parties, as long as I don't touch you sexually. But I can hug you, and kiss you occasionally?" he checked, grinning, seeming like he was struggling not to laugh. "It sounds like we're an old, married couple."

I chuckled and nodded. "You're old, I'm not," I joked, raising my foot and putting it on his chest, pushing gently. Where he was crouched on the balls of his feet, I caught him off balance and he fell back onto his ass, laughing. I giggled wickedly as he stood up and dusted the grass and dirt from his behind, before taking the swing next to mine.

I smiled over at him, only just realising how much I'd missed just joking around with someone and laughing. For the last three years I'd barely interacted with anyone, choosing to make myself a recluse as I rejected my friends and family. It was nice just having someone to talk to for a change.

His smile slowly faded as his shoulders tightened, so I knew we weren't done yet. "What now?" I prompted.

He sighed and looked down at his hands. "I have one last thing I want to talk to you about." I waited for him to speak again, wondering what else I could have possibly forgotten. I thought I'd reasoned it all out before knocking on his door, apparently I was wrong. His eyes came up to meet mine again. "I hate your nightmares."

I snorted. He knew nothing of my nightmares. "Join the club."

He nodded, his eyes not leaving mine. "I have two options for you, both of them are okay with me so you can choose," he continued. "One of them I've suggested already. I change my sleeping pattern and sleep while you're awake. It'll just be like me working nights," he suggested.

I frowned, shaking my head adamantly. "No. What's the other suggestion?"

He sighed. "I sleep on the floor in your room. Or we could get one of those pull-out sofas or something. For some reason, you seem to sleep better if I'm in the room."

The reason was obvious to me. His snoring. And yes, I did sleep better with him there. It was almost as if I could still sense his protective presence while I was asleep, and that stopped me from going to that dark and terrible place where my memories taunted me in the form of nightmares.

"I guess a sofa bed might work," I agreed.

A satisfied smile pulled at the corners of his mouth as he nodded happily. "Once we get to our apartment, we can order one. Until then, I'll just sleep on the floor," he agreed. I opened my mouth, about to suggest that he could just sleep on the bed with me until we ordered a sofa bed, but then I remembered what had transpired between us this morning and my lips pressed together tightly. "Are you all packed and stuff for college?" he asked, changing the subject.

Packed? I hadn't even started. "Not really. It won't take long to throw a few pairs of jeans and a few T-shirts into a bag though." I shrugged, using my feet to start my swing off again.

His gaze swept over me as he nodded. "Have you always been a tom boy?" he questioned. "Not that you don't look good, of course, because I'm pretty sure you could make a used garbage bag look hot. I was just wondering."

"Um... well, first off, thanks for the weird compliment," I joked, blushing profusely. I tugged on the bottom of my shirt, fingering the material that I purposefully bought three sizes too big. "It's just easier for me this way. If I wear something fitted then guys hit on me, and I just can't... I don't deal well with it." I shrugged.

He reached out, taking hold of the chain of my swing and pulling me to a wobbly stop. "You have me now. You don't need to worry about guys hitting on you. You could dress in whatever you wanted." He pulled his cell phone from his pocket, glancing at the screen. "It's only just lunchtime; want me to take you shopping?"

I raised one eyebrow at the offer. He was right, with this new arrangement and him attending school with me, I wouldn't need to worry as much. Maybe I could buy myself a few new things. When I was younger, I was always a girlie girl. Like any carefree sixteen year old, I liked summer dresses, skirts, shorts and heels. A small smile tugged at the corners of my mouth when I thought about having a tiny piece of me back again. Shopping sounded like a nice idea.

"Okay," I agreed, nodding gratefully. I looked out across the grass, seeing the house in the distance. "Race you back?" I challenged.

He frowned, looking over at the house too. "That's not fair, I've seen you run," he protested.

I shrugged. "It's my favourite way to exercise," I answered. I said the words but my mind flicked to my morning workout with him in my bedroom. I definitely had a new favourite now. I blushed at the thought. He looked at me curiously, making me blush harder as I worried that he knew what I was thinking. "Maybe you should try running with me sometime, it'll build up your stamina, you're a bit lax." The heat in my cheeks flamed hotter as I realised I'd unintentionally just flirted with him.

He raised a teasing eyebrow. Clearly he'd noticed. "I have a problem with my stamina?"

"Oh yeah, definitely," I joked, winking at him. I nodded back towards the house again. "Race? Come on, Pretty Boy, where's the inner tough guy? Scared you'll get beaten by a girl?" I teased, smirking at him.

He shook his head adamantly. "I'm not scared, I just don't think it's fair that-" Midsentence, he suddenly sprang from his swing and burst forward. "Go!" he shouted over his shoulder, chuckling wickedly.

I gasped, and my mouth popped open in shock as I jumped to my feet too. "You freaking cheater!" I cried, giggling as I sprinted after him.

"Oh, for the love of God, can we *please* be done? Seriously, when I suggested shopping, what I actually should have suggested was buying a tin of paint, slapping it on a wall and watching it dry!" Ashton whined, cocking his head to the side and pouting at me.

I chuckled wickedly. Things had started out fine at first, he'd followed me around, smiling and nodding as I picked up things or tried them on. Three hours later and he was checking his cell phone every ten minutes, grunting in response to my 'like this shirt' questions, and dragging his feet as he walked. I must admit, I did find it entertaining and was stringing out the shopping trip, purposefully picking up everything, silently considering it before setting it back down again. His reactions amused me.

I looked down at his hands that were laden with my shopping bags and smiled, knowing I couldn't push him any further. How he'd made it this long, I had no idea. He must have the patience of a saint because I'd been ready to go after an hour.

"So I've found your weakness. You're a shopping lightweight," I teased.

He blew out a big breath and shook his head. "A lightweight would have begged to go home an hour ago when you made me walk past that pizza joint without buying anything. Personally, I think I should get a medal for sticking it this long," he countered.

I grinned. "I made you walk past the pizza place because you'd already eaten your way through a whole supersized McDonalds, followed by an apple pie!" I'd never seen anyone eat as much as Ashton did. It was unnatural.

"I needed the calories so I could carry your bags!" He held up my numerous shopping bags in evidence and raised one eyebrow.

Finally conceding, I nodded. "Okay, let's just go home now then, your whining is giving me a headache," I joked. I'd bought enough new things to keep me going for a couple of weeks anyway.

He pumped the air with one fist, and a smile graced his face for the first time in two hours. "Yes, thank you!" he chirped. His eyes flitted over my shoulder and his smile widened. "Let's get some cookies to take back with us." I burst out laughing, shaking my head in disbelief.

Once we'd gotten back to the house and I'd hung all of my clothes up, I didn't want to do much other than just sit and chill, so I suggested watching a movie – and he suggested popcorn.

After finally seeking out popcorn from the cupboards and microwaving it, I slumped onto the sofa in the lounge, while he looked over the wall of DVDs that we had accumulated over the years. After making his choice, he put it on, turned off the lights and then dropped onto the sofa next to me, smiling wickedly.

"What'd you choose?" I asked, watching as the trailers started up.

"Mama."

I frowned and nodded, not having heard of it. "Is that a scary one?"

He chuckled and shoved his hand into the popcorn bowl. "I wouldn't hazard a guess."

Shifting to get comfortable, I twisted to the side and put my legs in his lap because there wasn't much room. He didn't seem to mind. In the flickering glow of the TV, I saw him smile as he laid his arm across my legs, scooting down in his seat to get more comfortable.

As the movie played, he started absentmindedly rubbing my feet and ankles, and eventually was massaging the back of my calves with his hands up the leg of my jeans. Out of nowhere the lights flicked on and I let out a little squeal because the movie was at a particularly scary part and my heart was already racing in my chest.

My mother stopped short, her hand still on the light switch as her eyes widened in surprise. "Oh! Sorry, I didn't realise anyone was in here," she apologised quickly. Her eyes flitted to my legs where Ashton's hand disappeared up the bottom of my jeans. Catching on to how it probably looked to an outsider, I moved my legs quickly and sat up, clearing my throat awkwardly.

"It's okay; we're just watching a movie. Want to watch?" I offered, feeling the heat creep up my neck and spread across my face.

A small smile tugged at the corners of her mouth as she flicked the lights back off again. "No thanks, I'll watch something in the other room. See you two tomorrow," she turned and left, closing the door tightly behind her.

I sank my teeth into my lip and turned to look at Ashton to see if he found that as awkward as I did, but apparently he didn't seem to care about the interruption and was just watching the movie again. Settling back down into the warm spot I'd created. I tried to watch the movie, but I couldn't get into it again. All I could think about was Ashton rubbing my legs, how nice it had felt at the time, and what on earth my mother had made of it.

When it was finally over, he turned the lights back on while I took the disk from the DVD player. "You like that?" I inquired, clipping it back into the case.

He shrugged, crinkling his nose. "Not really. It was alright," he answered, shrugging. "To be honest, I was expecting it to scare you; I was

100

hoping you'd be begging me to cuddle you or something. Plan didn't work." He smiled in my direction, so I slapped him in the stomach with the DVD case.

I laughed incredulously and rolled my eyes as I picked up the empty popcorn bowl. "It didn't work because you distracted me with all your foot rubbing," I joked.

He clicked his tongue in disapproval and shook his head. "I didn't even realise I was doing that until your mom came in."

I smiled weakly, heading out of the room and into the kitchen. "Don't whine, it doesn't become you. Besides, I'm sure I'll get plenty scared over the next eight months," I replied sarcastically, as I put our empty glasses and bowl into the sink.

He stepped up close behind me, his chest practically touching my back. His breath blew down my neck as he spoke, "You're finally convinced I'm not gonna quit then?" he asked.

A little shiver ran down my spine at how sexy he sounded. Gulping, I mentally chastised myself for still letting him affect me. I pushed my elbow back into his stomach, forcing him to step back and give me some personal space.

"I believe you won't quit," I admitted. "Your problem will be if I have to get you transferred," I warned.

He sighed and stepped back, so I chanced turning and looking up at him. He forced a smile. "You won't have to get me transferred, I promise." I smiled gratefully, and a large yawn escaped before I even had time to cover my mouth. He grinned and nodded over his shoulder. "Bedtime, Miss Spencer."

As we walked through the house, he was asking me what type of movies I preferred because I admitted that I didn't like horror or paranormal ones. By the time we got to my bedroom door, he frowned and kicked at the floor with his toe. "So, er, can I sleep in your room?"

I gulped, recoiling slightly but nodded in agreement. "I guess, yeah."

Not waiting for him, I marched into my room and grabbed some pyjamas before heading into the bathroom to change. I took my time, calming my nerves, mentally steeling myself against being in bed with him again. I wasn't sure this was a good idea after what had happened between us that morning.

When I'd finally worked up the courage, I left the bathroom, expecting to see him lying in my bed, half naked. But he wasn't. Instead, he'd taken one set of my pillows and the throw that covered the bottom of my bed and had made a little bed for himself on the floor next to my own.

My heart stuttered at the sweet move because I'd just assumed that he would expect to share my bed. He was lying on his back, his chest bare, one arm folded behind his head, and his other stretched across his stomach. He smiled as I stepped out of the room.

"I thought you'd fallen in or something," he joked, mocking the amount of time I'd been in the bathroom.

I laughed awkwardly and walked to my bed, climbing in but rolling so I was at the edge of the bed and could look down to see him stretched out on the floor. "You gonna be okay down there?"

He nodded quickly. "I'll be fine, don't worry," he vowed. "Goodnight."

"Night, Pretty Boy."

My eyes wandered to his chest as my body longed to move down onto the floor with him, to press against his side and let his warmth flood into my system. My scalp prickled as I imagined how soft his skin would feel under my hand if I just stretched out and touched him, or how his tongue would taste against mine. I longed for these things, but I refused to allow them to happen. Instead, I reached up and flicked off the light, submerging us into darkness.

Chapter Twelve

I cracked my eyes open, wincing as the light from the window made my eyes sting. I squeezed them closed again and rolled over, almost falling out of the bed as I was so close to the edge. Groaning quietly, I suddenly realised that Ashton wasn't snoring, or even breathing heavily. Frowning, I peeked over the edge of the bed, only to find that the place that he'd slept was now empty, his pillow and makeshift blanket folded and placed on my dresser chair. My eyes flicked to the alarm clock, it was only just after seven thirty. I groaned in frustration. I would have definitely preferred to sleep in longer than this! A small folded piece of paper on the side next to my alarm clock caught my attention. My name was scribbled on the front in typical boy's messy handwriting. I reached for it, opening it eagerly, already wondering why he'd gotten up so early.

Anna,

I went for a run in the gym to build up my stamina.

Ashton

A small chuckle escaped my lips at the stamina comment. I flopped back against the pillows and stared up at the ceiling. Today was my last day here because tomorrow was the scheduled trip to Arizona, ready to start my new school on Monday. There was nothing I wanted to do today, so I nibbled on my lip thinking of how I could whittle away the hours rather than having to spend time with my parents. If I kept myself busy then I wouldn't have to see them behave awkwardly around me all day while they tried to pretend like they understood how I was feeling. I hated that.

The only thing I could think of was something that Ashton had said yesterday. Shooting practice. Maybe if I was there with him and he was teaching me how to use a gun in a safe way, I would finally get over some of my fear of them. I wasn't stupid enough to believe that it would ever go away, I just wondered if him teaching me the basics of shooting might stop the complete blood-curdling terror from taking over whenever I came into contact with one. There was only one way to find out.

I sighed and pushed myself out of bed, needing to get this over with early if I was actually going to be able to go through with it. My nerve would deteriorate the longer I left it, so I needed to set the wheels in motion before it fizzled out altogether.

Stepping into my en-suite bathroom, my gaze landed on the mirror. The girl that looked back at me was unfamiliar and so incredibly different to what I'd been used to seeing for the last three years. My eyes had lost the tired look that they always had, probably because since Ashton came here, I'd slept better than the last three years put together. My skin looked like it had more colour, my posture wasn't as tight and defensive as usual. I smiled, perplexed that one person, and of course, some sleep, could make me feel and look so different.

I decided to try out how it felt to wear normal clothes. At least if I tried it out here and couldn't cope, then I could pack my usual stuff before we left. Not bothering to wash my hair again, I straightened it using the straightening irons that my mother had bought me two years ago that hadn't even been removed from their box. Afterwards, I looked through my closet for a solid five minutes before choosing a pair of cropped, fitted jeans, a fitted red shirt and a pair of red open-toed heels. When I looked in the mirror again, I looked even less like the girl that I had come to associate myself as. I wasn't sure I liked it.

Knowing I needed to take the plunge before we left, I pulled back my shoulders and raised my chin, trying to fake confidence as I left my room and headed downstairs. I didn't pull it off.

As I passed the entrance to the gym, I could hear the sounds of feet thumping on the treadmill. I smiled and slipped inside, seeing Ashton running with his back to me. He was jogging steadily in just a pair of black shorts. Sweat ran down his back and wet the hair at the nape of his neck. I gulped as I watched the muscles in his legs and back tighten with each stride. I couldn't take my eyes off him.

He was just slowing down, so I waited until he'd come to a stop before I spoke. "Hi," I chirped, smiling and trying not to blush and let on to the fact that I'd just been watching him with lust-filled eyes for the last couple of minutes. He spun around as if I'd made him jump. The shock was evident on his face as he stared at me with his mouth hanging open and his eyes wide. "I didn't think I was supposed to be able to creep up on you. I thought you were supposed to be some badass SWAT guy. Maybe I put too much faith in your ability to protect me," I teased, leaning on the doorframe, crossing one leg over the other.

"I... I..." he stuttered weakly as his eyes raked over my body slowly. *Oh, he likes my new clothes!* "You... You... what?" I asked, grinning.

104

He blew out a big breath and shook his head. "Shit, Anna, you look beautiful."

I blushed at the compliment. "Um, thanks."

"I'm not kidding. Damn. I think I'm gonna need to buy another gun," he shrugged, finally dragging his eyes up to mine.

"Another gun?"

He nodded, grinning at me wickedly. "Yeah, looks like I'll need the extra bullets to keep all the guys away from you next week."

"Well, thank goodness I have a badass boyfriend then," I joked, picking up the towel and throwing at him. "You have any plans for today? I've thought of something for us to do, if you're not busy."

A sceptical, worried expression crossed his face as he winced. "Please tell me it doesn't involve walking around any more clothes stores," he whined.

I couldn't help but laugh at his begging voice. "No more clothes stores," I confirmed. I swallowed around the lump that was rapidly forming in my throat. "I was actually thinking that you could teach me how to shoot, like you'd said. There's a shooting range that my dad goes to sometimes. It's about an hour away, I think. We could go as soon as you're ready."

His eyes widened as he walked over to me, reaching out and setting his hand on my waist as he bent and looked straight into my eyes. I could feel the heat from his hand seeping into my skin through my clothes. I gulped at the intimacy of this small touch. "I thought you didn't want to do that," he whispered, eyeing me worriedly.

"And I thought you said you wanted me to learn," I countered. I didn't want him to talk me out of it now. I'd been psyching myself up to it for the last half an hour. "It'll be fine. If it gives me nightmares then my big, bad bodyguard can protect me," I teased, grinning. He smiled at me cockily. "I may have to pay Dean overtime, but I'm sure he'll be up for it," I added quickly.

He snorted and rolled his eyes playfully. "You're gonna let Dean in your bed? Can't see that happening," he replied, grinning mischievously as he tickled my waist. I wriggled and twisted out of his grasp, laughing uncontrollably. I had a very ticklish spot on my ribs, and it appeared that he'd just found it.

He laughed and stepped back, letting his hand drop from my side. "I should shower. Why don't you go have some breakfast and then I'll meet you in there in a bit," he suggested. I nodded in agreement, and headed out of the room, holding the door open for him to walk through too. He shot me a little smile as he walked in the opposite direction to me.

As I stepped through the door to the kitchen, I groaned inwardly and wished I'd skipped food today. Both of my parents were sitting at the breakfast bar sipping coffee. They stopped talking and looked up at me as I walked in.

I forced a tight smile. "Morning." I kept my greeting short, not wanting to instigate a conversation with them.

"Annabelle, you look beautiful!" my mom gushed. "Did you get that shirt yesterday?"

I nodded, frowning as I strutted to the coffee pot and poured myself a cup. Did everyone know my every move? "Yeah. I got a few things to take with me to the new school. I spent on the credit card, hope that's okay." Too late if it wasn't. Maybe I should have asked first...

"Of course it is. It's your allowance, you never spend it," my dad answered. I turned back to see him smiling at me – a genuine smile. I hadn't seen one of those for a long time. Generally our relationship could be classified as 'strained' so I never really saw them smile much around me anymore. I could see the hopefulness in both of their eyes. Clearly they were reading something into the new clothes. I hated the little, meaningful smile they exchanged because they thought I wouldn't notice.

Roll on tomorrow, so I can get the heck out of here!

I pulled out a stool at the end of the breakfast bar and sat down, pulling a bowl and box of cereal towards me. The air was thick with awkwardness, and you could probably cut the tension with a knife as I sat there with them. It was probably strange for both of them to be sitting here having coffee with a daughter they had all but been estranged from for the last three years. It appeared no one knew what to say.

Needing to break the silence because it was practically deafening me, I cleared my throat and said the first thing that popped into my head. "Agent Taylor is taking me shooting today."

My dad's eyes widened as he regarded me quizzically. Either because I'd volunteered to start a conversation, or because of the topic. "Oh really? I didn't know you had an interest that that kind of thing."

"I don't. Ashton thinks it'll be good for me," I replied, shrugging and focussing on pushing my cereal around my bowl with my spoon.

"Well, maybe it would be a good idea," my dad agreed. I could practically hear the cogs of his brain ticking over, trying to work this all out and read things into it. "I'll put in a call to a friend and have you some guest passes ready so you don't have to join and fill in paperwork."

My mom chimed in then, asking my dad when the last time was that he went shooting, and thankfully the conversation required little to no input from me, so I sat quiet and chewed on my cereal, silently willing Ashton to hurry up.

After ten minutes I was all but ready to run from the room. Talk had been sparse, and the uncomfortable atmosphere had gotten so bad that I could barely sit still. When Ashton strutted into the kitchen, dressed and smiling, I practically jumped out of my seat and breathed a sigh of relief.

"Hi, you ready?" I asked hopefully.

"Er…" he looked from me to the food and back again. My heart sank. I'd had enough and needed to leave. "Yeah, sure." He turned to my parents and smiled politely. "Good morning, sir, ma'am."

I reached out and snagged him a bagel and an apple before stepping to his side and holding it out to him, praying he wouldn't suggest we eat it here. "Let's get going then, it's a little way away." He smiled sympathetically and nodded, before leaning over and picking up a granola bar too. "Bye. See you at dinner," I said to my parents, knowing that I would never get out of my last dinner before leaving.

Ashton bid his goodbyes as I was walking out of the room. I breathed a sigh of relief as I rolled my shoulders, turning to look at him as he bit into the bagel eagerly. "Thank you. That was… awkward."

He grinned. "No problem."

As we walked, I slipped my hand into his, partly because I wanted more practice at the fake boyfriend thing ready for next week, but mostly because I just wanted a little reassurance that everything was okay. I was extremely nervous about going shooting. He turned to face me, a smile twitching at the corners of his lips.

"What?" I asked, confused.

He lifted our hands, grinning. "That's the first time you've taken my hand."

"Um… Yeah, I guess it is," I admitted, squeezing his hand gently, willing him not to push the subject further. When we got to the carport, I pulled my car keys from my pocket, tossing them to him and nodding towards the driver's side of my Aston Martin again, watching as his eyes widened in delight.

"Hell yeah!" he cried, grinning from ear to ear.

"What is it with boys and cars?" I mused. "Hey, that reminds me, we'll have to buy a car when we get to Arizona. Unless you want them to arrange one for us."

He opened the door for me. "Never thought about that." He popped the rest of his bagel into his mouth before walking confidently around to the other side of the car and climbing in.

"What sort of car do you want?" I wasn't really into cars, as long as I got from A to B, that did me.

He shrugged. "I don't know. Something we can both drive."

"I can see you in a Porsche or Ferrari." I narrowed my eyes, picturing him getting out of a little, sexy sports car. *I bet that would be a good look for him!*

"Ooh, how about one of those yellow ones from the transformers movie?" he joked.

"You do know it wouldn't turn into a robot though, right?" I countered, poking him in the ribs.

"Aww man, really?" he frowned, faking disappointment. We laughed for a few minutes while I searched for the shooting range on the GPS. "Do we really need to choose a car?" he asked after a few minutes, when we'd finally gotten going. I nodded in confirmation. "Okay, how about a four by four then. You'll drive that, right? They're nice and safe. If you have an accident, you can pretty much just drive over the other car." His face was serious and thoughtful.

"Are you saying I'm a bad driver?" I gasped, faking hurt.

He laughed and nodded. "Yeah."

I rolled my eyes and shrugged. "Whatever. Like I said, you choose something you like. You can be my glorified chauffeur considering you'll come everywhere with me anyway." Then I had a thought, was he planning on coming *everywhere* with me? "Hey, what happens if I have a ladies appointment?"

"Ladies appointment? Like what?" he questioned, glancing at me curiously before concentrating on the road again.

Is he seriously going to make me spell it out? "I don't know, a waxing or something like that," I muttered, embarrassed. I forced myself to go for a bikini and leg wax every few weeks because sometimes the paparazzi liked to stalk our house and take shots for magazines. Especially with the election coming up, they would be all over my family soon; hopefully I would avoid all of that though being at school.

"A waxing? Why couldn't I come with you?" he asked, raising one eyebrow, looking like a little, confused puppy dog.

"Ashton, seriously?" I scoffed, shooting him a warning face. There was no way I was standing for that; I drew the line at that one.

He sighed in defeat. "Okay fine. I guess I can't really do things a boyfriend wouldn't do, so for things like that, you'd have to take Dean with you and get him to stand outside the door," he explained, shrugging.

That was what happened now, a guard waited in the car for me outside the building. "Outside the door? Well, what happens if the lady tries to kill me with hot wax?" I asked with mock horror.

"Don't start me worrying about that or I will come with you to your appointments," he replied, smirking.

"Oh shut up! Why can't I just go on my own? Nothing will happen at a beauty salon, for goodness' sake. I think you're taking this job way too seriously. So what if my dad needs to beef up his security because of the election, no one's seriously going to attack me," I scoffed, frowning. This whole thing was just stupid. He didn't say anything, so I looked over at him; he was frowning at something and looked a little unhappy. "What's wrong, Pretty Boy, cat got your talented tongue?" I flirted, and then blushed at what I had said. *Oh man, did I really just say that?* I turned towards the window and bit my lip to stop the giggle escaping at the obvious slutty comment I'd just directed at my bodyguard.

He burst out laughing. "Damn it, Anna, will you stop making me laugh? I'm driving!" he scolded, trying to be serious.

"I apologise," I said, still giggling. I glanced over at him, and he gave me a wicked grin and winked, making my face burn even more.

Despite the GPS, we still got a little lost on the way there so it took well over an hour before we pulled into the shooting range parking lot. The anxiety and worry had been building inside me the whole ride, so by the time he cut the engine, my stomach was churning so much that my cereal was threatening to come back up.

Dean's car pulled in and stopped beside ours, but he didn't bother to get out. As far guard, he was just to wait outside the building in the car and be on call to jump in and save the day if he was needed. Ashton smiled at me encouragingly as I forced myself to climb out of the car and look over at the large, and incredibly intimidating, brick building.

As soon as the door to the place opened, the noise made me want to run. There were already a few people inside, so a gunshot sounded every couple of seconds. Each shot made me squeal and press myself against Ashton's side as he spoke to the assistant and signed us in with the guest passes my father had arranged. Ashton was handed two black trays, and I could see a small handgun in each one as the assistant led us over to the last two lanes in the building.

My heart was crashing in my chest, and my breathing was shallow. I didn't take my eyes off Ashton the whole time; it felt like if I kept him in sight I would be okay. Once the assistant guy had left, Ashton turned to me and pushed some safety glasses onto my face before snapping a thick, heavy pair of headphones over my ears. Sound was instantly muffled, but I could still hear the gunshots ringing out in the background.

He gripped my hips, guiding me to turn and face the right way. Stepping close to my back, his arms circled around my waist as he clamped my back against his chest. "It's alright, Anna, I promise," he said loudly so that I could hear him through the huge ear defenders.

I pressed harder into Ashton's body, wanting to melt into him as another shot rang out somewhere in the building. I was struggling to stay in control. Deep down, I wasn't sure I could do this. My eyes locked on the black and white target of a body that was in front of me but about twenty feet away. There was a target on the centre with circles spreading outwards with little numbers in so you could obviously keep track of your progress.

He gently lifted one of my ear defenders off my ear, resting it on my cheek before his hands closed over my shoulders, squeezing supportively. "Okay, Baby Girl," he said. His voice vibrated against my head, making the hair on the back of my neck prickle.

Wait, did he just call me baby girl?

Reaching out, he gripped one of the hand guns, holding it out in front of me. I groaned and shied away from it, pressing back into him further. "It's fine," he promised. With his other hand, he took mine and placed the cold metal into my hand before forcing my other hand around it too so that I was holding it. His hands stayed firmly wrapped around mine. A pitiful whimper left my lips. "Do you know where the safety is?" he asked. Forcing myself to look at the killing machine in my hands, I spotted a small button on the side of it. I pointed it out with my thumb, taking a wild guess. I didn't bother trying to talk, my mouth was too dry; I knew nothing would come out if I tried to speak. "That's great, Anna," he purred in my ear. His praising, sexy voice almost distracted from the deep down terror that had practically consumed me – almost, but not quite.

Ashton then proceeded to give me a brief overview of how to line up my target and sight it properly; he went on and on about how I was supposed to squeeze the trigger, not pull it – which actually made no sense to me at all. Apparently, the gun would jerk in my hand a little when I shot it, so I had to expect that.

By the time I was ready to start, my breathing was coming too fast, and my heart was racing. He put my headphones back into place and then guided my hands out straight in front of me, still pressing into me from behind.

"Okay, click the safety off when you're ready, and then go," he instructed, holding my hands tightly on the gun. A long groan escaped my lips, but I moved my thumb regardless and clicked off the safety. When I squeezed the trigger, the gun did indeed jerk in my hand. I squealed and jumped at the sound and the fact that I'd just shot a gun. "That was fantastic. Go again," he encouraged.

As I squeezed off another shot, it dawned on me that it wasn't quite as bad as what I had been envisioning. After a couple more shots, Ashton took the gun from my hands, prising it from my stiff fingers as he clicked the safety back on.

I turned to look at him over my shoulder, chewing on my lip.

"That was great!" he cried excitedly. "You wanna have a go on your own?" he offered, raising one eyebrow.

"Okay," I agreed hesitantly. "But don't leave me."

He shook his head, raising his hand and crossing one finger over his heart. "I won't, I promise." He nodded back towards the target and held the gun out to me again. I gripped the gun, turning towards the target, trying not to notice that my hands were shaking. Once his arms encircled my waist, I closed my eyes, taking deep breaths. "Whenever you're ready, aim, take the safety off, and then go."

I concentrated on the safe feeling I felt with his arms around me like that; I focussed on the heat and hardness of his body as he held me tightly. Finally, my nerves subsided, so I took a deep breath and pointed the gun.

After four shots the gun was empty so he took it from my hands. I breathed a sigh of relief and felt my shoulders sag forward as I smiled, more than a little proud of myself for overcoming my fear like that. It was all because of Ashton though. I knew there was no way I would have even set foot in this place if he weren't with me.

"I am really proud of you for doing that," he said, bending forward and planting a soft kiss on my forehead. I gulped, feeling my smile grow

110

even bigger because of his praise. "Want to see how you did?" he offered, pointing to a button labelled target recall on the side of the booth we were in. I nodded eagerly and pressed it, watching as the paper target slowly made its way to us, on the little overhead track. Ashton smiled at it happily as it stopped next to him. I'd shot twelve shots in total. Nine of them had actually hit the paper, three of them were even on the shape of the body which I was surprised about. I hadn't thought I'd even hit the paper with my hands shaking like they were. "A few more times and you'll be a pro," Ashton joked.

"Are you going to have a go? Or are you scared you can't match my awesome skills?" I teased. I would actually quite like to see him fire a gun for some reason, maybe the horrible images would be replaced if I saw him do it.

He shook his head quickly. "Not today. Another time I will. I think you've been in here long enough already," he answered, picking up the gun and setting it, along with the extra clips we'd been given, into the black tray. "We should probably get going."

I nodded in agreement. That was probably a good idea. I didn't want to push it too far today and end up suffering the consequences tonight when my nightmares took over. Taking off my ear defenders and goggles, I dropped them into the tray too.

"I'll have you shooting like a pro by the end of my eight month assignment," he said as we walked to the reception desk to sign out.

I scoffed and shook my head. "I'd be happy just to get all of my shots on the paper by the time you leave." *Actually, I'd be happy just to be able to hold a gun without my hands trembling dangerously.*

As we walked out of the building and got in the car, I spotted Dean still sitting in the same spot. The boredom was easy to see on his face. Ashton nodded at him as he held my door open for me to get in. "It must be a really tedious job, being a far guard. I mean, he's always on his own, sitting around waiting for me," I mused once Ashton climbed into the driver's side and started the car. I actually felt a little sorry for Dean; he must be bored senseless watching me all day.

Ashton shrugged, pulling out of the parking lot. "That's his job. He gets paid for it."

A sudden thought occurred to me. "Do you get any extra money for looking after me? I mean, you're basically on duty for twenty-four hours a day, right? So are you getting double pay or something?"

A smile twitched at the corner of his mouth as he drove. "Nope, but I get the pleasure of your company, which is something I would gladly pay for. I actually think I'm doing them out of something," he answered. I blushed and shook my head, not knowing what to say to that. Thankfully, conversation flowed easily after that as he started telling me about his best friend, Nate Peters, who was apparently a bit of a ladies' man. Ashton assured me that if I ever met him that he'd try to get me into bed.

"So how does he get all of these women then?" I asked, grinning after hearing a tale of Nate scoring with three women in one night – and then it turned out that two of them were sisters, so he gotten a drink poured over his head.

He smirked in my direction. "It's the uniform. Girls like the uniform."

"Ahh." His meaning was clear. "So you score in yours too then I bet." My mind flicked back to the photo I'd seen of him in his uniform. He was right; the uniform was a definite pantie-moistener.

He shrugged awkwardly. "Sometimes I guess," he admitted.

"Did you bring it with you?" I asked. Immediately my face flooded with heat as my insides squirmed with embarrassment at asking that question. *Holy shit, Anna, you are on fire today!*

He grinned. "Why, do you want to see it?" he flirted.

I gulped; the answer to that question was 'heck yeah', but I refused to admit it. "Sure, why not. I can handle it, I have considerable self-control," I lied, shrugging.

He chuckled, grinning wickedly. "Yeah, much to my disappointment." He shook his head. "I didn't bring it. I'm undercover, remember? I'll show you some other time if you want," he offered, turning back to watch the road. *Oh heck yeah, I would certainly like to see him in that uniform!* I didn't say that though, and quickly changed the subject to his shooting.

Chapter Thirteen

When we pulled up at the house, I was a little disappointed. I genuinely liked spending time with him, but there was just too much pressure here.

"So, you wanna go do something? Swimming maybe?" he offered as we climbed out of the car. "In the indoor heated pool, I meant, not the ice water again," he added quickly, shuddering.

I laughed at that. "Er... there's something I really want to do first, so maybe in like an hour or something?" I suggested, raising my eyebrows. Yesterday, while shopping, I'd seen the Apple store and realised that Ashton needed an iPod if he was going to survive college. I was pretty sure he didn't have one, and I had a spare, brand new one that I'd bought for myself a few months ago when I thought I'd lost mine. Music was a college attendee's survival essential; he'd need that to keep himself sane.

He looked at me sceptically. "You're not leaving the house though, are you?"

"No, I'll be in my bedroom." I rolled my eyes at his assumption. He obviously took this guard thing way too seriously.

"Okay good. An hour's fine then, I'll go finish that book." He shrugged, smiling a half smile.

"I'll have to make sure to pack the other three for you if you're that into them," I teased.

He just rolled his eyes and didn't bother to answer me. On the way through the house, we stopped by the kitchen to grab a drink and sandwich for lunch. I said goodbye to Ashton for the hour, taking my food to my room. As soon as I was alone, I pulled out my laptop and started to sync my spare iPod to my iTunes, copying all of my music over to it for him. Having no idea what kind of music he liked, I had no clue if there was anything in my collection that he would like – it would be a start for him though, at least.

After exactly an hour, he knocked on my door. I winced and looked up worriedly because the music was still syncing. "Ashton, I'm not done, I'll be a bit longer then I'll come get you, okay?" I called, hoping he wouldn't just walk in and see me doing it. I wanted to give it to him tomorrow on the plane so he could listen to it during the flight if he wanted to.

"Are you okay?" he asked, sounding a little concerned.

"Fine," I answered, chewing on my lip, watching the grey bar at the top as it copied all of the music over.

"Anna, can I come in?" he asked, still sounding unsure.

I ran to the door and yanked it open before he just walked in and ruined my surprise. "What's up?" I asked, pulling the door close to my side so that he couldn't see into my room.

"Are you really alright? You're not freaking out because of the guns, are you?" he asked, reaching for my hand.

I smiled at his concern. I appreciated the thought actually. "No, I'm not freaking out. I just had something I wanted to do on my laptop before we leave tomorrow," I promised, shrugging.

His face brightened, and he seemed to visibly relax. "Oh, that's good, I was worried," he admitted, rubbing the back of his neck.

"Thank you for being worried, but I'm honestly fine." I shrugged.

"Okay, well, let me know when you're ready." He raised my hand to his lips, planting a soft kiss on my knuckle before turning and walking to his room next door.

While my laptop finished its task, I dug out another swimsuit and shrugged out of my clothes. By the time I had my clothes back on top of it, the sync was finished. As I walked to his room, I scraped my hair back into a bun before knocking politely on his door. He pulled it open as I was mid-knock so he must have been keen to go.

"Hey, I'm done," I greeted.

"Okay, great," he smiled and stepped out of the room, slinging a towel over his shoulder. As we stepped into the pool that we had at the back of the house, he raised one eyebrow in appreciation. "This is nice, I didn't even realise this was here."

"Yeah, I guess I should've shown you this on my tour of the house, huh?" I teased, grinning, remembering how I ditched him on his first day.

"Yeah, I still owe you for that," he warned, narrowing his eyes at me.

"I'm so scared," I mocked, stripping out of my clothes.

"You should be." His arms closed around me quickly, lifting me off my feet as he stalked towards the pool.

"No!" I shouted, just as he threw me into the water. I came up laughing and spluttering. "Asshole!" I cried, wiping the water out of my eyes. He did a cannonball into the pool, sending water everywhere. "Wow, you're such a child," I scoffed, trying to hide my grin.

We swam a few lengths, bantering back and forth. Ashton was a strong swimmer; apparently they had to swim a lot for training. He said that once, as a punishment for letting a chicken loose in the officers' lounge, he and Nate had to spend the whole night in the pool, swimming lengths and picking bricks up from the bottom.

"Wow, and you liked this place?" I asked, turning my nose up.

"Sure, it kinda saved me, I guess. When I was seventeen I didn't get many opportunities and I started hanging around with the wrong people. It was a toss-up for me between joining up with the force, or carrying on being that person who I was becoming. Thankfully I chose the academy."

I swam over to him and held onto the edge so we could talk. He grabbed my waist and pulled me to him. He was so close to me that the heat started up again. I had no idea how he did it to me. I moved closer to him, trailing my finger across his shoulder, looking at his tanned skin as lustful thoughts crashed over me in droves.

"You're looking like a prune," he teased, looking at my wrinkly fingers.

"You do too," I muttered, chewing on my lip. I knew I needed to get out of the pool, this was just plain wrong, and I shouldn't let this guy affect me so much. "Maybe we should get out." I didn't wait for an answer, just swam to the ladder and pulled myself out, grabbing my towel and drying my face.

When I turned back, he was just pulling himself out of the pool. My stomach tightened as he picked up his towel from the chair and started rubbing it over his chest. I watched the movements with interest; I'd never envied a towel before that moment.

Once I could bring myself to stop staring at him, I wrapped the towel around myself and we started walking back through the house. At my bedroom door, we parted ways. "I guess I should start packing after dinner," I mumbled, scrunching my nose up. Packing was the worst part about being kicked out of so many schools and having to start over.

"I can help you if you want," he offered. "I don't have that much to pack. If you have anything you want to put in with my stuff, you can."

I smiled gratefully. He'd already told me that he had a selection of clothes waiting for him at the apartment. Apparently they were supplying him with appropriate clothing; all he'd had to do was tell them his sizes. I dreaded to think what kind of clothing they deemed 'appropriate' for college.

I pushed my door open. "Okay thanks. I'll knock for you after I get back from dinner with my parents." I was going to do my best to enjoy my dinner tonight. As of tomorrow I would be leaving – and having a chef certainly was one thing I missed while at school.

~ Ashton ~

After I'd eaten dinner with the other agents and the other staff they had at the house, I'd packed up my own clothes before she finally knocked on my door signalling she was finished eating with her parents. As I lay on her bed with my arm folded behind my head, I couldn't keep the smile off my face. She was just so incredible. I genuinely didn't understand how there could be such a perfect creature like her in the world, and yet all those terrible things had happened to her.

My eyes were glued to her as she bent over, folding up her clothes. I could barely suppress my moan of desire for her. She obviously had no idea the effect she had on me, and I was pretty grateful of that fact. Clearly she needed a friend right now, so that was what I was planning on being for her. I'd do whatever it took to make her happy, even if this assignment ended up killing me. It was going to be incredibly hard on me to be so close, yet be so far away at the same time, but I could cope with it.

She turned and caught me looking straight at her, so I quickly flicked my eyes onto something else, knowing she was going to bitch me out about it. "You want to help me instead of just watching?" she teased, tossing a rucksack at me.

I laughed in relief. At least she didn't realise I was perving on her. Pushing myself up from the bed, I turned to her art materials that she had piled on her dresser and started putting it into the bag. When I got to her sketchpad, I wanted so badly to look at it, but I didn't know if she would want me to.

"Can I look through your drawings?" I asked hopefully.

She winced uncomfortably. "Um, okay. Some of them are a little… harsh."

Harsh. What is that supposed to mean? I sat down on the chair and started flipping through the pad. My mouth dropped open in awe as I looked at her drawings. They were incredible: the lake, the house, a tree, a sunset, one of her mom. I could tell which ones she called harsh. They were actually quite disturbing; blood, death, knives and guns. The same man was drawn over and over, looking menacing and angry. I recognised him from the photo in her file, this was Carter.

"These are really great. What do you want to do when you finish school?" I asked, pushing the book into the bag.

"Well, I always wanted to be a graphic designer, but I'm not sure that'll happen now. I'll just be happy if I can graduate and finish my course," she replied, looking a little sheepish.

I could feel my anger simmering just below the surface again. Carter had taken everything away from her. She just needed to get her confidence in people back though, that's all, I could help her with that. I'd do whatever it took to get her life back on track again.

"Well, don't give up on your dream, Anna. I'll help you," I promised, looking at her beautiful face.

She laughed quietly, and the sound made my heart beat faster. "You sound like Jack. He used to say things like that all the time."

I decided to take that as a compliment. Jack sounded like a good guy from what I'd heard, and he was a damn lucky one too to have her love him so much. "Smart guy," I commented, grinning.

I turned back to her stuff and picked up the sketch pad that she bought the other day when we went shopping. I flipped it open and on the first page was me again. I had to laugh at her portrayal of me. She obviously thought I was good-looking; I could tell by the way she seemed to skim over my flaws and drew me looking perfect, with not even a hair out of place.

"Do you like drawing me?" I asked, flipping the pad around so she could see what I was looking at.

"Sure, why not," she replied, shrugging.

I frowned, trying to work out what that meant. Women were incredibly hard to read; I'd never really tried to understand one before. It was a lot harder than it looked. I flipped to the next page – it was Jack this time, I recognised him from the photo next to her bed. He was covered in blood and looked like he was in pain; the picture was a little horrifying.

I groaned and shook my head. "Why don't you draw a nice picture of him, instead of this?" I asked, nodding down at the book. I didn't want to show her the picture in case it upset her, suddenly being confronted with it.

She sighed, and her eyes dropped to the floor; her whole posture was sad and defeated. "It makes me too upset, so I don't draw him anymore."

"Anna, surely it's harder for you to draw him like this," I protested, silently wondering if she just liked being sad.

"You'd think so, huh?" She took the pad out of my hand and put it in the bag, indicating the end of the conversation.

I sighed, angry at myself. *Way to go, Ashton, upset her again. Great job, asshole!* I reached out and put my finger under her chin, guiding her eyes up to meet mine. I needed to see her smile again, I hated that she was so sad all the time. "It's okay to miss him. You should remember the nice times and try to forget the bad stuff. It's not good for you," I whispered.

She smiled weakly, but it didn't reach her lifeless eyes. "I know, but I can't help it. When I close my eyes, that's what I see."

"In time the bad stuff will fade, and you'll just be left with the good memories," I promised, stepping closer to her and wrapping my arm around her shoulders. She fitted against my body perfectly. The smell of chlorine wafted up from her hair, making my scalp prickle. It was almost like torture. *If I can't have her, then why does she fit me so perfectly?* I wanted so badly to dip my head and kiss her cheek, so I could feel her soft skin against my mouth again. I hadn't been able to stop thinking about the taste and feel of her since what happened yesterday.

She pressed her face into my chest and her body accidentally brushed against mine. I gulped and willed myself not to get turned on by the tiny movement. "Everyone says that, but three years on and it's still just like yesterday," she muttered.

I sighed and closed my eyes, pressing my face into her hair, breathing her in. I had no idea how I could make her feel better. "Just take one day at a time, that's all you can do."

Her arm tightened on my waist for a second before she sighed and pulled out of my grasp, stepping back and frowning down at the floor. "Let's just get this stuff packed."

Two suitcases and a rucksack later, she was finally satisfied that she had enough clothes to last her. She seemed to have packed everything but the kitchen sink. I even saw her throw in the next three Twilight books for me. I'd never had someone think about me like that before. The guys at the academy were great, but guys just didn't do that sort of thing. It was weird for me to accept that someone could just genuinely be that kind and thoughtful. It amazed me that, although she was going through agony, she still had it in her heart to think of others too.

After we were done, she disappeared off into her en-suite to have a bath, so I sat on the edge of her bed, staring at the door, just wishing I could go and sit on the floor and talk to her some more. That was easily my favourite thing about her; she always had something interesting to say and could make me laugh like no girl I'd ever met. Sighing, I pulled out my cell phone, opening my email and finding the itinerary for our travel the following day.

When I knew it word for word, I stripped out of my clothes and took the spare pillow and throw off her bed, laying it out on the floor again. My back muscles were already protesting about sleeping on the floor, but it seemed to stop her nightmares so I could deal with it for a while. I'd already put in a request for a sofa bed to be put in the apartment we were to share.

A little while later I could hear her moving around in the bathroom. When the door handle twisted, I quickly lay down and closed my eyes, pretending to sleep. There was no need for me to make anything more difficult for her. She sighed and the light flicked off before the mattress creaked and the sheets rustled. As I lay there, I could hear her breathing as she rolled to the edge of the bed. It was one of the most precious sounds in the world to me.

Suddenly, I felt one of her fingers trail across the bridge of my nose and trace across my cheek before she swept the hair from my forehead softly. I desperately wanted to open my eyes and talk to her, hold her and kiss her, but she needed me to be the strong one, so I would be. Her hand moved down, resting on my chest, just above my heart. It was almost as if she wanted to check I was still there or something. It was nice, and I couldn't help the smile that crept onto my face – lucky for me, the light was off so she couldn't see how excited the small touch was making me.

I woke early again in the morning. I sat up, clenching my teeth so that I didn't groan as my muscles protested. I smiled over at Anna who was still in a peaceful slumber, so I pushed myself up to my feet, bending and planting a soft kiss on the top of her head before I silently folded up my makeshift bed. It was easier this way; there was no awkwardness for her if I snuck out while she slept. I sighed and went to my room for a quick shower, changing into my clothes for the day and packing the last of my things.

After taking my bags downstairs, I sought out Dean to check he was all set for today. We were due to be driven to the airport at nine, so there wasn't long to wait. Satisfied he was ready to go and knew what he was doing, I made my next stop the kitchen. My stomach was growling angrily as I looked at the stack of pancakes that Mary had made.

After gorging myself on a huge stack, I picked up an extra plate and loaded a couple on for Anna, carrying it carefully through the house and up to her room. When I got to her door, I knocked and waited for her to call me in. It was only just seven, so I was assumed she wouldn't even be up yet.

"Yeah?" she called sleepily.

I opened the door and strutted in, seeing that she was sitting up on the bed, yawning and rubbing her eyes. Her hair was all messed up from sleeping, yet she still looked like the most beautiful girl in the world. I smiled to myself. I could look for a thousand years and never get tired of seeing her face, I was sure of it. I knew that every girl I met from now on would pale in comparison to Anna.

"Hey, Baby Girl. I got you some breakfast." My eyes widened in horror at what I'd said. Baby Girl. I'd called her it a couple of times now by accident; I really needed to stop that.

Thankfully, she didn't seem to notice. "You did? Thanks," she smiled at me gratefully as she scooted back to the headboard, grinning when I passed her the plate.

I watched her in silence while she ate her breakfast, the whole time willing myself not to get turned on when she licked her lips and put her fork in her mouth. I had no idea how eating could be a turn-on, but she somehow managed it.

"You sleep okay?" I inquired when she'd finished eating. I knew the answer to that question already; I'd spent half the night watching her sleep.

She set her plate on the side and nodded. "Yep. You?"

Not really, no. "Yeah, fine," I lied.

She smiled and climbed out of the bed, stretching her body and groaning. I closed my eyes at the sight of her flawless body; I could already feel the tightening of the crotch area of my jeans, the sight of her stretching certainly wouldn't help at all.

"I'll take your bags downstairs ready. We're leaving in just under two hours," I suggested, checking the time on my cell phone.

"Okay, I'm just going to get dressed. Can you leave one of the bags so I can put my hairbrush and stuff in it?" she asked, bending over one of the suitcases, giving me a spectacular view of her ass and legs. Well, that did it; I got a full on hard-on and quickly turned to rearrange myself downstairs while she wasn't watching so it wasn't noticeable.

Fuck my life! This is going to be the longest eight months ever!

The next hour was pretty hectic and so I didn't get to see her much. When the car finally arrived to take us to the airport, her parents followed us outside, their expressions anxious and sullen.

I stood back and watched as she said her awkward goodbyes. Her back was stiff, and her weak smile was forced as they hugged her goodbye one at a time. I hated to see her so tense, it made my stomach ache. I wasn't close enough to hear what they were saying, but her mother had tears in her eyes, and her father looked like he was begging her to stay out of trouble.

Once they were done, her eyes flitted in my direction before she climbed into the waiting black Bentley. I stepped forward to go with her, but her dad stepped into my path and smiled warmly. I gulped. I was actually incredibly intimidated by him, after all, not only was he the probable next President and my boss, he was also the father of the girl I wanted to date. I wanted him to like me.

"Agent Taylor, I just wanted to say thank you," he said quietly. I could tell by his fierce expression that he meant the words.

"You don't need to thank me, sir. It's my job."

He shook his head. "Not just the job, Agent Taylor, I meant for what you're doing for Annabelle. She seems so much better. You're good for her." He held out his hand for me to shake. I grinned placing my hand in his. *Looks like I may get Dad's approval after all!*

"No problem, sir. Anna's a great girl who's been through a lot." I frowned at my words. 'Been through a lot' didn't even begin to cover what she'd had to endure.

"Yes, she has," he agreed, nodding. "Please take care of her. She trusts you, and so do I."

I felt immensely proud of myself. "Thank you, sir, that means a lot. You don't need to worry about her, I'll take excellent care of her," I promised.

He turned, nodding towards the waiting car. "You'd better get going or you'll miss your flight."

I nodded and started towards the car, but just as I was about to climb in the back, he spoke again, making me stop. "At the end of this assignment you can name the department of your choice, and I'll make it happen," he said sincerely. My insides knotted at the thought of any department, my hand gripping the door handle slightly too tight.

"Thank you, sir." I smiled gratefully and slid into the car with Anna, smiling broadly.

After being ushered through airport check-in and security, we were boarded in first class. Anna seemed both relaxed and happy to be away from the house and her parents. I had a feeling that it was difficult for her there with them, knowing they wanted the old Anna rather than this new version.

Once the plane was in the air, and the seatbelt signs went off, she stood and pulled down her inflight bag, rummaging through it. A smile crossed her face as she pulled out a rectangular box that had been wrapped in a sheet of her sketch pad. She grinned and held it out to me. "I got you something."

I frowned, a little taken aback. "You did? What is it?"

She grinned, pulling out a book from her bag before plopping herself back down in her seat and tossing the little hard box into my lap. "Open it and see."

I frowned and picked up the package. It was hard and about the size of my palm. As I unfastened the tape and pulled the paper off, my eyes widened in shock. It was a wicked-looking iPod. "Seriously?" I asked, looking at her face for signs of trickery.

She nodded in confirmation, smiling smugly, obviously pleased with herself. "I didn't think you had one, and I had a spare, so I figured you could have it to help keep you occupied during the boring lessons. It's a college must have."

I looked at her in awe. Her thoughtfulness and caring attitude amazed me; I'd never known anyone like her.

"Again with that face?" she teased, rolling her eyes. She reached out and took it from my hand, opening it and connecting the headphones before turning it on. "I didn't know what kind of music you liked, so I just put all of my stuff on here for you for now so you've got something to be getting on with," she rambled, flicking through a list of albums.

I gulped, unsure what to say. Could this girl actually be real?

"You'll have to set up your own iTunes account, but you can share mine for now," she continued, shrugging casually. I didn't think she had any idea how thoughtful and incredible she was.

I ran a hand through my hair, still struggling to come to terms with how crazy about her I was. "Thank you. You didn't need to do that, that's really sweet of you."

She smiled wickedly, handing the device back to me again. "Next week when I'm being all bitchy to you, just remember that I was nice to you... once."

Before I could stop myself, I'd leant in and pressed my lips to hers. She moaned in the back of her throat and kissed me back. My mind was racing a mile a minute. After her threat at the cemetery, I didn't think this would happen again. The feel of her soft lips on mine made the hair on my arms stand up on end. Her hand moved up, gripping the back of my head as her lips pressed against mine harder.

Although it only lasted a few seconds, the kiss was sizzling hot, yet, at the same time, chaste and sweet. She pulled away, blinking a couple of times before squirming in her seat uncomfortably.

121

"I'm sorry, I shouldn't have done that." I winced apologetically, waiting for her to lash out and tell me to keep my hands off her.

She cleared her throat, turning away and picking up her book. "It's okay. Glad you like it."

"I love it, thank you." My heart was killing me, I wanted her so badly, but her happiness was more important to me than mine and she didn't want to betray Jack. Maybe if we carried on being friends, she'd allow herself to fall in love with me. I hoped that was true. My stomach was churning as I watched her open her book to the right page. I was falling in love with her, I could practically feel it happening – another week or two and I'd be a goner.

During the two hour flight, she just sat there reading, munching on peanut M&Ms, and I sat there playing with my new gadget. As I scrolled through the music, I was pleasantly surprised by how similar our tastes were. It was easily the best present anyone had ever given me. I'd wanted to get one when I was training, but I'd never had enough money at the time. After a little while, she lifted the arm rest between our seats and shifted in her seat, leaning against me, getting more comfortable.

The flight ended way too soon for my liking. I was enjoying the casual closeness a lot more than I should.

Peter Burnet, the night time far guard, met us with a little sign at the baggage collection point. He was younger than I expected, probably only mid-twenties. Clearly he liked to work out, that was evident by his broad shoulders and thick neck. He smiled nervously when we stopped at his side; his eyes scanned the group quickly before coming to a rest on Anna.

After a brief round of introductions, he led us out the front where a sleek, silver Jaguar XF sat waiting for us. My eye twitched at the beauty of it, and my hands were already itching to touch it. A smile tugged at the corner of my mouth. If my best friend Nate could see me now, he'd probably scream like a little girl. Dean and Peter didn't get a flash car like ours though, much to Dean's obvious disappointment.

The drive to our new apartment wasn't that long. I tried to memorise the streets as I let the GPS lead me to the college campus. When we arrived, I pulled into an underground parking lot and cut the engine, surveying the area before walking around to her side and opening the door for her.

Peter and Dean had arrived by then too, so we all made our way to the elevator with Peter telling us about the security on the building. Other than the fire escapes that only opened from the inside, there was one way in and out, which would be advantageous for surveillance. You could only gain entrance to the building with a tag card, and then you also needed a pass code to use the elevator or stairs. The building itself had obviously been chosen carefully.

When we got to the second floor, I left Anna outside with Dean and Peter while I went into our apartment to check it was safe before I let her just wander in. My eyes widened in appreciation as I took in the expensive-looking hardwood floors, the perfect paint jobs and the enormous flat screen TVs that hung in each room. The fully-equipped, high-gloss, white kitchen was pure luxury. The apartment was huge and stunning.

After checking out all of the rooms and deeming them safe, I went back to get her and let her get her first look at our home for the next eight months. Peter went down to get the luggage from the car.

"Wow, this place is gorgeous," Anna enthused, walking in and opening all the doors that she came across, looking in them. When we got to the bedrooms, she turned and winced. "There's no sofa bed. We're gonna have to order one."

I frowned, flicking my eyes around seeing that she was right. I'd requested one, but perhaps the request had been overlooked. I'd have to make a couple of calls later. "Looks like it's the floor for me again then," I joked, trying not to wince, because sleeping on the floor made me feel like an old man.

She turned back to the bed and frowned. "You can just share with me if you want. I don't like you keep sleeping on the floor," she mumbled.

I waved my hand dismissively. "It's fine, don't worry about it. Shall we unpack then?" I suggested, dreading unpacking all of her stuff again.

She shook her head adamantly. "Nope. Something much more critical needs to be done before that," she answered, raising one eyebrow knowingly.

Hmm, what can be more important than unpacking? "What's that then, Baby Girl?" I asked curiously. *Damn, Ashton, again with the pet name? Stop it, dipshit!*

She smirked at me. "We need to go collect menus from all the takeout places that deliver because I'm not cooking for your pretty ass every night."

I burst out laughing. "Hey, I'll cook some nights," I protested.

She scrunched her nose up in distaste. "Tuna melt baked potatoes can get boring pretty quick." I smiled because she'd obviously listened to me carefully before; she seemed to remember everything I told her, no matter how insignificant it was.

"Tell me about it. Come on then, I'll call Dean and let him know we're going for a walk," I agreed, pulling out my cell and dialling his number.

"Tell him we're going for a drink after too."

I raised one eyebrow. College clearly had an effect on her – or maybe it was the freedom of being away from her parents. Whatever it was, she was smiling and it made my insides tingle with happiness.

Chapter Fourteen

~ Anna ~

After about an hour of wandering around picking up menus for the local takeout places, I decided we had enough. I really needed a drink. My eyes landed on a bar across the street, and I guided Ashton in that direction. I ignored the peeling paint on the sign and the broken glass panel on one side. They served alcohol, and that was all I cared about. I looked up at Ashton hopefully.

He frowned, his eyes flicking between me and the crappy bar. "You wanna go in here?" he asked, looking at it distastefully.

I laughed at his expression. "Snob."

"Anna, this doesn't look like a nice bar," he protested, narrowing his eyes at the door.

"Please?" I whined, pouting.

He sighed in defeat and pulled out his cell phone, calling Dean to tell him because he was standing at the end of the street, waiting for us. "Come on then, but stay with me, no bathroom breaks," he said sternly.

I nodded excitely. I hadn't been to a bar for ages. I went through a stage when I first got away from Carter of sneaking out and going to bars and getting drunk, but that had been well over two years ago now. Lately, I'd pretty much been a recluse.

The bar was an absolute dive, but the drinks were cheap. There was a load of people that looked like students, so they were probably from my college because the campus was only a couple of minutes' walk from here. The owner obviously didn't think twice about serving underage people.

"So, what do you drink?" Ashton asked, dragging me to the bar.

"Whatever's on offer."

"Orange juice?" he suggested.

I laughed and shook my head. "I want a real drink."

A disapproving frown settled on his forehead. "You're not old enough," he whispered, tracing his hand down my back. "I could get into trouble for buying you alcohol."

I pouted, begging him with my eyes. "Please? I have a fake ID. I always drink. Please?"

He rolled his eyes. "One drink," he conceded. "Want wine or something?"

I smiled and shrugged, but when the barman came over, I ordered two double Jack Daniels and cokes. Ashton looked at me shocked and then ordered an orange juice too. "Who's the orange juice for?" I asked, pushing one of the drinks towards him.

"For me. I can't drink while I'm on duty, so it looks like I'm t-total for the next few months," he replied, shrugging and pushing the drink back towards me.

I gasped. That wasn't fair at all. "Aww, come on, you can drink. Nothing's gonna happen. This whole freaking guard idea is just stupid anyway!" I ranted, feeling like a spoiled brat.

He looked a little pained about something before he rearranged his expression. "No, Anna, you need guards so you don't get expelled," he joked, chinking his glass against mine, grinning. "Cheers." I sighed and downed one of the drinks straight away; I didn't want to be carrying two glasses around with me. "Oh man, you're not one of *those* drinkers, are you?" he asked, looking a little horrified.

"One of *what* drinkers?" I grimaced from the alcohol after-burn.

He grinned, winking at me. "The ones that really can't handle their drink and throw up over their boyfriends when they carry them home."

I chuckled at his joke. "You never know, there's a first time for everything. Oh and, by the way, if you see anyone you like and want to go for a quickie in the bathroom then let me know first so I'm not wandering around looking for you," I said seriously, downing my next drink. We definitely needed to make that rule clear before it happened, because I didn't want to be looking for him all night long. His mouth dropped open, making a pop sound as he looked at me, stunned. I frowned. The two drinks in quick succession were already making me feel slightly tipsy. "Jeez Ashton, I won't throw up on you, I promise," I vowed, laughing.

"I wasn't thinking about that," he retorted, frowning at me, looking annoyed about something.

"Well, what then, Pretty Boy?" I asked, waving to get the barman's attention again as I ordered two more doubles and slid a twenty dollar bill across the bar.

Ashton shook his head in annoyance. "Anna, I'm not gonna leave you to go have sex with some girl at a bar! Is that what you really think of me?" he asked, looking a little hurt.

125

I raised an eyebrow. *Honestly? Yes.* He'd slept with me after three days and, technically, I was his boss, my guess was that he'd sleep with a girl he met in a bar – or wherever the hell else he met her.

"Oh come on, Ashton, we both know that you're a player. You're too damn pretty not to sleep around," I teased. "I mean, damn, you got me into bed after three days, and I can't even give out a handshake without flinching. You must be kick-ass at the art of seduction." I giggled and downed my next drink.

"Did you ever think that maybe that means something? That maybe we're meant to be together and that's why you let me touch you the first time I ever met you?" he asked, looking at me intently.

He looked so serious; a dark, sexy, brooding look was etched on his face. I smiled and stepped forward, putting my hand up to his face and smoothing out his forehead with my fingertips. "Careful, you'll get wrinkles on your pretty face," I teased, going up on tiptoes and kissing his cheek. "Pool?" I offered, walking off towards the back where the pool cues were mounted on the wall.

He laughed quietly. "You play pool?" he asked, wrapping his arm around my waist as I walked up the stairs unsteadily.

"Nope," I replied, popping the p and grinning. "Wanna give me a lesson on how to handle a stick?" I purred, holding it suggestively.

He smiled weakly. "Anna, please don't be getting all drunk and flirting with me, that's not on," he warned, grinning and shaking his head.

"You shouldn't be so sexy then, and then I wouldn't want to flirt with you."

He chuckled, smirking in my direction. "Right, I'll get to work on that and solve any issues you have with my sexiness."

I grinned. "Okay, if I'm not allowed to flirt with you, who should I flirt with? You scope out the bar and find me a suitable candidate," I joked, stepping to his side.

"Okay." He tapped his chin and looked around the bar. His eyes settled on an old man who was sitting in the corner playing chess with a friend. "Oh, old guy, three o'clock. He looks like he'd enjoy a bit of flirting from a pretty, young thing," he teased, grinning at me.

"Hmm, I do like an older man, but maybe I should go for someone younger than my dad? He does like to call people 'son', so I don't think it would go down terribly well if I brought home someone old enough to be *his* dad."

Ashton laughed and collected all of the balls, putting them inside a black, plastic triangle. "How about these guys right here, coming up to talk to you," he suggested, looking over my shoulder. I glanced around and, sure enough, two guys were coming over to us, both smiling. They were both about our age and judging by their ripped jeans and T-shirts, I would say they were college students too. One of them had strawberry blond hair and brown eyes, and the other was slightly taller than the first and darker in complexion, with brown hair and dark brown eyes. As they approached, I quickly moved to Ashton's side and he stood up straighter, a small smile playing at the corner of his mouth.

"Hey, wanna play doubles?" the strawberry blond asked, smiling and nodding towards the pool table.

Ashton smiled politely. "Anna? Wanna play doubles?" he asked, wrapping his arm around me. His touch made me feel better instantly.

"Um, yeah okay," I agreed, shrugging.

"Great, I'm Tim. This is Rich," the blond said, grabbing a cue.

"I'm Ashton. This is my girlfriend, Anna," Ashton replied, smiling and nodding.

The guy called Rich stepped forward. "How about loser buys the next drink?" he suggested.

I laughed. "Are you guys trying to hustle us for drinks?"

Rich laughed. "No way, babe. All the tables are taken, that's all. If you don't want to play, we'll wait until you're done. I was just trying to make the game more interesting."

"I don't think we should play for drinks, I've never played pool in my life," I admitted, downing my drink and pushing the glass onto the side.

Rich laughed. "You haven't? Then I think we should definitely be playing for drinks," he joked. "Or phone numbers?" he offered, raising one eyebrow.

Ashton's hand closed over mine, pulling me closer to him. "She has enough numbers," he answered for me. "Want to play or not because if you've just come over here to hit on my girlfriend, then you're shit out of luck because she's not interested." His voice was stern and warning. You could almost hear the cop in his tone, or maybe that was just me because I knew that's what he was.

Tim held up his hands innocently and shook his head. "Hey, no problem, we only want to play pool," he assured Ashton, jabbing an elbow into Rich's stomach in warning. "Ignore him, he can't help himself. When he drinks he gets verbal diarrhoea and tries to chat up anything that moves."

"I'll stay still then," I joked, which seemed to diffuse some of the tension in Ashton. He smiled and laughed, his shoulders loosening as he rolled his eyes.

Tim and Rich were actually quite likeable guys; after the flirting incident, things settled down and we all played pool, laughing and joking around. As it turned out, I wasn't very proficient at pool at all. In fact, I barely hit a ball, and all I kept doing was sinking the white. It was pretty good thing that we didn't agree to play for drinks because my lack of skills would have put a serious dent in Daddy's credit card.

Ashton had tried to teach me at first, showing me how to hold the cue, how to line up and where to angle it, but as soon as he leant over me and put his hands on mine, my mind was on other things. I couldn't keep my mouth in check and at one point pondered out loud if it would be comfortable to have sex on a pool table or if you'd get carpet burn on your butt. That had made the boys howl with laughter and Ashton look at me with a lustful twinkle in his eye that made my stomach flutter and my body temperature rise a few degrees.

After about an hour, a couple of girls joined us. Apparently they knew Tim from school. The girls were called Serena and Monica. I didn't like Monica. It wasn't that she didn't seem like a nice person, in fact, she did seem nice and friendly and funny… it was just that she couldn't keep her eyes off my bodyguard. Since she walked up the stairs to where the pool tables were, she had been eyeing him like a vulture waiting to pick his bones.

The more I drank, the more annoyed with her flirting I became. So when she put her hand on his arm, giggling profusely, I downed my drink and scowled. He was talking back to her but didn't really seem interested. In fact, mostly he didn't take his deep green, sexy eyes off me or the surrounding area, doing his job perfectly, but that didn't help with the annoyance I felt towards the large-breasted blonde that was hitting on him right in front of me.

Deep down, I knew that I had no right to be jealous of him, but I just couldn't rein it in. The alcohol in my system told me that what I was about to do was a terrific idea. Pushing myself up off my stool that I was perched on, I sauntered the three steps over to where Ashton was and smiled as I stopped in front of him.

His head cocked to the side, regarding me curiously. "Okay?" he inquired. I gulped and nodded, taking the final step towards him so that our chests were touching. His shoulders stiffened as I raised my arms and looped them around his neck. "Anna?"

I grinned and went up on tiptoes, pulling his head forward at the same time so that our lips connected softly. He made a small, startled grunt before he kissed me back enthusiastically, wrapping one arm around my waist and holding me securely against him.

I smiled against his lips, gripping my hand into the back of his hair as the kiss deepened and his tongue touched mine. I moaned into his mouth because of how nice it felt. Everywhere he touched on my body, little shots of electricity were sent into my system, and I actually forgot where I was. My whole body was burning for him; I couldn't get enough. The kiss wasn't nearly enough for me. I was so aroused that it was actually making my body ache.

He pulled back, making a moaning sound in the back of his throat. "Anna, stop it. Come on," he whispered, pleadingly. But I couldn't stop. I shook my head adamantly and pulled his face back down to mine again with such a force that I stumbled back on my drunken legs, pulling him with me as we bumped into the wall. The kiss didn't break though; instead, he pushed me tightly against the wall as he kissed me urgently. He kissed me as if he could devour my soul, making my knees weak. It was probably lucky that I had the wall behind me; otherwise he would have made me swoon like they did in the olden days.

I gasped for breath as his mouth pulled away from mine, travelling down my neck. With my eyes closed, my hands slipped down to his ass, squeezing gently as I tangled my legs with his. "Damn, you have such an incredible ass," I mumbled.

He chuckled, finally pulling his mouth away from my skin. Pressing his forehead to mine, his eyes locked onto mine as he cupped my face in his hands. His breathing was heavy; it blew across my face and ruffled my hair. "You need to stop drinking," he mused. "You're a damn horny drunk." He smiled his sexy smile at me and my whole body seemed to come alive with passion.

"Wanna take me home to bed, Ashton?" My hormones were raging. I needed him. I chewed on my lip as I started to play it out in my head. I couldn't help but wonder if it would be as enjoyable as last time, or whether I had maybe distorted the experience in my head, and it wasn't actually as mind blowing as I thought it was. Maybe I'd be disappointed this time.

"That's not going to happen," he answered, shifting so that there was an inch of space between us.

I raised one eyebrow suggestively. "Not even if I beg you on my knees?" I countered.

He groaned, looking like he was in pain. "Anna, please, you're making this hard for me," he whined, looking at me hungrily.

"Isn't that the point?" I joked, giggling wickedly. Actually, I would gladly beg on my knees if he'd enjoy that.

His fingers dug into my waist as he shook his head. "Enough," he said sternly, looking directly into my eyes. There was no wavering in his tone; he wasn't going to change his mind.

I frowned at his rejection. It felt like a slap in the face. *Did he not enjoy the other morning? Wait… am I terrible in bed or something? Had I done something wrong, or not done something?* My mouth popped open and my face flushed with embarrassment.

His hands slid down my neck, across my shoulders and down my arms until they got to my hands. I gulped, still embarrassed as his fingers tangled with mine and he stepped back, smiling weakly.

"You two need a room or something?"

The comment made me jerk back into reality, and I realised we were in a bar, and not in private. Everyone and everything else seemed to disappear when I was kissing Ashton. Flicking my eyes over Ashton's shoulder, I saw Tim and Rich fake gagging.

I giggled and bit my lip, unsure what to say. Ashton, on the other hand, obviously knew exactly what he should be saying. "Actually, yeah. I think I'm gonna take her home and finish this there. Nice to meet you guys." He turned back to me and gave me a little tug away from the wall, holding me steady when I swayed on my feet. "Can you walk in a straight line?"

I raised one eyebrow. Clearly, he was implying I was intoxicated. "Yes, Officer, I can," I flirted, winking at him. He chuckled but luckily no one else commented on the double meaning. He nodded and let go of my hands, watching me as my legs wobbled as if I was wearing high heels, even though I had flat sandals on.

Laughing, he quickly gripped my waist as the floor started to slope off to one side. "I'll give you a piggyback."

He lifted me, sitting me on the bar stool next to me before turning his back on me, bending and wrapping my arms around his neck. As his hands slipped under my behind, lifting me off the stool, fumbling to get a decent hold on me, I giggled wickedly.

"Not sure what you're looking for there, Pretty Boy, but it's slightly to the left," I joked. Everyone burst out laughing and I blushed. "Oops, did I say that out loud?" I pressed my face into his neck as everyone laughed harder.

After sending a triumphant smirk in Monica's direction, I waved and chirped goodbye to everyone else that we'd spent the evening with. The air was refreshing as Ashton carried me out of the bar and into the street. Dean was sitting on the wall outside the bar, playing on his phone under the haze of a street light. He looked up and stood as we walked out. His gaze wandered to me on Ashton's back, and a small smile tugged at the corners of his mouth.

I had no idea how long it took to get home. Most of the time I just had my eyes closed and my head resting on Ashton's shoulder as he walked with long, confident strides. He and Dean were talking about basketball.

As we got into the lobby of our apartment building, Peter, the night guard, came walking down the stairs to meet us. No doubt Dean had called him to tell him his shift was starting when we got back.

Ashton carried me right into my bedroom, finally setting me on my feet and looking at me worriedly. "Can you stand okay?" He reached out, gripping my elbow.

I giggled and slapped his hand away playfully. "I'm not drunk," I protested, plopping heavily down onto the bed and giggling as the mattress bounced, making me feel a little lightheaded. Raising one foot, I tried to unbuckle my sandals, but my fingers wouldn't do what I told them to do.

Ashton laughed loudly, taking my foot and easily pulling the strap off for me before doing the other. "Which case are your pyjamas in?" he asked, walking over to the two cases in the corner of the room.

I actually had no idea. *Did I even bring pyjamas? I guess I must have done.* "Um, I don't know. I'll just sleep naked," I suggested, waving my hand dismissively at the case full of clothes.

He closed his eyes for a couple of seconds. "Give me a break here. Do you honestly not know which one they're in?" he asked, shaking his head and rifling through the clothes carefully.

"Nope." I laughed, popping the p and smiling broadly. *Hopefully if I'm sleeping naked, I'll be able to convince him to ditch the clothes too.* He sighed and zipped the case back up. As he stood up, he gripped his T-shirt, pulling it off over his head, exposing those edible abs and chest that made my mouth water.

He threw the T-shirt at me, hitting me full in the face with it. "Sleep in that. I'm gonna go check the doors and windows and stuff." He turned and walked out the door, closing it behind him.

I burst out laughing at his second rejection. Embarrassment washed over me because I was just lusting after him and he wasn't even slightly interested. Obviously I hadn't learnt from my rejection at the bar!

Shaking my head at myself, I tugged off my clothes, leaving my underwear on, and slipped his shirt over my head. As soon as I had it on, I moaned in appreciation. It smelt incredible, just like he did. Pulling the neck of the shirt up over my nose, I climbed in the bed, surrounding myself with his scent.

He strutted in moments later, carrying the bedcovers from the room next door. His eyes were tight before he spotted me in the bed. I whipped my mouth and nose out of his shirt, but it was too late, he'd seen it. A smile slipped onto his face as I squirmed at being caught. It was almost as pathetic as if I'd just been leaning in and sniffing his hair or something. Bet his subconscious was screaming the word 'stalker' at him.

"Doors and windows all locked?" I asked, rolling onto my side to watch him take off his jeans and socks.

"Yeah, you're all safe," he replied.

"Of course I am, I have a big, bad boyfriend to look after me," I flirted, dragging my eyes down his body. He sighed and spread the sheet out onto the floor before walking around to the other side of my bed, picking up the spare pillow. Catching on to his intention, I shook my head. "You can sleep in the bed," I protested.

He shook his head, tossing the pillow down onto the floor. "That's not a good idea tonight."

I frowned. "Why not?"

"Because you, plus alcohol, clearly equals horny beast," he threw at me before flicking off the light, surrounding us with darkness.

I frowned, listening to the rustling of him settling himself down onto the makeshift bed on the floor. I rolled to my side, squinting through the darkness, seeing that he was lying on his back. "I was hoping you'd want to sleep in bed with me tonight," I whined, after a few minutes of silence.

"I do."

Fumbling with the bedside light switch, I turned it on, narrowing my eyes at the sudden brightness. He groaned, cupping his hands around his eyes too. "Then why don't you, if you want to?" I asked.

"There's a difference between what I want, and what can happen. You're drunk and you need some sleep. If I got in the bed with you, then stuff might happen and you'd hate me in the morning for taking advantage of you. I refuse to do that." His tone was final and stern. I pouted, and he chuckled wickedly. "You have the cutest little puppy dog face I have ever seen." He shook his head, smiling up at me.

"If I promise not to make a move on you, can I sleep with you?" I begged. After two rejections and someone flirting with him, the alcohol was making me insecure. I needed to know that he wasn't going anywhere; I needed reassurance that he wasn't going to walk out of my life like everyone else did.

He looked pained, like he wanted to but thought that he shouldn't. "I don't think you can keep that promise."

I scoffed, making my mind up that I was going to prove him wrong. "You're not that hot, Agent!" I protested.

"You think I am," he shot back cockily.

I gasped and shook my head. "I'm pretty sure I can resist your hot ass. And I'll prove it." I threw off the sheets and swung my legs out of the bed. He grunted when I almost stood on him and then stumbled, falling down at his side and accidentally bumping his head with mine. "Shit. Ouch. Sorry," I grumbled, sitting up and rubbing at my forehead.

He laughed, rubbing his head too, watching me curiously. "You alright? Where are you going?"

I rolled my eyes and pulled his pillow to the side so that there was some room for me to share it. "I'm proving my point that you're not, in fact, as irresistible as you think you are." I settled down on his sheet, and closed my eyes, waiting for him to lie back down too.

"Anna…"

I shook my head and patted the empty side again. "Lie down and shh. My hangover has started to kick in, so shut up and cuddle me," I instructed, trying not to laugh.

He chuckled, shifting onto his side before settling himself down so he was facing me. I held my breath and prayed that he couldn't see the effect that he had on my body. His beautiful green eyes were trying to hypnotise me, I could feel them pulling me in. I sighed deeply and scooted closer to him. The smile that graced his lips was beautiful as he shifted and moved one arm to the side, slipping it under my neck before wrapping it around me tightly.

With his beautiful, unique scent filling my lungs and the heat seeping from his skin to mine, my body relaxed for the first time in two days. Ashton just had this strange ability to make me feel whole, like I wasn't broken anymore, like he was some sort of magical cure that I just couldn't get enough of. He made all the terrible things seem to fade away, at least for a little while anyway. Setting my head on his chest, I tangled my legs in with his as he kissed the top of my head before turning off the light again.

It was easy to imagine while he was holding me like this that everything was normal, that he was really my boyfriend, that he wasn't just doing his job, and that I wasn't some screwed up, dirty piece of trash that would never be loved again.

When his breathing deepened and the soft snores resonated from his chest, I pulled back slightly so I could look at him properly. My heart was hammering in my chest as butterflies seemed to take flight in my stomach as I raked my eyes over his handsome face. I reached out a hand and brushed my finger tip across his cheekbone, tracing along the line of his jaw, smiling at the prickle of his five o'clock shadow. I'd done the same last night; it was like I just needed to touch him to make sure he was real or something.

He truly was handsome. I didn't think I'd ever seen anyone so perfect, and he was such a lovely guy to go with it. It would have been so much easier if he were a jerk. I really hoped that I could keep this boy out of my heart, otherwise in eight months when he left for the stupid front line or whatever the hell he wanted to do, I was going to have another serious problem.

Chapter Fifteen

As I slowly started to drift into consciousness, the first thing I noticed was that my head was pounding. I groaned and rolled over, pressing my face into the pillow, trying to block out the light. My stinging eyes cracked open and raked around the room. Not recognising anything, I jerked up quickly with a horrible sensation brewing in the pit of my stomach. The last time I woke up not knowing where I was, I'd been with Carter.

I jumped to my feet and pressed myself against the wall as my breathing started to accelerate. The muscles in my body ached, as if I'd slept awkwardly or something. Slowly, it started coming back to me. College, I was at ASU with Ashton, and this was our new apartment. I breathed a sigh of relief and relaxed, resting my head back against the wall. My eyes fluttered closed again and I groaned as another wave of pain started in my head. *How much did I drink last night? Jeez!* I remembered having about four or five doubles, then we met a couple of guys and played pool. What were their names? Tim and someone else, and two girls…

One of the girls was flirting with Ashton, and I got jealous and… oh no, I kissed him! I was all over him and begging him to take me home and… oh God no. I basically begged him for sex when we got back too! My cheeks flamed from the shame of what I'd done last night and how much I'd flirted with him. Thank goodness he'd said no though, not many guys would have turned down a free score, I'd bet. I'd have to thank him today for that because if I'd slept with him again, I was pretty sure I'd be feeling guilty over Jack again afterwards. I covered my face with my hands in disgust. I really had no self-control, and I should have been thinking about Jack last night, not myself.

After a few deep breaths, I decided I should go and see if we were okay this morning after that. Maybe my drunken antics had frightened him away and he'd request that transfer that he was so adamant he wouldn't be asking for. The smell of coffee and toast drifting from the kitchen made my stomach rumble as I made my way out of the bedroom and into the kitchen. As I stepped into the room, I stopped. It wasn't just Ashton in there, Dean and a guy I vaguely recognised as Peter, the night guard, were there too. They were all standing around the kitchen island, drinking coffee.

"Good morning," Ashton chirped, smiling as he spotted me.

I waved a hand in response. He grinned and nodded down at my legs for some reason as if trying to tell me something. My gaze drifted down, confused, until I spotted that I was only wearing his T-shirt. Heat flooded my face for the second time in a few minutes as I realised that they were all looking at me. I grabbed the bottom of the T-shirt, trying to pull it down further; it already came to my mid-thigh, but I felt exposed in front of the other two. I actually didn't care if Ashton saw me like this. He'd seen me in much, much less.

"Um, hi. Sorry, I didn't know you guys were here." I winced, smiling apologetically.

"Don't worry about it, Miss Spencer," the new guard replied, looking me over slowly with an appreciative look on his face.

I frowned at his obviousness. "My eyes are up here, Agent!" I snapped acidly, pointing to my face.

Ashton's body tensed as he stepped to my side, glaring at Peter warningly. I moved closer to him, trying to discreetly hide behind him as he spoke. "Agent Burnet, I appreciate that you might want to keep the relationship of bodyguard and client informal, but that shit stops right now, understand? Plenty of other Agents would love a cushy job like yours, so if you want to keep your position, I suggest you be a little more respectful," he stated, his voice angry and full of authority.

Peter jumped, looking a little taken aback as he nodded in agreement. "Right. I'm sorry, Miss Spencer," he apologised nervously.

I laughed uncomfortably. "Don't worry about it," I told Peter, waving it off. "But can everyone just shush, please?" I winced and looked longingly at the coffee, trying to decide if I could be bothered to make the four steps over to it to pour some for myself.

Ashton's shoulders loosened as he smiled down at me before picking up a glass from the side and pouring me a glass of water. "Suffering after last night?" he teased, nudging me in the side and setting the glass of water and two pills in front of me.

"Thanks." I smiled gratefully, swallowing them quickly.

"So, what's on the agenda for today? Do I have anything I need to do, or can I unpack?" Ashton asked, as he poured me a coffee.

I frowned. "I don't know. We need to go grocery shopping, I guess, but I need to unpack too, I don't have any clothes for today. I mean, why the hell am I wearing your shirt?" I asked, looking at him curiously. All three of them laughed again.

"You were drunk. I couldn't find your pyjamas, so I let you borrow my shirt," Ashton explained, shrugging casually, but the tiny tightening to his eyes showed me how uncomfortable he was.

Flashbacks of me suggesting we sleep naked flashed into my brain, so I quickly averted my eyes from his. *Dear God, what is wrong with me lately?* "Right okay, well thanks."

"No problem. So, if we unpack first, then maybe go grocery shopping this afternoon?" he offered. I nodded, liking the idea of having a few hours to chill in the apartment; hopefully my hangover from hell would be gone by then. "Did you want to go to that party tonight?" he asked curiously.

"Party? What party?" I didn't know anything about a party.

He shook his head, smiling. "Tim, the guy who liked you last night, asked us to go to a party tonight at a bar. You had a whole conversation about it with him. There's a band and DJ, apparently," he explained, shrugging easily.

I frowned. A party invite didn't ring any bells with me so I must have been more intoxicated than I thought last night. "Do you want to go?" I asked, watching his face. I didn't actually want to go, but I knew that I needed to start thinking of him more. I couldn't trap him in with me twenty-four-seven for the next eight months, he'd go stir crazy.

"I don't mind, whatever you want is fine with me," he answered noncommittally, finishing his coffee.

I turned to look at Dean and Peter. "Well, what about you guys? Do you mind if we go? I guess that means one of you has to go too, unless Ashton and I can go on our own and forget this whole guard business? After all, what my dad doesn't know won't hurt him. We could have a sweet set up here. You can do what you want, and so can I," I suggested, suddenly excited for a little piece of freedom away from prying eyes.

Unfortunately, they didn't look as if they were going for it. Peter gasped, looking at me in disbelief. "Are you kidding? What with everything that's going on, there's no way that's going to happen, Miss Spencer."

Ashton snapped his head around to look at him, giving him a warning look which made Peter shrink back and press his lips into a thin line.

"Everything that's going on? What does that mean?" I quizzed, confused.

Peter cleared his throat. "I meant with the whole starting college thing. We still haven't checked out everywhere. No one knows routines and stuff, that's all," he answered quickly.

I detected a measure of unease as he spoke, but decided to leave it. I didn't know him well enough to start second guessing what he was talking about. "Oh okay," I muttered. "Well, maybe we should go for a little while, just to see what it's like," I agreed. "I'll leave it up to you three to sort out the details; I'm gonna go start my unpacking." Before I turned and ran to the bedroom, I stole Ashton's toast from his plate, laughing as he complained about it.

We spent the whole day just lounging around and not doing much. Lazily, I'd unpacked my clothes, arranging my room how I wanted it, with my photo of Jack right beside the bed as usual. After we'd unpacked, we'd headed to the grocery store to stock up for the week. Even that was actually quite fun. I'd only ever been when I was a little girl with my mom. Since my dad had climbed higher up in his job, we weren't really allowed to do normal things and I enjoyed the day of just relaxing, and talking to Ashton about random things. He was incredibly easy to get along with, so easy that it almost frightened me.

After half an hour of watching him pull up the schematics for the bar that we were going to tonight, my tummy rumbled. I smiled, deciding to make some dinner. "Want to help me cook?" I offered, pushing myself up from the sofa I was slouched on.

"Sure." He closed the laptop and followed me into the kitchen, standing close to my back as I pulled open the fridge, looking at the array of meat, salad and vegetables that we'd bought.

"What do you want?" I pursed my lips, not sure what I was in the mood for.

He reached around me, making his chest press against my back as he picked up a pack of chicken. "Fajitas?"

I nodded, ignoring the butterflies in my stomach caused by the accidental brushing of our bodies, and we both set to work. The whole time he was pottering around behind me, trying to help, but actually just getting in the way. It was cute the way he was concentrating so hard on learning how to cook.

Surprisingly, despite Ashton helping, the food was nice. He'd cleared his plate of five wraps, and even finished the last of my second wrap when it appeared that my eyes were bigger than my belly. He moaned in appreciation, sucking the spicy juice from his fingertips one at a time with a satisfied smile on his face.

"That was good. I think I could make that on my own," he mused, eyeing the empty dishes and nodding to himself.

I raised one eyebrow in disbelief. Just from that one meal alone, I already knew that Ashton was a terrible cook. He'd been so slow slicing up an onion that, in the end, I had to take it off him and finish it, and then I'd left him in charge of stirring the pan while I set the table, and by the time I got back, the chicken was seconds from burning. No, Ashton would not be able to make fajitas all by himself. Frankly, I'd be worried that we'd die of food poisoning.

"Maybe you should start with something easier… like grilled cheese?" I joked, shaking my head.

"You doubt my ability," he observed, standing and picking up the plates.

I grinned. "I just think you shouldn't get ahead of yourself," I replied cheekily.

He grinned and leant against the counter, folding his arms over his chest. "Alright, admittedly, I probably need more practice at cooking, but I reckon that by the time we're married, I'll be able to lay on a full feast."

My heart jumped into my throat at that word. Marry him. It wouldn't even be possible. "Right, yeah, okay, that's not gonna happen. You're too pretty for me." I gulped and stood, squirming uncomfortably.

"Too pretty? Damn it." He clicked his tongue, smiling his heart-stopping smile. I forced a smile too, even though I could feel the emotion swelling inside me like a storm. I needed to get away from him before he saw it and questioned me on it. "You never know, I may be able to get you to overlook my prettiness and make you fall madly in love with me by the time I leave," he replied, smirking at me cockily.

I smiled back weakly as my heart started drumming wildly in my ears. I needed to leave. "Okay, Pretty Boy, I'm sure I'll fall madly in love with you, right about the time that you fall madly in love with me."

"About two more days then," he replied, winking at me playfully.

My mouth had gone dry, and my eyes started to prickle with tears. "I'm going to go in the shower and then get ready to go out." After excusing myself, I headed into the en suite bathroom and closed the door tightly. My breathing was coming out in short pants as I leant against the door, trying to calm myself. *Why the hell did he have to say that?* I looked down at my left hand and willed myself not to remember. *Just forget it, Anna, he was just joking around, stop being pathetic!* I mentally slapped myself and switched on the shower, trying to forget his comment.

The shower made me feel slightly better. Once dry, I searched through my closet, finding a black skirt and a cute baby doll top. After drying my hair and adding a few curls, I hesitantly picked up the make-up bag that I'd brought with me. During our shopping trip, I'd filled it with new make-up that I was yet to wear. Deciding to see how it looked, I swept on some chestnut eye shadow and a little mascara. Once I'd applied a small amount, I stepped back and frowned at myself with my hand poised over the face wipes. I hadn't worn make-up since my sixteenth birthday, and I wasn't sure if I was ready for it again.

At that moment, Ashton knocked on the door.

"Um, yeah?" I called hesitantly.

"Hey, are you nearly ready?"

"I guess." I picked up the face wipes, tearing them open and pulling one out. I gulped, looking back at my reflection, still undecided.

"Can I come in, Anna?"

I groaned and narrowed my eyes, hating that the smallest bit of make-up actually scared me. "Yeah, okay."

Behind me, the door opened and he walked in. I watched his entrance in the mirror. He was wearing dark blue fitted jeans and a black button-down shirt, open a little at the top; he'd left it un-tucked and rolled the sleeves to his elbows. *Wow* was all I could think. He actually hurt my eyes to look at because he was so incredibly mesmerising.

He strutted in, but stopped in his tracks when he was halfway across the room. His mouth popped open, and his eyes widened as he stared at me.

I swallowed around the lump in my throat. "Too much, right? I should take it off, shouldn't I?" I rambled, before realising he was still staring at me. "Why are you staring?"

He finally closed his mouth. "You just…" He blinked a couple of times, his eyes still wandering over me slowly. "You look stunning, Anna. So beautiful," he complimented.

A small smile tugged at my lips as I dropped my eyes to the floor. I hadn't expected that reaction. "I haven't worn make-up for years."

He walked over to me slowly, hooking his finger under my chin and lifting my gaze to his. "Anna, you look perfect, but if you're more comfortable without the make-up, then take it off. Either way, you are the most beautiful girl I've ever seen," he said, dipping his head and kissing my forehead softly.

His sweet words made my insides squirm. "You're such a charmer." I shook my head, smiling.

He shrugged. "I'm serious."

I took a deep breath and looked back at my reflection. "Okay, I'll leave it on then. You won't leave me tonight though, will you?" I asked, feeling slightly nauseous at the thought of being on my own looking like this while there were guys around.

His hand closed over mine as he pulled me closer to him. "I won't leave you, promise." I could hear the sincerity in his voice, and that gave me the confidence I needed.

"Okay, let's go then before I change my mind," I suggested, nodding at the door.

He grinned. "I honestly have the sexiest girlfriend in the world. I've got my job cut out for me tonight to keep the guys away from you," he teased, winking at me.

"I need to get you to earn your money somehow," I joked.

He stopped at the front door, his hand on the handle as his eyes turned to me. "Do me a favour tonight, huh? Try not to flirt with me as much as you did last night, because damn, I'm not sure how much I can stand with those sexy legs out like that," he growled, looking me over again, making me blush.

"Stop being a pervert, Ashton!" I scolded, slapping his chest playfully.

"Hey, a guy's allowed to perv on his girl!" he protested innocently before his famous smile slipped onto his face.

"Stop!" I warned.

He laughed and nodded. "Seriously though, try and tone it down tonight if you can, alright?" he asked, looking a little pained. I nodded and smiled apologetically. "Right then, let's go," he chirped excitedly.

The line for the bar was already about thirty people deep by the time we arrived. Dean and Peter joined behind us, not talking to us so that no one would know we were together. Thankfully, the line moved fairly quickly so we were ushered in within fifteen minutes. As we were let in, we had to show our IDs as proof of age. Ashton refused to allow me to drink again tonight, so insisted that I show my real ID that said I was only nineteen – which resulted in me getting an underage blue wristband so that the barman would know I wasn't allowed to be served alcohol. Ashton showed his fake ID that he'd been given when he started his assignment, so he was rewarded with an underage wristband too. Frowning, and not very happy with the colour of my bracelet, I folded my arms over my chest.

"Stop pouting. Do you want me to get in trouble for letting you drink whilst underage?" Ashton said in my ear, leaning in close so that I could hear him over the band that was already in full swing. Rolling my eyes, I shook my head. Of course I didn't want him in trouble, but it appeared that hanging out with an undercover cop for the next eight months was going to put a dampener on my college experience at ASU.

Not answering his question, I looked around. The club was a lot bigger than it looked from the outside. It was across two levels and had strobe lighting coming from the ceiling. A stage off to my right housed a live band that was slightly too loud, and slightly out of key as they jumped around excitedly. There were cheap carpets and cheap tables dotted around the edges. The long and well-stocked bar was five people deep, most of whom sported blue wristbands like mine. A smile tugged at the corner of my mouth. I actually quite liked it here. My hand slipped into Ashton's as I grinned and gave him a tug towards the bar.

Unexpectedly, I was actually having a nice time. It turns out that I didn't even need alcohol to enjoy myself. What did annoy me though was the fact that every now and again, my safety would be put into Dean's hands while Ashton went to the bathroom, or got stuck at the bar buying another round. Dean was trying to be discreet, I could tell that, but him standing close to me, pretending to look around while ignoring me completely was totally over the top and actually screamed 'bodyguard' – but maybe that was because I knew that was what he was. No one else seemed to bat an eyelid at him. Each time he had to leave my side for something, Ashton would call or text Dean and ask him to 'watch the jewel' for him for a minute. I couldn't help but roll my eyes at the stupid codename they'd obviously come up with for me.

140

After a couple of hours, a hand closed around my forearm. A little squeal escaped my lips, and my body reacted immediately, making me jump into Ashton as if a bomb had detonated near me.

"Whoa, sorry! Didn't mean to make you jump," Tim said, laughing hysterically.

My heart started to slow as Ashton's arm slipped around my waist. "Hey, sorry, you scared me," I admitted, smiling with relief.

"Hey, Ashton. How you doing?" Tim greeted, smiling warmly.

"Yeah, I'm good," Ashton replied, rubbing his hand up my arm; he was doing it to calm me down I presumed, and it was certainly working.

"I've been looking out for you two all night. We've got a table. You want to come and sit with us? We're upstairs," Tim offered, nodding towards the back of the bar. Ashton looked at me as if waiting for me to make the decision. I would honestly rather stay here with him, but, for his sake, I probably needed to start being more social.

"Sure, okay," I agreed, nodding. Ashton smiled and we followed Tim, weaving through the sea of people to the stairs.

At the bottom of the stairs there was a table that we had to pass to get to the next level. It was full of a group of laughing men, all of them wearing white 'adult' wristbands. My stomach tightened as one of them turned towards me and raised one eyebrow as we approached. A predatory smile crept onto his face. "Hey, sweetheart, I can show you a better time than that guy," he purred, nodding at Ashton distastefully.

I scoffed and shook my head. "I doubt that very much, *sweetheart*," I answered sarcastically, trying to appear confident even though my insides squirmed.

His smile grew bigger. "Well, you never know if you don't try," he flirted as he leant forward and landed a slap on my behind.

My nervousness suddenly gave way to anger and my hands clenched into fists, but before I had a chance to respond, Ashton whirled around, looking so angry that he actually looked like a different person as he pushed me in front of him, away from the guys. "Hands off my girl if you wanna keep them!" he growled.

The guy flinched. "Whoa, chill dude, I was just having a laugh with her," he said, nervously.

Ashton's shoulders were tense. "Oh really? I didn't realise. I tell you what, touch her again and then we'll see how fucking funny you find it," he suggested, smiling but at the same time looking at him menacingly. The guy held up his hands in protest, shaking his head quickly as his eyes widened at the threat. He actually looked frightened, even though he and his friends outnumbered Ashton five to one.

I gulped, looking back at the stairs that were only a few feet away. I didn't want him to get in trouble. "Let's go," I urged, pulling his hand. His jaw tightened as he nodded, putting his hands on my hips possessively as he gave me a little push towards the stairs to get me walking.

"You okay, Baby Girl?" he whispered in my ear.

I nodded. Spotting Tim already at his table, we wove through the crowd to get to him. Rich and Serena were already sitting there, along with Monica. I suppressed my groan as her predatory eyes landed on Ashton again. I had hoped that my jealousy would have evaporated, but she seemed to make it rear its ugly head again immediately.

Behind Monica there were three other people. Two new boys and one new girl. Tim waved a hand at each of them in turn. "This is Sam, Andrew and Rosie. Guys, this is Anna and Ashton."

"Hey, nice to meet you," I greeted as they all scooted over to let us sit down. Ashton nodded for me to sit in the booth first. I bit the inside of my cheek and looked at him pleadingly; I didn't want to sit next to the new guy I'd only just met. Ashton smiled, obviously understanding my silent plea because he sat down and pulled me onto his lap.

The new girl, Rosie, smiled warmly and leant over to talk to me. "So, you're new to the college? How come you're starting mid-semester?"

I smiled in return. She looked extremely nice. She was actually exceptionally pretty; she had long reddish-brown hair and brown eyes that were warm and welcoming.

"Um, well, I didn't like my old college, so we transferred here," I lied, shrugging.

Rosie looked at Ashton, raising one eyebrow curiously. "You came all the way here because your girlfriend didn't like her college?" she asked. Ashton smiled and nodded, which made Rosie make a cooing noise as she put her hand over her heart. "That's so sweet! Do you have a brother?"

"Nope sorry, only child," Ashton replied, laughing and tightening his arms around my waist.

Rosie sighed dramatically, looking disappointed. "That's a shame."

The three new people were really nice too; I liked the whole group of people if you discounted Monica's doe eyes that she directed at Ashton. Due to us all having blue wristbands, we were all on soft drinks tonight, but it was fun, I enjoyed it.

When the band finished their set, a DJ came on which seemed to get the crowd even more fired up. Serena looked at her watch. "Shall we dance, girls?"

I looked at Ashton questionably. I actually did want to dance, but I wasn't sure if that would be okay. Did that mean that he had to dance too, or could he wait here with the other boys?

"You can dance if you want," he confirmed, nodding. I smiled and stood up, downing the last of my drink as he pulled out his cell phone and sent a quick text. I rolled my eyes, seeing Peter appear out of nowhere and walk about five steps behind me as we made our way to the dance floor downstairs.

142

"So, how long have you two been together?" Rosie inquired as we danced.

Okay, time to remember all the lies we made up. "Just over a year."

"Where did you meet?" she asked, seeming genuinely interested.

"We met at a basketball game," I lied, shrugging.

She sighed, stepping closer to me. "He is so damn hot, Anna! Are you in love with him?" she asked, looking at me hopefully. She struck me as a bit of a romantic, the type of person that would cry at soppy movies and enjoyed a good love story.

My hands were getting sweaty, and my insides starting to tie in knots at the questioning. "Yeah," I lied, nodding.

Serena chimed in then. "I'd love him too if he were mine. He's so damn sweet!" Suddenly her eyes narrowed with interest. "He must have a flaw though; no one can be that perfect." She pursed her lips, waiting for my answer.

Flaws. Did Ashton actually have any flaws? I hadn't seen a single one, apart from… "He snores." I didn't class that as a bad thing though, after all, if he didn't snore I'd probably still be screaming myself awake, haunted by dreams of Carter's leering face.

Monica turned her nose up, obviously finally deciding that she didn't want him now that he was a noisy sleeper. "I hate guys that snore."

I smiled weakly, feeling the need to defend him in some way. "Yeah, but he wakes pretty easily, and if I wake him up then he always insists on apologising properly, if you know what I mean." I waggled my eyebrows suggestively.

"Oh well then, I'd definitely forgive him," she replied, laughing and looking at me enviously. Immediately, I wished I hadn't said my comment. I'd rather she kept her wandering eyes to herself, but stupidly I'd said the wrong thing. Suddenly she nodded behind me. "Speak of the devil."

I barely had time to turn and see he was walking up behind me before his arms snaked around my waist. "I figured I could steal one dance before we have to go," he whispered in my ear. His hot breath blew down my neck, and I shivered as his chest pressed against my back. My hands started to get a little sweaty as the temperature in the already warm room, started to climb. "Oh, and apparently these damn sexy legs are also driving the guys wild, so Peter tells me."

I frowned, confused by his statement. I knew Peter was watching, he was standing against the wall at the edge of the dance floor trying – and failing – to fit in. "What are you talking about?" I asked, confused, looking at Ashton over my shoulder.

He smiled teasingly. "You've not noticed?" We swayed to the beat of the song as one of his hands slid down to the outside of my thigh. "Young, impressionable, sex starved, geeky college guys are staring at you as we speak."

I frowned, looking around, seeing that he was right. There were guys looking in our direction, some of them looking at me, others looking at the other girls that I was dancing with. I guess a group of girls dancing would normally draw some male attention. I gulped as my back stiffened.

"It's fine, don't worry," he whispered reassuringly. Sliding his hand back to my waist again, he guided me to turn around to face him. "People just need to know that you have a boyfriend, that's all. It's easily sorted." He pulled me closer to him, wrapping his arms around me.

I nodded, keeping my eyes focussed on him as I looped my arms around his neck. As I looked into his deep green eyes, everything else seemed to fade into insignificance around us. They were beautiful and they trapped me there. He raised his hand and slid it slowly up my back before tangling his fingers into the back of my hair; his other arm wound around my waist and pulled me closer so that there was no gap between us at all.

I had no idea how long we danced like that for before he finally started to inch his mouth closer to mine, all I knew was that however long it was, it wasn't long enough. I wanted to live in that moment forever. Holding my breath in anticipation of feeling his soft lips against mine again, I closed the distance between us and then, I was lost.

When he moaned in the back of his throat, my heart seemed to do a little flip in my chest. His lips parted against mine and then his hot tongue slipped into my mouth, tangling with mine in a tantalising kiss that left me breathless and giddy. With his mouth on mine, I forgot everything else around us and what this kiss was probably for. In that moment, we could have been anywhere, we could have been standing in the middle of a stampede of wild horses, yet I wouldn't care, so long as he didn't stop kissing me. His kisses were addictive. My excitement was growing inside me, building like a raging inferno as I pressed my body against his, needing to be closer, to feel more of him, to be devoured and possessed by him.

But he broke the kiss and put his forehead to mine. A needy whimper left my lips as he breathed heavily and clutched me closer to him. Tilting my head, I captured his lips again, tangling my hands into the back of his hair, needing just a little more of his undivided attention. An involuntary moan escaped my lips as he kissed me back, sucking my bottom lip into his mouth and biting it gently.

Again he pulled away, shaking his head this time. "Enough now." His voice was husky and thick with lust as he swallowed and those sultry, heavily-lidded eyes met mine.

I blinked a couple of times and nodded in agreement, even though every nerve in my body was screaming for the opposite. I laid my head on his shoulder as he continued to dance, swaying to the slow beat of the song that the DJ was blasting out. His ragged breathing slowly returned to normal as I tried desperately to push the lustful thoughts away so that I could calm my jittery body.

As the song slowly filtered into another, his pace changed seamlessly to compensate. I smiled and looked up at him. "Are you good at everything?" I asked.

"No, why do you say that?"

I waved my hand at him as an explanation. "You're a really good dancer. I'm yet to find one thing you can't do."

He laughed and smiled at me. I tilted my face, rubbing my nose up the edge of his jaw, breathing him in as his hands stroked my back softly. "I would say the same for you, but the only thing I know you're not good at is letting people in," he said in my ear.

I pulled back to look at him. "Hey, I can let people in; I let you in, didn't I?" I was a little annoyed at his comment.

He shook his head. "No. You won't let me in; you barely even want to be my friend because you think I'm going to leave you. You close yourself off from everyone so that you don't have to feel anything again. You like to be numb," he said matter-of-factly.

I stared at him, dumbfounded. *How the hell does this boy know so much about me? Oh my God, does my file have my therapy tapes in there or something? Has that bitch of a therapist breached my confidentiality?*

"Have you been listening to my therapy tapes?" I snapped angrily, pushing myself out of his arms.

He laughed and caught my hands, pulling me closer to him again. "No, Anna. You're actually pretty easy to figure out most of the time," he replied, squeezing my hands gently. My body relaxed, and I rolled my eyes at his comment. "Now shut up and dance with me before the bar closes." He pulled me closer to him again and I laughed, smiling because somehow, he always seemed to make me feel better.

Chapter Sixteen

The sun beams down on me as I absentmindedly flip through the pages of a magazine. The strong scent of jasmine drifts up from the bushes that I'd not long planted, a few feet away from the swing chair I'm slouched on. I am just about to take a sip of my coffee when a slam of a door and a girlish giggle come from the house. A smile breaks out on my face as I look up, seeing a beautiful, little girl running towards me. I notice how tall she seems and how the smile on her face melts my heart. Her long, black hair is still damp and flows out behind her as she runs to me.

"Momma!"

I put my cup down just in time for her to jump onto my lap, laughing excitedly. "Hey! Did you have a good time? Did you jump in on your own?" I ask, excited to hear about it.

She nods enthusiastically. "Yeah, I jumped in loads of times, and I splashed Daddy right in the face," she chirps, laughing wickedly.

I grin. "You did? Good girl! Where is Daddy anyway?"

She shrugs, twirling a lock of my hair around her finger. "He's putting our swimming stuff in the laundry room."

"Hey, Baby Girl." I look up and my heart speeds at the sight of him walking across the garden to me. He is so handsome that my mouth waters.

As he gets to me, he bends and plants a soft kiss on the corner of my mouth before using the pad of his thumb to brush a smudge of dirt from my cheek.

"Hi," I breathe. It's almost a sigh of contentment because my whole world is now around me.

"Missed you," he whispers, before stealing my coffee cup from the side and downing the contents as he plops himself into the seat next to me and casually slings his arm around my shoulder.

I jerked awake, gasping, but for once, smiling as I roused from my dream. Ashton sat up quickly from his makeshift bed on the floor. "You okay? Nightmare?" Concern coloured his sleepy voice.

I opened and closed my mouth a couple of times, grateful that he hadn't turned on the light because my face was sure to be beet red. I had no idea what to say. *I've just had my first nice dream in three years… And it involved me having his child? Something is seriously wrong with me!*

Horrified, I lay back down. "No, not a nightmare. It's fine." A quick check of the clock told me it was almost ten in the morning. We'd not gotten back to the apartment until after one this morning, so I was still tired.

He didn't leave it though. Instead, he moved, climbing onto the bed and resting his arm across my stomach. "It wasn't a nightmare? What's up then?"

My embarrassment grew because the object of my desire in my dream was now too close to me as he looked down at me through the semi-darkness. "I was just dreaming. It wasn't a bad one. Actually, it was the first nice dream I've had since… since…" I frowned, not wanting to say his name again.

"You had a nice dream? That's great! What was it about?" He sounded ridiculously happy about it.

I winced, squirming under his scrutiny. *You,* wasn't exactly something I could answer. "Um…" I chewed on my lip, and he flopped down next to me, lying on his side and shoving his arm under the pillow as his other arm tightened around me, pulling me closer to his warm body. "I, er, had a little daughter. She was beautiful. It was just nice."

A dazzling smile crossed his lips as I spoke. "You did? Did she look just like you? If she did, then she'd have to be the most beautiful, little girl in the world."

My heart seemed to clench in my chest at his adorable words. The answer was no though, she hadn't looked like me, she'd looked like him! "She kinda did," I answered. The little girl did, in fact, have brown eyes like mine. Needing to make an escape from this awkward conversation before he probed further, I pushed myself up out of bed. "I'm going to make some breakfast. I'm thinking bacon and eggs. Sound good?" I didn't even wait for an answer before I practically ran from the bedroom, needing a few minutes away from him and the knowledge that I'd had a seriously inappropriate dream about him.

A little while after we'd eaten, I decided that I'd like to kill some time in the gym. According to the pamphlet about ASU that I'd read, there was a well-stocked gym on campus, so I was eager to check it out. As we pulled up outside and climbed out, another car pulled up next to us.

I groaned and threw my hands up in exasperation. "I *can* go on my own, you know!" I snapped, glaring first at Ashton, and then at my two far guards that had obviously followed us here.

Peter shrugged. "I actually just came to use the gym, I'm off duty. Please direct your glare at these two," he joked, waving a hand at Ashton and Dean.

I had to smile at that as I rolled my eyes and stalked into the building, not waiting for them. "You guys think I'm some pathetic wuss that can't defend herself. I could kick all of your asses," I muttered, shaking my head. I had no idea why I even needed a far guard; Ashton was surely more than enough to stop people from grabbing my butt or pushing me over into a puddle, which was all that would ever likely happen to me.

A scoffing noise came from Peter's direction, so I raised one eyebrow in question. "You think you could kick my ass?" he asked sarcastically, pulling his shoulders back and smirking at me as he opened the door to the gym and nodded for me to go first.

"Yes," I answered flatly. He was probably about six foot tall and easily heavier than Ashton because he packed in more muscle, but I was pretty sure I could take him.

When I stepped into the gym, I sighed happily. It was indeed as well-stocked as the pamphlet had promised. And another benefit it had was that it was empty. Being Sunday lunchtime, most students were probably still in bed, sleeping off the night before.

Peter scoffed again, following me into the gym and rolling his eyes, before nodding towards the padded mat area off to one side. "Want to try?"

A grin spread across my face as I nodded slowly. *Heck yeah, I want to embarrass you!* "Sure."

Ashton shook his head quickly, holding his hands up in protest. "That's not really a good idea, Peter."

I frowned angrily, clenching my teeth together. *He thinks I'm going to get hurt? Lousy pretend boyfriend! He's supposed to support me!*

Peter grinned, linking his fingers together, stretching out his arms and cracking his knuckles at the same time. "I won't hurt her, don't worry."

Ashton snorted. "I wasn't worried about *her*. You're supposed to be on duty tonight, and I don't think having a broken nose will go down well with the whole blending in thing," Ashton teased, chuckling. My anger evaporated immediately as I understood his hesitancy, and it wasn't because he was worried I'd get hurt.

"You think she could beat me?" Peter asked, clearly shocked.

Ashton shook his head in response. "I've seen her fight, she could *definitely* beat you, no thinking involved," he replied rather proudly, smiling over at me.

Peter just burst out laughing and slapped Dean on the shoulder with the back of his hand. "Can you believe this? As if she'd stand a chance."

Dean's smile was tight as he raised one eyebrow. "I've seen and felt her right hook. I wouldn't recommend you fight her."

I grinned happily and walked over to the treadmill. "I'm going to warm up for a while and then if you want, we can spar or something?" I offered, stepping on and turning it onto a slow walk.

Peter nodded in agreement. "Five minutes and then I'll wipe that smile off of your face."

Ashton didn't look too pleased as he walked over to the treadmill next to mine. His gaze was firmly locked on the speed control dial on my machine as I cranked it up a little faster. I would imagine he was waiting for me to go full pelt again – that wouldn't happen though, not if I was going to be sparring.

After a few minutes Peter called over to me from the weight bench he was at with Dean. "You ready to get your ass kicked, Anna?" he challenged, smirking at me confidently.

Trying to hide my smugness, I turned off my machine as I nodded over to the mats. "Sure, best of three?" I suggested.

"Anna, take it easy, okay? No broken bones," Ashton warned, following me over to the mats too with an apprehensive look on his face.

"I won't hurt her!" Peter protested sternly.

Ashton chuckled wickedly. "I wasn't talking about *her* bones."

Peter waved a dismissive hand. "Whatever. Best of three. No hitting in the balls, that's the only rule on my end. Other than that, you can do what you want."

I nodded in acknowledgment. "Okay. No taking it easy on me because I'm a girl, that's my only rule," I teased. He looked so overconfident; clearly he thought I was some little, delicate doll that couldn't look after herself. He was in for a shock; this was going to be fun.

"Right then, first down to the mat," Ashton said, blowing out a big breath. "No pinning down," he added seemingly as an afterthought.

I nodded and waited for Peter to come at me, standing with my hands down at my sides, not even bothering to defend myself. He wasn't even going to try and hit me, I could tell. He grinned and came towards me, moving to grab me. Casually, I knocked his hand away and moved to the side, smiling. His eyes widened a fraction before he came for me again. This time I ducked out of his way and kicked him in the leg – not too hard, but just hard enough so that he knew I wasn't playing around.

"Shit! You actually know how to fight?" he asked, his mouth popping open in shock.

I nodded, grinning. "Kickboxing or karate?" I changed my stance to show him I knew both.

His eyes narrowed as his shoulders tensed. "Er, I don't know that shit, I know how to street fight," he stated, coming for me again with his fists up to hit me this time. Effortlessly, I moved to the side, hitting him in the stomach and arm, spinning around low on the floor and sweeping his legs out from under him so he landed flat on his back. I smiled triumphantly as I offered my hand down to help him up. "Ouch, damn it! What was that?" he whined, rubbing his stomach.

"Karate. Want to go for kickboxing now?" I asked hopefully. If he really wanted to fight, that was undoubtedly my favourite.

"Er, I guess," he answered, looking a little uncomfortable as he glanced at Dean, who was just watching with a grin on his face.

I nodded and stood waiting for him to come at me. He seriously tried this time and managed to get a couple of hits in that would have been good if I hadn't gotten my guard up, but again, I easily put him down on his back.

"Enough, enough, I believe you. Jeez, you're a really good fighter," he admitted, shaking his head and rubbing his leg and arm where I'd hit him.

"Thanks, want to go again?" I asked hopefully. He shook his head quickly, so I looked at Ashton hopefully. "What about you, Pretty Boy?"

"You know you can't beat me," he replied, grinning cockily at me.

"I know, but I managed to split your lip last time. You never know, I might be able to get you on your back," I said shrugging.

He walked up close to me, encroaching in my personal space. "You could get me on my back anytime, Anna. You only need to ask… Oh, and be sober, of course," he whispered.

Blushing immediately, I laughed and pushed him away. A boyish grin broke out on his face as he kicked his shoes off and stepped onto the mats. He was watching me like a tiger stalking its prey. My insides seemed to squirm as I realised that watching him watch me like that was actually a turn-on. Plus, every time he looked at me, all I could see was the little girl from my dream and the way he'd looked at me when he'd walked up the path, and it was making it difficult to concentrate.

He shifted his weight to his other leg, ready to come for me, so I quickly ducked to the left and tried to hit him in the side, but he blocked it easily. I shifted to kick him, and he brought his leg up so I kicked his leg instead of his side. I smiled in awe; he was an incredible fighter. It was actually sexy to watch him in action.

He came at me again, and I threw a couple of punches and kicks that he deflected. He didn't once try to hit me, just defended and tried to grab me. As I raised my leg for a well-timed kick, his arm looped around my thigh. The air rushed out of my lungs as he swept my other leg from under me and we both fell to the mats in a heap.

He chuckled. "You're getting better. You nearly caught me a few times there," he said, looking at me proudly, still hovering above me. Every inch of his body was pressed against mine. My body started to react to how close he was, my heart was thumping, and my skin was starting to tingle.

"Are you gonna get off me or not?" I asked breathlessly, actually hoping for the second. He groaned before pushing himself off me, pulling me up off the floor as he stood up. His eyes were tight with frustration, and I couldn't help but smile. *At least I'm not the only one that feels this attraction!* "Wanna go again?" I asked, grinning.

"Yeah, if you want," he answered, instantly shifting into his sexy stance.

After an hour in the gym, everyone was all exercised out, so we went back to our respective apartments. I flopped down on the sofa, instantly grabbing the TV remote to see if anything good was on. Ashton took the seat next to mine, scooting down into the seat and watching as I channel surfed until we settled on a movie.

Watching him from the corner of my eye, I realised that I was actually getting used to how relaxed he was and how easy he was to be around. Since Carter, I'd never felt safe or normal in my own skin, but with Ashton it was like I didn't feel the need to be afraid or ashamed of who I was or what I felt inside.

He laughed at something, running a hand through his hair, making it stick up at the front. Perfectly at ease, I twisted to the side and raised my legs, stretching them out across Ashton's lap. Without taking his eyes from the movie, he placed an absentminded hand on top of my shin, holding my legs in place as his thumb drew a small circle around my kneecap. I sighed contentedly because it was extremely comfortable. I suddenly wondered why everything with Ashton seemed so effortless. It was weird because even with Jack there had been some awkwardness at times. Maybe it was because we were young; maybe things like comfort came with age. I could quite happily sit with Ashton, not saying a word, but with Jack, sometimes it had felt strained and uncomfortable. Sometimes we'd run out of things to say to each other – that would usually have been about the time that he would go home, or we'd just make out, or watch TV.

Discreetly watching Ashton instead of the movie, I thought about him having a girl of his own and sitting with her like this. He was going to make some girl incredibly lucky when he finally settled out of his player ways that he so vehemently denied. *Well, he'll make her incredibly happy until he's killed on some stupid SWAT mission, and then he'll destroy her soul and shatter her heart,* I thought. Everyone important left sooner or later. Nothing lasted forever. I'd had first-hand experience at that heartbreak and wouldn't wish it on anyone.

He looked over at me and smiled when he caught me watching him. "You okay?"

I nodded quickly, hoping he'd brush off my looking at him as a coincidence that we'd looked up at the same time. To help that excuse, I said the first thing that came to my mind. "Why did you make Dean and Peter come to the gym with us today? I would have been fine with just you." Suddenly I was slightly annoyed at his overprotectiveness. The three of them were going to drive me crazy.

151

He took a deep breath before answering as if expecting a scolding about it. "It's standard practice and what your father wants."

I frowned at that. My father wanted a lot of things, not all of them were possible. "Yeah, well I think you're all taking this too far. It's ridiculous. And that new codename you were all using for me last night... stupid." I folded my arms across my chest.

A small smile crept onto his face. "You would have preferred Rocky?" he inquired. I scoffed, trying not to smile.

"I would have preferred to be called by my given name, actually," I retorted.

He sighed and resumed drawing the little circle on my knee. "Look, one of us needs to be watching you at all times. In order for me to be able to look like your boyfriend and not some pervert stalker that follows his girl everywhere, we made up a code word so I could call if I needed one of them to watch you for a few minutes. It's not a big deal."

I did understand that. I'd had codenames before, but I still didn't really like them. With my father being who he was though, I should probably just accept it as part of the norm now. "Jewel is just pathetic. Who came up with that anyway?"

He shrugged, picking up the TV remote and flicking through the channels because the movie had finished. I hadn't even noticed because I'd been too busy staring at him and musing about things like his future girlfriend's broken heart. "We just went with Peter's suggestion in the end."

My ears pricked up, interested to know what the other suggestions were. "What were the other suggestions? Maybe we could change it?"

"Well, Dean wanted Regan."

"Regan?" I frowned at the randomness.

Ashton chuckled wickedly as he nodded. "That's what the little girl was called in The Exorcist."

I gasped in outrage. "No! That asshole!" I cried, though laughed at the same time.

"I thought it was pretty good," he countered. "But I figured that would be hard to explain when we put in the paperwork with your dad." He grinned at me, his eyes twinkling with mirth.

I had to smile at that too. My father would have been less than impressed. "What about your suggestion, what was that?" I asked, still hopeful that we could switch it to something less pretty and delicate.

His back stiffened as his hand stilled on my leg. "I didn't have one."

I cocked my head to the side, watching as his jaw tightened and untightened unconsciously. He was hiding something from me. "You're a terrible liar," I stated confidently. "I bet Regan was yours, wasn't it." I narrowed my eyes, resisting the urge to pout.

He shook his head in rejection; flicking through TV channels so quickly that you couldn't even see what was on. "I'm not. That wasn't mine, promise."

I nudged his leg with my foot to get his attention from the television. "Tell me yours then," I prompted.

He shook his head, smirking in my direction teasingly. My mouth popped open in dissatisfaction. I hated secrets. Pushing myself up onto my knees, I poked him in the ribs. Instantly he chuckled, gripping my hand, so I tried to poke him with my other hand instead.

"Tell me!" I demanded, poking him again, watching as he squirmed. That was when I came to the conclusion that my near guard was ticklish. A grin spread across my face as I decided to use it to my advantage. I launched forward, fighting my hands free from his as I started a tickle war.

It was pretty obvious within seconds though that I wasn't going to win. In mere moments, I was pinned to the sofa with him hovering above me, laughing excitedly as he returned the tickling treatment, making me giggle and squirm under him.

"Stop it!" I cried, struggling to fight free as I gasped for breath from all the laughing.

My wrists were pinned to the sofa as he looked down at me with mischievous eyes. He finally stopped, hovering above me, grinning happily. The smile faded from his face slowly as his eyes met mine. The burning passion was back inside me. I saw it cross his face too; and I *definitely* felt it stirring against my thigh. I didn't move. His restraining hold on my wrists loosened, but he didn't let go or get off me. I grinned, trying to slow my breathing and calm my racing heart. I hadn't laughed that much for years. It felt nice, kind of liberating.

"Please tell me yours," I begged.

He sighed, and his eyes tightened. "You don't want to know mine." I pouted, even fluttered my eyelashes as I silently begged him. A long groan escaped his lips as he looked down at me and frowned, clearly uncomfortable. "Damn that face, that's not fair!" he whined. Finally, he sighed. "Pacey. I wanted Pacey."

Not having a clue what that was about, I raised an inquiring eyebrow. "And what is Pacey? Some sort of sadistic killer?" I inquired.

A smile twitched at the corner of his mouth. "No. Have you seen The Peacemaker?" he asked, biting his lip. I shook my head in answer. I'd never even heard of it. "It's a movie, one of my favourites, in fact. There's this girl in it called Pacey. She's like a supreme being, perfect in every way, incredibly beautiful. She's kind of a badass like you. She saves the world and then gets the guy at the end," he explained. His eyes narrowed as if waiting for me to freak out or something.

His words repeated in my head. Incredibly beautiful and perfect in every way. And he'd wanted to name me that? My heart stuttered in my chest as the hair on the nape of my neck stood on end.

"Aww, that's really sweet. Are you sure that wasn't Dean's suggestion?" I joked, trying to keep a hold on the sensations that were flitting through my system as if they were on a freight train.

153

Ashton laughed uncomfortably. "Actually, yeah it was, I just wanted to steal his glory," he replied, avoiding my gaze and playing with a strand of my hair.

I smiled, watching him intently, loving how he looked so unsure and so vulnerable. "You're cute when you're nervous," I mused.

There was no sarcastic comment or anything, like I had expected; instead, his words made butterflies swoop around in my stomach. "What would you do if I kissed you right now?" He looked at my lips longingly.

I gulped, shocked at the turn in the conversation. What would I do? I was pretty sure I'd kiss him back, but part of me was screaming at me to push him the hell off me and be true to Jack.

"I'd kick your butt out of my apartment, and you'd have to sleep next door." I said the words and tried my best to make them sound true.

He shook his head slowly, his eyes never leaving mine. "No you wouldn't," he whispered, inching his lips towards mine.

My breath caught in my throat. "Ashton, don't," I rasped.

Ignoring my protests, he dipped his head and brushed his lips softly against mine. The kiss lasted barely a second before he broke it, but it was enough to send my body into overdrive as memories of his taste, his touch and his kisses flooded my brain. "Want me to sleep next door tonight?" he asked, his voice sounding husky. His lips brushed against mine softly as he spoke, sending a shiver of anticipation down my spine.

Deciding to answer truthfully, I shook my head, never taking my eyes from his. He smiled and closed the small distance again, pressing his lips to mine harder this time. My eyes fluttered closed as I revelled in the luxury of his lips on mine. Not even having to think about it, I kissed him back. His resulting moan made my skin prickle with excitement. My hands tangled into the back of his hair, pulling him closer to me as the kiss deepened and changed into something more urgent and passionate. Shifting slightly, I freed my legs from under him and gripped his hips with my knees, pulling his body on top of mine harder. The weight of him on top of me, as his hands wandered my body, almost made me dizzy with excitement. My whole body was aching for more of him.

A thought suddenly occurred to me – if kissing him was so wrong, then why did it feel so right? *Just once more,* I decided. I could make myself happy and give myself what I wanted, couldn't I? I deserved to be happy just once, didn't I?

I ran my hands down his back and pushed them down the back of his jeans, feeling his firm buttocks. I moaned at the feel of it. I could picture it when I closed my eyes, and I wanted to see it again. I wanted to have him, just once more. But would I be able to stop at once if it happened, or would I become addicted to his body just as I had done his personality and smile?

A knock at the door interrupted us, snapping us both back to reality. He broke the kiss and a little whimper escaped my lips as my grip tightened on him unconsciously, not letting him move away. A smile twitched at the corner of his mouth as he dipped his head again, pressing his lips back to mine as he cupped the side of my neck with one of his hands.

The knock sounded again, more insistently this time. He groaned against my neck, so I knew the moment was over. Unclamping my knees from his hips, I turned my head to the side and gulped in fresh air as he pulled back, looking down at me with hungry, lust-filled eyes that made my insides clench in excitement.

"I need to get that," he whined, looking back over his shoulder to the hallway and front door beyond. I nodded, unsure if my voice would work if I tried to speak. He sighed, putting his hand to his hair, smoothing it down because I'd had my hands tangled in it so it now stood at all angles. A blush covered my cheeks as he shoved his hand down the front of his jeans, rearranging himself so that his arousal was less noticeable as he walked to the door.

From the front door, I could hear him talking to someone, and then the voices got louder as they walked towards the lounge. I sat up quickly and smoothed my hair down too, praying my face wasn't flushed. The person with him was Dean, and judging by the no-nonsense look on his face, it wasn't a social call.

Dean smiled awkwardly. "Sorry to interrupt. Ashton and I just need to go over a few things before school tomorrow."

I nodded. "And by that you mean, 'get lost, Annabelle, we want to talk about secret agent stuff and you're not invited'," I guessed, rolling my eyes. "That's fine, I'm just going to go and see if I can make my head spin and vomit pea soup."

Dean's mouth popped open before he looked at Ashton accusingly.

Chuckling and waving over my shoulder, I headed into the bedroom, deciding to take a long soak in the tub. After running myself a bubble bath, I stayed in the water until it turned cold. The whole time I was in there, I couldn't stop thinking about that kiss with Ashton. Would I have had sex with him again if Dean hadn't interrupted? I genuinely didn't know the answer.

After I got out, I found one of Ashton's T-shirts hanging over the back of the chair, so I pulled it on, pairing it with some boy shorts. I sat on the bed and eyed the photo of Jack that sat on my bedside cabinet. I sighed and picked it up, running my finger over his face. He was so handsome, not in the totally hot way that Ashton was, but in the traditional, blue eyes, blond hair, type of way. I missed him terribly. Guilt built inside me because I had no right to yearn for someone else's arms to comfort me, yet I just couldn't seem to help it around Ashton.

My sketch book and pencils were by the bed, so I grabbed them and sat against the headboard. I drew the thing that had been on my mind since I woke up this morning – the little girl from my dream. In my sketch, she laughed and smiled excitedly. On the corner of the page, I drew Ashton as he looked in my dream: gorgeous, happy, and loving.

155

When I was done, I looked at the page for a long time, confused. It was almost like torture, looking at something that I wouldn't ever have. My eyes flicked back to the photo of Jack. *Why the hell am I obsessing over this little girl?* It was just a dream. My heart belonged to Jack and always would, just like we'd always promised each other.

A knock to the bedroom door made me jump. "Hey, can I come in?"

I quickly closed my pad so Ashton couldn't see the little girl. "Yeah sure."

He smiled timidly as he opened the door and stepped in. "You okay?"

I smiled, covering the confusion and pain I was feeling at the moment. "Yeah, I'm okay," I lied. "You get your secret stuff that I'm not allowed to know about done?" I asked, rolling my eyes.

He laughed and walked over to the bed, sitting on the edge. "You're so hostile! I don't tell you how to do your job," he replied.

I snorted at his comment. "Er, actually you kinda do. It's my job to be guarded, and you tell me what to do all the time," I countered, raising my eyebrows to make my point.

He grinned. "Not *all* the time," he repeated sarcastically. His eyes flicked down to the bed and the smile fell from his face as he picked up my photo of Jack. "So you go for blonds, huh? I've got no chance then, completely the opposite," he stated humourlessly, running a hand through his black hair.

I laughed awkwardly. "You're too pretty for me, remember?"

He pursed his lips, still studying my photo intently. "You look really happy here." He finally took his eyes off of it, holding it out to me.

"I was. That was before my life got blown to shit," I shrugged.

He sighed and scooted closer to me on the bed. "I upset you again because I kissed you, didn't I? I've made you sad again."

"No. I'm fine," I lied quietly. I didn't want to tell him about my personal debate as to whether I could sleep with him one more time or not, I was still undecided on the answer.

He sighed deeply and silence filled the room before he spoke again. "So, what are you drawing? Can I see?" he asked, holding out his hand for the sketchpad.

I laughed, blushing as I hugged the pad to my chest. "If you're thinking that it's some dark and horrible drawing that shows my inner turmoil, you're wrong."

There was no way I wanted him to know I was obsessing over this little girl, because technically, that meant I was obsessing over him and I didn't want to scare him away from me. I needed him now; I didn't want to go back to my life before him – alone and scared. I shuddered at the thought. I suddenly realised that I'd already done what I said I wouldn't do. I'd let him in. I liked him, cared about him even. Plus, I hadn't had nightmares for days because of him. What on earth was I going to do in

156

eight months when it came to the end of his assignment and he left me to go make some other girl deliriously happy? The thought alone hurt, and I'd only known him for a few days. What about when I'd known him for eight months? What would I do then?

Panic built inside me because I'd unknowingly made myself vulnerable by letting him close to me – but the thing was, I wouldn't actually change anything. I liked being around him, and I liked the person that he allowed me to be when I was around him. It was a glimpse of the old Anna, the one that was too frightened to make another appearance in case something went terribly wrong again. Ashton was slowly bringing that lonely, frightened girl back to life again. And I hadn't even realised until just now. I suddenly found myself wishing he would stay forever. I didn't want him to go and be reassigned somewhere else and get a girlfriend, I wanted him all to myself so I'd always have this contented, comfortable, safe feeling surrounding me.

"Anna?" he prompted, touching my foot tenderly.

I gulped, swallowing my feelings that didn't quite make sense to me. "What?" I answered, unsure what he wanted from me. Maybe he'd been talking to me while I was off trying to make sense of my emotions.

"I said, are you really okay? You ran off right after we kissed, and now you're all quiet and distant with me. Are you wishing that didn't happen?" he questioned, dipping his head so that my eyes had to meet his.

Again, I didn't know the answer. "I'm fine. It's all just complicated. I can't explain my feelings to you, I don't know how I feel," I admitted. I chewed on my lip nervously. My answer was the truth – how could I explain something that I didn't even understand myself?

He stood and looked down at me worriedly. "Well, if you need to talk to me, I'm here to listen, anytime."

I smiled gratefully at his back as he stalked to the door. "Ashton?" I called, needing to say something else, because it didn't feel right leaving it like that. He turned at the door, looking at me quizzically. "Thank you." The words seemed right, and the only ones that I could think of.

His answering smile was dazzling, and my tummy fluttered again. "No problem, ma'am," he replied. I groaned as he shut the door behind him. *How on earth can one word be so hot when it comes out of his mouth? How can one word make my insides melt? It just isn't fair.*

Chapter Seventeen

~ Ashton ~

For an hour, Dean and I planned out our positioning, ready for the first day of school. We'd gone over pretty much everything three times, but you couldn't be too prepared in my opinion. I'd also memorised the map of the school so that I knew where all the exits and meeting points were, just in case.

Over breakfast, I'd gone through the rules with Anna. She'd agreed to them all, not protesting, and actually looking a little happy with them. I'd insisted on a few changes to her normal routine which she seemed quite happy about. For one thing, no one knew who I was, so while the boyfriend cover worked, we were going to play it to the maximum. Dean would be in plain clothes the whole time, not even acknowledging us unless there was a huge problem that I couldn't resolve amicably. I had my gun and police credentials with me, but I was praying they wouldn't ever need to be of use, because that meant that Carter would never find where she is.

The school knew of our situation and that I wasn't actually a college student, so I wasn't going to be expected to hand in any masterpieces – which was handy considering I couldn't draw.

Anna had agreed, finally, to stay with me at all times – even bathroom breaks where I'd have to stand outside and wait for her. We'd already agreed that I could kiss her a couple of times throughout the day so that the boyfriend story stuck. She'd even consented to trying to meet up with the friends that we'd made over the weekend for lunch so that we could integrate with society better and move easier through the crowd.

Of course, Anna had scolded me a few times at how seriously I was taking this whole operation. She'd called it "going overboard." She'd accused me of acting too much like a SWAT officer rather than secret service, but I'd let it slide. She didn't know about Carter and his letters; if she did, then she wouldn't be as hostile about being guarded. She'd promised to be on her best behaviour and let me deal with any issues so that she wouldn't be kicked out of yet another school. I had high hopes for her at this one, hopefully my arrangements would allow her to finish her course and start to take a hold on her anger and insecurities that she had deep-rooted inside her.

While she was getting dressed, I put my hands on my hips and did a few stretches. My body was really starting to protest about sleeping on the floor, but thankfully I'd received an email last night saying that the sofa bed would be delivered this afternoon. Peter was going to take delivery of it for me, so at least I'd have something soft to sleep on tonight, which would hopefully make me feel less like an old man.

When the door handle of the bedroom moved, my stomach seemed to twist into a knot. I frowned and shook my head at myself. I knew I had it bad now, but this was bordering on ridiculous. I was so excited to see her, yet I'd only seen her over breakfast forty minutes ago. This didn't bode well for me.

As she stepped into the kitchen with a tentative, nervous smile on her face, my heart seemed to stop. She looked so hot that my mouth actually started to water. My eyes slid down her frame, taking it all in slowly as she played with her fingers and chewed on her lip, waiting for my opinion on her outfit. The insecurity about wearing normal clothes was clearly still there.

I gulped. The black shorts she wore came to about mid-thigh, showing off her long, gorgeous legs. My hands were itching to trace the line of them and feel the soft skin under my fingers. The tight, black top she had on clung to her flat stomach and pert breasts, showing a sexy, red bra-strap. The loose fit, red chequered shirt over the top completed the outfit and made her look so sexy it was starting to hurt as my jeans constricted across the crotch.

Stop, Ashton, focus! She's looking at you, you need to say something. You look like an idiot!

"Er… You look, er…" I stuttered. *Come on you stupid prick, think of a word!*

She raised one eyebrow in question as she looked down at herself and straightened her shirt. Clearly, she had no idea that she looked like a goddess and that all I wanted to do was crush her against me and run my tongue over every inch of her. I mentally groaned. I wanted to beg her for a chance; I wanted to be with her so badly that I could almost taste it.

I took a deep breath and tried to stop embarrassing myself. "You look stunning, and you're going to make this hard for me all day," I said honestly. There was undeniably a double meaning to those words, she certainly was going to make me hard all day, that was for sure.

Her shoulders seemed to relax at my compliment, and she looked at me gratefully. "Hard for you, why?" she asked, turning to get a glass of juice from the fridge.

I groaned quietly. From the back you couldn't see the shorts; it looked like she was just wearing a shirt and ankle boots. *Oh man, how the heck am I going to be able to do my job with her looking like that? Maybe I should ask her to change... Can I ask her to change without making myself look like a freaking pervert?*

"Ashton? How is it going to be hard for you? What are you talking about?" she asked, interrupting my examination of her legs.

I closed my eyes and willed myself to calm down downstairs. "You're gonna get hit on a lot today," I admitted.

She turned back and held out a glass of apple juice to me, making her bangles jingle as she moved. I smiled down at them weakly. I'd noticed that whenever she wore short sleeves, she always wore something on her wrists, covering up the scar from her suicide attempt and the various other small scars on her wrist where she had obviously self-harmed at some point in her life.

When she boosted herself up onto the kitchen counter, my body moved of its own accord. I stepped closer to her, setting myself between her legs. Her minty breath blew across my face as her breathing started to speed up. Her eyes widened a fraction as I leant in closer.

"With you looking like this, I may have to kiss you a fair few times today," I warned. I kept my eyes trained on hers, watching for her reaction as I reached out and traced the line of her cheekbone with one finger.

Her breath seemed to catch in her throat as she nodded slightly. "If you think that's necessary," she replied, not taking her eyes from mine.

I could feel the passion building between us and I knew she could feel it too because of the way she was looking at me. That look made the hair on the nape of my neck stand on end. There was no denying that she was attracted to me too, but she didn't like the fact that she was, I knew that for sure.

"With you looking like this, Baby Girl, I think it's going to be very, very necessary." My voice was so husky and thick with lust that it was almost embarrassing.

Her knees tightened around my hips as her gaze flicked down to my lips. All I could envision was pressing my lips to hers and tasting her again as I pressed every inch of my body against hers. Before anything could happen though and I could act on what my instincts were telling me to do, there was a knock at the door. My heart sank because I knew that the intimate moment was over. I seriously needed to get a grip on myself.

"That'll be Dean," I whispered, not taking my eyes from hers. "Are you ready to go?"

She blinked a couple of times as if coming out of a daze, and then nodded, clenching her teeth together. It was almost as if she was mentally scolding herself for allowing me close to her or something. She did that a lot after we'd almost had a 'moment'.

"Yeah, I'm ready," she confirmed. "Do you have your iPod? You'll need it."

~ Anna ~

As the rental car headed towards the school, I could still feel the residual ebb of the sexual tension from the apartment. I had no idea how he did it, but one smouldering look from Ashton seemed to reduce me to a needy, quivering mess.

I flicked my eyes over to him, trying to be discreet as I watched the way his muscles tensed in his arms while he drove. He looked particularly irresistible today. He was wearing blue again – I liked him in blue. My teeth sank into my bottom lip as a thousand lustful thoughts of him seemed to hit me at once. Clear as day, I could remember the feel of his skin under my hands, the taste of his tongue, and the sensations that his lips created with the smallest of kisses. A wistful sigh escaped my lips as I forced my eyes away from him, looking out of the windshield instead. I needed to stop this because it wasn't right, and it wasn't fair on Jack for me to keep lusting after another man.

After another five minutes, we pulled into the campus parking lot. Ashton turned to me. His eyes were stern and warning, just as they had been this morning when we'd discussed the rules of him guarding me. "Wait there for me to come around and get you. You stay with me at all times."

I nodded in agreement, trying to keep my breathing steady. This was my last attempt at school because I wasn't going to start over again. I was really going to try hard this time, just like I'd promised Jack I would. Hopefully, Ashton would make that possible with all the changes that he'd made to my usual routine.

As he opened my door for me, I took a deep breath and took his offered hand, closing my fingers around his tightly. He smiled reassuringly. "You'll be fine," he whispered, pulling me to my feet gently. "This'll be fun, and I'll look after you. You trust me, don't you?" he asked, bending his knees so that his emerald green eyes met mine.

An involuntary smile tugged at the corner of my lips. "I trust you with my life, Ashton." That was the honest truth. He was the only one that made me feel safe, but I didn't know why, there was just something about him that told me that I could put my faith in him.

161

A dazzling, proud grin spread across his face as his arm slipped around my shoulder, pulling me to him as he guided me across the parking lot and towards the large campus building in front of us. As we walked past people, I pressed against his side, trying to melt into him as inquisitive glances were cast in our direction. The tension was practically radiating off him in droves as he discreetly surveyed the area. Dean was doing the same thing about a hundred yards off to my right. I smiled because no one was paying the slightest bit of attention to my far guard, which meant that maybe the undercover thing would work here like Ashton kept assuring me.

A group of girls fell silent as we walked passed, all of them eyeing Ashton like he was their next meal. "You could get a lot of action here, Pretty Boy," I teased, shaking my head in awe. He wasn't even trying, yet it looked like girls were willing to throw themselves at his feet.

His forehead creased with a frown as he shook his head. "I'm not interested in any of these girls, Anna." His tone was a little brisk, as if I should have known better or something. He opened the door to the building and pulled me inside with him. "Come on then, let's get to our first class," he whispered, guiding me down the hallways as if he knew exactly where he was going.

"Don't we need to go to the office first? How do you even know where our first class is?" I asked, confused. Usually I had to book in at the office and someone gave me a tour of the school before showing me the way to my classes.

"They sent me everything already, and I spoke to the dean this morning while you were getting dressed. Plus, I have the map, remember? You know, the one I was looking at this morning when you said I was taking this too far," he mocked, smirking at me.

I laughed, slipping my arm around his waist. "Okay, I guess your memory will come in handy for finding our way around then."

He stopped walking, pulling me to a stop too. "Wow, that's almost an apology."

More people were watching us now. I shook my head in rejection. "No it wasn't, I don't do apologies very often," I denied, shrugging and narrowing my eyes at him teasingly.

He grinned, cupping my face gently as he stepped closer to me, so close that my skin prickled with sensation. "Oh, I know that," he purred as his mouth closed over mine, claiming my lips in a kiss that made my tummy flutter with excitement.

Waves of desire crashed over me; they were so powerful that I was surprised we were still standing. I moaned in the back of my throat and wrapped my arms tight around his neck, trying to get closer to him, tangling my fingers in his soft hair. When he nibbled on my lip, wanting to deepen the kiss, I kissed him with everything I had in me. The passion from the kitchen was spilling over as he ran his hands down my back, gripping fistfuls of my shirt, clamping me to him. A small moan escaped his lips that set my heart soaring.

I wanted him. I needed him. When Ashton's mouth was on my body, everything felt right and whole again, like all of that awful stuff with Carter hadn't happened. But the kiss didn't seem enough for me, I wanted more. I wanted him to lavish attention on my body like he had done that one time at my parent's house. I wanted him to make me feel like that special, beautiful girl that he looked at with those sultry eyes that shone with desire. My whole body ached for it.

By the time he pulled away, my head was spinning with need. He pressed his forehead against mine, still holding me against him as our breathing slowed to normal. His eyes that met mine were dancing with excitement too. He looked like he was fighting for control. I could see the conflict across his face; he wanted to drag me to the nearest supply closet too, just like I was silently envisioning.

"What was that for?" I whispered, raising my chin and brushing my nose against his softly.

He swallowed loudly as his hand slid down my back, coming to rest on the small of my back. "Just wanted everyone here to know that you're mine."

Mine. The word made a shiver of something run down my spine as I pressed myself closer to him. "Why don't you just take me against the wall or something then with everyone watching?" I joked.

A smile twitched at the corner of his mouth as he dipped his head towards mine. "Gladly." His lips met mine again, and I sagged against him in contentment. The kiss didn't deepen though, it was just a little chaste kiss before he stepped back and ran his hand down my arm, taking my hand and interlacing our fingers. "We should get to class before we're late."

I swallowed the lust that had built inside me and nodded in agreement, letting him give me a gentle, little tug to get me moving again. Now that I was out of the little bubble that he seemed to create around me, I could see people watching us again. Clearly, being new and having a major make-out session in the middle of the hallway was drawing peoples' interest. As we walked, I tried my best to ignore the stares and whispers. I cringed into Ashton's side as a couple of guys let their eyes wander over me just that little too long.

Finally, after lots of twists and turns, he stopped outside a classroom. I peeked in, seeing people already sitting on desks, chatting amongst themselves as they waited for lessons to start. The teacher was perched on the edge of her desk, sipping coffee. I scanned her, making my estimations of how good she would be. She was thin and wearing all black and her brown hair, flecked with the occasional grey, was pulled back into a severe ponytail. If I had to guess, I would put her at mid-fifties. She looked friendly enough, and just the right amount of eccentric to teach art at college.

"Ready?" Ashton asked, squeezing my hand gently.

I gulped. "Not really."

He chuckled and pulled me into the room and up to the teacher. Ashton cleared his throat. "Mrs Donovan?"

She turned and smiled, setting down her cup. "Good morning. You must be my new students," she greeted.

Ashton nodded, and I let my gaze rake over the class. Most of the students were girls and all of them were now eyeing my near guard with undisguised lust. One of them was staring with an open mouth. My back stiffened as panic set in. What if Ashton wanted to hook up with one of these girls? What if he started to like one of them and wanted to bring her back to the apartment? How was I going to cope with that? Jealous anger and resentment settled in the pit of my stomach, and I felt the frown tug at my forehead.

"Yes, ma'am. I'm Ashton, and this is my girlfriend, Anna." He squeezed my hand so I looked up at him, seeing that he had one eyebrow raised in question.

I shook my head quickly, not wanting him to know that my mind was running rampant and thinking up scenarios where he fell in love and I had to watch it happen. I definitely didn't want him to know about the jealousy that was eating me up inside because of it.

"You like Anna and not Annabelle?" the teacher inquired, her tone warm and welcoming.

I turned and forced a smile. "Yeah, Anna is fine." My parents were the only ones who had ever called me Annabelle.

She nodded in acknowledgement and waved a bony hand towards two empty seats at the back of the classroom. "Take a seat, and then we can get started." She clapped her hands and the whole room seemed to come to attention, ready to start the day, as Ashton and I wove to the empty seats at the back.

By the time the class was finished, my stomach was hurting from all the giggling. When Ashton had said that he couldn't draw, I hadn't thought he meant that all he could muster up was barely more than stick people. My cheek muscles were aching from smiling and laughing so much. I'd never seen anything so terrible, and it was lucky we were sat at the back so that no one else could see and ask what the heck he was doing in an art class. The teacher turned out to be quite nice though, and I actually had fun in class which wasn't something I was used to.

As soon as the class ended, Ashton screwed up his paper into a ball and tossed it towards the trashcan, holding his hands up in celebration when it went straight in without touching the sides. "Three pointer," he chirped, grinning. I chuckled at how childlike he was sometimes – it was incredibly cute.

"Maybe you should stick to paper basketball instead of art," I teased, shoving all of my stuff back into my bag.

He nodded, taking my bag off of my shoulder and holding his other hand out to me. "Let's go eat, I'm starving."

I rolled my eyes. "You're always hungry. I'm surprised you're not as big as a house." I'd definitely never seen anyone eat as much as he did.

"I've got hollow legs," he joked, leading me out of the classroom.

I kept my head down as we made our way to the lunchroom. I'd promised him that I would try to integrate into the school and be more sociable, but I wasn't sure I was ready for it today. After buying two plates of some disgusting-looking pasta and a wilted salad, I sat down at an empty table. Ashton sat opposite me, and I saw Dean in line to buy food too. I smiled. With him dressed in normal clothes instead of a suit, he blended in so much better. He actually passed as a mature student, and no one was batting an eyelid at him.

The chair next to me scraped, so I looked up to see a guy sitting himself next to me. My back stiffened automatically as my hand tightened around the fork I was holding. A predatory smile crossed his face as he leered at me. "Hi, sexy, what's your name?" he asked.

"Well it's not sexy, that's for sure," I scoffed.

He grinned, opening his mouth to answer but before he could, Ashton leant forward over the table. "Her name is back the fuck off." He was smiling politely, but the tightness around of his jaw and the hardness to his eyes showed that it wasn't a friendly smile.

The guy recoiled slightly before standing up and holding his hands up defensively. "Easy. I didn't realise she was taken," he shook his head, shifting nervously on his feet, clearly intimidated by Ashton, who had that menacing agent look back on his face again.

"Right. Well, now you do. Why don't you go back to your table and tell your boys that she's taken too," Ashton instructed, nodding at the table of guys that were all staring in our direction, watching their friend make his move on me.

The guy smiled sheepishly before turning his attention back to me again, ignoring the obvious possessive vibe that Ashton was radiating. "If you ever ditch this loser, my name's Colt," he said, grinning at me.

"Not planning on ditching the loser, Colt, sorry." I looked at Ashton, seeing the angry expression on his face as he watched the guy strut back across the lunchroom to his friends. "Back the fuck off? Could you have been any ruder?" I muttered sarcastically.

Ashton's frown deepened. "What? I thought I was extremely polite."

I burst out laughing. "Extremely polite, yeah," I choked out.

"Well, what do you want me to say?" he countered.

I shrugged, spearing some of my pasta with my fork. "Just try not to be so overprotective. I'm sure there's a nicer way. Besides, there's like ten of them over there. If they wanted to, they could kick your ass," I said, glancing over to their table, noticing that actually there were twelve of them, but I didn't bother correcting myself.

Ashton sighed dramatically, faking hurt. "You doubt my skills."

"You could fight ten guys?" I asked sarcastically.

"Sure. They're college students who have probably never been in a real fight in their lives. I bet you could take at least five of them on your own," he answered confidently.

I smiled because he never seemed to doubt my ability. "Well, let's not find out, I like our apartment, I don't want to be kicked out of school just yet," I suggested, grinning and eating my food while he laughed.

From the corner of my eye I saw Tim and Rich bounding over, arms laden with food. "Hey, we've been looking for you. How's your first day going?" Tim asked, smiling as he sat down next to me.

"Yeah great, we're making friends already," I joked, making Ashton almost choke on his food.

"Yeah? I'll bet you are with those legs on display like that," Rich flirted, grinning at me as he sat next to Ashton.

I rolled my eyes. "Whatever. Where's everyone else?" I asked, mostly meaning Rosie. I'd gotten on remarkably well with her on Saturday night.

Tim rolled his eyes. "They're in the food line. Those damn girls take a ridiculous amount of time to choose a salad."

When the girls finally graced us with their presence, Monica was again flirting with Ashton but thankfully, the same as usual, he didn't seem interested. Rosie and I chatted easily throughout the rest of lunch. She was extremely easy to get along with, and incredibly funny most of the time. Her smile was infectious.

When lunch was over, Ashton and I made our way to Graphic Design, which was our afternoon class. I didn't hold out much hope for Ashton in there though, he didn't seem to be the artsy type so no doubt he would be doodling stick people and cars like he was all morning.

I actually loved the class. We were given a week long project which we had to pair up to do, of course, I was paired with Ashton. We'd been given a slogan of a company that was rebranding, and we were to come up with a new design and company image to fit their needs. My teacher, Mr Wilson, informed the class that the designs would be sent on to the actual company and if they liked one then they could potentially use it.

Throughout the class, Ashton was no help. Most of the time he'd sat there watching me with one of his iPod earphones in his ear, making stupid jokes with a goofy grin on his face. By the time the lesson finished, all I'd managed was a brainstorm of ideas because he'd been so distracting.

I sighed happily as we stepped out of the building. In my year that I'd been trying to go to college, I'd never once enjoyed being there, until today. Ashton's hand closed over mine as he nodded towards the car. I squeezed his hand in silent thanks because his presence seemed to be making everything easier for me. *Maybe, just maybe, it will work out here.*

166

After a few hours at home, everything was getting on top of me again. Sitting around and watching TV was making me think too much. Sitting with Ashton, I couldn't but long to be closer to him. I wanted to snuggle against his side and let his heat envelope me. I wanted to press my lips against his and lose myself in the bliss of his kissing. But I knew I shouldn't want those things at all. Guilt and shame were building up inside me because I felt disloyal to Jack for wanting things from another man that I promised would be his and his alone. Self-loathing was making me twitch in my seat. I needed a distraction and something that would make me think clearly again instead of lusting after my near guard.

"Do you mind if I go to the gym for a bit?" I held my breath, hoping he would say I could go on my own. I needed a release, and I knew he would complain and tell me to take it easy if he came with me.

He nodded immediately. "Yeah, sure. I'll just get changed and call Dean."

My heart sank but deep down I knew he wouldn't have let me go on my own anyway. I followed him into the bedroom, grabbing some sweatpants and a T-shirt before heading into the bathroom to change.

Ten minutes later, we arrived at the gym with both Dean and Peter in tow. As soon as we were in, my eyes settled on the treadmill. My shoulders ached with tension as I shoved my bottle of water into the hole and tied my sneakers tighter before stepping on. As I fiddled with the buttons, turning it on to a gentle walk, my gaze flicked to Ashton. He'd chosen the rowing machine. My eyes seemed as if they were glued to him as I watched the muscles flex in his arms and legs. He'd removed his T-shirt so all of his glorious body was on display. Something deep down in my belly clenched as my mouth went dry. He looked beautiful.

He looked up then and his eyes met mine. A small smile crossed his lips, and I forced myself to turn away and stop looking. I really needed to get a grip of myself and this lust that seemed to come out of nowhere and consume me, leaving me a quivering mess. It just wasn't right that he could make me feel like this, I hated it.

Shoving my iPod headphones into my ears, I took a deep breath and put my hand on the speed dial, slowly cranking it up until I was running as fast as my legs would carry me. I ran away from my problems and everything that was bad in my life, focussing only on the music and putting one leg in front of the other. I ran until I couldn't even think about Ashton's gorgeous body anymore – which took a surprising amount of time.

Having no idea of time, I could have been running for either five minutes or five hours. All I knew was that my hands started to tingle and sweat was trickling down my back, making my T-shirt stick to me. As per my usual routine, I sped up for about another minute before slowing right down, barely able to breathe.

167

Once I'd stopped, I slumped to the floor with my heart crashing in my ears. Knowing I was close to passing out, I put my head between my knees and took deep breaths through my nose as I squeezed my eyes shut. When my fingers finally stopped tingling and the acidic taste in my mouth started to subside, I flopped down onto my back and groaned.

When I opened my eyes again, I noticed all three of my guards were staring down at me. Both Dean and Peter wore shocked expressions, but Ashton looked incredibly angry.

I frowned, turning off my iPod as I pushed myself up to my feet, ignoring how my legs shook from the effort of supporting my weight.

"You feel better now?" Ashton snapped.

I snorted, frowning at him. "For goodness' sake, *this* is why I wanted to come on my own! Don't start giving me lectures on what's good for my body," I retorted, walking past him to the punch bag that was hanging in the corner of the room.

"Anna, you can't keep doing this! That was fucking ridiculous. You were running like that for almost thirty minutes, I'm surprised you're not dead!" Ashton shouted.

The anger in his voice made me slightly nervous, but I tried to ignore it as I slipped on some training gloves and started hitting the bag. I let out all of my frustration and annoyance. Each hit made my muscles in my arms ache. Just as I was about to throw another punch, a hand closed over my arm, pulling sharply so that I had to spin around. My eyes flicked up to Ashton's face. He looked so angry that the frightened, little girl that I tried so hard to bury inside me surfaced immediately. I flinched, cowering away as I closed my eyes and waited for him to hit me.

His hold on me ceased immediately, and nothing happened. Tentatively opening my eyes, I looked up at him, seeing a horrified, devastated expression on his face as he stepped away from me and shook his head in disbelief. "You actually think I would hit you?" he asked weakly.

I winced, knowing that I'd offended him. "I… I… No, I just…" I looked at the floor, not wanting to admit that yes, just for a second, I thought he would hit me.

"I would never do that, ever." He stepped back again, shaking his head. "I'm sorry, I can't do this. I can't watch this anymore."

My mouth popped open in shock as he turned on his heel and walked out, leaving me with Dean and Peter. As the door slammed behind him, I jumped as a huge lump seemed to form in my throat. *He left me. He promised he wouldn't leave me…* My heart immediately hurt in my chest as my stomach tightened. Deep down, I'd known it was only a matter of time before he left because everyone did eventually, I just hadn't realised that it would happen so soon or so suddenly. I wasn't even close to being prepared for it.

I stared at the door, willing him to walk back in and shout at me some more, to tell me that I'd upset him but that he'd been hasty in deciding to leave. He didn't come back though. My whole body seemed to go cold as my heart sank. My vision became a little blurry and I realised that I was about to cry. I swallowed my sobs and raised my chin as I took a deep breath, trying to calm myself. I refused to cry over another man.

Knowing that Dean and Peter were still watching me and waiting for some sort of reaction, I forced the devastated feelings aside and turned back to the punch bag and hit and kicked it until I hurt all over from the effort. By the time I finished, my legs were wobbly and my fingers were numb.

Dean and Peter were sitting on the chairs, waiting for me in silence. "I'm done," I muttered, walking past them and not waiting for them to catch me up.

The ominous silence continued as they walked me to my apartment. When I stepped through the front door, Dean followed me in and headed into the lounge while I went straight to the bathroom for a shower. He would be the one that would move in and take over as near guard until they found a replacement for Ashton. I couldn't even bring myself to care about the fact that I didn't want him here.

The hot water of the shower did nothing to help the crushing feelings I had inside. I felt terrible, the loss of him was painful, and all I could see was his devastated face when he said that he would never hurt me. My insides were hurting, my head was throbbing, and my whole body was aching.

When I got out of the shower, I pulled my hair into a ponytail and found one of his T-shirts that he'd left behind. I pressed it against my face, inhaling deeply. A little whimper left my lips because it still smelt like him. Needing the comfort, I slipped it on over my head and climbed into the bed, hugging myself tightly. Feeling cold and lonely, I cried for him until I fell asleep.

"Come on, Princess, it's fun, you'll like it. I've played lots of times. Take the gun, take a deep breath and then pull the trigger," Carter insists, waving the gun towards me again.

My whole body is shaking as I wring my hands, ignoring the pain in my wrists caused by the deep cuts I'd made there the week before. I feel nauseous.

Carter raises one eyebrow. "Come on, we'll make a deal. You wanted to die last week; if you die, then you'll be getting what you wanted. If I die, you then can go free, and if neither of us dies, then you'll stay here with me. Forever," he suggests, grinning wildly.

Silent tears fall down my face as I look at the shiny, little silver gun balanced on the palm of his outstretched hand. "That's not a deal! I don't have a choice!" I cry.

"You have a two in six chance of not being here with me. That's what you want, isn't it?" he retorts sarcastically.

"Please don't make me do this, Carter. Please?" I beg. He sighs and moves the gun; using two fingers, he spins the cartridge.

As I realise that this is my only way out, I silently pray that either I die or he does, because the alternative, staying here with him, doesn't bear thinking about. Fear runs through my veins, causing my hands to shake violently. I watch as he pulls some kind of straw out of his pocket, bends towards the table and the line of white powder that I'd watched him make, and snorts it all before grinning at me wildly.

Because I've not moved, he rolls his eyes and points the gun at his own temple. "I'll go first," he states, as if this is an everyday occurrence.

I hold my breath. He smiles and winks at me as he pulls the trigger. Vomit rises in my throat, but nothing happens, the gun doesn't go off. Overwhelmed, I turn to the side and am violently sick over the expensive-looking rug.

He smiles at me tenderly, clearly planning on ignoring the fact that I'm still retching. "Well then, I guess the best you can hope for is that you die, Princess," he states, shaking his head sadly. He holds the gun out to me again, nodding encouragingly. I raise a shaky hand, and whimper as my fingers close around the cool metal of the gun. Carter's hand closes over mine as he guides the gun up under my chin. I swallow, feeling the hard metal pressed against my skin. "You can do it, Princess." The tone of his voice is kind and loving; it doesn't match the fact that he is making me pull a gun under my chin. I take a deep breath and pray for death. I don't want to stay here. "Count to three," he whispers.

"One... Two..." My voice is shaking as I count slowly. My heart stops just before the last word comes out as a broken whisper. "Three." I pull the trigger.

CLICK.

"I guess you're mine to keep now, Princess," Carter gloats. His eyes are dancing with delight as a large, lopsided, drug-induced smile creeps onto his face.

I sat bolt upright as my piercing scream tore through the air. Ashton's T-shirt was stuck to me where I was sweating. My lungs were tight so I couldn't breathe properly. I just couldn't get enough air in, so it felt like I was suffocating.

Seconds later, the door burst open, slamming against the wall loudly. "Anna! Shit, it's okay, Baby Girl, it's okay. I'm so sorry, I fell asleep on the sofa, I'm so sorry," Ashton cooed. My eyes widened in shock as I looked up at him, still struggling to breathe. He sat on the bed and wrapped his arms around me, rocking me gently. "I'm sorry. I didn't mean to fall asleep out there, I'm sorry," he whispered, stroking my hair.

I couldn't focus on anything other than my dream and the crushing horror that was eating me up inside. Carter. Carter's face. His voice. His wicked smirk. His excited eyes. All of it swam before me, taunting me, hurting me, killing me.

Vomit rose in my throat, so I clamped one hand over my mouth and shoved myself out of his arms. I staggered out of the bed and ran for the bathroom, barely managing to make it before I emptied my stomach into the toilet. While I was being sick, Ashton rubbed my back and whispered soothing words. I pushed on his legs, pointing to the door, signalling for him to leave.

"I'm not leaving you like this," he stated, getting a washcloth and wetting it, before placing it across the back of my neck as I retched and retched.

170

I squeezed my eyes shut, gasping for breath. *Why that one? Why did it have to be that dream?* Other than seeing Jack die on that fire escape, this one was the worst dream that usually haunted me – because right after the incident with the gun, Carter had pinned me to the floor next to the pile of my own vomit and had taken my virginity.

My whole body was shaking as I wiped my forehead, sitting back on my feet as I gasped for breath.

"Calm down, Baby Girl. Take deep breaths and calm down. Everything's fine, I promise you," Ashton whispered, adjusting the cool cloth on my neck.

My chin wobbled as I looked over at him sitting on the floor next to me. I could see the pain on his face; he looked helpless, like he didn't know how to help me. At that moment, my body reacted instinctively. I whimpered and threw my arms around his neck, holding him tightly as I sobbed against him.

He groaned, wrapping his arms around me and rocking me gently until I finally managed to calm down. When he moved to pull back, I shook my head in protest, clamping myself against his chest. "Don't leave," I begged. I couldn't let him go anywhere. I couldn't go back to dreaming like that again every night, I didn't want to be without him.

"Anna, let go," he whispered, reaching up and unclasping my hands from his neck.

Rejection made my eyes sting as I clenched my teeth together and dropped my eyes to the floor. As he stood up, I realised that this was entirely my fault. He was leaving because I'd pushed him away by not trusting him. I'd pushed him out of my life, and I was now going to have to deal with the consequences of that.

Instead of leaving though, he bent down and slipped his arms around me, lifting me easily off the floor and holding me tightly against his body. I looked up at his face, shocked as he pushed the bathroom door open and carried me over to the bed.

Wordlessly, he laid me down and curled around me protectively. Not daring to hope that this meant what I thought it meant, I burst into another round of sobs and scooted closer to him, burying my face into his chest.

"I'm so sorry, Ashton. Please don't leave, please?" I begged, clutching him tightly.

He stroked my hair. "I'm not leaving," he murmured, kissing the top of my head. My heart skipped a beat at his words, and I pulled back to look at his face to check if he was just saying that to calm me down. "I'm not leaving," he insisted, kissing my forehead and cheeks.

"Really?" I whimpered. He nodded in confirmation as he bent and kissed my forehead. I closed my eyes, and a small smile twitched at the corners of my mouth as his words sank in. "I'm sorry," I croaked.

"I know. It's alright. Just go back to sleep. I'm staying right here, I promise." His arms tightened around me as he rested his chin on top of my head. Closing my eyes, I pressed my face into his chest and let his smell waft over me. My heart seemed to slow down as the dread and loneliness slowly receded. As his hand stroked my back softly, I realised that I actually loved Ashton's smell.

Chapter Eighteen

I woke in the morning trapped underneath him. I was on my back, and he was lying on me, his head on my chest, his arms either side of my body and his bottom half between my legs. He was heavy, but, in a weird way, it was actually a pleasant weight. A quick glance at the clock told me it was only six thirty; I could let him sleep for another thirty minutes. I wrapped my arms around him and ran my fingers through his messy, black hair.

Shame washed over me because I'd doubted him at the gym by thinking that he'd hit me. I should have known better and had more faith in him. My eyes raked over his handsome face and I felt the frown slip onto my face. I was so attached to him already; I really shouldn't have let this guy past my defences. It scared the life out of me that I needed him. I deliberately pushed everyone away so that I would never have to feel loss again, but I'd felt it last night. I had known him just a week, yet I'd felt it when he'd walked off, and this dependency would only get worse.

After half an hour, the alarm buzzed so I quickly silenced it, but it was too late, he'd woken. His eyes fluttered open as he lifted his head, looking down at me.

"Hi," I greeted sheepishly.

He smiled sadly "Hi, you okay?" he asked.

I winced, knowing that I'd probably never be able to take it back or make it better. He'd always know that I didn't have faith in him when it mattered. "I'm really sorry, honestly, I'm so sorry, Ashton."

He sighed and shifted on top of me, pulling himself higher so he was hovering above me. "I would never hurt you." Sincerity dripped from every syllable as he looked directly into my eyes.

My heart throbbed painfully at the intensity of his look and the way he said the words. "I know. I don't know what I was thinking. You were just so angry and then you grabbed me, and I just… I don't know," I swallowed, trying to keep the tears at bay again.

"Anna, no matter how angry I was, I would never do that. I promise you." I nodded, unable to speak. "You thought I was gonna leave?" he asked, stroking my hair away from my face.

"I thought you'd already left," I admitted.

He shook his head, frowning. "I won't leave you. Even if we had a huge fight, I still wouldn't leave you," he promised.

With his eyes blazing with truth, I believed him. The only way he would leave before his assignment was over was if I had him transferred, because he wouldn't quit. I looped my arms around his neck, smiling happily now.

"Thank you," I whispered, gratefully.

"You don't have to thank me, Baby Girl." He bent his head and planted a soft kiss on my lips, pulling back after a fraction of a second. I didn't even have time to react before he pushed himself up off me, straddling my hips as he grinned down at me. "I guess I'm squashing you, huh?"

"I liked it," I muttered, chuckling as heat flooded my face at my admission.

He grinned too and dropped down onto the mattress next to me instead. "Guess I didn't even get to try out the new sofa bed." He nodded towards the new addition to my room. Apparently it had been delivered while we were at school.

I smiled and shrugged. "It looks like it would be comfy too," I teased. "Probably more comfortable than sleeping on top of me." I frowned at the sofa bed, resenting it a little because I would actually rather him sleep in my bed with me, especially after last night – so long as I could manage to keep a hold on my slutty side that only ever seemed to come out when I was around him.

He laughed. "Doubt it." His arm wrapped around my waist, pulling me tightly against him as he looked at me intently. "Anna, will you tell me why you train like that? I can understand you pushing it with the self-defence stuff, but the running I just don't understand."

I sighed, I'd never talked to anyone about this before, but I felt like I owed him an explanation for it. "It takes my mind off everything. It gives me something else to think about. The more it hurts, the easier it is to forget everything else and just focus on the pain. It's just something I've done since... well, since Carter." My voice cracked when I said his name.

He nodded sadly. "I can't stand to see it though. I know you like to run, but do you have to run for thirty minutes flat out like that? I mean, you ran so damn fast that I don't think I would have been able to keep up with you. And that last minute," he blew out a big breath, "damn, you looked like you were ready to die, and yet you went faster? It was awful to watch," he winced, swallowing hard.

I frowned. When you looked at it from his point of view, it did sound kind of over the top. "Okay. I'll try and tone it down. Can we just leave it?" Not liking the turn in conversation, and wanting to think of more pleasant things, I leant in closer and pressed my face into the side of his neck. I sighed in contentment as I inhaled his delicious smell. There was nothing else like it in the world.

"Do I smell bad or something?"

I jumped back, realising what I was doing. "Sorry." I chuckled nervously, looking anywhere but him.

He laughed. "Are you telling me I should go for a shower?"

"No!" I protested. "You smell good. It's soothing. You smell like-" I stopped quickly when it dawned on me what I was about to say. I gulped, sitting up. "Never mind. Do you want breakfast?"

As I scooted towards the edge of the bed, his hand closed over my arm, thwarting my escape. "Hey, not so fast! I smell like what?" he asked.

I winced. "I don't want to say," I whined.

One of his eyebrows rose playfully as he tugged on my arm so I fell back onto the bed. He grinned as he quickly manoeuvred himself so he was pinning my arms above my head and my body was trapped underneath his. "If you don't tell me, we don't go to school today." I chuckled and shook my head. I didn't want to go to school anyway, I would rather he pinned me to the bed all day. "Please tell me," he breathed, pulling out the puppy dog face.

I groaned, done for. "Oh, for goodness' sake, fine! You smell like safety, like home," I admitted, turning my head to the side so that I wouldn't see his face as I said it.

His grip loosened on my arms as he pushed himself off me, sitting up. From the corner of my eye, I could see him looking at me. "You want to know what you smell like to me?" he asked quietly. I nodded without looking at him. "Your smell scares the life out of me. You smell like commitment and marriage," he said simply.

The air rushed out of my lungs as I sat up and looked anywhere but him. I knew he was joking, but his casual joke about marriage made my stomach twist into a knot. "That's not funny. I told you mine seriously," I muttered, shaking my head and climbing out of bed. He didn't answer as I headed out of the room, already deciding that I'd make bacon for breakfast. I needed the energy today and cooking it would be a welcome distraction from the thoughts that were trying to force their way into my head.

In typical guy fashion, he was showered, dressed and looking like a Greek God by the time the food was ready. As he walked out of the bedroom, I set bacon and eggs in front of him. "Wow, that's great service," he joked, sitting himself at the kitchen island. "By the way, are you busy Friday night?" he smiled a little nervously.

Busy? If I was busy then he'd already know about it. "No, why?"

He cleared his throat, rubbing at the back of his neck absentmindedly. "How about we make Friday nights our date nights?"

175

My ears picked up the plural of that sentence. Did he mean every Friday was date night?

He grinned. "I was thinking dinner and a movie. That's a good first date, right?"

I smiled at how unsure he looked. "What would you normally do with a girl if you took her out?" I asked, curious as to why he seemed to be asking for my input.

He grimaced a little. "Er, a bar then her place, probably."

"Wow, and you don't think you're a player?" I teased. "Why her place? So you can leave when you want and don't have to stay the night?" I continued, giggling at how uncomfortable he looked. I had completely hit the nail on the head; clearly that was the exact reason. "So, what would you do for a second date then? Because, technically, the lake was our first date, you said so yourself," I said matter-of-factly, enjoying him squirming.

He cleared his throat. "Well, on a second date, we'd probably skip the bar and just go to her place."

"And the third?" I inquired, grinning.

"I've never been on a third date," he shrugged, shovelling his food into his mouth.

My mouth popped open at this admission. "Seriously? When you said you'd never had a girlfriend, I thought you meant like a serious one, not like you'd never been on more than two dates."

"I've never met a girl I wanted to date. I told you that," he replied, finishing his food in record time and heading over to the sink.

I rolled my eyes. "Right, I know, you're not a player, just misunderstood," I mocked, grinning as I finished up my food too. I held out my empty plate for him to take. He seemed remarkably domesticated, aside from cooking; he was very adept at tidying up after us both.

"Hey, you want to go shooting tonight? While I was on the net last night, I found one that's not too far away. We could go join," he called as I walked to the bedroom.

I gulped. I wasn't actually sure if I could see a gun again after my dream last night, but I didn't want to have to explain that to him. "Um, sure."

School was good, just like the day before. As promised, Ashton's presence kept all of the guys away from me so I didn't need to worry about anything. Again, we had lunch with what was fast becoming our group of friends. Before the end of lunch, I exchanged numbers with Rosie. I could see the disapproval on Ashton's face – probably because of the 'safety factor' as he so often called it, but to me it was no big deal. Rosie was actually a genuinely nice girl, I liked her.

Throughout the day, Ashton kissed me a few times again. Each kiss seemed to spark something deep inside me. It was like some sort of age-old primal instinct that I had no control over. I both liked and hated it at the same time.

Too soon though, we pulled up at the shooting range that Ashton had found. Nerves were churning in my stomach, and I wrung my shaking hands, chewing furiously on my lip as he cut the engine in the parking lot. I wasn't sure I could get out of the car. My whole body was stiff, frozen in place as Ashton climbed out and walked around the car to my side.

This was all because of the dream last night. The dream was the whole reason that I was terrified of guns. During my time with him, I'd seen Carter shoot people, but that was the only time I'd ever had a gun put into my hand. The experience had scarred me deeply.

"You okay?" Ashton asked, as he opened my door and bent down to see why I hadn't moved to get out. I shook my head in answer. He reached in, unbuckling my seatbelt before taking both of my hands and squeezing them gently. "I promise it's fine," he cooed.

I flicked my eyes up to his face, seeing the concern in his eyes. "I don't think I can," I whispered, shaking my head.

Without answering he leant forward and planted a soft kiss on the corner of my mouth, squeezing my hands again. All of my worries seemed to melt away as his warmth and safety washed over me, giving me the confidence to move my heavy legs and let him help me out of the car.

"You can," he replied, nodding sternly. "But if you don't want to, then we'll just go home. It's your choice."

I closed my eyes, taking a couple of deep breaths before clasping his hand in a vice-like grip as I nodded in agreement. With him at my side, I could do it, and if I couldn't, then I'd just ask him if we could leave. "I want to. Just don't let go."

"I won't," he promised. I gulped, swallowing the squirming terror that was building in my chest as he led me inside.

I pressed into his back as he filled out a couple of forms, signing us in and setting us up a membership so we could go whenever we wanted to. When he was finally done with the paperwork, the guy led us to one of the lanes in the middle. Thankfully, we were the only ones in there, so it was quiet apart from the radio humming old eighties tunes in the background.

I whimpered and turned to Ashton, watching as he sent off one of the little target sheets the same distance away as I had it last time. When he was satisfied with the sheet, he turned and put my goggles on for me before he covered my ears with the headphones. He smiled and reached behind him, unclenching my hand that I had fisted onto the back of his shirt, holding him tightly.

"You sure you want to do this?" he checked, rubbing my knuckles with his thumb as he straightened my aching fingers for me. I hadn't even known I was holding him that tightly until then. I nodded weakly, eyeing the door warily as I decided if I should run or not. Before I could make up my mind, he moved behind me, pressing his chest against my back as his arms wrapped around me tightly. "Breathe, Anna," he instructed. I gulped and sucked in a ragged breath as he picked up the little, black handgun from the box he'd been given. Immediately, I shrank back away from it, trying to melt into his chest. He rested his chin on my shoulder as he held the gun out in front of me. "Take it when you're ready."

My hands were sweating, so I had to wipe them a couple of times on my jeans before I reached up and let him put the heavy gun into my hand. "Oh God," I whimpered.

His hands closed over mine, holding them tightly. "Remember the safety button, and whenever you're ready, go."

I took a couple of deep breaths to try and steady my nerves. When I realised that it wasn't going to get any better, I flicked the safety off, aiming for the target and shot all six bullets in steady succession. It actually wasn't as bad as I had expected it to be. The whole dream thing must have distorted it in my head. Deep down though, I knew that having Ashton there was the key, he was the only thing keeping me together.

Wordlessly, he took the gun and changed the cartridge for me. The whole time, his arms were around me securely. After shooting another six rounds, I finally put the gun onto the counter and breathed a sigh of relief. Ashton turned me around and hugged me tightly, grinning from ear to ear. "I'm so proud of you. I didn't think you'd be able to do it when we were at the car," he congratulated.

I smiled back. "Neither did I."

"Let's see your skills." He pressed the button, calling in my sheet. I smiled, not actually that bothered where my shots had gone, I was just happy to have overcome my fear and not crumbled under the pressure of it. As it turns out though, I'd done pretty well considering my hands were shaking. Almost half of my shots were within the outline of the body.

"Are you gonna have a go?" I asked, eyeing the gun cautiously. It was weird but I wanted to see him in action. The couple of times that I'd seen him with a gun he'd looked menacing, yet sexy in a weird way.

He shook his head. "Nah, it's okay," he replied, shrugging.

I wasn't expecting the disappointment that settled over me. "Oh come on, I haven't seen you shoot yet."

His head cocked to the side, regarding me curiously before he finally nodded. "You," he pointed to me, "there," he continued, pointing to the side of the booth where we were standing.

I grinned at his order and did a mock salute. "Yes, sir."

He laughed and walked over to me, taking my ear defenders and putting them back on for me before trailing his fingers across my cheek softly. "Don't move."

I gulped and nodded in agreement as he walked back to the counter, sending off a fresh target off into the distance. He didn't stop it at the point I had mine at; instead, he sent it all the way back to the other wall, a solid sixty feet away.

178

The way he stood was sexy as hell: one leg back, knees a little bent, slightly turned to the side and arms out front. I could just imagine him standing like that in his uniform that I'd seen in that photo. *Talk about mouth-watering,* I mused.

I saw him glance at me from the corner of his eye before he picked up the gun, aimed and squeezed off six shots, changed the cartridge and then shot the other six, all in the space of about fifteen seconds.

My mouth popped open in shock because it had all happened so fast. He turned back to me and laughed. I was vaguely aware that my eyes were wide and that my mouth was hanging open in awe of what I'd just seen. I'd actually never seen anything so sexy in my life.

He put the gun down and motioned me over to him. "Go on then, pull it in." He nodded at the recall button.

I pressed it and we waited while the paper made its way all the way back to us. When it stopped, I was a little lost for words. Every single shot that he'd made was on point. In fact, he had made two little groups of shots, one on the centre of the chest and the other in the centre of the head. He had grouped the shots so closely that it actually looked like two large holes instead of twelve little ones.

"Holy shit, that was incredible," I gushed, still looking down at the paper in awe.

He shrugged as if it were nothing. "You forgot I was a badass?"

I chuckled, shaking my head. "How did you even do that so fast?"

"Practice, lots of practice," he winced as he spoke, probably at the memory of being made to shoot continuously or something, like when he'd told me about having to swim all night as punishment for pulling a prank.

The training academy that he went to sounded like torture; I had no idea why he'd liked it there so much. "And you can honestly say that you enjoyed your training?" I asked incredulously.

He nodded, putting all of the guns and equipment back into the box. "Yep, best time of my life," he confirmed. "Well, up until that point anyway."

I raised an inquisitive eyebrow. "Up until that point?"

"Yeah. You're the best time of my life now," he replied, closing his hand over mine and walking off to the reception without waiting for me to answer.

A blush crept over my face as I bit my lip, fighting a smile. My heart was crashing against my ribs because of how sweet that comment was. I knew he was only joking around, as usual, but for some reason his comment made my skin prickle with excitement.

The days passed quickly. Ashton and I were growing closer and closer the more time we spent together. I was just so comfortable with him now that I didn't even pay attention to how close he was to me. The pretending to be a couple charade seemed to be getting easier and easier, and I actually

179

couldn't seem to get through the day without a few of his hugs. His arms were comforting to me in a way that I never expected.

Since that night when I thought he'd left, Ashton and I had shared a bed a couple of times. Of course, we had the swanky new sofa bed in my room, but that night after going shooting, I hadn't wanted to be alone so I'd snuck over into the sofa bed with him, just needing to be comforted. The next night I just asked him to sleep in with me because I was actually becoming addicted to that safe, contented feeling that I got whenever his arms were around me. I slept so much better when he was snoring in my ear. Luckily, I'd managed to contain my slutty side that liked being in his arms *way* too much.

Before I knew it, Friday arrived, which also meant our 'date'.

Unfortunately, I was still tired because the night before it had taken me hours to fall asleep because I'd never been on a proper date before. Jack and I had been out to places, but because we were just kids, we only went to fast food restaurants or the movies or something.

I stood in front of the mirror, staring at the skin just under my eye, squinting, trying to see if I needed to add a little make-up to hide my sleepless night. A knock at the bedroom door made me jump. "Anna, I'm just gonna go next door and speak to Dean about tonight. I'll be back just after seven, alright?" He actually sounded a little nervous, probably because he was leaving me in the apartment on my own. He took his job extremely seriously.

"Yeah, sure," I called, grinning at his overprotectiveness. Turning back to the mirror, I decided that I could forgo the extra make-up. I'd already applied a little and done my hair into a cute little up-do. As I skipped over to my wedge heeled, cherry red sandals, I smiled, excited to go to this restaurant that Ashton had adamantly refused to tell me about. Much to my disgust, it turned out that the boy liked surprises.

Just before seven, I adjusted the red belt that accompanied my little, black dress and headed out to see if he was ready, but the apartment was still empty. Sighing, I sat down at the kitchen counter, waiting for him to come back. Less than a minute later, there was a knock at the front door. I glanced at it hesitantly. Ashton had strictly forbidden me to answer the door, ever. When the knock sounded again, I decided that I could take the risk. It was probably him, but if it wasn't, then no doubt I'd get scolded for it and a stern warning about my 'safety being of utmost importance to him'.

I pulled the door open quickly, and my heart jumped up into my throat. Ashton stood there looking incredibly handsome. The clothes that he'd chosen for our date fitted him perfectly, clinging to him in a way that would have any designer begging for him to model their clothes. His jeans were faded and just the right amount of scruffy, a white T-shirt clung to his body, and he accentuated it with a chequered blue and white shirt over the top, which he wore unbuttoned. My mouth started to the water at the sight of him. I was very aware that I was practically ravaging him with my eyes, so I reluctantly dragged my gaze up to his face.

As excited as I was about the date, I actually didn't want to go anymore. In fact, I wanted nothing more than to drag him inside and take his clothes off him because I knew they would look even better in a heap on my bedroom floor.

When I looked back at his face, I realised that he was still staring at me; doing exactly the same thing I had been doing moments before. I hid my grin and cleared my throat dramatically. "My eyes are up here, Ashton," I stated, trying to sound annoyed, even though I was actually flattered he was paying so much attention to my body.

He jumped, as his eyes flicked up to meet mine. "Right, yeah, sorry. I… er… I was just, er…" he gulped, shaking his head, clearly flustered at being caught.

"Checking me out?" I offered, shrugging.

He grinned sheepishly. "Right. I was just checking you out," he confirmed guiltily. I chewed on my bottom lip, tasting the sugary sweetness of my strawberry lip gloss that I'd applied. "You look stunning, Anna. You take my breath away," he breathed, letting his eyes wander my body again.

I internally swooned at his sweetness. *Does he just pull those comments straight out of a how to make a girl fall for you book or something?* "You look extremely hot too," I replied. He didn't take my breath away exactly; it was more like he made it speed up with excitement. I grabbed his hand and gave him a little tug into the apartment. "Come on in, my boyfriend's just popped out so he won't even know," I joked, breaking the tension.

He laughed and brought his hand out from behind his back, producing a beautiful bouquet of white roses. I gasped, shocked. "Second favourite after dandelions, right?" he teased, grinning. I smiled weakly. I remembered telling him that in our little 'getting to know you' session on the dock when he'd first started. "I didn't want to give you dandelions because I thought that was Jack's thing, so I went for these instead," he added, looking a little uncomfortable as if he thought he was going to upset me or something.

Overwhelmed by emotions, but for once, not in a bad way, I did the only thing I could think of in that moment. I stepped forward and kissed him, slipping one arm around his neck as I pressed my body against his. Silently, I wondered how on earth one person could be so sweet. He was killing me with kindness. I was so confused that, at this point, I almost didn't even know which way was up.

After a small intimate kiss, I pulled away and smiled gratefully. "Thank you, they're beautiful." I headed over to the sink and picked up a jug to put them in.

"I got Peter to buy us a vase for you to use. I put it under the sink yesterday," he said easily. I smiled over my shoulder because of how thoughtful that was. This was already the most perfect date I'd ever been on, yet we hadn't even left the apartment. Leaning down, I found the glass vase and filled it with water before putting the flowers in so they wouldn't die. I'd arrange them properly later. "I got you something else too, but this wasn't specifically for our date, I just waited to give it to you until today," Ashton said behind me, sounding a little uncomfortable.

I turned to see him holding out a small, rectangular red velvet box. I gulped; already knowing that the box contained jewellery because of the name on the top of the box was the one from the jewellers in the shopping mall near the lake house. I hadn't seen him buy anything, but then again, he had left me with Dean for a few minutes while I was trying on clothes, so maybe he'd snuck off to buy it then.

"You shouldn't have bought me anything."

"Open it," he instructed, holding his hand out to me again.

I stepped forward and took the box from his hand, prying open the lid, holding my breath the whole time. Inside was a breathtaking, thin and delicate gold chain. Attached to it was a little, round pendant set with a green stone. It was so beautiful that my vision blurred as my eyes filled up.

"You said green was your favourite colour." He took the box from my hand, fiddling with it and removing the chain. "Did you know that the colour green is supposed to make you feel calm and safe? I thought it was appropriate for me to give you an emerald considering it's my job to keep you safe." He stepped behind me, setting the chain around my neck before fiddling with the clasp.

I opened my mouth, but nothing came out. He'd brought me an emerald necklace? He seemed too good to be true, this boy. Once he'd secured it, I turned and shook my head in awe, reaching up to grasp the little pendant in my fist carefully. I couldn't help but notice how he seemed a little unsure of himself, his smile a little weak.

"It's so perfect. Thank you," I whispered, knowing that my voice would crack if I tried to speak properly.

His shoulders relaxed and his smile turned more genuine, and in that second it dawned on me that he was worried I wouldn't actually like it.

"You're very welcome, Baby Girl." He held out a hand for me to take. "We'd better go so we don't lose our table."

I sighed happily and placed my free hand in his, letting him lead me out of the apartment and to the car. I couldn't keep the smile off my face as he drove to the surprise restaurant; not once did I let go of the little pendant. I was already in love with this necklace and didn't ever want to take it off.

When we pulled up outside where we were eating, I burst out laughing and turned to him to see if this was a joke. "Seriously? You're taking me to eat at... Harvest Grill?" I asked, grinning from ear to ear as I read the sign above the awful-looking restaurant. It actually looked more like a truck stop café than a restaurant you would go to on a date.

He held up one finger to silence me. "Ah, just wait and see! You think I'm crazy now, but keep an open mind, okay?"

I shrugged, already feeling overdressed as a guy wearing a pair of jazzy, green board shorts and a string vest walked out. I sat in the car, waiting for him to come around and open the door for me. That was another one of his 'rules' that was apparently for my safety. I didn't see the point in it all, but he seemed more relaxed if I just went along with what he wanted.

As we walked into the place, I grinned, biting my lip so I didn't laugh. The place was practically empty aside from two other people. Casting my eyes around, I noticed that the tables were covered in some sort of plastic cloth, the chairs were old and had a worn covering on the base of them, and as Ashton pulled me forward, my foot stuck to the floor in a couple of places. I was definitely overdressed.

In the corner of the restaurant, there was a reserved tag on the table. "Lucky we got here on time, wouldn't want them to be overrun and have to give our table away," I joked.

Ashton laughed, waving for the waiter's attention. "Open mind, remember?" he muttered as the guy walked over to us.

By the time I was done eating, my cheeks hurt from all the smiling. As it turns out, despite the lack of ambiance in the place, I was actually having a fantastic time. The food was merely average, my chicken was a little rubbery and the fries were a little cardboard-like, but the company was faultless. Ashton and I chatted easily the whole time, laughing, joking and even flirting a fair bit too. It was the best date I'd been on by a clear mile.

When the waiter came and cleared our table, he and Ashton exchanged a secret look before he turned to me and grinned. "Now for the real reason we came here." He nodded over my shoulder and I twisted in my seat, seeing the waiter coming back. On the table in front of me he set down a ginormous slice of chocolate fudge cake and a little pot of hot fudge sauce. My eyes widened in surprise as my mouth immediately watered. Ashton had remembered my favourite dessert and pre-ordered it for me?

Ashton leant back in his seat with a smug smile. "I asked around, apparently this is the best chocolate fudge cake in the whole of Arizona."

I shook my head, bemused. He was so incredibly thoughtful. I hadn't expected anything like this in the slightest. "Seriously, I just… you've put so much thought into this, huh?"

He shrugged as if it was no big deal. "Well yeah, I guess. I just wanted to make it special," he explained. "Well try it then," he laughed, pointing to my cake.

"Aren't you having anything?"

"Nah, I need to watch my figure," he joked, winking at me playfully. More excited than I should be over a piece of cake, I grabbed my spoon and cut off a huge mouthful. "Wait, wait!" he cried, as my spoon was half way to my mouth. "You have to try it properly," he smiled and picked up the little pot of sauce, and poured it over my dessert before waving his hand, giving me the go-ahead.

After scooping a little of the sauce onto my spoon too, I greedily shoved it in my mouth. The sickly sweetness and richness of it made me moan in appreciation. It was easily the best thing I'd ever tasted. "Oh my God, you have got to try this!" I mumbled with my mouth full.

He chuckled wickedly. "Very lady like," he teased, grabbing a fork and cutting off a piece, shovelling it into his mouth. "Holy shit, that is good!" he agreed with his mouth full too. I burst out laughing, covering my mouth with my hand as I laughed so hard I thought I was going to choke.

When we finished eating, I thought we were going home, but instead of walking left to the car, he turned right and led me down a darkened side street. "What's down here?" I asked, confused.

"Just wait and see," he answered as we carried on walking. At the end of the little street, we rounded a corner and the place opened up into a sort of square. There was a small marquee covering a makeshift dance floor, with little fairy lights covering the ceiling as couples slow danced underneath. A live orchestra played classical songs nearby.

My eyes widened, stunned by the intimate little setting. "Did you know this was here?"

He nodded. "Yeah, I found it on the 'what to do in your town' tourist website," he answered, smiling at my astonished face.

He took my hand, laughing, and gave me a little tug towards the dance floor. His arms wrapped around me, and I smiled as we swayed slowly to the beautiful, yet haunting music that surrounded us. It was perfect. As I looked up and his eyes met mine, my stomach fluttered erratically, and my heart started to race.

We danced for about an hour before I started to feel slightly chilly. He frowned, chafing his hands up my arms as I shivered. "Want to go?" he asked.

I shook my head quickly. I didn't ever want to leave, actually. "Not yet. Can we just stay a little longer?" I pouted, not wanting this night to end.

He smiled sadly before pulling out of my arms. I sighed, knowing the experience was over. But instead of leaving, he stripped out of his shirt and wrapped it around my shoulders instead, helping me put my arms into the holes before fastening a couple of the buttons for me.

My heart melted at the thoughtful gesture. "You're just too sweet, Ashton. Seriously, you're going to make some girl really happy." I stepped back into his body, resting my head on his chest.

"Yeah? Some girl like you?"

I sighed wistfully. "Yeah, maybe not as screwed up as me though. You need someone who'll treat you right, and not give you shit," I answered. I closed my eyes, enjoying being close to him.

184

"Maybe I like being given shit," he joked, tracing his hands up my back.

"What are you, a masochist?"

"All things worth having are worth fighting for," he replied firmly. I didn't know what to say in response to that. I agreed with his statement wholeheartedly, but some things were just not worth having, and I was certainly one of those things.

We danced for another few songs before the cold seemed to seep into my very bones and I could no longer repress the shivers, even with his shirt and arms wrapped around my body. "Wow, I'm really cold now," I admitted. "Maybe we could come back another time, and I'll bring a jacket," I suggested, smiling at him hopefully. I loved it here; I would definitely like to come back again with him.

He pulled back and smiled apologetically. "I'm sorry; I should have thought to bring you a jacket."

I rolled my eyes. "Hey, don't do that! You've been so thoughtful, and I've had a great night," I insisted, hugging him tightly.

"Me too." He kissed my temple as he wrapped his arm around my shoulders, guiding me back down the windy street to where we'd parked the car. During the drive home, I watched him from the corner of my eye, just wondering what it would be like if things were different and if this were real, instead of being a ruse to fool people into believing we were dating instead of him guarding me.

When we pulled up at home, Dean's car rolled into the space next to ours. My mouth fell open in shock. "Was Dean following us?"

Ashton grinned and nodded. "Yeah, of course," he confirmed, opening my door for me.

"Why?" I asked, slightly annoyed that he had watched our private date.

"That's his job, Baby Girl," he replied casually.

I sighed and shook my head; they really were taking this too far. As Dean caught us up and stepped into the elevator, I forced a smile. "You did a great job tonight. I didn't even see you once," I congratulated, trying to keep the irritation out of my tone.

He nodded and smiled as the doors slid open on our floor. "Thanks, Annabelle, I'll see you tomorrow."

Ashton stepped out first, looking around. "Tell Peter that we're back and his shift starts now, so he's to get his ass downstairs in the lobby quick smart." His face showed he was joking, but the tone of his voice showed that he meant every word. Dean nodded and watched us walk into the apartment.

Once we were safely inside, I turned and smiled tentatively at Ashton. My daring side was coming out because I wanted this perfect night to end the perfect way. "So, do I get a goodnight kiss then?" I asked shyly. His eyebrows rose in surprise, but he didn't say anything. I smiled. "What,

185

you wouldn't kiss me at the door if this was under different circumstances?" I teased.

"Yeah, I guess I would," he smiled and stepped closer to me, putting his hands on my waist and pushing me back gently so that my back was against the wall. I couldn't breathe as my eyes settled on his luscious lips. I gulped, forcing myself to meet his eyes as he started inching his mouth towards mine. The passion was building inside me.

His lips brushed against mine gently for just a couple of seconds. My whole body tingled and heat spread through my veins, warming every part of my body. His eyes were shining with excitement and happiness as he pulled away.

I fought the urge to throw myself at him, to wrap myself tightly around him and ravage his mouth with mine. He always seemed to make me lose myself, this boy. It was like he had a secret power over me that made all of my inhibitions and worries fade into insignificance.

"Thank you for an incredible night, Anna."

I smiled. It had been incredible, and I was glad he'd had a nice time too.

He sighed, tracing his finger across my cheek. "I like it when you smile. Your whole face lights up." His hand dropped from my face as he nodded over his shoulder towards the bedroom door. "Go get changed, I'll check the windows and stuff."

Once in the privacy of the bedroom, I shrugged out of my clothes and into a pair of pyjamas, and then used a wipe to remove my make-up. When I was ready for bed, I sat down on the corner of the mattress and looked at my photo of Jack on my bedside cabinet. I sighed; I just didn't know what to feel anymore. I didn't want to go back to the life I used to have before Ashton. I was enjoying college, I loved my classes, the people here were nice and made me laugh, and of course, I had Ashton. He made my life easier. He was great. Actually, he was *really* great, and he made me happy.

My gaze locked on my fifteen-year-old carefree face in the photo; I was smiling so happily with Jack. I hadn't ever expected to feel happy again after what happened, but I just couldn't help it lately. There was just something about Ashton. He was slowly fixing me, I could feel it. The trouble was though that I actually felt guilty for letting him. My head was telling me that I should stay the broken girl that walked through life alone, that I shouldn't be allowed to be happy after what had happened to Jack and that he'd died because of me. But my heart was telling me that I was being irrational and that just because he was gone, didn't mean that my life had to be over.

I just didn't know the answer anymore. Everything that I knew and was absolutely sure about before I met Ashton was now a little fuzzy and confusing.

Behind me, the bedroom door opened, and he walked in with a smile on his face that made my heart stutter – which, in turn, made me feel even guiltier because I just didn't have any control over my body at all anymore. I hated that. Control was something that Carter had taken away from me, and I'd fought with everything I had in me to regain it. But Ashton took it with just one of his smiles.

He smiled and started stripping off his clothes while I just stood there watching him unashamedly. *Why is every move he makes so freaking sexy?* My eyes took in every inch of him. His body was amazing; I'd never seen anything like it. Jack's body had been nice because he'd been captain of the football team, but it was nothing like Ashton's. Ashton was just flawless, not too much muscle but clearly defined, and wasn't too bumpy to lie on comfortably. When he started unbuttoning his jeans, I had to look away, because my body was starting to long for things that I shouldn't and couldn't have.

When he picked up the spare blanket and started walking towards the sofa bed, the words tumbled from my mouth before I could stop them. "Will you sleep with me again tonight?" I winced, turning and climbing into the bed as my face flamed with heat. I hated the fact that I wanted his presence around me all the time.

"You want me to?"

I nodded in response, flopping down onto my front and burying my face into the pillow. Moments later, the bed dipped next to me. I turned to the side and smiled gratefully as I scooted closer to him, melting against him and pressing my face into the side of his neck as his arms circled around me. I loved him touching me, everywhere he touched, my body would tingle. His attention made me feel special and needed. At times like this, with his arms looped around me tightly, I pretended that he really was my boyfriend instead of just doing his job. I pretended that he really did want me and that he saw past the broken, dirty and used girl, to see the real me inside. The girl that I didn't let anyone else see.

"Ashton?" I mumbled against his skin, half asleep already.

"Mmm?"

"That was the best date I've ever had," I admitted.

His arms tightened around me, pulling me impossibly closer. "Good."

Chapter Nineteen

Six weeks passed in a blur of school, drawing, laughing and flirting. The days and weeks passed so fast that I could barely keep up; somehow, Ashton made every day seem better than the last. He was always sweet and kind and considerate, always had something to talk about, or some way to make me laugh. He would kiss me occasionally, making me yearn for him so badly at times that I swore it would kill me soon. Every time it would be him that broke off the kiss first and not the other way around. Another thing that had changed in the last six weeks: I no longer slept alone. I gave up fighting the fact that I liked his hugs way too much, and in the end just suggested that we forgo the sofa bed in favour of sharing. So far it had worked out perfectly and I revelled waking each morning being wrapped up tightly in his arms.

Of course, Ashton was doing his job perfectly. I no longer had problems with guys hitting on me because he was the perfect, little, possessive boyfriend when someone got too close to me. Our 'relationship' was blossoming too. Every Friday we would go out for date night, going to different places like the movies, dinners or walks in the park. It was lovely. Another thing that was in our routine now was the shooting range and with each passing session it seemed to affect me less and less. I still hadn't gotten a better shot though, much to his amusement.

We were hanging out with our group of friends a lot too. Usually every Saturday, we would go to a bar or a party or something. Rosie was my favourite; she was adorable and funny and our personalities seemed to click instantly. I was even getting more comfortable with the guys of the group too, so much so that when Tim put his hand on my shoulder whilst laughing one night, I didn't even freak out and want to break it. I owed everything to Ashton, if he wasn't here I would still be an aggressive, quivering wreck.

I thought of Jack less often – which did make me feel guilty. Sometimes it seemed like the guilt would crush me. Whenever I was feeling down though, Ashton would always cheer me up with a joke or a hug, or a little gift. He was terribly romantic at times, downloading songs he thought I would like, or writing me little messages in the mirror so I would see them when I had a shower. He'd honestly make the perfect boyfriend for someone one day.

Today I was repaying him a little for his kindness that he'd shown me over the last few weeks. It was his birthday in a couple of weeks, and although I'd already arranged most of his gift by phone, I still had a little bit of shopping to do for it. The only problem was how I was getting away from him so I could surprise him. Of course, I'd debated sneaking out when he was in the shower, but I had a strong feeling he would freak out and worry himself to death about me. So instead I'd opted for a little white lie that Dean and Peter were helping me with.

"Hey, Pretty Boy, I'm going out with Dean today," I said casually as I made my way up the hallway on Sunday afternoon. I'd left it until now to spring it on him; otherwise he would use the advance warning to come up with some way to ensure he came with me. He was obsessive about not leaving my side even for a minute.

"What? Why? Where?" he asked, walking up behind me and taking my hand, stopping my escape.

"I have an appointment," I lied, shrugging and looking longingly at the door.

He frowned; his body tensing. "Your legs don't look that hairy to me," he joked, looking me over in my cropped jeans.

I laughed weakly. "Well, maybe I'm not having my legs done." I smirked at him, tapping his nose with my finger.

He groaned, turning to grab his car keys. "I'll come with you."

I shook my head sternly. "No way! You'll look like an obsessive stalker boyfriend that can't let his girl go to get waxed without him being there! You said I could have some privacy for this," I whined, pouting. I'd become pretty adept at getting what I wanted from him. He didn't seem to be able to tell me no very easily, unless it was something about my safety and then he would refuse point blank and not budge an inch.

"Well, you can't go with one guard so…" he trailed off, shrugging as if it was decided.

I rolled my eyes. "Peter's coming too." I pushed him away from the door gently and took the keys from his hand, tossing them back onto the side. "I'll see you later." I grinned, knowing I'd won. As I turned to make my exit, his hand closed over my arm, holding me in place as he put his cell phone to his ear.

"Hey, Dean, are you taking Anna for her appointment? Yeah, Peter's going too though, right? Okay, well I should have been told. I don't know why I wasn't informed earlier. Look, just stay with her. I want you inside

189

the store. No, inside! Peter can be outside. Right, I know. Yeah fine. Call me when you leave there," he growled into the phone sounding a little grouchy and extremely authoritative. There was no doubt that Ashton was in charge out of the three of them; even though he was only twenty-one, the other two really respected him. He disconnected the call and looked at me sternly. "Anna, you do not leave Dean's side. You do as you're told, and you call me and let me know you're okay when you get there and as you're leaving," he ordered, his face stern and warning.

I giggled. I love the sexy SWAT agent mode he switched into sometimes. "Yes, sir," I purred, pursing my lips. I could see the smile tugging at the corner of his mouth.

"I'm serious, Anna," he stated, looking me straight in the eyes.

I sighed. "I know you're serious. You only call me Anna when you're serious. I promise I will stay with Dean at all times, and I'll call you when I get there," I reassured him, smiling.

He frowned, still looking annoyed. "And when you leave," he added.

I nodded, grinning. "And when I leave," I agreed. "If you're really worried, you could always call me." I stepped forward and kissed his cheek softly.

When he hugged me I could feel how tense he was all over, his muscles all bunched up and tight. "Be safe, please?" he begged.

"I will," I promised. "Make sure you do something fun while I'm not here. Sleep with some girls, walk around naked, call Nate, I don't know," I suggested, waving my hand in an example of the various things he could do while he was free.

"Sleep with some girls? You know you're the only girl I sleep with."

"Sorry, bad choice of words. Go get laid, Ashton, and chill out," I replied grinning.

"Maybe I will, what will you say then?" he teased.

My heart suddenly stopped, and I got so jealous that I could feel the anger bubbling up inside me, bursting to come out. *Holy crap, he's not yours, Anna! The man has needs, stop being an idiot; you don't want to be with him.* However, my mental scolding didn't stop the jealousy from brewing inside me.

"I would say, use protection and don't make my bed smell like sex," I lied, frowning, trying to sound blasé about it.

He sighed deeply and frowned; I got the distinct impression that wasn't the answer he wanted. "Right. Well, be safe," he muttered, pulling open the front door.

I frowned angrily at myself. What the heck was wrong with me? Why was I so jealous? I wanted to wait outside the apartment, stalker-style, and wait to see if a girl showed up and if she did, I wanted to rip her head off. I took a few calming breaths and forced myself to stop being possessive over a man that wasn't actually mine. As I walked out of the apartment, I could see Ashton in quiet talks with Dean and Peter. They both looked appropriately abashed so I would imagine they were being berated for not telling him we were planning on going out for a while.

Without waiting for them, I pressed the call button on the elevator and stepped in when it opened. "You two coming or am I going on my own?" I called teasingly as my finger hovered over the close doors button. Ashton's hand slammed against the door frame, holding it open as he raised one eyebrow in silent warning and then ushered my two far guards in with me.

As the door closed, I winced in Dean's direction because he was the one that seemed to have taken the brunt of Ashton's annoyance. "Sorry. Thanks for doing this guys, I know he's gonna be calling and being a general pain in the butt until we get back." I smiled apologetically at the pair of them.

He shook his head and smiled back. "Don't worry about it, Annabelle, he's harmless. Well, as long as we bring you home in one piece," he joked as the elevator lurched down towards the parking lot floor.

An hour and a half later, I had everything that I wanted. "Do you guys mind keeping all of this stuff at yours?" I asked as we pulled up at our apartment.

Dean shrugged. "Yeah, no probs," he agreed, picking up the numerous bags containing my shopping. "Come on; let's get you back with Ashton before he has kittens. He's already called me eight times," he suggested, grinning.

As soon as I walked through the door of our apartment, Ashton grabbed me into a huge hug; I laughed and hugged him back as he lifted me off my feet so he didn't have to bend. My legs seemed to act of their own accord as they wound around his waist, clamping myself to him tightly. He carried me into the lounge and sat on the sofa with me still wrapped around him, not wanting to let him go. It was weird being without him actually; I'd missed him so much more than I thought I would. I was certainly used to being around him all day everyday.

"Does our bed smell like sex?" I mumbled into the crook of his neck.

"No. I did her up against the wall," he answered. I laughed, but part of me was crying out for reassurance. I pulled back to look at him and he put his hands either side of my face, looking me right in the eyes. He looked stressed; his hair was extra messy where he'd probably been running his hands through it a lot. "I missed you," he whispered. I could see by his fierce expression that he meant it, and it made my heart throb.

"I missed you too," I admitted. He smiled and pulled my face to his, planting a soft kiss on my lips for a few seconds before pulling me into another hug.

I sighed contentedly against his skin of his neck as I ran my tongue over my bottom lip, wanting nothing more than to press my mouth against his again. His kisses sparked this needy reaction in me every time. "So, what did you do with yourself?" I asked, making no moves to get off his lap.

"Not much. I watched a bit of TV, then worried about you. Went on the internet, then worried about you again. Spoke to Nate, and oh yeah, I worried about you some more."

I smiled and pulled back to look at him. "You are such an overprotective guy. Seriously, what are you going to do with yourself in six months when you don't have me to worry about anymore?" I asked, genuinely curious as to what he would do with his spare time.

"I'll still be worrying about you, trust me," he answered, stroking my face.

At that moment, my stomach growled loudly. "Wow, embarrassing. Shall we order a pizza? Or maybe Chinese?" I asked, not wanting to cook.

"Yeah okay, I'd probably prefer Chinese," he agreed.

A little while later the food arrived; I'd already changed into my lounge clothes of tank top and sweats. We ate sitting on the sofa, watching TV, joking around and flicking rice at each other. I hadn't mentioned his birthday and neither had he. He'd probably forgotten that I even knew the date. Based on what he'd said before about not celebrating Christmas or birthdays, I had the distinct impression that he wasn't expecting anything for his birthday from anyone.

When we'd finished eating, he settled onto the sofa and found an old horror movie for us to watch while I took the empty plates back to the kitchen. "Come lie with me," he suggested, holding his arms open for me as I walked back into the room. I went to him immediately. My body just seemed to respond to his every request; it was like I didn't really have a choice. Smiling to myself, I lay down next to him on the sofa. His arms wound around me tightly, holding me against his chest so that his whole body pressed against mine from behind.

"I really missed you this afternoon," he whispered.

His words hit me harder than I ever expected them to. "I missed you too, Pretty Boy," I replied, snuggling into his embrace.

About half way through the movie I lost interest in it, all because Ashton was trailing his fingers along my upper arm. I didn't think he was even aware he was doing it, but my whole body was almost vibrating with excitement. I couldn't concentrate on anything other than the smooth silkiness of his fingertips against my skin. I moved my hand back and rested it on his thigh. Scooting backwards, I tried to get impossibly closer to him. Because of the position we were in, I could feel that he was starting to get a little excited downstairs. I gulped at the feel of it as my body seemed to come alive. The desire that I felt for Ashton frightened me, but when it hit me it was almost as if I had no control over myself.

Holding my breath, I rolled over to face him. He smiled that little smile that seemed to make my stomach flutter and my body ache. Needing to be closer, I bent my head and pressed my lips against his. As soon as the kiss started, something inside me snapped, and all my restraint seemed to fly out of the window. He made no moves to do anything else other than kiss me back, the same as always, but I needed him tonight, I couldn't take it anymore.

Seemingly of its own accord, my hand slid down his chest. A little shiver of anticipation overcame me as my hand got to the waistband of his jeans. When I pushed one finger inside, following the outline of it across his skin, he broke the kiss and pulled back, his eyes wide and wary.

I gulped, meeting his bewildered eyes as the temperature in the room seemed to increase by ten degrees – or maybe that was just my body. I nodded in encouragement and bent forward, pressing my lips against his again. As soon as it started, I knew the kiss was different. It wasn't just the usual soft, chaste kisses that he gave me occasionally when we were at school or sometimes at home when he seemed to forget himself, no, this one was full of fire and passion. The small moan that he made in the back of his throat made my body go into some sort of frenzy.

When the kiss deepened, he moved so that he was half hovering above me, but he still didn't make any moves to take things further. Knowing I needed to spell it out for him, I slid my other hand down his chest too and got to work on his belt buckle, pulling it open before starting on the buttons.

He grunted and pulled back slightly, his eyes wide and shocked. "Anna… what?"

I smiled and bit my lip; the need for something else was making me ache. I wriggled under him. "It's okay," I whispered, reaching up and gripping the back of his head, guiding his mouth back to mine again.

Obviously taking the hint, he kissed me back desperately as his hands finally seemed to catch on to what I wanted. I whimpered under him, closing my eyes as his hands traced my body slowly, slipping under my top and finding their way to my breasts.

I couldn't keep still as he kissed down my neck, biting my overheated skin gently. As I finally got the last button on his jeans undone, he groaned, pressing against my hand. My mouth watered as I felt the hardness of him through the material of his boxers. Thoughts of the one time I'd been with him bombarded my brain as I longed to get closer, to be consumed by him, to have him possess me completely.

My fingers traced the outline of his erection as his hot mouth wandered my body before latching onto my nipple through my bra. I gasped, arching my back, loving the feel of it. My shyness and overthinking mind was long gone now, only to be replaced by a needy, desperate being that needed this to happen more than anything in the world. I pushed my hand inside his boxers, closing my fingers around his shaft. His whole body seemed to stiffen as he groaned. With my free hand, I gripped the back of his hair and pulled his mouth up to meet mine again.

As I got to work, stroking him softly, his hand seemed to be hovering at the waistband of my sweatpants as if undecided if he should do it or not. I squeezed my eyes shut, lifting my hips in silent invitation.

Just as I thought his hesitance would drive me insane, he pushed his hand inside slowly, trailing his palm over my thigh and squeezing my ass gently. The kissing turned a little animalistic then as he practically devoured me, kissing me with such intensity that if I'd been standing, it would have knocked me clean off my feet.

He moaned into my mouth and slipped his hand inside my underwear, tracing his fingers over my wet folds. I wriggled, gasping as a little burst of pleasure erupted inside me. Tingles spread across my body from every place that his hand touched. I continued to pump him while his hand slid further down and he slowly pushed two fingers inside me. I moaned his name, before biting on his lip roughly in an attempt to try and get a hold on the pleasure he was creating as he slowly worked his fingers inside me to the same rhythm than I was stroking him.

When he flicked his wrist the other way around, massaging me with his thumb at the same time, I almost lost my mind as the pleasure became almost too much to bear – almost, but not quite.

His movements were speeding up, his breathing coming quicker and shallower as I sped up too, squeezing gently with each stroke. "Anna," he murmured against my lips as he kissed me passionately, almost making me dizzy. I was almost there, I could feel it building. With each thrust of his fingers, he was pushing me closer and closer to the edge of that cliff.

My pulse was drumming in my ears; I was barely able to breathe. Suddenly, my body felt like it exploded with pleasure, making me arch my back into him. I threw my head back and cried his name as my body vibrated and convulsed around his fingers. Wave after wave of pleasure washed over me, dragging me under, drowning me in it. I'd heard girls talk about seeing fireworks when they climaxed, but I'd never actually believed them until now. Ashton's body tensed against mine as he pressed his face into my neck. He made an incredibly sexy, little grunting sound as he came onto my hand.

I sighed and closed my eyes as my body slowly came down from the extreme high. I couldn't keep the smile off my face. My body felt relaxed and satisfied. When he eased his fingers out of me, my body jerked from the after effects of my orgasm. Forcing my eyes open, I saw him grinning down at me before he dipped his head and kissed me softly.

I smiled against his lips as he settled down next to me on the sofa, propping himself up on his elbow. He looked just as I felt: happy, contented and tired.

Scooting closer to him, I closed my eyes and breathed in his delicious smell that always made me feel safe and protected. His lips pressed to my cheek softly before trailing little kisses down the side of my neck. I giggled and squirmed as he nibbled on my earlobe. Finally, he pulled away and laid his head down next to mine, just watching me silently. I had the distinct impression he was waiting for me to speak first.

The edge of sleep was already tugging at my eyelids making them heavy. "Thanks," I mumbled.

He burst out laughing at my comment. "You're welcome, ma'am," he whispered, causing goosebumps to break out over my skin. His heavy arm was placed over me as he pulled me closer to him, stroking my back until I was asleep.

I woke up cuddled in his arms. My body was draped over his chest; we were both fully clothed. I raised my head and realised we were in bed. Silently, I wondered how on earth we got there. I definitely fell asleep on the sofa.

"Good morning, Baby Girl," he said quietly.

I blushed as suddenly all of the memories from last night washed over me. I moved off him and rolled back onto my own pillows, leaving a bit of space between us. When he didn't move to me, disappointment washed over me. *Did he not enjoy last night? Is he not even going to try and kiss me this morning?*

"Morning," I replied sheepishly, unable to look into his eyes because I was a little embarrassed.

"You okay today?" he asked, watching me nervously.

I gulped. What was I supposed to say? Was I okay? I felt okay. Actually, I felt fantastic; my body was, for once, relaxed and satisfied. I had a feeling he was asking because of Jack. The last time something had happened between us, I'd freaked out and ran off to the cemetery. But this time my confusion and unease wasn't just because of Jack and the fact that I felt disloyal to him for wanting someone else, there was something else this time too.

"Um, yeah, I'm fine. You want some breakfast?" I climbed out of bed quickly, wanting to avoid this conversation. I had no idea what I actually wanted or what I felt about last night, and I knew I wouldn't be able to think about it while he was there. Whenever he was near me, all I could think of was him.

He sighed deeply. "Yeah sure."

I couldn't look at him. I left the room quickly and headed straight to the kitchen, pressing my forehead against the fridge to try and calm myself. Confusion was making my head swim. I'd enjoyed last night, *really* enjoyed it, in fact, and my body was begging for me to go back to the bed and do it again – and an awful lot more, too. But my head was telling me that I needed to keep him at a safe distance from my heart. I just couldn't stand anymore heartache, and Ashton Taylor was not the commitment kind of guy. He'd be with me just long enough for me to really fall for him before he would run away screaming, taking my heart with him. I couldn't feel heartbreak again; I wasn't strong enough to lose someone again. I needed to tread extremely carefully here because I was in some real danger of being crushed beyond repair by him.

Absentmindedly, I scrambled some eggs and made some toast, deliberately taking my time so he could shower; that way I could go in and get dressed and hopefully avoid being alone with him until tonight at least. Maybe I would figure out what I was going to say to him by then. Last night was entirely my fault again. *I* was the one making all the moves. *I* was the one who touched him and gave him the green light. I'd instigated it all, and this confusion and awkwardness that I felt inside was all of my doing.

"Stupid, stupid idiot!" I scolded myself, shaking my head.

"Who's a stupid idiot?"

I spun on the spot, gasping in shock as he emerged from the bedroom, dressed and ready to go, looking every inch the gorgeous man that he was. "Er, no one. I was just thinking about something," I lied, shaking my head dismissively and quickly serving up two plates of food. I set one on the counter for him and picked up the other, deciding to eat in the bedroom today so that I could be alone.

As I walked past him, he held his arm up, blocking my path. "Why aren't you eating out here with me, like normal?" He sounded so terribly sad that it made my eyes prickle with tears.

"No reason. I just want to finish some stuff for our class this afternoon, so I thought I'd make a start while I'm eating. It'll save some time," I lied.

He sighed deeply and let his arm drop down to his side. "Right."

Clearly he knew I was lying, but neither of us said anything. I made my way to the bedroom quickly, sitting on the bed and stuffing my food down my throat even though I didn't actually want to eat. I felt strange inside. Although I didn't actually feel bad when I thought about what had happened between us last night – maybe that was the problem.

I showered and dressed in black leggings and a tank top, throwing an oversized blue and white checked shirt over the top, leaving it undone. I put on my bangles too. I didn't bother with any other jewellery anymore, the only necklace I ever wore was the one that Ashton had given me on our first date; I hadn't taken it off yet and had no plans to either. I pulled my hair into a pony tail for the day and pulled on some ballet flats. When I was dressed I didn't want to go back to the kitchen, I wasn't ready to see him again yet. So instead, I sat on the bed, watching the clock, waiting for the time we would need to leave.

At exactly eight thirty, I made my way to the kitchen, where he was standing reading the newspaper. "Hey, I'm ready to go," I mumbled, grabbing my bag and turning for the door. I heard him walking behind me, and I knew that he was waiting for me to bring up the subject first. I silently wondered how long he'd wait before he cracked and said something; hopefully I'd at least have time to figure out what I want to say.

"Morning guys," Dean greeted us happily, waiting outside the door for us as usual.

"Morning," I grunted, going to the elevator and letting them lag behind me. Usually Ashton would be holding my hand by now and making me smile, but today there just seemed to be this colossal rift between us.

I dropped my eyes to the floor and stood there in silence. Ashton didn't even glance at me, well, at least I didn't think he did, but I didn't dare raise my eyes to him in case he caught me looking. The car ride to school was silent too. When he came around my side of the car to open my door for me, he didn't take my hand like he usually did.

I gulped, hating the change in routine. I was missing his contact, missing his presence at my side. Even though he was still there, it felt like he was too far away from me. He sat next to me in classes, not speaking to me apart from when he asked to borrow my pencil sharpener. My stomach was really hurting now. I felt incredibly rejected and lost without him being his usual self. Every time I looked at him, he would smile weakly at me, but it didn't reach his eyes, it wasn't a real smile. I hated those smiles with a passion.

At the end of our morning classes, I threw my stuff roughly into my bag, not caring if my sketches got ruined or my pencils spilled from their cases. I was getting angry; I hated this cold, distant guy. I needed the old Ashton back, the one that could make me feel better in an instant by smiling or saying something silly, or flirting his butt off with me. I'd ruined everything for a quick thrill, and I hated myself for it.

I followed him down to the cafeteria, buying a sandwich and plopping down at our table of friends, making sure to choose a seat that was a couple of spaces away from him, knowing he would hate it.

"Anna, why don't you come sit next to me?" he suggested politely, but looking at me with a small warning gesture.

"I'm fine here, thank you, Ashton," I replied, using his name as he'd done to me. He hardly ever used my name, and it hurt my insides that he was doing it now. I turned away from him to talk to Rosie.

She raised one eyebrow in question. "Trouble in paradise?"

I sighed. What was I supposed to say to that? *'Yeah, he's just pissed because I finally let him touch me last night, and then refused to speak to him this morning.'* I had a feeling that wouldn't go down remarkably well.

I shrugged. "I guess."

A frown lined her forehead. "You two are perfect for each other! What's happened? He can't have cheated on you; I've never even seen him look at another girl, not once," she shook her head sternly.

I smiled sadly. "No, nothing like that. It's just little things at home, that's all." I picked my sandwich apart, not hungry in the slightest.

Ashton leant over Rich so he could talk to me. "Anna, want to go for a walk before next class?"

I shook my head quickly. "No thanks. I really need to talk to Rosie about something," I lied, looking at her pleadingly. She nodded in confirmation, helping me out, but looking a little uncomfortable because of it.

"Anna, please?" he asked.

I huffed angrily and dropped my ruined food into the carton. *Why can't he just let me have some time?* "Ashton, for goodness' sake, I said I need to talk to Rosie about something. Why don't you go do something with the guys?" I snapped.

He recoiled instantly, and a hurt expression spread across his face. Guilt settled in the pit of my stomach. I hated being a bitch to him. This wasn't his fault, it was mine. He hadn't done anything wrong; this was my problem and my mistake.

I sighed and stood up, walking over to his side. "Sorry, I didn't mean to yell at you. Maybe we should go for a walk," I agreed, looking anywhere but him because I didn't want to see the hurt on his face. Wordlessly, he stood up and followed behind me, putting his hand on the small of my back as we walked past a group of rowdy guys.

As we got outside, I instantly headed towards the picnic benches out the front, sitting down and staring at the sky. It was a really nice day, the sky was a beautiful shade of blue and the clouds were white and fluffy, but it could have been raining for all I cared at the moment.

Instead of sitting next to me, he squatted down in front of me, putting his hands on my knees. "Anna," he said quietly, trying to get my attention. My heart was racing. I had no idea what to say to him. I reluctantly dragged my eyes to meet his and saw what I hadn't wanted to see there all morning: hurt and confusion. "Anna, talk to me. Don't shut me out like this, please, I can't stand it," he begged.

My chin trembled as my emotions threatened to boil over. I fought desperately to keep them in check and not break down and weep. "I don't know what to say," I admitted weakly. "I guess I should say that I'm sorry. I should say that I shouldn't have done that last night and that I won't do it again. But I don't want to say that. I'm *not* sorry. I enjoyed it." I frowned, not knowing how to express this conflict that was going on inside me. I decided to tell him the truth – well, half of it at least. I figured it was best to leave out the fact that I was frightened to death that he'd break my heart. I took a deep breath before I spoke, "Look, I like you. You are the sexiest damn thing I have ever seen, and I want you so badly that it hurts sometimes. I've never wanted anyone the way that I want you, not even Jack. But the fact is that I love Jack, and I shouldn't be doing this when I'm not over him. And the thing that is tearing me up inside is that I know I'll never be over him," I winced, dreading his reaction. This was the first time I'd ever let him into my messed-up head. Maybe this would send him running from me. He'd finally see how screwed up I was and he'd bolt.

He didn't bolt though; instead, he put his forehead to my knees and sighed. "I knew that was it. I knew this was about Jack," he mumbled, his voice muffled against my knees. "Anna, do you really think that because you don't know what to say to me, that saying nothing is better?" he asked sadly, not raising his head.

I couldn't stand the pain in his voice; I tangled one hand in his hair. "I'm sorry, but you didn't say anything either," I countered, trying to make him shoulder some of the blame that was clearly all mine.

He sighed. "I wanted to give you space, Baby Girl, I knew you needed space. I figured you'd come talk to me when you were ready, but I just can't wait any longer." He lifted his head from my knees and looked at me intently. "I really like you," he whispered, trapping me in his eyes so I couldn't look away.

My breath caught in my throat. I liked him too, but I just couldn't let him in, I couldn't. Even aside from the fact that I was still messed up over Jack, I couldn't go through another heartbreak. Everything I touched turned to shit and left in the end, and I couldn't stand for that to happen to him. Having him in my life as a friend, or even as an acquaintance, was much better than not having him at all.

"I like you too," I muttered, "but I just want us to be friends. There's something between us though, I don't know if you feel it too, but it's like a need, like something I long for, but I can't have it. I can't let you in, I'm sorry." And I truly was sorry. Sorry for all the times I may have led him on and used him for a quick bit of self-pleasure, support and comfort. That wasn't fair of me, I knew that. The words were painful to say; it felt like I was ripping my heart out, and the pain that I felt scared me even more. It was then that I realised that I'd already let him in to a certain extent.

"You can't let me in, or you won't?" he countered, not taking his eyes from mine.

"Both." I was fighting the urge to cry, I could feel my eyes prickling with tears.

He sighed. "I don't like hurting you. I think I should just request a reassignment so it'll make things easier on you."

Panic surged through me at the thought of being without him. I couldn't do it. I needed him way too much for my own good. I threw myself at him, knocking him flat onto his back as I wrapped my arms around his neck tightly, afraid to let go. The emotions that were threatening to break free merely seconds before now hit me full force.

"No! Oh God, please don't go. I'm so sorry. I won't shut you out again, I won't. Please don't leave me," I choked out between sobs, gripping fistfuls of his T-shirt.

He gasped, wrapping his arms around me tightly too, stroking the back of my head soothingly. "Anna, shush. It's okay. I won't leave if you don't want me to. That was just a suggestion, that's all. I just don't like hurting you all the time. You're killing me, I swear."

I sniffed in a very unladylike fashion and pulled back so I could look at him. "I'm so sorry. I just need you around me. Please don't leave," I begged. "I just can't be with you in that way. I can't do that to you or Jack, please understand."

He sighed, cupping my face in his hands. "I understand. Just don't put me through this again, alright? I hate seeing you upset and knowing that I caused it."

"You didn't cause it. It was my fault. I'm so sorry. Please say you forgive me?" I begged. The emotional pain at the thought of him leaving me was crushing me inside.

He tilted my head down and kissed the tip of my nose tenderly. "There's nothing to forgive, Baby Girl. I enjoyed last night as much as you did." He wiped my tears off my cheeks using his thumbs. "Just promise me we'll talk through stuff in the future. Don't shut me out again, promise?"

I nodded quickly. "I promise."

A gorgeously wicked smile crossed his face. "Good. Now, how about we skip the rest of the day and go catch a movie or something?"

I laughed, wiping away the last of my tears; he always did seem to know how to make me feel better. "You're a bad influence on me, Agent Taylor," I scolded, grinning now too.

"Yeah, but you love it," he teased, rolling so that I was under him and then pushing himself up to his feet.

"Yeah, I do," I admitted. I smiled and took the hand he offered, letting him pull me to my feet. We walked hand in hand to the car as he called Dean to tell him we were leaving. As we climbed into the car, I silently prayed I could always keep Ashton in my life somehow.

Chapter Twenty

~ Ashton ~

I woke in the morning with Anna nudging me gently in the ribs. I smiled and opened my eyes. She was wide awake, looking at me, grinning like the Cheshire cat. The same as every morning, her eyes were still droopy from sleep and her hair was messy and sticking out. Still, she took my breath away.

"Hi. What are you grinning at me like that for?" I asked, confused. Had I done something to make her happy? I thought back over the last few days but couldn't think of anything specific, today was just a random Thursday, so nothing was going on that I could think of.

"Well, I've got you something for your birthday on Saturday, but I need to give it to you now."

"What? How do you know it's my birthday on Saturday?" I asked, rubbing my sleepy eyes and propping myself up on my elbow.

She chuckled. "You told me, remember? When we were at my parents' house, when you first started," she explained, shrugging and leaning away from me. My stomach clenched as it always did when she was about to move away from me. I reached out and put my hand on the small of her back so I could savour the last touch before she got dressed and we were back to just being bodyguard and client. When we were all cuddled up in bed, I liked to believe we were more than that.

Instead of getting out of the bed though, she reached into her bedside cabinet and pulled out an envelope with her name on the front, but I noticed that it was addressed to next door, to Dean and Peter's apartment.

She sat crossed-legged on the bed and held the envelope out to me, grinning wildly. I smiled. Anna liked to do things for me; even just little things like making my favourite food seemed to make her happy. I loved it when she smiled.

"Here." She bit on her lip like she always did when she was excited.

Seeing her lip in her teeth like that made my mouth water. I wanted to bite her lip like that. Thoughts of her lip between my teeth and her tongue in my mouth started to play out in my mind. I felt a stir in my boxers, so I quickly looked away from her, taking a deep breath and forcing myself to think of other things.

I took the envelope from her hand and frowned uncomfortably. This was my first birthday present since my parents had died over eleven years ago and I didn't really know how to deal with it. "Baby Girl, you shouldn't keep buying me things."

She didn't need to spend money on me; to be honest, the best thing she could give me, she gave me every day – just a smile, a laugh, and her time. All I ever wanted was just to be with her. It almost killed me just to be her friend, but that was what she wanted and needed, so I tried my hardest every day to make her happy. She was everything that was good in my world, the most important and precious thing in my life, and I would always love her, even if she couldn't feel the same about me.

"I like to buy you things. Now, will you just open it before I do?" she cried, practically bouncing on the bed with excitement.

I laughed and opened the envelope, pulling out a sheet of paper. It was an itinerary for tomorrow. I frowned, confused because we didn't have any plans for tomorrow. I scanned the details quickly. At eight in the morning we were to be at the airport, ready to fly to her parents' house on the lake. Apparently a helicopter would meet us at the airport, transfer us to the Lake House, where I would deliver the jewel. The helicopter would then take me back to the airport in time for flights to LA.

My mouth was dry. "What's this?" I asked, not liking the sound of delivering the jewel and then leaving without her.

She laughed happily. "I got you the weekend off and booked you flights to go home for the weekend so you can spend your birthday with your friends!" she chirped, her eyes dancing with delight.

No. Fucking. Way!

"Anna, what?" I gasped, reading over the paper again. Apparently I was to deliver her to her parents, then fly to LA. She'd booked a rental car too for me to pick up at the airport that I would use all weekend. On Monday morning I had flights to go back to the Lake House to pick her up again and escort her back to college.

"I'm going home for the weekend, and you, Dean and Peter get the weekend off. The only trouble is that you'll be travelling most of Friday and Monday because they're being all pathetic and won't let me fly on my own, I'm sorry," she said, frowning angrily.

She's planned for me to spend the whole weekend without her? No way, I'm not doing that! "You want to go home and send me off for the weekend?" I asked, shocked. I was actually a little hurt because she looked so happy about being away from me for the weekend. *Does she not feel anything for me at all?* I immediately mentally chastised myself for that thought. I knew she felt something for me, and that she was doing this for me. Maybe she didn't realise that it would almost kill me to be away from her for that long. I couldn't do it, not for a whole weekend. I physically didn't think I was strong enough to be away from her, not just because I was desperately in love with her, but because I'd be worrying about her too damn much. What if something happened to her? What if that was the day they came for her, and I wasn't there to protect her?

She cocked her head to the side, looking like a curious puppy. "Why are you not looking happy about this? I thought you'd want to see your friends for the weekend." Her face fell, and I immediately felt terrible because I was obviously hurting her feelings.

I grabbed her and pulled her down next to me. "Baby Girl, this is really thoughtful of you, really, no one has ever done anything like this for me or put themselves out so much for me, and I love it, I do," I started, unsure how to word it. I took a deep breath, composing my thoughts. "But I just can't do that," I added, looking at her intently.

Confusion crossed her face. "You can," she insisted. "I've arranged everything; you just need to take me back to my parents first."

I shook my head. "Anna, you're not understanding me. I love the gift, but I can't go. I can't leave you," I stated, willing her to understand and not be upset.

She rolled her eyes. "Pretty Boy, seriously, you worry about me too freaking much. There are over ten guards at my parents' house, you know that. Plus, they have all the security on the house too. There's nothing that can hurt me there," she countered. "I promise I won't sneak off without guards," she said sarcastically. I smiled at her blatant lie. We both knew she would sneak out to see Jack; there was no way she'd take a guard there.

I shook my head in rejection. "I'm sorry that I'm ruining your gift, but I'm not going," I said sternly.

"Why?" she cried, looking hurt and a little annoyed.

"Anna, I don't want to be without you for the weekend. You've done this so that I'll have a nice birthday, am I right?" I asked, waving the itinerary at her, watching her face. She nodded and pouted, shooting me the begging face that I had zero resistance to. I groaned. *Oh shit, not the face! Please don't use the face on me because I can't give in on this!* "Well, I won't have a nice birthday without you. I can't leave you," I explained, trying not to sound too much like an obsessive stalker.

A smile played on the edges of her mouth. She obviously liked what I'd said about not leaving her, and it made my insides do a flip. "But you'll get to see your friends, go out with them and get drunk. You'll probably get some birthday sex," she teased.

I mentally sighed. It was so hard being in love with this girl when she had no idea. She was making a casual comment about me getting laid, when in all honesty, I was pretty sure that I'd never want sex again if it wasn't with her. I just didn't even see other girls anymore, everyone just looked so plain compared to her and I knew they always would.

"Anna, I'm not going. Thank you for the thought, it's honestly the most special thing anyone has ever done for me, but I'm not spending my birthday without you." That was the end of it. We were staying here and I would have the best birthday ever, even if I just got to hold her for a couple of seconds. Her eyes started to fill with tears and I felt my heart break. "Aww shit. Please don't cry. I just want to spend my birthday with you," I insisted, wiping her tears quickly and kissing her cheek tenderly. She was fighting for control; I knew she didn't like to cry.

"I just wanted to give you a nice birthday," she explained, her voice breaking.

"It'll be the best birthday I've ever had, as long as I'm with you," I promised. Nothing would ever top that; just waking up next to her on my birthday would make it the best ever.

She smiled weakly. "You're just too damn sweet, Pretty Boy," she whispered, making my heart beat faster and my hands itch to touch her soft skin, to hold her and caress her, and to finally be able to tell her that I loved her.

"You know they say that it's the thought that counts? Well that's true, and this thought blows my mind, so thank you." I smiled, pressing my body against her side lightly, feeling her warmth seep into my skin and my legs brush against hers. Goosebumps broke out all over my body at the small contact of her skin on mine. I lay down next to her and sighed contentedly.

"Please think about it," she begged, taking my hand and interlacing our fingers.

I shook my head. "I can't. I don't even want to think about a weekend away from you, I'd miss you too damn much. I'd be pining for you the whole time, which would suck big time."

"But you'd get to see Nate," she countered, obviously still trying to persuade me.

"Anna, the only way I'm going to LA is if you come with me," I rebutted. *Wait, that's a great idea! I can take her with me to LA and introduce her to my friends, show her around where I live and the places that we've talked about!* Excitement started to build in my chest at the thought of it. "Come with me," I suggested, pushing myself up so I could look at her face. She laughed, obviously thinking I was joking. I raised one eyebrow, waiting for my offer to sink in.

Her smile slowly faded. "Seriously?"

I nodded eagerly. "Hell yeah! You want me to see my friends, and I want to be with you, so that's a great solution." I was already starting to

204

plan it out in my head. I'd have to keep Nate and Seth away from her, they were total players and probably wouldn't care that she was mine.

"Ashton, I can't," she laughed nervously, looking at me like I was crazy. She playfully pushed on my chest, so I grabbed her wrists, pinning her arms above her head. I rolled on top of her, being careful to keep my weight off her. My heart swelled at the fact that she let me do this to her. If anyone else – even her own mother – pinned her to the bed, she'd be going crazy, but she was smiling at me while I did it, her trust in me evident in her eyes. She wasn't scared of me, and I loved it. She was meant to be with me, I just needed to make her see it too.

"Sure you can. I'll get to introduce you to my friends. We'll have to keep up the girlfriend charade though because they don't know I'm assigned to you, they think I'm in Washington in Division Two," I explained, grinning happily. This was going to be great. I could tell she wanted to, her eyes were excited, but she was trying to hide it from me.

"I'd love to come, but I can't. Dean and Peter are getting time off too, I can't ask them to give up the weekend, it's been planned for weeks. We can't even stay here, we'll have to go to the lake house if you won't go to LA," she protested, shaking her head firmly.

I smiled persuasively. "How about I make you a deal?" I offered, smiling and pulling her arms higher above her head so her hands were touching. She looked so incredibly hot and trusting under me like that. I wanted to kiss her so badly that it was almost painful, but I wouldn't, she wouldn't want that.

"What kind of deal?" she asked.

She shifted one of her legs out from under me, only to hitch it over my hip and lay it across my ass so my crotch was pressed against hers. My body reacted immediately to the intimate position. I gulped and scooted down slightly so that my groin was pressed into the bed between her legs rather than onto her. She didn't need to know just how freaking crazy she drove my body. The girl had some talent, that's for sure; she could turn me on just by looking at me in the right way. It was ridiculous. I'd never felt anything like this attraction for her, it was almost animalistic, and if we were dating for real, I'd probably want to make love to her for twenty three out of the twenty four hours in the day, only allowing her time off for eating and bathroom breaks.

My brain was like mush as I struggled to remember what we were talking about before she moved and made me think of other things.

I cleared my throat as I finally composed myself. "Here's the deal. You come with me to LA if I can get them to agree to it, or if I can't, then we both stay at the lake house," I offered. "Either way, I'm spending my birthday with you," I tagged on the end.

She sighed sadly. "Ashton, I'm not gonna be able to go. It's not fair to pull Dean and Peter out of a weekend off. Dean's going home to stay with his mom; he said he hasn't seen her for almost a year."

"Is it a deal or not?" I asked, grinning slyly. I was pretty sure I could convince them to let me take her, but even if they refused, it was a win-win situation for me. Whatever happened, I would get to be with the love of my life.

"Okay, deal," she agreed dejectedly. I could tell she was disappointed; clearly, she wanted me to see my friends and was feeling bad that it wouldn't happen now. I bent and kissed her lips lightly just for a second, pulling away before I wouldn't be able to. She whimpered unconsciously as I pulled away and I couldn't help but smile. I loved that she wanted me, even if she wasn't interested in a relationship.

I climbed out of the bed, being sure to keep my back to her so she wouldn't see my painful arousal. That was another thing she did to me, she made me so damn hard that it hurt. I was literally stiff as a board, and probably spent a solid three to four hours that way every day. Not that Anna knew that, of course, I did well to keep it from her. I pulled on a pair of jeans, arranging my erection so it wasn't too noticeable.

"Where are you going?"

I turned to look at her over my shoulder and quickly looked away because she was doing the face. The pouty, pleading, hurt face that made me want to throw myself at her feet and beg her to take me, to let me spend my life making her happy, to give her any damn thing in the world. I'd known her for two months now, and in that time I'd fallen so in love with her, it was ridiculous. I would do anything for her, absolutely anything.

"I'm going to see if I can get us to LA for the weekend," I replied, smiling to myself as I imagined her waking up in my tiny apartment.

I walked out of the room and pulled the door tightly shut, unlocking my phone and dialling Maddy's phone number. "Senator Spencer's office," she answered immediately.

"Hi, ma'am, it's Agent Taylor. How are you?" I asked, being polite. I needed to get her on my side; hopefully if this went well, she would need to rearrange a lot of things for the trip tomorrow.

"Oh, Agent Taylor, I'm very well. How are you and Annabelle doing?" she asked cheerfully.

"We're both really good. Actually, I was hoping to speak to the Senator, is that possible?"

She tapped away on her keyboard. "Well, according to his schedule, he's free for the next fifteen minutes. Let me buzz you through," she chirped, putting me on hold.

I waited a few seconds, heading over and boosting myself up onto the kitchen counter. "Agent Taylor, is everything okay? How's Annabelle?" the Senator asked as he came onto the phone.

"She's very good, sir. I just wanted to talk to you about this weekend." I mentally crossed my fingers that he would say yes.

He laughed. "Ah, she's finally told you."

I smiled. "Yes, sir, she did." I winced, praying he'd consent. "Sir, Anna and I have been talking and we wondered if it would be possible for her to come to LA with me."

"To LA?" he repeated.

"Yes, sir. Anna really wants to go. I think it would be good for her, she's doing so well here." Anna was actually doing brilliantly at the moment; she loved school and was settling in really well and making friends.

"Agent Taylor, that's not possible. Your far guards have been given the weekend off, as have you. You should make the most of it. It's not a scheduled school break, but I won't ask the far guards to give up a weekend that's been promised to them," he said sternly, his tone implying that I was crazy even to suggest it.

"Sir, I wasn't asking for the far guards. I could take Anna to LA on my own. She would stay at my apartment with me. I live with another agent, his name is Nate Peters. He graduated second under me at the academy, and I know that he would be willing to protect Anna with me if I needed him to. She really would like to go," I persuaded. I had no doubt in my mind that Nate would protect her if the need arose.

"Agent Taylor, are you seriously asking me to let you take Annabelle to LA without a far guard? Do you understand what you're asking of me? Carter Thomas' organisation has been threatening her constantly and the trial is only three months away," he replied condescendingly.

I frowned angrily. Did he think I didn't know that? Did he not know that I thought about that asshole constantly and that if I ever saw him, I would rip his heart out, and wrap it in gift wrap for her?

I took a deep breath, trying not to growl my answer. "I am very well aware of the situation, sir. But I will be able to protect her; you know I can. I would die for Anna, and I would never let anything hurt her. Sir, I think you should let her go. In a little under a month's time, there's a very good chance that you're going to be elected President. Once that happens, Anna will probably never get the opportunity to be normal again. You can trust me, Sir. I give you my word that she'll be safe with me," I promised. Nothing would hurt Anna as long as I had breath in my body.

He took a deep, shaky breath, and I squeezed my eyes shut. *Please, come on, please!* He was quiet for about thirty seconds, and disappointment ran through my veins. Lake House it was then. At least I'd get to spend time with her there, and she'd get to go and visit Jack, she'd like that.

"I'll ask Maddy to arrange the details," he answered and my heart leapt into my throat as my mouth popped open in shock. "Agent Taylor, please take care of my little girl," he begged, not sounding like the next President, but like a worried father.

"I will, I promise." I jumped off the stool, fighting the urge to do a happy dance in the middle of the kitchen.

"I know you will, son, and if it was any other Agent asking for this, then I'd say no, I just want you to know that. She trusts you, and so do I," he stated. The hairs on the back of my neck stood up at his words.

"Thank you, Sir. I won't let you down," I vowed, grinning from ear to ear.

Instead of going straight in to tell her, I grabbed some bagels and spread them with cream cheese. I made two cups of coffee, putting it all on a tray, along with one of the roses from the bunch that I had bought her last week. I'd been buying her flowers every week, trying to be romantic. I grinned as I made my way back into the bedroom, seeing it empty.

I set the tray on the bed and walked over to the bathroom door, hearing the shower running in there. "I made breakfast. Are you gonna be long?"

"No, I'm just about to get out," she called back as the water snapped off.

I shivered as I imagined her standing naked in that room, just a few feet away from me, her glorious body all wet and dripping. I groaned at the thought. "Damn it," I mumbled, quickly coming away from the door and taking deep breaths, trying to calm myself.

She came out a couple of minutes later, a towel wrapped around her body that came to her mid-thigh, her legs still glistening. I reluctantly dragged my eyes away as she walked to the bed, pulling her pink robe over the top. A cute, little confused expression crossed her face as I placed the tray on her lap. This wasn't the type of thing I usually made her for breakfast; I usually stuck to fruit salad, toast or cereal, because everything I cooked burnt to a crisp for some reason.

I grinned smugly. "It's a typical LA breakfast."

She looked even more confused for a couple of seconds, before understanding and then excitement shot across her face. "I can go with you?" she cried, spilling half a cup of coffee all over the tray as she jerked up excitedly.

My heart leapt at her excitement. I nodded in confirmation, grinning like an idiot. "Yep, you can come."

She squealed and grabbed me, spilling the other half of the coffee over the tray in the process. As she clung around my neck, I lifted the tray off her lap and set it on the bed. Suddenly her body stiffened against mine. "Oh," she said quietly, pulling back. I looked at her beautiful face, watching the excitement fade. She looked a little sad, guilty even.

"What's up?" I asked, reaching out and brushing a loose hair up into the towel she had twisted on top of her head.

"I just feel bad for Dean, that's all."

I laughed quietly. She really was incredible this girl, always thinking of other people. "You don't need to feel bad for Dean, he's not coming. He and Peter still have the weekend off," I informed her, smiling proudly.

Her eyes narrowed. "Well, who are they sending? Not Mike, I hate Mike," she sneered at his name.

I laughed at her reaction. "No, not Mike. You don't need to worry, you like who you're going with," I said confidently. She raised her eyebrows, clearly not believing me. She didn't like any of the other guards. She had warmed to Dean, and I think she quite liked Peter too, but she hated the guards at the lake house.

She eyed me suspiciously. "Well, who's taking me then?"

I grinned proudly. "Me."

She looked at me expectantly. "And…"

"And me," I replied, grinning at her.

She gasped. "Just you? Are you freaking kidding me? No far guard?" she cried with wide eyes.

I nodded. "Just me, no far guard," I confirmed, smiling, my chest throbbing painfully because of how excited she was.

She squealed and threw herself at me; the force of it caught me off guard and threw us both off the bed. I twisted so I took all of the impact of the floor and held her protectively to my chest. It hurt a little but not too bad. I laughed as she gasped, obviously shocked at what had happened.

She cupped her hands around my face, looking at me worriedly. "Oh God, I'm so sorry. Are you okay? Did I hurt you?"

I shook my head, laughing. "I'm fine."

A smile spread slowly across her face as she took in the news again. "I really get to come to LA? Just with you?" she asked, pressing her perfectly toned body to me tightly.

I nodded. I couldn't speak; I was incredibly turned on by this position. She was straddling me and leaning over me so our chests were pressed together. Her robe had opened at the bottom, and I could see one of her legs right up to the top of her thigh. I was rock hard, and there was no way to disguise it this time, she was sitting on top of it, for goodness' sake.

"Thank you," she breathed as she bent her head and kissed me, hard, making my whole body yearn for her.

I brought my hand up to the back of her head and tried to get her closer, moaning in the back of my throat as the desire took over my body. I had the bare minimum of control when she jumped on me like this. Most of the time I could manage to keep in my mind that I couldn't upset her. If I didn't love her so much then I wouldn't even try to stay away from her. It was weird, but because I loved her, I almost didn't want to be with her, because I couldn't stand to see her upset afterwards. It was impossible to reconcile, the need to be with her, but yet, at the same time, wanting to stay away.

As she nibbled on my bottom lip, wanting to deepen the kiss, I shook my head which made her whimper with disappointment. The sound nearly killed me inside. I hated myself sometimes, I really did; I was putting her through so much. I twisted and rolled so that she was underneath me, and then kissed her again, taking control this time. When she parted her lips, I kissed her passionately, sucking on her tongue and exploring every inch of her mouth, lighting a fire deep within me.

I had more control of myself when I was on top, I knew when to stop. I pulled out of the kiss as she ran her hands down my back, scratching with her nails, making me moan breathily. I groaned. Everything about her was incredible. She was perfect for me. If I could only get her to see that I was perfect for her too, then we'd be set for life. I looked into her gorgeous brown eyes, almost losing myself. I kissed her nose gently as her breathing slowed down.

"Maddy's changing the flights and stuff and she's going to let me know the new details," I told her, brushing the damp hair from her face where it had escaped the towel.

She looked at me curiously. "How did you manage to do this?"

"I asked your father."

She gasped. "You asked my dad? And he agreed to this? Seriously?"

"Yep."

She looked at me proudly, making me feel like I was a hundred feet tall. "He must really like you," she smiled, her eyes shining with pride and happiness.

"I guess so." I shrugged dismissively, but her words were hitting me hard. Of course I wanted him to like me; I was in love with his daughter.

She grinned. "Wanna skip school today so we can pack?" she asked excitedly.

I laughed. "Whatever you say, ma'am," I replied, climbing off her quickly before she grabbed me again. I knew she liked it when I called her that, so I did it occasionally just to tease her. I pulled her to her feet and kissed her forehead, then turned and reached up, grabbing one of the suitcases from on top of the closet. "Want to share one of these?"

She nodded, already digging in her drawers and pulling out underwear and toiletries. "Sure," she agreed. "What kind of things should I pack? What kind of clothes do girls wear there?"

I smiled at her flustered face as she walked to the closet, opening it and peering in. I walked up behind her, wrapping my arms around her waist, sighing at just how perfectly she fitted me. "People wear all kinds of different stuff. How you normally look is incredible, so just take what you want. Whatever you wear, I'm sure you'll be the most beautiful thing in the whole of Los Angeles." She didn't need to dress up to look stunning, I'd never seen a girl rock a pair of sweats and a hoodie like she did, whatever she wore she looked beautiful.

She laughed. "Do you get these lines straight out of a how to pick up women book, Ashton?" she asked, elbowing me gently in the stomach.

I chuckled. "Yeah, is it working?"

"Most definitely," she answered, winking at me playfully.

I grinned. "I'm gonna go make you some more breakfast, seeing as you spilled coffee over the last one," I scolded playfully. A grin stretched across my face as I stepped away from her quickly. The hormones were raging through my body and demanding that I grab her again, so I needed to get some space to calm myself. I picked up the tray and headed back out to the kitchen, deciding on a fruit salad this time.

About an hour later, Maddy emailed me a new itinerary for the weekend. Everything was different. We still had to go to the Lake House on Friday so that Anna could see her parents for a couple of hours, but then we were to fly to LA from there. It would be a long day, but worth it by the time I got to show her off to my friends.

I dug my cell phone out of my pocket and dialled Nate, my best friend and roommate. "Hey, Taylor, what's up, bud?" he chirped happily.

I grinned at the sound of his familiar voice. I'd missed the guy like crazy these last couple of months. "Hey, I just wanted to let you know that I'm coming home for the weekend. I'll be there tomorrow night, around six-ish, I guess."

"Yeah? That's great, bud! We can go out on the hunt. I've missed having you as my wingman. Seth's such a damn player that we always end up going for the same girl," he laughed.

I smiled. "Actually, I'm bringing my girlfriend with me."

"WHAT?" he almost screamed down the phone.

"Whoa! Take it down an octave there, Nate," I joked, laughing at his surprise. Nate knew nothing of my undercover assignment with Anna, as far as he was concerned, I was working in Washington somewhere. I'd told him I met a girl on a night out with the boys.

"You're really serious about this one? When you kept talking about her, I thought it was just a phase you were going through," he said.

I rolled my eyes. "It's not a phase. I'm crazy about her, so you'd better warn the guys to stay the hell away from her," I frowned, thinking of Seth hitting on her or trying to touch her, not that she couldn't set him straight on that.

"Seriously? This is it then? Ashton Taylor, settled down, in a relationship? You're totally serious? Not bullshitting me or anything?" he asked, sounding like he didn't believe me.

I laughed. "I'm totally serious. Anna's incredible, and I guarantee you'll be in love with her too by the end of the weekend," I stated confidently. She just had a power over men that made them fall for her. It wasn't her looks either; she just had something else, an inner beauty – a charm – that you just wanted to be around.

"In love with her *too*? Are you in love with her?" he cried, sounding shocked again.

I grinned, nodding to myself. "I'm totally in love with her. So tell the guys to keep their distance."

"Wow, possessive. Must be love then," he teased, chuckling. I sighed; I didn't care how much the guys teased me, I was in love with Anna and that was all there was to it.

"Listen, just make sure the apartment looks okay, will ya? Have a bit of a clean-up," I winced. Nate wasn't exactly the best housekeeper, I could just imagine the dirty plates in the sink, and the dirty clothes over the floor.

"Taylor, I'm not a freaking maid!" he retorted.

I chuckled, rolling my eyes. "For me? Please? It doesn't have to be spotless, she won't care. Just no used condoms down the toilet, or dirty plates in the lounge, that kind of thing," I suggested.

He sighed dramatically. "Fine, I'll have a clean-up," he agreed, somewhat reluctantly. "I won't be here tomorrow at six though, I'm working until twelve. I'm covering for one of the guys and pulling a double shift."

"Okay, well I'll see you Saturday then." I slid my phone back into my pocket and couldn't keep the ecstatic grin off my face.

Chapter Twenty-One

Once the plane had touched down and the seatbelt sign had finally been turned off, she twisted in her seat and smiled up at me. "Hey, have a nice sleep?" she teased, reaching up and wiping something from the corner of my eye.

I smiled sheepishly. Admittedly, I had dozed off during the flight. It wasn't really my fault though; the first class seating was extremely luxurious and comfortable, and it was made even better by the fact that she'd been leaning all over me and snuggling into my side while she read her magazine. Plus, I'd barely slept the night before because I was so excited to take her home with me and show her off to my friends. I'd lain awake most of the night, watching her sleep peacefully in my arms. I couldn't imagine an angel would look more beautiful than her.

"Yeah I did. Sorry I didn't talk to you for the whole way," I winced, hoping she didn't mind. She was still smiling so I couldn't have annoyed her too much.

She shrugged casually, shoving the last of her candy wrappers into her inflight bag. "Least you weren't snoring."

I rolled my eyes but didn't answer. I didn't snore, but she was always trying to make me believe that I did.

As soon as we disembarked the aeroplane, we were ushered through the airport like royalty. Dean was with us because there always had to be two guards with her, but Peter had already started his weekend off. The helicopter was waiting for us a short car ride away and half an hour later, we arrived at the lake house.

I raised one eyebrow in awe as I looked up at the building. It looked even bigger than I remembered. Practically as soon as we were out of the chopper, Anna's parents both hurried out of the house to greet us. In a seemingly unconscious move, she stepped closer to me and my heart leapt in my chest because she obviously needed my support. I smiled reassuringly and put my hand on the small of her back.

As they stopped in front of us, both grinning happily, Anna plastered on what seemed like a fake smile as she stepped forward and wrapped her arms around her mother. I watched as her mother's eyes widened in surprise before her whole body relaxed and she threw her arms around her daughter and hugged her back like she was a long lost child. Anna's dad was watching them both with his mouth hanging open and tears glistening in his eyes. When she broke the hug and engulfed her father in a hug too, his whole face showed his elation.

As soon as the embrace broke, she stepped back to my side again. I smiled and stuck out my hand towards her father. "It's nice to see you again, sir."

He cleared his throat, finally dragging his bewildered eyes away from Anna. "You too, Agent Taylor," he replied, shaking my hand firmly in greeting. He turned to Dean who was standing slightly behind. "Agent Michaels, you have plans for this weekend?"

"Yes, sir, I'm going to visit my mother," Dean answered.

"Good, sounds good," Senator Spencer nodded.

I turned to Dean and smiled. Now that we were here, his vacation could finally start. "I guess I'll see you at the airport Monday."

"Yeah, have a good birthday tomorrow," he replied, grinning and grabbing one of the two cases he'd brought with him.

I reached for the other one to give him a hand, but Anna was quicker. She gripped the handle and pulled it to her side. "This one's mine."

I frowned. "No it's not, we shared," I countered, shaking my head.

She smiled wickedly and shrugged. "This one has all my girlie stuff in it," she replied, waving her hand dismissively. She turned to Dean, obviously wanting to change the subject. "Have a nice time," she called as he was putting his case in the trunk of the car he was using.

"You too, Annabelle. Don't give him too much grief, okay? I don't want him whining to me about it on Monday," he joked, waving as he slid into the car.

I looked down at the case, confused. She had plenty of clothes in with my stuff. What could she possibly need another case for? Her hand closed over mine, squeezing gently as she gave me a little tug towards the house. As I opened my mouth to ask what was in there, she shook her head and grinned. "Don't ask. It's none of your business."

I rolled my eyes and smiled, letting her lead me along.

As we walked to the house, I noticed that her mother was looking at me as if I was some sort of God and at Anna like she was a total stranger. My back stiffened, praying they wouldn't keep looking at us like that for the next couple of hours because it would surely make Anna uncomfortable.

Anna cleared her throat. "Um… I was wondering if anyone would mind if I went to see Jack?" she said quietly. "I could be back within half an hour. I just want to take some flowers; I haven't been there for two months." She chewed on her lip, her eyes tight with worry.

I knew that she felt guilty about not being able to go there to see him, but she thought of him a lot. He must have been a great guy to have her love him so much. I was a little sad that I didn't get to meet him actually; my guess is that we would have gotten along.

Melissa recoiled as if expecting some sort of meltdown from her daughter at any moment. Admittedly, the last time that they had seen her, something like this may have caused one, but Anna was much stronger now.

Senator Spencer frowned, looking a little concerned. "Yeah, that's a really great idea," he agreed. "But you need to take guards with you though, Annabelle. You can't just go on your own."

She smiled and her shoulders seemed to relax, as if she'd been expecting a protest and for them to insist that she spent the whole two hours here with them. "Ashton will come with me." She turned to me, and suddenly looked a little worried as if she doubted that I would. "Won't you?" she asked, looking at me hopefully.

"Of course," I agreed. She smiled gratefully and squeezed my hand.

Melissa cleared her throat nervously. "Maybe when you get back, we could have a coffee or something? You could tell me about your new school and your apartment," she suggested hopefully.

Anna nodded easily. "Sure, I'd like that." Both of her parents seemed shocked at her answer; I watched as slow smiles spread across their faces.

After finding another guard to come with us to replace Dean, we made our way to the cemetery, stopping to buy some flowers on the way. As we walked through the cemetery, she stooped to pick up any dandelions from the grass. There were a couple on my side of the path, so I bent and picked them for her. When I handed them to her, her eyes widened in surprise.

"Thank you," she murmured gratefully.

"Sure," I shrugged casually. Clearly she appreciated the small gesture. When we got level with Jack's gravestone, I stopped on the edge of the path so that she could approach it on her own. I wasn't allowed to give her any more privacy than this because no matter how close we got, I was first and foremost, her near guard. I felt awful that she would have to talk to him in front of me. For all I knew, maybe she wanted to talk to him *about* me. I stood silently and watched as she brushed all of the dead leaves and flowers from his grave before replacing them with hers and sprinkling the little yellow dandelions on top of his headstone.

As she sat down, she brushed her fingers across the lettering of his name. "Hey. I'm really sorry I couldn't come sooner, I wanted to, but it's just too far away from my new school." She ran her hands over the grass absentmindedly. "I'm doing really good. I haven't said that in a long time, but I really am." My heart throbbed in my chest as I listened to her admit that. "I love my school. The teachers are great, and I've even made some friends," she smiled weakly.

"I brought someone with me today. He's my new near guard, the one I told you about the last time I came. He seems to be lasting well so far," she joked, laughing quietly. "He's really great, and I know you would've liked him if you'd gotten the chance to meet him. We're going to Los Angeles for the weekend. I always wanted to go there, remember?"

When she sighed deeply, my heart started to race. This was it. This was the part where she would get upset and sob, and I would have to watch it while my heart broke in two.

"Jack, I know a lot of stuff has happened that you've probably seen from where you are, and I'm sorry, but I need him. He makes me feel better, so that's not bad, right? You forgive me for trying to be happy, don't you?" she asked quietly, picking a blade of grass and rolling it around between her fingers.

I winced, shifting on my feet uncomfortably. Had she forgotten I was here? Surely I wasn't supposed to be hearing this one-sided conversation.

"People always say that you wouldn't want me to be sad, but it's really hard to believe that after what happened to you and then… after. I don't know what to think anymore. Everything is so confusing now. I hope you forgive me for letting someone else make me happy."

I swallowed the lump in my throat. I couldn't watch from a distance any longer; I walked up behind her and sat down, spreading my legs either side of her and scooting close to her back. As I was doing it, I was mentally shouting at myself for intruding on her private moment. No doubt she was going to freak out because I was doing this, being close to her in front of Jack's grave.

But, much to my surprise, she didn't freak out.

Instead, she pressed back into me and put her hands on my knees. I literally stopped breathing because she was showing me some affection in front of Jack's grave. Was that supposed to mean something? I didn't even know anymore.

"Hey, I'm nearly done." She turned her head and smiled at me over her shoulder, her face inches from mine. I nodded, unable to speak. Even if I could force a word out, I wouldn't know what to say. She turned back to the gravestone. "This is Ashton Taylor; he's been looking after me for the last couple of months. He's a great guy." She squeezed my leg affectionately, but I still couldn't speak. "So, my dad might get elected in a month and then I could officially be the President's daughter. I guess I'd better shape up my act, huh?" she joked, chuckling to herself, changing the subject. "And Carter's trial starts again in three months' time, but you don't need to worry about that, he won't get out. There's still a lot of evidence and stuff, so he'll pay for what he did to you, don't worry, okay?"

216

I scowled at the sound of his name. I silently wondered if she realised that she didn't mention what Carter had done to her at all. It was a little scary how she just blocked everything out like that; it couldn't be healthy for her.

She sighed deeply. "I'm sorry that I can't stay longer, but my parents are insisting I spend some time with them before we leave." She leant forward and trailed her fingertips across his name once more. "I'll come back next time I'm here, okay? I miss you. Bye." She pushed herself up and turned back to me, holding out a hand to help me up.

She didn't look too bad as we made our way silently to the car. She didn't look like the other two times we had walked away from here, like she was dying inside.

No one spoke as we climbed in the car, and I signalled to the other guard that we were ready to leave. After a couple of minutes of driving silently, she turned to me. "So, are you going to take me to this Denny's place that you keep going on about?"

I looked at her smiling face, shocked. My insides started to hurt. We'd just visited Jack's grave, she'd let me sit with her, and she didn't look like her heart was breaking. Was she finally letting go of him? Was she finally ready to move on?

I gulped. "Yeah, I'll take you to Denny's at some point before we leave LA," I promised. Anna would love it there; they served the best chilli cheese dogs in the world. After Nate, it was the thing I missed the most about not living in LA.

When we got back to the lake house, her parents had arranged lunch on the terrace for the three of them. As I was about to leave, Anna clung to my hand and silently begged me with her eyes, thwarting my escape. I smiled weakly as I sat down at the table with them, watching silently as her mother ordered another place setting because the table had only been laid for the three of them. I shuffled uncomfortably in my chair, knowing that they would probably prefer to have time alone with her, but the way Anna was clinging to my hand told me that she didn't want me to leave.

For the first ten minutes, talk was a little strained as they caught up on how her course was going and what the apartment was like. After that though, she seemed to relax and her forced smile turned into a genuine one as her dad reeled off stuff about his campaign and her mother talked nonsense about the prize begonias she was growing.

By the end of the second hour that we were scheduled to stay at the lake house for, I was slightly less intimidated by her father, and actually having a nice time. It was heart-warming to see their reactions to her smile and her laugh. It was like they were seeing her for the first time in years – well, technically, they probably were. The happiness that I could see in her mother's eyes made my skin prickle.

217

When the time was finally up, Maddy called Senator Spencer to tell him that the helicopter was ready for boarding. As we walked towards the noisy chopper, her father placed his hand on my arm, pulling me to a stop and letting the girls go ahead.

"Agent Taylor, I've not seen my daughter this happy in years. I don't know how you're doing it, but thank you," he said, smiling gratefully.

I grinned and shook my head. "You don't have to thank me, sir." I didn't do it for my job. Whenever she was happy, my heart would melt into a puddle on the floor, it was like this was the reason for my existence – to make her happy.

"Well, I want to. Anyway, have a nice weekend, and happy birthday for tomorrow."

I smiled uncomfortably. *Does everyone now remember my birthday?* I mused. "Thank you, sir. And don't worry about Anna, I promise to take care of her," I vowed, wanting to add 'forever' on the end. I ran to catch up with her, and we climbed in the helicopter, setting off for the airport, both of us grinning excitedly.

The flight to LA was good. As we walked through the airport at the other end, I was careful to keep her close and check for danger. The thought of not having a far guard was a little worrying, but I didn't doubt my ability to protect her. Also, it would help that no one knew she was here with me, apart from her parents and a few guards. As far as everyone else was concerned, she'd dropped off the face of the earth; even the name she travelled under today was fake.

As we made our way over to the car rentals desk, Anna was grinning like crazy. "Hi, we have a car reservation under the name of Taylor," she informed the attendant.

His face lit up. "Ah, yes! Very unusual request for a rental. It's right outside in bay two. Here, I'll get the keys." He turned and fished through the cupboard.

Once he'd found what he was looking for, he slid a form across the counter to me. I looked it over, noticing there were no details other than 'special request' written across the top. I signed it wearily, and he led us back through the depot. Anna was practically skipping at my side. I frowned, wondering why she looked so excited.

As we walked out of the door, I burst out laughing when I saw what she'd done. She'd rented me a brand spanking new yellow Camaro, an exact replica of the one from the Transformers movie. That was something else I had said to her when we'd joked around about buying a car for us to use at school. The car was beautiful, and my hands were itching to run across the top and feel the shiny paintwork.

"Seriously? You rented this for the weekend? Damn, these are expensive!" I laughed, shaking my head at her thoughtfulness.

"Unfortunately, it doesn't turn into a giant robot though. I tried my best…" she shook her head, faking sadness.

I pulled her into a hug. "You are too funny. This is incredible. Honestly, I've never met anyone as thoughtful as you. Thank you," I gushed, holding her tightly against me.

She hugged me back. "You're welcome. No speeding though," she replied, giggling.

I grinned and popped the trunk, putting our suitcase inside. When I went to pick up the other one containing the 'girlie stuff', she pulled it away and lifted it herself, carefully setting it next to the one we were sharing. "That one's mine, so hands off, okay?" she instructed, playfully tapping her finger on my nose.

"What the hell is in there?"

"None of your business," she replied, grinning wildly.

I frowned but decided to let it go. "Let's get to my place then, and we can order some food."

She rolled her eyes. "You ate two hours ago."

Pulling open her door for her, I shrugged. "What can I say? I'm a growing boy."

She chuckled, and I pushed her door closed before practically skipping around to the driver's side.

As I drove down the familiar streets, worry started to settle into the pit of my stomach. My place wasn't exactly a palace, and Anna was used to living in luxury, I definitely should have booked a hotel or something for the weekend. "Um, Anna, my place isn't exactly what you're used to. It's not really what you'd call a nice place," I said, grimacing.

"You think I care where you live?" she frowned, looking a little hurt because I was kind of implying that she was shallow.

I shook my head quickly. I didn't think of her like that at all. "No, I know you don't. It's just a little embarrassing, that's all. I mean, it's okay, but it's nothing like our place," I explained, shrugging and pulling into an empty space in the parking lot outside my apartment block. I winced as I looked around at the other cars; this car was going to stick out like a sore thumb. "This car is insured, right?"

She laughed at me. "Yeah, Pretty Boy, don't worry."

I sighed as I climbed out; waving her out of the car after checking it was safe. When I popped the trunk, she was too preoccupied with looking around and smiling to notice me get her case out of the trunk too. My hand closed over hers, pulling her close to my back as I led her across the parking lot and towards the rickety, old elevator in the lobby of my apartment building.

When we got to the third floor, I guided her along and stopped outside the door to my place. I held my breath as I pushed the key into the lock, silently praying that Nate had tidied up a little. Once the door was open, she stepped in first, and I followed behind, barely able to breathe. Nate was a total slob and liked to live in his own filth. For the last few years that we'd shared a place, I'd been the one to tidy up. The images I had in my head of what we were going to walk in on were horrifying. But, much to my surprise, it actually didn't look too bad.

As I stepped into the lounge, I felt my body relax. There were no dirty dishes or clothes anywhere, and no slutty magazines on the table; he even looked like he'd run the vacuum around. It wasn't too bad at all for a bachelor pad; I was actually quite impressed with him.

Anna smiled as she looked around. "I thought you said it wasn't a nice place, this is great." She went straight over to the photos on the wall and started looking through them. "Are these your friends?" she asked, motioning to one of me and my boys at the races last year.

"Yeah. That one's Nate," I confirmed, pointing out my best friend.

She whistled appreciatively. "Right, I can see why he gets the girls."

My heart stopped. I hadn't even thought about the possibility of her liking Nate. He was a good-looking guy and all the girls fell at his feet. I felt sick, jealousy coursing through me. What the hell would I do if she liked my best friend?

She turned back to me. "What's wrong?" Concern coloured her tone as she reached up and touched my cheek.

"Nothing," I lied, stepping away from her.

"Hey, don't lie to me. I can see that something's wrong. Tell me," she demanded, grabbing my hand.

"Nothing. All the girls like Nate. He's your typical heart throb – blond hair, blue eyes, every girl's dream. Just your type," I stated, shrugging, trying to appear unconcerned.

Understanding crossed her face as she giggled wickedly. "Are you jealous about what I said?"

I jumped. *Shit! What the hell do I say to that?* "No," I lied.

"You're a terrible liar," she teased, stepping forward and putting her hands on my chest.

I groaned. "Okay fine. Yeah, I was jealous," I admitted uncomfortably.

She smiled again. "You don't need to be. He's not right for me at all. Besides, I already have a boyfriend, and he's extremely hot," she flirted, running her hands down my chest and catching hold of my belt loops.

My body was going crazy at her casual, playful touch. "Right, yeah, I forgot you already had someone," I grunted, my voice sounding thick with lust. I wanted her so badly that it was almost driving me insane.

"You forgot? Maybe I should remind you more often."

I gritted my teeth. "Maybe you should."

She smiled seductively and stepped closer, pushing me down onto the sofa, falling on top of me. She kissed my forehead and nose. "You don't have anything to worry about, boyfriend. You're the only one I could ever let this close to me," she promised, kissing along my cheek. Her breathing was speeding up with excitement, making me long for things that I shouldn't even think about.

How could I have been so stupid? She couldn't even let other men close to her, that was how I knew I was the one for her. When her soft lips connected with mine, I kissed her back, hard, rolling so that she was trapped underneath me. As the kiss deepened, one of her legs wrapped around my waist and clamped me against her. I moaned into her mouth, enjoying the last few seconds before I knew I had to pull away.

"Anna, come on, Baby Girl, let's stop now, huh? I can't have you getting upset," I rasped, breaking the intense kiss but staying on top of her.

She sighed dramatically. "Yeah, I know. Sometimes it's just hard to resist you. You're so goddamn sexy, Ashton," she frowned, looking slightly annoyed about the fact that she couldn't resist me.

I grinned at her comment. "Thank you, Baby Girl, and you're so goddamn sexy too." I sighed and looked up at the clock on the wall. "It's getting late. How about we make some food and then unpack and go to bed?" I needed to get off her because my traitorous body was begging for me to upset her again.

"Yeah, okay." She actually looked both sad and relieved at the same time.

After eating a grilled cheese sandwich that I'd burnt beyond recognition, we unpacked. While she went to the bathroom to change, I stripped down to my boxers and climbed into my bed. She strutted out a couple of minutes later in the tiny, little shorts and tight tank top pyjamas that I both loved and hated at the same time. I loved them because they clung to her body and made her look so freaking hot it was unreal, and I hated them for exactly the same reason. As she slipped into the bed next to me and scooted over against me, tangling her legs in with mine, I sighed as desire for her started to build. It looked like this was going to be another long night for me.

In the morning my eyes fluttered open, seeing Anna's beautiful face just inches from mine. Smiling happily, I dipped my head and kissed her forehead gently before moving back so I could watch her sleep. About twenty minutes later, she stirred and moved closer, pressing herself to me and burying her face in my chest. This was my favourite part of everyday – the time when she was just waking up and she would always try to get closer to me, no matter how close she already was. This small little bit of attention got me through the whole day. I smiled to myself. *Yep, best birthday ever!* She opened her eyes, a slow smile spreading across her face.

"Morning," I greeted, brushing the hair from her face.

"Good morning. Happy birthday," she sang, happily.

I laughed. Those two words sounded a little weird to me. "Thanks. So, do I get a birthday kiss?" I asked hopefully.

She nodded, smiling teasingly. "Sure, who from?"

I grinned as I leant forward and kissed her softly. She responded immediately, kissing me back and tangling her fingers in my hair. I pulled away after a couple of seconds, not wanting to push my luck too far. She didn't take her hand out of my hair as she looked at me excitedly. "Want your presents now?"

I groaned in exasperation. "Anna, you didn't buy me anything, did you? Seriously, this was already too much," I whined. I hated that she spent money on me, I didn't need it, the only thing I needed was her.

She didn't answer, just pulled out of my arms and jumped out of bed, skipping over to the suitcase that Dean had brought. She hadn't unpacked it last night, and now I knew why – she'd hidden my gift in there. I sighed as she wheeled the case over and lifted it up onto the end of the bed.

My brow furrowed as she lifted the lid. I had known there would be a gift when she jumped out of the bed, but instead, the case was almost full. I could clearly see two large boxes, a medium sized one, and three smaller ones.

"I don't want you to keep buying me things," I grumbled.

She flopped down onto the bed beside me and leant in, kissing me softly on the mouth, silencing my protest. "Please don't start. You'll hurt my feelings. I put a lot of thought into each one, and I wanted to get you them, so please just shush," she ordered, smirking at me. I groaned as she picked up the three smaller packages, placing them in my lap. "Open them, and smile please?" she pouted and gave me the damn face that I couldn't resist.

I rolled my eyes and ripped open the first one. Out fell James Patterson's new book. I grinned excitedly. We'd spoken about this a couple of weeks ago and I'd told her I wanted to read it. "This is great, thank you." If she'd only bought me this, it would have been the best gift I'd ever had.

She smiled. "I thought you'd like that one. Open the next one," she breathed excitedly, motioning towards my lap. I grinned and opened the next one; it was The Peacemaker on DVD. I laughed as I looked it over. "I didn't know if you already had it, but I saw it and wanted to get it. I hope it's the right one. You said it was your favourite movie," she waffled, playing with her necklace like she did when she was a little nervous about something.

"It's definitely the right one, and no, I don't have it." I turned it over, looking at the back. I genuinely loved this movie.

"Next one," she prompted.

I laughed at her enthusiasm and tore the paper from the last small package, revealing a black square jewellery box. I frowned down at it curiously as I lifted the lid. A chunky silver watch was nestled inside. My eyes widened at how expensive it looked. I flicked my eyes up to her and shook my head because it was too much, I couldn't accept it. Before I could say anything though, she held up one hand to halt my protest. "Before you say no, hear me out," she pleaded. "You don't have a watch. You're always checking the time on your cell phone. I really wanted to get you something you could use, and I saw this and really wanted to get it for you. Everyone

222

needs a watch. Please just accept it in the manner which it was given. I want you to have it."

I gulped. "Anna…"

She pouted. "If you don't like it, you can change it," she offered.

I looked down at the watch. It was perfect, incredible even, and something I would never have purchased for myself in a million years because I'd never have this kind of money to spare. "I love it, it's just-"

Her hand closed over my mouth. "If you love it, then just put it on and smile. I wanted to get it for you."

I could see how much she wanted me to accept it, clearly it meant a lot to her, and she'd obviously put a great deal of effort into buying it and choosing it. I sighed and pulled her hand from my mouth. "Thank you," I conceded.

She squealed happily, clapping her hands excitedly as she nodded towards the medium sized package. "Great! Now do that one."

"These were enough, you shouldn't have bought me anything else," I scolded, leaning over and kissing her lips gently. In all honesty, that kiss would have been more than enough for me.

"Just open it or I will. I'm not good at waiting for presents to be unwrapped. You should see me at Christmas, I can do a pile of presents in like a minute flat," she stated proudly. I didn't doubt her words at all.

"Calm down, anyone would think it's your birthday," I joked.

Her face fell, and her eyes tightened. "I don't like my birthday, so I like to celebrate other people's."

Understanding hit me like a ton of bricks. Her boyfriend had been murdered on her birthday, and she'd tried to kill herself for the last two years on the anniversary of it. *Christ, how stupid could a guy get?* "I'm sorry, I didn't think. I shouldn't have said that." I took her hand, looking at her apologetically.

She shook her head and smiled again. "Just open it!" she cried, pointing excitedly at the present.

I laughed and ripped open the packet. My eyes went wide at the picture on the box. A camera. I couldn't speak. This was just the perfect gift; no one could have picked anything better for me. I desperately wanted a photo of us two together, I had a couple of my cell phone but I couldn't print them off.

"Oh shit, this is incredible. Thank you so much," I gushed. "But you know I'm gonna be taking photos of you though, right?" I added.

"If you're thinking I'm gonna be posing naked for you, you're wrong," she teased, sticking her tongue out at me.

I laughed wickedly. "Well, I wasn't thinking that, but I definitely am now."

She laughed and shook her head. "Whatever, pervert." She slapped my arm playfully.

I leant over and kissed her lips, just once. "Thank you, I love this, it's incredible." I looked back at the box in my hands, not actually believing that this girl was real.

She picked up the last two boxes and put them in my lap. "These two go together, but open this one first," she instructed, pointing to the flatter of the two. I was still in shock over the camera, I couldn't wait to take it out tonight and get some photos of us together. I looked over at her and noticed that she was watching me expectantly, so I reluctantly dragged my eyes from her and ripped off the gift wrap.

My breath caught in my throat, and my body jerked – as would any red-blooded male that got this for their birthday. On my lap sat a PlayStation 4. They weren't even out yet. "Anna, what the actual fuck? How did you get this?" I gasped.

"I had my dad pull a few strings. He's old friends with someone who works for Sony," she answered happily. "I knew your face would look like that!" she grinned smugly. "Open the other box. They go together."

Still in shock, I unwrapped the other gift, tearing the tape off the cardboard box, seeing an extra controller and six games inside. She settled herself against my side and waved her hand at the box. "I didn't know what games to get, so I asked the guy what a twenty-two year old male would like, and these are what he came up with. I hope they're alright," she winced, looking a little worried.

I grabbed her waist and pushed her down onto the bed, pinning her underneath me. Could I tell her that I loved her? Would it ruin everything? I couldn't risk it, she'd undoubtedly freak out. "You are the sweetest, kindest and most thoughtful girl I've ever met, Anna. Thank you so much for everything, and for coming to LA, and for just being with me. I really, really appreciate it."

She grinned. "You're welcome. Happy birthday."

I kissed her again, setting my body on fire as I pressed against her tightly, relishing in the feel of her curves. When I pulled away, we were both breathless. I sat up, looking back at the PS4. "I can't believe you got me this," I breathed, shaking my head in awe. I was already itching to play it and eyed the soccer game on the top of the pile.

"Actually, I didn't buy these for you," she replied, shrugging and pointing to the console and games.

"Oh yeah? Did you get it for yourself?" I grinned. I'd love to play against her. Girls playing videogames was sexy!

She shook her head. "No, I got this for Nate," she answered, grinning smugly.

I raised one eyebrow. "For Nate? I don't understand."

She smiled and reached for the box that had contained the games. She tipped it up and a little headset thing fell out onto my lap. "You miss your friends, so I got this for Nate. The games are interactive which means you can play against other people. This little headset means you can talk to each other while you're playing. I got one for Nate, which is this one, and I left your one at home. They're exactly the same," she explained.

Oh my freaking God! Not only did she buy me this, but she bought the same for my best friend so we could play against each other because she knew I missed him? Damn it, I need to marry this girl! Please let her fall in love with me, I promise I'll make her happy, please! I begged silently.

"Anna, this is incredible. So thoughtful. I'm kinda speechless."

She grinned and shrugged as if it was nothing. "I wanted to do something for you. I owe you more than I could ever give you for what you do for me. I just wanted to make up for that in some small way so you know I appreciate you."

"You don't owe me anything," I countered, frowning. Everything I did for her, I did because I wanted to. I wanted to be there for her and make her happy; I knew deep down inside that was what I was made for.

"I feel like I do," she shrugged.

I sighed and looked deeply into her chocolate brown eyes, wishing I could make her see that we were made for each other. "Well you don't," I dismissed.

She smiled and shrugged, reaching for my book. "Let's just agree to disagree." She flopped back against the pillows, flicking through the pages.

I shook my head, wondering if she'd ever see how special she was. I didn't think she would. I settled back against the pillows too, looking through the games with a huge grin on my face. They were all things that I would choose for myself, and I couldn't wait to play them. After a couple of minutes, I rolled on to my side, resting my arm over her stomach, just taking her in.

"Thank you," I whispered, snuggling closer to her.

She turned her head to the side and smiled that mesmerising smile that melted my heart every time. "You're welcome, Pretty Boy."

Closing the distance between us, I pressed my lips to hers, kissing her softly.

Chapter Twenty-Two

~ Anna ~

After a couple of minutes of kissing, I pulled away. He looked so incredibly happy and heart-stoppingly handsome this morning. Twenty-two certainly suited him.

"I'm gonna go make some coffee. Maybe we could get some breakfast out or something?" I suggested.

"Sure," he agreed, before looking down at the items in his lap. "What the hell am I gonna tell Nate?"

I smiled. "Well, I thought about that a bit, and figured maybe you could say that you won two in some competition. Tell him that you're giving him one so you could play against each other." That was the only thing I could come up with that fitted; he couldn't exactly tell him that the Senator's daughter bought it.

He laughed, his green eyes sparkling with happiness that made my heart soar. "You've covered all bases here. You're a devious planner, huh?"

I nodded, rolling my eyes. "Oh yeah, I'm pretty sneaky, you need to keep your eyes on me."

"Oh, I plan to keep my eyes and anything else that I can on you, don't worry," he flirted. I laughed and pushed him away from me playfully before jumping out of the bed and running across the room before he could stop me. At the door, I turned and blew him a kiss, grinning.

I practically skipped to the kitchen. As I flicked on the kettle, I let my eyes wander around his apartment. The place was actually extremely sweet. It was a total guys' place though. The furniture didn't match, and was all designed for practicality and not for how it looked, as with any bachelor pad. I smiled as I looked through his cupboards, finally finding what I was after and grinned as I pulled out two mismatched oversized mugs. I loved it here; his apartment made me feel safe and calm. This place was Ashton all over.

"Well, that's definitely a nice view to wake up to in the morning," a male voice purred behind me.

I grinned as I turned, knowing this would be the famous Nate Peters, Ashton's best friend. As I expected him to be, Nate was gorgeous. All blond, spiky hair and blue eyes, tall and toned. The cocky, confident smile that was stretched across his face made him look just the right amount of cheeky. He was currently only wearing boxer shorts and a white vest. I could see why the girls apparently went crazy for him. In my opinion though, as hot as Nate looked, he had nothing on Ashton.

"Well thanks. I presume you're talking about the fact that I'm currently making coffee, and not the fact that I'm not wearing very many clothes at the moment," I stated, raising my eyebrows innocently.

He was smirking at me. "Of course I was," he replied, just as innocently.

"Good." I turned and grabbed another mug from the cupboard so I could make him one too.

"You must be Ashton's girlfriend, Anna." He moved so he was leaning against the counter next to me and folded his arms over his chest as he looked me over.

"And you must be Ashton's best friend, Nate," I answered, giving him a cocky smile.

"Yep," he confirmed, popping the p. I rolled my eyes and went back to the coffee. "You know, Ashton said you were hot, but damn, that's the understatement of the century," he continued.

"Well, he told me you were a flirt who would try and get me into bed, but damn, I didn't realise you'd start before nine in the morning." I smirked back at him, chuckling. I liked this guy already; it was probably the fact that he was Ashton's best friend. Ashton loved this guy, and anyone that got Ashton's respect, got mine.

He laughed and shook his head. "That's what he told you about me? I'm a womaniser?" he asked, faking hurt.

"Big time," I confirmed, laughing.

"Maybe I'm just waiting for the right girl to set me on the right track, make me want to settle down," he purred suggestively.

"Right, you know what? I can help you with that," I answered, looking at him through my eyelashes.

He raised his eyebrows and smirked at me. "Oh really?" he asked, obviously interested, leaning in closer to me.

"Yeah," I breathed, nodding and leaning in closer to him too, watching as his eyes widened and he flinched back slightly. I smiled. Clearly he was regretting flirting with his best friend's girl now that I was playing along too. "I'll help you find a girl tonight when we go out," I added, winking at him and laughing as relief washed over his face.

He chuckled and shook his head. "You're funny, no wonder he likes you. Mind you, I can think of a few other reasons too," he muttered as his eyes skimmed my body again.

"Well at the moment, Nate, I'm struggling to find anything that he'd like about you," I teased.

"Ouch, Anna, you wound me." He put his hand over his heart, faking hurt.

The kettle boiled, so I spooned the cheap instant coffee granules into the mugs, plucking the milk from the fridge. "So how do you take it?" I asked, putting sugar in my coffee and extra milk in Ashton's.

"I'll take it and give it any way you want, baby," he flirted again.

He's an even bigger flirt than Ashton! Can he just not help himself? I wondered. "Right, well how about I give it to you strong and straight?" I offered, putting a strong black coffee down in front of him. He laughed in response. "I'm gonna go take this into my man, and start his birthday off right for him," I winked at him and picked up the two coffees.

"Well, I will definitely see you later, Anna."

I rolled my eyes as I stepped back into Ashton's bedroom and kicked the door closed behind me. "Hey, Nate's here," I chirped, as I plopped back on the bed.

Ashton's body seemed to stiffen as he frowned. "He's up already? He was working until twelve."

"He's up; I just met him in the kitchen. He's a funny guy," I shrugged.

Ashton's eyes tightened. "He hit on you, didn't he?"

I smiled at his question. He was so overprotective of me, sometimes he seemed to forget that I wasn't actually his girlfriend, although most of the time lately, I wished I was. "Yep, but don't worry, I told him I wasn't interested," I promised, scooting to his side, setting the coffees on the bedside unit.

"I think you're the first girl I've met that wasn't interested in him," he smiled, wrapping his arms around me, pulling my body closer to his.

I waved my hand dismissively. "Nah, I told you, I already have an extremely hot boyfriend," I stated, smiling before continuing, "even if he is an old man now."

He scowled jokingly. "Hey, don't start with the age jokes; I'm a little sensitive about it."

"Well, we could always say you're twenty-one and three hundred and sixty-six days," I offered, shrugging.

He laughed again. "Yeah, that definitely sounds better than being an old man," he answered, trailing his fingers up my arm, making me ache all over. He grabbed his new camera off the bedside unit and held it out in front of us, snapping a photo before I could even protest.

228

"Hey! I haven't even brushed my hair," I whined.

"You look beautiful, Baby Girl. I love your messy bed hair."

I smiled at that. I had a feeling he wasn't joking either, I loved his messy bed hair too.

After drinking our coffee, I headed into the shower, and he went out to talk to Nate. I could hear him laughing and catching up with his friend; mostly they were talking about me. I showered and went back to his room to get dressed, pulling on a pair of cropped skinny jeans and a white tank top, slipping a black waistcoat over the top. After pulling on a pair of black wedges, I quickly dried my hair, scraping half up and leaving the rest half down. I didn't bother with make-up today.

When I walked into the lounge, the talking stopped immediately, and two sets of eyes fell on me. I frowned at the abrupt change of mood and looked down at myself, wondering if something was wrong. "What? Should I change? Is this not appropriate LA clothing?" I asked, concerned because I didn't bring lots of clothes with me, so I was limited on options.

"Damn, you look so damn hot that my mouth's watering," Ashton practically growled, looking me over slowly.

I laughed with relief and felt the blush creep onto my cheeks. When my gaze fell on Nate, I saw he was looking at me too. I raised one eyebrow, knowing I needed to show him that I wasn't interested. As the plan formed in my head, I didn't even think twice about it as I strutted over to Ashton and plopped myself down on his lap, straddling him. Dipping my head, I pressed my lips against Ashton's, wrapping my arms around his neck. He kissed me back, moaning in the back of his throat. The small sound he made seemed to set my body on fire and turned me on more than anything else.

His arms circled my waist, pulling me tightly against him as the kiss deepened. My whole body seemed to pulse with desire as his taste and the warmth of his tongue resonated through my senses. As I pressed myself against the hardness of his body, all I could think about was getting closer and melting into him. Every nerve ending in my body seemed to come alive as an uncomfortable ache seemed to be building inside me. I needed him.

I was so thoroughly lost in the moment that someone clearing their throat next to me made me jump and come back to reality with a bump. I reluctantly pulled my mouth away from Ashton's, dragging in a ragged breath. Ashton's eyes shone with excitement and lust – as I would imagine mine did too.

"Happy birthday," I whispered, making no moves to get off his lap.

"Definitely the best birthday ever," he breathed, resting his hands on my hips.

He moved me slightly, but the small movement made us rub together in places that were already way too excited for my own good. A little zap of pleasure pulsed through my body. I gasped, tightening my hold on him as I wriggled, trying to ease some of the tension and pressure from my body.

His lips found mine again, and in that moment I was lost all over again. His fingers bit into my thighs as another little bolt of the same sensation washed over me. I couldn't take any more teasing, my body needed relief. It felt like I would spontaneously combust if I didn't release this tension from inside my body. It was then that I decided that I would make this weekend special for him.

"Er... you two need a room? Hello, best friend here!" Nate teased. "Not that this isn't hot to watch," he added, laughing.

Ashton groaned and pulled his mouth from mine, somewhat reluctantly. "Dude, seriously, go away!"

Realising this was inappropriate for their lounge sofa, with Nate watching, I blushed and gulped. "Let's go eat. I'm starving," I suggested, changing the subject. I smiled over at Nate. "You coming?"

A devilish grin broke out on his face. "Not yet, but you can help me with that if you want," he purred, winking at me.

Ashton suddenly punched him in the arm. "Mine!" he growled warningly, looking like he was only half joking.

Nate gasped, rubbing his arm as he winced. "Ouch, dude! I was kidding."

I giggled uncontrollably at his put-out face. He looked like a kid that had gotten caught with his hand in the cookie jar.

Ashton scooted forward on the sofa, still holding me on his lap. "Come on, Baby Girl, Nate doesn't want to go where we're going, I already asked him."

Nate shrugged. "Actually, I think I'll come for breakfast, but I'm definitely not coming to the museum," he chimed in, standing up.

I frowned, confused. Ashton wasn't into that kind of thing, so that was a weird choice of thing to want to do. "Museum? What museum?" I asked curiously.

"There's a really cool museum I thought you'd like," he explained, shrugging.

I shook my head incredulously. "What? We're not going somewhere for *me* on *your* birthday," I protested, attempting to push myself off his lap, but he held me against him tightly.

"Aww, come on. You'll really like it there, I promise," he whispered, leaning forward and kissing my cheek before trailing little kisses down my neck.

My body tingled. "Maybe I like it right here," I mumbled, closing my eyes and enjoying the sensations his mouth was creating within me.

I felt him smile against my neck. "Well, maybe I like it right here too," he replied, nibbling on my earlobe.

"Maybe I'd like to go eat," Nate chimed in, laughing.

Ashton sighed and moved his face away from my neck; I bit my lip so I didn't whimper at the loss of contact. "Come on then. Let's go eat," he agreed, rolling his eyes and finally letting go of me so I could stand up.

We walked to a little café down the road from their apartment, talking casually about nothing in particular. As we walked inside the café, Ashton mumbled 'shit' under his breath as a waitress came over, smiling broadly at him.

"Well hi there, Ashton. How are you doing? Long time no see," she breathed, setting her hand on his arm as she batted her eyelashes.

"Er, hi Kelly," he greeted, clearly uncomfortable.

An angry expression crossed her face. "It's Shelly," she growled. I burst out laughing but quickly turned it into a cough when she turned to glare at me, which of course, made Nate laugh. Ashton was just staring at me in horror as the waitress looked me over distastefully. "Who's this?" she asked, obviously trying to be polite, but failing miserably.

Ashton took my hand and pulled me to his side as he spoke, "This is my girlfriend, Anna."

I winced at the furious expression that crossed her face. She looked like she wanted to kill me. I had the strong feeling that this girl was going to spit in my food. I inwardly sighed, but decided if she was going to do it anyway then I may as well have some fun too.

"Nice to meet you, Kelly," I greeted, trying desperately to hide my grin.

"It's *Shelly*!" she snapped.

"Oh, right yeah, sorry." I grinned, looking anywhere but Nate, who was clearly trying to hold in his laughter.

One of Shelly's eyebrows rose wickedly as she turned her attention back to Ashton. "I didn't know you had a girlfriend. Does she know we slept together?"

I smiled as Ashton seemed to squirm on the spot. I nodded in confirmation, deciding to help him out. This girl was clearly trying to cause trouble between the two of us. "Oh yeah don't worry, I know my boy's slept with half of LA," I dismissed. "Hey, were you the one that taught him that thing that he does with his hand? Because damn, if you did then, I owe you a big thanks," I added, grinning. Nate lost the battle and his laughter rang out as he shook his head, clutching at his side.

Shelly's nose scrunched up distastefully as she snatched three menus from the side, obviously dissatisfied with my reaction. "You want a table?"

She didn't wait for an answer as she turned around and strutted off, practically throwing the menus down onto an empty table. Ashton's hand closed over mine, squeezing tightly as we crossed the restaurant to get to the table she had stopped at. As I slid into the booth, Ashton slid in beside me, still looking extremely uncomfortable and apologetic.

Shelly seemed determined to ignore me as she took our drinks order. As soon as she was gone, Nate shook his head, still chuckling to himself. "Oh God, that was freaking hilarious," Nate laughed.

Ashton groaned. "I'm really sorry. I forgot she worked here."

I smiled and waved my hand dismissively. "Ashton, if I got annoyed or upset every time I met a girl you'd slept with, I'd be upset all damn day," I joked, shrugging.

His anxious eyes softened, and the tension that was in his shoulders seemed to fade as he smiled gratefully. "I guess. That was a class way to deal with an ex though. That was awesome," he congratulated. His head cocked to the side, and his eyes turned playful. "But what thing are we talking about that I do with my hand?" he asked, raising one eyebrow knowingly.

I grinned. "I think you know," I replied, feeling the blush creep onto my cheeks. He chuckled and leant in, kissing my burning cheek before brushing a loose strand of my hair back into place.

"Wow, she's a firecracker, Taylor. No wonder you're in love with her," Nate said, looking at me in awe.

My heart stopped as my eyes widened in surprise at the revelation. *Ashton has told Nate that he's in love with me?* But then I realised that this was all part of the charade and undercover assignment. Of course, he had to lie to his friends about me. He was just playing the part of loved up boyfriend like he was supposed to.

When my eyes flicked to Ashton, I noticed he was glaring at his best friend for some reason. Thankfully though, the waitress chose that moment to come back with our drinks.

Shelly was still ignoring me as she started taking our food order. After scribbling down what the boys wanted, she turned her evil eyes on me. "And you?" she asked impatiently.

"I'll have chocolate chip pancakes, please. Oh and Shelly, I'll leave you a fifty dollar tip if you don't spit in my food," I smiled sweetly, handing her my menu. Nate was laughing again now.

She laughed and for the first time, smiled at me. "Right okay, I'll go get your order."

Nate was practically crying with laughter as she walked off. "You know, I think you should leave Taylor and be with me, Anna," he said, winking at me.

"Hmm, I don't think you could handle me," I countered. That was the honest truth; he would probably crumble under the pressure of one of my meltdowns.

"Oh really? I would definitely like to try," he purred suggestively.

Ashton's body seemed to tense up at my side. I smiled, placing my hand over his because for some reason that I couldn't fathom, Ashton seemed to be jealous and worried that I was going to fall for his best friend. "I'll tell you what, Nate, if he screws up," I nodded my head at Ashton, "then I'll give you a go."

"Sweet!" Nate chirped.

Ashton shook his head adamantly and slung his arm over my shoulder. "I'm not gonna screw up, Baby Girl," he said, leaning in and planting a soft kiss on the base of my neck. I whimpered and tipped my head to the side as his lips left a burning trail against my overheated skin. In that moment, I wanted nothing more than to drag him to the bathroom and have him consume me completely.

"Seriously, you two need to cut that out!" Nate ordered, flicking a couple of drops of water at us from his glass.

I laughed and Ashton pulled away, groaning. He seemed to be enjoying that as much as I was. Knowing I needed to change the subject because my body was already aching for Ashton's touch, I turned back to Nate. "So, why don't you want to come to the museum then?"

"Boring! How about we go do something fun instead?" he suggested, raising his eyebrows excitedly.

"Like what? What do you two boys like to do for fun?" I asked curiously.

He grinned at me over the rim of his glass before he jerked in his seat and his eyes lit up excitedly. "Ooh, how about we go Go Karting?"

Go Karting? I'd never done that before. "Sounds fun. Want to?" I asked, turning back to Ashton.

He shrugged easily. "Sure, if that's what you'd rather do."

I nodded eagerly, snuggling into his side. Nate pulled out his cell phone, already tapping away on the screen. "Great. I'll call some of the guys and we can meet them there."

Ashton's mouth closed over mine, kissing me almost desperately as his arm tightened around my waist, crushing me against his side. I moaned into his mouth. This was going to be a long day, I could feel it. However, before it could get too heated, our kiss was interrupted by Nate flicking more water at us. "Right then, Seth, Wayne and Ryan are going to meet us there in an hour," he said happily.

I smiled. I was actually excited to meet the rest of Ashton's friends and see how he spent his time when he wasn't worried to death about me. As we sat there talking about racing and who was the best driver, the food arrived. Shelly set a plate of pancakes down in front of me, and I looked at her hopefully. "Do I owe you a fifty or not?" I asked, watching her face, trying to read if she'd really spat in my food.

She laughed. "I didn't spit in your food," she promised, looking like she was actually telling the truth. "I spat in his," she added sweetly, plopping Ashton's food down.

"Oh, he won't mind. You've shared saliva before, it's no different," I joked, nudging him playfully.

She laughed and sat down next to Nate. "So, how long have you two been together?"

Ashton grinned. "Two months."

She looked at him disbelievingly. "Seriously? I didn't think you'd ever settle down. You told me that you didn't do relationships," she pouted, seeming a little hurt.

"I didn't. Not until I met Anna," he replied casually.

I smiled and shrugged. "Yeah, I think I may have curbed his player ways for a little while. I'll enjoy it while it lasts, he's picked up a lot of tricks from screwing all of those girls," I joked. Everyone laughed at that.

"I'll bet he has. There have been a lot of them," she smirked at him, obviously still trying to get him in trouble with me. "Enjoy it while it lasts, he'll kick you to the curb soon enough," she added, pushing herself to her feet.

I nodded in agreement. "No doubt about it. I'd say I have at least another six months though. I can keep you interested that long, can't I?" I asked, grinning slyly at Ashton – he had that long left before he would be reassigned.

He chuckled and nodded. "Definitely," he replied, rubbing his hand up my back softly.

Obviously disgruntled, she huffed and strutted off towards the kitchen again. I smiled at her back. "Well, I don't think her plan to make me jealous worked the way she wanted it to," I stated.

Nate's eyes were wide as he regarded me with a bewildered expression on his face. "What the hell kind of girlfriend are you if you don't get jealous?"

"The best kind," I answered, cutting off a large chunk of pancake and stuffing it into my mouth. Ashton hadn't started eating; he was just frowning down at his plate distastefully. "You not gonna eat, Pretty Boy?"

He winced. "Do you think she really spat in my food?" he asked, turning his nose up. Nate and I burst out laughing and I didn't stop until my sides were hurting.

The rest of the time we talked and laughed. When we were done, we took a leisurely stroll back to their apartment so we could pick up the car. I smiled happily. Nate was actually a really nice guy, other than the fact that every word out of his mouth was suggestive. He got on exceedingly well with Ashton, and it was nice to see him joking around with his friend. It made me extremely glad I'd arranged this. Ashton grinned at me as we approached the car, pressing the button on the key, making the lights flash.

Nate stopped dead in his tracks as his mouth popped open in shock. "Holy shit. You have got to be kidding me!" he cried.

"I know right? Anna rented it for me for the weekend as a birthday present," Ashton boasted, grabbing me and pulling me in for a hug.

Nate practically choked on fresh air as he shook his head. "Anna, I really think we need to hook up, my birthday is in like a month."

Ashton punched him playfully in the arm again. "I told you, she's mine," he stated, laughing because Nate still hadn't taken his eyes off the car. "I'm assuming you're riding with us in this instead of taking your car?" Ashton pulled open the passenger door for me, ushering me in as he smirked at his friend's astonished expression. Nate nodded, running around to the driver's side and wrenching the door open. "Back seat! I'm driving!"

Ashton protested as Nate went to slide into the driver's side. I grinned to myself. Boys were too easily impressed by a flashy car.

As we made the short drive to the Go Kart track, Nate was sitting in the back, gushing about the car and how beautiful it was. Ashton held my hand the whole time, shooting me sly glances with a big grin on his face. When we pulled in, the car was immediately swarmed with guys. Well, that was a slight exaggeration, there were three of them. I recognised them from the photo I'd seen back in the apartment.

We all climbed out, and Nate was raving to the three newcomers about the car. Ashton stepped to my side and grinned as they all exchanged the typical man hug thing. He turned back to me and smiled proudly as he wrapped his arm around my waist. "This is my girl, Anna." He gave me a little tug forward, smiling reassuringly as I tried not to show my unease at being surrounded by three unknown men that were all looking me over like vultures look at a wounded animal. "Anna, this is Seth, Wayne and Ryan." He waved his hand to them in turn.

"Nice," the guy called Seth purred under his breath. He was gorgeous too, and I silently wondered what they put in the water here in LA. He had light brown hair and brown eyes and when he smiled, he got dimples, making him look cute. I had a feeling it would be the innocent little boy dimples that the girls were attracted to.

"Hi," I smiled; trying not to show them how nervous I was. It had been different meeting Nate because that was one-on-one. This situation frightened me a little.

"How you doing, Anna? I'm Seth, and it is definitely my pleasure," the dimpled guy flirted, holding out his hand to me. I forced a smile and shook his, attempting to let go quickly, but when he didn't release my hand my heart took off in a sprint. I dug my fingers into Ashton's side, silently telling him that I was uncomfortable.

"Seth, remember I said this is *my* girl?" Ashton growled warningly. Seth looked at him and grinned sheepishly, releasing my hand quickly.

Instantly Nate punched Seth in the arm. "His," he pointed at Ashton, "and then mine when he screws up," he joked, grinning.

And just like that, the tension was broken and I laughed as Ashton's arm tightened on my waist. "Right, that's enough flirting. Let's go race," Ashton suggested, nodding at the large metal building.

The boys were obviously regulars here because they greeted the instructor like an old friend and were led through to the back where the helmets were. As we stepped through the door, the noise of the engines and the smell of exhaust fumes that lingered in the air actually made the hair on the nape of my neck stand up on end. I turned to Ashton, seeing his big bright smile and my nerves instantly started to fade. I knew he wouldn't let anything hurt me, so this had to be safe. My heart rate slowly started to return to normal as a helmet was pushed onto my head and I was led over to a large blue Go Kart and shown how to drive it.

Once I was going, however, I actually loved it. Although, much to my embarrassment, I was a total disaster at it. After crashing into the tyres for the sixth time in three laps, I decided to give up and just watch. As I pulled into the makeshift pit lane and climbed out, Ashton pulled up behind me. I frowned as I pulled the helmet off and breathed a sigh of relief because they were heavy and constricting.

"Hey, don't stop, I just want to watch you," I protested, waving him back into his car.

He shook his head, pulling off his helmet too. "I'm not leaving you on your own."

I sighed dramatically. "Ashton Taylor, get your perfect ass back in that Go Kart and finish your time. You've only got a few more minutes. I'll be fine here, I promise. I won't move from this spot until you come and get me," I vowed, crossing my heart with my finger.

He smiled and walked over to me, kissing me quickly. "Okay, but you'd better not move from this spot, Miss Spencer." The words were said in a joking way, but his eyes were serious; I knew it was an order and not a request.

"Yes, sir," I answered, grinning.

His mouth closed over mine again, kissing me fiercely as he stepped up against my body, clutching me close to him. My heart sped uncontrollably as the lust from earlier spilled over and built into a raging inferno. I threw my arms around his neck, kissing him back desperately as one of his hands slid down my back and cupped my ass.

I groaned, breaking the kiss but leaving my lips against his as I spoke, "If you don't go right now, I'm not gonna be able to let you go," I admitted. My eyes were locked onto his as my hormones spiked to preposterous levels. He grinned and bent his knees slightly so that his face was level with mine, his arms tightened around me as he stood back up, lifting me off my feet. I gasped, a little shocked, but caught on immediately, wrapping my legs around his waist, clinging to him tightly.

"I don't want to drive anymore," he whispered, kissing me again, sucking lightly on my bottom lip.

A needy whimper left my lips as I gladly opened my mouth, eager for his taste. He kissed me deeply and my world seemed to spin just that little bit too fast. Rough brick scratched at my back through my shirt as he pressed me against the wall. I completely forgot where we were as he kissed down my neck, sucking gently on the skin under my ear. My fingers tangled into the back of his hair, tugging gently, which made him bite my neck gently. Everything about this moment was incredible, from the rough wall scratching at my back, to his hard chest pressed against mine, to the slim line of his hips that seemed like they were just made for my legs to fit perfectly around.

Suddenly he pulled his mouth away from mine and groaned. I gasped, shaking my head as I looked at him pleadingly, silently begging him not to stop. "What the hell are you stopping for?" I whined, pouting.

He laughed and used his head to motion over his shoulder. Confused, I looked in that direction only to see that his friends were all standing there, watching, whistling and shouting rude comments about how we should get a room. Nate was shrieking in a high pitch voice, "Oh! Yes, Ashton, yes."

I blushed and buried my face in his neck as Ashton just laughed. "Holy shit, that's embarrassing," I whispered, reluctantly unwrapping my legs from his waist.

He smiled and set me down onto my feet as the boys all strutted into the office, still making jokes about us and laughing wickedly. "You look so adorable when you blush," he mused, brushing his finger across my cheek.

Rolling my eyes, I grabbed his hand and followed his friends into the office so we could give our helmets back. Nate grinned as we walked into the room. "So, what are we doing now? Or are you two going home to have some fun on your own?" he asked, smirking at me.

I shrugged, hoping to appear confident. "I don't mind, whatever Ashton wants to do."

"Well, I'm all for going home and having some fun," Ashton teased, grinning at me devilishly.

I giggled at the lustful expression on his face. "Oh, you're always up for that, Pretty Boy."

He laughed and pulled me closer to his side, winding his arm around me securely. "Seriously though, I actually I don't mind what we do now. How about we go to the races or something?" he suggested.

My heart leapt in my chest. I could barely suppress my girly giggle of delight. "The races? Really? That'd be great!" I enthused, bouncing on the spot with excitement.

"It's dog racing, not horses," Ashton mumbled apologetically.

My excitement jumped up another level. "Well that's even better. I've never been!"

Ashton grinned and pulled me into his embrace, our chests pressed together. "You're so very easy to please," he whispered, looking at me gratefully.

I smiled and wrapped my arms around his neck, going up on tiptoes and pressing my lips to his again softly, just once before pulling back. He made a growling sound in the back of his throat before his lips claimed mine in a scorching kiss that made the hair on the back of my neck stand up.

"Holy fuck, would you two cut that out? Jeez, I'm all for a live porn show but damn," Nate scolded.

Ashton groaned and pulled his mouth from mine, not letting me pull away from him as he scowled at his best friend. "I hate you," he grumbled.

The boys behind me laughed. "You love me, Taylor, don't even try to deny it," Nate joked. "So, are we invited to the races or what?"

Ashton sighed and rested his chin on my shoulder. "Yeah sure, if you want to."

Three hours later, and collectively a couple of hundred bucks down, we were all crammed into Ashton's lounge eating Thai takeout while the boys argued over the PS4. I'd had a fantastic day with them, and even losing on the races didn't put a dampener on the day. Los Angeles was, so far, surpassing my expectations. I loved it here.

As I sat there watching him quietly, seeing him fool around with his friends, laughing and joking, I realised that my insides felt a little weird. Ashton Taylor actually frightened me witless. I cared about him way too much for my own good. Seeing him happy seemed to make me happy, and that wasn't a good thing in my book. I just loved having him in my life. I was starting to depend on him too much already. I had no idea what I was going to do when his assignment was over. I had no idea how I would cope without seeing his smile or hearing his voice. I was already in too deep.

Forcing my eyes away from him, I looked up at the clock. It was almost nine in the evening. They had all arranged to go to some bar at ten, so I knew it was probably time for me to start getting ready for that.

"I'm gonna go get dressed," I announced, standing up and stepping over Wayne, who was sprawled out on the floor, his eyes glued to the TV.

Seth frowned and pouted. "I should probably go too," he agreed, looking at the controller in his hand and frowning as if he didn't want to leave it.

I smiled and left them to it, heading in for a quick shower but being careful not to wet my hair. As I stood in front of Ashton's closet, deciding what to wear for the night, I felt the excitement bubbling up in the pit of my stomach. I was actually genuinely looking forward to going out tonight, and I had a plan to finally see Ashton drunk. He didn't know yet, of course, but I'd use bribes if necessary to get him to have a few drinks with me on his birthday.

After pulling on a pair of black shorts and a blue short-sleeve top with blue heels to match, I sat on the bed and started to curl my hair. Just as I was finishing up, Ashton came in with a towel wrapped around his waist and water glistening off of his well-sculpted chest.

"Do you mind if I get dressed in here? It'll be a bit weird if I get dressed somewhere else; Nate thinks we're a couple, so…" Ashton explained, looking a little uncomfortable as he grabbed some clothes from his drawer.

I laughed at his awkwardness. "Ashton, I see you in your underwear every night, I think I can cope."

A dazzling grin split his face. "Yeah I guess, sorry," he replied sheepishly, carefully tugging on a pair of boxer shorts under his towel. As he pulled the towel off, I grabbed his camera from the side and snapped a couple of photos of him in his underwear. "Hey! I hope I get to take underwear shots of you too," he protested, closing his hand over the lens to thwart my efforts.

I giggled and shrugged. "Maybe if I get drunk you might," I flirted, raising one eyebrow at him suggestively.

He groaned. "Anna, no begging me for sex if you're off your pretty face tonight, okay?" he whined, pouting.

I grinned wickedly as I shrugged. "I never agree to a deal that I know I won't be able to keep." That was the truth. I wouldn't be able to agree to that because whenever I was drinking, I couldn't seem to stop flirting with the boy. I guess the drink made me shed my inhibitions, and my sense of right and wrong, because flirting with him was always such a terrific idea at the time.

He laughed at my comment. "Yeah, I guess you wouldn't be able to keep your word," he agreed, pulling on a black button-down shirt and dark blue jeans. I groaned as he clipped on his little gun holder around his ankle.

"Aww come on, you won't need that!" I whined.

He sighed. "Look, I already got rid of one of the guards for you; I can't get rid of the gun too."

Knowing he was right and that I couldn't actually protest when he was already breaking the rules by bringing me to LA on his own, I stood and decided to change the subject. I did a little twirl. "Do I look okay? I could dress up a little more, I brought a dress with me," I offered nervously. I had no idea what the girls in LA wore to a club.

"You look beautiful," he promised, taking my face in his hands and looking into my eyes. My stomach clenched at his compliment. The way he looked at me so adoringly made me feel as if I was flying. As he stared into my eyes, I could feel the passion building; I'd been feeling it all day. He bent his face towards mine slowly, and I held my breath waiting for his soft lips to touch mine. They were millimetres away when a loud banging on the door ruined the moment.

"Come on, let's go already!" Nate shouted, sounding bored.

"I'm really starting to hate my best friend," Ashton muttered, sliding his hands down my neck, across my shoulders and down my arms. When his hands got to mine, he interlaced our fingers and gave me a little tug towards the door.

Nate's eyes widened as we walked out of the room. "Damn, Anna, you look sexy as hell," he growled, looking me over slowly. I giggled as Ashton punched his arm again in reprimand. "I know, I know. Yours!" Nate grumbled, turning for the door.

Chapter Twenty-Three

As soon as we arrived at the club we would be going to, we were ushered through because apparently Ashton and Nate knew the guy on the door. The security guy didn't even look twice at me, which was fantastic considering I wasn't actually old enough to be in the club in the first place. As we made our way through the crowd, Ashton seemed a little tense; he practically stuck himself to my back as we walked past a group of guys who were eyeing me. I wasn't quite sure if he was trying to do his job properly, or if he was just being possessive, I had a feeling it was a mixture of both.

I followed Nate to the far side of the club, seeing Seth, Wayne, and Ryan standing there flirting with a couple of girls. Even though he'd only left us just over an hour ago, Ryan's lopsided smile told me he was already slightly tipsy.

When we stopped and exchanged pleasantries, I spotted a pretty blonde girl standing alone at the bar. I touched Nate's arm. "Right then, let's find you a woman," I chirped. "You like blondes, I bet."

"Yeah, I like anything that's female," he agreed, laughing.

"Okay, I've got you a suitable candidate. Try not to make a fool of yourself, alright?" I joked. "Who wants what to drink? My round," I offered, looking around at them all. Everyone answered with beer, apart from Ashton who just took my hand.

"I'll come with you."

I tugged my hand out of his and stepped closer to him, smiling reassuringly. "But I'll be right there. There's no need to worry, I promise. You can even still see me," I murmured, going up on tiptoes and planting a chaste kiss on his cheek. "Please? No one even knows me here," I whispered so that no one else could hear. He sighed, and his shoulders tightened as his eyes scanned the bar before he finally nodded in agreement. I grinned triumphantly. "Great, what do you want to drink then?"

"Orange juice."

I frowned at that. "Can I put vodka in that?"

Ashton shook his head sternly. "No, Anna," was all he said. I knew that was a definite no, he only used my actual name when he was serious.

Walking off before he could change his mind, I made my way to the bar, squeezing in next to the blonde girl I'd scouted for Nate. I smiled at her. "I love your dress, it's gorgeous."

She smiled before brushing the skirt of her red dress gently. "Thanks! I got it on sale. It only cost thirty-five bucks, can you believe that?"

"No way, that's awesome," I gasped, looking down at it enviously, wondering if I could ask Ashton to hunt out this mystery store so I could buy one before we left to go back to school. The barman stopped in front of me and smiled expectantly. "Hey, can I have four beers, an orange juice and a rum and coke?" I asked, praying he wouldn't card me.

He didn't even bat an eyelid as I reeled off my alcohol order. While he was making it, I turned my attention to the girl again. "Are you here on your own?"

She sighed and frowned, looking around quickly. "I'm supposed to be meeting friends, but I'm a little early."

"Do you want to come over and wait for them with us?" I asked, raising my eyebrows innocently. "I'm with my boyfriend and his friends." I nodded over to where they were. They'd snagged a table, so were now sat around it, laughing and chatting.

Her gaze flicked in that direction and her eyes widened. "Wow, they're freaking hot!" she gasped. I chuckled and nodded in agreement. "Which one is your boyfriend? Ah, I bet it's the one with black hair, he hasn't taken his eyes off you yet." She nudged me in the side, smiling.

I grinned, looking over to see that Ashton was indeed watching me like a hawk to make sure I was alright. "Yep, that's him," I confirmed. "You can wait with us if you want, it's no problem. It's better than standing here on your own."

She nodded in agreement, smiling gratefully as she picked up her drink. "I'm Michelle, by the way."

"Anna." When the barman set a tray down on the bar, I slid my money across the wood and then we made our way across to the boys' table. "Guys, this is Michelle, she's going to wait with us for a bit for her friends," I introduced, nodding at her.

Nate's face lit up as he stood. "Hi, Michelle. I'm Nate." He took her hand and looked straight into her eyes, leaning in a little too close for an informal greeting. A blush spread across her cheeks.

I laughed and turned my attention to Ashton, who looked like he was finally relaxing now that I was back at his side. On quick inspection, I noticed that there weren't enough chairs with Michelle here too, so I smiled and sat myself on Ashton's lap, placing his orange juice down in front of him.

"So, what will it take for me to get you to drink and enjoy your birthday?" I inquired.

He grinned, shrugging. "I don't need to drink to enjoy my birthday. I've had the best day of my life with you today."

My insides melted as I pressed myself closer to him. I still wanted to see him loosen up though. "Please? Just a drink or two, I'll do anything you want," I offered, raising one eyebrow suggestively.

He gulped, and I could almost see the dirty thoughts running through his mind. "I don't want anything," he protested, but at the same time he licked his lips. I was no body language expert, but that subconscious move told me that he wanted something.

Raising my hand, I ran one finger around the collar of his shirt, tracing his skin with my fingertip. "There must be something that you want, or that I can do for you," I whispered in his ear. My skin prickled as I thought about all the things that I could do as a bribe for getting him to have a drink with me. There wasn't that much that I wasn't up for tonight. Tonight I would make sure he had a spectacular birthday. I smiled and pulled away teasingly, making him groan. "One drink and you can name your price," I offered, smirking at him.

"Baby Girl, come on, I can't. It's not that I don't want what you're offering because damn, that sounds like the best offer I'm ever going to get in my life, but I can't do that, I won't," he answered sternly.

I sighed and shook my head. I'd keep working on him; he'd cave eventually even if I had to insist that he suck a shot from my belly button. "You will by the end of the night," I disagreed knowingly. He shook his head sternly and smiled confidently, both of us sure of the outcomes. He'd give in though, I was sure of it, he wasn't that strong.

Giving up for now, I turned my attention back to Nate. He and Michelle were locked in the middle of a full scale makeout session. I smiled and shook my head incredulously. The stories that Ashton had told me about his best friend being the master of seduction were clearly not exaggerated.

Two hours later and I was having a fantastic night. Michelle's friends had turned up a little while later, so she'd made her exit – not before keying her number into Nate's cell phone and telling him to call her later. I'd made sure not to drink too much; I'd only had three drinks before moving onto orange juice too. Nate and Ashton's other friends were growing on me more and more by the second. Los Angeles was turning out to be everything I thought it would be, and more.

"Ashton, your turn for drinks, bud," Nate announced, knocking on the table to get his attention. Ashton groaned and stood, sending me a meaningful look that told me to stay put and not move. I watched as he deliberately walked to the corner of the bar so that he could still see me easily. I grinned and shook my head at how overprotective he was. Nate turned to me and smiled. "So, where did you two meet anyway? Ashton never said."

Okay, time for some fun; let's see how gullible Nate is! "We met in a strip club, I gave him a dance," I lied, shrugging casually.

"Shut up! You're a stripper?" Nate cried with wide eyes.

"No!" I snapped, faking horror.

"Oh, sorry, I just thought when you said... oh, never mind," Nate stuttered, smiling apologetically.

"I'm most certainly not a stripper. I'm a lap dancer," I replied, trying not to laugh as he choked on his beer.

"A lap dancer?" he asked, shocked.

"Yep, there's a big difference."

Ashton came back then, setting the drinks down on the table. He smiled but didn't ruin my game as he slid into the seat next to mine.

"Really? You're serious?" Nate inquired.

I grinned. It looked like Nate was extremely gullible after all! "Yep," I nodded, trying to keep a straight face.

"Well, how much, Anna? I'll take one," he chirped, grabbing his wallet out of his pocket, grinning like crazy.

"How much you got?" I leant in as he opened his wallet.

He counted for a couple of seconds. "Fifty eight dollars and twenty five cents," he answered, looking at me hopefully.

I waved my hand dismissively. "Nowhere near enough," I replied, scrunching my nose up. Ashton laughed, so I turned to him and raised one eyebrow. "You, on the other hand, can get one for one drink. Two drinks will get you a private one. And for three drinks, I'll do it in my sexiest underwear," I offered. He groaned and a pained looked crossed his face.

"I'll buy you three drinks, Anna," Seth interjected, jumping up quickly.

I shook my head, smiling apologetically. "Sorry, Seth, your price is much higher. This one's just for my man," I explained. I scooted to the edge of my seat, pressing my side against Ashton's as I leant in closer, leaving our mouths millimetres apart. "Three drinks is all it takes. I might even forgo the no touching rule, seeing as it's your birthday." My body was begging for him to accept, I would definitely forgo the no touching rule they usually had for lap dances.

"I can't," he whined, looking at me pleadingly.

I shrugged nonchalantly. "Offer expires at midnight, that's when your birthday is officially over." I ran my nose up the side of his, listening to my heart thumping wildly in my chest.

"Anna, please?" he begged, closing his eyes.

"Anna please... what?" I asked, nibbling on the edge of his jaw.

"You're killing me," he moaned, shaking his head. I pressed my lips to his, kissing him gently before pulling back and grinning wickedly.

From the corner of my eye, I saw Nate stand and walk off. A minute later he came back and set three shot glasses down in front of Ashton. "You've only got until midnight before the offer expires, Taylor. If I were you, I would drink them the hell down, right now," he suggested, looking at me longingly.

Ashton glanced at his watch and groaned. "It's ten to twelve now."

I smiled. He was definitely wavering. "Well, how about you do one shot and I give you a taster, and if you like it you can do the other two," I offered. I watched his face as the offer sank in. He wanted it badly. As if unable to help himself, he picked up one of the glasses. My stomach clenched in anticipation of having to give him a lap dance in front of everyone, but the alcohol in my system was giving me the confidence. Putting my hand on the bottom of the glass, I guided it towards his lips, watching his face as he tried to decide.

Before he could make up his mind though, a fight broke out in the bar. I didn't even get the chance to flinch before Ashton was out of his seat and had yanked me to my feet, pushing me against the wall as he stepped in front of me protectively. As sounds of a struggle rang out, I hooked my fingers into his belt loops and stayed still and quiet, just like he had taught me to.

Within minutes, it was broken up and two drunks were thrown out of the bar. Ashton turned to face me, cupping my face in his hands as he bent and planted a sweet kiss on my forehead. "I'm not having a drink. Now don't ask me again," he said sternly. His tone told me that this was the end of the conversation. I nodded in agreement, knowing he wouldn't change his mind now. That little fight had spiked his protective instincts, he wouldn't waver again.

When we got back to the table, he took a seat and gripped my waist, pulling me down onto his lap. Nate shook his head and laughed. "Bud, talk about overreaction. That fight was never coming over here," he mocked.

"I don't care. I'm not having Anna near anything like that," Ashton replied, shrugging.

Reaching out, I picked up one of the shots, pushing another towards Nate. "Cheers." I chinked my glass against his and then knocked back the shot.

Nate smiled and downed the drink at the same time I did. "Is it after midnight already?" he asked, grinning as he rolled his eyes at Ashton. "I can't believe you blew your chance."

"Maybe another night then," I said shrugging. I hadn't ruled out the possibility of giving him one anyway if he asked me nicely. After what he was doing for me, I owed him something. If I wasn't here with him tonight, he would be drinking with his friends, instead of working. I was ruining his birthday celebrations. Ashton looked like he wanted to say something. His mouth opened, but nothing came out. "Cat got your tongue, Pretty Boy?" I teased, looking into his beautiful green eyes.

244

He nodded. "I guess. It's just… what's got into you today?"

I smiled and shrugged. "I don't know. I'm just having a great time here in LA with you."

He grinned at me happily. "Well I'm having a great time here in LA with you too," he replied, kissing my cheek.

"Hotties at three o'clock!" Nate announced, nudging Seth in the side.

"I call the redhead!" Seth said quickly.

"Damn it! I was gonna call the red!" Nate grumbled, clearly annoyed. I laughed and shook my head as they stood up and walked over to the girls with their game smiles plastered on their faces.

"Wanna dance?" Ashton offered, nodding at the busy dance floor. His hand traced my back slowly, causing my skin to break out in goosebumps. I nodded in agreement, and we wove through the crowd.

Dancing with Ashton seemed to spark something in me every time it happened. Maybe it was just the way that his body fitted so perfectly against mine, or maybe it was the close proximity, or maybe it was that his hands rested firmly on my ass. Whatever it was, it seemed to send my body into a frenzy of excitement.

As we swayed to the heavy beat of the song, his eyes never left mine. Everything around us faded into insignificance as I lost myself in his gaze. My heart was racing in my chest as my stomach fluttered with excitement and longing. Raw passion was building inside me, and this time I wouldn't be able to contain it or stop it. Tonight I was giving him the best birthday ever, and at the same time I was going to allow myself to be happy for once. I wanted one night of pure, unadulterated bliss in his arms, with no guilt about it after, and no regrets. Tonight I was thinking of myself and putting aside what always held me captive to my emotions. Tonight I was going to pretend that what Ashton and I had was real, instead of just being for his job. If we made some rules, and agreed on one night, tomorrow we could pretend this never happened and we could both move on from it.

When the song changed to a slow one, he pulled me closer to him. His eyes didn't leave mine as the desire raged inside me. My heart clenched as a small smile tugged at the corner of his mouth. He really had the most incredible smile I'd ever seen. Dancing with him in the semi-darkness, with his body pressed against me and his face inches from mine was easily the most romantic moment of my life and my whole body was tingling.

I gulped, swallowing the lust that made my mouth dry. "Ashton, will you take me home please?" I tangled my fingers into the back of his hair and pulled his forehead against mine.

He nodded, kissing the tip of my nose before pulling back and taking my hand. He led us back to the table, smiling at Wayne and Ryan. "We're leaving, see you tomorrow. Tell Nate and Seth we said bye," he said. I waved and let him lead me out of the bar. As we walked the short distance to his place, neither of us spoke, but it wasn't an uncomfortable silence.

Once we got back to his apartment building and climbed the stairs to his door, he fumbled in his pocket for his keys. I couldn't wait any longer. The ache for him was actually painful, and I felt like I was trapped inside my own body and I needed to get out. Stepping between his body and the door, I went up on tiptoes and pressed my lips to his. His body stiffened, but he kissed me back immediately, pushing me against the door, pinning me there with his body. I moaned into his mouth as the kiss deepened. My whole body was throbbing with excitement.

When his hands slid down to my rump, lifting me off my feet, I wrapped my legs around his waist and kissed him passionately, releasing all of the feelings that had been trapped inside me since this happened two months ago. He fumbled with his keys and then we were inside the apartment. He kicked the door closed behind us and carried me to his bedroom, never once breaking the kiss as he pressed me into the soft mattress.

My hands wandered his back, pulling him impossibly closer as his mouth ravaged mine. Little sparks of pleasure were popping and fizzing inside me, his hands left a burning trail on my overheated skin as they slid down my bare legs, kneading my thighs.

Rules, Anna. Set the rules! My brain was screaming it at me, but my body was lost. My trembling fingers worked the buttons on his shirt, pushing it down over his shoulders as my eyes wandered down his chest and my mouth watered in anticipation.

My mind was whirling: Was it going to be as enjoyable as I remembered? Had I distorted the memory of it and I was thinking that this mind-blowing thing had happened to me, when in reality I was just setting myself up for disappointment? The real thing couldn't have been as good as I remembered it.

He caught the bottom of my shirt, slowly pulling it up as if waiting for me to protest. I smiled reassuringly and arched my back to make it easier for him. There was no way I was stopping tonight. He groaned and pulled my shirt off, tossing it carelessly over his shoulder as his eyes dropped to my chest.

Wait, rules, sort the rules before this ruins everything!

"Ashton," My voice was so thick with lust that it didn't sound like mine at all.

"Mmm?" he murmured, dipping his head and licking the skin between my breasts as his fingers went to the button of my shorts, tugging eagerly.

I gulped, swallowing my lust. "Ashton," I repeated, trying to get his attention. I shook my head quickly, closing my hand over his and stopping him from unfastening my shorts. Once my shorts were off and his hands were there, I would surely forget what I needed to say.

He stopped immediately. His eyes widened in horror as he pushed himself up off me, rolling to his side, holding his hands up innocently.

246

"Shit, I'm sorry! I got carried away. I didn't mean to take it that far, I'm really sorry. Are you okay, Baby Girl?" he apologised, wincing.

I smiled reassuringly because he'd clearly jumped to the wrong conclusion about why I asked him to stop. I rolled to the side, pushing him onto his back before swinging my leg over his body, straddling him. As I looked down at him, I tried extremely hard not to notice how excited he was downstairs or how nice he felt between my thighs. I needed to concentrate, and that thought wouldn't help at all.

"I need to talk to you," I muttered.

"Okay," he nodded, moving to sit up but I put my hands on his shoulders, pushing him back down onto the bed.

I took a deep breath to calm myself and my raging hormones. I silently prayed that he was agreeable because I needed him tonight. "I want you right now," I admitted.

A breathtaking smile stretched across his face. "I want you right now too."

He moved to sit up again, so I pushed him back down, leaving my hands on his shoulders. I needed to explain before this went any further, he needed to understand and agree to it before this could happen. "I just want you for tonight, that's all. Tomorrow we pretend like this never happened," I offered, biting my lip, begging him with my eyes to accept.

He frowned. His expression was like I'd just slapped him in the face. He looked both hurt and shocked. "Anna, what? I don't want to pretend that it never happened."

My heart sank. "Please?" I begged. "I need you. Ever since that first time we were together, I just can't stop thinking about it. Sex, no strings, one night, I'll do whatever you want. It's your birthday, so you name it and I'll do it," I bargained as I ran my fingertips down his chest.

"Anna, I don't just want you for one night." His voice was a little strained and the sad tone of it made my heart ache.

"I just want to make myself happy, just for one night. I promise I won't feel guilty about it tomorrow and get upset. I promise, please?" I leant down so our faces were inches apart. Indecision was clear across his face. "Please? I want you and I know you want me too. Just for tonight?"

"Tell me why you won't let me in," he said suddenly. "Try and explain it to me." His eyes searched mine for answers that I myself didn't even know.

I blinked, a little shocked at his request and the sudden change in conversation. I sighed, feeling dejected. Clearly my request was ruining the easy relationship we had. I shouldn't have wished to be happy, even for one night, because I obviously didn't deserve it.

"I just… can't. I let Jack in and when he died, it killed me inside. I'm broken. I don't have anything to give you. Jack took all of me when he died," I whispered, closing my eyes. I knew that wasn't true though, Jack didn't take everything, I thought for the longest time that he had, but since

247

I'd met Ashton, I'd started to feel again. I couldn't be dead inside because I could feel the tug at my heart when Ashton looked at me just as he was looking at me now: pleading and hurt. I wanted to make him feel better; it was almost painful to see that look on his face. So that was how I knew that my heart didn't die when Jack did. The trouble was, I couldn't let Ashton have my heart. I couldn't feel heartbreak again; I wouldn't live through it a second time. I wasn't strong enough to go through another man leaving me; I couldn't open myself up like that again. But I could give myself to him physically and give us what we both wanted.

"But if you could just give me a chance…" He looked at me pleadingly, begging me with his sad puppy dog face.

I shook my head fiercely. "No. I've been there and felt what it's like to have your heart ripped out. I won't ever let myself get in that position again, not ever. I can't." I swallowed the lump in my throat. "But I just want to feel happy for one night. I want to be normal and not worry about anything or anyone. Please? Will you just… make me forget everything, Ashton?" I begged.

I could feel the disappointment and devastation building inside with each passing second. Tears welled in my eyes as I pressed my face into the side of his neck, willing them not to fall as I breathed in his smell that I was fast becoming addicted to. His arms wrapped tightly around me and hugged me to him while I fought for control.

After a couple of minutes he spoke, "This is what you want? Just one night? Sex, no strings?" I nodded, not taking my face from its nice little hiding place; I could feel my cheeks burning with embarrassment. He rolled suddenly so I was under him again. "You know I want more than that, don't you?"

My eyes widened in surprise. Was he about to say yes? "I can't give you more than that," I whispered in answer. His eyes fluttered closed as he sighed. I waited, feeling hope building in my chest. When his eyes opened again, they burned with a passion that made my stomach twist into a knot. After a slight nod of his head, his lips claimed mine in a scorching hot kiss that resonated through every single cell in my body.

I whimpered as the excitement became almost too much to bear. I smiled against his lips as my hands hurriedly went to his belt buckle. My fingers were shaking, making the process hard as I unfastened the buttons on his jeans and pushed them down slightly, sliding my hand down the back of his underwear, feeling his tight little behind. A moan of appreciation left my lips as the kiss deepened and turned into something that burned through my senses, leaving me barely able to breathe.

As he unfastened my bra and slid it off, his heavily-lidded eyes showed his appreciation. "You are so beautiful, Anna," he whispered, dipping his head and flicking his tongue over the tip of my nipple. I moaned and arched my back, trying to get closer to him as his tongue lavished attention on my sensitive skin. He smiled and blew gently across

248

the wet trail, making my skin tighten and my arousal bump up another notch.

While his hands worked the buttons of my shorts and pushed them down, his mouth travelled further down, sucking on the skin of my stomach, dipping into my belly button. His weight shifted off of me as his thumbs hooked into the side of my panties, easing them down my thighs teasingly. His hot tongue made its way down my leg before coming back up again. He nudged my thighs apart as he settled himself between them and looked up at me with a devilish glint to his eyes.

My body jerked involuntarily as he dipped his head and his tongue traced my wet folds. Gasping from both shock and pleasure, my fingers fisted into the sheets as I squeezed my eyes shut tightly. This was pleasure like I had never experienced, it was concentrated and strong; waves of it were rolling over and over me in time with the movement of his tongue.

I whimpered and tried to squirm away from him because it was too much, too good, and I couldn't cope with it. But before I could get away, his arms wrapped around my thighs, clamping me in place as he carried on with his beautiful, yet torturous assault. My moans bordered on obscene as I raised my hips, trying to get closer to his mouth, yet at the same time I wanted to be further away from it. At this point I didn't know which I wanted more. As his fingers pushed into me at the same time, he made a deep moaning sound in the back of his throat.

I gasped his name as the pleasure suddenly took me to new heights. My body felt like it was on fire as he pumped his fingers at the same rhythm as he was working his tongue. I could feel my climax building; my whole body trembling and shaking. When his teeth nipped me, it felt like I shattered inside and everything came to a glorious and beautiful head. My body jerked as I cried out his name breathlessly.

He chuckled, easing his fingers out of me as I lay there panting for breath. I blinked a couple of times, trying to come back to reality as I looked up in time to see him sucking on his fingers. "Was that the thing that you liked that I did with my hand?" he teased, smirking at me confidently.

I giggled and nodded, chewing on my bottom lip. His eyes flashed with excitement as he hovered over me, just looking at me with that soft and tender look that he always had for me.

I smiled happily. "My turn now," I announced, pushing on his body and guiding him onto his back. My eyes flitted down his body, taking in every glorious inch of it before I bent and trailed my tongue across his abs, following the lines of his muscles. His skin tasted delicious and made my scalp prickle. As he put both hands behind his head and smiled down at me in obvious enjoyment, my tongue and lips worshipped every line of muscle on his sculpted chest, every bump, every groove. He was perfection, and I had never seen anything more beautiful. His jeans were already loose around his hips so I tugged them off easily, along with his boxer shorts.

The sight of him naked made my ache inside me come back with a vengeance. I sat up, just looking him over unashamedly, taking in every beautiful inch of him and memorising it so I could see it when I closed my eyes at night.

When I couldn't stand not touching him any longer, I reached out and closed my hand around his erection. My breathing sped at the feel of it and memories of how good it felt inside me surfaced and made my stomach quiver with anticipation. But first I owed him something. I bent my head and licked the drop of wetness from the tip, before tracing my tongue down the underside and back up again. Taking the tip of it into my mouth, I sucked gently before pushing down further, sucking harder as my hand started to move too. I wasn't even there a minute though before he groaned and gripped the tops of my arms, pulling me up his body as he shook his head.

My face filled with embarrassed heat. "Did I do something wrong?" I asked, horrified because he hadn't liked what I was doing.

"No, of course not. The opposite, in fact." His hand tangled into the back of my hair. "I don't want this over too quickly and your hot, little mouth sucking on me like that is gonna make me finish way too soon," he answered, grinning wickedly.

I giggled, wriggling on top of him as a sense of pride swept over me because I'd clearly pleased him. He guided my mouth back to his again and as my tongue touched his, I could taste myself on his tongue. Strangely, it made the kiss even better, even more erotic and sexy. His hand trailed down my back, cupping my ass and shifting me so that we rubbed together. A breathless moan erupted from within me as I bit on his bottom lip roughly.

"Do you have a condom?" I asked breathlessly, genuinely not caring if he didn't.

He nodded in answer, reaching over towards his bedside drawer and pulling it open. As he fumbled in there and pulled out a strip of condoms, I moved off him, watching as he ripped off a packet and tore it open with his teeth. He got to his knees, carefully rolling it on before looking back to me with a stunning smile that I couldn't help but return. When he grabbed my thighs and jerked me forwards, I fell back into the pillows and giggled. He laughed too, manoeuvring himself on top of me as he kissed me again.

The air in the room seemed to be getting thicker as I wrapped my arms around his body, digging my fingers into his back. His hand gripped the back of my knee, guiding my leg up around his waist as he pressed forward gently, easing himself into me so slowly that it made every nerve ending in my body scream. I was so on edge that I accidentally bit down onto his shoulder and dug my fingers into his ass as I raised my hips to meet his.

He groaned as he buried himself into me entirely. "Shit. So good. I forgot," he moaned, kissing me deeply as he moved slowly, starting up a rhythm that made my heart hammer in my chest.

It was strange when I was like this with Ashton; it was like it was meant to be. He fitted me so perfectly, and everything in my world seemed good, healed, and incredible. He was the only one in the world I could be this close to, and let have this power over me. I trusted him and only him.

I couldn't keep still under him as he controlled my body perfectly, strumming it, playing it like we had done this hundreds of times before. It seemed like he knew exactly how and where to touch me. My mind was slowly melting at his touch. Sweat covered my skin in a thin sheen as I raised my hips to meet his and clawed at his back in ecstasy. My body was racing towards its climax; with every thrust he was pushing me towards my end. His mouth lavished attention on my body, driving me into a state of wild abandon.

As my body seemed to get hotter and hotter, my pulse drummed in my ears and finally my body shattered, coming apart under him and his expert touch. I cried out his name as my eyes filled with tears because of the intense sensations. My whole body was quivering in pleasure and my heart crashed in my ears. It felt like heaven, like a waking dream. His lips claimed mine in a kiss that felt like it could devour my soul as he let out a long groan. His body stiffened on top of me and he thrust another couple of times as he reached his end too.

When he pulled back slightly, I looked up into his face. He was smiling down at me, his eyes filled with passion, tenderness, and something that I could easily mistake for love, but it couldn't be that. I dismissed it as gratitude because he hadn't had sex for two months.

"Holy shit, Baby Girl, that was incredible," he growled, kissing along my cheeks to nibble on my earlobe as he eased out of me.

"You were just okay," I joked breathlessly as he rolled to the side and pulled the condom off, throwing it into the trashcan before turning back to me to wrap me in his arms.

"Don't tell me… you've had better," he said sarcastically, rolling his eyes jokingly. My heart stopped at his words. I'd only ever been with him and Carter. Tears stung my eyes as my throat seemed to tighten. Ashton's eyes widened as he gasped and shook his head, cupping my face in his hands. "Fuck. I'm so sorry. I didn't think, I didn't mean it like that. I was just kidding. I'm so, so sorry!"

I forced a smile even though my heart now hurt at the reminder. It seemed like I would never escape the fact that I was dirty and used, not even for a moment. "It's alright. Don't worry," I lied.

He grimaced and kissed the tip of my nose. "I'm sorry," he murmured, kissing my nose.

"Just forget it, it's fine." I knew he hadn't meant it that way at all, but it was just the reminder that hurt. I didn't for a second think that he had meant to bring up Carter; it was just a joke than he hadn't thought through. "Just for the record, I think you were incredible too, and I'll never have better," I said honestly. I knew that for a fact because I'd never have anyone else. I kissed him again, cuddling close to his side as I buried my face in his chest, breathing in his delicious smell. I instantly felt better. His body didn't relax at my reassurances though. His muscles were still bunched; his arms were too stiff around me. I moved back, looking up to see his tense face. He was clearly angry with himself. Reaching out, I smoothed his frown line from his forehead. "It's okay, I promise."

He sighed heavily. "Man, I'm such a douchebag. I can't believe I said that to you."

I smiled. "Just forget it. I have." I decided then that I refused to think about anything bad after I had just had the most incredible sex ever. He rolled to his side so we were facing each other. His body was still tense, so I snuggled closer to him and kissed his lips softly. For a few minutes, we just lay there in silence, looking at each other as his fingers tickled up and down my spine. Finally, he spoke, "Thank you for today, I've honestly had the best birthday ever," he said quietly.

I smiled. "I had a great day too," I replied. "Although I feel guilty because you've technically been working and couldn't drink and stuff because I'm here. You really should have just come on your own; you would have had so much more fun."

He shook his head in protest. "Baby Girl, *you* are what made my day great. I don't care if I don't drink," he countered. I smiled and he leant forward, kissing me again hungrily. He moaned in the back of his throat and tightened his hold on me. Where we were pressed so tightly against one another, I could feel that he was starting to get excited again. I grinned against his lips, and he pulled back, smiling at me tenderly as he combed his fingers through my hair. "What's funny?" he asked.

"You're like some kind of machine. It's lucky we agreed on one night, and not one time, huh?" I teased, running my finger down his chest and raising one eyebrow when I got to his groin. He grunted, obviously shocked, but a slow smile spread across his face before he covered my mouth with his and we started all over again.

Chapter Twenty-Four

I woke in the morning, naked and wrapped in his arms. He was stretched out behind me, spooning me. One of his hands rested on my hip, and the other was cupping my breast. The thought of being naked in his bed and us being in such an intimate position made a blush creep up onto my cheeks. Not that I had to worry about him seeing me naked though, after all, he'd probably kissed every inch of my body last night during the three times that we'd had sex.

A satisfied smiled crept onto my lips. I refused to feel guilty about it today, I was entitled to one night of pleasure after the years of misery I'd had recently. I pressed myself back into his body, wanting to melt into him. I loved waking up next to him in the morning, he was so warm and comforting and the fact that he had never spent the night with another girl made me feel special.

He moaned sleepily and wrapped his arms tighter around me, lazily kissing the back of my head. I turned my head to look at him, leaving my body pressed against his, not wanting him to let go yet.

"Hi," I murmured sheepishly.

He grinned not making any moves to let go of me. "Hi. How are you feeling this morning?" He looked a little worried, as if he were waiting for a meltdown at any moment.

"Happy and satisfied," I confirmed, smirking at him.

He burst out laughing and kissed my cheek. "Hmm, what a coincidence, me too." I felt a stirring against my thigh as he started to get excited again; he moved his hips away from me so that I didn't feel it – the same as he usually did in the morning when it happened.

I grinned and raised one eyebrow. "This could still count as last night if you want," I suggested, wriggling back into his body and smiling at him over my shoulder. His erection prodded into the back of my leg, and my whole body seemed to thrum with excitement.

He grinned. "Oh it can, can it? So, what you're asking is if I want to have sex with you again. Hmm let me think," he teased.

I tried hard not to laugh. "Well if you don't want me then…" I trailed off and scooted away from him.

He gripped my hips tightly, thwarting my efforts to get away. "I never said that I didn't want you. I don't think I'll ever say that, Baby Girl," he whispered. His lips pressed against the back of my neck, his teeth nibbling gently and I felt goosebumps break out on my whole body. "Can you pass me a condom from the drawer?" he murmured, still kissing the base of my neck.

I nodded quickly, scooting to the edge of the bed and pulling open the drawer where he'd got them from last night. The empty box stared back at me, taunting me. I groaned when I realised what that meant. "Damn it! There's none left," I whined. I felt so disappointed that I could cry.

He pulled me back to him again. "I'll go get one from Nate's room, he didn't come home last night so he won't even know," he said grinning. He pulled away from me and I whimpered at the loss of his contact, feeling empty and needy. He chuckled at my face and kissed my nose. "I'll be right back, I promise."

I watched as he jumped up and ran out of the room, butt naked. I laughed at how eager he was, he'd almost run into the door because he didn't wait for it to open fully. He was back within about ten seconds and pounced on the bed, grinning.

"I brought two, just in case, maybe, in a little while, that might count as last night too," he explained, looking at me, hopefully holding up the two packets as evidence.

"Don't push your luck, Pretty Boy," I teased, grinning.

An hour and a half later, we were both exhausted. I flopped off him and lay on my back, trying to catch my breath. He rolled onto his side, moving closer to me, putting his arm over my stomach and nuzzling into my neck. I was sweating. My whole body felt weak and like I'd been on a thirty minute sprint. That last time was extremely tiring, and I could do with going back to sleep for a couple of hours.

"So tell me, how come you'll let me do that until I nearly pass out, yet I can't run on the treadmill like I want to?" I asked, grinning.

He bit my neck lightly. "Because I don't get anything out of you running on the treadmill," he joked, laughing.

I laughed and slapped his hard chest playfully before rolling onto my side and sighing contentedly. "Thank you," I said gratefully.

He raised one eyebrow in question. "For what?"

"For last night, well and this morning, that was the best night of my life. Thank you." I kissed his soft full lips, marvelling over how they seemed to be my exact match.

"Well in that case, thank you for the best night of my life too, ma'am," he replied, smiling at me.

I groaned at the word 'ma'am'. That word from his lips did strange things to my insides. "Ashton, don't keep calling me that. My body is already aching all over, I can't go again," I whined.

"Well, maybe later," he shrugged, looking at me hopefully.

I winced at his expression, praying that this didn't ruin our friendship because I needed him in my life. "Ashton, we agreed…" I trailed off uncomfortably.

He sighed. "I know. I had to try though, right?" He kissed the tip of my nose. "You want me to run you a bath, and I'll make breakfast for when you get out?" he offered. He glanced over at the clock and laughed. "Well, actually it'll be lunch," he corrected.

I smiled at how thoughtful and generous he was. "Sure, that'd be great," I answered, biting my lip at how adorable he was. He certainly was going to make someone incredibly happy one day. The thought made me so jealous that it actually hurt. He looked me over slowly and laughed at something. "What?" I asked curiously.

He shook his head and climbed out of the bed; he pulled on his jeans and made his way to the bathroom. I winced and bit my lip when I saw he had some red scratches on his back. I could hear water running, so I got out of the bed and stretched my tight muscles; it genuinely did feel like I had been working out.

When I looked in his mirror, I gasped. "Holy shit!" I cried, as I looked at the red marks on my neck and breasts. Immediately, Ashton ran back into the room, looking around worriedly. "Ashton, seriously, what the hell?" I asked, rubbing the marks as if they would come off.

He laughed and wrapped his arms around me. "I'm sorry, I didn't realise I did it. I guess I got a little carried away," he explained, grimacing.

I laughed and slapped his arm. "A little carried away? There are five hickeys on me!" I scolded, laughing incredulously.

"Six actually. I've just seen another one on your cute, little butt," he stated, slapping my behind gently. I gasped and turned to look in the mirror and sure enough, there was another hickey on my butt cheek.

I giggled. "Well, at least I can cover that one up."

He grinned sheepishly. "Sorry."

I rolled my eyes and pushed him away gently. "Go turn off the bath, Pretty Boy, before your apartment floods," I suggested, grinning. He jumped like he'd forgotten it and ran out of the room quickly. He called me in there after a couple of minutes, and when I walked in I saw that he'd drawn me a bubble bath. I couldn't hold the little 'aww' that escaped my lips as my heart skipped a beat at the thoughtfulness of him. I climbed in and sighed as my strained muscles started relaxing. I closed my eyes and replayed some of the memories of last night; I had a feeling I would be revisiting those memories a lot.

255

After a little while, I forced myself to focus and washed my hair and body before getting out and wrapping myself in a towel. Once I was back in the bedroom, I looked through the outfit choices I'd brought with me. Settling on something casual, I dressed quickly in black leggings and a fitted white shirt. Not wanting to spend too much time on my hair, I pulled it over one shoulder and braided it. Happier than I had felt in years, I practically skipped to the lounge. My whole body was relaxed and contented. My need for Ashton's body that I had been struggling with for the last two months was finally satiated.

Ashton paused his video game that he was playing as I walked in the room. "Wow, you look beautiful."

Seeing him sitting there, smiling at me, and with the memories of last night still fresh in my mind, the need for his body came back with a vengeance. "Thanks." I walked over and sat next to him on the sofa. "Can I play too?" I asked, nodding at the TV screen, needing a distraction before I dragged him back to his bedroom again.

He grinned. "Actually, I'd love that. That's every guy's fantasy, a girl that plays video games, did you know that?" he replied, winking at me playfully before standing up and getting another controller for me, adding me on to his game.

I smiled. "Oh really?"

He nodded in agreement, passing me the controller and restarting the game as he sat at my side.

As it turns out, I sucked royally at video games. We were playing some kind of war game, but all I was doing was running around aimlessly and getting killed. Ashton seemed highly amused by my lack of ability though.

After about half an hour, the timer on the stove beeped and he paused the game, setting his controller onto the sofa. "I'm gonna go get lunch, no cheating while I'm gone," he teased, kissing me quickly on the lips but pulling away way too quickly for my liking. I watched him go into the kitchen, and a few minutes later he returned with the only thing he could cook without cremating it – tuna and cheese baked potatoes.

I smiled gratefully. "Thanks, Ashton."

"So, what shall we do today?" he asked, digging into his food.

I shrugged. "I don't know, what is there to do?" I smiled down at my full plate. I was actually ravenous after all of the exercise this morning.

"Do you want to see my training academy? I'm sure my captain would like to meet you."

"Sure. Sounds great," I agreed, grinning. I would love to see the academy he raved about so much.

"I'll have to call my Captain to see if I'm allowed to take you in there," he winced as he pulled out his cell phone, dialling quickly. After a couple of seconds the line obviously connected, so I listened to his side of the conversation. "Hi, sir, it's Ashton Taylor. No, everything's going great actually. I'm in LA with Miss Spencer and she's requested to see my academy, do you think that would be possible? Yeah, she's good. No, she's not being difficult at all," he smiled at me, so I blushed and looked away. "She'd really like to come, sir. No, but I can get the senator's permission if it's needed." He looked at me with wide eyes before his face relaxed. "Yeah great, we'll be there in about half an hour or so. Thanks, g'bye, sir." He grinned happily and pushed the phone back into his pocket. "It's all arranged, so whenever you're ready."

I smiled and tucked into my food. I had a feeling he would enjoy showing me around there. When he was done eating, he showered quickly and threw on his clothes while I did the dishes.

When we got there, Ashton was beaming his kilowatt smile. He grabbed my hand, dragging me in behind him. A balding older man wearing a black SWAT T-shirt and black pants came over. The warm smile and the way he shook Ashton's hand told me that they liked each other.

"Officer Weston, this is Anna. Anna, my old captain," Ashton introduced, waving a hand between us.

The man turned to me and smiled, somewhat nervously. He had obviously read my file too and was erring on the side of caution.

I held my hand out to him. "Nice to meet you, Officer Weston," I greeted politely. His eyes widened in surprise as he glanced at Ashton, who nodded and smiled encouragingly.

Officer Weston tentatively shook my hand with his rough calloused one. "You too, Miss Spencer," he replied, his face betraying his total and utter confusion.

I waved my hand dismissively. "Anna's fine, not Miss Spencer."

He nodded. "Well, I wasn't expecting a visit from you. What are you two doing here in LA? And where's your far guard?" he asked, glancing behind me.

"We're on our own for the weekend, sir. It was cleared by Senator Spencer," Ashton answered quickly.

The older man's eyes snapped to Ashton. "Seriously? He let you bring her to LA on your own?" A proud smile tugged at the corners of his mouth. Ashton nodded and smiled down at me, squeezing my hand that he was still holding. "You must be making an impression there, Taylor."

I laughed at that. "Oh he is," I chimed in, smiling suggestively at my pretend boyfriend.

Ashton choked back a laugh and nodded. "Well, I'll be showing Anna around then, sir," he chirped happily. Officer Weston nodded and handed me a visitors' badge as Ashton dragged me off up the hallway, grinning like a mad man.

His tour was pretty thorough. As we went into the swimming pool, combat rooms and gym, Ashton was telling me little stories about what him and Nate used to get up to in there and how many ways they got into trouble with their superiors. It sounded like they were a nightmare to control. It surprised me that Officer Weston seemed to like him; actually, it surprised me that they graduated at all, what with all the pranks and practical jokes they'd pulled.

After we'd seen practically everything, he smiled excitedly at me. "Wanna see the shooting range?"

"Sure." I shrugged. I didn't want to, but he looked so excited about it that I didn't want to ruin his fun.

Instead of taking me to some dingy room like we'd been shooting in, we went outside. "Hey, Carl, let me borrow your gun, would ya?" he shouted over my shoulder. I turned to see a guy decked out in full SWAT uniform.

My breath caught in my throat because it was even hotter than I imagined it to be. If I saw that on Ashton, I was pretty sure I would just burst into flames, and all that would be left of me was a pile of dust on the floor. "Ashton, why the hell didn't you put that on for me last night?" I whined, digging my fingers into his waist as a thousand fantasies of him calling me ma'am in the hot uniform flooded my brain. I squeezed my eyes shut and moaned, the thought alone made my legs feel weak.

He chuckled wickedly. "Whoa, chill, Baby Girl. I have mine at home if you want me to show you," he whispered, his teeth nipping my earlobe as he wrapped his arms around my waist. My mouth started to water. That was definitely something I would be requesting before we left LA. He winked at me and turned back to the guy, who had now reached us.

"Hey, Taylor, what are you doing back here? I thought you were in Washington," the guy called Carl said as they shook hands and did the one-armed man hug thing.

"Yeah I was. I've got the weekend off, but they just called me in at the last minute to sign for something. We were on our way out, so I had to bring my girlfriend in too," Ashton lied, rolling his eyes, faking exasperation.

Carl looked me over and grinned wolfishly. "I didn't know you did girlfriends."

I smiled suggestively. "Oh, he does them alright," I interjected, winking and holding out my hand to him, smiling. "Anna."

He shook my hand. "Carl."

"So, can I borrow your gun for a sec? I just want to show off for my girl," Ashton repeated. Carl nodded, swinging what I assumed to be an assault rifle off his shoulder.

I jumped and jerked back away from it. My breath seemed to catch in my throat. Ashton took the offered gun and moved it away from me. "It's alright, I promise," he smiled reassuringly at me. Carl took off his ear defenders that were hanging loosely around his neck and held them out to me. I took them and nodded a thanks, though my eyes were still firmly fixed on the gun.

"Use Station Four, it's just been set up," Carl instructed, nodding off to the right.

Ashton grinned. "Cheers, man." He pulled me over to the grass next to a number four sign, and laid himself down on his stomach, fiddling with the gun for a few seconds before patting the grass next to him. Taking the hint, I lay down at his side and looked out into the direction that he was looking in. I couldn't see a thing, only grass and more grass. "You ready? Put those on," he instructed, nodding at my ear defenders that were in my hand. I nodded and slipped them on, not knowing what to expect. He let off a series of shots in bursts of two, and then clicked the safety back on less than a minute later. "What do you think?" he asked, smirking at me.

I shrugged in response. "It's a big gun?" I offered, not sure what else to say.

He laughed and wrapped his arm around my waist, pulling me closer to him. "Look through the eyepiece."

Confused, I did as I was told. At first I had no idea what I was looking at, but then I spotted it. There was a target out there, one of the paper ones like we usually practiced with. Pulling my eye away from the eyepiece, I squinted off into the distance. I couldn't see it at all. When I used the eyepiece again, I noticed that the black shape of the head had two eyes, a nose, and a mouth all made out of bullet holes.

I burst out laughing. "I can't even see that! How far away is it?" I asked, searching the horizon for it again.

"Five hundred yards," he answered, shrugging.

I gasped in awe of his talent. "You shot a smiley face from five hundred yards away?"

"Yeah, but you should see Nate shoot. He could literally shoot a fly if it landed on that target," he said, shaking his head in disbelief.

"You're incredible. Honestly, your talent just boggles my mind," I breathed. *How on earth can one man be so skilled at his job, yet look and act the way he does?* I turned my head to see his face inches from mine; his beautiful green eyes sparkling. I moved my head closer and pressed my lips to his softly. Instead of it being a chaste kiss though, it turned into something else. His hand went to the back of my head as the kiss deepened and he moved so that I had to roll onto my back with his body half over mine. When I seemed to lose all control of myself, he took my hands off his butt and pinned them above my head, smiling against my lips.

"You're so adorable," he purred, pressing himself to me tighter as his lips found mine again. Someone cleared their throat behind us, and Ashton groaned. "Go away, Carl. Can't you see we're busy?" he muttered, kissing me again.

"Agent Taylor, that's not exactly appropriate behaviour. If you were still under my charge, you'd be doing kitchen duty for a week!" Officer Weston growled.

Ashton jumped up quickly. I'd honestly never seen anyone move so fast in my life. He turned, standing straight and saluted his officer. The sexy little display of respect made my stomach quiver. "I'm sorry, sir. I was just showing Miss Spencer how to shoot, sir," he lied, holding down a hand to help me up while still standing straight as a poker.

"Really? Showing her how to shoot, is that what you kids call getting it on nowadays?" Officer Weston countered. An amused smile played on his lips. My face burned with embarrassment at being caught and I pressed into Ashton's back, trying to hide.

"Yes, sir," Ashton answered, his tone amused.

"Well, I'm glad you're taking your role as boyfriend seriously, Taylor," Weston said, shaking his head and walking away, chuckling to himself.

Ashton turned to me and winced. "Oops."

"That was so embarrassing!" I giggled.

"Embarrassing? I thought he was gonna have my balls," Ashton countered, shaking his head in amusement. He leant down and grabbed the gun from the floor, folding in the little legs before holding his hand out to me. "Come on, let's go to that museum I was telling you about. I'd really love to take you."

I smiled at his thoughtfulness. "You'll be bored," I countered.

A heart-stopping smile crept onto his face as his hand squeezed mine. "Not if I'm with you, I won't."

I didn't think it was possible to have a better day than the one we'd had previously, but I was wrong. After a few hours at the museum, we ate ice cream in the park while he told me little stories about living in LA, what he loved and hated about it. The more he'd spoken about it, the more in love with it I'd fallen. I'd decided there and then that if I managed to graduate and get a job, I would try to relocate to LA. Maybe then Ashton and I could hang out occasionally. Of course, that was three years into the future, and I still had a long way to go before I could think about graduating at all.

Once we'd finally grabbed one of the hotdogs that he raved about, we headed back to his apartment. He even allowed me drive, much to his horror and white knuckles. Ashton drove all the time usually, he said it was in case he had to take evasive action, but I knew it was just my driving he hated. I must admit, maybe I did drive a little too fast at times and tended to stomp on the brakes a little too hard occasionally.

We'd already arranged to go out again with his friends tonight. One of Nate's cousins was a doorman at a bar that had a live band playing, so that was where we were heading tonight.

Once we were back at his apartment, I changed into a little black dress and some hot pink heels. My hair was unsalvageable, so I just unfastened the braid and clipped it up in a little twist at the back of my head. While Ashton dressed next to me, the red scratches on his back came into view again.

I winced. "Did I hurt you last night? I'm really sorry," I muttered, nodding at his back when he seemed confused.

He twisted, looking in the mirror before laughing. "Looks like you marked me too then," he mused. He slipped on a shirt, covering it up and smiled over at me. "You weren't hurting me, trust me."

I chewed on my lip and stood up, smoothing down my skirt. "Look okay?"

"You look stunning." His eyes shone with adoration as he held out one hand towards me. "Ready?"

I nodded and grinned, excited for my second night out with him in LA.

When we arrived at the bar, Ashton led us past the huge line to the front and gave his name to the doorman. Much to my amazement, we were waved straight through.

Ashton scanned the bar from the doorway. I assumed he was looking for his friends, but couldn't rule out the possibility that he was surveying the area for hostiles because he never seemed to relax. Nate's blond head caught my attention, and I frowned as I spotted Seth standing a few feet away from him with his tongue down a girl's throat already. I looked back at Ashton and felt unreasonable jealousy settle in the pit of my stomach as I wondered if he had a different girl every night like his friends seemed too. If he did, it would explain why he was so killer in bed.

"They're over there," I stated, pointing towards Nate.

He smiled and took my hand as he guided us through the crowd. Nate's eyes widened as we stopped next to him. "Wow, you look hot Anna. Fuck me," he said, looking me over slowly.

"Thanks for the offer, but I think I'll pass," I joked, shrugging.

He grinned. "You're funny."

"Did you have fun last night? I was worried when you didn't come home," I teased.

"Aw, that's sweet. Were you concerned about little old me? Or did you just want someone to rock you to sleep?" he asked, winking and smirking at me.

"Yeah, you know anyone?" I shrugged, playing along.

Nate looked at Ashton and grinned. "You know, Taylor, you said I'd be in love with her by the end of the weekend and damn, I think you're right." He slapped Ashton on the shoulder proudly.

"Too bad I'm taken, huh?" I joked.

Nate stepped closer to me. There was a calculating edge to his eyes that made me slightly nervous, not in the frightened way, but in the 'he's up to no good' way. "I think we should play a little game," he suggested, grinning wickedly.

"What kind of game?"

261

His smile widened. "A dating game. Let's see who can get the most phone numbers from the opposite sex tonight."

I laughed and shook my head, stepping closer to Ashton. "I have all the phone numbers I want, thanks," I declined.

Nate pouted. "Oh come on, a little competition. If I win, then I get to drive your rental car for an hour tomorrow, and if you win, hmm well, what do you want?" he asked, narrowing his eyes at me.

I laughed wickedly as a plan formed in my head. "If I win, you get up on stage and sing a song of my choice," I bargained.

He laughed, looking way too overconfident in his ability. "Deal. There's no way I'm losing this bet. Getting girls' digits is my specialty," he announced proudly.

I turned to Ashton and raised one eyebrow. "You okay if I play this, Pretty Boy? You know I'm coming home with you, right? Not gonna have a jealous hissy fit?" A jealous hissy fit wasn't actually what I was expecting, more like a panic attack because I would be more than four feet from him while out in the open.

"As long as you know you're mine, we're all good," he answered, bending and kissing my cheek. He turned to Nate and smirked confidently. "You really shouldn't play against my girl, buddy. She's gonna kick your ass."

Nate made a scoffing sound in the back of his throat and waved his hand dismissively. "Winner is the one who has the most numbers by the end of the night," he explained with a confident smile plastered on his face. His eyes were already scanning the area for potential girls.

I shook my head quickly. "I don't want to play all night. Let's make it an hour instead." Nate nodded in agreement, looking at his watch. "By the way, are there any rules as to how to get these phone numbers?" I asked curiously. I didn't want to be accused of cheating.

"Nope, no rules. Anything's allowed. Hour starts now." He winked at me and then strode off into the crowd and up to a couple of girls that were giggling off to one side, dancing drunkenly. They didn't stand a chance against him. He was a serious charmer, and his awesome personality was matched by his good looks. I smiled and shook my head at his slutty behaviour, but I just couldn't bring myself to dislike him for it. He was such a great guy, women were clearly his downfall.

Turning back to Ashton, I smiled. "Wanna dance?"

He frowned. "You're not doing the game?"

I nodded, taking his hand and giving him a little tug towards where some other people were dancing already. "I am. I just don't need an hour to kick his butt."

After about half an hour of us dancing and flirting, Nate stopped at my side and grinned. "I've got four so far, how many have you got?"

"I haven't started yet." I shrugged.

He frowned, looking slightly annoyed. "Are you not playing?"

"Yeah, I'm playing. I'm just about to make my move actually, wanna watch?" I asked, winking slyly at him. I strutted confidently through the crowd and up to the bar. I leant over to the barman and gave him a seductive smile. "Hi, I need a favour; do you have a microphone I can borrow?"

"Er yeah, I've got one here so I can announce the band," he replied, picking up and microphone, looking a little baffled.

"Any chance I can borrow it and stand on the bar?" I asked hopefully, pouting and trying to be persuasive.

He blinked a couple of times and nodded, handing me the microphone. "Er... sure."

I put a twenty dollar bill on the bar. "Can I get a shot of whatever you have there," I asked, pointing to the nearest bottle. While he poured it, I lifted myself up onto the bar, trying to be ladylike considering my dress was relatively short. I grinned as I spotted Ashton and Nate both watching me with confused looks on their faces.

I stood up and took the shot from the barman as he held it out to me. After flicking the on switch on the microphone, I tapped the top of it, making a loud noise and a little screech. "Excuse me? Hi. Can I have everyone's attention, just for a minute?" I said into the microphone, making my voice ring out through the bar. People stopped and looked at me, obviously wondering what was going on. "So, my name's Tracey, I'm twenty-one, and I'm only in town for the next three days. I'm a part time lap dancer, and I've just found out my boyfriend cheated on me with my sister!" I lied, downing the shot. "He's here tonight. His name's Nate. He has blond hair and blue eyes; he's wearing a blue shirt. So, girls, if he comes up to you, I'd think twice about it, fucking asshole!" I scowled, trying to sound annoyed. "So anyway, I'll get straight to the point. I'm looking for some no-strings-attached rebound sex. If there are any single guys in here interested, then come and give me your number. I'll be over in the corner with my gay friends." I pointed over to the corner where Seth and Wayne were. "Thanks for your time." I sat down carefully and then eased myself off the bar. I smiled gratefully at the barman and placed the microphone onto the bar.

"I'll give you my number," he said quickly, scribbling on a napkin and holding it out to me.

"Great, I'll give you a call tomorrow," I looked down at the paper, "Paul," I added, reading his name off it. He grinned, and I walked back over to a shocked Ashton and Nate. "Beat that," I teased. "Oh, and I think something by Queen would be good." I patted Nate's chest, giggling at his astonished, yet slightly proud face.

"I told you not to play against my girl," Ashton chimed in, shaking his head in disbelief.

By the time I got back to where Seth was standing, I already had six numbers. Nate shook his head in protest. "You cheated," he accused.

"No way! I asked you if there were any rules and you said that anything was allowed. Isn't that right, Wayne?" I asked, grinning.

Wayne nodded. "Yep, dude, those were your exact words," he agreed, laughing as Nate punched him in the shoulder.

I grinned at Nate triumphantly. "So, how many do you have? Can we stop now?" I asked as another guy came up to me and handed me his number.

He sighed dramatically. "Yeah, okay. You win, I guess," he grumbled dejectedly.

I grinned and turned to Ashton, cupping his face in my hands. "What? You're secretly in love with me, and you're not really gay?" I cried. He flinched, taken by surprise at my outburst, but I didn't give him time to recover before I pressed my lips to his, kissing him passionately.

Chapter Twenty-Five

~ Ashton ~

As we walked back to my apartment, I held Anna's hand tightly. I'd had another incredible night. The band had been great, dancing with her was great, and Nate singing at the end of the night was priceless. Nate was easily the worst singer I had ever heard in my life, so Anna couldn't have chosen a better forfeit for him to do.

Nate was coming home with us tonight too. Due to Anna's little *'he slept with my sister'* stunt, he hadn't managed to hook up with anyone tonight, much to his disappointment. From the corner of my eye, I glanced at Anna and silently wondered if she was going to want me to make love to her again tonight. Every part of my body hoped that she did. The girl literally blew my mind. Last night and this morning was the best sex I'd ever had in my life, and I'd savoured every last second of it in case I never got to do it again.

In a way, Anna had ruined me. I couldn't even look at other girls anymore; they were nothing in comparison to her. She was just incredible inside and out and what we had was more than just sex, it was everything that was good in my world. Being that close to her and knowing she would never allow another in my place made me feel as if I were the only man in the world.

When we got to my apartment, it was a little after one in the morning. "Hey, wanna play PlayStation?" Anna chirped.

I grinned; she honestly was the perfect girl. "Yeah, if you want to."

Nate jumped over the side of the sofa. "First game!" he called excitedly. I rolled my eyes; he was such a kid at times.

"You two play first, I'm gonna go change," Anna suggested. As she walked past me, she trailed her hand across my ass teasingly. I had the strong urge to follow her into the bedroom, but I wasn't sure she'd want that. Instead, I plopped down onto the sofa next to Nate. We were in the middle of a mission on Grand Theft Auto when Anna walked out of the bedroom. She'd let her hair down so it fell messily around her shoulders. She had on one of my T-shirts and nothing else. Her long, toned legs were bare and begging to be touched. I couldn't take my eyes off her.

"Holy shit, come sit by me, Anna," Nate suggested, smirking at her and patting the chair next to him. Jealousy reared its ugly head, as it kept doing when he hit on her, so before I knew what I was doing, I'd punched him in the arm.

Anna giggled and shook her head. "I'm gonna make a sandwich or something, you two want anything?"

"Yeah, sounds good. You need a hand?" I asked, silently adding 'or any other body part' on the end.

"Nah, I think I got it, Pretty Boy," she smiled her sexy smile and disappeared into the kitchen.

Instantly, Nate turned to me with wide eyes. "How the hell do you cope with that all the time?" he asked, shaking his head.

"Cope with what?"

"With dating Anna. I mean, damn, she's so hot, I'd just want to bone her all day. You really like her, huh?" he questioned. He wasn't teasing, which was surprising.

"Yeah, I'm so totally in love with her that it's not even funny."

"You'd better not screw this up, bud, because seriously, I'm gonna ask her out if you do," he said, looking at me warningly. His serious expression told me he wasn't joking.

"I won't screw it up," I promised. I just prayed that at the end of my assignment she'd still want to be around me.

"Good, because I really like this one, I think she's a keeper."

"Who's a keeper?" Anna asked as she strutted back into the room with a plate of sandwiches, which she set on the coffee table.

"This girl on the game," Nate lied quickly.

Anna looked at the screen, and a little frown lined her forehead because we were driving down the street in a stolen police car, no girl in sight. She picked up a sandwich and sat next to me, swinging her legs up into my lap. My attention was now solely on her bare legs and not on the game at hand so, of course, I was killed within a minute and passed my controller on to her. The position certainly wasn't helping with my inappropriate arousal that seemed to happen all the time around her, and she was sure to feel it poking her in the leg but, thankfully, she didn't mention it.

Unable to resist, I traced my hand up her leg, marvelling over the feel of her soft skin. My heart started to race as my hand reached her inner thigh. Her leg twitched, and her breath seemed to catch in her throat as she looked at me and sank her teeth into her bottom lip. I gulped loudly as she sat up and manoeuvred herself onto my lap. Her hand fisted into the back of my hair as her eyes locked on mine. The pure, unadulterated lust that I saw on her face sent shockwaves through my whole body. She leant in, pressing her chest against mine tightly as her mouth inched towards mine before stopping a hairsbreadth away.

"Bedroom, Agent Taylor. Now." Her lips brushed against mine as she spoke.

I grinned, catching on immediately. "Yes, ma'am," I answered, taking the controller from her hand and tossing it to a shocked and envious Nate. I gripped her pert little ass and pushed myself up off the sofa, taking her with me. Her lips crashed against mine as I carried her to the bedroom and kicked the door closed behind me.

As the kiss deepened, I pressed her against the wall. My fingers dug into her thighs, trying to cope with the sheer luxury of having her body wrapped around mine again. Slightly confused as to what she wanted, I broke the kiss and put my forehead to hers. "Anna, what are-"

Her lips pressed against mine, silencing me before I could voice my question fully. Her hands immediately went to my belt buckle, pulling on it frantically. My excitement bumped up another level as she wrenched the buttons open and slipped her hand inside, releasing my now painful erection. I groaned as her small hand wrapped around me tightly.

"Now, please, right now," she begged breathlessly.

I nodded and fumbled in my pocket, pulling out my wallet intending to find the condoms that I'd purchased from the bathroom of the club, but her mouth closed over mine and she shifted her hips on me, crushing herself against me tightly.

"What are you waiting for, you want me to beg?" she asked breathlessly.

I grinned against her lips. "That would be pretty hot," I admitted.

Her teeth sank into my bottom lip in reprimand as her thighs tightened around my waist. I chuckled wickedly, but her hand started stroking my erection gently and I knew I was done for. Now almost desperate, I dropped my wallet carelessly and took hold of her hips, lifting her higher and positioning myself at her entrance. I could feel the heat that was waiting to envelop me. I held my breath, waiting for the intense pleasure of her as I pushed her panties to the side and pulled her down onto me, forcing my body inside hers. She threw her head back, accidentally banging it on the wall behind her as she moaned my name. I hissed through my teeth as her inner muscles instantly gripped me in a vice-like grip. She fitted me like a glove. It was like she was made for me. Slipping one arm under her ass, I held her still as I used my free hand to tug off the T-shirt that she was wearing. She squeezed herself tighter to me, forcing me in another inch, taking my whole length inside her. The pleasure of her was so immense that it was almost dizzying.

She gasped and gripped the back of my head as she pressed her forehead to mine, looking me directly in the eye as she spoke. "This still counts as last night."

Disappointment rushed through me at the thought of not being with her like a real boyfriend tomorrow, but the disappointment soon faded as she shifted her hips, making me move inside her.

I groaned and lifted her hips, starting up a rhythm that seemed to suit her. I kissed her passionately, wishing I could make her love me like I loved her – even half as much would still be more than I thought it was possible to love anyone. I loved her with everything I had; everything that was important to me just disappeared in a puff of smoke when she came into my life. I would do absolutely anything for her. She felt something for me too, deep down I knew it, but she was just scared of getting hurt again. I could wait though; I'd wait as long as she needed.

Her inner muscles started to tighten with each thrust; it was getting harder to move inside her as her moans became louder and more frequent. Suddenly her hips bucked and her whole body jerked as her eyes squeezed shut. Her inner walls tightened and convulsed around me, trying to force me to finish too, but I couldn't allow that to happen. In the back of my mind, I was acutely aware that I hadn't put on a condom, so I needed to be careful. At the tip of her climax, she gasped my name. The sound of it made my heart ache. I panted through her orgasm, trying to remain in control as the pleasure of her coming apart at my touch was becoming almost too much to bear.

Once her body started to relax and she slumped against me, I held her still against me and carried her over to the bed. Laying her down gently, I pulled out of her and just stared down at her in awe. She was gasping for breath with a look of pure pleasure and happiness stretched across her face. Pride swelled inside me that I had made her, the broken and emotionless girl, feel happy. Reaching out, I snagged my camera from the side and took a picture of her face.

"Hey! What are you doing?" she protested, trying to grab it from my hands.

I smiled and held it out of reach. "I just love that look on your face, and if I'm not gonna get to see it again after this trip, then I want to be able to have a picture of it," I explained, shrugging. I didn't need a photo though, I was confident that I'd be able to see that face every time I closed my eyes. As she smiled up at me and ran her fingers through my hair, I silently wondered why I couldn't have met her four years ago before all that terrible stuff happened to her. Maybe then I could have stolen her from Jack, and she wouldn't be afraid to fall for me.

Suddenly her smile faded, replaced by a horrified expression. "Oh no! We didn't use a condom!"

I smiled reassuringly. "It's okay, I didn't finish." I brushed her hair from her sweaty forehead.

She gasped. "You didn't?" She looked both relieved and angry at the same time.

I winced, knowing that she was going to chew me out for not using a condom. "I was going to put one on, and then I got distracted. You said now, and I just, I don't know, I lost my thoughts. I remembered though, I didn't finish, it should be fine," I rambled, trying to explain my irresponsible act.

She put her hand over my mouth, stopping my garbled excuses. "Just shush," she whispered, lifting her head and brushing her nose up the side of mine. She gripped my shoulders and pushed me onto my back, moving to straddle me. "So you haven't finished?" she asked, grinning wickedly.

I shook my head, watching her, waiting for her reaction and scolding. Instead, she stood up on the bed above me, one foot either side of my hips. She unclasped her bra, sliding it off slowly, making my breath catch in my throat as her breasts came into view. She swung her bra on one finger teasingly before dropping it in my face. I groaned and moved the material quickly so I could watch her. She was grinning as she ran her hands across the waist of her panties before slipping her hand inside the hips of them, pulling them down slowly, running her hands down her legs as she did it. With every inch that the panties moved down, my heart rate seemed to speed up. With every inch of creamy flesh that her hands traced over, I felt my arousal heighten. She didn't once take her eyes from my face. This was killing me slowly; it was the hottest thing I'd ever seen in my life. I moaned as she kicked them off, standing stark naked above me, making my mouth water as she exposed all of her brilliance.

"Anna," I breathed, I couldn't summon any more words than that, my brain was like mush. Clearly I'd unleashed a sex-crazed freaking monster. Whatever the hell she was doing was almost painful. I gripped my hands around the back of her knees and pulled, making her knees buckle. She fell onto me, giggling. I could feel her naked skin pressing on every inch of my chest making me tingle with excitement. I ran my hands up her legs, from her knees, following the curves of her body, all the way up to her breasts.

She pushed herself up to sitting, straddling my chest, looking at me sternly, grabbing my hands from her body and pinning them above my head. She shook her head forcefully. "No, Agent Taylor, I'm in charge, and you'll do as you're told," she scolded, grinning wickedly. My stomach clenched and, impossibly, my dick got even harder.

"Yes, ma'am. I'm sorry, ma'am," I replied, knowing she'd like that.

She narrowed her eyes and moaned breathily. "That is so damn hot, Ashton," she purred, licking her lips slowly. I smiled at how turned on she was too, it seemed like she was loving this just as much as I was. "Now, where are your handcuffs, Agent?" she asked.

269

Holy fuck. "Seriously?" I asked breathlessly. My excitement was spiking to new heights at the thought alone.

"I'm serious, Agent. Where are your handcuffs?" she repeated, biting her lip.

"Over in my top drawer on the right," I answered quickly. I was so excited that I could barely breathe. She grinned and climbed off me, walking naked to my drawers. I watched her pert ass sway as she walked. The little red hickey that I'd put there the previous night actually made my mouth water. As she pulled the drawer open, she giggled excitedly as she reached in and produced my SWAT tactical waistcoat. Her eyes lit up as she looked back at me and raised one eyebrow as if silently asking my permission. I gulped and nodded. Almost instantly, she slipped it on and zipped it up. I groaned loudly because of how hot she looked in that. I'd never be able to look at my uniform the same way again. She sashayed her way back to me, crawling on all fours over the bed, her eyes playful. Every nerve in my body was on fire with desire as she climbed onto me, straddling me before kissing me deeply. She held up the handcuffs and smiled as she reached my hands, pushing them through the bars on my headboard before clipping the handcuffs around my wrists. I'd honestly never seen anything more beautiful than her sitting on top of me, wearing just my waistcoat, and that sexy smile.

She grinned at me wickedly. "I'm gonna go play PlayStation with Nate," she smiled teasingly, and I couldn't help but laugh.

"Don't you dare," I warned.

She laughed and put her finger to her chin, pretending to think. "Hmm, actually I think maybe I'll have more fun here with you," she purred. "I'm gonna tease you until you beg for mercy." She grinned wickedly, and I knew then that I would probably die before this night was over.

"As long as you fuck me after, I don't mind," I answered.

She bent forward, tracing her nose along the edge of my jaw. "Oh I will, don't you worry about that, Agent Taylor."

My heart was crashing in my chest. I loved this girl so much; I really wished she knew it.

Once she'd finished with me, she slumped down against my chest, pressing her face into my neck, breathing heavily. Our bodies were slick with sweat. I bit my lip when I wanted to confess my love for her, she really didn't need to know that.

I turned my head and kissed her temple, still feeling my heart fly in my chest. "That was freaking awesome," I muttered breathlessly. Annabelle Spencer certainly had a wild side, and although some of the time she'd looked a little insecure and had silently asked my permission for stuff, she had undoubtedly been liberated by what we had just done.

She sighed happily and ran her hands up my arms, pushing her hands through the bars of the headboard and interlacing our fingers. "Mmm," she mumbled.

I gripped her hands tightly, afraid to let go. The sad truth was that I wanted her forever, but she just had no idea.

After a few minutes, she raised her head and smiled lazily at me. "That was the most fun I've ever had," she whispered, kissing my mouth.

I grinned; she'd taken the words right out of my mouth. "I'm glad, Baby Girl. Now, can you take these damn cuffs off me so I can wrap my arms around you?" I asked, looking at her longingly. I needed to touch her, hold her, make the most of every second of her before this agreement was over.

She laughed and sat up on me. "Hmm, I'm not sure I want to let you go just yet. Where exactly did you put your camera?" she teased. I looked at her warningly, and she giggled. "Okay, okay. Where are the keys?" She bent down and kissed me, making my world spin faster. I needed to get these cuffs off and hold her, my whole body was aching for that closeness, that reassurance that I wasn't going to lose her.

"Same drawer where you got the cuffs," I mumbled against her lips. She climbed off me, looking somewhat reluctant, and went to the drawer. I glanced at the clock, shocked to see that it was quarter to three in the morning, which meant that we'd been at this for over an hour and a half.

She came back with the key, smiling teasingly. "So, what's it worth, Pretty Boy?"

"Whatever you want." I'd give her anything she asked for – not that I'd tell her that though because she already ran rings around me.

"How about I have a girls' night at our place when we get back," she blurted quickly, a hopeful expression on her face.

I looked at her curiously. *She wants some girlfriends over? I don't mind that.* "Sure." I shrugged. I was getting off easy with that one.

"You're not allowed to be there. You have to wait next door with Dean and Peter," she added, grimacing.

"What? No way, that's not happening!" I said sternly.

Her shoulders slumped with disappointment as she crawled to my side. "Please? Not all night, just for a couple of hours. Maybe a movie and some drinks?" she suggested, pouting and shooting me the face that I had serious issues saying no to.

I swallowed hard, trying not to give in. "Anna, I can't do that," I said apologetically praying she wouldn't keep asking.

She sighed sadly, and my heart sank. I hated telling her no. "Okay, never mind, it was just a thought," she muttered, reaching out and unlocking my hands.

As soon as I was free, I grabbed her into a hug and rolled to my side, pulling her close to me. I ignored the fact that her naked body fitted perfectly against mine and that her breasts were pressed tight against my chest. "Please don't be upset, Baby Girl. I just can't let that happen," I whined, feeling awful.

"I know. I shouldn't have asked. I just wanted to be a normal girl for a change. Don't worry about it; it was a stupid idea anyway. I knew you wouldn't go for it," she shrugged, smiling weakly, but it was a forced smile and I could see the disappointment in her eyes, even though she was trying to disguise it.

I groaned, knowing I shouldn't allow it but not being able to stand the look on her face. It wasn't even as if she was asking for the world, it was only a couple of girls. I'd just have to pray her father didn't hear about it, otherwise I'd be in trouble for neglecting my duties.

"Okay fine," I agreed. "But not all night," I added quickly.

Her head snapped up. "Seriously?" A smile crept onto her lips and her eyes widened with excitement.

I grinned; I loved seeing her happy. "Seriously," I confirmed, nodding and hooking my leg over hers, pulling her closer to me.

She kissed me gratefully. "Thank you so much, Ashton. I really appreciate it, I know you're gonna hate doing it," she said, looking a little guilty.

"I know, but it's worth it to see that look on your face." I would walk through fire to see that look on her face.

She kissed me again before pulling back and resting her head on my chest. I sighed and ran my hands down her back, relishing in the feel of her naked skin against the pads of my fingers. But a nagging sensation in my bladder had to ruin the moment. "I need to pee. I won't be long," I whispered. She nodded and moved off me, curling onto her side. I smiled at her as she started to fall asleep almost immediately; she looked so peaceful and adorable. I sighed happily and pulled on a pair of boxers, heading out to the bathroom.

"Finally, you two are finished," Nate said, smirking at me. He was still sitting in the exact same spot, playing the same game.

I grinned. "Yeah, she's a freaking beast," I replied, laughing quietly at how much that statement just didn't even begin to describe Anna and what had just happened to me. I ran my fingers through my hair and turned to go to the bathroom.

"Wow, Taylor, she got you a bit there," Nate called, laughing and nodding at the scratches on my back.

I shrugged. "That was last night."

He pointed to my hand and frowned. "What the hell happened to your wrists? Those look like handcuff marks!" he stated, frowning. I looked down to see a small red ring around each wrist; it was my own fault from where I was pulling, trying to get my hands out so that I could touch her.

I smiled wickedly. "None of your business, man. A gentleman never tells."

His eyes widened in awe. "Screw that, you're not a gentleman! We always share details," he whined.

I laughed and shook my head. "Not this time. She's not some one night stand, Nate; she wouldn't want me to say anything."

I said goodnight to Nate and slunk my way back to the bedroom. I looked at her sleeping form for a few minutes, feeling the love simmer inside me. I sighed and flicked off the light, pulling my boxers back off. I figured that if she was sleeping naked, then I could too. I climbed in the bed next to her, and she instantly shifted in her sleep so I could wrap my arms around her.

"Mmm," she mumbled as she snuggled into my chest.

"I love you," I whispered, knowing she was asleep. I quite often told her when she was asleep; saying it out loud made me feel better.

"Mmm. Love you too," she murmured, tightening her arms around me.

My heart stopped. *What the… did she just say that to me?* I shifted so I could look at her, she was definitely asleep. "Anna, are you talking to me?" I asked quietly.

She didn't answer, she was sound asleep.

I sighed and closed my eyes. All I could think about was those three little words she had said. *Love you too.* They sounded incredible in her voice, and I would kill to hear them again. My heart was trying to escape out of my chest, and my stomach was clenched up tight. She wouldn't have been talking to me though, I was being stupid, she was probably dreaming about Jack or something. Disappointment washed over me, killing my happy mood and making me feel slightly nauseous. I sighed and kissed her forehead, snuggling into her warm naked body, making the most of my time with the most perfect girl in the world.

Chapter Twenty-Six

When I woke in the morning, my eyes still stung with tiredness. It had taken me hours to fall into slumber because I couldn't stop thinking about what she'd said while she was asleep. A quick glance at the clock showed me that it was almost ten in the morning. I decided that I needed to wake her. We only had a few hours left before we needed to head out to the airport, and I wanted to spend some more time with her here. It felt different being just the two of us here with no other guards; it was more like we were a real couple. Of course, I had still been extremely vigilant and doing my job as well as I would normally, but I didn't want to leave here and go back to the reality of being just her bodyguard and nothing more. I'd had a taste of what it would truly be like now, and I wanted it so badly that I would do anything for it.

"Baby Girl, it's time to wake up," I whispered, reluctantly untangling my body from hers and moving my hips back so that she wouldn't notice my inappropriate morning glory.

She stirred and snuggled back into my embrace. "Mmm, I'm still tired," she mumbled, kissing my shoulder.

"We'd better get up, it's almost ten. We need to pack and stuff."

She pulled the pillow out from under her head and hit me with it. "Shh, still tired!"

I laughed as she pressed the pillow over her face, blocking out the light. "Want another half an hour then?" I offered.

"Mmm hmm," she confirmed, rolling to put her head on my chest. "Wait, why the hell am I naked?" she asked quietly, a couple of seconds later.

Oh my God. Was she drunk last night? Shit! Did I take advantage of her? "Anna, I thought… we… you… we were," I stuttered, lost for words.

She laughed and pinched my stomach playfully. "I'm just kidding, I won't be forgetting last night in a hurry."

274

My body relaxed as I shook my head in reprimand. "Damn it, that wasn't funny! I thought I'd taken advantage of you or something."

She giggled. "You were the one in handcuffs, so I'd say I took advantage of you."

I laughed and trailed my hands down her back, savouring the feel of her skin against mine as I looked at her hopefully. "So, last night was a one off again then? Nothing's changed?"

She bit her lip and squirmed uncomfortably. "Ashton, nothing can change. I thought we agreed." She swallowed loudly. "We both got something out of it, didn't we?" She frowned nervously as her fingers traced patterns on my stomach.

I sighed and nodded. "Yeah, we both got something out of it. It's fine. Forget I said anything. From now on then, we're back to normal. What happens in LA stays in LA, yeah?" I suggested jokingly, trying to lighten the mood. I'd made her happy, I'd given her what she wanted, so I'd just have to live with it and be thankful that I had my time with her. I could wait until she was ready; she was letting me closer and closer with every day. I still had time to make her fall for me before the end of my assignment.

"Yeah, and I loved LA," she flirted.

That sounded so much like the words from last night that my insides squirmed. "I loved LA too." I loved it more than I could ever tell her. "So, what were you dreaming about last night?" I probed, trying to go for the casual approach in finding out if she'd been talking to me when she said those three little words.

She shrugged and pushed herself up to a sitting position, holding the sheets to her chest. "No idea, why?"

"You were talking in your sleep," I explained.

She raised one eyebrow inquisitively. "Really? What did I say?"

"You said something about Jack," I lied. "Were you dreaming about him?" I asked, hoping to be able to get the answer I wanted without having to ask outright.

She pursed her lips, obviously thinking back. But then she shrugged. "I honestly don't know. Maybe, but I don't usually dream of Jack unless it's a nightmare," she winced.

I sighed and pulled her back down next to me. My heart was thumping wildly in my chest. If she didn't usually dream of Jack, then was she talking to me last night? Deep down I knew that she may have heard me say it and subconsciously thought I was Jack. I'd probably never know so I should stop stewing over it before it drove me crazy. "You didn't have a nightmare, Baby Girl. I just thought I heard you say Jack, that's all."

She shrugged one shoulder. "I don't remember dreaming anything."

I smiled. That answer was good enough for me.

"I'm gonna go make you some breakfast. Do you want scrambled eggs or something? I'm in the mood for something hot." She climbed out of the bed and pulled on my boxer shorts and shirt that I'd worn the previous night.

A lump formed in my throat. She looked seriously hot in my clothes. I laughed at my excited body, and she looked at me weirdly. "I think that is the sexiest outfit I've ever seen you wear," I explained, raking my eyes over her slowly, taking in every delicious inch of her.

She looked down at herself and laughed incredulously. "Yeah, okay, Ashton." She shook her head dismissively, blowing me a kiss at the door as usual and heading to the kitchen.

Once I was alone, I looked down at my crotch and sighed heavily. Another cold shower was needed. They were becoming pretty normal for me in the last two months. As much as I loved waking up next to the girl of my dreams, a wood that wouldn't go away and aching balls really wasn't something that I enjoyed very much.

After an extremely quick shower, I dressed and then headed out of my bedroom, stopping in the kitchen doorway. I leant on the door frame watching Anna make breakfast in my oversized clothes. I'd never seen anything so sexy in my life – and Nate obviously thought that too because he was leaning over the counter, watching her legs while she cooked with her back to him.

"So, do you have a sister you could hook me up with?" he asked her.

"Nope, and even if I did, I wouldn't let you hook up with her," Anna replied, laughing.

"Hey, why the hell not?" he cried, sounding a little hurt.

"Because you're a player, and players break girls' hearts," she answered, shrugging, totally oblivious to him checking her out.

"Well Ashton's a player too, and you're dating him," he countered. I got a little uneasy at that statement. I'd changed; there was no way I was going back to that life again. I wanted her and only her.

"Well, Ashton's special," she answered. I smiled at that.

"Special, huh? You love him?" Nate asked.

Her back stiffened as her hand stilled on the eggs she was stirring on the stove. "Do you want two slices of toast?" she asked, totally avoiding the question.

Please say yes, please say yes! My head was screaming, begging her to answer the question.

"Don't change the subject; do you love my best friend? I need to know what your intentions are, young lady," Nate teased, using a father figure tone of voice.

She shrugged. "We've been going out for two months. That's not long enough to fall in love with someone." Her tone was uncomfortable and tight.

"He loves you," Nate stated.

Fuck! What did you say that for? Shut the hell up, big mouth! That was the second time he'd told her I was in love with her this weekend.

She shook her head, moving three plates onto the counter next to her as she started to butter the toast. "No he doesn't, he just thinks he does. He doesn't know what a bitch I am; when he finds out, he'll leave me. They all do. I'm cursed," she joked, laughing.

"Well, if he does, you give me a call," Nate replied, looking over her legs again.

As I stood there, dumbfounded, I slowly processed what she'd said. Clearly she still thought I was going to leave her. Maybe if I showed her I wasn't going to, then she'd finally open up to me.

Clearing my throat, I stepped into the room, forcing a smile. She grinned at me, her eyes twinkling with that little spark that she'd had all weekend. As I got to Nate's side, I slapped him on the back of the head. "Stop staring, it's rude."

He groaned and rubbed the back of his head, wincing. "Shit, Taylor, when the hell are you leaving? I'm gonna come out of this weekend covered in bruises!" he whined.

I grinned and sat on the stool next to his. "About four," I answered, pouring myself a glass of milk.

Anna smiled as she set a steaming pile of eggs in front of me. My stomach growled and my mouth watered as the smell wafted up. As we all dug in, Anna sat next to me. "What are we doing today?" she asked.

I shrugged. "I don't know. Whatever you want. We need to pack though and leave for the airport about four, but we'll have a few hours here at least."

She pursed her lips and nodded. "We don't need the car for the next hour or so, do we?"

"I guess not," I answered, confused as to where this was going.

Anna grinned and closed her hand over the keys to the rental car, sliding them across the counter towards Nate. "Go on then, Nate, knock yourself out," she chirped.

He gasped. His eyes widened in shock. "You're kidding me. Seriously?" he asked, grinning and jumping off his stool, abandoning his half eaten breakfast.

"Sure," she agreed. "And don't worry about scratching it or anything, it's in Ashton's name," she joked, winking at him.

I scoffed and shook my head quickly. "You'd better freaking worry about scratching it!" I warned.

He actually giggled like a little girl as he practically ran for the front door. "I'll be careful," he promised, slamming the door behind him.

I groaned. "I love that car," I whined, making Anna laugh.

She chuckled and stood up, scraping the last bits of her food into the trashcan before turning back to me. "So what shall we do for our last couple of hours?"

Deciding to make the most of our last few hours of freedom, I strode over to her and grabbed her waist, lifting her easily and throwing her over my shoulder. She squealed and giggled as I carried her into the lounge and plopped her onto the sofa. "Cuddling, making out and getting naked sounds good," I answered, settling myself down at her side.

She giggled and poked me in the ribs, which just started a tickle war that she most certainly lost before she begged me to stop, claiming she was about to pee herself. Happier than I had been in a long time, I settled down on the sofa next to her, just breathing her in as we talked about nothing in particular. In the back of my mind, I knew that I had to be the luckiest guy in the world because Annabelle Spencer was in my arms.

When the sound of the front door opening cut through the happy cloud I seemed to be floating on, my heart took off in a sprint. Reacting instinctively, I jumped up and wrenched my gun from my ankle holster, pointing at the door ready to shoot if it was Carter or one of his men.

Instead though, Nate gasped and his hands flew up innocently. "Whoa shit! It's me. Damn it, Ashton, calm down!" he shouted, shaking his head in disbelief.

I recoiled quickly, immediately clicking on the safety on my gun. "Shit, sorry, I wasn't expecting you back so soon," I admitted sheepishly.

"Soon? Dude, I've been gone an hour," he grumbled, frowning at me as if I'd lost my mind.

"Oh, I didn't realise," I admitted, running a hand through my hair. I hadn't realised we'd been cuddling and talking for that long. My eyes flicked down to Anna; she was sitting up, seemingly frozen in place, her eyes wide, and her mouth agape. I knelt down next to the sofa and shook my head. "I'm sorry, Baby Girl. Are you okay?"

She nodded, finally closing her mouth. She pushed herself up to her feet, not looking at me. "I'm gonna go take a shower."

As she walked off, my gaze dropped to her hands, noticing that they were shaking. I frowned, hating myself because I'd frightened her. Following her up the hallway, I slapped Nate on the shoulder apologetically. My hand closed over hers as she got to the bathroom. "Are you really okay? I'm so sorry that I scared you. It was a shock, I wasn't expecting anyone, I just reacted," I explained.

She nodded. Her face was pale, and her eyes were a little vacant. "It's fine."

I traced my hands up her arms, gripping her shoulders. "If it's fine, then why are you shaking all over?"

A tear escaped down her face. "I… I just thought, when you jumped up like that, I thought for a second he was there and he'd come back for me," she whispered. Her lip trembled as she spoke.

I groaned, looking up the hallway to see that Nate was watching us curiously. I couldn't have this conversation in front of him. Reaching behind her, I pushed the bathroom door open and guided her in there, closing the door tightly behind me. "He won't hurt you again, I promise. You don't need to be scared anymore. I won't ever let him hurt you," I vowed, kissing the top of her head as I pulled her in for a hug. She nodded and clung to me tightly. "I'm so sorry I upset you, this is my fault."

She shook her head quickly. "It's not your fault, it's mine. I'm such a stupid idiot." She pulled away from me and swiped at her face roughly, wiping the telltale tears away.

"You're not an idiot, Baby Girl. You're perfect." I hated the way she thought of herself so badly. She always seemed to turn everything bad around and make it her own fault. It was no wonder she didn't cope particularly well sometimes; she shouldered too much guilt and blame.

She sniffed and looked over at the shower. I took that as my cue to leave and dipped my head, kissing her cheek before walking to the door. "I'll just be outside," I muttered.

"Wait!" she called just as my hand closed around the door handle. "I don't want to be on my own. Will you stay with me?" she begged. "Please? Just sit on the toilet or something."

She wanted me to stay in here while she was in the shower? "Er, yeah, sure okay," I replied, nodding. I made my way over and sat on the toilet, watching as she brushed her teeth before turning on the shower. I groaned internally because I was about to be in the same room with her, naked. As my shirt that she wore fluttered to the floor, I closed my eyes so that I wouldn't see.

"You're really going to sit on the toilet with your eyes closed?" she chuckled weakly.

"Mmm hmm," I mumbled, not trusting my voice to speak. The sound of the water changed, so I knew she was under the spray. I put my head in my hands and tried to think of something else other than the water caressing her flawless body. This felt like torture.

"Ashton?"

"Yeah?"

"We're still in LA, you know," she giggled.

My body jerked. *Does that mean what I think it means?* "And?" I prompted, not wanting to get my hopes up.

"And, get your hot ass in this shower with me and make me think about something nice instead of what I'm thinking about right now."

I stood so quickly that I almost stumbled as my hands went to the bottom of my T-shirt. She didn't need to ask me twice. Once naked, I stepped into the shower and groaned because of how stunning she looked.

She smiled weakly. "That was fast," she teased.

"Well, that was an offer I couldn't refuse," I answered, my voice husky and thick with lust. I watched as the water ran down her body, caressing every inch of her. She gave me a sexy smile and stepped back further into the spray, holding out one hand towards me. I gripped her trembling hand, vowing to take her mind off what happened even if it killed me.

The day passed incredibly fast. While she packed her clothes, I hung out with Nate in the lounge. Although we were playing a video game, I couldn't keep my mind off the hot, little shower scene that had gone down hours before. I'd probably never be able to take a shower again without thinking of it. That was another thing she'd ruined for me.

Suddenly, Nate groaned and looked down at his watch. "I have to leave for work. Where's that sexy ass of a girlfriend you have? I want to say goodbye."

"Bedroom, packing." I pushed myself up and he followed me into the bedroom, where she was still gathering stuff up. I noticed that she'd started packing my clothes for me too.

"Hey, Anna, I've got to go to work now. It was really good to meet you," Nate said, walking up to her with his arms out. I stiffened, knowing that she wouldn't want to be that close to him.

I saw her hold her breath as she hugged him. "Yeah, you too, Nate. Thanks for letting me stay in your bachelor pad."

He grinned wolfishly. "You know what, you can come and stay anytime you want." He turned back to me, slapping me on the arm. "Seriously, Taylor, bring her back here, she's a lot of fun." I could tell by the way he said it that he'd meant it, he genuinely liked Anna.

"I will," I confirmed. I would certainly be working on her, trying to convince her to come back here with me in her next scheduled school break. Hopefully her father would go for it a second time, seeing as this trip was so successful.

He gave me a hug and slapped me hard on the back. "I'll give you a call, we can arrange a time for playing," he chirped excitedly. I grinned and nodded in agreement, thinking lovingly about my PS4 that I had waiting for me at our apartment.

"Yeah, definitely. I'll call you."

Anna smiled and waved as he left the room, closing the door behind him. "Nate's a great guy. I can see why you like him."

"Yeah, he's cool, all the girls think so," I replied, grinning at her.

"Hmm, that's funny; he just doesn't do it for me," she winked at me, and we both laughed and packed up our belongings. Before we left the apartment, I took a few shots of the place. I already had the exact pictures that I wanted on here. There were at least fifteen good photos of me and Anna, and more than that of just her on her own, looking like a goddess.

On the way to the airport, we stopped by Denny's to get another chilli cheese dog. That was another thing I would miss about LA. Before we boarded, I called Dean to make sure that he knew where and when to meet us on the other side of the flight. Once everything was set, we were ushered through and seated in first class. As soon as we were in the comfy chairs, she scooted closer to me and I wrapped my arm around her tightly. Within minutes, my eyes became heavy due to my lack of sleep the previous night.

When I knew I couldn't fight it anymore, I rested my head back on the chair and just let myself doze.

"Ashton, help me please!" she begs. I can hear that she's crying, her breathing is hitching somewhere off in the darkness, but I can't see her. I turn, running in the direction that I think she is, but I can't find her. Doors and corridors stretch off into the distance, and her crying seems to echo from the walls so I can't get a sense of direction. The place is like a maze. "Please, he's coming. Please help me!" she screams.

Desperation makes me feel sick as I run and run, crashing through door after door, trying to get to her. "I can't find you, Anna! Where are you?" I shout, spinning in a little circle as I grip my hands into my hair, totally panic stricken.

"Please help me," her voice is a whisper and it breaks my heart as I start running aimlessly again.

A wicked laugh echoes down the corridor and my hair stands up on the back of my neck as I hear his voice. "Well hello, Princess, long time no see."

I jerked up, gasping for breath as my hand shot straight down to my ankle, fumbling as I reached for my gun. But it wasn't there, my holster was empty. I'd had to check it in, so it was locked in a little box in the cockpit with the pilot because of the standard air travel procedure. Sweat beaded on my brow as I looked around quickly, realising that I wasn't in some darkened maze trying to find her; I was, in fact, still sitting in first class. Anna looked up at me worriedly, her sketchpad balanced on her knees.

"Ashton, what's wrong?"

"Nothing, Baby Girl. I just had a bad dream." As soon as I said it, I wished I hadn't.

"Really, what about?" she asked, snuggling against me. Her touch made my panic fade marginally.

I grasped wildly at anything that wasn't to do with Carter. "Car crash."

She recoiled, scrunching her nose up. "Maybe I should drive when we land," she replied, raising one eyebrow teasingly.

I shook my head and laughed, feeling my tense body relaxing. "No. You were driving in my dream."

She slapped my chest playfully. "I'm not a bad driver!"

"Yeah right, I won't trust you to drive our kids around," I joked.

She poked me in the side playfully. "I'm not having your babies, Pretty Boy."

I shrugged casually. "Hopefully you'll change your mind. I still have time to make you fall for me. I predict we'll be engaged within a year," I teased, pulling her body closer to mine, noticing how she tensed at my words.

Her forehead creased with a frown as her eyes tightened. "You still under the impression that I'm gonna fall in love with you?" she replied sarcastically.

"I'm hoping." I smiled and couldn't help but laugh; if she knew I was serious, she'd freak the hell out! Knowing I needed to change the subject before she saw though my playful joke that wasn't actually a joke, I nodded at her sketchpad. "What you drawing?"

She smiled and turned it around so I could see. On the page was a perfectly drawn portrait of Nate and me sitting on the sofa in my apartment.

"That's incredible." What she could do with a piece of paper and a pencil amazed me.

"Thanks," she nudged my shoulder with hers. "So, that girls' night…" she trailed off, looking at me hopefully.

I suppressed my groan and forced a smile. I had agreed to it after all, so there was no backing out now. "Yeah, whenever you want."

She beamed at me and her whole face seemed to light up. "I'll talk to them about it tomorrow then, maybe we'll arrange it for Friday night?" she suggested, watching my face.

I nodded and looked away so she didn't see that panic that was starting to burn inside me at the thought of leaving her alone. Technically, I wasn't allowed to leave her alone if there was someone else with her, but I would be right next door. I could maybe have a background check done on them before they came, just to make sure nothing flagged up. Today was only Sunday, so I had a few days to get some searches run before Friday. I'd definitely keep that secret though, she'd probably kill me if she knew I was screening her friends.

Chapter Twenty-Seven

~ Anna ~

As I slowly started to wake up on Saturday morning, I realised my head was pounding. I groaned and put my hands up to my head, squeezing my temples, trying to get the pain to subside. The previous night had been girls' night, and I had certainly made the most of it. Though my head was now telling me that there had been way too much giggling, pizza, popcorn and vodka.

"Suffering?"

I groaned again because of the loud voice that was almost gloating near my ears. I squeezed my eyes shut tighter, nodding. He laughed and my ears instantly rang. "Shh!" I mumbled, rolling onto my front, pressing the pillow over my head. "Ugh, don't let me drink ever again!" I moaned.

He laughed, and the mattress dipped next to me. "Here, I brought these in for you, I thought you'd be a little delicate this morning," he whispered, sounding amused. I lifted the pillow off my head to see him sitting up, fully dressed, holding out a glass of water and two pills.

"Thanks," I mumbled gratefully, pushing myself up and swallowing them quickly. Looking down at myself, I saw that I was still wearing my shirt that I had on last night. My jeans were in a pile on the floor though. I didn't even remember coming to bed, but clearly I'd been too intoxicated for pyjamas.

Ashton smiled widely. "Come on then, get up and get dressed, I'm taking you out for breakfast to make you feel better."

I looked him over while he spoke. He looked super sexy today. He had on a pair of light blue ripped jeans and a white T-shirt with a black hoodie over the top. I swallowed my wave of desire quickly. It had been almost a week since we'd been back from LA, and keeping things on a purely friends' level had been a struggle. Now that I knew how good being with him could be, I couldn't help but wish for it to happen again and again, but we were managing to move past it and behave in a respectable manner.

"You look nice today," I muttered, lying back down and throwing my arm over my eyes to keep out the light.

He laughed and lay down next to me. "Are you still drunk? I thought you would have cut out the flirting now that you aren't stumbling all over the place," he teased, moving my arm and smirking at me.

I shook my head. "Was I drunken flirting with you again?" I asked, smiling apologetically.

"Oh yeah, Baby Girl. After I carried you to bed, you begged me to fuck your brains out, you cursed angrily because my belt buckle wouldn't unfasten and, therefore, must have been made by ugly goblins that didn't agree with sex, and then in the end you made me go to sleep right on top of you when I turned you down," he said, chuckling.

I smiled sheepishly, feeling a blush creep up my face and neck. "Sorry. I guess I forget myself when I'm drunk."

He grinned and nodded in agreement. "Don't worry though, I was a perfect gentleman. I didn't even let you blow me like you were begging."

I squealed and threw my hands over my face. "Oh God, stop. There's a reason that people don't remember these things in the morning, you're not supposed to remind me! The alcohol induced memory loss is a form of protection from all the stupid things you did the night before."

He chuckled wickedly. "Alright, fine. I won't say another word." He sat up. "Can we go eat? I'm starving."

I sat up and winced as the movement made my head a little fuzzy. "You're always starving," I teased. He grinned and leant in, planting a soft kiss on my forehead before standing up and leaving the room.

Forgoing the shower because I didn't have the energy, I dressed and then put on a large pair of shades to keep the brightness of the day out of my eyes.

"Hey, you ready?" he chirped as I walked out of the bedroom. I nodded, picking up my purse. "I'm in the mood for bacon, what about you?" he asked, taking my hand and interlacing our fingers.

I shrugged. "Anything, as long as it's greasy and bad for me."

In the local café that was a five minute drive away from our apartment, I ordered a huge plate of bacon and eggs, and surprisingly, it did make me feel better. Or maybe that was the two espressos that I had to accompany it.

"So, about our date tonight, I know where I want to go. Make sure you dress casual and warm, and no heels," Ashton instructed, grinning as we waited for the waitress to bring his change. I frowned. Our date night was usually on a Friday, but because I'd had my girls' night, we'd shifted our date to tonight instead.

I cocked my head to the side. "Where are we going?"

He shook his head, smiling teasingly. "Surprise."

"Oh come on, tell me, please?" I whined. I hated surprises, and he knew it.

"Nope," he answered, popping the p. The bell above the door rang, signalling someone either coming in or leaving the café. His eyes flicked to the door and his body stiffened. I glanced over my shoulder in time to see a group of five guys walking in. They were all loud and boisterous, like they were still drunk or high from the night before. "You ready to go?" he asked, still discreetly watching the group of guys as they started harassing a couple of women a couple of tables away. I nodded, standing up. Ashton's hand wrapped around mine as he pulled me close to his back on the opposite side to the men than were laughing and jeering, pushing each other playfully.

When we were about four feet from the door, one of them stepped in front of us and smiled. "Leaving so soon?"

"Yeah, excuse us." Ashton smiled politely, tightening his grip on my hand.

"Well, maybe your lady would rather stay here," the guy suggested, smiling at me.

I snorted in disbelief. "No thanks."

Ashton shifted on the balls of his feet. "Seriously, bud, excuse us before you get yourself hurt," he growled. The guy laughed but stepped out of the way, waving us through. As soon as we walked past him, he grabbed my hand, yanking me backwards. My instincts took over and I turned, throwing my knee up into his groin. He groaned in pain and Ashton shoved me towards the door as one of the other guys stepped forward.

"Son of a bitch!" he ranted.

"Leave with Dean!" Ashton growled, pushing me towards the door again.

"What? No!" I cried, horrified. There was no way I was leaving him here with five guys.

"NOW, ANNA!" he ordered.

I flinched at the authority in his voice and quickly turned for the door. As soon as I was outside, I ran to Dean, who was about a hundred years away, leaning casually against the wall. "There's a fight. Go help him!" I shouted, pointing frantically at the café. I felt sick with worry. He was going to get hurt, I just knew it. My heart was pounding out of my chest.

Dean's eyes widened as he looked back at the café but didn't move. Suddenly he shook his head. "No. I need to take you away." His hand clamped around my elbow, starting to drag me forward.

What the hell? He's going to leave Ashton on his own? "Dean, what the hell are you doing? Ashton's in there with five guys!" I screamed, trying desperately to shake off his hold.

"Then I feel sorry for the five guys. My orders from him are to take you away if there's trouble," he replied simply.

I didn't want to hurt him, but if he carried on dragging me away then I was going to break his face. "For God's sake! You can't just leave him in there. Get the hell off me! Dean, will you stop? Ashton's in there on his own, please go and help him!" I shouted, struggling to a stop.

Another pair of hands gripped my hips, and I squealed from the shock. "Chill out, Baby Girl, I'm here," Ashton said in my ear.

My breath caught as my heart stuttered. I turned to face him and threw my arms around his neck, hugging him tightly. "What happened? Are you okay?" I asked, gripping onto him for dear life, probably choking the life out of him.

Instead of answering, his arms circled my waist and he lifted me off my feet. "Dean, let's get her to your car," he ordered. He moved one hand to my ass and forced my legs around his waist with the other as he started to jog in the direction of the car.

"I can walk, Ashton," I protested, unwrapping one of my legs, but he just hooked it back there again and continued to jog towards the parking lot where we'd left the cars.

"I know you can, just humour me, okay?" he countered, gripping me tightly. My breathing started to slow, and my stomach unclenched now that he was here with me. When we got to Dean's car, Ashton set me in the passenger seat and slammed the door, talking to Dean outside. I took the opportunity to look at every inch of his exposed skin, trying to see a red mark or blemish that indicated that he'd been injured, but there was nothing.

Suddenly, he slapped Dean on the shoulder and turned on his heel, running off towards the café again. I gasped and tried to open my door so I could follow him, but Dean pushed me back into the car and locked the door before running around to the driver's side.

"What's going on? Where's he going? Is he okay?" I shouted as he started the car, pulling out without even buckling his seatbelt.

"He's fine. Someone called the police, he needs to go and handle that. It's best that you're not there so he doesn't have to explain the whole undercover thing," he explained.

I gasped, looking back over my shoulder, hating that we were driving away and leaving him. "Someone called the police? Well, what happened?" I cried, wiping my face, I didn't even realise I was crying until I did that.

Dean shrugged. "He took care of it.

Took care of it? What the heck does that mean? There were five guys in there for goodness' sake! "What? How?"

286

Dean grinned and shook his head as if I'd said something silly. "Annabelle, he's an excellent Agent. You shouldn't worry about him."

I scowled at him. "I'd worry about you too, you know. I just don't think you should have left him like that! He wouldn't do that if that was you. He wouldn't have left you!" I ranted angrily.

He laughed loudly. "Annabelle, Ashton would kill me himself if it meant he could stop you from getting hurt. I have no doubt in my mind about that," he replied, still laughing.

I sighed angrily and looked out the window, not wanting to talk to him anymore. I hated the thought of Ashton just being left like that on his own. Anything could have happened to him, he could have been seriously hurt and that thought made my whole chest tighten with worry.

When we arrived at our apartment, Dean walked me in, doing a quick survey of the rooms to check they were empty before he left to wait outside the door. I sat down on the sofa and put my head in my hands. The silence was deafening as I sat there watching the clock tick around slowly. My nerves were making me feel sick. I couldn't seem to stop myself from crying silently as I imagined all of the horrible things that could have happened to Ashton today. I could barely breathe. Unconsciously, my hand went to the inside of my elbow, pinching and picking at the skin there as I tried to regain control of my emotions.

Well over an hour later, the front door opened. I jumped up with my heart crashing in my chest. My trembling legs barely supported me as I rushed around the corner and looked up the hallway. When I saw his black head of hair, I dashed to him, jumping on him. I obviously caught him off guard because he staggered back under my weight and we both crashed into the door with a loud bang. My lips slammed against his as I kissed him fiercely. He seemed shocked but kissed me back after a second or two, wrapping his arms around me as we slumped to the floor in a heap of tangled limbs.

"All I needed to do was get in a fight to have you throw yourself at me like this? I wish I'd known that two months ago," he joked. My tears were flowing uncontrollably again as I kissed every square inch of his face before burying my face in his neck and sobbing in relief that he was unharmed and safe. Thoughts of losing him, of him leaving me just like Jack did made my heart ache so much that it was almost unbearable. I dug my fingers into his shoulders as I pressed myself to him tightly, completely lost in my overwhelming emotions. "Hey, come on, Baby Girl. Shh, everything's okay," he said as he stroked my hair soothingly.

Suddenly anger boiled inside me as I realised that he'd made me feel like this. By not letting me stay and help him, he'd put me through this. It hadn't needed to be like this, I hadn't needed to feel this pain again.

I pulled back and smacked his chest as hard as I could which resulted in making my hand sting. "Don't ever do that to me again!" I shouted angrily. His mouth dropped open in shock as he looked at me like I'd lost my mind. "You stupid damn boy! Don't you realise how worried I was about you? You couldn't even wait long enough to tell me you were okay before running off?" I shouted, pushing myself off him as he opened and closed his mouth again, looking a little lost for words.

"Anna, calm down," he finally said, clambering to his feet. I scowled angrily. I was so mad that I didn't even want to look at him. I turned and stormed off to the bedroom, but he followed me in there. "That's my job," he said sternly.

"That's your job?" I repeated incredulously. "Your job is to leave me fucking worried sick about you? You couldn't have stayed there for one minute to show me you were okay? You couldn't have just left the car door open while you talked to Dean so I could hear what was going on?" I almost screamed. I was so angry that I wanted to smash something.

"Anna, calm down! My job is to get you as far away from trouble as possible," he countered, reaching for my hand.

I jerked it away from him before he could touch me, glaring at him. "There was no damn trouble! You carried me to the car like a fucking child!" I spat, wiping my traitor tears away angrily.

He threw his hands up in exasperation. "What the hell do you want me to say? Do you want me to apologise for doing my job?" he asked desperately.

I growled in frustration. "Oh, just go away, Ashton! Thank you for doing your job. Thank you for making sure I was safely away from trouble. Thank you for making me worry so damn hard about you that I felt sick. Thank you for thinking so little of me that it didn't even occur to you that I would be worried about you. Just thank you, Agent Taylor!" I shouted almost hysterically. My breathing was shallow. A full blown panic attack was building up inside me as the feelings of being powerless, abandoned, and helpless resurfaced and started trying to drag me under. My hand flew to my elbow that was already red raw from what I'd inflicted on myself earlier. Using my nails, I pinched the skin there as hard as I could, feeling them cutting into my flesh, but not caring in the slightest.

Ashton groaned and stepped forward, wrapping his arms around me and crushing me against his chest. "Please calm down, Baby Girl," he begged, gripping his hand into the back of my hair, holding my face against his neck securely. "I'm sorry. I should have stayed and showed you I was okay. I didn't think about that. All I could think about was my need to have you safe and as far away from trouble as possible," he whispered, rubbing my back soothingly. As if he knew what I was doing to myself, his hand closed over mine that was pinching my inner elbow and he pulled it away, guiding my arm around his waist instead. "Stop that," he whispered. "I'm fine, I promise. Please just breathe properly and calm down."

"I hate you," I mumbled against the skin of his neck.

"No, you don't," he whispered, pressing his mouth into my hair.

I sniffed and wrapped my arms around him tightly, letting his familiar smell fill my lungs. "I hate that I care about you," I admitted, digging my fingers into his back and pressing myself closer to him.

He laughed quietly. "I know." He kissed my temple softly.

I whimpered and clutched him tightly. "You're really okay?" I asked, trying to regain control of myself.

"Yeah, I promise. I'm so sorry, I didn't think," he whispered. His hands traced a circle on my back as my breathing started to slow. His arms wrapped around me, lifting me off my feet as he walked to the bed and sat down on the edge, pinning me on his lap and rocking me gently. When I pulled back to look at him, he smiled sadly and wiped my tears away with his thumbs. "I hate myself for making you cry."

I sniffed loudly as I took hold of his chin, turning his head one way and then the other, checking for bruises. "You really didn't get hurt?" I asked, finally satisfied as I pressed my forehead against his.

"I didn't get hurt."

I closed my eyes, and a little whimper left my lips. "Don't ever do that to me again. I was so worried about you. I started thinking all these terrible things, and imagining you being hurt. I couldn't stand to see anything happen to you, Ashton. Please, don't do that to me again," I begged quietly.

"I won't, I promise. I didn't mean to upset you," he whispered, holding me tightly, stroking my hair. He moved under me and took hold of my wrist, straightening my arm and looking down at the damaged skin on the inside of my elbow. A bruise had already formed, blood was just under the surface, and there were little scratches there oozing with blood from my nails digging into my flesh. "Jesus, Anna," he groaned, shaking his head. "Why do you-"

"Don't," I interjected. I reached up and tugged on the sleeve of my shirt, covering it as best I could. I didn't want to talk about it. I couldn't explain to him that sometimes pain was the only thing I could control in my life, or that pain was the constant that never left me, and was the one thing that made me think about something else when all else around me crumbled.

His eyes closed and his jaw tightened as his arms looped around me again, crushing me against him. Silence lapsed over us as I just let myself relax into his embrace. My body sagged against his with relief as I rested my head against his shoulder. I was emotionally drained.

"What happened in the café?" I asked a couple of minutes later.

He lay down and rolled onto his side, holding me tightly to his chest. "I arrested them," he said simply.

I couldn't help but laugh. There were five guys in there, all looking to smash his face in. "You're a badass," I chuckled. He just smiled and kissed my nose and we just lay there for a few minutes, looking at each other in silence. It was nice just being close to him, we only really did this at night time and then we were usually trying to go to sleep. After a couple of minutes, his cell phone rang.

He laughed and shook his head. "Wow, good timing, Dean," he grumbled, looking at the screen. He answered his phone, still holding me tightly. "Hey, what's up?" he asked, rolling his eyes. I didn't hear Dean's answer, but I felt Ashton's body jerk in response. "Really? Yep, okay, that's fine. Yeah, in a bit. Absolutely." He disconnected the call. His face was tight with worry, but he was trying to disguise it.

I smiled and reached out, brushing a lock of his hair back into place. "If I wasn't allowed to hear the conversation, maybe you should have gone outside," I said sarcastically, rolling my eyes at him.

He chuckled and rolled so that he was on top of me. "Hmm, you know you're not interested in the secret agent's stuff," he teased, smirking at me.

"Yep, totally boring stuff," I confirmed, gripping his hips with my knees, stopping him from going anywhere.

He laughed and brushed my hair back from my face tenderly, smiling at me. "So, about that date… shall we say seven?"

I sighed dramatically. "Can't you just tell me what it is now? You know I hate surprises."

"Nope," he answered, kissing my nose and pushing up off me.

I tightened my grip on his hips, smirking at him. "If you don't tell me, then I'm not letting go."

He shrugged as his emerald green eyes sparkled with mischief. "Hmm, well maybe I don't want you to let go. This is a kind of nice position to be in," he retorted, waggling his eyebrows.

"Pervert," I scolded, slapping his chest as I released my grip on him.

He stood, bending to grab my hands as he tugged me to my feet. "I'm only a pervert around you," he replied, laughing sheepishly.

"Yeah right, player." I scoffed sarcastically as he pulled me from the room.

"I'm not a player!" he protested.

"Mmm hmm, yeah, whatever."

As I turned to walk off, a small slap to my behind made me squeak in surprise. "I'm not a player! I'm a one woman man," he stated, shaking his head.

"Oh really? So that just means that you've never had a threesome?" I joked.

He rolled his eyes at my comment. "Miss Spencer, you are the only girl for me," he answered, bowing theatrically.

I giggled. "Whatever you say, boyfriend." I blew him a kiss and headed to the lounge to work on my project for school. I didn't bother to try to listen when he slipped out of the front door to talk to Dean about the secret agent's stuff that I wasn't allowed to know about.

~ Ashton ~

I smiled to myself. The word 'boyfriend' was bouncing around in my brain as I made my way to the door to go and speak to Dean. When I stepped into the hallway, I saw him standing there waiting for me, his face pale and worried.

I slapped his shoulder and took the letter from his hand, trying to appear unconcerned. "This it?" I asked, swallowing my anger. He nodded in confirmation. I looked at the address on the envelope. It was addressed to Anna but had been sent to the College's office address, so at least he didn't know the address of our apartment.

"The school just sent it over by messenger," Dean replied, shaking his head nervously. I scowled when I flipped it over, seeing the prison address on the back. I didn't want to read it, but I had to. "Maybe we should send it on to Senator Spencer and not open it."

"No, I'll send it on to him after," I disagreed. I needed to know what he said. If this was a threat against her, I would be wasting time sending it over to the Lake House and back again. I tore it open and held my breath while I read it, thankfully it was fairly short.

Dear Princess,

I see you've started a new school. You've already been there for a couple of months from what I hear, so hopefully you'll stay at this one longer than the last.

I miss you and can't wait to see you. The trial is less than three months away now, and I can't wait for us to be together again. I dream about you every night, how I want to run my tongue over every inch of your body and hear you call my name. God, I've missed your beautiful face so much and I hope that you've missed me.

Maybe once all of this is over, we can move away somewhere nice. I know you didn't much care for

291

Miami, so we can talk about it. I hope you're behaving yourself while I'm not there. If I find out that you've been with anyone else whilst I've been locked in this shithole, I will be very angry, Princess. You're mine, and mine alone. I can't even bear to think about you with other men, but I know you wouldn't do that to me, so I try not to dwell on it too much. I guess that's just me being my usual jealous self. I've just been apart from you for so long now that it's starting to drive me crazy, I can barely think about anything other than holding you in my arms and taking you into our bed again.

Life here is much the same as usual, nothing ever changes in this place, I guess that's why I hate it so much – well, that and being away from you. I wish you would visit me, even just for a few minutes so I could hear your voice and see your face again. Sometimes I think I'm losing grip of you, at times I cannot picture the exact shade of your hair, or the exact fragrance of the perfume you favoured. All of that will change soon my Princess, just a few more months and then we'll be reunited, and nothing will keep us apart this time.

Well, I'll write you again next week. Good luck in your new school; see you in a couple of months.

As always, I love you.
Carter
xxx

I could barely breathe through my anger. Dean was watching me curiously, so I shook my head. "It's not a threat. It's a love note from Carter," I stated, almost spitting his name. Dean's face turned angry too. "I'd better call her father. You tell Peter about this when he gets up. Don't say anything to Anna, I'll ask her father again if she can be told, I really think she should know about this." I shoved the note back into its envelope and slid it into my pocket. I didn't offer to let Dean read it, there was nothing of interest in there, and if these notes ever did get back to Anna, I knew she wouldn't want people to know about them anyway. She valued what little privacy she had.

Dean was watching me, waiting for more directions; I closed my eyes and thought everything through. He wouldn't get to her; if anyone came anywhere near her, then I would kill them. He was talking about seeing her at the trial and about the future, so he wouldn't order anyone to hurt her in any way. He loved her.

I opened my eyes. "Okay, she already has pretty tight security; I think we need to pull in a little further. We'll cut far guard distance from a hundred yards, to fifty instead. Make sure you have your gun with you at all times. We'll still go tonight otherwise she might get suspicious, but I think that both you and Peter should come, if you don't mind. I'll authorise overtime payments for you both for any extra hours that we need when we go out and stuff," I instructed. Forcing a smile, I tried not to show the panic that was building inside me because she was in the apartment on her own, even though I was standing outside the only door.

Dean nodded, so I pulled my cell phone from my pocket and dialled Maddy's number. "Senator Spencer's office," she answered cheerfully.

"Ma'am, it's Agent Taylor. I need to speak to the Senator, please."

"That's not possible, Agent Taylor. He's in a meeting at the moment," she replied apologetically.

"Ma'am, please put me through immediately and tell him I need to speak to him," I ordered sternly.

"Um, okay, hold on," she answered nervously. I was put on hold for a minute then he came on the phone, sounding slightly panicked.

"Agent Taylor, what's happened?"

I took a deep breath. "Sir, we've received a letter from Carter here at the college. It was addressed to the college offices, thankfully, and not the apartment, so there's a good chance he doesn't know our exact location. It's another love note, not a threat," I stated.

He drew in a sharp breath. "Oh God. Do you think she needs to leave school and come home?"

"No, sir, I don't. I don't think he wants to hurt her at all. He refers in his note to seeing her at the trial; I honestly don't believe that he would actually strike against her."

He sounded like he breathed a sigh of relief. "Okay, so what do we do?"

"Well, I've already tightened her security. I'd like your permission to authorise overtime payments for times when I want to take extra agents out with me. Like tonight, for example, it would be helpful to keep Agent

293

Michaels on for an extra couple of hours because we're going out in public. That kind of thing," I explained.

"Yes, yes of course, you authorise whatever you need. Do you want me to send you another agent as well?"

"Not at the moment, sir. If a threat comes in then I may request one, but at the moment I don't believe the danger is any greater than it was," I admitted. Sure, he knew which college she was in, he obviously had someone keeping tabs on her because he knew that she'd been here for a couple of months – but that didn't mean that he was going to do anything about it.

"Okay. Let me know if there's anything that you need," Senator Spencer sighed heavily.

I cleared my throat. "Sir, I really feel that now is the time to tell Anna about these letters. It would make her safer if she understood why we're always being so cautious with her security," I explained, closing my eyes and hoping he would say yes. I knew she'd worry, but at least she would be more responsive to us guarding her.

He was quiet for a minute, obviously thinking about it. "No, I really do think it's best if she's kept unaware. She doesn't need to be worrying that he's coming after her."

I sighed and ran my hand through my hair. Part of me wanted to argue the case that it was morally wrong to keep this information from her, but the part that loved her and wanted to shield her from everything bad, was actually a little relieved that she would still be in the dark. Her reaction to me drawing my gun on Nate was in the forefront of my mind. She'd been terrified that Carter had come back for her. I didn't want her to start to worry about that now. I decided not to push him to change his mind.

"Okay sir, it's your decision. I'll have this letter forwarded to you and keep you apprised of the situation." I couldn't help but feel slightly annoyed with him because he was making the wrong decision. As just her guard though, it wasn't my place to make that kind of decision and I had to go with what he said.

"Okay, thank you, Agent Taylor."

He disconnected the call and I sighed, looking over to Dean. "We still can't tell her. Let Peter know that we're going out at seven. If you could both be ready, that'll be great. If this gets too much for you two then let me know, I've been authorised to bring in another agent," I stated, grimacing, because I had no idea how I would explain another agent to Anna.

"Right, I'll see you at seven then," he nodded, and headed over to take his position in front of the elevator again.

I took a few deep breaths to calm myself and went back into the apartment, praying that nothing would ever hurt my girl. In the kitchen, I sought out an envelope, shoving Carter's note into it and addressing it to the lake house. Peter could arrange for it to be sent special delivery tomorrow.

I hung around in the kitchen for a while, trying to calm my nerves. Anna was like a mind reader at times, she could tell just by looking at me if something was wrong. When my body relaxed, I made two coffees and went into the lounge, watching her work on her project for college. My heart was throbbing painfully with the need to wrap her in my arms and keep her safe and never let her go, but I refused to make this any harder for her than it was every day. She needed to have fun, and tonight I would give her exactly that.

Chapter Twenty-Eight

~ Anna ~

At six o'clock, I went for a quick shower. I dried myself quickly and straightened my hair, putting on a bit of make-up. Then the long process of choosing something to wear to our date started. Casual and warm, he'd said. I chewed on my lip as I settled on a pair of jeans and a fitted black shirt, pairing it with some black converse.

Once satisfied with my choice, I made my way out to the lounge where he was already waiting for me. "Wow, you look incredible," he purred, looking me over slowly. I smiled and blushed under his intense inspection. "You'll need a sweater though, it might be cold."

I frowned; confused as to where we would be going that would require warm clothing. "Where are we going, Ashton?" I called as I strutted back into the bedroom and found a hooded sweatshirt.

"It's a surprise, stop asking."

I rolled my eyes and slipped the sweater on, going back out to the lounge again. "Do I pass the examination this time?" I asked sarcastically, twirling on the spot.

He grinned and nodded. "Trust me, you pass every time, but I want you to be comfortable so…" he trailed off, taking my hand again and leading me to the kitchen. Sitting there on the counter was a dozen white roses; he hadn't given me any for two weeks because last date night we were in LA. He handed them to me, grinning.

I smiled gratefully as I smelled them, breathing in their sweet aroma. "You're so romantic, Ashton. Thank you," I gushed, running my finger over the soft petals. He opened one of the drawers and held out a rectangular silver tin. "What's this?" I asked curiously.

"Open it and see," he instructed, leaning on the counter next to me.

I opened it to see a brand new set of inks, the professional expensive kind that would be perfect for my project at school. I gasped from the surprise. "My God, these are perfect!" I cried excitedly. "Thank you!" I threw my arms around his neck, hugging him tightly.

"You're welcome, Baby Girl," he answered. He pulled out of my arms and picked up the bouquet of flowers, putting them into a vase and filling it with water. "I'll let you arrange them later. Come on then, let's go before the suspense kills you," he teased.

The drive to the secret location for our date took about forty minutes, and he even overstepped the mark by making me sit with my hands over my eyes for the last couple of minutes. "Oh come on, you're taking this a little far," I complained.

"Will you stop whining? Jeez," he scolded, laughing. I huffed and sat in silence. It was killing me, but I actually didn't peek like I normally would have done, he was so excited about it that I didn't want to ruin anything for him. The car rolled to a stop, and his door opened then closed. A couple of seconds later, my door opened too. "Keep your eyes closed," he instructed as he took hold of my elbow and helped me climb from the car.

Sounds of screaming and laughing filled my ears, and in the background there was soft music playing. The air smelled sweet, like popcorn. I grinned, not having a clue where we were. The suspense was killing me. "Ashton, come on, please?" I whined, bouncing on the spot.

He chuckled wickedly. "Okay fine." His hands closed over my shoulders, turning me the other way. "Open your eyes."

Pulling my hands from my face, I blinked a couple of times as bright lights and colours overwhelmed me. I gasped as it all started to make sense. A fairground. I could see the Ferris wheel going around with twinkling fairy lights looped around every post. There were guys dressed up as clowns walking around on stilts, roller coasters, stalls where you win prizes, food stalls. I laughed excitedly and turned to Ashton, grinning, finally understanding the reason for the warm, casual clothes.

"Ashton, this is awesome," I chirped, grabbing his hand and stepping closer to him.

"Do you like fairground rides?" he asked as he guided me over to the ticket booth, paying for two wristbands.

"I love them," I admitted. "Provided you hold my hand," I added quickly.

He smiled as he wound the blue plastic band around my wrist before holding my hand tightly. "Now that would definitely be my pleasure," he flirted, dragging me into the park. We both ignored Dean and Peter, who paid for entry only behind us and followed us in.

Deciding to do the scarier rides first, Ashton and I went on a couple of rollercoasters which, of course, made me scream like a little girl. My near guard had found my high pitched girlie scream extremely amusing. After, he led me to a hot dog vendor.

"Hungry?" he asked.

"Yeah, they have a Denny's chilli cheese dog here?" I joked, slipping my arm around his waist.

He just laughed and kissed the top of my head. "I wish."

Taking our food into one of the large marquees, we ate and chatted at the same time, joking around and flirting. A brass band was sitting in the corner, playing old fashioned show tunes and people were dancing on the grass. I couldn't wipe the smile off my face. Every date night seemed to get better and better. Ashton surpassed himself on the thoughtful, romantic stakes every week. I knew he was still doing his job perfectly but, even so, he always managed to make me feel as though I was the most important girl on the planet.

When we'd finished eating, he took my hand and gave me a little tug in the direction of the makeshift dance floor. We danced for a couple of songs, fooling around and laughing the whole time before I stopped and nodded over my shoulder towards the exit.

"Let's go do some other stuff. I want to make sure we do everything before we leave."

As we stepped out of the marquee, the Ferris wheel caught my eye, so I dragged him over to it. Sitting on the Ferris wheel with him was extremely romantic. The fairy lights twinkled, the stars were out in force tonight and the music could still be heard from the marquee. I sighed in contentment and sagged against him. He grinned down at me before placing his lips over mine softly. I whimpered against his lips and kissed him back, reaching up and tangling my hand into the back of his hair. I hadn't kissed him like this since LA; we'd toned it down a little at school this week because people already knew we were together, so we didn't have anything to prove now. When he nibbled gently on my bottom lip, I gladly deepened the kiss. Our tongues danced together in perfect unison, and I moaned at the taste of him. I'd missed this more than I realised.

The moment was perfect, and I actually didn't want it to end. When the ride stopped, I looked up at the operator and pouted. "Can we go again?"

The guy laughed and flicked the switch, starting the ride again. Ashton moaned in the back of his throat and instantly crashed his lips back to mine. After a further two rides, we finally climbed out, and Ashton bought me a pink cotton candy. As I bit into it, he looked over my shoulder and laughed as he gripped my hand and tugged me over to a shooting stall. A wicked grin stretched across his face as he handed the guy five bucks and picked up the gun.

The old man that ran the stall smiled, tipping the brim of his cap. "Five shots. Get three on the target to win a small prize, get five on the target and you get one of the big ones. You ever done this before, son?" he asked Ashton.

"Nope," he lied, grinning.

"That's cheating," I whispered, giggling.

He laughed. "Mmm," he winked slyly at me before looking at the target and shooting his five shots – only getting one in. "Damn it," he mumbled, smiling.

The guy laughed. "Aw, never mind, son. I'm sure your girlfriend's not too disappointed, are you, darlin'?" he mocked, winking at me jokingly.

I smiled. "Never mind, Pretty Boy, you can't be good at everything," I teased.

Ashton laughed and slid another five bucks across the counter. "Let's win her one of these damn things then," he stated as he raised the gun again and shot all five directly into the centre of the target. The guy's mouth dropped open as his eyes widened. Ashton shrugged innocently. "Beginners luck?"

I burst out laughing and the guy shook his head, looking a little bemused. "What'll it be then, darlin'?" he asked, smiling kindly at me.

Glancing at the prizes that hung from the sides of the stall, I spotted what I wanted and pointed to a green monkey. The guy pulled it down and handed it to Ashton, who immediately passed it to me.

I smiled gratefully; hugging it to my chest and feeling the soft fur of it tickle my skin. "Thanks."

Ashton looked down at his watch and frowned. "It's getting pretty late. We've probably got time for another ride before we go if you want," he offered, pushing a stray hair behind my ear.

I looked around to see if we had missed anything. "We haven't been on the ghost train or the swan boats yet, so you choose."

"Hmm, well I like the sound of both," he replied, wrapping his arm around my waist and guiding me to the ghost train first. After the ghost train we went to the swan boats. It was a slow, lazy ride. Basically, you just floated around a shallow canal with the current. Ashton's arm was wrapped around me, so I twisted in my seat, swinging my legs over his lap, just enjoying being close to him. After a minute or so, we started heading towards a makeshift plastic cave. I giggled as I read the sign that was over the top.

"Tunnel of Love?" I giggled.

"I didn't know that's what it was, I swear," he replied, holding his hands up innocently, looking a little uncomfortable.

I laughed as our boat floated in. It was dark inside, and the only light was coming from the water that was illuminated underneath. Soft music was playing. I sighed and pulled him closer to me by his shirt. You couldn't really go into a tunnel of love without making out, there had to be some law against that, surely.

"Well, it is supposed to be romantic, after all," I mumbled as I pulled his lips to mine.

I kissed him hungrily. It wasn't sweet like the Ferris wheel, I think it was the darkness; it made it hot as hell. As he kissed me back, it was almost frantic and desperate. My desire spiked as he moaned into my mouth. I pushed myself up and sat on his lap, straddling him as he kissed down my neck. When his hands slid up the back of my shirt, I moaned and pressed myself closer to him. Underneath me, I could feel how excited he was getting, and the feel of it was driving me into a state of wild abandon. My body ached for relief that I knew wouldn't come.

"I hope they don't have cameras in here," I breathed as he bit my neck gently. I felt him smile against my skin as he pulled the hood up on my sweater, shielding my face. I giggled, closing my mouth over his again as he pinned me onto his lap and kissed me as if he could devour my soul.

The tunnel was getting lighter now as we neared the exit. I sighed, frowning because the ride was over, and so was our intense make out session. He slid one hand up and cupped my cheek, just looking at me adoringly before bending forward and kissing me again softly. His eyes sparkled in the semi-darkness and my heart stuttered in my chest. The way he looked at me sometimes made me feel as if I was flying. It was incredible how one look from him made me feel so free and unshackled. I had no idea that people like him even existed in the world.

As we got out of the boat, he grabbed my stuffed monkey from the seat, handing him to me. "I think he saw more than he bargained for," he joked, grinning. "We should probably get going. It's after midnight."

"One more cotton candy?" I pouted as we walked past the little stall. He grinned and purchased one, handing it to me and rolling his eyes. Happiness bubbled inside me and I practically skipped to the car, swinging our hands between us.

I must have fallen asleep on the drive home because I woke up as he was lifting me out of the car. "Hey," I mumbled sleepily.

"Hi," he whispered, picking me up bridal style and carrying me as if I weighed nothing at all. I wrapped my arms around his neck and closed my eyes again, drifting back to sleep. I vaguely heard the door click shut and then I was laid onto something soft. He tugged at my jeans, pulling them off before lifting the sheets up under my chin. After pulling off his clothes, he slipped into the bed next to me and wrapped his arms around me tightly, pulling me against him.

A sleepy smile crept onto my lips as I buried my face into his chest. "Thank you for tonight. That was the best date ever. I know I say that every week, but that beat all of the others, hands down," I yawned.

"Yeah, I agree," he whispered as he pulled himself up to kiss me.

The remainder of the passion from the tunnel of love ride was boiling up inside me as I pressed myself against his body. I bit my lip, fighting with myself as to whether I could beg him for sex. The week since

LA had been a long one, and I missed his body and the physical intimacy terribly.

"Can we go back to the fair another time?" I asked, hoping to distract my body that was itching to take things further.

"Sure, Baby Girl, anything you want."

I closed my eyes and smiled. I actually felt happier than I had ever felt in my life. I knew everything was down to him. He truly was an amazing guy, probably the nicest and sweetest guy in the world, and I was immensely lucky to have him. Right then and there, I decided to make the most of every single second with him because every minute took us one step closer to when he would leave me.

The following three weeks were extremely eventful and seemed to pass in a blur. That wasn't something that was going on in my life though, that was something that was going on with my father. Election Day. The event that he had been building up to practically all of his life finally arrived. In the lead up to it, I saw him everywhere I went – in newspapers, on TV, posters on walls, magazines. I couldn't escape it. But it all paid off in the end. He won the election by a landslide, as most predicted he would. My father would become President Spencer in just a few short weeks.

My pride was something that I hadn't expected. I had actually burst out crying when I got the call from him moments after the results had been announced. For years, he and my mother had worked tirelessly towards his goal, and now it was paying off.

It also meant, however, that come January when he was inaugurated, I would officially be the first daughter. That thought I wasn't as keen on, but I couldn't begrudge my dad his dreams, so I'd plastered on a fake smile and told him how happy I was about it.

The week following the election was actually my father's birthday, so they had organised a rather large soirée to celebrate, which would also serve as a kind of victory party for him and his staff too. Ashton and I were told we had to attend to show a united front, so we were flying over there for the weekend. Personally, I was dreading the party. No doubt, everything would change now. My life was about to spiral out of my control once again, it seemed.

Chapter Twenty-Nine

~ Ashton ~

I tried again to tie the silky material into some semblance of a bowtie, but I just didn't have a clue. A loud groan escaped my lips. I was going to look like a first class prick at Anna's dad's birthday party. I was sure to embarrass Anna because I had no idea how to behave and integrate with the class of people that were sure to attend. I had even heard this week that there were going to be actual celebrities attending too, friends of Senator Spencer's.

Giving up, I sighed and grabbed the corsage off the side that I'd bought for her, and made my way downstairs, hoping to find Dean or someone to fix my tie for me. As I got to the bottom of the stairs, Anna's mom, Melissa, looked up.

She smiled warmly at me, and nodded at my bowtie that was hanging loosely around my neck. "Let me give you a hand with that," she suggested,

My pride sank to a new low. "Er, that'd be great, thanks," I replied, stepping closer to her, hating the fact that I was so out of my depth and it was probably glaringly obvious for all to see.

She laughed quietly as she fiddled with it. "Don't be embarrassed, I just had to tie Tom's too," she winked at me conspiratorially. At least the future President of the United States couldn't do it either.

"You did? Well that makes me feel better," I admitted, laughing. "You look very nice tonight, Mrs Spencer." She looked radiant in her gold gown; she was undoubtedly where Anna got her looks from. But Anna just had something else, an inner beauty that just burst from every pore.

"Thank you. You look exceptionally handsome in your suit. My guess is that you'll make Annabelle swoon," she said, grinning. I smiled, silently hoping she was right.

302

Senator Spencer came down the stairs then. "Melissa, are we ready to go?" he asked, smiling lovingly at his wife.

"I think so, we're just waiting for Annabelle," she answered, looking expectantly at the stairs. "Annabelle, are you almost ready? We need to leave, the car's here!" she called up the stairs.

"You look nervous," Senator Spencer observed, smiling warmly at me.

I nodded. "I am, sir. I've never been to an event like this."

He laughed at my remark. "You'll be fine, son. Just start the cutlery from the outside, and smile. If you have no idea what you're doing, just smile and pretend you do, that's how I get through these things," he admitted.

"I'll do that. Thank you, sir."

Footsteps to the side caught my attention. "You look great, Annabelle," Dean's voice drifted down the stairs.

"Thanks, Dean, you look pretty good yourself. I haven't seen you in a suit for a while," Anna replied, her voice teasing and light.

"Yeah, it feels a bit weird to be wearing it actually. It's been almost three months since I've been made to wear this uniform. Thank goodness for undercover assignments, is all I can say," he replied, chuckling.

She laughed in response and my heart throbbed at the sound of it. No matter how many times I heard it, I just couldn't get enough of her happiness.

I looked up at the stairs expectantly, waiting. As soon as I saw her, my legs felt weak. She looked stunningly beautiful, and that was exactly how I felt, stunned. I couldn't move. I couldn't even breathe. I'd never seen anything so perfect in my life, all she was missing was the wings and she would look like the angel that she was.

The plum coloured ball gown that had been specially made for her tonight clung to her, showing off her perfect, flat stomach and tiny waist. The top was a halter neck, so it showed off her flawless creamy-white shoulders. And the cleavage... I had no idea how I was going to keep my eyes away from it tonight. The dress showed just enough to tease and hint at what was underneath, making me feel hot and horny as hell. The skirt of the dress flowed out all the way to the floor, hiding the toned long legs that I knew were underneath. Her hair had been pulled up and was pinned in curls at the back of her head, hanging down her back.

I sucked in a ragged breath as I looked at her face. She looked radiant, her skin almost shining. Her make-up was different tonight; she had on some grey eye shadow that made her brown eyes look like they were shining with an excitement and joy, that made my world stop spinning. She always took my breath away, no matter what she was wearing, even if it was baggy sweaters or one of my T-shirts, but tonight she was almost killing me. She was walking towards me and looking me over slowly; a small, sexy smile played at the corners of her mouth.

I swallowed, wondering what I was going to say when she got to me. My mouth was so dry, I wasn't even sure I could speak. I couldn't take my eyes off her as I shifted from one foot to the other, trying to get my brain to form an articulate sentence so that I wouldn't embarrass myself. The trouble was, the only word that I could think right now was: wow.

"Hi," she greeted, smiling as she stopped in front of me.

"Hi," I managed to choke out. I looked into her eyes and felt her pull me in. I loved this girl with all of my heart. I cleared my throat, knowing I needed to compliment her on how she looked. "You look incredible; I've never seen anything more beautiful in my life."

She blushed and smiled her sexy smile, making my insides flutter. "Thanks. And you look extremely smart in your tux," she countered, as she ran her hand along the edge of the jacket that I was wearing, making my body yearn for her in the normal way.

Calm down, Ashton; do not get a boner in front of her parents! I swallowed the lump in my throat. I was behaving like a love-struck moron, I could feel it, but I just couldn't help myself. *Just give her the damn corsage, Ashton!* "I... er... I got you this," I muttered.

Her eyes dropped to the box and her teeth sank into her bottom lip as she looked at the little white rose corsage bracelet I was holding out like a complete and utter moron. "Ashton, that's gorgeous," she gushed, smiling gratefully.

I smiled awkwardly. "If I'd known you would look this beautiful tonight, I would have gone for something a little bigger and more expensive. This is gonna pale in comparison to you tonight, Anna," I admitted, frowning at the thing that I thought was beautiful until I saw her.

"Jeez, Ashton, seriously, do you just get these lines straight from a how to make the girls melt handbook?" she teased, grinning at me. I couldn't help but laugh. I genuinely didn't understand how she could look the way she did but still have the greatest personality in the world. From my experience, it didn't usually work like that. People were usually blessed with either looks or personality. Yet Anna had an abundance of both. I slipped back into our easy flirty mode as I remembered that I loved her personality even more than I loved her body.

"Yeah, is it working yet?" I joked, grinning wickedly.

"Definitely," she giggled, nodding.

I plucked the corsage from the box. "You don't have to wear it." I fiddled with it, embarrassed, giving her another chance to change her mind if she didn't like it. She stepped closer to me, and her perfume wafted around me, filling my senses and making me forget my protests.

"I love it. Thank you," she whispered, looking into my eyes. I could see the honesty there, she really did love it. When she offered her arm to me, I slipped it on her wrist, trailing my fingers across her soft skin afterwards.

Movement from the corner of my eye snapped me out of the little fantasy I was slipping into, and I remembered that we weren't alone in the room. Anna just had the power to make everything else disappear in an instant. Dropping her hand quickly, I stepped back, hating that her father was close enough to have heard every single word I said.

Her father stepped forward, grinning proudly. "You look beautiful, Annabelle."

"Thanks, Dad. You look good too," she replied, smiling warmly at him.

He shifted uncomfortably on his feet. "Thank you, sweetheart." He brushed his hand over his jacket before his easy smile faded from his face. "So, I've just spoken to Reginald, my publicist. Apparently word has gotten out about the party tonight, and someone has leaked the venue. There are some press and a couple of TV crews that are converging around the entrance to the hotel. It's nothing to worry about," he stated, smiling reassuringly. "Reginald has made a few quick adjustments, and nothing needs to change too much apart from maybe posing for a few photographs at the entrance and answering a couple of questions to placate them. He'll guide you through everything when you get there, just remember to smile for me, alright?"

Anna's shoulders seemed to tighten as he spoke. I knew she was unhappy about losing her anonymity, but there wasn't much we could do about that now, apart from roll with it and hope that it all worked out.

I placed a hand on the small of her back, forcing a smile when she looked up at me. "It'll be fine. You knew this might happen. I'll be right there, just smile for the camera, that's all."

She took a deep breath and nodded, stepping closer to my side as she fiddled with the little gemstone necklace I'd bought her that I'd never once seen her take off. "Hold my hand though, okay?"

"Definitely," I nodded in agreement. That wasn't a chore on my behalf.

"Right then, let's go," Senator Spencer suggested, nodding at the crowd of staff and secret service that were waiting by the front door for us. We weren't coming back to the Lake House tonight; for ease, we were staying at the hotel where the party was being held. Our overnight bags were already there. As we walked towards the door, Anna slipped her arm through mine. A black limousine was waiting out front for us. I watched as her parents climbed into the car first and then Anna and I followed suit.

The car journey was only about ten minutes, but Anna didn't let go of my hand the whole time. She didn't even seem to notice or care that her parents were watching us. Since we'd come back from Los Angeles, she'd been unconsciously seeking out contact with me all the time. She hugged me a lot, wrapped her arm around my waist, held my hand or just plain old pressed herself to my side. I loved it and didn't even think she knew she was doing it half of the time.

305

When we pulled up outside the hotel, the crowd of reporters were easy to see. The staff had cordoned off an area and they were all lined up ready with their cameras and microphones. Luckily, due to the tinted windows, they couldn't see us yet. On the opposite side to the reporters, a gathering of onlookers waited excitedly too. Obviously word was spreading beyond just the press that this event was happening.

Anna winced and leant forward in her seat. "Are you sure that Ashton and I can't sneak in through the back?" she asked her dad hopefully.

He sighed and shook his head apologetically. "I'm sorry, Annabelle, I need you to come in the front. We need to show a united front. I know it's going to make things more difficult for you."

I knew she didn't want to do this at all; everything was going to change for her now. Once it was common knowledge who she was, her normal life that we had tried to build would change completely. Until now, her father had people managing the press so that it made it possible for her to remain in the shadows. Now that she was about to step out of this car with him, there would be no more paying off photographers to keep her name out of the tabloids and magazines. I squeezed her hand gently, trying to reassure her that everything would be fine. We'd spoken about it a lot recently, so I knew exactly how she felt about it; she was putting on a convincing show for her parents though.

"It's fine, don't worry," she smiled, waving her hand dismissively. She squeezed my hand tighter, so I knew she was lying through her teeth. Her parents looked like they bought it.

As soon as the car rolled to a stop, someone opened the door and waved her parents out but then held up a hand to tell us to wait in the car. People cheered, shouting their names excitedly as the cameras flashed in a nonstop stream. I took a deep breath and snapped my business head back on. I turned in my seat.

"You don't leave my side, and you stay within my reach at all times," I ordered, trying to sound stern with her. I hated telling her what to do but I needed to keep her safe, she was the most important thing in the world.

She grinned. "Yes, Mr Sexy SWAT Agent," she flirted, raising one eyebrow at me. I couldn't help but smile. Before I could answer, the same guy stuck his head in the door and waved us out of the car too. I climbed out first, doing a quick survey of the area. Dean was already out of the car that had travelled in front of us; I could see he was scanning the crowd for trouble too. He nodded discreetly, so I turned and held out a hand to Anna.

Her hand closed over mine, gripping so tightly that my fingers mashed together. She stepped out; biting on her bottom lip so hard that I was afraid she'd bite it in two.

"Miss Spencer, Mr Taylor, if you would just follow me, and pose for a couple of photos?" the flustered organiser guy requested, ushering us forward. This was probably Reginald, the publicist.

We both followed behind him, stopping where he pointed before he announced our names and that Anna was Senator Spencer's daughter. As soon as he said who she was, the cameras started flashing in our direction, so many flashes that I could barely even tell where they were coming from. I pulled Anna closer to me.

She turned to look at me, smiling her beautiful smile. "Oh my God, this is crazy," she whispered, laughing. I grinned and nodded. Crazy wasn't exactly the word I would have used. A piece of her hair blew across her face, so I brushed it back into place, smiling down at her.

"Totally freaking crazy," I confirmed.

Reginald stepped in front of us, holding up a clipboard, trying to shield us from the continuing flash of the paparazzi. "Okay, that's great. The reporters are going to want to ask you a few questions," he said, as he pointed to a huge line of people with microphones and video cameras. Anna tensed next to me as we followed him over to the right place. Nerves settled in the pit of my stomach. "Just a couple of questions, guys. One at a time, alright?" he instructed, pointing to the first person standing there.

Anna tightened her already vice-like grip on my hand. I smiled, silently wondering if she thought I was going to run away and leave her here. The first reporter, a woman in her early thirties I would guess, grinned excitedly as she looked Anna over quickly, clearly debating on her one question so that she didn't waste it.

"Miss Spencer, who designed the dress? It's beautiful."

I laughed. *Of all the things she could ask, and she asks about the dress. Typical woman!* Anna smiled and looked down at herself. "I know, it's incredible. It's by an English designer called Mary Shaun; I think she's going to be the next big thing. I love her designs," she answered easily, as if she was expecting this to be like torture or something. I was half a step behind her.

Reginald pointed to the next reporter who was obviously more prepared than the first and wasn't as concerned about fashion. "Miss Spencer, what do you think of your father being elected?"

She beamed a killer smile. "It's great. He's worked extremely hard and his policies are worth supporting. I'm immensely proud of him."

"Miss Spencer, who's your date tonight?" the next reporter asked.

My back stiffened because I wasn't expecting to be mentioned at all. I was a nobody. Anna laughed and tugged on my hand so that I had to take a half step forward to be at her side.

"This is my boyfriend, Ashton Taylor," Anna answered, smiling up at me. I couldn't help but smile back. I was so proud to have those words come out of her mouth, even if they weren't strictly true. My boyfriend, Ashton. I loved that.

"How long have you two been together?" the next reporter asked quickly, using up their question.

"A year and three months," Anna lied quickly. That was how long we had told people at college that we were together, so we needed to keep up the pretence for them.

"Miss Spencer, will you be working for your father's administration?" the next one asked.

She shook her head in response. "No, I'm actually in college at the moment."

My stomach clenched, and I squeezed her hand warningly, praying for her not to elaborate. While we'd discussed possible scenarios about what would happen once people knew who she was, I'd already instructed her not to give away any details of her life. Thankfully, she didn't elaborate though, so I breathed a sigh of relief. We were on the last reporter now, and then I could get her inside and stop being so damn worried about her safety. We both looked at the last reporter expectantly.

The lady smiled. "Mr Taylor, what's it like dating the future President's daughter?"

Anna laughed, and I smiled at her nervously. I had no idea why this woman would waste her question on me. Not having practiced anything for myself, I decided to answer her question with the truth. "Well, to be honest, it was a little intimidating being taken home to meet the parents," I joked. Anna laughed, as did half of the reporters who were still filming and taping us. "Honestly though, it's been the best time of my life. She's the best thing that ever happened to me," I said honestly. I bent my head and kissed her on the forehead.

Anna's eyes shone with happiness and joy as she smiled up at me, clearly impressed by my answer.

Reginald stepped forward once more. "Okay, that's it folks. Only one question each. Miss Spencer and Mr Taylor would like to get inside and enjoy the celebrations." He waved us towards the door so I pulled her inside quickly, happy that it was all over.

My body relaxed as we made it through the doors. From the corner of my eye, I saw Dean slip into the building behind us. He nodded at me discreetly, signalling that everything was satisfactory.

"That was insane," I muttered, wrapping my arm around her waist and pulling her body close to mine.

"I know, but it's done now though," she sighed deeply, looking relieved. She nodded towards the sign that was sitting in the foyer of the hotel, announcing the way to the private function in the ball room. "Think that's us," she muttered, slipping her hand into mine.

Formal didn't quite cover the posh party that I was currently in the midst of. The dinner had been exquisite; on the small side though, so I was glad I'd eaten a sandwich beforehand. After dinner, there were a couple of speeches and people wishing Anna's father happy birthday and offering stories of him when they first met or witty anecdotes on something he'd done or said at some point in their friendship. It was nice and intimate. Of course, because Anna was underage, and I was pretending to be, we had to toast with non-alcoholic champagne.

Finally the speeches finished, and a big band started to play. I smiled, wanting to escape the stuffy people that were seated on our table with us. "Want to dance?" I asked Anna.

She smiled happily and nodded. "Sure," she replied, taking my hand. I stood up and proudly led her to the dance floor, pulling her as close as I could without being all over her.

"You're amazing, you know that?" I whispered. I didn't just mean how she looked tonight; I meant how she was conducting herself with grace and poise when she probably hated this whole thing and the attention that was being directed at her. I was immensely proud of her right now.

She smiled. "You're not too bad yourself," she teased, tightening her grip on my shoulder.

Dancing with Anna made me feel amazing, like I was the most important man in the world; she wouldn't dance with anyone else like this and I loved that fact. I could see some of the guys in the room watching her like vultures. I smiled to myself smugly, setting my hand on the small of her back as we sashayed around the dance floor.

After a few songs, her father walked over, smiling happily. He looked every inch the President tonight, and I was honoured to be in his presence; he truly was a brilliant man who would do well for the country.

"Do you mind if I cut in?" he asked. I resisted the urge to say no. I didn't want to let go of her tonight. Well, that wasn't strictly true, I didn't want to let go of her *ever*, it wasn't limited to tonight.

Anna shrugged. "Sure, if you want to dance with Ashton, then I'll go get a drink or something," she teased, making both me and her father laugh.

I stepped back as he held his hand out to her in invitation. She took a deep breath, seeming to steel herself before she stepped closer to him, placing one of her hands into his and the other onto his shoulder. I grinned proudly and made my way back to the table, sipping my water but not taking my eyes off her the whole time. Anna's father looked like the proudest and happiest man on the planet as he paraded his daughter around the dance floor.

When the song was nearing completion, he bent and kissed her forehead. Surprisingly, she didn't flinch away from him the way I had seen her do in the past. She detested all forms of affection or closeness with other people. Her father looked up and caught my eye, giving me a small nod. He had things to do tonight, and people to speak to no doubt, so their dance was probably limited to one because of that. I smiled and headed over to them.

I caught the end of their conversation. "I know this is going to be hard for you now with my new job, and I'm sorry. But I'm glad you have him. He's a really good guy," Senator Spencer told her quietly. I slowed my approach so that they could finish talking. I had a feeling that the 'him' was me.

"It's fine, Dad, honestly. I'm really proud of you," Anna replied.

Her father beamed down at her. "Thank you, Annabelle. That means a lot to me," he answered. I couldn't put it off any longer. I stepped to her side, and she instantly melted against me. I smiled and wrapped my arm around her waist affectionately. Her father smiled at me before looking back at his daughter. "I won't see you again tomorrow because your mom and I are heading out early to catch a flight to New York, so make sure you say bye to your old man before you leave tonight, huh?" She smiled and nodded in agreement. "Thank you for the dance," he said happily.

Anna laughed. "Anytime, Mr President."

He grinned. "That's going to take some getting used to," he stated, shaking his head, looking a little bemused. He turned to me and held out his hand, smiling warmly. "Look after my little girl," he pleaded.

He really didn't need to ask me that, I would look after Anna forever if she'd let me. "Of course, sir," I promised, nodding and tightening my other arm around her waist as I shook his hand. As soon as her dad left, I pulled her into another dance, eager to have her in my arms again. My mouth was itching to be on hers. She looked exquisite tonight; she was so beautiful that it honestly hurt to look at her. I couldn't seem to get close enough to her. "I don't suppose I can kiss you in front of your parents," I whispered, already knowing the answer was no.

She shook her head and winced. "I don't think I'd ever hear the end of it."

"Yeah, that's what I thought," I admitted, trying not to show her how disappointed I was that I couldn't kiss her soft lips. As her eyes drifted over my shoulder, her whole posture changed. She stiffened, her hand tightened on my shoulder, her nails dug into the back of my hand that she was holding as we danced. My body tensed too in response, but I had no idea what, or who, had caused her reaction. Just as I was about to turn and look, she twisted my body and ducked her head so that she was hidden from view. Whoever she was looking at, she obviously didn't want them to see her.

"Holy shit, Jack's family are here," she whispered.

My eyes widened in surprise. No doubt, she was going to have a full scale meltdown now, just like last time she'd seen Jack's mother. My arm tightened on her as she pressed her body closer to mine, peeking over my shoulder. "They are? You want to leave?"

She gulped but didn't answer. Slowly, her hand loosened on mine and her shoulders lost the tenseness to them. "Actually, I'm alright," she replied, seeming a little shocked about it herself. I looked down at her, stunned. Her eyes told me that she was telling the truth, she really was okay at being confronted by Jack's family. *Is she finally getting over him? Is she finally ready to move on?* I wondered.

310

"Yeah?" I asked, watching closely to see if her mask slipped.

"Yeah," she nodded. "Actually, I want to go say hi," she added, as a smile tugged at the corners of her lips.

Pride swelled inside me. I actually wanted to jump up and down in celebration, doing my victory dance because she was clearly making some progress with her grief.

She pulled out of my arms and sidestepped me, walking confidently over to a table at the back of the room. I followed behind her with my heart still slamming in my chest. "Hi, I didn't realise you guys were here, otherwise I would have come over sooner," Anna said, smiling happily at them as we got to their table.

I glanced around the table quickly, taking them all in. When my eyes landed on the blond guy, I felt sick. It was Michael, Jack's brother. Last time she'd lost control because he looked so much like his brother. Maybe she hadn't seen him yet? I flicked my eyes over to Dean, seeing that he was watching the scene unfold with wide eyes. He was clearly expecting her to freak out at any second too.

A blond guy, probably in his early forties, stood and smiled at Anna affectionately. "Hi! Oh you look beautiful, Anna," he cooed as he stepped forward and wrapped her into a tight hug.

She smiled as she stepped back after a second. "Thanks, Steve, you're looking pretty good yourself there," she answered, looking him over. She turned as Jack's mom stood too. "It's so nice to see you again. It's been a while."

The lady engulfed her in a hug too, patting her back as she closed her eyes and clearly cherished the affection from someone whom she cared about deeply. "It's been way too long," the lady gushed. I tried desperately to remember her name, but I couldn't recall it. When I was introduced to her in the café, I'd been too concerned with Anna to listen to her name.

"This is Ashton Taylor," Anna smiled, motioning towards me.

The guy she'd called Steve smiled. "Right, yeah, we've heard about him. He's the one with you at college?"

"Yeah, he is," Anna confirmed.

I reached out a hand towards him. "It's nice to meet you, sir," I greeted politely.

He grinned, placing his hand in mine and shaking it firmly. "You too. You can call me Steve," he replied, waving a hand dismissively. I nodded. He seemed like a nice guy.

My body unconsciously stiffened as Michael jumped up from his chair. He looked so much like Jack that it was scary. I was pretty used to what Jack looked like from the photo Anna had in our bedroom – even though it wasn't on the bedside unit anymore. She'd moved it onto one of the shelves, and the photo on the bedside was now of me and her and my friends in LA at one of the bars we went to.

"Hey, Michael," Anna greeted, smiling.

311

I frowned in confusion, again flicking my eyes over to Dean, who looked just as stunned as I felt. I had no idea what was going on. This wasn't how I would have predicted that this meeting would have gone.

He pulled her into a hug and said something in her ear which made her chuckle in response. When the embrace broke, he stepped back and motioned towards a young girl who was sitting at the table with him. "This is my date, Lisa. Lisa, this is Anna," he waved a hand between his date and Anna in introduction.

"Hey, it's nice to meet you," Anna said.

Lisa stood, looking a little awed, probably by the ambience, the setting, the celebrities and the sheer luxury of the party. "Hi. I love your dress," she replied, looking Anna over a little jealously. I wasn't surprised that the girl was jealous; Anna's dress was killer and made her look like a runway supermodel.

Anna nodded quickly in agreement. "I know it's hot, right? Did you see my shoes? I *love* my shoes," she gushed, lifting her dress up past her knees. I looked down at her perfect legs and groaned internally because dirty thoughts immediately clouded my mind. Jack's mom and the girl gasped as they both stared at her shoes longingly. I noticed Michael was looking too, but I didn't think he could even tell you what colour the shoes were – he was looking at her legs the same way I was.

"Oh goodness, those are beautiful," Jack's mom gasped.

"I know. I have to return the dress and shoes, but I'm going to accidentally lose the shoes in my suitcase," Anna stated. I grinned at that. She was totally serious – I could tell by her voice.

"I'd lose them too," Lisa chirped, laughing.

Anna nodded, dropping her dress back to the floor again. "Well, it really is great to see you. I'm going to go dance some more, but I'll come and see you again before you leave."

Jack's mom reached out and touched Anna's face adoringly. "I'd like that, honey. I've missed you."

Anna nodded sadly, before slipping her hand into mine and giving me a little tug in the direction of the dance floor as she waved over her shoulder to Jack's family.

I watched her warily as she wrapped her arms around me. She looked happy though, and I just couldn't comprehend it. "You really okay?" I asked.

Her lips pursed as she seemed to think about it for a few seconds. Finally, she nodded, seeming a little shocked about her own feelings. "Actually, I'm fine. Strange as it may seem, I really do feel fine."

Happiness exploded within me, because maybe, just maybe, she really was getting over him... maybe I did have a shot after all. "Great. That's really great, Baby Girl," I said, rubbing my hand across her skin on her back, sending little tingles of pleasure through my hand. I was so proud of her, I could barely stop myself from grabbing her and spinning her around in a circle. She truly was getting over him, and I didn't even think that she realised it.

We danced for another couple of songs in silence before she set her head on my shoulder and sighed deeply. Tracing my hands up her back, I gripped the back of her head, feeling her soft silky hair under my fingertips. My heart sank, knowing what this would be about. The Jack thing was finally catching up to her. "What's wrong?" I whispered, bending and resting my head on the top of hers.

Her arms tightened around me as she spoke with her face pressed into the side of my neck. "Nothing's wrong. I'm just having a nice time with you tonight."

It hadn't been a sad sigh. It was a sigh of contentment. My heart started back up in double-time. "I'm having a nice time here with you too," I replied, pressing my nose into her hair, breathing her in.

It wasn't too much longer before the party started to wind down. I followed behind Anna as she said goodbye to Jack's parents, promising to stay in touch and visit next time she was in town, before seeking out her own parents and bidding them farewell too.

I nodded to Dean who immediately headed to the door and stopped, waiting for us. As we stepped out of the hotel ball room, we made our way across the foyer and over to the elevators. Two secret service agents that I recognised from the lake house were waiting outside it, they waved us through quickly.

As the elevator sped us up to our desired floor, I felt slightly sick. I wasn't staying in with Anna tonight. The accommodation was prearranged, and it would look weird if we changed them, so the agents were to be sleeping two floors below the family tonight. The night guards would take over their protection duty. I'd been dreading this part all day. I hated being separated from her; I worried about her like crazy when she wasn't at my side. Thoughts of Carter haunted me when she wasn't with me, but spending the night away from her would be even worse because I knew she would dream about him and there would be nothing I could do to prevent it.

I tried not to show Anna how worried I was as we walked to her hotel room. "Can I come in and check your room?" I asked, needing to make sure that she was safe. I knew that her room was okay because there had been guards outside it all day, but I knew I wouldn't be able to settle if I didn't look for myself. Realisation hit me that maybe I really was too overprotective, just like she always said I was.

"Sure," she agreed, looking amused as she gave me a little tug into her suite.

My eyes widened at the luxury of the place as we stepped inside. She had a separate living area with a ginormous flat screen TV on the wall, sofas, and even what looked like a little kitchen area. She plopped down on the sofa as I headed to the bedroom and checked under the bed and in the closet and bathroom to make sure nothing or nobody was hiding in her room. When I had satisfied myself, I sat down next to her on the plush sofa. This situation was killing me. I knew she was going to be annoyed with me if I didn't stop stressing out, but I couldn't calm my jangled nerves.

One of her perfectly plucked eyebrows rose in question. Silently, I waited for her to scold me for treating her like a child or something, but she didn't. Instead, she looked like she understood. "Ashton, I'll be fine, will you stop worrying?"

I sighed. I really wished I could. My life would be so much easier if I'd never met her and didn't have her to worry about. "I know you'll be fine, I'm just worried about how many bad dreams you're gonna have without me there," I admitted. "And also, I'm gonna miss you in the bed," I added, smiling weakly.

She laughed quietly. "I'm gonna miss you in the bed too," she shrugged before continuing, "And maybe I won't even dream, you never know. I haven't had any nightmares for three months. Maybe they've stopped?" She looked like she didn't believe a word of that statement at all.

"Yeah, I hope so. If it gets bad, then please call me," I begged. "I'll come up if you need me." I took her hand, just needing to touch her before I left her.

A reassuring smile graced her lips. "I'll be fine, but if I'm not, then I'll call you," she agreed.

I sighed, knowing that it was time to go. "Well, I guess I should let you get some sleep then. I'll see you for breakfast, yeah?" I asked hopefully.

She nodded. "Yep," she agreed and I kissed the back of her hand as she walked me to the door. She nodded tersely at the guy who was sitting in the chair outside her bedroom door. By her tight and defensive posture alone, I could tell she didn't like him. I smiled and shook my head; she really had a problem with guards.

"Goodnight then, Anna," I whispered, watching her face, silently wishing she would beg me to stay with her, screw the guards and her parents and their opinions.

"Night, Ashton." She shook her head, and an amused smile pulled at the corner of her mouth. Probably because of me and how pathetic I was. I sighed as I stepped out of the door and closed it behind me. Every muscle in my body was tight, wanting to run into her room and throw her on the bed and never let go. I pushed the thought away and turned back to the agent outside her door as I reached into my pocket, fumbling for the scrap of paper that I'd written my cell phone number on.

"Hey, here's my number. If there's any trouble with Anna tonight, then give me a call. Any time, I don't care," I instructed, holding out the paper to him.

He grinned. "I think I can handle Annabelle's trouble," he replied sarcastically, sneering at me like I was a three year old.

I bit back my angry retort. "Look, I'm sure you think you can handle her, but I've been working with her for the last three months, if she freaks out or has a nightmare or something, then call me, okay?" My anger was growing by the second.

"Screw it, man. If she has a nightmare, then that's down to her. You've got the night off, go enjoy yourself, you don't get paid enough for her shit," he said, shrugging arrogantly.

Fucking asshole! My hand was itching to punch the smirk off of his face, but I swallowed my anger and tried to keep my voice normal. "What's your name?" I asked politely.

His smile faded. "Mike."

Clearly, my tone hadn't been as polite as I'd intended. "Well, Mike, if I find out tomorrow that she had a bad night and you didn't call me, you and I are going to have a big fucking problem. You understand what I'm saying?" I growled, looking at him warningly.

He flinched, so he obviously got the point. "Right, whatever you want," he answered as he snatched the note from my hand and shoved it into his pocket.

"Thanks, I'm glad we understand each other," I replied, staring him down for a couple of seconds before I left for my floor. My rage was simmering on a slow boil, and I knew I wouldn't be getting much sleep as I stewed on what an uncompassionate jerk Mike was. When I got to my own room that I was sharing with Dean, I noticed that he was already in his bed and sound asleep.

As I shrugged out of my clothes and slipped into my own bed, I knew then that I was in for a sleepless night as I worried about the girl I was hopelessly in love with.

Chapter Thirty

~ Anna ~

I sighed as the door to my hotel room clicked closed. As soon as I was on my own, I missed him; I didn't want to spend the night alone at all. I'd lied and reassured him that I wouldn't dream tonight, but I knew that wouldn't be true. I was probably in for a bad night tonight, but I knew that it was only eight hours and then I'd be able to see him again. That thought was comforting.

I sighed and headed to the bedroom, slipping out of the dress that my mother had commissioned specifically for this event. Smiling to myself, I slipped the shoes into the bottom of my travel bag so I could keep them; there was not a chance I was giving those back. When I had on my pyjamas, which consisted of a pair of boy shorts and the T-shirt that Ashton wore yesterday, I climbed into the cold bed. It was so weird lying on my own, the bed felt too big somehow, I had too much leg room and no one was crushing me. I laughed quietly to myself and thought about my evening.

I'd had an incredible night tonight, and although things were going to change now that people would know who I was, I wouldn't have missed this party for the world. Seeing Ashton in that tuxedo had given me many new fantasies to think about. I pictured his face as I had walked down the stairs to meet him. The way he'd looked at me made my heart flutter erratically. I had never seen anything more heart-stoppingly gorgeous in my life than Ashton Taylor standing there with that familiar smile on his face. He'd certainly given all of those celebrities a run for their money tonight; he was undeniably the hottest guy in the room. I sighed contentedly and pulled Ashton's T-shirt up to cover my nose so I could breathe him in while I fell asleep, hopefully that would be enough to stop the dreams.

Pressing tighter against the wall, I silently pray he won't see me. I am going to pay for disobeying, I know this, but still I stand there, motionless, instead of running back to the yard and pretending that I hadn't moved from where he'd told me to wait.

As I peek around the corner of the wall and into the lounge, I see Carter standing with his back to me. At his feet, someone is on their knees. "Please, I'm sorry, it won't happen again," the guy begs, his voice breaking through fear.

"Not good enough, Mario. I lost two mil in coke because you couldn't keep your fucking dick in your pants long enough to make the fucking exchange!" Carter growls, his voice hard and angry. He moves to the side, and I see the guy on the floor. I recognise his face but know nothing about him; Carter always keeps his business away from me. A gun resides in Carter's hands, his favoured silver pistol with the ivory handle. It is his preferred gun, he tells me this often. Mario's eyes flick to me for a split second, and I freeze. Carter, seeing Mario's attention diverted, turns and looks at me. Anger crosses his face before his usual loving expression masks it.

"What are you doing here, Princess?" he asks, waving his hand for me to go to him.

I gulp. "I'm sorry, Carter. I just needed the bathroom," I explain apologetically, walking over and taking the hand that he is offering.

"It's okay. Take a seat there, I'm almost done," he instructs, nodding towards the couch.

I gulp and obediently sit. Mario's shoulders loosen as some of the tension leaves him. Clearly he thinks he is safe now that I am here, possibly thinking that Carter won't kill him in front of me. Obviously, he doesn't know Carter very well.

"I'm sorry, boss, it won't happen again," Mario apologises.

Carter nods in response, bringing the pistol up and aiming for the middle of Mario's face. "I know," he states as he pulls the trigger.

As the shot rings out, I whimper and try to look away, but I can't. It is the single most disgusting and horrifying thing I have ever seen in my life. In an instant, half of Mario's face disappears to be replaced by a bloody, soft, ragged, oozing mess. His body twitches a couple of times before falling backwards to the floor, making a loud thump.

Carter touches my face. I can barely breathe. "Princess, I told you to wait outside for me," he coos lovingly as he leans in and kisses my cheek.

"I… I know, I… I'm sorry," I stutter.

"Hmm, it's no problem. I missed you anyway," he purrs as his fingers move to the zip of my dress, tugging on it gently. While he slides the straps of my dress over my shoulders and kisses the side of my neck, I can't focus on anything other than the pool of blood that is forming under the dead body. "Mmm, you are so fucking hot. I love you," he whispers as he pushes on my shoulders, guiding me to lie back onto the sofa. The buttons pop on his jeans as he wrenches them open before settling himself on top of me. "Do you love me?" he asks, slowly lifting the skirt of my dress so that the material bunches around my waist.

The pool of blood is so big now that it is almost touching the rug on the floor. As I ponder over how much blood can be left inside him, a sharp pain resonates across my ribs and I gasp, whimpering. "I said do you love me?" Carter repeats, pressing on the bruises that I already have across my ribcage.

"Of course I love you, baby," I lie quickly. The words still feel as though they rip my heart out, even though I've said them every day for the last six months.

"Hmm, good," he whispers, easing my legs apart and settling himself between my thighs. When Mario's leg twitches, I squeal and look at it with wide eyes, knowing I will have a fresh nightmare tonight instead of the usual ones. "It's normal," Carter says quickly. He grips my chin between his thumb and forefinger, turning my head towards his and crashing his lips to mine.

As he uses my body, pleasuring himself like he does every day, all I can see is the dead man's foot twitching, his one lifeless eye staring up at the ceiling, and the dark blood that is slowly congealing on the tiled floor.

Finally, he reaches his climax and slumps down on top of me, crushing me with his weight. When his breathing has slowed and the dead man's blood has reached the edge of the expensive-looking cream rug, Carter moves to nibble on my earlobe. "I love you so much, Princess."

Numb. I'm numb and emotionless. I barely even feel the pain between my legs where he's just used me for his own sick satisfaction.

He smiles against my neck. "You know, I was thinking about something earlier." He pulls back and grins down at me, his eyes sparkling with excitement. "I think we should get married."

My mouth is dry. I have no words.

He strokes the side of my face softly. "Annabelle Thomas. I like it. Maybe we'll go to Vegas tomorrow," he suggests, grinning at me.

I don't feel anything. I am dead inside. He has killed me. I honestly don't care if I am married to him or not, there is nothing I can do about it either way.

Screaming, someone was screaming. I jerked up in the bed, only to realise that it was me. Fumbling behind me, I grab the pillow and press it over my face to muffle the sound as the scream slowly subsides. I didn't want any guards to burst in and see me like this, and I also didn't want it getting back to Ashton in the morning that I'd had a nightmare. Helpless tears flowed down my face at the memory. I panted, trying to calm down. My heart was crashing in my chest. After what seemed like forever, my body slowly started to return to normal. My muscles unclenched, my jaw loosened and my tears dried up. Glancing over at the clock, I saw that it was only three in the morning. I groaned and rolled over, squeezing my eyes shut, hoping for more sleep to find me.

"So, all we need is some identification, and then you're all set to go," the guy says from Carter's window.

Carter grins at me excitedly as he squeezes my knee. I smile automatically, knowing that is the response he wants from me. He grabs his driving licence and my fake one that Jack got for me for the club, and then he hands them to the guy at the drive through, along with a wad of cash.

I stare at my nails, picking aimlessly at the skin down the side, making it bleed. When the car rolls forward a few minutes later, I glance up, emotionless. This was what it had come to. Getting married in a drive through chapel in Vegas because he doesn't trust me to get out of the car, so he'd found a place where minimal contact with people was needed.

As we pull up at the next window, a guy stands there in a white robe. As he talks, I can't even pay attention, so I pick aimlessly at the skin on the edge of my nail again. A sharp sting on my wrist distracts me from my task. I look down, seeing that Carter is squeezing my wrist, digging his nails into my skin.

"Say your words, Princess."

I look up expectantly at the man in the booth, not even bothering to beg for help. If I did, Carter would shoot him dead – he'd already told me that several times on the way here.

I repeat the words after him. "I, Annabelle Spencer, take you, Carter Thomas, to be my lawful wedded husband. To have and to hold from this day forward. For richer, for poorer, in sickness and in health, until death do us part." As I say it, I pray the last part, the part about death, comes soon for either me or him. At this point, I'm past caring who.

I feel nothing. Ever since he'd made me lose the baby, something had been terribly wrong with me. I just don't care anymore, nothing matters to me. I don't even feel pain like I used to. Sometimes I long for pain to give me something else to think about, so I provoke him into beating me. Even that pain doesn't last long enough anymore though.

Carter grins and I plaster on a fake smile as he says his words to me and slips the expensive-looking gold wedding band onto my finger. I study it, emotionless. It is set with little diamonds all the way around it, and probably cost him more than the car we were driving in.

"I now pronounce you husband and wife. You may kiss your bride," the man says happily, utterly oblivious to my waking nightmare that I can't escape from.

Carter lets out a triumphant growl and grabs me, kissing me, hard. After a few seconds, he pulls back, grinning from ear to ear, looking happier than I have ever seen him. "You're officially mine now, Mrs Thomas."

I gasped and sat up. I was sweating so much that the bed was damp, and the sheets were stuck to my body. My hand was hurting for some reason. I turned the light on and looked at my left hand; it was clenched in such a tight fist that my fingernails had cut into my palm, drawing blood. Groaning, I pushed myself out of bed and take a deep breath. Dizziness overcame me, so I put my hand on the bed to steady myself as my legs wobble. I hated to think of the fact that I was married to the man that caused my life to spiral out of control. No one knew. I had never told anyone, not even my parents, and I didn't ever plan on it either.

I knew deep down that the marriage wasn't legal. I was sixteen when it happened and we'd used a fake ID. I could easily have it annulled, but that would mean I would need to tell people, and I didn't want to do that. I couldn't talk about it, I couldn't tell people what I went though, couldn't admit the shameful things that had happened to me under his hand. There was no way I was strong enough to look my parents in the eye and tell them that I'd married him. I couldn't ask them to help me get it annulled because I didn't want to see that pitying, horrified look that made everything worse. So I buried it so deep that the only outlet it had was through my night terrors. I hid the shame and the terror, and I never let it out. Not ever.

Once my dizziness had subsided, I headed to the bathroom and ran my hand under the cold water, rinsing the blood away, and then pressed it onto a towel until the bleeding stopped. My gaze drifted up to the mirror behind the sink. I frowned at my own reflection, hating myself. I looked like a complete mess. My mascara was smeared under my bloodshot eyes, and my face was pale and sweaty. I splashed some cold water over my face; it felt so good that I decided to go for a shower.

After a long shower, I stepped back into my room. It was barely five in the morning, but I didn't want to go back to sleep, I couldn't dream again tonight. Throwing on some jeans and a new shirt, I grabbed my iPod and then headed out of the room. As I opened the door to my hotel suite, I stopped short as Mike looked up at me with wide eyes.

"Annabelle? Is everything okay?" he asked, frowning down at my fully dressed body.

I nodded, sidestepping him and heading for the elevator. "Fine. I'm just going for a walk. I won't leave the hotel, don't worry." I waved my hand over my shoulder dismissively.

He made a kind of scoff sound in the back of his throat as he stepped to my side and reached out, pressing the call button for the elevator for me. "Not on your own, you're not," he stated flatly.

I didn't bother to protest, I knew it was useless anyway. As soon as the elevator arrived and the heavy doors slid open, I slipped in and pressed the lobby button and tried to ignore him as he stepped in beside me.

Unfortunately for me, because of the early hour, the salon and spa were all shut, so the only thing I could do was sit in the lobby and have a drink while Mike went to stand against the wall about twenty feet from me.

After three coffees, it was finally seven o'clock and the place started to wake up a bit. People were coming down for breakfast, and the night staff were going home, to be replaced by new morning staff.

The new barman kept looking over at me somewhat excitedly. I smiled warmly as he brought me another coffee that I hadn't ordered. He had a newspaper tucked under his arm. "Excuse me, Miss Spencer, do you think I could get your autograph?" he asked nervously.

I burst out laughing. "My autograph? What for?"

He smiled, confused. "Well, you are the President's daughter, are you not?"

I nodded, frowning. "I guess, but why would you want my autograph?"

320

He grinned as he pulled the newspaper out from under his arm and held it out to me. "You're all over the paper."

I gasped, practically snatching it out of his hand as my heart jumped into my throat. "No way! Seriously?"

He nodded. "Yeah, front page and pages four, five, six and seven," he stated, shrugging. My eyes wandered the paper as my breathing seemed to falter. On the front page there was a huge picture of my parents as they posed on the red carpet. Just underneath their picture, was one of me and Ashton. My eyes widened as I sat back in my chair, dumbstruck and lost for words.

"Can I read this?" I asked, scanning the text quickly.

"Yeah, sure. When you're done would you sign it for me?" he asked. I nodded, still not quite knowing what to say. He turned on his heel and strutted back to the bar, leaving me there with my heart in my throat.

I scanned the article quickly. It was all about my dad's birthday celebrations and a rough guide to what we ate and the decorations inside the ball room. Once I was done with the first page, I flicked through to the continuation part. The next couple of pages were more about the celebrities who attended and who wore what. As I turned the page again, I gasped, and my eyes widened in horror. Pictures of me and Ashton were splashed everywhere. The headline above it: *New Celebrity Couple 'Annaton'.*

Chapter Thirty-One

~ Ashton ~

To say that I'd not slept well would be a ridiculous understatement. I hadn't been able to switch my brain off and stop worrying about Anna all night. My cell phone hadn't rung though, so either Mike decided not to call me, or she'd had a good night.

Pushing myself out of bed just after seven, I snuck into the shower. My eyes stung with tiredness as I stood under the spray and let the powerful jets loosen my bunched up, tensed muscles.

When I was finished and dressed, I headed back into the room, seeing that Dean was just waking. I forced a smile, hoping I didn't look as rough as I felt. "Morning, sleep alright?"

He snorted and narrowed his eyes at me. "Not really."

One of my eyebrows rose in question. "No? How come?"

He sat up, running a hand over his face. "You fucking snore like an elephant with the flu!"

I recoiled, shaking my head and rolling my eyes. "Let me guess, Anna told you to tell me that, right?" She was always trying to make out that I snored; now she obviously had Dean in on it too.

He blinked a couple of times, not answering as he swung his legs out of the bed and trudged into the bathroom, sighing tiredly. My gaze fell on my cell on the side, so I sat on the edge of it, bringing up her number and debating whether I could call her or not. I decided against it, she was probably still sleeping anyway. Our flight wasn't until twelve, so she could have a longer lie-in. I flopped back onto the bed, playing around with the apps on my phone as I tried not to clock watch. Just as Dean walked out of the bathroom fully dressed, there was a soft knock on the door.

"I'll get it," he muttered, already heading over there and pulling the door open. "Oh, good morning, Annabelle."

My heart leapt in my chest as I shoved myself up quickly and headed over there, practically pushing Dean out of the way as I wrenched the door open further. There she stood. My frayed nerves finally settled as I laid eyes on her beautiful face. Stepping closer to her, I wrapped my arm around her shoulders, pressing my face into her hair and breathing her in. I'd missed her so much that it was actually painful.

She hugged me back immediately. From the corner of my eye, I saw Mike standing in the hall behind her. His posture was awkward as if he was trying not to watch or felt like he was intruding. I forced myself to pull back and smiled down at her. "Hey, how did you sleep? Okay?" I put my hands on either side of her face, and felt my eyebrows knit together. She looked extremely tired. Her eyes were bloodshot, either from lack of sleep or she'd been crying. My jaw tightened as I glared at Mike. We would have words later.

"Fine," she answered, shrugging as she dropped her gaze to the floor.

I shook my head and sighed as I gave her a little tug into my room and closed the door. I didn't know why she bothered trying to lie to me, I could always tell. "No you didn't, Anna."

She groaned and shook her head. "Whatever, doesn't matter now," she replied. "Anyway, I have something that you need to see. Don't freak out, alright?" she raised her hand, holding out a newspaper to me.

I frowned, confused as I took it from her hands. My mouth popped open when I saw the two photographs that were splashed across the front page. "Fuck me, there's a picture of us there!"

She sighed and flopped down onto the little sofa in our room. "More than one. There's a whole two page spread just dedicated to us," she muttered.

My mouth had gone dry. I couldn't take my eyes off the photo on the front page. Anna looked just as incredible as I remembered. But then my mind was back on business again. Carter. He could see this and make a move against her in anger. Of course, her father and I had already preempted this kind of thing happening, and he'd arranged for a heavy duty block to be put on information going in and out of the prison, limiting the number of magazines and papers going in if she was featured or mentioned at all. Also, *all* personal letters going into the prison, not just Carter's, were being screened in a bid to keep this information away from him for as long as possible. It wasn't an indefinite thing, but hopefully it would hold for a few weeks at least until all the attention around Senator Spencer and his family died down. The trouble was, we had anticipated that Anna would be featured, but not us as a couple. Anna posing with me and claiming me as her boyfriend was sure to anger him.

I didn't take my eyes from the paper as I sat on the sofa next to her, scanning the words for anything important. It all seemed to be trivial stuff about the party. I bypassed the second and third pages of the article too because they all seemed to be more about fashion successes for the night and who should fire their stylists. I could feel Anna staring at me, clearly waiting for some sort of reaction to all of it.

I forced a smile. "Apparently you should keep your stylist," I muttered weakly.

She chuckled and nodded. "Keep reading. Did you get to the body language bit yet?"

I shook my head in answer as I turned to the last two pages. My heart stuttered in my chest. Lining a whole two pages were various photographs of me and Anna. The headline insinuated a new hot couple. My eyes flitted over the photos, loving every single one of them. Deciding I should read the article because there was clearly something that Anna didn't like in here, I folded one leg over the other and set to work.

Apparently they thought that Anna would be the hottest 'First Daughter' that there ever had been. I wholeheartedly agreed with that statement. There was a mention of me and my joke about being intimidated to meet her parents. The journalist thought I was adorable.

When I got to the part she was referring to, I felt my back stiffen in shock. The paper had a body language expert analyse some of the photographs that had been taken. His findings were printed next to each one. The first was of future President Spencer shaking my hand. The expert had analysed his smile and the way he was leaning in towards me. He concluded that it meant he liked me and trusted me with his daughter. The caption was that I was 'already well in with the future in-laws'. Pride swelled in my chest as I read it. If only I could get Anna to actually date me, I'd already be in good standing with the family. The next one they looked at was of me and Anna dancing and laughing. According to the professional, the way that one of her hands was loosely placed in mine and the other tangled into the back of my hair, how close our bodies were, and the 'small knowing smile' that lined our lips all meant one thing in his opinion – we were very in love.

Shock resonated through my body, making me jerk in my seat. I couldn't breathe. They actually thought she was in love with me? I flicked my eyes up to hers, seeing her furiously chewing on her nails. *Is she in love with me?* I wondered. I would give anything for it to be true. I knew she was starting to get over Jack, and I was certainly in love with her, but according to this expert, she loved me too. Maybe she didn't even know it herself. That revelation wouldn't have surprised me in the least; Anna's brain might be refusing to even contemplate it. If she even was in love with me, then she wouldn't want to be, I knew that for a fact. Anna didn't like to feel

324

vulnerable and didn't want to get hurt again. I knew that she hated the fact that she even cared about me; if she loved me, then it would be a whole new ball game and one that would probably terrify her to the very core.

I knew I couldn't push it at all because it would probably frighten her and make her retreat back inside herself and shut me out again. I tried desperately not to react as I forced myself to carry on reading the article.

The body language expert wasn't done with us yet apparently. He analysed another photo and came to the conclusion that I was fiercely protective over her and that she trusted me completely. A small smile crept onto my lips at that last part. Then the part that made an excited shiver tickle down my spine. He stated that ours was a serious long term relationship that would continue to blossom. He predicted wedding bells within the next three years. I gulped and blinked a couple of times. Wedding bells. If I had my way, I would marry her tomorrow if I had the chance.

Apparently, we were the hottest couple that attended the party – outshining even the A list celebs that had attended. The paper had already come up with a trashy couple name too.

I laughed incredulously, shaking my head. I hated couple names. "Annaton? That is lame," I muttered. Nate was going to ridicule me about this forever; I could already see it happening.

Anna groaned and leant forward putting her head in her hands. "I'm so sorry. I can't believe they've printed all of that. Everything is going to be so much harder for you now."

I smiled weakly and scooted closer to her, slipping my arm around her shoulder. "Everything will be fine. It'll settle down in a couple of days. It's not like they're going to be following us around college or anything." At least, I prayed that wouldn't happen. Clearly I'd already underestimated the reaction to us. I figured it would just be a photo of her with her father, they would name her, and that would be it. I hadn't expected her to be highlighted this much at all. "Of course, it'll be a little harder at school now that people know who you are. But it's not that bad. The boyfriend cover still held so no one will know I'm an agent," I squeezed her shoulder gently and she looked up at me with apologetic eyes. "Everything is fine. Don't stress."

She sighed and nodded, chewing on her bottom lip. "You're not going to request a reassignment now then?"

I raised one eyebrow. Was there something I was missing? "Why would I?"

She shrugged, still gnawing on her bottom lip.

I sighed and rolled my eyes. "I'm not leaving you. I promised, didn't I?"

She blew out a big breath and nodded as the corner of her mouth twitched with an unwanted smile. "I know you did. I just wondered if your player instincts were going to make you run away screaming like a little girl now that the papers are insinuating that I'm in love with you."

I laughed as realisation washed over me. She thought I was a commitment-phobe and would leave because of what they'd printed. She had no idea. "I don't scream," I replied, winking at her playfully. "Besides, I kinda like our apartment."

She chuckled; her eyes sparkled as her tense posture seemed to relax. "Glad to hear it."

I smiled, knowing I needed to change the subject quickly. There was only so much teasing she could take before she started to freak out or panic and overthink things like she usually did. I didn't want her getting upset because, in some dark recesses of her mind, she thought that Jack would disapprove of a tabloid rumour.

"Some of these photos are great. We should try to get some of these and put them up in our apartment," I mused and held the paper out to Dean because he was trying to read it over my shoulder.

Anna nodded. "I love the one on the first page, the one of us on the red carpet."

"I like the dancing ones too. And the one with your dad in it," I replied, grinning proudly.

She giggled and slapped my stomach gently with the back of her hand. "Don't start getting all high and mighty just because the future President likes you."

I grinned. I couldn't care less if the President liked me or not, I cared that the father of the love of my life liked me. There was a vast difference in those two things in my eyes. "I'm allowed to brag a little, surely?" I joked.

She laughed and stood, looking down at me. "I'm starving. I'm assuming you haven't eaten yet?" I shook my head in response, now feeling my stomach grumble because she'd mentioned food. "Breakfast then?"

I stood and nodded eagerly. "Hell yeah. Coming, Dean?" I offered, turning to see him still scanning the paper.

He nodded absentmindedly. "Sure, breakfast with celebrity couple Annaton, every guy's dream," he joked, closing the paper and tossing it onto the bed. "Can I get your autograph?" he joked, grinning widely as he walked towards the door and pulled it open.

Anna winced, scrunching up her nose. "Don't joke about it, I already signed one."

I looked at her, shocked. "You already signed one? When?"

"When I was in the bar this morning," she shrugged and turned for the door to follow Dean out of the room.

I grabbed her hand and made her stop as I scowled at her. "When you were in the bar? You went to the bar without guards? Damn it, Anna!" Why did she have no regard for her safety? Did she not know that it would kill me if something happened to her?

She frowned and shook her head. "I took a guard."

326

"When were you in the bar?" I asked, frowning and hating the fact that no one had called me.

She shrugged casually. "This morning. I couldn't sleep, so we went for a tour of the hotel and then had a coffee, or four, in the bar."

My heart sank. "What time did you get up, Baby Girl?" I asked, pulling her to me. I raked my eyes over her face, noticing again how tired she looked.

"I don't know. About five? Can we go and eat, please?" she whined, begging me with her eyes to let it go.

I sighed deeply as I traced the shadow that resided under her eye. That shadow broke my heart. "Okay," I agreed. "Maybe we could get an early night tonight or something? I didn't sleep too great either."

She groaned and wrapped her arm around my waist, pressing herself to me. "You weren't worried about me all night, were you?"

"Nah, bed was lumpy. You really do think too much of yourself," I joked, turning her towards the door and pushing her out as she burst into a fit of giggles. When we got to the end of the hallway, Dean pressed the button for the elevator, and we all headed in and downstairs to the restaurant for breakfast.

As we stepped into the restaurant and were shown to an empty table, I tried extremely hard not to notice that the tables closest to us had stopped eating and that the middle aged lady had her forkful of eggs halfway to her mouth as she stared at us unashamedly.

Anna squirmed in her chair, so I slid my hand across the table and took hers, squeezing gently. I was graced with a dazzling smile in return. Breakfast was awkward, to say the least. While we were eating, we were approached several times by other guests who were gushing about how excited they were to meet us, and how they had voted for Anna's father. After posing for a couple of shots on people's cell phones, I finally decided enough was enough and discreetly nodded to Dean. He then kept everyone else at a respectable distance, but that didn't stop the whispering, staring, pointing or discreet photos where people were taking selfies with us in the background.

Anna hardly ate anything, just pushed her food around her plate and kept glancing around nervously. When I finally realised that this wasn't going to get any better, I stood and held my hand down to her. "Let's go get a coffee in the bar area. Hopefully no one will be in there at this time of day. It's got to be better than this," I suggested.

Her hand slid into mine as she smiled gratefully. "Hope so." She sidled up to me and leant her head on my shoulder as we walked through the lobby, again trying to ignore people that stopped walking just to stare at us. Thankfully, when we got to the bar, it was fairly empty, apart from two or three people that I recognised from the party last night. They didn't pay a blind bit of notice to us as we slipped in and sat on one of the plush comfortable sofas. Dean and Mike stopped at the door, shoulder to shoulder, clearly blocking the entrance so that we could have some well needed privacy.

After ordering a couple of espressos, I took Anna's hand again, this time noticing how she winced slightly. I frowned, confused as I pulled her hand up, meaning to look at it. "Your hand okay?" She nodded, tightening her grip on me so that I couldn't let go. Her eyes told a different story though. I gently pulled my hand out of hers and groaned when I saw four little crescent shaped cuts on the palm of her hand.

She tugged her hand out of my grip and sighed. "It's fine," she mumbled.

My heart sank as I looked at her, silently begging her to stop shutting me out and telling me she was fine when, clearly, she wasn't. "Bad dream?" I inquired, not actually wanting to know the answer but, at the same time, needing to. She nodded, and my stomach clenched with anger. If I ever managed to get within a few feet of Carter Thomas, I would beat him to death without hesitation. I swallowed the raw anger that tasted so acrid in my mouth. "Want to talk about it?"

She closed her eyes and shook her head, picking up her coffee and wrapping her hands around it as she blew the steam from the rim. "No."

I nodded in acceptance. Silence washed over us for a minute before I decided to change the subject. "So, do you have much to pack?"

She smiled gratefully. "Not really. It'll only take like ten minutes. I'm keeping those shoes from last night; I think they'll look super cute with a pair of jeans. What do you think?" she asked excitedly.

I grinned because she could get so excited about a pair of shoes. "Yeah, I guess. I didn't really see them."

Her eyes narrowed. "I showed you them."

I nodded. "Yeah you did, but you also showed me your legs at the same time. My eyes didn't make it down as far as the feet."

She giggled and slapped me on the shoulder. "You're such a pervert!" she scolded, shaking her head, trying to look like she disapproved but failing miserably.

I grinned and nodded. "Only around you, Baby Girl." She rolled her eyes. She never believed me when I said that, but it was true. Since I'd met her, I hadn't even looked at another woman, and I just didn't want to either.

Behind us, Dean walked over, talking into his cell phone. "Yeah, I'll tell them. Yeah, I'm sure we can get it on, it's fine. Thanks, Cindy." He slid his cell phone back into his pocket and winced. "Cindy from the press office just called to let me know that the news channel had a reporter at the party, and they'll be on in five minutes," he nodded in the direction of a large flat screen TV that was mounted on the wall. "I'll go see if we can get that turned on." He strutted off to the bar, talking to the barman for a minute before the black screen flickered to life and then settled on the news channel.

Anna pulled her knees up to her chest, and we both sat watching it, expecting it to be about the party and her dad's birthday. On the screen came the host of the show, and seated next to her was one of the reporters that had waited outside on the red carpet, who had inquired about Anna's dress.

The host smiled warmly, doing her introductions, before turning to the reporter. "So, Judy, you were at the party at The Wiltshire last night. What's the gossip? The papers are raving about Annabelle Spencer this morning, and I must say, she's very beautiful," the host of the show said, smiling broadly. Anna gulped and shifted uncomfortably in her seat. Placing my hand on her knee, I squeezed supportively. They would just talk about her for a minute and then they'd move on.

Judy, the reporter, put her hand over her heart and beamed. "Oh my gosh, she was so beautiful in person, and so sweet. And that boyfriend of hers is incredibly good-looking! I can see why the papers are flagging them as the new celeb couple of the year," she answered. I couldn't help but grin. Everyone seemed to think we made a marvellous couple, apart from Anna.

Anna laughed awkwardly, wincing in my direction as if she was now waiting for me to run away screaming again, like she had suggested earlier. "Sorry."

I rolled my eyes, but didn't get a chance to answer before they started the excited chatter on the television again. "I know the party was actually to celebrate the birthday of the President-elect, but my goodness, when Annaton stepped out of that limo, all of the attention just shifted to them. It was like some sort of eclipse. And I got the first question!" Judy gushed excitedly.

The pair of them then went on to analyse every detail of Anna's dress, hair and make-up, before moving on to me. They somehow even knew who made my tuxedo – even I hadn't known who made my tux. After, they showed a clip of me helping Anna out of the car and us walking up the red carpet. They ooh'd and ahh'd when Anna turned to me and smiled as we were having our photographs taken and when I brushed her hair back. I had to admit, watching it from the outside *did* make us look like a loved-up couple. The next clip was me joking about meeting the parents; they slowed it down, showing Anna laughing and looking at me with a gorgeous little smile on her face. When it got to my next line about Anna being the best thing that had ever happened to me, they showed that twice, gushing about how sweet I was and how lucky Anna was to have me.

For a further ten minutes, they somehow found more things to talk about before finally changing the subject back to what the show should have been about all along – Anna's father. When Dean finally turned off the TV, I grimaced over at Anna. She was wincing, hiding behind her knees and just peeking over the top. I laughed before I could stop myself.

She groaned and shook her head. "It's not funny, Ashton! Did you not just watch the same programme as me?" she whined, pouting at me as if

I could somehow make all of this better and make it disappear in a puff of smoke. "And what the hell is Nate going to say? And Rosie, and the rest of the guys at school?"

I smiled weakly and got off of my chair, squatting in front of her and taking her hands in mine. "Anna, calm down. Everything will be fine, and we'll get through it together. If Rosie and the guys from school want to treat you any different after this, then they're not worth having in your life and you've lost nothing special anyway." I didn't mention Nate. I was pretty sure I was in for some mocking about the name, and a decent amount of ridicule for looking like a soppy jerk on TV, but he was my best friend, and there was no doubt in my mind that he wouldn't treat me or Anna any differently.

She took a deep breath and closed her eyes before nodding, seeming to visibly calm herself. "Okay, fine. Let's just go pack or something. I want to go home. I'm done with all this stuff."

Leaning forward, I wrapped my arms around her tightly and hugged her, letting her delicious smell waft over me. Her arms wrapped around my neck too, hugging me back. Not ready to let go of her yet, I slid my arms down her back and under her ass as I leant back and pushed myself to my feet, lifting her with me and holding her tightly against me.

She giggled, and her legs automatically wrapped around my waist, clamping herself to me as she buried her face into the side of my neck and finally seemed to relax. A contented sigh left my lips because she was back in my arms again, right where she belonged.

As I carried her through the foyer and headed towards the elevator, someone shouted our names from my left. I turned my head in that direction, seeing a photographer on his knees snapping shot after shot of me carrying her before Dean and Mike both rushed forward and intercepted him, blocking his view.

Anna gasped and I quickly set her down onto her feet, ushering her towards the now open elevator. Not waiting for Dean, I pressed the button for her floor and looked out, seeing them guiding the photographer out of the front door without actually touching him.

"Shit," I growled under my breath as the doors closed and left us alone. "Sorry. Hopefully they were able to intercept before he got a decent shot?" I offered weakly.

She sighed and nodded, gripping my waist and pulling me towards her as she pressed herself against my chest. As the elevator travelled upwards, I dipped my head and captured her soft lips in a gentle kiss. She seemed to melt against me as her grip tightened on my waist. A small moan escaped her lips as she kissed me back. When the doors to the elevator slid open, I reluctantly pulled my mouth away from hers, smiling when her eyes took a few seconds to open again. When they did open, they latched onto mine and seemed to burn with a passion that made the hairs on my arms

330

stand on end. An agent stuck his head around the door, seeing that it was us before nodding in acknowledgement and going back to his lookout post.

Gripping her hand tightly, I gave her a little tug towards her hotel room door. "Let's pack your stuff and then you can come to my room while I do mine."

There wasn't much to collect really. All of the party clothes had been provided for us, so it was only what we travelled in yesterday and our sleepwear that needed to be packed. She was done within three minutes and then we headed down a floor to pack my belongings.

She lay on my bed while I threw my clothes into a bag. When I was done, the need to hold her was just too great, so I gave in. I crawled up the bed, hovering over her as I smiled down at her underneath me. I didn't touch her as her gaze came up to meet mine. I searched her eyes, desperately trying to see if what the papers had printed was true. Her full lips curved up into a smile as she reached up and traced the line of my jaw with one delicate finger.

I was almost so lost in the moment that I missed the click of the door as the handle twisted, but thankfully, I still had some degree of control over myself. I rolled off her quickly, tensing, watching the door, but relaxing when I saw Dean saunter in.

By his tight jaw alone, I knew something was wrong. "Car's here when you're ready to leave. But, there's a slight problem."

I raised one eyebrow in question as I stood. "Problem?"

He nodded, running a hand through his hair. "Yeah, there are some reporters out front waiting for you two. Probably a good fifteen or twenty of them all crowded out there. There's probably about the same amount out the back too. There's no way to get out of the building without going past them," he stated.

Anna groaned behind me. I nodded, this was just something we had to deal with, it'd be over soon and then we'd be away from it all. "It'll be fine." I put my hand on top of Anna's head, stroking her hair as I kept my eyes firmly on Dean. "We'll go out the front, just make sure the car is parked there waiting. Also, ask that Mike guy to follow us to the airport, just in case."

Dean nodded in acknowledgment before picking up his overnight bag from his bed and sauntering out of the room to get to work. I turned back to Anna. "Once we get back to campus, everything will settle down and they'll lose interest. It's only because we're still in the hotel." *At least, I hope it is!* "Come on." I picked up her bag and mine, and waved for her to follow behind me.

By the time we got down to the lobby and had checked out, passing our luggage to one of the concierges to take to the car, Dean had arranged the cars and had rounded up two extra guards along with Mike. They were all standing by the door waiting for departure.

331

My hand closed around Anna's as I pulled her close to my side. "Don't leave my side. If anyone grabs you or anything, I'll handle it, or Dean. You just smile and we'll get to the car."

She nodded in understanding, chewing on her bottom lip furiously. We walked over to Dean, and I nodded discreetly, watching as they pulled the doors open for us to exit.

As soon as we stepped out, the fifteen or so people started shouting our names and cameras started whirling. Dean and Mike stepped to our sides, arms outstretched, keeping the crowd back as they surged forwards, trying to get the best pictures. My eyes scanned the crowd, looking for anything untoward or suspicious, but they were all just reporters after a scoop.

One of the reporters quickly shoved a Dictaphone towards us, leaning in as close as she could even though Dean was holding her back. "Annabelle, Ashton, what do you think about what the papers are saying about you two this morning?"

Anna looked up at me quickly as if she wasn't sure she should answer. I shrugged. I had no idea what the protocol was for it, she should probably have had a press agent here with her or support, but that was too late now. No one predicted anything like this would happen.

She cleared her throat and smiled. "It's crazy, this is all just crazy," she answered, waving her hand around at all the people as her hand tightened on mine.

Another reporter tried to bustle forward. "Ashton, what do you think of the body language expert saying that the President-elect liked you and trusted you with his daughter?" he shouted.

I shrugged awkwardly. I didn't want to answer any questions; all I wanted was her safely away from this crowd. "I'm glad, of course. What boyfriend wouldn't like to hear that his girlfriend's dad likes him?"

Anna laughed at my answer, and we carried on walking, but it was a slow feat because they were all crowded around the path to the car. We were about half way to the car now.

"Annabelle, now your father has been elected, do you think your relationship with Ashton will change?" another asked.

Anna smiled. "I hope not, I don't want it too. Hopefully he won't see me as a different person now. What do you think, Pretty Boy, you gonna see me any different?" she asked, turning to look at me, smiling affectionately.

I grinned and pulled her closer to me. "I won't see you any different, Baby Girl," I promised.

"Can you two kiss so we can get a photo?" one of the reporters pleaded.

I groaned inwardly. She wouldn't want to do that. If we were to kiss, then her parents would find out and she would hate that. I looked down at her and was just about to tell the reporters that that kind of thing was private, when Anna gripped the front of my T-shirt and pulled my mouth down to hers.

My whole body stiffened from shock, but I kissed her back immediately, very aware that the cameras were clicking like crazy around us as they took their shots. As she tried to deepen the kiss, I pulled back and shook my head discreetly. Clearly, she had forgotten where we were and that everyone was watching. She whimpered as I pulled away, but then blushed as she seemed to come back to reality. I smiled and brushed my finger across her pink cheek as I nodded my head in the direction of the car, signalling for her to start walking again.

"Do you think you two will get married?" someone questioned.

I grinned sheepishly. *I would marry her right now if I could!* I squeezed her waist, she probably knew what my answer would be to that because I'd made a couple of little marriage jokes to her already. Anna winced, recoiling slightly at the question. "We're pretty young to be thinking about marriage," she answered weakly, shaking her head in rejection.

"Ashton, what do you think?" the same guy probed.

I laughed and shrugged, deciding to answer honestly. "Well, I don't think we're too young, let's leave it at that."

Anna gasped, slapping me on the shoulder playfully before pushing me towards the car. "What the? Seriously, Ashton, you should get in the car before you drop us in anything!" she scolded nervously, blushing profusely. The reporters around us laughed too at her embarrassed outburst.

I grinned and grabbed her hand, pulling her forwards the last couple of steps as the cameras started up again. Dean opened the back door of the car, so I manoeuvred behind Anna so that she had to get in first, discreetly positioning my body so that I was between her and the reporters. Once she was safely in, I slipped in behind her and Dean slammed the door before climbing in the driver's seat. Twisting to look out of the back window, I saw Mike and the other guard climb into the car behind us and follow as Dean pulled out and sped off down the road.

Anna slapped me on the shoulder again. The blush was still prominent on her cheeks. "What the hell was that?" she asked, shaking her head in disbelief. A small smile twitched at the corners of her mouth though, so I knew I wasn't in too much trouble.

I smirked at her. "Oh come on, if I asked you flat out, you'd say no. Maybe I need to trap you into it," I joked, winking at her.

The smile faded from her face instantly. "Don't ever trap me into anything, Ashton. I don't like being forced into things," she mumbled. Her chin trembled as she spoke and I suddenly realised this wasn't just about me making a joke, this was something deep-rooted to do with Carter and her not having control of her life.

I cupped my hands around her face, making her look at me as I smiled apologetically. "I was playing around. I would never do that to you," I promised.

"Good," she sighed and nodded. Her heavily lidded eyes met mine and she scooted closer to my side, setting her head on my shoulder. "Let's go home," she whispered.

Chapter Thirty-Two

The trip home was uneventful; no one was waiting for us at our end of the airport. I was hopeful that no one would know where we lived or even which state we were in. Her father was still going to limit press access to her as much as possible.

By the time we got back to our apartment, it was after two in the afternoon. Anna immediately headed off saying she wanted a nice, long soak in the bath, and I headed to the lounge and flopped on the sofa, exhausted. I hadn't slept well at all in the last couple of days, and my body was definitely feeling the ill effects of that now. My nerves finally settled, and I relaxed now that we were home. It was so much easier when we were on our own and could behave like ourselves rather than putting on an act for her parents so that they wouldn't look at us strangely. As far as they were concerned, they thought I was doing my job and playing the role of attentive loving boyfriend, no one knew that it carried on when we were alone. Dean had some idea. He'd certainly shot me a couple of looks that suggested he knew how I felt about her. That didn't matter though; the only one I wanted to know how I felt was still entirely oblivious.

After ten minutes of me sitting in silence and fighting my stinging eyes, my cell phone started to buzz in my pocket. As I pulled it out and looked at the screen, I groaned. I was too tired to be dealing with this already.

"Hey, Nate," I greeted, putting it to my ear. "I know what you're gonna say."

He laughed excitedly in response. "Fuck me, Taylor; you're dating the President's daughter? I met the President's daughter and saw her semi-naked! I drank and flirted with the President's daughter!" he chirped.

"He's not President yet, but yep," I agreed tiredly.

"You're all over the papers. Every channel I put on the TV, the two of you are on there." I could just imagine his face, shocked and amused, one eyebrow raised like he did when he tried to tease the life out of me.

"I know, man, weird huh?"

"So seriously, what's he like? Is he a nice guy? Did you know who Anna was when you met her? How come the papers said you had been together for a year and three months?" he fired off the questions, one after the other.

My breath caught in my throat at the last one. Nate knew we hadn't been together that long, but we had to say that because of her college. "I don't know, that must be a misprint, it's three months," I lied. "And no, I didn't know who she was when I met her. She didn't tell me at first. But yes, I have met the President-elect. He's a good guy," I said, trying to answer all of his questions briefly.

"Why didn't you tell me who she was? Her dad was Senator when I met her, you could have told me."

I sighed. He was such a good guy, he wouldn't even mind when this was over and I told him about my assignment. He'd understand, I knew that, but I still didn't like lying to him. "Nate, I couldn't. I wanted too, but she had to try and blend in for her security and stuff. I'm not allowed to do anything without her bodyguards say so."

"Yeah, I get it, bud, don't worry, I thought it was something like that," he admitted. He made a strangled laugh. "You do know that if you screw up and hurt her, he has the power to have you killed," he joked.

A tired grin covered my face. *Trust Nate to think of it that way!* "Lucky I'm not gonna screw up and hurt her then."

"I saw you two getting interviewed outside the hotel. I didn't realise you were so serious about her. I knew you were in love with her, that much was pretty damn obvious by the love-sick puppy eyes you shoot her, but I didn't realise that you wanted to marry her. It came across on TV like you were trying to make a joke, but I know you too well, Taylor. You were serious, weren't you?" he asked.

I smiled. Nate always had known me well. "Yeah, but I don't think she's up for it yet. I'm working on it though. Listen, Nate, I need to go, I haven't slept in forever and my head is killing me."

"Sure, I'll speak to you in the week, say hi to Anna for me when you see her, okay?" he instructed.

"I will. See ya," I disconnected the call and switched on the TV, flicking onto the news channel, only to see me and Anna plastered all over the screen. There were clips of us leaving the hotel and answering questions. They still loved us as a couple and were talking about our nicknames for each other. A proud grin slipped onto my face when they played the bit of her pulling me in for a kiss. Admittedly, it looked just as hot as it had felt.

In my hand, my cell phone rang again. My body jerked in my seat when I saw the number that was flashing on the screen. I answered the phone with wide eyes.

"Hi, Agent Taylor. Please hold for the President-elect," Maddy stated formally. I swallowed the lump that was building in my throat. No doubt Anna's father was calling to reprimand me for what I'd said about wanting to marry her outside the hotel.

Moments later, his firm voice greeted me. "Agent Taylor, I just wanted to check how Annabelle was holding up after the reporters hounding you two at the hotel."

"She's fine, sir. She was shocked and nervous about it, but she's fine now."

He sounded like he breathed a sigh of relief. "That's great. Melissa and I were concerned that she'd be under too much pressure with everyone thinking you were dating," he said.

I grimaced, knowing this was where he was going to warn me to do my job and to keep my hands off his daughter. "She's fine, sir. You don't need to worry."

"Good. At least people still aren't aware that you're an agent. The boyfriend cover seems to be working well so far."

I smiled. *Well, it definitely works well for me.* "Yes it is."

"Well, call me if you have any problems on your end, or if you need to up the security and I'll make the arrangements," he suggested easily.

I frowned. *Okay, where's the speech?* "I will, sir. Don't worry about Anna, I'll take care of her," I promised.

"I know you will, son," he replied as he ended the call.

I stared at the phone, my tired brain not quite able to work out what just happened. I'd expected at least a warning that I should back off and do my job properly, but there had been nothing at all. He hadn't even mentioned the fact that she kissed me in front of the reporters.

I sighed as I pushed the phone onto the side, deciding to give up trying to second guess everything. People never seemed to react the way I thought they would lately. When my eyes started to get heavy, I rested my head back on the sofa.

Just as I was about to fall into slumber, the sofa dipped next to me, so I forced my stinging eyes open. Anna smiled sadly at me, her hair was still wet and scraped back into a bun. She was wearing one of my T-shirts again. "Lie down," she cooed, pushing her hand under the back of my head and pulling it towards her gently. All that came out of my mouth was a strangled gargle as she pulled a little harder and smiled. "Lie down, Ashton." I gave in fighting and twisted, lying down and setting my head in her lap as I swung my legs over the arm of the sofa and fell into a peaceful sleep.

~ Anna ~

When my alarm sounded in the morning, I cracked my eyes open, wincing as the light from the window made my eyes sting. I squeezed my eyes closed again and rolled over to cuddle into Ashton; I was actually pretty surprised he wasn't all over me already. I rolled onto his side of the bed, instantly noticing that the sheets were cold against my skin. I pushed myself up, frowning at the empty space beside me.

The alarm was still beeping loudly, so I turned it off, wincing because I was still tired and didn't want to go to college today. My heart sank when I remembered that this was the first day since the party so the cat would be out of the bag about who I was now. Things were going to change today, no doubt.

After slipping on a bath robe, I headed out of the room and made my way to the kitchen, needing a strong coffee. My eyes settled on Ashton sitting there with both Dean and Peter. I frowned as I poked Peter in the back as I walked past. "Shouldn't you be in bed? Don't night shift workers usually sleep during the day?" I teased.

"Hey, Anna. Yeah I should, but my boss is a real hard ass," Peter answered jokingly, motioning towards Ashton who was sitting there with a pencil and paper and a stack of notes and diagrams in front of him.

I waved my hand dismissively. "Don't listen to him, he's a pussy cat. Just go to bed."

Peter laughed, and Ashton rolled his eyes. "We're just going over some stuff for today as a precaution," Ashton explained.

I had to scoff at that. "Just chill, will you? Everything's fine. Jeez, you're going to work these two to death. Nothing's going to happen. Maybe I'll have a couple more people talk to me today, or maybe they'll all avoid me like the plague. Nothing to be dramatic over," I shrugged, genuinely not knowing what to expect.

Ashton cleared his throat loudly and turned back to Peter and Dean. "Ignore the interruption," he stated, waving dismissively at me.

I laughed incredulously. "Interruption? Wow, rude much?"

A smile twitched at the corner of his lips as he carried on planning with the agents, obviously trying to ignore me and not react.

"Anyone want coffee? I'm making eggs if there are any takers," I smiled wickedly as I interrupted again on purpose.

"No thanks. We're working," Ashton replied tersely before the other two could answer.

I grinned. *Wow, serious Ashton is here today!* I waited for him to start talking again before I spoke, "Orange juice, Dean?"

Ashton sighed dramatically. "Seriously, Anna, are you trying to annoy me?" he asked, raising one eyebrow in warning.

I nodded, smiling sweetly. The idea of Ashton getting annoyed with me was actually pretty funny; I didn't even think he would. I could see Dean and Peter trying to hide their smiles. Ashton shook his head at me, obviously trying terribly hard not to smile and turned back to them, starting to plan again.

"Cereal anyone?" I asked, laughing wickedly.

Ashton jumped out of his chair so fast that I barely saw him move. He grabbed me from behind, wrapping one arm tightly around my waist, pinning my arms to my sides and covering my mouth with his other hand. I laughed against his hand as he shushed me and pinned my body against his so I couldn't move.

"Right, we're done now anyway but just to recap, Peter, you'll come meet us at the end of school. Dean will move a little closer, and if I call, then you'll adopt near guard position and ignore me completely," Ashton ordered. I squirmed in place as I started to find it incredibly sexy the way Dean and Peter were hanging on Ashton's every word. I could see the respect for him and it made me practically overflow with pride. "I've already spoken to the school office this morning and told them that additional arrangements may need to be taken, and they were fine with it. There should be no problems, it's just business as usual, but Dean can show his presence from now on seeing as everyone will expect Anna to have a guard with her now." His grip loosened slightly around my waist, but I didn't move away from him, I liked having him this close; I shifted my weight to my other leg and discreetly ground my ass across his crotch. His arm immediately tightened back up again, pinning me against him. "If there are any problems at all, I need to maintain cover, so you take her away. Don't wait for me to make the first move, I'll only move if I have to because I need to look like a boyfriend and not an agent. Right, well, Peter, you'd better go get some sleep," he said sternly.

Dean and Peter nodded, both standing to leave. "Got it, boss," Peter answered, nodding as both of my far guards left the apartment.

After the front door shut, Ashton kissed the side of my neck softly, still holding his hand over my mouth. "Now, Miss Spencer, you need to stop interfering with my job, or else," he growled sexily in my ear. My whole body started to throb at the sound of his husky voice as he held me tightly against him. When he bit the back of my neck playfully, I whimpered with desire and instantly regretted teasing him because now I was going to be fantasising about him all day. "Is that understood?" he whispered against my neck, sending his hot breath blowing down my back. I couldn't answer; my mouth was dry and my body practically vibrating with excitement. "I said, is that understood, Miss Spencer?" he whispered in my ear. I grinned against his hand and nodded. "Hmm, good," he purred as he moved his hands from their restraining positions and rested them on my hips gently. I didn't move away from him, I couldn't. I loved the feel of his body against mine, I would be quite happy just to stand here like this all day. "How about I make you breakfast?" he offered, his voice still thick with lust.

How about we skip breakfast and school and go to bed? It was on the tip of my tongue, but somehow I held it back. I squeezed my eyes shut, trying to block out the lustful thoughts that seemed to come to me so frequently lately. "No, it's okay. Thanks for the offer though, I thought I would make something hot today," I said, finally able to drag myself out of his embrace. "You hungry?"

"Of course," he grinned, watching as I pulled out a packet of bacon from the fridge. He nodded eagerly. "You know you're the best girlfriend anyone ever had, don't you?"

I smiled. "Well, I do now that you've told me," I replied, shrugging. I did already know that actually, he told me a lot.

When we arrived at school, the whole parking lot seemed to turn in unison to watch us. A hushed silence settled over the crowd, and I shrank into Ashton's side, already wishing I was somewhere else. This was going to take a lot of getting used to.

Ashton's arm tightened around me as the excited whispering started. "Relax, Baby Girl, it'll die down," he said, squeezing my waist affectionately.

As we made our way to the building, my eyes settled on Rosie and the rest of our friends that were standing in a little huddle outside the front entrance. I sighed, feeling my shoulders slump in defeat. I knew this would happen; clearly they would all treat me differently now that they knew who my father was. It was inevitable. However, the wide eyes and tight lips that looked back at me made my insides ache. I should have taken more time to prepare myself for this kind of public rejection, I wasn't ready at all.

But as we got to the last step, a cheeky grin broke out on Rosie's face as she produced a pen and paper from behind her back. "Can I get Annaton's autograph, I heard they're going for ten bucks on eBay," she teased, before bursting out laughing.

My shoulders relaxed as she shook her head grinning happily. Maybe I'd underestimated them a little. I smiled, grateful for their acceptance. Rosie York was an incredible person, and an even better friend, I would have been extremely sad to lose her because of this. We'd gotten incredibly close.

"Ten bucks, really? Maybe we should sign a load and sell them ourselves?" I joked, turning to Ashton. He laughed in response.

Serena smiled. "I can't believe your dad is going to be the next President. My dad's a paint salesman," she said, grinning.

I shrugged, wincing apologetically. "I didn't really want to announce it to everyone. People can be a little standoffish when they find out your father's running for office."

Rosie nodded and stepped forward; linking her arm through mine. She gave me a little tug away from Ashton and made me start walking up the hallway with her. "On to more important things," she whispered, looking over her shoulder at Ashton conspiratorially. "I saw you two get interviewed. Do you think he's going to propose?" she asked, grinning excitedly as her eyes sparkled happily.

I chuckled awkwardly. "I hope not. We're too young."

She sighed and nodded in agreement. "True, but he's so yummy. Imagine being married to that," she said, fanning her face dramatically as she winked at me. "You should accept if he does."

I dropped my eyes to the floor. I hated marriage talk, it made me uncomfortable and brought back feelings and memories that I tried extremely hard to bury. "He won't," I assured her. I didn't want to plant false hope there for her by going along with her excited chattering; after all, he was just a bodyguard who had become my friend, nothing more.

For the rest of the day, a few people came up to speak to me, most seemed a little intimidated. A rare few asked for autographs or a photo, which was more than awkward considering they were in my classes and had been talking openly to me for the last couple of months.

By the time the end of day came around, I was grateful to be out of the spotlight for a little while. As we stepped through the door to our apartment, I breathed a sigh of relief that the day was over and done with. There were only a couple of weeks left of school anyway, and then the semester was over. Hopefully, by the time we came back in the New Year, everything would have settled and people would be used to it even more and not bat an eyelid at me.

I flopped down on the sofa while Ashton headed to the kitchen to make coffee. When he set my cup on the side next to me, I smiled. "Thanks. I'm glad that's over with," I admitted. "Just another couple of weeks and then we can get away from all of this for Christmas."

I frowned as I said it. I wasn't actually looking forward to Christmas at all. Of course, I was looking forward to not getting up for classes and not having assignments to finish, but I wasn't looking forward to being away from Ashton for two weeks. Because this one was a scheduled school holiday, he got the two weeks off, so I would need to brave it on my own with my parents at the Lake House.

He nodded thoughtfully and sat down next to me. "Yeah, Christmas. I wanted to talk to you about that actually, but there never seems to be the right time because we've been so busy lately."

I nodded, already knowing what this would be about. "Yeah, we can go tomorrow or something. There are still a few bits I need to buy, but I've got most of mine already," I stated, pre-empting him suggesting we go gift shopping soon. I'd been very organised and had already arranged the more important things that I wanted to get – like Ashton's gift that Maddy had arranged for me.

"Go where?"

I smiled, confused. "Shopping. Weren't you just about to say that you needed to buy gifts?"

He shook his head. "No actually, but I do need to do that," he admitted. "Actually, I was going to ask what we're doing about Christmas itself." He frowned as if he was trying to work out a complicated algebra problem.

"What's that supposed to mean?" I asked, picking up my coffee and blowing it gently to cool it before taking a sip.

He shrugged. "Well, I'm guessing that you'll want to spend Christmas day with your parents. But maybe we could spend New Year in Los Angeles. What do you think of that?"

I almost choked on the coffee as he spoke. *Spend New Year in LA? With him?* "What? I don't…" I stared at him, waiting for him to say something that made sense.

"If you don't want to come to my place again, that's fine, I just thought that you liked it last time and figured I'd suggest it."

I smiled gratefully. "That's a really nice thought, Ashton, but you should just go out with your friends. That way you won't have to worry about me, and you can just have a good time."

He frowned, looking a little angry at my answer. "I'm not going without you."

I raised one eyebrow in question, confused by the turn in the conversation. "What are you going on about? I'm totally lost, Pretty Boy," I admitted.

He sighed dramatically, as if I was missing something that was obvious. "What exactly do you think is happening at Christmas?"

I frowned, setting my cup down and tucking my legs up underneath me. "Well, I'm going to the Lake House with my parents and the house guards, and you're going home…"

He shook his head. "Not happening, Baby Girl."

"What's not? I'm freaking confused! Ashton, will you just spit out what you're trying to say already?" I grumbled, starting to get annoyed because I didn't like being confused.

He laughed wickedly at my outburst. "I love it when you're feisty," he teased, smirking at me. I rolled my eyes and waited for him to explain what on earth he was getting at. "Okay, so I'll put it simply. I want to spend the school break with you. If you want to spend the time with me, then we just need to figure out what we're doing," he explained, shrugging.

I gasped as it clicked into place. *Mr Overprotective strikes again! He doesn't even trust his job to anyone for two weeks.* "You've got two weeks off, Ashton. Stop worrying about me, I'll be fine!" I snapped, frowning.

He laughed and shook his head at me. "Anna, I'm not talking about my job. I'm talking about wanting to spend Christmas with you," he said simply. I recoiled at the honest revelations, too shocked to speak. His smile fell from his face. "You don't want to spend Christmas with me?" he asked, looking hurt and embarrassed.

"I… I, Ashton, of course I do, but…" I shook my head because that couldn't happen. They wouldn't let me go with him, not now that my dad was President-elect. Dean and Peter would have time off so we couldn't stay here, and I couldn't very well invite him to spend Christmas with my parents because they would certainly read something into that.

His hand brushed across my cheek as I stared at him, lost for words. "Anna, just forget everything else for a minute, okay? If you could, would you want to spend your winter break with me?" he asked, looking at me a little pleadingly.

Damn, I would love that. "Yes," I managed to get out; I was still shocked that he even wanted to do that in the first place. This was his first scheduled break away from me; he could hang out with his friends, laugh and joke around. Yet, he was telling me that he'd rather spend time with me. My heart was aching in my chest because of how much that meant to me.

A dazzling grin stretched across his face. "Okay, great. Well, I want to spend my two weeks off with you too. So now we just need to figure out what to do." He took my hand, playing with my fingers gently. "So would you prefer to go to LA or stay with your parents?"

I frowned. "Um… I don't really think either one is possible, is it?"

He sighed. "I know it'll be hard to convince your father to let me take you to LA again, but maybe he'll go for it. Or I could come home with you," he shrugged as if the thought of spending Christmas with the next President of the United States was something he did every day. I closed my eyes and thought about it; I honestly didn't care where I spent Christmas. If I could spend it with Ashton I'd go anywhere. "There's a third option," he added, sounding a little excited.

I opened my eyes. "What's the third option? Because LA doesn't seem likely, and going home sounds like it would be uncomfortable with my parents watching our every move and smiling at us all the time," I admitted.

He pursed his lips before speaking. "Well, how about we go away?"

"Like a vacation?" I asked, a little confused.

"Yeah, like a vacation. Somewhere where people don't know you. Maybe I'd be able to convince your father to let me take somewhere where there's no risk to you and no one knows who you are."

Excitement suddenly bubbled up inside me, but I tried hard to contain it. A vacation didn't sound like something my father would consent to. "I like option three," I admitted quietly.

"Hmm, what a coincidence, I like option three too," he grinned, tucking a loose strand of my hair behind my ear. "Hot or cold then? What's your preference?" he asked, smirking at me excitedly. "Beach or snow?"

"I don't care. What do you want?" In all honestly I would follow him anywhere he wanted, it didn't really matter.

"Well, I like the idea of snow for Christmas and maybe you'd get cold and would cuddle up to me," he mused, smirking at me.

I rolled my eyes at his train of thought. "Right, Pretty Boy, because otherwise that wouldn't happen," I stated sarcastically. We hugged all the time; it didn't need to be cold for that.

"I also like the idea of the beach, because you'd be wearing a bikini a lot," he continued, waggling his eyebrows at me.

I raised one eyebrow teasingly. "I guess… unless I went topless."

His back stiffened as he nodded eagerly. "Beach then, definitely."

I laughed and slapped his arm playfully. "Pervert!"

"Only around you," he replied, winking at me. He stood up quickly, fumbling in his pocket and producing a cell phone. "So that's what we'll try for first then? I'll ask to take you away somewhere hot," he said, looking at me hopefully.

I frowned, wanting to check he wasn't doing this for the wrong reasons. "Are you sure you don't just want to go hang out with your friends on your own and get drunk every night? I'll be fine with the temporary guards if that's what you're worried about," I protested.

He sighed deeply and bent, pressing a soft lingering kiss on my forehead before standing up again. "I want to spend the holidays with you. It's nothing to do with work, trust me." The way he looked so deeply into my eyes made me feel like I was the only girl in the world.

"Okay," I replied breathlessly.

He smiled, already thumbing through his contact list. "I'll see what I can do then, okay?" He turned and headed into our bedroom, closing the door tightly behind him so that he could speak to my father about it and reason out his case for wanting to take me away.

I smiled broadly. Worst case scenario, he would come and spend the holidays at the Lake House. At least then I would still get to see him every day. The thought of seeing him open his gifts on Christmas morning made my stomach quiver with excitement.

Chapter Thirty-Three

~ Ashton ~

Once in the solitude of the bedroom, I closed the door tightly behind me. I didn't want to make this call near Anna in case I had to bring up Carter in the conversation. As I pressed the connect button and put the phone to my ear, I silently prayed that he would go for one of the three options because I didn't want to spend two weeks pining for her.

Maddy answered on the third ring. "Hi, ma'am, it's Agent Taylor. How are you today?" I asked politely.

"Oh, Agent Taylor, I'm good. How are you and Annabelle?" she asked happily.

"We're great, thanks. Is it possible for me to speak to Senator Spencer?"

"Sure. He's free right now, I'll buzz you through."

The line beeped, and he answered a few seconds later. "Agent Taylor, is everything alright?" he asked quickly.

"Yes, sir, everything's fine. I just wondered if I could talk something through with you. It's about Anna's winter break." I tried to sound confident when all I wanted to do was beg this man to let me spend Christmas with his daughter.

"Okay, I'm listening."

"Well, sir, Anna has just asked me if it would be possible for her to go away for winter break. She said she wanted to get away and have a break somewhere hot," I lied, blaming the whole thing on her. Hopefully, if he thought it was her idea and something she really wanted, he would be more likely to accept it. This was one of the reasons why I wanted to speak to him in private.

"She wants to go on vacation?"

"Yes, sir, she said she'd like to," I confirmed, trying to sound casual.

"I'm not sure that's possible, I mean, with the whole guard situation…" he trailed off, sounding like he was thinking about it.

Okay, Ashton, now sell it. "I'd be happy to take her. We could go somewhere where she's not going to be recognised. The risk will be minimal to her. Less than here actually," I countered, trying to convince him.

"You would take her? What about your time off?" I could clearly hear the shock in his voice.

I smiled. "That's fine, I don't need time off. I'd be happy to take Anna."

He was quiet for a while, obviously thinking about it. "Well, where were you thinking?" he asked.

I smiled. *Okay, I'm half way there, he hasn't said no!* "I'm not sure where she would want to go, sir. Somewhere far enough away that she wouldn't be recognised, somewhere quite remote," I suggested, thinking of lying on a quiet beach with her.

He sighed. "Can I call you back? I'll speak to Melissa about it; she was looking forward to having Annabelle home for Christmas as much as I was." The disappointment in his tone was obvious.

"Okay, sir." I closed my eyes and prayed that her mother would say yes.

"You think she would like that? It would make her happy?" he asked quietly.

"Yes, I'm positive it would."

"I'll call you back in a bit." He disconnected the call.

I physically crossed my fingers, just hoping that he'd agree to it. My mind wandered to all of the places we could go. Of course, I couldn't afford five star luxury, but since I'd been guarding Anna I'd had nothing to pay out for because they paid my rent and expenses. I had some money saved, so we could certainly go somewhere nice.

About fifteen minutes later, my cell phone rang. I was still in the bedroom because I didn't want to go out and get Anna's hopes up by saying he was thinking about it, just in case it didn't happen. If he said no, then I would move onto option two of her coming to LA with me. I didn't think she'd actually want me to go to her parents' house with her, they would be cooing over our 'relationship' and she hated that, it would make her feel uncomfortable.

"Agent Taylor," I answered, knowing it was Maddy's number.

"Agent Taylor, please hold," Maddy instructed.

The phone clicked, and he came on. "Agent Taylor, I've spoken to Melissa, and we've agreed to her going on vacation if you're sure that you don't mind taking her," he said casually, as if we were discussing the weather. My breath caught in my throat because I was seriously expecting him to say no.

"Absolutely," I confirmed, grinning from ear to ear.

"Okay, great. We were thinking that Melissa and I would book the trip as her Christmas present."

My mouth popped open in shock. "Sir, that's nice of you, but I can cover it."

He laughed a booming hearty laugh. "That's not in your job description, son."

"I know that, sir, but Anna and I have become friends, it wouldn't really be like working. I guess it would kind of be a vacation for me too, so I'm more than happy to pay for us," I explained.

He laughed again. "Agent Taylor, it's terrific that you two are friends, but you're not paying for the trip. Melissa and I will book it for the two of you."

"Sir, honestly. I can't let you do that-"

"Son, I appreciate your position, but at the end of the day, you're going to be working, aren't you? You *do* plan on protecting my daughter, don't you?" he asked, amused.

"Of course."

"Well then, it's settled. As part of your job, you'll be accompanying my daughter on vacation. You won't be paying for it," he stated, ending the discussion.

"Thank you, sir," I replied, frowning. I felt a little deflated now because I'd actually wanted to book it and take her. I didn't want it to be like I was working, even though I would be.

"You're welcome, son. Thank you for doing this for Annabelle; if it wasn't for you, then she wouldn't even be thinking about a vacation. We really appreciate what you're doing for her," he said gratefully.

I smiled. "You're very welcome. Like I said, Anna and I have become friends."

"Well, is there anywhere you two would like to go? Did she mention anywhere?" he asked curiously.

"Not really, she just said somewhere hot. Are you planning on sending a far guard with us?" I asked curiously. *Please say no, I want her to feel completely comfortable...*

"I was under the impression that you meant just the two of you," he answered.

I grinned, fist pumping the air. "Yes, sir, I did mean just the two of us. I just wondered if that was alright with you." My insides were going crazy as I thought about rubbing lotion on her body with no one else watching, and no act to keep up.

"Son, can you protect my daughter on your own?" he asked.

"Yes, sir," I answered confidently.

"Well then, that's good enough for me. I trust you, Agent Taylor. If you say you can protect her then I believe you," he replied just as confidently.

Wow, he genuinely does trust me with his daughter! "Thank you, I appreciate your confidence."

"Like I said when you took her to LA, if it were any other agent then I would say no." The hair on the back of my neck prickled at his proud tone. I'd never had a father figure in my life, so I really appreciated that this man was so confident in my ability.

"I won't let you down," I promised.

"Good. Well, Melissa and I will have a think about it and get it arranged, if you really have no preference as to where you go…"

Jeez, I would follow that girl to the ends of the earth, I don't care. "No, sir, anywhere is fine. I would ask for an apartment though, instead of two hotel rooms. That way it would be easier for me to do my job without having to worry about another entrance to her room. Also, if you could book all the travel plans under another name, like LA, that way it would just cover the trail further," I suggested.

"Good idea. I'll let you know what we come up with and hopefully we'll have it booked by the end of the day. I'm sure Annabelle will want to go shopping for vacation clothes," he laughed, and I felt the predatory grin slip onto my face as I imagined all of the beachwear outfits she'd wear.

"Thank you, sir." This seriously was the best four months of my life, probably the best four months of anybody's life.

"No. Thank you, son," he countered as he hung up.

I stared at the phone for a minute in shock; Anna was going to flip when she heard this. I rearranged my expression before I exited the bedroom. She looked up expectantly with a hopeful expression on her face. I tried my best to look sad, and it must have worked as her expression faded and was replaced by a fake smile that clearly meant she thought we were headed to her parents' house.

"So?" she prompted as I sat next to her on the sofa.

I sighed dramatically. "Well, we can't go to LA."

"Oh man, I'm sorry, Ashton! You should just go on your own, you'd get to hang with your friends, go out New Year's Eve, and have fun," she smiled, trying to look enthusiastic.

"No, I want to spend winter break with you," I refused, trying desperately to keep the smile off my face.

She sighed. "Ashton, come on, be serious. It's going to be so awkward for us at my parents' house, how am I supposed to explain you being there instead of going home?"

"Yeah, you're right. I don't want to do that," I nodded in agreement.

She smiled sadly. "So just go to LA. Spend time with Nate."

"I don't want to do that either."

She took my hand, squeezing gently. "I'm sorry," she muttered.

348

"Yeah. So, about that shopping trip for Christmas presents…" I trailed off, fighting my urge to grin like a moron.

"Yeah?" She looked really sad, but she was obviously trying not to show me.

"Well, do you think we could go somewhere that sells skimpy bikinis and sun cream?" I asked, laughing.

She gasped as her eyes widened from shock. "Bikinis and sun cream? You mean? No way! Are you serious? But… but… really?" she cried.

I nodded, grinning ecstatically. "I'm serious. Your parents are booking the vacation as your Christmas gift. They're getting it booked by the end of the day, apparently," I confirmed, watching as her face went from shock to complete happiness. I chewed on the inside of my mouth because of how beautiful she looked when she smiled.

"You mean we get to go away? Really? You're not tricking me, are you? Because if you are, that's seriously mean," she asked, eyeing me curiously.

"I'm not tricking you, Baby Girl, I promise. I get to take you somewhere hot, with a beach. Just the two of us and no far guard," I confirmed.

She squealed excitedly and jumped up and down on the spot. "Oh my God! No far guard either? I can't believe you! How did you do that?" she cried as her eyes filled with tears.

"I must be the best boyfriend in the world," I joked, shrugging as if it was nothing.

Before I could either react or prepare myself for impact, she jumped onto my lap and hugged me tightly. "Thank you, Ashton. Oh God, this is going to be great! Thank you, thank you, thank you!" she squeaked, hugging me as I grunted from the sudden weight being thrust upon me.

"You're welcome, Baby Girl," I replied, grinning. In all honesty, I couldn't wait for some me and her time, with no one to act normal or pretend for. This was going to be the best Christmas ever.

Suddenly, her eyes widened and she pushed herself off my lap. "Oh man, I need to go to the gym!" She didn't even wait for an answer as she turned and streaked into the bedroom.

"Anna, where the hell did that come from?" I asked, getting up to follow her into the bedroom. She was just pulling on a pair of sweats and riffling through her drawer, coming out with a tank top. She was still practically bouncing on the spot. "Why are you going to the gym?" I asked, confused.

"Oh, come on. We're going to lie on a beach, I need to look good in my bikini," she explained, grinning like a mad woman.

I practically choked on her absurdity. "Look good in your bikini? Are you joking?"

She shook her head. "Are you coming or can I go on my own?" she asked as she walked past me.

I grabbed her hand, making her stop as I stared down at her in disbelief. "Are you serious? You're going to the gym so you'll look good in your bikini?"

She nodded and shrugged. "Well yeah. I know I can't do much in a week, but I've put on like four pounds since you stopped me running like I used to."

I scoffed and shook my head in disapproval. "You have got to be kidding me! You're perfect; you don't need to suddenly start running off to the gym! Honestly, you're the most beautiful thing in the world, Anna. And I happen to like the extra four pounds." I wasn't just saying that because I was in love with her.

She made a little aww sound as she went up on tiptoes and planted a little kiss on the corner of my mouth. "You're so sweet sometimes with these little comments of yours," she mused, pinching my stomach gently. "But of course you think I'm perfect, you're biased and are probably paid to say that," she replied. She nodded over her shoulder towards the door. "We would have gone to the gym later anyway, so what's the problem?"

I groaned and rolled my eyes. She never seemed to take me seriously when I told her how I felt about her. Maybe one day the information and hints would finally sink in.

"Are you coming or not?" she asked, stepping away from me and grinning.

Admitting defeat, I nodded in agreement. "Fine, just let me change first. I suppose I need to look good on the beach too."

She grinned. "Pretty Boy, you look *way* better than good all the time!"

After an hour at the gym, we were back at our apartment. Anna went in for the first shower while I opened my laptop because Maddy had texted to tell me that she'd emailed me the itinerary for our trip.

Agent Taylor,

Please find below details of your trip. Tickets will be waiting at the check in desk; passports will need to be shown to obtain them. As you will notice, I have amended Annabelle's name, as per her father's instructions. I have arranged for some local currency to be delivered to your apartment tomorrow. I trust that you can get a ride to the airport from one of the far guards, if not then let me know and I will book a car for you. Transfers have been arranged for when you get there. Weather should be delightful, so make

sure you take plenty of sunscreen. No injections
required. Have a marvellous time.

Maddy.

Duration: 14 nights
Flight time: Depart :10:45 Saturday 21st Dec
Return :14:00 Saturday 4th January
Destination: Maldives (South Male Atoll)
Hotel: 5* Deluxe Over water suite
Board: All inclusive
Transfer's: 20 minutes by speedboat
Passengers: Mr Ashton Taylor. Mrs Annabelle
Taylor

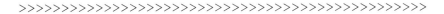

My breath caught in my throat at the last line. They'd put us as married? I
actually loved the sound of that. Annabelle Taylor. I'd never heard of
anything more perfect in my life. But I knew Anna wouldn't like it. For
some reason, she was really touchy about marriage and always seemed to
clam up or go quiet whenever I made jokes about it. Needing to sort it out
before she saw this email, I grabbed my cell phone and was just about to
dial Maddy's number, but Anna walked out of the bedroom behind me.

I closed the laptop quickly as she walked up behind me. She placed
her hand on the small of my back and smiled up at me. "Did you get it?
Where did they book?" she inquired excitedly.

"Um, yeah, I got it." I swallowed the lump in my throat.

She grinned and reached for the laptop, lifting the lid and looking at
me expectantly so I could enter the password. I typed it in quickly, wincing
as she opened my emails and double clicked on the one that Maddy sent.
She looked so excited that I didn't have the heart to stop her. I'd just have
to deal with the fall out and hope that she didn't think this was my idea.

She slid onto a stool as she read it. I held my breath, waiting.

"Speed boat transfer?" she asked, practically bouncing in her seat.

I winced, knowing she was almost done. I knew the exact moment
that she got to the last line because her body seemed to tense. Her eyes
flicked up to me. "Did you see the passengers?"

I nodded and waited for her reaction.

"That's…" she stopped talking, her mouth opening and closing a
couple of times before she frowned at the screen.

"I can ask for them to change it. I asked for them to change your
name, I didn't think they'd change it to mine," I chimed in, wanting her to
know this wasn't my idea.

She shook her head in rejection. "It's done now. Just leave it," she muttered.

"Are you sure?"

Her smile was forced as she nodded. "What's the matter, Pretty Boy, don't you want me to be Mrs Taylor?" She was trying to come across as playful, but I could see she was uncomfortable with this.

I decided not to answer that question honestly because clearly something was wrong that I didn't understand. "Anna, seriously, I can get Maddy to change it if you want."

She shrugged. "It's fine. Do you care?"

Hell yeah I care, I love it! I shook my head. "No, I don't care, Baby Girl," I lied smoothly.

"Don't worry about it then. It's kinda cute in a weird way. Plus, it'll help with people not following us around. I'm up for anything that means I won't get asked for my autograph!" she joked, shrugging nonchalantly.

Just needing to check that she wasn't putting on a brave front, I wrapped my arm around her waist and stepped between her legs, looking at her intently. "You're really okay with it?"

She shrugged easily. "I don't mind. It's just a name; as long as your player side isn't going to come busting through and make you run off," she teased.

"I'm not a player!" I cried, annoyed that she didn't seem to notice that I didn't see anyone else in the room but her.

She smiled tenderly at me as she nodded. "I know, I was just teasing," she whispered, wrapping her arms around me tightly. I stood there like that for a couple of minutes, just letting it all sink in. Finally, she pulled away and grinned up at me. "I'm going to go look through my clothes and see what else I need to buy before the trip!"

I chuckled as she jumped off the stool and practically skipped to the bedroom to look through her clothes.

Chapter Thirty-Four

~ Anna ~

After a seemingly never-ending flight, and then twenty minutes on a speedboat skimming over perfect, crystal clear ocean, we finally arrived at the island that we would call home for the next two weeks.

Almost as soon as we stepped onto the jetty, a tall man with golden, tanned skin and sun bleached, blonde hair walked over, smiling warmly and holding his hand out to Ashton. "Mr Taylor?" Ashton nodded in confirmation, shaking his hand firmly, and then the guy turned to me. "Mrs Taylor," he greeted.

A nervous giggle slipped from my lips at the sound of the name he'd used. When I'd first heard that they'd changed my name to that, it had taken me by surprise, and I hadn't liked it at all. Seeing my name attached to someone else's surname had brought back a lot of unpleasant memories for me. But having Ashton's name attached to me was different somehow; it wasn't as horrifying as I first thought it was. In fact, I even kind of liked it. In a strange way, it was almost as if the name change had given me the freedom to be normal for a little while. After all, nothing bad had ever happened to Annabelle Taylor.

"Nice to meet you," I replied, nodding in greeting.

"My name is Kyle, and I am the manager of the resort. If there is anything that you need during the duration of your stay, please let me know," he said.

Ashton smiled, slipping his hand into mine. "Thank you. You can call us Ashton and Anna, not Mr and Mrs Taylor."

Another unconscious giggle slipped out, so I chewed on my lip and looked at the beautiful scene that stretched out before me. It was like paradise, like a postcard, and I'd never seen anything more majestic in my life. The sand on the beach was pure white and powdery, and bright, blue sea lapped at it lazily. Little beach hut cabins were dotted along the tree line with hammocks hanging in the shade of palm trees outside. A little further up the beach, a wooden dock went straight out to the calm ocean, with villas each side of it. A little happy sigh left my lips as I imagined staying here for the next two weeks. It was going to be bliss.

Kyle smiled and motioned up the beach a little way. "I will show you to your villa. Hassan, bring their luggage," he instructed to the guy that was already unloading our bags from the boat. "Please follow me." Kyle walked off quickly, with his flip-flops slapping against the bottom of his feet with each step.

I grinned and squeezed Ashton's hand excitedly as we both followed behind him. When I realised he was walking towards the little wooden dock and the water villas beyond, I let out a little squeal of excitement.

"The main reception is located where we were just speaking. There are three restaurants inside, snack bars, two swimming pools, a spa, a couple of stores, and three bars. Up the beach, we run various water sports, including kayaking, snorkelling and windsurfing. On the edge of the beach here, each night from eight until midnight, we have an outdoor grill. They'll cook anything you want – steaks, fish and lobster. If they have it, they'll cook it," Kyle boasted. He stepped up onto the wooden walkway and waved out to the eight or so villas on stilts that sat directly over the sea. "These are our overwater villas. The one at the very end is yours." Kyle pulled two key cards from his pocket. "The one next door to you is empty for the next two weeks so you'll have privacy up there. The ocean on this side is restricted access for the villas only so you shouldn't have people swimming there. No boats or water sports allowed in this area so you can use it freely."

I swallowed noisily. Clearly my father had thought of everything because no one was even allowed to swim near our apartment.

As he stopped at the little wooden door and scanned the key on the black electronic box on the side, the door clicked and he pushed it open, waving me inside. As I stepped over the threshold, I had to gasp at the sheer luxury of the place. It was stunning.

In the centre of the large room was a ginormous cream sofa with a canopy hanging from the ceiling that was draped around it. Next to it was a little table with a large bouquet of flowers set in the middle and two cosy-looking arm chairs. The walls on three sides were wooden, but on the wall opposite the front door it was floor to ceiling glass that looked out over beautiful, calm, uninterrupted ocean.

Ashton walked in behind me, and I heard his gasp of shock too. Kyle waved at a little white box mounted on the wall. "The air conditioning operations are here." He walked in a little further and motioned to a door on the right. "This is your bathroom, complete with whirlpool bath. The glass in there is privacy glass, which means that you can see out, but no one can see in. It's totally private."

"It's incredible," I mumbled, shaking my head in awe.

Kyle nodded in agreement and pushed open another door, waving me in. "This is the largest of the bedrooms."

The bedroom was just as glorious as I thought it would be. The covers on the four poster, king sized bed were pure white. Two red towels had been folded and arranged into the shape of a heart, and little red rose petals were scattered over the white sheets. The bed faced another wall of glass so that the first thing you would wake to in the morning was ocean, as far as the eye could see.

"Over there is my favourite part of this whole villa," Kyle said, pointing to two armchairs. I frowned but walked over, shocked to see that a large part of the floor had been removed and replaced by glass. The water below was so perfectly clear that you could see every stone that graced the bottom and every fish that swam. So far, it was easily my favourite part of the villa too.

"Let me show you the terrace, and then I'll leave you two to get settled."

As we walked back through the lounge, I noticed that our bags had been placed just inside the door already. As Kyle slid open the heavy-looking glass doors, the warmth from outside hit me full in the face. I sighed contentedly, squinting outside and unable to keep the smile off my face.

Ashton busied himself quizzing Kyle about when the maids would come, and how to call for room service; so I walked around the deck, touching the little table and chairs, and the sun loungers. As I leant against the bannister and took in the magnificent view, I spotted a little set of steps to my right. We had our own access to the sea right from our terrace. With that and the room service, I didn't even need to leave our villa for the next two weeks.

"Well, I'll leave you to get settled. Good bye, Mrs Taylor. I hope you enjoy your stay here with us," Kyle called, waving as he stepped back into the villa.

I grinned. "Thanks. I'm sure we will."

Ashton followed him back inside, and I eyed the sun lounger, unable to decide if I wanted to bask in the sun, or swim first. Just as I was making up my mind, Ashton walked back out with a dazzling grin on his face. "It's really hot out here. You should come inside and put on some sun cream."

I nodded in agreement. "I know." My eyes again flicked to the sea, and I finally made up my mind what I wanted to do first. Swimming.

Unfortunately, there was the menial task of unpacking to get to first. It seemed to take forever to find places for everything that we'd brought. As I unpacked my sixth bikini, I realised that, in my excitement, I may have gone a little overboard with the packing.

As I watched Ashton silently unpacking his clothes and setting them in the drawers next to my own things, I realised something. This place was so remote, beautiful and romantic, that with the idyllic surroundings, and minimal clothes covering his incredible body every day, I knew I wouldn't be able to fight my attraction to him for the duration of this vacation. Just like in LA, the passion and desire were already building inside me. There was no point in trying to fight the inevitable. Now that we were away from school and on our own, there was nothing to stop us from giving in and having a little fun for two weeks. As I came to this realisation, my stomach clenched with anticipation and a little smile slipped onto my lips. It had been so long since his hands had been on my body that I was almost buzzing with excitement.

Finally, after what seemed like a lifetime of unpacking, I was finished. Picking up the first bikini that I got my hands on, I smiled over at him. "I'm going to change. I need to see if that water feels as good as it looks," I grinned happily, snagging a bottle of sun lotion from the side and skipping off to the bathroom.

Once I'd stripped out of my clothes, I pulled on my black bikini, tying little bows at my neck and hips. Twisting this way and that, I looked at myself in the mirror and chewed on my lip. It was incredibly revealing, and not something I would usually choose, but I'd picked it because it would be the one that would allow me to tan without getting huge tan lines on my back and shoulders. I made a mental note not to wear this one on the beach, I couldn't have other people see me in this; I almost felt indecent in it even though I was entirely covered.

After spreading on a layer of sun cream to all the places I could reach, I strutted out of the bathroom, seeing Ashton in a pair of black swim shorts and nothing else. I stopped short, my mouth popping open in shock and awe as I watched the muscles ripple on his chest and arms as he smothered white sun cream over his chest. My mouth was dry. My hands were itching to take the bottle from his hands and smooth it over his soft skin for him. I realised then how crazy I was about him.

He looked up as I walked out, and his hand stilled on his body. His eyes widened as they raked down my body slowly, his bottom lip rolled into his mouth. The blush crept over my face as he carried on staring, not seeming to care that I knew he was looking. "Want me to do your back?" I offered, nodding at the lotion bottle in his hand.

He swallowed loudly, looking down at the bottle in confusion as if he'd forgotten it was there. "Er… yeah. Thanks."

I walked out to the terrace, knowing he would follow me. When I turned back, he was standing by the sun lounger, still watching me avidly. I smiled and took the bottle from his hand, nodding towards the sun lounger, motioning for him to sit.

Rubbing sun cream on his back was a sensual act in itself. I did it slowly, letting my fingers explore the tanned skin of his back and shoulders, making sure not to miss a spot. The simple action of rubbing cream on his body was making me tingle all over and a burning ache start between my legs.

The whole time I was fighting my inner slutty side that just wanted to push him down on the sun lounger and ravage him until I passed out from exhaustion. There was a fairly good chance that I wouldn't get a tan at all on this vacation if my hormones had anything to do with it!

When I was done, I pulled my hair into a messy bun and held out the bottle of sun cream to him as I turned on my seat and offered him my back. "Will you do me?"

He didn't reply, just squeezed a blob of cream into the palm of his hand before rubbing it into my back in small circles. I closed my eyes and focussed on my breathing, trying not to let his touch send me over the edge. Finally, he was done, so I turned back and smiled. "Thanks."

He stood. "No problem. Can't have you burning on the first day, can we?" he joked. Ashton turned and stalked off towards the stairs, leaving me there with my insides melted and my heart beating excitedly in my chest as I watched the muscles in his back and legs tense as he took a step. As he dipped his toe into the water, he moaned in appreciation. "It's so warm. You're gonna love this!"

As he dove off the first step and into the water, I sighed dreamily. This place, his touch, the thought of his hands on my body and his mouth on mine, all of it was so overwhelming that it almost felt like a dream. After Jack had died, I never thought I would be happy again, but Ashton just seemed to be able to make everything better with one of his little smiles.

I stood and walked to the edge of the terrace, leaning on the wooden railings. The water was about five feet below, kind of like a second diving board at a pool. As Ashton resurfaced and shielded his eyes from the sun, looking towards the beach, I smiled and raised my foot to the bottom railing. Leaning over slightly, I looked towards the beach but couldn't see anything at all. Our villa, as Kyle had suggested it would be, was totally cut off from everyone and private.

"Is it deep?" I called.

He looked down and then disappeared beneath the water before few seconds before he broke the surface and whipped his head back, flicking the water from his hair. My stomach fluttered, and a little moan of appreciation slipped from my lips. "It's probably about ten feet," he shrugged, looking unsure. I smiled excitedly. Ten feet was adequate. As I raised my bare foot and started climbing up the railings, Ashton gasped. "No, Anna! What the hell?"

As I got to the top railing, I held my hands out for balance and shook my head at his overprotectiveness. "Chill, Pretty Boy." After taking a deep breath, I linked my arms over my head and dived off the side. As the warm water touched my skin, I closed my eyes at the sheer luxury of it. It was perfect, like diving into a warm bathtub. Kicking my legs, I swam a little way underwater before breaking the surface, rubbing a hand over my face. As I opened my eyes I couldn't help but laugh at the stern and disapproving expression that was plastered on Ashton's face.

"Don't do that again. Jesus, Anna, what if you'd cracked your head or something? I was only guessing at how deep it was," he scolded, scowling at me.

I bit my lip and nodded, trying to appear appropriately abashed as I swam over to him slowly. It was time to set the rules. I didn't want any body guarding crap on this vacation. Ashton needed to loosen up and have fun too. "Ashton, seriously, I can dive off the railing. Come on, lighten up. We're on vacation, just the two of us, privacy, views of the ocean, room service. Please relax and have a good time," I begged. As I spoke, I wrapped my arms around his neck and pulled him closer to me. *It's time to start the fun right now!* As I thought about what was about to happen, my whole body was thrumming in need.

His face softened the closer he got to me. "I still need to do my job," he protested.

I nodded slowly, wondering how on earth to seduce him without flat out begging like last time we went away together. "Mmm hmm, your body guarding job," I whispered.

He gulped noisily. "Yeah. So don't make it hard for me."

In one swift movement, I wrapped my legs around his waist, clamping myself to him. I could already feel his excitement pressing against me. *Too late, he's already hard!* I giggled excitedly. I could barely wait any longer, but I just wanted to have a little fun with him first. Tightening my legs around him and trusting that he'd keep us both afloat, I moved my hands behind my back, quickly untying the knots of my bikini top. Once it was unfastened, I pulled it off, lifting it out of the water and showing him it before tossing it in the direction of the terrace, not even caring if it made it. He groaned and his eyes immediately dropped downwards as his eyebrows furrowed.

I smiled wickedly. "And what if I want to make it *hard* for you?" I flirted. While he was distracted, I shoved my hands down, getting to work on the knots at my hips, tugging quickly.

"Well, I guess life is supposed to be a little hard," he muttered breathlessly.

A little hard, jeez, it feels like he's smuggling an iron bar to me! I giggled at the thought and tugged the bikini bottoms free, again lifting them out of the water to make sure he saw them before tossing them to the terrace. A pained expression flitted across his features. I couldn't stop the smug smile that stretched across my face.

"A little hard?" I inquired, raising an eyebrow suggestively as I looped my arms around his neck again.

His fingers bit into my back as his eyes came back to meet mine. "Maybe a lot hard," he growled, crashing his lips to mine.

My whole body immediately felt alive as the passion woke inside me. I pulled back quickly though, breaking the kiss. There was something I wanted him to do before this happened. I quickly unwrapped myself from him and swam away a couple of feet, smiling teasingly. He was begging me with his eyes to go back to him and finish what I'd clearly instigated, but I knew he would never utter the words.

"Oh, don't give me the puppy dog eyes," I said, laughing as I almost gave in. I nodded towards the terrace before my will crumbled. "I want to see you dive. You need to loosen up too."

He groaned and looked back at the terrace where I'd dived from. Wordlessly, he turned and swam to the steps, climbing and walking to the railing, his eyes not leaving me as he raised his foot.

I shook my head quickly. "Lose the shorts. You won't need those," I called, winking at him playfully.

As he pulled his shorts off, letting them drop the ground in a soggy pile, I bit my lip as he exposed all of his perfection. My insides fluttered as he climbed to the top of the railing, standing there in all of his naked glory. My heart raced as I watched how the sun reflected off his wet body and how his hair glistened in the sunshine, like it was covered in a thousand little diamonds.

When he smiled down at me, my whole body seemed to tingle as it suddenly dawned on me. I wasn't just crazy about him; I was totally, utterly, and devastatingly in love with him. I didn't think I'd actually loved anything or anyone more, maybe not even Jack. I loved Jack so much, I still did, and he would always have a piece of my heart, but impossibly, I'd fallen in love with Ashton so hard that it actually hurt. It was like he was my everything, my sun, my air, my whole life rolled up into one six foot package. Time seemed to stand still, and it felt as if my whole life had been building up to this moment here with him, as if the sole purpose for me being on this earth was to love this boy. Ashton completed me, and I'd only just realised.

He dove off the railing, disappearing into the ocean, and I came back to reality with a bump. My eyes widened as panic started to build inside me. How had I let this happen? What was I supposed to do with this knowledge now? Maybe I'd always been in love with him, but I was too afraid or stupid to admit it. I was in some serious trouble because he didn't love me. Yes, he lusted after me and we were friends, but someone like him would never be content with someone as broken as me. He deserved far better and far more than I would ever be able to give him. I would never be good enough for Ashton Taylor.

A whimper escaped my lips as I looked back at the stairs. I contemplated running, just climbing out of the water and running as fast and as far as I could. The feelings inside me were crushing me, squeezing my heart and making my skin prickle with fear. Since Jack, I hadn't allowed myself to care about anything for fear of being hurt again, but somehow, Ashton had broken down my barriers and had set up camp in my heart without me even being aware what he was doing. The boy had totally stolen my heart without my permission.

Before I could even get a grip on the thoughts that were circling around my head, hands gripped my thighs and he broke the surface of the water just in front of me. When he smiled and wiped the water from his eyes, my heart thumped in my chest and I no longer wanted to run. In fact, what I actually wanted was to be closer to him, so close that I melted into him.

Knowing I couldn't let on how I felt, I decided to act casual and pretend that this whole devastating realisation hadn't just happened, that my world hadn't just shifted, that my heart didn't belong to him and him alone. If he knew the crushing feelings I had for him, it would probably terrify him to the very core just like it did me. Ashton Taylor was not the commitment type of guy.

Forcing a smile, I wrapped my arms around his neck. "Well, I liked your form," I joked, noticing how my voice sounded strained and not like mine at all.

His answering smile dazzled me. "I'm glad I impressed you."

"You always impress me." That was the truth. Giving in to the passion that was consuming me, I gripped the back of his head. "Kiss me then." Not giving him the chance to answer or turn me down, I pulled his mouth to mine. He kissed me back so softly that it made me want to cry. It was beautiful. His touch was soft and gentle as his hands wandered down my body, pulling me closer to him and guiding my legs around his waist. My hands twisted into his wet hair as I kissed him with everything that I had inside me, showing him that I loved him without actually saying the words.

My stomach fluttered as I clamped myself to him, revelling in the feeling of his skin against mine. I needed him. I needed more than this kiss. I needed to be completely at one with him, consumed by him, and possessed by him. My whole body ached with a desperate longing that I'd never felt for anyone else.

I broke the kiss and put my forehead to his. "Make love to me, Ashton," I begged.

His lips parted as he looked at me curiously for a few seconds before pressing his lips to mine softly again for a split second. "I can't. I don't have any condoms," he whispered. He actually looked a little annoyed with himself as he said it.

I sighed and tightened my grip on him. I didn't even care. If I got pregnant, I would love his babies just as much as I loved him. "I don't care. Make love to me, please? I need you to." I looked into his beautiful green eyes, and my insides did a little flip. His eyes were easily my favourite part of his body – and that was saying something because his body was flawless, so his eyes were nothing short of spectacular. I could look into them forever and it still wouldn't be long enough.

A smile twitched at the corners of his mouth before he kissed me again, nibbling on my bottom lip gently. As the kiss deepened, I realised that every touch and every kiss was different now. I silently wondered if it was because I knew now what 'making love' truly was. Was that why being in his arms like this, surrounded by beautiful paradise as far as the eye could see, felt so intimate and amazing? Every touch of his hands was like he was touching my heart and soul; my whole being was aching for him.

I wriggled my hips, trying to get impossibly closer to him. My love for him overwhelmed me as I whimpered into his mouth praying that this moment would last forever. I didn't ever want to come out of this little Ashton bubble that I was trapped in. We'd been on this island for less than an hour, and already it was the best time I'd ever had in my life.

When he broke the kiss and trailed little kisses down the side of my neck, I gasped and squeezed my eyes shut. "This is gonna be the best Christmas and New Year, ever," I mumbled. I would do everything in my power to make sure this was the best time he'd ever had too. It frightened me to think just how far I would go to make him happy.

"Yeah, it is," he agreed huskily. His grip tightened on my hips, moving me a fraction so that our bodies lined up. When I felt pressure at my entrance, I kissed him desperately as he pulled me down gently; entering me so slowly that it was almost maddening.

I moaned at the sheer ecstasy of having him inside me again. It was almost as if I'd been holding my breath for the last two months and now I could finally breathe again. His breath blew across my lips as I pressed my forehead to his and looked into his eyes as he built up a slow and steady rhythm, forcing my pleasure higher and higher with each gentle thrust of his hips.

While we made love, I savoured every second of it, committing every detail to memory. It was beautiful, and the most bitter sweet moment of my life. Everything about it was perfect, from the place, to the warm water that covered our bodies, to the way his hands and mouth seemed to worship my body as he made love to me. Every move was so sweet and tender that it made my heart throb in my chest.

When he held me still against him and swam for the villa, I thought he was going to get us out of the ocean, but he didn't. Instead, he pushed me up against one of the wooden stilts and continued his beautiful, yet torturous assault. I rested my head back on the post and just looked into his eyes. A strange thought suddenly occurred to me. I was almost grateful for everything that had happened to me in my past. If Carter hadn't done what he'd done, then I probably wouldn't have met Ashton. As his mouth closed over mine and his taste filled my senses, I knew that I would go through all of that stuff with Carter in a heartbeat, just for this one perfect moment with Ashton.

A small smile resided on his lips the whole time that he made love to me, his whole face beamed with happiness. The pleasure he was giving me was building to impossible heights. I closed my eyes, tipping my head back, losing myself in the moment and the sensations.

"Look at me, Baby Girl," he said breathlessly. "Please look at me." I forced my eyes open, looking back to his angelic face as he smiled and put his forehead against mine. His eyes locked on mine as he continued to take my body and soul to heaven. "That's better," he whispered, kissing me softly.

I moaned into his mouth so loudly that it was almost embarrassing, but I couldn't contain it. My heartbeat was pounding in my ears as was the whoosh of my own blood that was pumping through my veins. Suddenly it hit me, an orgasm so powerful that it made me bite down onto his lip roughly as my whole body shook and convulsed. His fingers dug into my thighs as his mouth claimed mine in a kiss that felt like he was trying to devour my very soul.

His body tensed too, and he pulled out of me, moaning into my mouth as he found his release too.

I gasped, and my eyes fluttered closed again as my head tipped back lifelessly against the hard, wooden post he was pinning me against. A tired smile twitched at the corner of my mouth as I looked back at him, seeing that his eyes were shining with passion as he brushed my wet hair back gently.

I wanted so very much to tell him that I loved him, but I couldn't. Instead, I swallowed the words, knowing that if I said them, it would ruin everything and that he would run away from me as fast as his legs would carry him. I needed him now; I needed him in my life, so I knew I couldn't risk confessing my feelings for him. I was just content in making him happy, and giving him what he wanted. I would take as much as he would give, for as long as he was willing to give it for.

Tears welled in my eyes as the vulnerability of being in love again overwhelmed me. Questions consumed me, worries, insecurities, fears; all of it surfaced and actually terrified me to the very core. How could I possibly have let this happen? How could I have given this boy the power to kill me? What would I do if something happened to him now? I would be lost.

A frown pulled at his forehead as he cupped my cheek in his hand and brushed his thumb under my eye, wiping away the tear that must have leaked out.

I forced a smile, knowing that he was probably worried that he'd upset me again. "That was perfect, Ashton. It was honestly the most beautiful and special thing that has ever happened to me. Thank you," I whispered, praying that my words wouldn't scare him away from me. I leant forward, pressing my forehead against his as I tightened my arms around his neck, hugging him tightly.

362

I would remember this moment forever. It would always be the best thing that had ever happened to me. He bent his head and kissed the tears from my cheeks, but didn't say anything. He didn't need to, I knew that he didn't love me like I loved him, and that was okay. As long as I could make him happy in a small way, even for a little while, I would do whatever it took.

He held me close to him, pressing me against the wooden post gently while treading water for ages, but it still wasn't long enough. Neither of us had said a word since I said about how perfect it was. When he pushed us away from the post and swam for the stairs, still holding me close to his chest, I smiled and wrapped my legs tightly around his waist. He strode effortlessly out of the water, carrying me over to one of the sun loungers on our terrace before lying down at my side. There was a strange look on his face, almost like he was trying hard to think of something to say, or to stop himself from saying something. Maybe he didn't want to ruin the moment, just like I didn't.

Sighing contentedly, I combed my fingers through his hair. My mind drifted to the little girl that I'd once dreamt of, the one with the exact same shade of hair as his. I wanted that dream to be real so badly. I wanted that little girl with him, and the way he looked at me so tenderly as he'd walked across the grass to me. But I knew I couldn't have it. Ashton would never want anything serious, what he wanted was the physical stuff and nothing more.

The solution was simple. I wouldn't tell him how I felt, and I wouldn't let him into my heart any more than he already was. Deep down I knew I needed to be careful and guard myself a little more because otherwise he would crush me completely. I couldn't let myself build a life with him, only to have him leave me in four months to go back to Los Angeles. Even as the thought formed in my mind, I knew I was only fooling myself. My whole world revolved around him already and always had done since the first time I saw him, but I'd refused to see it. Even my parents had seen it. Now I understood the knowing smiles and the little looks that they gave each other – they could see what I refused to see, that I was falling for him hook, line and sinker. I'd never even stood a chance.

As my eyes met his again, my whole body started longing for him immediately. The way his sensuous lips curved up reminded me of the little smile that had graced his lips while he'd made love to me in the water. My skin was tingling all over as my finger traced the line of his jaw before trailing down his neck. This was such a nice position to be in, that part of me didn't want to move, but another part, the playful side that he brought out in me, was urging me on.

"I'm gonna go get in the shower. Want to come and wash my back?" I asked, raising one eyebrow in clear invitation.

His eyes flashed with excitement as he nodded eagerly, so I knew we would be on the same wavelength. Ashton never was slow on the uptake.

"Hell yeah I do." I giggled at his enthusiasm and pushed myself out of his arms quickly, running for the door as I grinned over my shoulder, knowing he would follow me. He laughed wickedly as he pushed himself up too. "I do enjoy the sight of you running naked, Baby Girl." My excitement bumped up another level as he jumped to his feet and gave chase.

Chapter Thirty-Five

After an exhausting shower with him, I quickly dried my hair and pulled on a short, yellow sun dress and some white flip-flops. When I glanced over at him, I internally swooned because of how handsome he looked. He was merely wearing a pair of beige shorts and a white T-shirt, but he was just so captivating that it took my breath away.

"You ready, Baby Girl?" he asked, holding out a hand to me. I nodded and took his hand, allowing him to pull me up from the dresser chair. "You look so beautiful, Anna," he whispered as he bent his head and kissed me. My body reacted immediately to his touch, so I pushed him away quickly before I threw him on the bed and had my way with him again.

"Come on, I know you're hungry, let's go eat. You'll need to build up your strength if you're hoping to keep up with me on this trip," I teased playfully.

The lustful look that crossed his face made my body tingle. "In that case, I'd better eat twice as much as normal if I'm going to be burning off a lot of energy," he answered, smiling at me. I rolled my eyes, fighting to keep the smile off my lips, but failing miserably.

"Come on, before all the cocktails are gone." I looped his camera over my wrist as we stepped out of the cool air conditioned room and into the fresh muggy air of paradise. His hand closed over mine as we walked along the little pathway towards the beach. The sun's rays were bouncing off of the ocean making it glitter and sparkle.

The water sports hut caught my attention. "Want to try snorkelling tomorrow?"

He shrugged easily. "Whatever you want, Baby Girl."

Of course, he led us over to the outdoor grill that the manager had mentioned. His eyes lit up like a starving man that had just been given his first meal in a year when he saw the array of foods being cooked on the four large open grills. It took a surprisingly long time for him to make up his mind, and once we had two enormous plates laden with food, we headed off to the side so we could sit on the beach and eat.

As I sat, he smiled down at me and held out his plate. "Hold this for me. I'll be right back," he stated, grinning. I frowned, confused, but took his plate anyway, watching as he strutted off towards a little beach hut about twenty yards away. His eyes never left me for more than a couple of seconds the whole time he was away from me. When he turned back to me, I smiled at the two coconuts in his hand.

"What's that?" I asked, eyeing them curiously. Fruit skewers, curly straws and mini umbrellas poked out of the top of each one.

Ashton sat beside me and held one of the coconuts out to me. "It's a cocktail. This one is called sex on the beach," he replied.

I raised one eyebrow, holding my laugh at bay. "Seriously?" I took the drink, swishing the orangey-red liquid around with my straw.

"Yep."

I giggled. "Well, I think I'm gonna like these."

One of his eyebrows rose as he nodded and let his eyes slip down to the V at the front of my dress. "Me too."

Trying to hide the blush that I could feel creeping over my cheeks, I took a sip. The sweetness of it made my taste buds tingle and my eyes widen in shock. It was delicious. "Holy crap, that's good! Has it got alcohol in it?" I asked, taking another mouthful.

Ashton nodded and laughed, pulling the straw from between my lips. "Yeah, so slow down. There's quite a lot of alcohol in it."

While we ate, I pressed against his side and looked out over the sea as the sun started to set even though it was still very early evening. The sunset was so romantic and breathtaking that it made my heart throb. The dazzling colours in the sky were reflected in the ocean making it twice as spectacular. The whole time, Ashton's arm was wrapped around me tightly.

Once the stars started to make their appearance, tinkering, tinny music caught my attention; the beautiful sounds floating down the beach towards us. I laid my head on his shoulder and sighed contentedly.

"Want to go check out that band?" he offered.

"Sure." Without another word, he eased my head off his shoulder and pushed himself to his feet, holding his hands down to me. I smiled up at him, slipping my hands into his. "You're so damn romantic, Ashton. Are you sure you've never had a girlfriend before?"

He grinned. "You're my first and only," he answered, looking into my eyes, making my heart melt.

We held hands as we walked to the largest building that Kyle had pointed out as being the hub of the resort. The reception was beautiful, rustic and entirely made of wood. The music was luring us in from the back, and we followed a couple of other guests through the reception to a door at the back signposted as the lounge. I gasped as I stepped outside. It was unlike any lounge I'd ever been in before; in fact, how it could be classed as a lounge when it was outside was beyond me. It was essentially a clearing in the trees large enough to fit about twenty candle lit tables. A little wooden staging area had been constructed off to the right, and a steel band were currently playing some gentle melody that brought a smile to my face. People swayed to the music on a makeshift dance floor that was made of decking. The whole place was lit by gas lamps that hung from the trees and fairy lights that had been wrapped around tree trunks. A little hut with a straw roof served as a makeshift bar, and I could see people sipping on coconut cocktails like the one I'd had earlier.

"Wow. This place is beautiful," I murmured.

Ashton's hands cupped my face gently before his lips claimed mine in a kiss that was so heartfelt and special that it even made the magical place fade into insignificance. "It's incredible," he confirmed. "In fact, the only thing I've ever seen that is more beautiful than this place, is you." My heart melted at his words, and I bit my lip so I didn't let my confession of love accidentally tumble from my lips. "Let's dance," he whispered, tugging me forward gently as he pulled me flush against him.

I beamed up at him, wrapping my arms around his neck as we stepped up onto the decking and started swaying to the beat of the music. His arms were looped around my waist the whole night, holding me tightly against him. His eyes seemed to have me hypnotised because, while we danced, everything else and everyone seemed to disappear, leaving only us in our own little island paradise. In Ashton's arms, nothing else was important, and I knew it would feel that way for me forever.

The disappointment I felt when the band played their last song was so overwhelming that I felt the pout slip onto my face as we all applauded. Ashton smiled down at me before nodding over his shoulder at the door that led back to the reception area. "We should really get going, it's pretty late."

I sighed and nodded. "Where did the time go?" I mused.

He shrugged, brushing one finger across my cheek gently. "Time flies when you're having fun."

I smiled at that statement. "Did you have fun?"

He grinned. "I had the time of my life, Mrs Taylor." The sound of the name made my heart clench. Now that I knew how I felt about him, I desperately wanted a future with him – and for him to possibly give me his name one day – but it would never be able to happen because of Carter. Anger settled into the pit of my stomach because even now, after three years, I still wasn't free to live my life. Ashton's hand slid down my arm before getting to my hand and threading his fingers through mine, snapping me out of my train of thought. "Come on, Baby Girl, let's go." I nodded reluctantly, silently hoping that the rest of the vacation wouldn't fly past as quickly as our first night had. As we walked back through the reception, Ashton looked over at the store and then stopped walking. "Wow, the store's still open. They certainly cater to their guests here, huh?" he joked.

"I just need to get something." Without explaining what it was that he wanted, I was gently tugged in that direction. "Wait here. I'll just be one minute," he instructed. His face had turned serious, so I knew that was a bodyguard order and not just a general 'I'll be right back' remark.

I grinned and nodded. "Yes, sir!"

A lustful expression crossed his face before he shook his head and rushed off to speak to the guy behind the counter. They both disappeared from sight for a minute, and then Ashton was back at the register, paying for whatever it was that he'd bought. I didn't see what it was that he'd purchased because whatever it was, it was small, and he slipped it into his pocket. When he got to my side, he held out a single red rose to me. "They didn't have white," he said, almost apologetically.

I sighed dreamily at his thoughtfulness. "Thank you, I love it," I cooed, smelling the rose as we walked back to our villa, hand in hand. When we got back to our apartment, I pushed the bloom into the vase of flowers that sat on the table. The terrace and the stars beyond caught my attention. "Let's go sit outside for a bit," I suggested. On the way out of the door, I grabbed two bottles of water from the mini fridge that was in our room, and then headed out to the nearest sun lounger, settling down and then scooting over so we could share it.

Ashton stretched himself out on it next to me, pressing against my side and pushing one of his arms under my body as he pulled me even closer. A satisfied, euphoric smile crept onto my face as I rested my chin on his chest and looked up at him. It was so quiet that you could hear a pin drop. Neither of us spoke, but it wasn't an uncomfortable silence by any means; in fact, it was almost as if words were unnecessary.

In the moonlight, he looked devastatingly beautiful. His eyes were shining, his black hair had a faint blue hue from the reflections of the moon, and his smile made my whole body ache. I wanted so incredibly much to say those three little words, but I couldn't. I couldn't risk him not wanting to be in my life now. I'd never been this happy, and it was all down to this boy at my side.

Unable to fight my desire any longer, I raised myself up, leaning over him and kissed his lips. He responded immediately, pulling me down on top of him as his hands slid down my back and cupped my ass. His hands roamed further down, and slowly, oh so slowly, my dress was lifted. It was almost as if he was waiting for me to stop him or something. I smiled against his lips knowingly. I wouldn't be stopping him for this whole vacation, but clearly he was still unaware of that fact.

I pulled back, looking down at him as I unbuttoned his shirt, giving him the clear go ahead. One side of his mouth pulled up into a predatory grin, and before I had time to react, he'd grabbed me and flipped us so that I was now trapped underneath his body. I giggled breathlessly as he looked down at me and shoved his hand into his pocket, producing a box of twenty condoms.

368

I gasped. "That's what you just bought?" I inquired, giggling at his guilty expression. "Were you expecting to get some tonight, Ashton?" I teased.

He winced and shook his head. "No, not expecting. Just hoping," he replied, looking slightly embarrassed about it.

I grinned and raised one hand, gripping it into the back of his hair. "Well, I'll let you into a little secret, Pretty Boy," I purred, pulling his mouth closer to mine so that our lips brushed together as I spoke. "If you want, you can get *a lot* of action on this trip."

His whole body tensed on top of mine. "Oh yeah, I definitely want that," he growled, nodding enthusiastically as he bent his head and kissed me, ending the conversation.

After he had made love to me under the stars, he carried me into the bedroom and we started all over again on the bed covered in rose petals.

I woke in the morning with my whole body aching from our physical endeavours. Ashton's deep rumbling growl-like snore was coming from behind me, so I knew that he was still fast asleep. A quick glance at the clock told me it was almost ten in the morning. My overused muscles protested as I rolled slowly in his arms so we were facing each other. I smiled at the sight of him. His hair was sticking out in all directions where I had been running my hands through it last night, and his lips were slightly swollen from all of the kissing. Dark, short stubble lined his jaw, and I couldn't help but reach out and run the pad of my finger over it, smiling at the slight scratch.

My teeth sank into my bottom lip as a rush of emotion made my heart speed up. It was an unfamiliar sensation to me, but I knew what it was. It was love.

I swallowed the lump that formed in my throat. It terrified me, being in love again. I didn't like it. Most people would say that being in love was the best feeling in the world, and to some degree, I would agree with them, but not when all you could think about was losing it or watching something awful happen so that your heart shatters into a thousand tiny, jagged little pieces. No, being in love was more frightening than gratifying.

As I looked away from him, my gaze settled on the wall of glass opposite the bed. Looking out over the ocean that sparkled like a thousand diamonds sat just below the surface, I realised that as magnificent as the view was to wake up to, it actually had nothing on waking and seeing Ashton.

His arms tightened on me in his sleep as he fidgeted, let out a rather loud, nasal snore, and then licked his lips a couple of times, blissfully unaware that I was awake and panicking about being in love with him.

As I lay in Ashton's arms, my thoughts turned to Jack. I had never thought I would have someone in my life again after him, in fact, I thought he was *it*. My one true love. But maybe, as a silly immature sixteen year old girl, maybe I didn't have any idea of what true love really was back then. This felt different with Ashton, *I* felt different. Maybe this was a different kind of love than what I had for Jack. Somehow, it felt deeper. I loved Jack so incredibly much, but I was *in love* with Ashton. To me, there was a gulf of a difference. Ashton was just special, he was the one I needed and the one that understood me and accepted the messed up girl that I was now. He was the one that I felt totally and utterly at home with. He was everything that was good in my world. If I had to choose a cliché term, I would say that Ashton Taylor was my soul mate, and the one that was designed to be my other half.

After almost half an hour of just lying there, worrying about things, going over things and realising that I had no control over my emotions anymore, I decided that the best thing I could do now was to try and ignore it and to order him some breakfast – after all, the way to his heart was *certainly* through his stomach.

Getting out of bed without him noticing was always a tricky affair, and it took a lot of wriggling and slow movements. As I finally managed to worm my way out of his arms, I shoved my pillow back into my place, watching as his arms immediately hugged the pillow to his chest, completely unaware that it wasn't me.

I slipped on his shirt from the previous night and then padded into the lounge, finding the menus for the little café that apparently delivered the food straight to your villa. After scanning it for a few seconds, I picked up the phone and ordered what I guessed he would want.

The food didn't take long to arrive, and the waiter guy carried in a large tray, setting it on the table for me. Once he was gone, I made sure to lock the door, just like Ashton would want me to, and then I carried the heavy tray into the bedroom. He was still asleep, hugging the pillow to his chest affectionately.

"Ashton?" I whispered.

His arms tightened on the pillow. "Mmm?" he mumbled with his eyes closed.

"Pretty Boy, wake up. I ordered breakfast," I cooed, stopping at the foot of the bed.

His eyes snapped open at the mention of food, and he looked straight down at the pillow in his arms, clearly confused because it wasn't me. I chuckled wickedly at his bemused expression and finally his sleepy eyes settled on me. "Hey," he rasped.

I grinned, nodding at the pillow as he dropped it back onto the bed and sat up. "Who's your friend?" I joked.

He laughed and swung his legs out of the bed, throwing off the white sheet that covered his body. My eyes widened and I seemed to lose control of them as they immediately flitted down his body, taking in every glorious, naked inch of him.

"Pervert," he scolded playfully.

I shrugged unashamedly. "So arrest me," I replied breathlessly, sinking my teeth into my bottom lip as I imagined running my tongue across the V line at his hips and following it all the way down…

The tray was taken out of my hands and set on the bed, and then strong, tanned arms wrapped around my waist, pulling me against his hard body. "Good morning," he whispered, bending his head and capturing my lips in the first kiss of the day.

I sighed dreamily and nodded. "It is now."

He grinned boyishly and pulled back. "So where shall we eat?" he asked, pulling on a pair of shorts from the drawer, thwarting my inappropriate examination of his body.

I gulped, snapping out of my little fantasy and forced my eyes back to his again. "Terrace?" Any place with him would be fine with me.

He nodded, picking up the tray and we both made our way out to the terrace, sitting on the little table. I clipped up the umbrella to provide some shade while we ate so that we didn't burn. As Ashton lifted the two silver lids from the plates, he moaned in appreciation at the pile of French toast that sat there for him. It was his favourite by far, and something I usually only made for him at the weekends.

As he poured two cups of coffee, his hand suddenly stilled and he frowned over at me. "Wait, where the hell did you get this food from?"

"Room service?" I answered, unsure what I'd done to spark his angry expression.

His mouth popped open as he shook his head in disbelief. "You ordered room service and answered the door while I was still asleep?" he asked incredulously.

I smiled sarcastically. "Well, duh, that's how room service usually works."

He snorted and put the coffee pot down forcefully, still frowning at me. "Anna, you don't do that! Something could have happened, you can't answer the door like that," he scolded.

I sighed because he hadn't relaxed at all. "Ashton, seriously, chill out. You really think someone's gonna jump me posing as a waiter?" I giggled and shook my head at his overprotectiveness.

He didn't look amused at all. "Miss Spencer, you can't-"

I held up my hand and interrupted him.

"Er, *Mrs Taylor*, if you please," I corrected, knowing it would ease some of his tension.

His face softened for a fraction of a second before he put his stern face back on. "Fine, Mrs Taylor, you don't do that again. I'll answer the door," he barked, using his SWAT Agent voice on me.

I rolled my eyes. *Maybe in a couple of days he'll relax.* "Okay, Mr Overprotective," I stuck out my tongue.

He sighed and took my hand. "Look, I'm sorry. I hate telling you that you can't do things, but it's my job, okay? If we were home, you wouldn't answer the door to someone who you didn't know," he explained, looking at me apologetically.

I shrugged. "I guess, but no one knows I'm here."

He frowned down at his plate. "I still need to do my job. I need you safe."

I nodded, seeing that this conversation was making him uncomfortable. He was right, he genuinely didn't like to tell me no, I already knew that. "I'm sorry. I won't do it again," I agreed. "Do you want some of my pancakes?" I offered, changing the subject.

Our day was spent on the beach, snorkelling, sunbathing, and generally fooling around and laughing. The cocktails that the beach bar served were delicious, though we both opted for virgin ones this time. Ashton was snacking on the free cupcakes and doughnuts the whole day, claiming that he needed a sugar boost because I was wearing him out.

That night we dined in the more upmarket restaurant that was located just off the reception. The food was so incredible that I actually ended up eating three desserts. Afterwards, we went to the little lounge clearing in the woods where we went last night. Instead of steel drums, there was a pianist this time. The whole night, Ashton and I chatted and laughed while holding hands, or danced. It was perfection.

At closing time, Ashton suggested that we walk a little way up the beach before returning to our villa. As I slipped off my shoes, he took them out of my hand. The sand was nice and cool now. The moonlight reflected off the sea, sparkling and shimmering. I internally swooned at how romantic it all was. The beauty and tranquillity of it was astounding.

"It's nice here, huh?" Ashton stated when we stopped and threw a couple of seashells into the water.

I laughed at his choice of word. "Just nice? Are we at the same place?"

"Okay yeah, it's incredible," he amended, laughing.

"This is the nicest place I've ever been. It's amazing here. I want to come back some day." I stooped and picked up another couple of shells and a pebble, throwing them into the water too, watching the ripples.

"I'll bring you back one day," he promised, wrapping his arms around me and pressing his chest to my back. My breath caught in my throat. I would love that! Maybe, if we managed to stay friends after his assignment finished, we could vacation again together one year.

"Yeah? Cool," I replied, trying not to show that I was affected by what he'd said.

He kissed the back of my neck, just once, before moving away. I turned back, seeing that he'd sat on the sand a couple of feet behind me. His legs were stretched out in front of him as he just watched me with a smile on his face.

"Why so happy?" I inquired.

He shrugged easily. "I love to make you happy, it makes me happy."

My heart melted as I dropped the last couple of shells and pebbles I had and walked over to him, settling myself on his lap, straddling him. My stomach fluttered because that was just how I felt about him. Seeing him happy made me happy too.

I pressed my lips to his, seeming to light a fire inside myself that only he could extinguish. His arms looped around me, pulling me closer to him as the kiss deepened, and then I was lost.

Chapter Thirty-Six

Over the next few days, I had the time of my life. Each day was different to the one before, we snorkelled, sunbathed, hiked, hired a pedal boat, and even took a ride over to the next island on a speedboat and did a little shopping. We spent a lot of the day just holding hands and talking. Ashton had finally relaxed, and even let me go to the bar on my own a couple of times. The evenings were spent either in the lounge bar watching the entertainment that the hotel laid on, or just lying on our terrace, eating dinner under the stars. The whole vacation had been spectacular. And the sex; my whole body ached in a satisfied way that it had never done before. The thought of going back to school was almost painful because I knew our 'relationship' would have to come to an end.

On Christmas morning, the sun shone through the window, heating my back. My head was on Ashton's chest, and his arms were securely around me. A happy sigh left my lips. *This is already the best Christmas ever, and I've only been awake for ten seconds!*

I snuggled closer to him and looked up at his face. He was still asleep and looked like a dream because he was so beautiful. Pressing my face into the side of his neck, I breathed him in. It was like sensory overload as his unique scent filled my lungs and made me moan breathlessly.

He shifted slightly, and a lazy kiss was planted on the side of my head.

Excitement bubbled up inside me because he was awake and I could give him his presents. I'd already forwarded the other gifts that I'd bought – the main one being to all of his friends back in LA. The gift that I'd bought for Ashton would be better with a group of friends going too. I had no doubt in my mind that he was going to love it.

I pulled back to look at him again, and he grinned at me. "Good morning, Baby Girl. Merry Christmas," he whispered as he bent his head to kiss me. I smiled against his lips and rolled on top of him, before sitting up and smiling excitedly.

"Merry Christmas to you too. Can I give you your present now?" I asked excitedly.

A wicked smile crept onto his lips as his hands slid up my thighs, over my hips, and settled on my waist with his thumbs on the skin just under my breasts. "Oh yeah, I would love my present," he purred suggestively. Desire built inside me quickly, and the gift giving was long forgotten as I dipped my head and captured his lips in a soft kiss. Before things could progress, he rolled so that he was hovering above me. "I was joking, you know. I'd like to give you your gift too," he said, laughing.

I nodded, too lost in the moment to stop. "Maybe later," I muttered, guiding his mouth down to mine again as I wrapped my legs around his waist.

One intense lovemaking session later, I watched as he climbed out of the bed and fumbled through one of our suitcases before plucking something out of the side pocket and strutting back to the bed. I'd been more organised and already had mine placed under the bed where I could reach them. I leant down, picking them up, unable to keep the smile off my face.

As he settled back into the bed, we exchanged gifts. I nodded to the two things in his lap. "Do yours first, I want to watch you open them." I didn't actually care what he'd bought for me, he didn't need to have gotten me anything at all, I already owed him more than I could ever give him for what he'd done for my life in the last four months.

He smiled worriedly. "You promise that you didn't go crazy? You agreed not to go overboard."

"I didn't go overboard," I confirmed. Well, I didn't think I did anyway, but he may have a different idea about boundaries and limits. I pointed to the cheaper one. "Do that one first," I chirped.

He picked it up and slid his finger under the tape. My nerves were frazzled; he was being so slow, I was sure he was doing it on purpose. As he pulled the paper off, his eyes widened and a beautiful smile stretched across his face. "Oh God, Anna, I love this!" he enthused. I smiled down at the photo of us that I'd put into a silver frame. It was one of the ones from my father's birthday party; I'd purchased it from one of the photographers.

I grinned. "I have a couple of others at home too, but I only brought one with me because of the ridiculous baggage allowance restrictions," I chimed in.

"This is the best thing that you could have gotten me," he gushed, leaning in and kissing me softly.

I chuckled knowingly. "Yeah, until you see that one," I teased, pointing to the rectangular, gold, flat present. He picked it up quickly, ripping it open. As he pulled out the sheet of paper inside and saw that it was a trip itinerary, he looked up at me warningly. "I hope that you've included yourself on whatever this is," he said before he even unfolded it.

I sighed, knowing he would be difficult about it at first. "Ashton, don't start freaking out and panicking. No, I'm not going because it's really not something that I'd enjoy. Just get over it, alright?" I stated, trying to look stern but probably failing miserably because I actually loved the fact that he worried about me so much. "Smile, please? I'm so excited about this, please don't ruin it for me," I begged.

He sighed and nodded, finally looking down at the printed sheet in his hand. As he read it over, I saw the tension leave his face as he read the details of it. "Holy shit! You've arranged for a driving weekend for me and my friends? Shit, Anna, this is incredible!"

I grinned and chewed on my lip as I nodded enthusiastically. I knew he would love it. It was a weekend of driving in a Formula 1 car, with actual tuition and lunch with one of the McLaren-Mercedes drivers. Once I'd had the idea of it, my father had pulled in a lot of strings to make it possible. Luckily, it was off season for the Grand Prix, so that made it possible.

"Tell me that's not better than a photo," I prompted, smirking at him.

He laughed, shaking his head. "Okay, yeah, you got me. Thank you so much for this, it's amazing, seriously overboard, but amazing," he sighed, and his eyes tightened. "But you'll come too, right?"

I groaned, knowing that this was where it got difficult. I knew he wouldn't like being two and a half hours' flight away from me. "I don't want to go. I booked this for you and your friends, and you can relax without me being there. This really isn't something that I'd enjoy."

He reached out and touched my cheek softly, his eyes betraying his anxiousness. "I don't want to leave you."

I sighed at the puppy dog face that he pulled. "Please don't do that face at me! I've arranged for a guard to come and replace you for the weekend. It's just two nights. Please? Come on, you love this, right? Your friends are gonna love this too," I pleaded desperately.

He sighed and looked down at the paper. "I really, really love this. Thank you," he said gratefully.

An excited squeal left my lips as I threw myself at him, wrapping my arms around his neck tightly. "Yes! I knew you'd love it!"

He laughed quietly. "Why are you so excited? This is my gift, not yours."

I sighed happily and pulled back to look at him. "Yeah, but I love giving you things."

He nodded. "Yeah, don't I know it," he muttered sarcastically. "But you know what?" He bent forward and cupped my face in his hands. "This," he said, kissing me on the lips tenderly, "this kiss would have been enough to make this the best Christmas I've ever had," he stated, his eyes sparkling and showing me the truth of his words.

My heart melted to a puddle at his sweet words. "Well, in that case, now you've had the kiss and get to go to drive a fast car!"

He shook his head, laughing incredulously. "You are just too perfect, Baby Girl," he stated, looking at me softly. *Perfect? Yeah right, I'm not; I'm moody, bitchy, needy, and aggressive!* "Your turn," he said, handing me a flat present the size of a birthday card.

I smiled gratefully. "Thank you." I silently prayed this would be something we could do together. Tearing it open eagerly, I saw a Christmas card inside. When I opened it, two tickets for Usher's concert tumbled out into my lap. Shock resonated through my body as my mouth dropped open. They must have cost him a fortune. "Ashton..." Tears welled in my eyes because of how thoughtful this was. Usher was my favourite. "This is..." I was lost for words.

He smiled, leaning forward and wiping the tear away as it fell down my face. "You're very welcome."

I swallowed, running my thumb over the little official silver hologram. "You are so thoughtful; this is fantastic. Thank you."

"So, who you gonna take?" he asked, smiling at me.

I laughed and pretended to think about it. "Hmm, I think maybe I'll ask Rosie," I joked.

"Good choice. I would have gone for Rosie too," he winked at me playfully.

I literally threw myself at him, knocking him flat onto his back as I kissed him passionately. When I broke the kiss, I looked at him in awe because he was just so special. "This is the best Christmas, ever," I whispered truthfully.

He stroked his hand down my back softly. "I'm glad you're having a good time."

"I'm not having a good time, I'm having the best time of my life here with you," I corrected, smiling ecstatically.

His hand tangled into the back of my hair as he tilted my head back and kissed the tip of my nose. "I got you something else too," he whispered.

My overeager, hormone ridden body was already imagining things that he could do for me as a present. I raised one eyebrow, pressing closer to him. "Oh really? And would this thing involve your tongue doing sinful things to my body?"

He laughed wickedly and shook his head. "No, pervert!"

My mouth dropped open in shock as heat spread across my face because obviously I'd taken his comment the wrong way. "Oh."

He was still laughing as he rolled us to the side and reached into the drawer beside his bed, producing a little, red velvet jewellery box. "That wasn't the gift that I had planned, but I can absolutely do that after if you want." He grinned at me and my blush deepened. "This is what I actually meant."

My breath caught in my throat as he held out the box to me. "Why did you buy me something else? The concert tickets were already too much," I whispered, watching his face, just marvelling over him like I had done hundreds of times before.

"Just open it," he instructed.

I gulped and took the box, sitting up on the bed as I ran my fingers over the soft, velvety material. Lifting the lid slowly, I saw a beautiful pair of emerald stud earrings. My hand unconsciously went to my matching necklace and rubbed over the emerald stone that I hadn't taken off since the day that he'd put it around my neck. Air rushed out of my lungs because of how precious the earrings were. The sun shining through the window made them sparkle and cast green shadows over my chest and wrist. I looked up at him and couldn't speak. No one could be this perfect, could they?

"You like them?" he asked, looking a little unsure. "You can change them if you want to. Don't say you like them if you don't, I mean, I'm not good at picking out jewellery or anything. You probably hate them."

I put my hand out, covering his mouth to stop any more ridiculous words tumbling out. "Thank you. I love them," I whispered. The word didn't even cover how much I was in love with the earrings.

He smiled against my hand. "You're welcome," he mumbled through my hand, his voice muffled.

I sighed happily and swung my legs out of bed. "I'm going to put these in," I stated, unable to take my eyes from the little green stones nestled in the cream folds of silk.

"Hey, I thought I was doing sinful things to your body with my tongue!" he called as I walked out of the room towards the bedroom.

I grinned over my shoulder. "Hold that thought for two minutes while I put on my gift, and then maybe I'll let my tongue do sinful things to your body too, to show you how grateful I am."

That day was the most magical, lazy Christmas I'd ever had. Ashton and I lay on the beach in a hammock, listening to my iPod, sipping cocktails. It was pure perfection.

Unfortunately, our time in paradise seemed to whizz past all too quickly. On our last day, my heart sank with every item of clothing I packed into the suitcases. I didn't want to leave. I didn't want to go back to reality or back to our friends. The most special thing about being here with him wasn't the view or the sea, or even the whirlpool bath with the one way glass wall that looked out over the never-ending ocean. No, it was the fact that I had Ashton Taylor all to myself, and his undivided attention. Here, I could love him without the pressure or the barriers, but once we went home again, that would have to change. I couldn't let this carry on. I couldn't build my life around him any more than I already did. I couldn't allow him any closer.

Of course, I was hoping that once his assignment was finished, he'd want to remain friends, talk on the phone, maybe visit occasionally. I already had a secret fantasy where I finished my college course and moved to LA to get a job, and then I could hang out with him and Nate all the time. The only trouble with that idea was that maybe he'd already be taken by then. Maybe I'd have to watch him play house with some other girl and spoil her rotten with his little romantic gestures that make my heart ache. The thought of him with another girl brought tears to my eyes.

The vacation was the best thing that ever happened to me, but in a way it was also the worst too. If we'd never come here then maybe I never would have realised my love for him. Maybe I would be staggering along in blissful denial, and then I wouldn't be feeling like this inside. Life was so much easier when I had nothing to lose. No matter how hard I tried, I couldn't seem to force him out of my heart, and that terrified me because he could be taken from me at any minute and I would be powerless to shield myself from the pain and devastation. The pain doubled in my chest and I sniffed and wiped my teary face, taking a few calming breaths, knowing I was now going to have to have that painful and awkward conversation with him.

~ Ashton ~

Anna had been quiet all morning. Distant. It scared me. I wanted to ask her what she was thinking about, but something told me it was best to let her work it out. She liked to be in control and do things for herself. If she needed to talk to me or ask for help, she would.

"I'm gonna go shower, Baby Girl, then I'll help you pack, okay?" I suggested, wanting to give her a little space.

"Sure, I'll make a start," she replied, turning her back on me. The disappointment that settled in the pit of my stomach made me feel nauseous. I made my way to the bathroom, shrugging out of my clothes and tossing them carelessly onto the side as I switched on the water. The spray pounded down onto my shoulders as I looked out over the ocean. I would definitely bring her back here one day as I'd promised. My mind was preoccupied with thoughts of going home, back to normality, school and far guards, so I didn't even hear her come into the room.

"Hi, got room for one more?"

My heart leapt in my chest. I turned to see her standing in the doorway, naked. Her glorious body made my mouth water, but her face made my heart stop. She'd been crying. Her eyes were red, but she was faking a smile to cover whatever she was feeling.

I held out a hand to her and nodded. "Definitely."

As her hand closed over mine, allowing me to help her into the shower, I looked over her face worriedly. The hurt and sadness was easy to see. When her big, brown eyes met mine, the tenderness I could see there made my heart race. I could see in her eyes that she loved me, she was scared, but she loved me. I knew it now, even if she didn't.

Her eyes filled with tears as she reached out a hand and traced her fingertips across my chest. She pulled my face down to hers. I kissed her desperately, showing her how much I loved her, wanted her and needed her. She kissed me back with the same intensity; the kiss was so sweet it was almost too much to bear.

Every time I had been with her was incredible, but this was simply mind-blowing, it was more than sex, it was everything to me, so tender and perfect. It was as if she touched every part of my body, mind and soul, and I knew that I would want her and only her, forever. There was no doubt in my mind that we were made for each other.

I didn't ask her what happened now, or why it happened. I didn't need a label or anything this time. I knew she loved me, so I could give her all the time in the world to realise it.

It didn't matter that she was about to tell me this was a mistake, that it couldn't happen again and that things would go back to normal once we were home. I knew she was trying to let me in, she was trying to let herself love me and that was a gargantuan step for her. Even if I had to wait forever for her to realise that she loved me, I would always be grateful for this vacation. I'd got to make her blissfully happy for two weeks and that would see me through a lifetime full of hurt.

After we'd made love in the shower, I held her in my arms, not wanting to let go.

"We'd better go pack," she said quietly after a few minutes of silence. I nodded, not wanting to make this any harder for her because she was obviously struggling with the fact that she had feelings for me. I could see how torn she was inside, and her internal conflict made my heart ache. "Ashton, when we get home…" she trailed off, looking at her feet as she wrapped the towel around herself.

"Yeah, I know, you don't need to say it," I said honestly. I could tell by her face what she was going to say, and that was fine, she needed time after what she'd been through.

She looked up at me, her eyes full of sorrow. "Okay good. Let's go pack then, we need to leave in an hour or so, right?" she replied, changing the subject.

"Yeah we need to be at the boat in an hour and twenty minutes," I confirmed, looking at my watch. She turned her back on me and walked out of the bathroom. Once I was alone, I closed my eyes and prayed with all my heart that she was strong enough to let herself love me. I'd wait as long as it took.

Chapter Thirty-Seven

~ Anna ~

I felt slightly awkward after the talk, or I should really call it the 'non-talk' because he knew what I was going to say before I opened my mouth. Frankly, I was grateful, because saying the words would have felt like cutting my heart out. We fell back into the usual friendly routine pretty easily as we packed and joked around and he seemed to snap his business head back on as soon as we stepped out of the villa with our luggage. He was making sure I was close to his side and moving me so I was half a step behind him. The chilled and relaxed version of the bodyguard was completely gone now. I missed him already.

The flight was good. Long, but good. After hours and hours of doing nothing on a plane, we finally touched down. The stewardess came up to us immediately. "Excuse me, sir, I have Dean Michaels on the phone for you," she said to Ashton, leaning closer to him than necessary and putting her hand on his shoulder. I tried my hardest not to get jealous, but I just couldn't help it.

"Stay right there, Anna," he instructed, looking at me sternly. I fought a smile; he really was sexy when he was all bossy like that. I nodded and he hurried off to the front wall of the plane, not taking his eyes from me once as he spoke quietly on the phone. He pulled out his cell from his pocket and looked at it, frowning. I couldn't hear what he was saying, but he looked worried and slightly annoyed. After a minute or so he came over to me, his eyes tight with stress. "Right, Baby Girl, there are some reporters waiting for us just outside arrivals. Apparently, the paparazzi found out where we were staying, and somehow they've gotten hold of some photos of us on the beach," he explained, watching me as if I was about to go into meltdown.

"Okay, and?" I prompted, waiting for him to continue. There had to be more, this wasn't enough for him to look this troubled.

He sighed deeply, running a hand through his hair. "They know about the names we booked in under, and there have been a couple of stories in the papers today about our secret wedding," he stated uncomfortably. "I'm sorry we've only just found out but my cell's not working," he said apologetically.

I gulped as every hair on my body stood on end. My mind was whirling a mile a minute. The air in the cabin seemed to be getting thicker as I looked at Ashton with wide eyes. "Why would they even print that? It's not true! They can't print stuff that's not true!"

He sighed and cupped my cheek gently. "I don't know, Anna. They're paid to sell papers, that's all. Everything's fine. We'll get all of this sorted out. All we need to do is show them we're not wearing wedding rings," he smiled reassuringly as he took my hand. "Dean and Peter are meeting us at the gate. Our bags will be collected after, so all we need to do is get to the car. Apparently there are a lot of reporters."

I nodded in acknowledgment, trying not to worry as he led me out of the plane. As soon as we stepped out of the exit tunnel and into the arrivals lounge, Dean and Peter strutted over to us quickly. Both of them were wearing a professional black suit and white shirt, and looked every inch of secret service agents.

"Hey, happy new year," I greeted, forcing a smile.

"Happy new year," they both replied.

Then it was down to business. They both looked to Ashton for guidance. Although they took a couple of steps away from me, I could still hear them planning. My name was mentioned a couple of times, but I tuned them out and looked out over the runway, watching the planes line up and taxi along the tarmac as I tried not to panic.

After a minute or two, Ashton's hand closed over mine, squeezing gently. "Okay, we're ready to go. The reporters are just outside the lounge so we have to walk past them to get to the car out front. You stay with me. I've called in Airport security; they're going to walk us to the car too. If there are any problems, then you go with Dean," he ordered in his stern SWAT voice.

I smiled and nodded as six burly security guys stepped through the side door, they walked over and Ashton relayed the plan again before nodding for one of them to open the double exit doors.

As soon as the door opened, all I could see was flashing lights. People were shouting our names from all directions. It was almost deafening. Ashton's arm snaked around my waist tightly. "Everything's fine," he whispered. As one, the airport security, my two far guards, and Ashton and I took a few steps out of the door. I tried to smile, but the thirty or so cameras and reporters were overwhelming. Some of them were even on stepladders and chairs so that they could get a better shot.

My mouth went dry as Ashton smiled down at me reassuringly. It all went quiet for about two seconds and then the questions started all at once, people shouting louder and louder, trying to be heard over the din. The questions were all jumbled into one, but were all essentially the same. "Were we married? What was the ceremony like? What designer did I wear? Were we going to sell the photos? What did my father think?" It was endless.

Ashton held up one hand and they all stopped talking immediately. "Anna and I aren't married. We went on vacation, that's all. We changed her name to get a little privacy. It was a private joke between the two of us, this is all a misunderstanding," he said calmly. People immediately started shouting questions at the same time so all we could hear was a buzz of noise. He held up his hand again. "Look, we'll answer some questions, I guess, but you need to go one at a time," he suggested, laughing.

"You're not married?" one reporter shouted quickly.

I shook my head. "Nah, he's too pretty for me," I joked, trying to sound blasé when all I wanted to do was run. I didn't like this confrontation. I didn't like people assuming I was married, even if it was to Ashton. Marriage was a serious sore spot for me. The freedom that I'd felt over the last two weeks as Annabelle Taylor was now long gone.

"Why did you book the vacation under the name of Mr and Mrs Taylor?" another reporter asked.

Ashton shrugged. "We were just fooling around; it was a private joke which we don't really want to explain. Nothing was meant by it, so please don't read anything into it," he answered. He was so calm; this didn't scare him at all.

"Are you two expecting a baby?"

I gasped at the question. "What? No!" I cried, shocked. Ashton laughed wickedly and kissed the side of my head affectionately.

"You're not pregnant and you're not married?" someone clarified.

Ashton shook his head. "No baby, no wedding. Sorry guys, this is all just a misunderstanding," he stated easily.

"How was your vacation?"

I looked at Ashton, signalling for him to answer. I wasn't nearly as cool and collected as he was, in fact, I could feel the sweat breaking out on my forehead because of the pressure. "Fantastic. Shame to be back," he answered, tracing his hand up my back softly.

"Do you think you two will get married? Ashton, do you want to marry Anna?" one guy shouted.

Ashton laughed and looked at the reporters. "Who asked that?" A guy that looked to be in his mid-thirties raised his hand. Ashton grinned at him wickedly. "Well look at her, wouldn't you want to marry her if she was your girl?" he replied, grinning. All of the reporters laughed as I gasped and elbowed him in the ribs in reprimand. Thankfully, at that moment Dean walked up, standing in front of us as he motioned for us to start walking again, signalling that question time was over. Ashton's arm snaked around my waist again immediately as we were marched to the exit. Reporters ran alongside us, cameras snapped and they shouted last questions, but airport security and Peter held them back as Dean led us along quickly.

As we slid into the back of the waiting car, I blew out a big breath. "Damn, that was a lot of people!"

Both Dean and Peter slipped into the front seconds later, and as we pulled out of the space, Dean twisted in his seat. "Want to see these?" he asked, holding out three tabloid newspapers.

I nodded and took them off him. We were on the front page of each one: *'Annaton Secret Marriage And Baby Shocker'* and *'First Daughter Elopes'* and *'Shotgun Wedding Shock'* were plastered across the papers.

"This is just stupid!" I huffed, scanning over the first one. They were basing everything on the fact that we had booked our hotel and plane tickets in the name of Taylor. I looked over the photos that they had of us. There were a few different ones: us lying on the beach drinking cocktails, us swimming in the sea and playing around, Ashton rubbing sun cream onto my stomach whilst kissing my shoulder. There was even one of me lying on top of him on the sand; he had his hands on my derrière as we laughed about something.

They all seemed to be taken on the same day because I was wearing my red bikini and had my hair tied up. "Was this yesterday?" I asked, looking at Ashton.

He nodded. "Yeah, I think so," he agreed. A smile broke out on his face. "Nice photo," he added, pointing to the one of his hands on my butt.

"Yeah, way to get us in trouble, Pretty Boy," I teased.

He shrugged unashamedly. "You shouldn't have such a nice ass, maybe then I'd be able to keep my hands off it."

I rolled my eyes. "How did they get these photos anyway? I didn't see any photographers."

Ashton shook his head, frowning, and looking quite annoyed about it. "There weren't any. They must have had a boat or something with a long lens camera. Reporters and photographers aren't allowed on the resort."

I silently sent up thanks that they hadn't managed to get any photos of us in our villa, or even worse, doing naughty things in the sea. A blush spread across my face at the thought of those kind of pictures being in the papers. I turned to the next page to read what they had written about us.

Clearly, they still adored us as a couple. They speculated that I was pregnant, which was the reason for the young marriage. As evidence of me being 'with child', they reprinted the picture of Ashton rubbing sun cream on my stomach, pointing out how he was 'caressing it lovingly'.

I ground my teeth in annoyance. "Jeez, I know I've put on a couple of pounds in the last couple of months, but pregnant?" I grumbled.

Ashton burst out laughing. "Don't start with that! You don't have an ounce of fat on you," he chimed in, shaking his head, chuckling. I closed the paper, not wanting to read anymore.

384

When we finally arrived home, Ashton and the far guards were talking and planning in the kitchen, so I strutted into the bedroom and over to the full length mirror that hung on the wall. I lifted my top, turning to the side, squinting and trying to see why they had printed that I was pregnant. Since Ashton had stopped me running like a crazy person I'd put on a few pounds, but I hadn't thought it was noticeable.

The door clicked open behind me, but I wasn't fast enough in pulling my shirt down before Ashton groaned loudly. "Anna, be serious! You don't look pregnant. You're perfect and beautiful and girls would kill to have a body like yours," he scolded, looking slightly annoyed.

I sighed, defeated. "Well, where the hell did it come from then?"

Before I knew what happened, my feet were knocked out from under me as he pulled me into his arms. I squealed and threw my arms around his neck as he carried me bridal style over to the bed, sitting on the edge and settling me in his lap.

"People make stuff up in the papers everyday. It's probably our age; pregnancy is a reason some people get married young. They're just clutching at straws. That photo probably just added fuel to the fire. If I'd been rubbing cream on your back or shoulders then they might not have even printed it. Trust me, you are just perfect, I promise," he vowed, kissing my nose.

I sighed and tightened my arms around his neck breathing him in. "This will all die down, won't it? All of this attention."

He rubbed my back gently, soothing me. "I'm sure it will after a few weeks," he replied, his voice soft and tender. I pressed myself closer to him and tried desperately to ignore the way my body was reacting to the contact with him. "You tired?" he asked, as I failed in stifling a large yawn. I nodded and glanced over to the clock, noting it was almost midnight. "Let's go to bed then," he suggested, helping me off his lap. "I'll be right back." He headed out of the room to check the doors, the same as he did every night. I grabbed a pair of pyjamas and headed to the bathroom to change and wash my face.

Once I'd changed, I stopped short with my hand on the door handle. Ashton was probably waiting in bed for me. Tonight was going to be hard because we had to get back some semblance of normal. But, however hard it would be, it needed to be done. I needed to at least try and limit the damage he would do to my heart when he left.

After taking a couple of deep breaths, I tugged the door open and forced a smile. I was right. He was sitting up in the bed, his chest bare. *Oh God, please let him be wearing shorts or I'm done for!*

He watched me as I walked over to the bed. "Hey," he smiled.

"Hey," I replied as I climbed in next to him. When he didn't make any moves to come to me, I scooted closer to him. His arm immediately lifted and pushed under my neck, hugging me to him tightly. I sighed contentedly as I snuggled against him, loving how our bodies fitted together as if they were designed that way. Ashton kissed the top of my head softly, sending a wave of desire through me that made my whole body ache. Over the last two weeks, we had barely made it a few hours without making love; the physical contact was going to be a hard habit to break. I bit my lip and closed my eyes tightly, praying for sleep to take me quickly because the desire for him was almost too much to bear.

Within a week of being home, the attention surrounding us started to die down. The press had finally realised that we weren't married or expecting a baby, so they started to lose interest a little. Well, only a little, because we were still plastered all over the papers and magazines. The girlie magazines in particular liked to feature Ashton, he'd clearly woven his spell over them too because he'd actually been voted torso of the week in one magazine. He actually seemed pretty proud of himself when he saw that.

School was awkward again for a couple of days, but even people there were getting used to who we were again.

Today though, we had something different to worry about, other than just what magazines we would be featured in. Today was the day that Ashton was going with his friends to use his driving day experience. That was if I could calm him down from his latest panic attack about leaving me in someone else's care.

"You sure you can't come with me?" he asked, shooting me the begging eyes that usually made me melt inside.

I forced a smile. We'd been going over and over this all week long and he still didn't like the idea of it. "I don't want to go. Besides, you'll have a better time without me being there. You'll be able to relax with your friends and not have to work all the time. I've got Cohen here now, and Dean's moving into the other bedroom," I assured him.

He groaned and set his head on my shoulder. "I hate this," he mumbled.

I giggled at his overprotectiveness. "Look, just chill out. Nothing's gonna happen. You go have fun with your friends and enjoy your Christmas present, okay? If you need to, then you can call me," I suggested, wrapping my arm around his shoulder and stroking the back of his hair.

He looked up and his pained eyes met mine. "But what about the lawyer guy? You sure you can't reschedule him coming over so I could be here for that?"

I sighed. The prosecution lawyer for Carter's case had called and was in town this weekend. He wanted to talk to me and go over a few things in case I was actually called up to give evidence at Carter's retrial. This was the only weekend that he had free to see me before then, and Ashton knew that too.

"I told you, this is the only time he has before the trial. I can't reschedule." I frowned, actually wanting to give in and just go with Ashton or let him stay here with me like he was trying so hard to convince me on. I didn't want to see the lawyer guy again on my own. A deep frown lined Ashton's forehead and I reached out, smoothing it away with my thumb. "Careful, wrinkles," I joked. "Just go, I'll be fine."

"You'll call me and let me know what he says?"

I nodded in agreement. "Promise."

His heavy sigh blew across my cheek. I could see his internal struggle brewing in his eyes. "Be safe this weekend. If you go anywhere, then stay with Dean. No doing anything stupid like going off without a guard, okay?"

Without answering, I cupped his face in my hands, leant in, and kissed him. The heat of his lips felt like he'd set me on fire. I'd avoided kissing him whenever possible this week because it just reminded me how good it would be with him. He kissed me back, moaning in the back of his throat as the kiss deepened. My hands tangled in the back of his hair, pulling him closer to me and showing him how much I was going to miss him as our tongues tangled together.

He pulled away after a couple of minutes and set his forehead against mine as his ragged breath blew across my lips. My whole body was throbbing with need. "I'm gonna miss you so much, Anna. Please be safe and do everything that your guards tell you. If you need me to come back, call me, and I'll be on the next plane," he promised.

"Stop worrying!" I laughed, brushing my nose against his softly. "You try and enjoy yourself, alright?"

He nodded wearily. "I will. I guess I'd better go. Try not to dream, okay?"

"I won't dream." I smiled reassuringly. "It's just two nights, and then you'll be back." As a key twisted in the front door, Ashton groaned and my arms moved from his neck, dropping down into my lap. His eyes didn't leave me once as Dean strutted into the lounge. "Dean, tell Ashton that you're perfectly capable of looking after me while he's away having fun for the weekend," I instructed.

Dean grinned. "Yep, perfectly capable. The new guy is here now so we're all set up and ready. You should go; you'll miss your plane."

Ashton's eyes finally left me as he nodded and pushed himself up to his feet. "I'll see you in a couple of days then. I'll call you in the morning," he promised, bending and planting a soft lingering kiss on my forehead before righting himself and turning to Dean. "Can I have a word with you outside?" he asked, nodding at the front door.

I watched as he left, sending me a little defeated wave at the door. My heart ached. I was going to miss him so terribly much, but I was happy that he was going to have fun for the weekend. He deserved to.

To pass the time, I picked up my sketchpad and drew a few scenes from our vacation. Lately I'd been drawing our trip a lot, probably because it was on my mind a lot. I missed the freedom that the place afforded me, I missed the closeness of Ashton and our togetherness, and I certainly missed his body. It felt like an age since we'd been back but, in reality, it was only a week.

My routine for this weekend without him was slightly different. Dean was moving into the other bedroom to replace Ashton, and my father had sent over another far guard, Cohen, to replace Dean as daytime guard. Dean seemed slightly nervous about acting as near guard for the duration of Ashton's trip, but he was the only one that I trusted to do it and be that close to me.

After I'd made dinner for us both, I went for a long soak in the tub. My day dragged but, to be honest, I didn't want the evening to come too quickly anyway. I wasn't looking forward to a night without Ashton again.

The water was cold by the time I was out of the bath. I dried my body and hair slowly, taking as much time as possible so that I could avoid going to bed.

Finally, at half past eleven, I could avoid it no longer. I called goodnight to Dean and crawled into the bed, lying on Ashton's side. The pillow still held his scent, and a little feeling of contentment washed over me. My eyes flicked to the bedside unit and the photo of me and Ashton on our trip that one of the staff had taken. His handsome smiling face stared back at me, and I sighed, silently hoping he was having a nice time. He'd be there and settled in to his hotel room by now. I tried desperately not to think of him sleeping with other girls this weekend, even though I knew it was pointless to hope he wouldn't, after all, he wasn't mine and he was a player, so of course he would be with other girls. I closed my eyes, thinking of lazing on a hammock in the shade of a palm tree and hoping that the nice memory would ward off the bad dreams that were bound to plague me tonight.

I sit as still as I can. His anger is easy to see. "For fuck's sake, Mark, go fucking take care of it for me! Make him realise he can't rip me off and get away with it," Carter spits.

Mark smiles, sending chills down my spine. He is evil incarnate, and revels in doing his job. He is Carter's second in charge and delights in torturing people and inflicting pain. "Absolutely, how about I bring you his head?" he offers.

Carter laughs and shakes his head. "Nah, too messy," he jokes. I heave but due to not having eaten for a day and a half, I have nothing to bring up. When Mark leaves the room, Carter turns to me, smiling his loving smile. "Sorry about that, Princess. My business talk's all done now. Where were we?" he asks, taking my hand and pulling me from the edge of the bed so I have to stand. His hands slide down my body, catching the bottom of his T-shirt I am wearing. I don't resist as he lifts it over my head so I am naked. I don't resist anymore, I am all out of fight. "Right about here, I think," he coos, grinning and looking at my body lustfully. His hands run over my bruised body, and I whimper when his fingers touch a bruise I have on my stomach. "Get down on your knees, Princess," he whispers, unzipping his pants as a predatory smile creeps onto his face.

I sat up and screamed as the horror washed over me again. Reality tugged at my brain as it slowly registered that I was in my own room, that it was just a dream and that it was over. I put my head between my knees and tried to calm myself, wincing as the memory of it carried on playing in my head. I gripped my hands in my hair, biting my lip as I tried desperately to think of something else.

Loud knocking on my bedroom door made my breathing falter. "You okay, Annabelle?" Dean called.

I sucked in a ragged breath, knowing he would be worried if I didn't calm down. "Yeah, I'm okay, sorry," I called breathlessly. A quick glance at the clock showed me that it was past two in the morning.

"Is there anything I can do?"

I closed my eyes and wiped my sweaty brow. There was nothing anyone could do apart from the love of my life, and he was miles away. "No thanks. I'm sorry I woke you. Goodnight, Dean," I called, ending the conversation.

I fell back against the pillows and fumbled blindly on the bedside unit before finding the little switch I was after and flicking on the lamp. My gaze found the picture of Ashton again, and I stared at it until my heart started to slow to a normal pace. A little blue flashing light on my cell phone caught my attention and a little spark of hope started inside me as I reached for it. As I flicked the screen and unlocked it, I saw a message sitting on there from Ashton, sent earlier on in the evening around about the time I was in the bath. A smile crept onto my face as I opened it.

```
'Hey, Baby Girl, we're still on the plane.
You're probably going to bed soon, I just wanted
   to say goodnight and I miss you. Call you
            tomorrow, sleep tight x'
```

I grinned happily and put my phone back on the side. Just that small text from Ashton was enough to make me smile, even after the nightmare memory I'd just had. I closed my eyes again, leaving the light on as I drifted off to sleep, hoping he was enjoying his weekend off with his friends.

"Princess, I've got something for you," Carter says, smiling excitedly.

Forcing a smile, I look up at him. "What is it, baby?" I ask sweetly, trying to stay in his good books.

He turns and opens the door; immediately, Mark walks in and throws someone at my feet. I squint down at the broken person. I can't tell who it is; his face is all smashed and bruised. His body is twisted unnaturally as he struggles to move from the heap he's been thrown into on the floor. Blood is everywhere, dripping from his clothes, and covering his skin. Nausea hits me in waves and sympathy for the man makes my knees weak. My heart feels like it is breaking for him because of how much pain he is probably in. The man is someone's son, maybe someone's husband or father, yet he is lying here in front of me, completely and utterly helpless. Because he is here, in Carter's house, I already know they will kill him. Carter doesn't bring people back here unless it is the end for them. But why would he say it was a surprise for me?

"You don't recognise him, Princess?" Carter asks.

I look down again and squint, trying to make out the face behind the layer of blood. The guy is mumbling something incoherent; to me, it is more like a long groan of agony. I shake my head in response to Carter's question, but I can't take my eyes off the broken guy on the floor.

Carter laughs and bends down, grabbing hold of the guy's hair and turning his face to mine more. A scream of pain fills the air as the guys eyes open.

His green eyes lock onto mine, and I literally feel my heart break as my world shatters around me. "Run, Anna. Go, now!" Ashton orders, his voice thick with pain.

Carter laughs wickedly and pulls out a gun, pointing it directly at Ashton's face. "She's not going anywhere. She's mine, she stays with me. And you need to pay for touching my wife," he growls as he pulls the trigger. I watch in horror as Ashton's handsome face that I know so well, just folds in and disappears. He slumps back to the floor with a sickening thud. I drop to my knees, screaming his name as I cradle his broken body in my lap, but I can do nothing but watch as the love of my life bleeds out onto the floor. In the background, Carter and Mark laugh and laugh and laugh.

I screamed and screamed; helpless, heartbroken tears fell down my face as the horror of what I had just seen consumed me entirely. I couldn't breathe. I was suffocating. I pushed myself up and put my head between my knees.

"Annabelle, can I come in?" Dean called from the other side of the door.

I gasped for breath as my whole body shook. Sick. I needed to be sick. Swinging my legs out of bed, I stood but my legs shook so much that I almost fell. Sweat beaded on my brow and wet the back of my hair.

That was the worst thing I could have ever dreamed. At least when I had dreams about things that had already happened, I knew it was over, I woke up safe, but that dream… what would I do if that happened? If Ashton was ever hurt, I knew it would crush me inside, beyond repair this time.

"Annabelle?" Dean shouted from the hallway, banging on the door loudly.

I couldn't answer; my heart was crashing loudly in my ears. I still hadn't taken a breath. I couldn't calm down. Black spots started to appear in my vision as I stumbled blindly towards my bathroom. When my head started to spin, I felt that weightless sensation take over, and suddenly I was falling, falling into the blackness.

Chapter Thirty-Eight

As my heavy eyes blinked open, a guy in a green uniform was hovering over me, touching the side of my neck. I gasped, shocked and confused, and thrashed, slapping his hand away from me.

As I scooted up the bed and hit the headboard, Dean stepped forward, holding his hands up to halt me. "Annabelle, calm down! He's a doctor, it's okay," he said quickly, setting his hand on my shoulder. I flinched, flicking my eyes between the two men in my bedroom, only now noticing that my head was pounding and that my whole body felt weak. "It's okay. You passed out. I called an ambulance," Dean explained soothingly.

I nodded weakly, suddenly remembering the feeling of weightlessness moments before the blackness. Movement from the doorway caught my attention, and I looked over to see that Peter and the new far guard were both standing there, watching me anxiously.

"How are you feeling, Miss Spencer?"

I shook my head, dazed, and looked back to the newcomer in the green uniform who'd spoken. "I'm alright. A little fuzzy," I admitted, rubbing my forehead. My throat hurt and scratched as I spoke and I knew it was from all the screaming.

"What happened?" the guy asked.

I squeezed my eyes shut against the pictures of Ashton's broken face that were trying to force their way back in. The way his eyes had locked on mine. The sound of his pain filled voice as he told me to run. The sickening thud as his lifeless body slumped back against the floor. The hysterical laughter of the man who ruined my life…

"Miss Spencer?"

I gulped, coming back to reality. "I… I had a panic attack, I couldn't breathe," I explained. "I'm okay now."

"Maybe we should take you to the hospital and get you a thorough check up, just to be on the safe side," he replied, packing up his equipment into his little green bag.

I frowned in protest. "I'm not going to hospital. I just passed out, that's all. Nothing to worry about. This has happened before, a long time ago; there's nothing wrong with me that a couple of painkillers and a good night's sleep can't fix."

He pursed his lips, obviously displeased with my answer. I didn't break eye contact with him, letting him know I wasn't backing down. There was no way I was going to hospital because of a panic attack. Finally, he nodded. "Okay, well try and get some sleep. You may have a headache in the morning." He stood and looked down at me with his stern eyes. "You'll need to take it easy, and if anything like this should happen again, then you'll need to come to hospital for some in-depth tests."

"Absolutely. Thank you." I scooted down on the bed, tugging the covers up to my neck because I felt a little exposed in front of three males while just wearing Ashton's T-shirt. I watched as he walked over to the door with Dean, talking quietly with him, obviously relaying instructions on my care to him.

As they all stepped out of my bedroom, Dean smiled kindly at me before closing the door behind him, leaving me in the darkness. I leant over and flicked on the light, seeing the red numbers flashing on my alarm clock. 4:26am.

I sighed heavily and swung my legs over the side of the bed. There was no way I was going to sleep again tonight, not after seeing that dream. I never wanted to see that again, I couldn't. Luckily, my wobbly legs seemed to hold my weight as I stood and walked awkwardly to the door. Voices from nearby told me that they were all still outside, discussing me. I pressed my ear to the door, trying to hear, but it was no use, I couldn't make out a single word.

When I heard the front door open and then close, and then Dean's bedroom door close moments later, I crept out of the bedroom and tiptoed my way to the kitchen in the darkness. As I reached for the coffee pot, Dean cleared his throat behind me. I jumped, almost dropping the glass jug, and spun on the spot, seeing him standing there with one eyebrow raised and his arms folded across his chest.

"What are you up to? He said rest and sleep," he stated, his tone accusing.

I smiled weakly. "I'm not tired anymore. Don't worry, I'm fine," I promised. As I lied, I noticed that my hands were shaking so I quickly put down the pot and clasped my hands together out of sight. The last thing I needed was a lecture, or him insisting that we take an early morning trip to the hospital.

He sighed, raking a hand through his short, sandy hair. "Annabelle, you should rest."

"I will. I'm going to make some coffee and then lie on the sofa for a bit." I gulped, knowing I needed to broach the subject of Ashton. I just prayed I could say his name without scenes of the dream surfacing again because if they did my emotions were sure to betray me. "Dean, you didn't call Ashton, did you?"

"No, not yet. I'll call him in a bit, he'll be asleep now," he replied, looking at his watch.

I groaned and shook my head quickly. "Don't tell him. Please, Dean. If you tell him this happened, he'll cut his trip short and he'll come back," I begged. My eyes filled with tears. I desperately wanted Ashton to have a nice time with his friends; I didn't want to be the one that ruined all of his fun all the time.

"Annabelle, I need to tell him. He specifically made me promise to tell him if you had a bad night," he smiled apologetically.

My eyes widened fractionally at the revelation that Ashton had made Dean promise that, but to be honest, I wasn't that surprised about it. He did take overprotective bodyguard to a whole new level, after all. "Please don't. We don't need to tell him that this happened. He deserves to have this weekend. He works all the time, he even gave up his Christmas for me. Please?" My tears were falling now.

He closed his eyes and blew out a hefty breath. "If he finds out I didn't tell him, he'll give me hell," he explained.

I winced at that. I could just imagine how furious Ashton would be. "He won't find out," I pouted, silently begging him with my eyes.

Finally, he sighed. "I'm going to bed, I'll think about it," he mumbled as he shook his head and walked to the other bedroom.

My shoulders relaxed because hopefully he'd make the right decision and let Ashton have his time off. Turning my attention back to the discarded coffee pot, I made a strong black coffee, adding extra sugars, because I already felt exhausted and listless.

Just after eight in the morning, I was sitting and playing on Ashton's PS4 when my cell phone rang. My heart leapt into my throat because I already knew it was him calling me, just like he'd promised he would. I jumped to get it, almost knocking it off the side in my haste. I was ridiculously eager to hear his voice and reassure myself that he was alright and that it was, in fact, just a horrible dream I'd had last night.

I forced my most cheerful voice as I answered so that he wouldn't know anything was wrong. "Hey, Pretty Boy."

"Hey. Did I wake you?"

My heart thumped at the sound of his sexy voice. I smiled sadly. "No, I'm awake. How are you? Plane ride okay? Did you meet up with the boys alright?" I asked, trying to steer the subject from sleeping.

"Yeah, the flight was good. Met up with everyone here at the hotel. Nate and Seth were practically buzzing by the time I met them, I'm supposed to give you a thank you hug from them both for putting them in first class with the free champagne and peanuts."

I chuckled. "Those peanuts are good," I joked, grinning.

He laughed too. "So, how did you sleep?" he inquired, sounding almost afraid to ask.

I winced and flicked my eyes towards Dean's bedroom door. *Well, he didn't specifically say no, he said he would think about it...*

"I slept good," I lied, cringing. "I slept on your side, maybe that was the key."

"Yeah? That's great, Baby Girl. I was so worried about you all night," he admitted.

I closed my eyes, trying to ignore that nagging feeling inside me that told me that I shouldn't be lying to him. But my intentions were good, I was lying so that he wouldn't abandon his life, yet again, and come to my rescue. "You shouldn't worry about me, I'm fine. So, are you looking forward to today? What time are you going to the race track?" I asked, needing to change the subject.

"The tour starts at one, so we need to leave here about quarter to, I guess. The hotel you booked for us is literally on the edge of the track. It's so nice, you'd love it here. Maybe we could come here one time, and we could actually watch the Grand Prix race? Maybe I could convert you to a race fan," he teased.

I laughed. "I don't think so, you've got more chance of making me a football fan," I joked, smiling.

"Right, I guess you get to look at the guys' asses then."

"You know I like a nice ass," I joked.

"Yeah, I know," he replied, sounding amused.

Dean's bedroom door clicked open, and my eyes widened in horror. He would take one look at me and know that I was talking to Ashton and he'd tell him, without a doubt. "I'd better go, I've got breakfast in the pan," I lied, needing to get off the phone.

"Oh yeah? And what are you making for my replacement?" Ashton asked curiously.

"French toast," I teased.

He groaned. "Baby Girl, that's not fair, you know I love your French toast!" he whined.

"I'm sure they have French toast in your hotel." I watched as Dean strutted out of his bedroom, rubbing his eyes roughly as he stalked towards the kitchen. When his gaze flicked in my direction, I cringed and bit my lip. "I've got to go; I'll speak to you later, okay? Call me when you get time and let me know how you all got on driving," I suggested, watching as Dean changed his course and strutted over towards me, his eyes accusing and hard.

"Okay, I will. And if the lawyer guy comes before I call you, then you call me instead and let me know what he said," he instructed. "I miss you, Anna."

My insides tingled, and my heart skipped a beat at hearing those words in his silky smooth voice. "Miss you too, bye." *Wow, if only he knew how much I missed him, he'd be frightened to death.*

I disconnected the call just as Dean reached out to snatch it from my hand. He was glaring at me. "You have got to be kidding me! You called him and told him you were fine?" he growled angrily.

I shook my head innocently. "No, he called me," I corrected, but his glare seemed to deepen at my sarcasm. "I did tell him I was fine though," I admitted. "He's having a really nice time. Please don't ruin this for him? He'll never find out, just tell the other two not to say anything, and we'll pretend that everything was fine," I begged.

He huffed angrily and scowled at me. "Well, I don't suppose I have a choice now, considering you've already made the decision for me, do I?" he snapped, shaking his head disapprovingly.

I jumped up, smiling with relief. "Thank you! As payback, I'll make you breakfast, anything you want, you just name it." I practically skipped to the kitchen.

He followed behind me with a scowl still plastered on his face. "Annabelle, if he finds out, I expect you to back me up and tell him this wasn't my idea and that you railroaded me into it."

I nodded enthusiastically. "Absolutely, I promise." I crossed my heart with one finger and grinned. "But he won't find out anyway. I won't say anything, I swear." I smiled reassuringly and stopped in front of the fridge. "So, what's it to be? Eggs, pancakes, waffles?" I offered, waving my hands at the stove.

He shrugged and his scowl fell away, now replaced by a smile. "No wonder Ashton's crazy about you if you treat him like this all the time." I recoiled, taken aback by his words. *He thinks Ashton is crazy about me?* I shrugged it off and looked at Dean expectantly; he still hadn't answered the question. "Pancakes and bacon?" he suggested. I grinned and pulled the stuff from the fridge, getting to work.

Later that afternoon, I was chewing on my nails so much that they were starting to bleed, but I couldn't seem to stop myself from doing it. The man with the greying, thinning hair in the expensive suit sitting opposite me on the sofa looked just the same as he did three years ago, although maybe a little thicker around the middle. This was the man that had sat me down and convinced me that I needed to give evidence at Carter's trial the first time. I hadn't wanted to, in fact, I'd adamantly protested, but he'd talked at me and talked at me until I'd given in. Of course, there were restrictions on what I would give evidence on. I'd point blank refused to tell anyone what really went on between me and Carter at his house, so none of the abuse, rapes, or kidnapping charges were ever filed against him, much to this man's disgust.

My evidence hadn't actually helped much the first time around because I'd refused to press charges against Carter, so whenever someone asked me how I came to be at his house, or what happened to me there, it was quickly objected by Carter's team of highly priced lawyers, and then the jury were told to disregard anything they'd heard that did not relate to the actual murder of Jack.

As a matter of fact, Carter's team of three lawyers, had practically ripped my evidence to shreds, making me look like an immature, jealous girlfriend who barely understood what was being asked. It hadn't helped matters that I hadn't slept for three days prior to the trial, so I looked and acted like an emotionless zombie while I was being questioned. In the end, I actually felt as if I'd done more harm than good.

"The court are obviously understanding of your father's position now. We have the evidence that you gave last time on video. If we need to refer to anything, we can refer to transcripts of it." He unclasped his briefcase and pulled out a stack of papers, thumbing through them. "Of course, I have you on my list of vetted witnesses, but I'm not going to call you to the stand again," he assured me. "The only thing that's happened in the last month is that the defence has also put you down as a witness for their side this time."

My mouth fell open in shock. "The defence have? What the hell for?"

He frowned and nodded. "I'm not quite sure what they hope to achieve, but the judge will not allow them to call you in on a whim. With your father being who he is, and you being in the public eye too, they won't just be able to call you to trial without due cause. I'm assuming that they've added you onto their list as a publicity stunt. If they bring you in, it will draw attention to the case because of your social standing."

I ground my teeth in frustration. "I won't give evidence to help him," I spat.

Mr Stanson nodded, still shuffling his papers. "I don't believe it will come to that at all. As I said, I won't be calling you again but may refer to your testimony. And the defence will only be allowed to call you to stand if they can prove that you can provide something new and enlightening. I strongly believe this is all just a stunt, possibly to rattle you before the trial." He held out a stapled piece of paper to me. "Just in case though, let's go over a few things that you said in the last trial, and I'll brief you on any questions that you may be asked. We don't want you to be tripped up like you were before. After that, I'll describe what it's like inside a court room. I'm assuming that you've never set foot in one before?"

I shook my head. The only court case I had ever been involved in was Carter's, and then I'd been a minor so I was in a separate, normal room, while the lawyers asked me questions through video link.

I took the offered paper, noticing that it was a transcript of my evidence from last time. My head was buzzing with thoughts. The one that was the most prominent was that Carter had put me on that list just because he could. He was sending me a message that he could still get to me and have an effect on my life, even behind bars. This was a control thing all over again. I raised my chin, vowing that I wouldn't let him or this trial get to me like it did last time. Last time I'd fallen to pieces while being questioned, this time would be a different story.

When he finally left, an hour later, my heart was heavy and my brain fuzzy. For the rest of the day, it was like I was sitting under a raincloud and I just couldn't lift my spirits. My tiredness didn't help my situation. Dean was blissfully unaware of what I was doing as I sat in my bathroom, using a razor to make four small but precise cuts on the inside of my forearm. The pain helped marginally, but it still wasn't enough. I longed for Ashton. I longed for his arms, and his smile, and the silly things that he said to cheer me up when I was sad. I was counting down the hours now.

Ashton called me just after suppertime, asking about how it went with the lawyer, and what he'd said. I'd made light of it, not giving him the full story because I knew that he would just get angry if he knew that Carter's side had me on their witness list too. I'd tried to remain emotionless, but Ashton just seemed to bring something out in me that I couldn't control. In the end, I'd sat there, silently crying while he'd whispered soothing words down the phone, telling me that everything was fine and that I wouldn't even get called up.

When I finally got a hold of my emotions, I sniffed loudly, wiping my nose on the back of my hand. "So tell me about your day, was it fun?" I asked, needing to hear something positive for a change.

"Fun doesn't even cover it," he answered. "The tour was great, and the cars… my God, I wish I'd trained as a driver when I was younger instead of SWAT. They clocked me at 143mph on the straight," he boasted.

My heart leapt into my throat and I immediately berated myself for buying him something so dangerous as a gift. "Damn it, Ashton! Were you supposed to go that fast? You could have been killed!"

He chuckled wickedly. "I knew that would be your reaction when I told you that. You worry about me too much too, you know," he teased. "Anyway, thank you so much for arranging this."

"You're very welcome," I replied, chewing on my lip. "So, are your boys having fun too?"

"Heck yeah. Nate and Seth are talking about having me killed so they can have you to themselves."

"Those boys don't interest me," I answered honestly. Nothing and no one would ever steal my heart from Ashton.

"Good girl." I could practically hear the smile in his voice.

"So, what are you doing tonight? Getting drunk I hope."

He laughed. "You're always trying to get me drunk," he teased. "I might have a couple, I won't be getting smashed. You think I could call you when I get back and talk to you again before you go to sleep?"

My lips twitched with a smile. "If you want to. But how do you know you won't have some girl in your room?" It was half a joke, half serious. I knew there was a very good chance he would be sleeping with some random girl tonight. I couldn't stop the jealousy that was coursing through my veins. Deep down, I knew I had no right to be jealous, we were just friends who pretended to be more – but that didn't stop the ache in my heart when I thought about it.

He sighed. "I won't, Baby Girl."

I laughed incredulously, remembering something he'd told me once before. "Right, I forgot, you'll be in her room so you don't have to spend the night."

"Anna, seriously, will you stop? I don't want another girl! Christ!" he snapped.

I recoiled, shocked that he'd shouted at me. "I was just teasing," I muttered. I hadn't been, we both knew it, but suddenly I felt guilty for doubting him.

"Look, just stop thinking like that, alright? I really hate it. I don't want you thinking that I'm gonna be sleeping around just because I'm not there with you. I won't." His voice was sincere, and my guilt flared up again.

"Okay. Sorry," I frowned down at my bitten nails, chewing on my lip.

"Don't worry about it. Let's change the subject, alright?" he suggested. I smiled and closed my eyes, grateful that the awkwardness could be brushed under the carpet.

Our phone call lasted almost an hour, but it felt like merely minutes. At the end, he'd promised to call me later on, as soon as he was back in his hotel room. Once I put down the phone to him, I decided I would forgo sleep once again that night. I couldn't take another nightmare on top of everything else, and I certainly couldn't risk having another dream of Ashton, all broken and bruised.

I busied myself sketching while Dean watched TV. From the corner of my eye, I could see him yawning but trying to cover it up. I closed my book and stood. "I'm going to bed, Dean. Goodnight," I lied.

He stood too, stretching. "Yeah, I think I will too. I'll see you in the morning."

To keep up the act, I headed to my bedroom and changed into a pair of loungewear pyjamas before quietly listening to my iPod for an hour. When I figured that Dean would be asleep, I hesitantly crept back out into the kitchen, making coffee before sneaking back into the lounge to watch TV.

At just after midnight, I got a text from Ashton.

*'Hey, Baby Girl. I'm sorry this is so late.
If you're still awake, call me. If I'm too late,
then I'll call you in the morning. Missing you
like crazy x'*

A goofy smile stretched onto my face as I dialled his number as quickly as I could. He answered immediately. "Hey! I didn't wake you did I? I'm sorry it's so late. Seth wanted to stay for another one, which then turned into two," he grumbled.

The sound of his voice made my sour mood lighten. "I told you that I didn't care if you woke me up. You should have just stayed out and got smashed, made the most of your time. You haven't had a drink for over four months."

He sighed deeply. "I didn't want to stay out. It's not the same without you there. I really missed you tonight."

"You did?" I snuggled down on the sofa, unable to curb my ecstatic smile.

"Yeah. It was weird tonight. Usually when we go out, I have you to laugh and dance with but, towards the end of the evening, all the guys went their separate directions and I was left on my own talking to the barman," he chuckled awkwardly.

I frowned. "They left you? What for?"

"They all went out on the hunt," he replied casually.

The hunt? Oh, like hunting girls! "Right, and you didn't want to?" I asked quietly.

"No, I didn't," he answered, just as quietly.

I smiled as happiness built inside me because of his answer. We chatted easily for about an hour, about nothing in particular, he was just so easy to talk to. "I guess I should let you get back to sleep," he said, just after half past one in the morning.

I sighed. I hated lying to him but I was doing it for the right reasons. "Yeah. I miss you. Can't wait for you to get back tomorrow." That was the truth. Eight o'clock Sunday night couldn't come soon enough in my opinion. I closed my eyes and imagined his handsome face as he walked through the front door.

"Shall I bring us in some takeout?" he asked excitedly.

I laughed wickedly. "You're so excited about food!"

"I'm not excited about the food, Anna; I'm excited to see you."

My insides fluttered. "Ashton, seriously, sometimes you are just too damn sweet."

"It's true. Right then, I'll call you tomorrow when we get to the airport," he said, sounding like he genuinely didn't want to hang up.

"Okay, sleep well."

"I'll try. Goodnight, Baby Girl," he sighed. I disconnected the call and went into my bedroom, grabbing my vanity bag, deciding to paint my toe and finger nails, just so I would have something to do.

I managed to keep myself awake all night, but I was really suffering by the morning. My eyes were stinging, my body was aching, and I'd already had about eight cups of coffee. Ashton texted me in the morning, hoping that I'd slept okay and telling me he missed me. I text him back, lying that I had slept fine.

Dean looked at me a little concerned when he got up. "You sleep okay, Annabelle? You look like crap," he commented at breakfast.

I laughed weakly. "Thanks, that's what every girl likes to hear. You should know I slept fine last night, I didn't wake you up, did I?" I retorted sarcastically.

He shook his head but continued to look at me strangely. Clearly he knew something was up.

That day I did everything and anything in a bid not to sit down. I went to the gym and then I cleaned the whole apartment, scrubbing out the stove and even washing the windows, just for something to do. Ashton called briefly at four pm, but we barely spoke for five minutes because they called his plane.

The time seemed to take forever to pass. Finally, at 8:17pm exactly, I heard the key twist in the lock and I got so excited that I thought I would die.

Chapter Thirty-Nine

~ Ashton ~

As soon as I was off the plane and out into the warm Arizona air, I hailed a cab and headed straight for Anna's favourite Chinese restaurant. Thankfully, we came here a lot, so I didn't even need to place an order, just request our usual with the guy behind the counter.

While I was waiting for my order, I sent a text to Peter and Dean, telling them I was back and that I'd be along in about ten minutes and that business was to be as usual once I arrived. I struggled not to tell Dean to get the hell out of my apartment so I could spend some alone time with Anna. I sat there watching the minute hand on the clock tick around. I was so excited to see Anna again that I could barely breathe properly. Finally, after forever and a day, the food was done and stacked into two bags.

By the time I got back to our apartment building, Peter was standing in the lobby where he was supposed to be. A grin stretched across his face when he saw me. "Hey, have a good time?"

I nodded. Of course I'd had a fantastic time, how could I not, but at the same time I'd missed Anna so much it was as if I'd left a piece of me behind. I hadn't been able to stop thinking about her and worrying about her. A thousand scenarios had rushed through my brain every hour of every day – every single one of them bad. I hadn't been able to relax the whole time.

"It was fantastic, nice to be back though," I answered. "I got Chinese food. Why don't you go up and eat with the other two then come back down again once you're done?" I suggested, holding out the far guards' bag of food to him.

His eyes lit up. "Yeah? Great, thanks!"

"Call Dean. Tell him that the food's here and to get the hell out of my place," I instructed, only half joking as we stepped into the elevator. I didn't want to have to share Anna with Dean.

Peter laughed, immediately pulling out his cell phone and dialling. "Dude, Ashton's here. He bought Chinese food, and he said to get the hell out of his apartment so that he can seduce his woman," Peter joked, laughing wickedly.

I smiled down at the floor. He had no idea how close on the money he was there with that statement.

As we stepped out of the elevator on our floor, I tried extremely hard not to speed walk with a huge grin on my face. My heart was slamming in my chest with apprehension. My hands were shaking with excitement as I balanced all of the bags in one hand and slid the key in the lock with the other. As I pushed open the door, Dean was walking towards me, smiling.

"Hey, Ashton, you have a good time?"

"Incredible," I confirmed. "Any problems?"

He shifted on his feet, flicking his eyes over my shoulder for a split second before shaking his head. "Nope, nothing," he replied.

I detected his unease, but at the same time, movement behind him caught my attention and my eyes landed on her. My world seemed to stop spinning as she leant against the wall, sinking her teeth into her bottom lip and fiddling with her hands. Air rushed out of my lungs. She was so damn beautiful. It seemed like every time I looked away from her and then saw her again, I fell more in love with her. They did say that absence made the heart grow fonder, but I'd never quite understood that phrase until now.

"Good. Food is next door. We'll catch up later." I put my bags down by the door and motioned for him to leave, but I was unable to take my eyes from the most beautiful thing in the world.

"See you later then," he chuckled to himself as he left, closing the door behind him.

Bending down, I dug around in the top of my weekend bag, finding the single white rose that I'd bought for her at the airport. It was a little squashed and wilted from the trip, but hopefully she'd appreciate the gesture. Her gaze didn't leave me as I walked towards her deliberately slowly, letting my eyes wander over her, taking her all in again, as if for the first time. She had a dazzling smile on her face. Her eyes shone with love and tenderness; I couldn't look away from them. I stopped directly in front of her, our bodies merely inches apart. Neither of us spoke; I could feel the love swelling inside me, making my whole body tingle and my stomach tie up in knots.

Raking my eyes over her face, I realised then how tired she looked. Her eyes were slightly pink and shadows resided underneath. She hadn't slept well at all this weekend, and had lied to me to cover it up. That knowledge almost killed me. The thought of her having a nightmare was tearing me up inside.

She was wearing one of my T-shirts and a pair of leggings, her hair was pulled back into a messy twist. Even sleep deprived, she looked incredible. Before I'd left, I'd memorised every little detail, every curve and line, the exact placement of the five little freckles she'd gotten from the sun on our vacation. But seeing them in the flesh now, I realised that the memory version of her didn't even come close to doing her justice.

"Hi," I whispered, knowing my voice wouldn't work if I tried to speak properly.

Her smile grew even bigger. "Hi."

I held out the rose. As her hand closed over it, she didn't even look at it, her eyes never left mine. Unable to stop myself, I bent my head forward and captured her soft lips with mine just for a second, before wrapping my arms around her and hugging her tightly. Her arms looped around my neck, and her body sagged against mine as she pressed her face into the side of my neck and inhaled deeply. I smiled at the reason behind it. She'd once told me that I smelt like safety and home.

Her breath came out in a contented sigh as her arms tightened around me, clamping herself to my chest. "I missed you so much, Ashton," she mumbled against my neck.

I grinned. "Not half as much as I missed you."

"Really? Well then, you missed me a lot," she teased.

I nodded in confirmation. "Hell yeah I did." I bent my knees and held her tighter as I stood back up, lifting her off her feet. Instantly, her legs wrapped around my waist. I stalked across the lounge to the sofa, laying her down and settling myself on top of her, loving the feel of her under me. I had missed her so much that I couldn't even put it into words.

With her fingertip, she traced the bridge of my nose, across my cheek and then her hand tangled into the back of my hair. "Did you have fun?" she asked, smiling.

I nodded. "I had a great time, Baby Girl. Thank you." Lying on top of her was far better, if I was honest.

"I'm glad. So, are you not hungry for a change? You left the food by the front door," she teased.

I shrugged, pressing down onto her, pinning her underneath me as I brushed her hair away from her face. "Yeah I am, but I'd rather lie here with you."

Her eyes sparkled. "Wow, you did miss me, huh? Thank you for the rose," she whispered, finally looking at it.

I laughed quietly, proud that it had taken her this long to actually look at it because she was too concerned with looking at me. "You're welcome. So, you slept okay then?" I inquired, raising one eyebrow in challenge. I actually wasn't sure if she would lie right to my face.

She bit her lip and nodded, averting her eyes. "Yeah, fine."

I sighed and shook my head. "No you didn't, Anna."

A frown lined her forehead as her hand tightened in the back of my hair. "No, you're right, I didn't. But it doesn't matter anymore. You're home now," she stated, tickling her fingers on the back of my neck.

I decided to let it go, there was nothing I could do about it now and I didn't want to ruin the reunion by getting angry and lecturing her about something I couldn't change. Sure, I wished she'd called me and I would have gladly come home to be with her, but I understood why she didn't. Her selflessness was one of the things I loved the most about her.

"Yeah, I'm home now," I whispered. I was definitely home, *she* was my home.

She smiled gratefully, and her shoulder relaxed as she guided my mouth down to hers. I moaned in the back of my throat, kissing her back immediately. The kiss was getting hotter and hotter by the second as our tongues danced in perfect synchronism. My body was on high alert, wanting things to go further. I longed to peel her clothes off and run my hands and mouth over every inch of her, but I knew that wouldn't happen. My jeans were becoming tight across the groin as I struggled to contain my excitement. The way that Anna managed to wrap me around her little finger with one kiss should surely be illegal.

When I pulled back and broke the kiss a couple of minutes later, my lips were still tingling. Since the vacation, I'd been trying to keep my distance and give her space to miss me, trying to make her see that she wanted to be with me – but, much to my frustration, it hadn't worked at all. My body was screaming at me, demanding that I lean in, close the distance and kiss her again, carry her to the bedroom and have her moan my name in that sexy way that she does. She was looking at me tenderly, her gaze travelling over my face. I smiled at the love and passion I could see shining in her eyes, the kiss had excited her too. I could practically feel the sexual tension in the air. I brushed a loose hair off her forehead, savouring the feel of her flushed skin under my fingertips. Just as I was about to give in to my body's urges and kiss her again, her stomach rumbled loudly.

I laughed, grinning down at her. "Come on, let's eat. I got you chicken chow mein," I offered, pushing myself off her.

She smiled excitedly and followed me out to the kitchen, wrapping her arms around me from behind as I served up the food. "Next time I buy you something that you have to travel for, I'm coming with you, okay?" she mumbled into my back, slipping her hand up my T-shirt and teasing the small patch of hair beneath my navel.

I smiled at her words. "That's absolutely fine with me, Baby Girl." She sighed contentedly. She was pressed so tightly against me that I could feel her heart beating against my back. I turned and wrapped my arms around her waist, dipping my head and kissing her forehead. Everything fell back into place. The piece of me that had been missing over the weekend had now returned, making me whole again.

Chapter Forty

~ Anna ~

The call for our flight cut through my fuzzy, almost asleep brain. I raised my head off Ashton's shoulder and looked up at the TV screen that now showed our flight was finally ready to board. We'd been camped out in the airport for the last three hours because it was delayed. My head pounded because I'd just dozed off for ten minutes before the screechy speakers had announced we were ready to board.

Ashton smiled over at me sadly with those beautiful eyes that I would give anything to pass onto my children. "Won't be long now and then we'll be at the Lake House, and you can go to bed," he encouraged, as he stood and held down a hand to help me from my seat.

I hadn't slept very well again last night. This time it wasn't due to Ashton not being there though, it was merely because of what day it was tomorrow. Jack's birthday. That was where we were off to now, the Lake House. I was going to pay my respects and visit his grave on his birthday. Of course, not everyone had wanted me to go there. My father was being sworn into office the day after Jack's birthday, so I was expected to attend the ceremony. Plans had been made, without my agreement, for me and Ashton to fly into Washington tomorrow so that we could both attend a dinner party the night before my father was inaugurated. No one understood when I refused and said that I had to go and see Jack first. Everyone – even Jack's parents – had assured me that Jack wouldn't mind if I didn't go this year and that I could go the day after, or just think about him without being at his grave. The only one that seemed to listen to me was Ashton. When I'd gone to him, crying, telling him how much it meant to me that I visit Jack, he'd arranged everything, talked my father into it, and even called Maddy to rearrange our flights. He'd been a superstar campaigning for me and what I wanted. As usual, I owed him a lot.

Even though it was going to mean a lot of travelling, Ashton and I were heading to the Lake House tonight so that I could go and see Jack for his birthday for a few hours, and then tomorrow night we were flying into Washington so that we could attend the ceremony the following day. After the ceremony we would jet back to Arizona again to carry on with life as usual – except this time I would officially be the First Daughter.

As Ashton and I made our way onto the plane, I pressed myself tightly to his side and wove my fingers through his. All week I'd been clingy and extra cuddly. I knew I was doing it, but I just couldn't help myself. Luckily for me though, he'd not complained and asked me for more space or told me I was stifling him. In fact, I think he'd quite liked me hanging on him and cuddling up to him all the time.

By the time we arrived at the Lake House, it was after ten in the evening. My parents were already in Washington, preparing to move into the White House. Therefore, the Lake House looked a little bare and lifeless. The only people here were the caretaking staff.

Silently, I led Ashton up to my bedroom and curled in my bed without even taking my clothes off. I was exhausted, not so much physically, but mentally. It was hard being back here. It was hard knowing that tomorrow I would have to go and wish happy birthday to a boy that I had gotten killed. It was even harder knowing that I had promised to love him forever, when I was now hopelessly in love with someone else.

Behind me, Ashton climbed into the bed, wrapping his body around mine. As usual, his touch made me feel better and took some of the edge off the sadness that was creeping over me and slowly pulling me under. It was almost as if Ashton had some kind of magic spell over me that could calm my nerves.

"Goodnight, Baby Girl," he whispered, kissing the top of my head.

"Night," I replied, trying not to feel guilty for loving him so much.

When I woke in the morning it was early, in fact, it wasn't even six o'clock. Ashton's low snore was still rumbling behind me, so I crept out of the bed, unable to lie still now that I was awake. My body was twitching with unease and anxiety, and I knew there was only one way to calm myself down. After pulling on a pair of leggings and a T-shirt, I silently slipped out of the bedroom and made my way down to the gym.

When I stepped through the door, I stopped. The place that I used to frequent daily, now seemed a little weird and unfamiliar. It seemed like a lifetime ago that I used to exercise away my problems.

Out of habit, I cranked up the air-conditioning and headed over to the treadmill, starting off on a slow walk to let my muscles warm up. Once I was ready, I started building up speed until I was at a slow, leisurely jog. I stared at the speedometer as my finger hovered above the plus button. I knew that I shouldn't go faster, something inside me was telling me no, but I just couldn't stop myself. I pressed the button over and over, making the belt at my feet turn faster and faster until I was at a flat out run.

Within ten minutes, my muscles were screaming at me to stop, my breath was coming out in pants and sweat ran down my neck and back. I knew that Ashton didn't like me to run like this… but Ashton wasn't here right now, and I didn't want to keep thinking about Jack and how he should have been twenty today. I didn't want to think about how he should be half way into his medical degree, or how he probably would have joined the college football team. I didn't want to think about the fact that he was gone and that it was entirely my fault. I sped up a little on the treadmill, running as fast as I could to block out the grief and the thoughts that were trying to pull me under, but this time I was unable to outrun my problems.

When my knees wobbled and I almost fell, I knew it was time to give up. As I slowed down to a walk, I gasped for breath, pulling at the neck of my T-shirt because it felt tight all of a sudden. Once the treadmill came to a standstill, my legs gave way and I slumped to my knees heavily. Instantly, my whole body hurt and my leg muscles cramped and seized. Pressing my forehead to the floor, I gritted my teeth against the pain, gripping my thighs as tears slid down my face and fell onto the floor.

"Shit," I hissed.

"You okay, Baby Girl?" Ashton asked suddenly, reaching out to rub my back and legs.

I jumped and let out a little squeal because I hadn't realised that he was in the room. "Shit, it hurts so much!" I hissed through my teeth, unable to move from the little ball on the floor that I'd curled into. He sighed and continued to massage my thighs. After a few minutes, I twisted my head to the side to look at him. The sad and disappointed look on his face made my heart sink and guilt twist in my gut. The disappointed look on his face was so much worse than the disapproving scowl that usually followed one of my intense sessions. "I'm sorry, I didn't mean to," I apologised. I hadn't walked into the gym planning on running like that, I'd just needed a distraction and my old habits and coping methods had taken over.

Ashton nodded sadly. "I know. It's okay; I know why you did it."

"Please don't look at me like that, I can't stand it," I begged, feeling my chin tremble as I looked away from him. "I'm sorry," I whispered. He let out another heavy sigh as he tugged on my hand and tried to pull me into his lap. I shook my head in protest. "I can't I'm all sweaty."

He laughed incredulously as a playful smirk slipped onto his face. "I like you sweaty," he replied, tugging on my arm again. "Just do as you're told for once and come here."

I sniffed, swiping at the tears that were now falling down my face and complied with his request, manoeuvring myself into his lap and setting my head on his chest as his arms engulfed me. His hands resumed massaging my thighs softly.

"Are you okay? You want me to run you a bath or something?" he offered.

I lifted my head, looking into his caring eyes. "Why are you not shouting at me for doing that?"

He sighed, his forehead lined with a frown. "Anna, I understand why you do it. You haven't done it for so long so something must really be bothering you."

I closed my eyes, not being able to look at his face anymore. "I was just thinking about Jack's birthday. He would have been twenty today." He pulled me closer to his chest, wiping the sweat from my forehead, but not saying anything. When I opened my eyes, I saw that same disappointed expression on his face. My chin trembled, and I silently wished he'd just shout at me, it would be easier. "Please don't keep looking at me like that. I'm sorry, I won't do it again," I promised, feeling the tears welling up in my eyes.

"Looking at you like what?" he asked, confused.

I shook my head. "Like you're disappointed. It's not nice to see, I can't stand it."

"I am disappointed, Anna," he replied, closing his eyes and shaking his head.

A lump formed in my throat at his admission. "I know, I'm sorry." I turned my face into his T-shirt, trying to block out the sight of his face.

"I'm not disappointed in you, Baby Girl. I'm disappointed in myself," he said sadly.

I snapped my head up to look at him. *Disappointed in himself? What on earth does that mean?* "What? Why?"

He sighed and ran a hand through his hair, making it stand up on end. "I try to make you happy, I try to help you, I try to stop you hurting so badly that the only release is for you to kill yourself through exercise. I try, but I'm just not good enough," he stated, looking at me apologetically.

Disbelief almost made me gawk at him. He honestly thought he wasn't good enough to stop me hurting? I sat up, shocked, and looked at him in disbelief. How could this boy, who had saved my life and made me live again, possibly think that he wasn't good enough?

"Ashton, seriously, what the hell are you talking about? Not good enough? Are you crazy? If it wasn't for you, I would be hiding in one of the bedrooms in the White House, expelled from yet another school, screaming myself awake every night, afraid to let anyone near me, wearing baggy clothes, and drawing pictures which, quite frankly, scare the shit out of me. I didn't have a life before you, I had an existence, and I didn't even want that," I admitted, blurting out more of my feelings than I had ever done before.

His hand closed over mine as I unconsciously started pinching the skin on the inside of my elbow. "But you still won't talk to me, Anna. You'd still rather come down here and make your whole body hurt, rather than talking through your feelings with me," he explained, rubbing his thumb over the back of my hand.

"I don't want to scare you away," I admitted, looking away from him.

"You won't scare me away. Please talk to me. Nothing you could do or say would make me leave you," he vowed, putting a finger under my chin and making me look at him.

I gulped. *Does that mean forever, or for the next three months?* We just sat there looking at each other for a couple of minutes. His eyes were narrowed in a silent plea for me to open up to him, to finally let him in once and for all. The trouble was I didn't want to do that. It wasn't that I didn't trust him, it was more that I knew that if he knew even half of the stuff that went through my head, he'd finally know how fucked up I was and he'd run for the hills. But the soft, tender, pleading look to his eyes told me that he wasn't ever going to think badly of me, or judge me, or think I was a bitch or coward.

I sighed and decided to take a chance for once in my life. Ashton was worth taking a chance on. "What do you want to know?"

His shoulders seemed to relax as a dazzling smile crept onto his face. For some reason, he looked extremely proud of me. "What college were you and Jack planning on going to?" he asked.

I smiled. That one was easy. "We wanted different ones. He wanted to be a doctor, so he wanted Harvard, and I wanted MSU," I answered, shrugging.

His eyes widened with apparent surprise. "You would have gone to separate schools?"

I smiled sadly. "Yeah, we were very confident that nothing could break us up. Neither of us saw Carter coming," I said grimly.

His expression hardened in an instant. "You were with Carter for ten months?" The way he said Carter's name was almost a growl.

"Yeah, just over. I banged my head and passed out at the club, and woke up in his house in Miami," I replied, frowning, trying not to think about it too much.

His hand slid to my elbow. "This self-harming thing that you do, I've read about it. People that self-harm sometimes feel that they lack control in their lives. Is that why you hurt yourself?"

I blew out a big breath and turned my arm over, seeing the numerous little white scars that lined the inside of my forearm and the red patch at my elbow where I was pinching myself earlier. "Kind of. I don't actually know why I do it. It's like an outlet for pain sometimes is the only way I can describe it to you. Sometimes I get so overwhelmed that I can't cope and doing that can sometimes help me focus or can clear my mind. I don't know why I do it. I don't do it often anymore," I answered. That was the truth. I'd only done it a few times since Ashton had been with me.

Ashton was watching me, absorbing everything I was saying with a thoughtful look on his face. "I don't like you hurting yourself."

I swallowed noisily. "I know."

"I can be your outlet. If you just talk to me, maybe I can help you clear your mind from now on," he suggested hopefully. Unable to answer, I set my head on his shoulder and nodded. I knew there would always be times in my life that I would do it, I couldn't promise it would never happen again, but I would try

His hand slid down my arm, over the bumpy scars that had gone white over time and settled on my wrist as his thumb traced the biggest, jagged scar across my wrist. "You tried to kill yourself the first time by slitting your wrists." It wasn't actually a question and I realised that he was prompting me to talk about the more difficult things that had happened.

I didn't raise my head from his shoulder as I answered. "Actually, that was the second time. I tried to jump from the balcony at the club when they threw Jack off, but Carter stopped me. He said it was a waste," I admitted, swallowing the lump in my throat. That was the first time I had told anyone that, ever.

His angry silence filled the room for a few seconds before he spoke again. "You tried to kill yourself two other times, on your birthday."

I nodded. "Yeah, I took some pills." *Please don't leave me after this, Ashton!*

He took a deep breath, seeming to choose his next words carefully. "You actually wanted to die? You told me when I first started that you had nothing left to lose and that you wanted to die because you had nothing to live for," he winced, as if the memory hurt him.

I nodded. "Yeah, I wanted to die. I remember waking up after each time I'd tried to kill myself and feeling so disappointed that I was alive. I thought I was being punished for what I did to Jack," I admitted.

He gasped. "Punished? You thought living was punishment?"

"I guess." I shrugged. "Every time I tried to kill myself it never worked, I thought that someone wanted me to suffer, to feel the pain every day. Death would have been easier than going through that. The pain, the grief, it killed me inside," I explained.

He held my hand tightly in his. His eyes were concerned as he tilted his head so I had to look at him. "Your birthday's coming up," he whispered.

I nodded and smiled reassuringly. "I won't do it again, I promise." I didn't want to die anymore. I wanted to live my life. I wanted the day when Ashton would want to settle down and have a girlfriend; I wanted the one day that he might look at me and fall in love with me.

"You won't?" His voice was pleading and hopeful.

I smiled. "No, Ashton, I won't," I confirmed, looking into his beautiful green eyes. His whole face relaxed as relief washed over it, he blew out a sharp breath as if he had been holding it a long time.

"Why not?"

Because I'm in love with you. Because I love my life with you in it. Because a world where someone as special as you lives, can't be the horrible place I once thought it was.

All of those answers ran through my head at the same time. But what I actually said was, "Because you gave me my life back."

His lips parted as a muscle in his eye twitched. I pushed myself up from the floor. He didn't move.

I held down a hand to him. "Come on, Pretty Boy; let's go get some food, all that exercise has made me hungry," I laughed uncomfortably. I'd never openly had a conversation with anyone like that before, my therapist had always tried to get me to talk, but I either made bitchy comments or lied.

"Why did you tell me all of that?"

I looked up at his stunned face and shrugged. "Because I trust you, and I could see it was important to you that I opened up."

He stood up and a grin stretched across his face. I knew there and then that he wasn't running anywhere, not yet, at least. "Thank you," he rasped, his voice thick with emotion.

"No. Thank you," I whispered gratefully.

A couple of hours later, our hire car rolled into the cemetery parking lot. Ashton's hand was tight in mine as we walked through the graveyard. As per my usual routine, I stooped and picked up any dandelions that I came across on the way. About ten feet away from his grave, I stopped and looked at Ashton. "Do you think maybe I could be on my own for a bit? I promise I won't go anywhere."

He sighed deeply, shaking his head. "Anna, I can't. I'm sorry."

I stepped up and put my arms around his waist, setting my head on his shoulder. "Please?"

"Anna, I can't," he whined.

"Please, Ashton?" I begged, trying not to cry. I needed to talk to Jack about everything that had happened and beg for his forgiveness. I couldn't do that with Ashton watching over me and listening.

His arms tightened around me as he groaned in defeat. "I can move a bit further away, I guess," he conceded, pulling back and looking down at me with a suddenly stern expression. "You do not move from this spot. I'll still be able to see you, if anyone approaches you, *anyone*, you get up and you run as fast as you can to my side, understand?" A muscle in his jaw clenched as his eyes narrowed in warning. From his expression, I could see it was hurting him to do this.

I nodded and smiled gratefully, watching as he closed his eyes for a second or two and then let his arms drop from my side before he stalked off to a tree that was about fifty yards from Jack's grave. He pulled his gun from the leg of his pants and stood perfectly still, scanning the area over

411

and over. A little chuckle escaped my lips because he took his job so seriously. It was terribly cute.

Getting back to the matter in hand, I turned back to Jack's marble headstone and sprinkled my dandelions over the top before setting my lilies down next to the fresh flowers and the unopened birthday card that had his mother's handwriting on the front. I sat on the grass and pushed my hand into my sweater pocket, pulling out the card that I had made for Jack. I'd drawn it myself. It was him playing football and it was from the last game that he played. He'd just scored the winning touchdown and had kissed his hand and thrown it to me. It was sweet, a typical Jack moment, and one of the many happy memories I had of him. It had taken me a long time to draw the card. It was harder than I thought, but I'd gotten through it. In almost four years, this was the first picture I had ever drawn of him that wasn't of that night or him covered in blood.

I swallowed around the lump in my throat. "Hi. Happy birthday," I whispered. "You would have been twenty today. No longer a teenager. I don't know what we would have done for your birthday, maybe a party or something. Tomorrow my dad will be the President so, to be honest, we probably could have done anything that you wanted in the world," I smiled weakly. "My life is pretty crazy right now; I have a lot of stuff going on. I'm not sure if you can see me from where you are or if you know what I'm thinking or how I'm feeling, but I have some things I need to talk to you about." This was even harder than I thought it would be.

"I, er, have someone in my life that I didn't expect to ever have. His name's Ashton Taylor. I brought him with me when I came here last time." I glanced up to see Ashton shifting from one foot to the other, nervously scanning the area. "He's right over there. He's a little crazy. Look at him, waiting for someone to hurt me in the middle of an empty cemetery." I shook my head at his overprotective nature.

"Anyway, he's a really good guy, Jack. We've become close. He's the only one I can be myself with, I trust him and… I'm so sorry, but I've fallen in love with him." Tears pooled in my eyes. "I never meant for it to happen, I swear. He just kind of snuck behind my defences and wormed his way in." I never stood a chance against his charm really. I thought back to the first time that I'd walked into my father's office and saw him. I thought then he was the most beautiful boy in the world, and I had shaken his hand.

I sighed sadly. "Everyone's always telling me that you would want me to be happy. They say that you wouldn't want me to go through life on my own and that you would want me to move on. I'm praying that it's true, because he makes me so happy. I feel incredibly guilty about it. I don't think I should be allowed to be happy if you can't be," I frowned. "But I know that if I'd died, I couldn't bear the thought of you being unhappy, and I would want someone else to make you happy," I said honestly. I wouldn't want him to suffer; I'd just never been able to apply the same concept to myself.

"I will always love you, Jack, always. And I'll never forgive myself for what happened to you." If I hadn't suggested we went out to the club that night, if I hadn't worn that short dress, if I'd just gotten some help, then he would still be here. "I'm so sorry. This shouldn't have happened to you. You were such a good guy and had everything going for you, and you would have been a brilliant doctor." Jack had been terrific at whatever he put his mind to. "It should have been me who died that night, not you. I wish I could take it back and change it around, but I can't." A tear fell down my cheek so I wiped it away quickly. "I really hope that you can forgive me, even though I'll never be able to forgive myself."

I glanced over at Ashton again, seeing that he was watching an old couple who were sitting at a grave about a hundred yards away from me. He was glaring at them murderously as if he would shoot them if they made one move in my direction. I smiled weakly, knowing that I'd put him through enough. I'd said my piece, hopefully now that it was off my chest, some of the guilt would fade over time.

"I'd better go. Ashton's going to have a heart attack if I stay away from him for much longer." I pushed myself up to standing and brushed the grass off of the rear of my jeans. I smiled at Ashton and waved him over. Relief washed over his face as he jogged towards me. Kissing my fingertips, I traced the letters of Jack's name. "G'bye. I'll come back soon and see you. Sleep tight."

Ashton stopped at my side and smiled down at me sympathetically as he touched the small of my back. "Okay?"

I nodded. "Yeah. I'm ready to go." I took one last look down at the gravestone as I slipped my hand into Ashton's. "Bye, Jack."

As we walked back towards the parking lot, I nodded down at the gun that was still gripped in Ashton's other hand. "You can put that away now, Pretty Boy, that old couple aren't here to kill me," I joked.

He laughed sheepishly. "Well you never know, those wrinkles could have been a disguise," he teased, as he stopped and pushed his gun back into his ankle holster. I rolled my eyes at him. "So, are you okay?" he asked, squeezing my hand tightly.

I nodded. "Actually, I am. Thank you for letting me have some time, I really appreciate it. I know that was hard for you."

He sighed. "Yeah, I don't like to not be able to do things for you, but I can't do that again, especially with your dad being sworn in to office tomorrow. I need to be close to you out in the open like this. We've already lost the far guard for the day; I can't push the boundaries too far."

I blew out a big breath, resisting the urge to make a sarcastic comment about him being an overprotective control freak just like my father. I hated the whole guard situation, but I'd never really had a say in it. "Come on, we have a few hours before we have to be at the airport, why don't we go down to the lake or something," I suggested, changing the subject. I'd love to go back there, where I'd first started getting to know him. It seemed weird that it was just over four months ago that he'd waltzed into my life, blown everything up in the air and made me re-evaluate the way I lived my life.

Ashton nodded enthusiastically. He seemed almost as happy as me to be going back to the place where we'd had our 'first date'.

Chapter Forty-One

~ Ashton ~

Our time at the Lake House had ended all too soon. We'd barely had time to hang out before we had to make the trip to the airport so that we could fly to Washington, ready to watch her father be sworn into office. Anna had been quieter than usual, but that was probably down to it being Jack's birthday.

By the time we arrived at the hotel we were staying at, we didn't even get time to change our clothes or freshen up before a little man in a penguin suit and too much gel in his hair ushered us into the private dining room, where her parents and a few close family and friends were gathered.

We were the last to enter, and everyone else was already seated and dressed impeccably in smart suits and evening dresses. I couldn't have felt more out of place in my jeans and T-shirt if I'd tried. Anna's dad stood as we entered, smiling warmly. "You made it. I'm afraid we had to start without you, so you've already missed the chicken liver pâté." A shudder tickled down my spine at how disgusting that sounded.

"Thank God," Anna whispered, not even bothering to disguise her distaste. I chuckled, poking my finger into her ribs in reprimand.

Her dad grinned and walked over, and I noticed that the rest of the room had gone silent and were watching the exchange. "How was today?"

Anna's body tensed as she raised her chin. Her hard exterior was back again, she never seemed to like anyone getting behind her defences. Thankfully, she had been allowing me to lately. "Fine."

Her dad nodded, obviously catching on that she didn't want to talk about it to him. "Good. I'm glad you're here. Thank you for coming."

She shrugged, finally now letting a beautiful smile creep onto her lips. "Of course, I wouldn't miss it. Shall we sit and get on with dinner, Ashton hasn't eaten for two hours, he'll be passing out soon," she joked, grinning up at me.

"Two and a half," I corrected, winking at her playfully. Her dad chuckled at my side, so I turned to him. "It's nice to see you again, sir. Thank you for allowing me to crash your family dinner."

"Anytime, son, anytime."

Dinner was… small. Even after five courses, my stomach was still trying to eat itself. How upper class people survived eating a tiny piece of fish drizzled in oil and laid on a bed of asparagus, I would never understand. Thankfully though, Anna had said the same thing once the evening was over and we were finally dismissed. To make up for it, I'd followed her to the family floor and her suite, and we'd ordered Sloppy Joes.

The dinner conversation had been a little too high brow for me, and I'd struggled not to show my boredom. It was nice though, being included in Anna's family. And it wasn't even Anna that had requested my presence; it was her father that had asked for me to attend with his daughter. After the 'hands on ass plastered all over the tabloids' mistake of our vacation, I had been worried that he would have had a problem with me, or told me to keep my mind on the job, but it hadn't even been mentioned at all.

After two Sloppy Joes, I was finally satiated, but it was now almost midnight. "I should really go and let you get some sleep, we have an early morning call tomorrow," I begrudgingly said, pushing myself off her sofa and wiping my hands on a napkin.

She frowned, and her eyes flicked to the door. Just like when we'd attended her father's birthday party, I'd been booked a room that was three floors down with the other agents, and the Spencer family and other close-knit members of her father's cabinet had this floor booked out to themselves.

"I don't want you to go," she whispered, pouting.

"I could stay if you want, but I'm not sure how we'd explain it to anyone that asks why I spent the night in your room," I shrugged. I didn't want to leave either, especially not after everything that she'd been through. No doubt she would be suffering tonight.

She stood. "Stay then. I don't care what anyone else thinks about it. I don't want to be on my own, not tonight." She took my hand and nodded back towards the four poster bed behind us in the large room. My heart leapt in my chest because she clearly didn't care about the subsequent rumours it would generate. When we got to the bedroom part of her suite, she picked up her pyjamas from the bed and smiled at me tentatively before silently turning and waltzing into the bathroom.

Watching the door for her return, I slipped out of my clothes, laying my gun and holster on the bedside unit before climbing into her bed. She came out a few moments later, dressed in a killer red silk negligée that made every male part of me wake up and jump for joy.

A small smile graced her lips as she slid into the bed next to me and scooted up close to my side. As I wrapped my arms around her, I sighed contentedly. She felt so incredibly right in my arms. Every inch of her silk-covered body pressed against me as she just looked up into my eyes. The way she gazed at me made me feel like the most important man in the world. It was almost as if I was the only thing that she could see, and, in that moment, I knew we were meant to be together forever.

Her hand tangled into the back of my hair as the weightless feeling consumed me. "Ashton, can I talk to you about something?" she asked quietly. I nodded. She took a deep breath before she spoke. "It's something I've been thinking about a lot lately, and because you asked me to open up to you more, I figured that maybe I should talk to you about it."

I smiled encouragingly and reached out, brushing my fingers across her cheek. "You can talk to me about anything."

Her eyes fluttered closed as she dipped her head and pressed her face into the side of my neck. "Carter's trial starts in just over three weeks," she mumbled against my skin.

Anger boiled inside me, the same as it always did when I thought of him. "Yeah," I managed to force out.

"I know the lawyer guy said that I probably won't get called to give evidence again, but I was wondering," she gulped, "if I *do* have to go to court, would you come with me? Maybe you could sit somewhere where I can see you?"

I bent my head and kissed her hair. It actually hurt a little that she felt she needed to ask. "Of course I will."

Her small body relaxed against mine as she pulled her head back and smiled up at me gratefully. "Yeah? Thanks. I think that'll really help me if I can see you."

Her comment made me feel a hundred feet tall. "Whatever you need, Baby Girl. Though I'm pretty sure you won't get called."

She nodded in agreement. In her eyes, I could see the love burning and swirling as she stroked the back of my neck with one finger. I desperately wanted to lean in and kiss her, but I forced myself to remain still. After a few minutes she moved forward and snuggled into my neck again. Her leg tangled in with mine the way it always did when she wanted to go to sleep, so I knew the conversation was over. The next three weeks before the trial were obviously going to be a distressing time for her, but hopefully she'd allow me to help her in any way I could and not close herself off from me like she did everyone else.

Her father's inauguration ceremony went exactly to plan. Anna, her mother, and I had stood on the sidelines, watching as he'd stood in front of the

White House and had been sworn into office, taking the pledge and promising to serve his country.

Security had been immense. Police on motorbikes lined the streets, secret service were out in abundance too, issuing commands and checks through their ear pieces. I'd never seen so many guns all in one place.

Cameras buzzed and flashed everywhere, people stood and watched, soldiers lined up to salute and show their respect to their new commander and chief. The whole thing had been mind-blowing, and although I'd seen previous Presidents sworn into office on the TV, it was different being part of it and actually knowing the man that was going to lead his country for the next four years. An immense pride had swelled inside me as he'd been bestowed the title. Anna's hand had tightened in mine as she watched with wide eyes and an even wider smile. She looked so proud of him that she was practically bouncing on the spot. Melissa was even worse and had a hankie at the ready, dabbing under her eyes as she cried happy tears.

As he'd stood at the podium and given his speech, people had listened, enraptured, and transfixed with every word. He certainly had the heart of the nation behind him and, to me, it was a momentous occasion, just to say that I was there the day that President Spencer was sworn into office.

Then there was the parade where people cheered as we all walked behind her parents. Afterwards, we'd all been led into the White House and given a tour of the private residence. Anna, being given her choice of bedrooms for when she stayed here in the school holidays, chose a blue room that overlooked the grounds at the back. The whole time we'd wandered around, my heart had been in my throat because of the sheer luxury and intricacy of the building.

After spending a few hours with Anna, getting lost within the corridors, secret passages and large expansive rooms, we'd finally had to leave to catch our flight back to Arizona, leaving her parents to go through the motions of the rest of the ceremonies and galas that were scheduled over the whole week. The Spencers' goodbye had been a teary one, especially on Melissa's part who hadn't managed to contain her emotions all day long.

By the time we arrived back at our apartment, we were both exhausted and fell into bed without even unpacking our bags.

Chapter Forty-Two

The next three weeks before Carter's trial seemed to pass in a blur. Thankfully, and quite rightly, the press were now more interested in President Spencer than they were me and Anna – though the gossip magazines still chose to feature us both on a regular basis.

Security had tightened around Anna now that the trial was so close. I'd already pulled Dean and Peter in closer as a precaution.

Anna herself had changed slightly in the last couple of weeks. As the trial drew nearer, she became a little flaky and kept going off into her own little world, often completely oblivious to everything around her. Her school work was suffering, deadlines were being missed, but luckily her professors were already going easy on her because of who her father was. For the last two days, Anna had barely eaten anything, barely spoken, and I'd almost forgotten what her smile looked like. But, true to her word, she hadn't shut me out. We'd spoken numerous times about the trial and what would happen. Although she'd been quieter, and was clearly suffering inside, she hadn't had the breakdown yet that I was sure would come. I'd been keeping a close eye on her, even to the point of checking her arms while she slept to make sure that she'd not been hurting herself, but thankfully, she hadn't.

The day before the trial was due to start, the prosecution lawyer paid us another visit, again reassuring her that she shouldn't be called into court. He'd predicted that the retrial would last no longer than a week and then it would all be over. She'd just nodded politely the whole time, holding my hand in a vice-like grip that almost cut off the circulation in my fingers.

That night, we finally went to bed. That seemed to be where most of her talking was done. It was almost as if she waited for the lights to go off or something. I figured it was easier for her to talk about it when no one was looking at her.

419

As she scooted over to me and set her head on my chest, I wrapped my arms around her tightly. "Are you okay, Baby Girl?" I asked quietly.

"Yeah, I'm good," she whispered.

Frowning into the darkness, I rolled to the side and tangled one hand into the back of her hair, holding her securely against me. "Everything's going to be fine tomorrow," I assured her, dipping my head and kissing her cheek softly. That did it, the floodgates finally opened and she burst into tears.

I stroked her hair, knowing that there was nothing I could say or do to make her feel better as she sobbed uncontrollably onto my chest. Her whole body hitched and shook as her tears pooled on my skin and her breathing came out in ragged gasps. Her fingers dug into my back, clutching me closer to her as she cried her heart out.

After almost an hour of heart breaking sobs, she finally drifted off to sleep in my arms. I already knew I wouldn't be able to sleep well tonight. Anger simmered inside me as all I could think about was the photos that I'd seen in her file. The bruises and broken bones that had been documented on the day that she'd been rescued flashed before my eyes. I felt sick. I rolled onto my back, keeping one arm around her, and then I just lay there, staring at the ceiling for a couple of hours before I fell into a restless sleep.

I woke early in the morning. It was only just after six. Anna was stretched out across my chest, still sound asleep. It made a change for her to be lying on me instead of the other way around. I trailed my fingers up and down her back, enjoying her closeness. This week was going to kill me. Seeing her upset like that every day was going to be pain like I'd never experienced. I lay there, watching her for another hour until she stirred, scooting closer to me and making a little sleepy groaning sound as she kissed my chest softly. When she tilted her head up, I saw that her eyes were a little bloodshot and slightly puffy from crying for so long.

I reached out and brushed her hair from her face. "Morning, Baby Girl," I greeted, smiling sadly.

Her eyes flicked away from me as a subtle blush crept over her face. "I'm sorry I cried all over you last night, Ashton. I'm so pathetic." She ground her teeth and frowned as she absentmindedly traced my belly button with one finger.

I closed my eyes and shook my head at her. She truly was absurd sometimes. "You're not pathetic, and I don't care if you cry all over me, Anna. I want to be here for you," I promised.

She hugged me fiercely and made a strangled sound in the back of her throat. "You know, I'm going to miss you so much when you leave." Her voice was husky and full of emotion.

I frowned at her statement. "Leave? Where am I going?" I didn't have any planned trips or anything.

She smiled sadly. "When you leave, when your assignments done. You're only guarding me until after the trial is finished," she explained, rolling off me and lying close to my side.

That was true. My assignment was due to finish just a couple of weeks after Carter's trial ended, which potentially meant that I could have a new job in just three short weeks' time. I smiled sheepishly because I didn't intend for that to happen and had planned on speaking to her about it. It looked like now was going to be that time, seeing as she brought it up first. "I wanted to talk to you about that, actually," I admitted.

"Yeah?" she chewed on her lip as if she was trying to hold herself together.

I nodded, swallowing my nerves, knowing that the time had come for me to finally admit my feelings for her. "Yeah. I was thinking, once I'm not your guard anymore, I could request an assignment near your school." I watched her face to see what she truly thought.

A confused frown lined her forehead as she looked up at me. "Here? Why?"

I chuckled awkwardly because she just had no idea of the power that she had over me. Now I just had to suck it up and bite the bullet. It was now time for me to tell her that I loved her and pray that she didn't freak out.

"Well, I want to stay here with you. I was wondering if I get an assignment here, maybe we could still live together?" I suggested hopefully.

She gasped and shook her head, looking extremely angry. I winced immediately, scolding myself. She obviously wasn't ready for me to be getting this heavy with her. I should have waited another couple of weeks.

"I'm not some charity case, Ashton! God, you need to chill out, for goodness' sake! Other agents can look after me, you know," she cried angrily as she pushed herself up, about to get out of bed. I groaned. *Again, she thinks I'm only interested in her safety. Why can't she see that I'm head over heels for her?* I grabbed her hand before she could get out of the bed. "Get off, Ashton! Seriously, I'm really annoyed with you. You think other people can't look after me so you have to stay here and babysit me, even when it's not your job anymore?" she spat, struggling to pull her hand from my tight grip.

I tugged on her hand, making her fall down onto the bed beside me before I rolled so that I was half hovering over her. "Anna, calm down! Jeez, let me explain, will you?" I pleaded desperately. She sighed and a muscle in her jaw twitched angrily as she narrowed her eyes but stopped struggling. Nerves were making me feel sick. "I'm not worried about your safety, well actually that's not true, I'll always be worried about your safety. But that's not the reason I want to stay here." I begged her with my eyes to hear me out before she had whatever panic attack she was going to have. One of her eyebrows rose in prompt, clearly not believing a word of what I was saying. I took a deep breath. *Please God, please don't let her freak out.* "I want to stay here with you, I… I…" I stuttered. *Wow, the words are hard to say when you didn't know how they're going to be received.*

"What? Just spit it out!" she snapped angrily.

I fought a smile. I loved it when she was feisty. "I love you, Anna." The anger faded from her face to be replaced by shock. Her mouth dropped open, and her eyes widened as she looked at me. I nodded and smiled, watching it slowly sink in. "I've fallen so in love with you that it's unreal. Honestly, I want to stay here with you because I love you more than anything in the world," I explained, biting on the inside of my cheek, waiting for her to react.

It felt like an enormous weight had been lifted off my shoulders now that she finally knew how I felt. She was just staring at me like I had grown a second head, so I let go of her hands and pushed myself off her, sitting up on the bed next to her, feeling the panic brew inside me because her silence started to become deafening.

~ Anna ~

Stunned into silence was probably the phrase that would best describe me in that second. I had no words. Had he seriously just told me that he loved me? Me, messed up, damaged, broken Annabelle Spencer? Someone like Ashton couldn't love me, could he? What on earth would he even see in me? Ashton was a player; he didn't love girls… did he? My heart constricted. I wanted so badly for that to be true. I'd dreamt of him saying those words to me hundreds of times. Never, in any of my dreams, had they sounded so sweet.

He pushed himself up off me as he stared down at me, seeming to be gauging my reaction. His emerald green eyes were searching my face. They shone with tenderness and passion, and the sight of it made my heart ache. Could it be? Could someone as sweet, adorable, smart and funny, really want me?

My body seemed to belong to someone else, my limbs were not responding as I struggled to take in and believe his confession. It took a great deal of effort for me to push myself up to sitting too. His face was merely inches away from mine as his eyes narrowed, silently begging me to speak.

"You love me?" I whispered disbelievingly.

He nodded. "Yeah, I love you," he confirmed. That was when I saw it in his eyes, the truth, the depth of his feelings, the devotion. Suddenly it all made sense, his actions, his attentiveness, his affection. He wanted me. A sad smile twitched at the corner of his full lips. "It's okay; I know you're scared to let me in, Anna. After what happened with Jack, I know you need time before you can make yourself vulnerable again. I'll wait for you, as long as it takes," he whispered, looking at me fiercely.

My heart melted into a puddle in my chest. My muscles seemed to unfreeze, so I bent forward and pressed my lips to his, knowing that nothing I could say would explain it better than that. He didn't kiss me back though; he just stayed still as if shocked. When I pulled back, I looked up into his eyes, and I saw my whole future there.

"I love you too, Ashton," I whispered. Air rushed out of his lungs, blowing across my face in one large burst. His eyes widened in shock as his whole body stiffened. "I've known it for a while but I didn't really know how to deal with it, and I didn't want to tell you because I didn't think that you felt the same."

He groaned, leaning forward and pressing his forehead against mine. "Really?"

I laughed nervously and nodded. "Yeah."

His hands cupped around my face as he tilted my head slightly. His eyes met mine. "Let's try this again then, huh?" he whispered. His lips brushed mine when he spoke and my skin prickled with excitement. "I love you," he repeated, grinning.

I grinned. "I love you too," I replied immediately, feeling my heart skip a beat.

His lips crashed against mine forcefully; kissing me so fiercely that it was like he was unleashing all of his passion in one go. My arms looped around his neck and we fell back into the pillows, not breaking the kiss. His love for me resonated through every cell in my body, overwhelming me, consuming me, owning me. When the kiss broke, I was breathless. His eyes glittered with excitement and joy as he grinned down at me.

"Sorry, I need to hear it again," he stated, looking at me hopefully.

I giggled wickedly, tangling my hand into the back of his hair. "Wow, you're needy."

He laughed and kissed me again, making my world spin faster. Little kisses were planted across my cheek. "I love you, Annabelle Spencer," he purred in my ear. My whole body tingled as I gripped his hips between my knees, pulling him closer, needing him closer. I pressed my hand against the small of his back, pinning him against me. There was no way I was letting go now.

"I love you so much, Ashton," I promised. If he knew how much, I would be in serious trouble. I had a feeling he could do anything and I would still take him back. He had my heart; I just prayed he wouldn't break it. He smiled and let out a victorious growl as he crashed his lips back to mine, kissing me fiercely, setting my whole body on fire. I needed him. I needed that closeness, that intimacy that I only ever had with him. "Make love to me," I begged, running my hands down his back, clutching him closer to me.

Raw desire was almost killing me. He moaned and started to peel my clothes off, slowly, trailing his fingers over my body, making me shiver. I smiled against his lips, and he pulled back and smiled too, his green eyes shining with excitement and lust, and most importantly, love.

Everything was slow, tender, perfect. Every touch filled with love, need and want. It wasn't sex, we were making love, and we both knew it. Everything was beautiful and all consuming. He completed me, this boy. He was my life and the very thing I needed. The passion brought tears to my eyes because it was so perfect. After, I held him close on top of me as we both struggled to breathe. I was exhausted, not just from the physical exertion but from the feeling and the emotions that went into it.

He loves me…

He was kissing my neck as I combed my finger through the back of his hair, smiling contentedly.

He loves me…He really loves me. I still couldn't quite get my head around it.

After a few minutes he shifted off me, lying down at my side and brushing my hair from my sweaty forehead. He kissed me gently, just once, a soft, chaste kiss, before propping his head up on his elbow and just smiling down at me. Neither of us spoke, it was just the perfect moment, and I didn't ever want it to end.

After an eternity of comfortable silence, he spoke, "I want to ask you something," he whispered.

"Oh yeah, what's that?" I asked, smiling, feeling happier than I had ever felt in my life.

"Will you be my girlfriend? Like, for real? Be with me, be mine," he asked, looking at me hopefully.

Mine. That word had never had much meaning in it before, but hearing Ashton asking me to be 'mine', I knew I would never hear that word the same again. "Of course I will."

"I promise I'll be the best boyfriend in the world," he replied, looking at me tenderly.

I had no doubt in my mind about that. "You already are."

He smiled and kissed me again. "I love you, Baby Girl."

My heart skipped a beat at the sound of those words from his mouth; they were the sexiest damn words in the history of the world. I could feel him starting to get aroused again against my thigh, and I felt the blush creep onto my cheeks. He was like some kind of machine.

"Well, I love you back," I said playfully as I rolled him under me and kissed him, starting all over again.

Chapter Forty-Three

For two full days and nights, I felt like I was walking on air. They describe being in love like being on cloud nine, but to me, it felt almost like twelve or thirteen at least. But, of course, something had to come along and ruin it. It was as if the universe refused to allow me to be happy. Maybe I didn't deserve to be happy, just like I always thought. Ashton and I had barely left the apartment for two days since we first made the L-word confession. At my request, we'd skipped school and it wasn't only because we were too wrapped up in exploring each other's bodies, though that certainly was a part of it, but it was also because of the trial. I didn't want to go anywhere in case I was called up suddenly and had to jump on a flight to go and give my evidence. The trial weighed on us both, casting a shadow over everything that should be wonderful and full of roses. It seemed that Carter still had a way of ruining my life, even without knowing he was doing it.

On the third morning, we didn't even bother setting an alarm. It surprised me when I woke to the sound of Ashton's cell phone ringing loudly from the bedside unit. I nudged him with my elbow as I eyed the alarm clock, seeing that it was half past ten in the morning.

He let out a loud, sleep-filled groan as he pushed himself up off me and fumbled for his phone. I rolled over to face him, feeling the smile creep onto my face because he just looked so mouth-wateringly gorgeous in the morning. Knowing that the boy was mine literally made my heart pick up in double-time.

"Hello?" he muttered into the phone, running a hand through his messed up, I-had-a-lot-of-mind-blowing-sex-last-night hair. His eyes immediately widened as the muscles in his shoulders tightened. He practically jumped out of the bed, pulling on yesterday's jeans. "Yes, sir," he said, zipping them up with one hand. His eyes flicked to me. "No, she's right here. Yeah okay, one moment, sir," He pulled the phone away from his ear, frowning. "It's your father, Anna. He wants me to put the call on speaker so he can talk to both of us," Ashton explained, fiddling with his phone.

My mouth popped open, immediately knowing what this would be about. Somehow, he had found out that Ashton and I were together. He was probably calling to express his displeasure and to tell us to cease the relationship and for Ashton to pack his bags. My back stiffened at the thought. There was no way I was allowing my father to send him away from me.

Ashton set the phone on the bed. "Okay, sir, go ahead."

I glared down at the phone challengingly, waiting for him to say the words and for us to start the almighty argument that I knew would come once he tried to split us up. My dad cleared his throat. "Okay well, I have some news, I've just heard, it's literally just happened," he said, uncharacteristically stumbling over his words.

"What, Dad? Spit it out," I instructed, already exasperated with all of this pussyfooting around. Yes, it was probably wrong for Ashton and I to be involved because he was my guard, yes, we had probably gone about this the wrong way, but hadn't my parents been telling me to let go of Jack and be happy for the last three and a half years?

He sucked in a ragged breath before he spoke the words that I had never expected to hear in my life. "I've just been informed by the court that they've had to release Carter Thomas."

My breath caught in my throat as I registered his words. He was out? He couldn't be. He'd killed Jack. I'd watched him do it. How could he have been released? The trial had only been going for two days.

Ashton gasped. "What the? They released him? How? Why? When?"

My dad sighed. "This morning, less than five minutes ago. They overturned his conviction. He's been cleared of all charges. Apparently yesterday was a disaster. His lawyers ripped all the previous evidence to shreds, had crime scene experts come in and testify against their own colleagues. Apparently it was ruled that the DNA samples, fibres and fingerprints that they found on Jack's body were collected incorrectly. There was a risk that they were contaminated, something to do with not using a sterile bag. Because there was a slight chance that they were contaminated, the Judge had no choice but to deem them all inadmissible," my dad explained.

I closed my eyes. It was just too much to take in. The man who had killed Jack and tortured me for months on end, who had raped me repeatedly and beat me, was free. My husband. He was out. There was no justice. Jack was dead, and Carter, his murderer, was walking off scot-free. That wasn't right; this wasn't how it was supposed to be. Tears stung my eyes.

"Anna, are you okay?" Ashton's hands cupped my face gently, forcing my head up so I had to look at him. His eyes were flashing with anger, but still managed to look at me tenderly, like I was the only girl in the world.

I nodded awkwardly. "I didn't even get called. Why didn't they call me in to testify again?" I croaked.

My dad answered that question. "Late yesterday afternoon, Carter's lawyers also presented some new evidence. I've been told this morning that it was some kind of CCTV footage that was date stamped from that night. It showed him half way across town the night it happened. They even had an expert come in and verify it. Without the fibres and fingerprints, it would have been your word against his plus the CCTV footage. That wasn't enough to continue with the trial. The Judge had no choice but to rule in his favour." My dad sounded like he'd aged ten years in the last couple of minutes.

Ashton made an angry growling sound in his throat. "What? How the hell can they do that? How the hell can there be CCTV footage?"

I smiled at him sadly; he really had no idea who Carter was. "Carter can do whatever he wants. He has people everywhere; if there's something he wants, he won't stop until it's his. These experts, they can be bought. Hell, he probably had someone in the police tamper with the evidence so it couldn't be used," I explained, shrugging.

Ashton looked at me like I had lost my mind. "You're saying that he paid someone to fabricate some CCTV of him across town to give him an alibi?" he asked, shocked.

"Sure, why not. Hell, I'm surprised it's taken him this long to get his conviction overthrown," I replied matter-of-factly.

He shook his head fiercely. "But what about the fact that Anna was there at his house? Doesn't that prove what she's saying is the truth? That he killed Jack and kidnapped her? How can they just dismiss that?" Ashton asked, glaring at the phone on the bed.

I gulped. I knew the answer to that, and it was my fault. I hadn't wanted to press charges; I refused to give any statements about what he did to me because I couldn't bring myself to talk about it. During the first trial, it was recorded that I refused to make a comment, and Carter's lawyers claimed that I was there of my own free will, that we met, that it was pure coincidence, that I was drunk that night and confused. They made me out to be some kind of scorned girlfriend that was trying to pin something on Carter as some sort of payback for some undisclosed incident. They even had someone question my sanity. It wasn't my evidence that secured the conviction; it was the fibres that they found on Jack's body that put him away for murder. My evidence had just helped; it was never me that made a difference.

"That was ruled last time as inconsequential. What he did to Annabelle was never brought into question, the fact that she was there was marked as coincidence, but it couldn't be used against him," my dad explained, skirting around the issue.

427

"So that's it, after everything he's done, he gets to walk away?" Ashton growled. His hands tightened into fists. "You can't do anything, sir? You're the President, for goodness' sake, you can't let this happen!"

"Son, you need to calm down. I hate this situation as much as you do, but just because I'm in a position of power doesn't mean that I can break the law! If I force the issue then I'd be no better than he is. My whole campaign was based on truth and justice, I can't very well force them to hold him if there's no evidence," my dad answered, his voice stern and final.

Ashton sighed and closed his eyes, running a hand through his hair, his whole posture agitated and alert. "Sorry, sir. I didn't mean to suggest…" he trailed off, his hands still in tight fists, his knuckles white.

"I know. Let's just look to the matter in hand here, shall we?" my dad suggested.

Ashton plopped down on the bed next to me and took my hand. "I won't let him hurt you, I swear," he told me fiercely, his jaw tight, his whole body tense.

I smiled sadly. "He won't hurt me, Ashton; he won't have the slightest interest in me at all. All he'll be worried about is getting his power back and showing people he's back in charge. I wouldn't be surprised if some big deal's not being arranged as we speak," I said honestly. If I knew Carter at all, he'd want to gain his respect back. Respect was always the most valuable thing to him.

Ashton looked at me desperately before turning back to the phone. "Sir, surely it's time now?"

I raised one eyebrow in question.

My dad sighed. "Yes, I guess it is," he muttered. I looked up at Ashton, confused about the turn in the conversation. What was it time for? My dad groaned. "Annabelle, Carter's been sending you letters every week since the time he was arrested."

Bile immediately rose in my throat. Carter was still interested in me? How? Why? And why the hell would they not tell me this?

"I thought it best to keep it from you at first because you just weren't coping, then I didn't want to put any more pressure on you. You were so fragile," my dad explained quickly, answering my unspoken question.

I glanced up at Ashton's guilt-stricken face and realised that he already knew about this. Suddenly, everything clicked into place. "This is why Ashton's here, a SWAT guy. I finally get why he was assigned to me. Carter wants me dead, so you bring in a guy like Ashton to protect me. Now it makes sense," I said, shaking my head, frowning as the reality of it sank in. I'd always wondered how on earth someone like Ashton could get stuck in a dead-end assignment like this one.

"He doesn't want you dead, Annabelle," my dad said grimly.

"Well what does he want?" I asked, confused.

There was silence on the end of the phone for a few seconds and in those few seconds, I think my heart stopped beating. "He wants you back," my dad answered quietly.

I gasped and jumped out of bed. My body reacted of its own accord. My back slammed against the wall as my eyes darted around the room, suddenly afraid that he would jump out from some darkened corner. Memories of the rapes, the beatings, the isolation, the way he looked at me... all of it rushed back to me at once, making me dry heave. I wanted to scream. I wanted to run. I wanted to hide under the bed and never come out. He wanted me back...

A heavy weight pressed me against the wall tightly. My numb brain came back to the present a little and I realised it was Ashton. He'd pinned me against the wall, his body pressing against mine. It was a protective pose.

"Shh, it's okay, shh," he whispered, smoothing my hair away from my face. His hand gripped the back of my neck, guiding my head to his chest. I closed my eyes and listened to his heart, forcing myself to breathe in and out, in and out. My fingers dug into Ashton's back, and I was sure to be hurting him, but I couldn't let go.

"You knew but didn't tell me." My voice was barely more than a whisper.

His arms tightened around me as he pressed his cheek against the top of my head. "I wanted to, Baby Girl, I promise. It wasn't my call," he explained.

My chin trembled as I pulled back, looking up into his eyes. I could see the truth in his words, this wasn't his idea, this was my father's half-assed idea of keeping me safe and shielding me from more harm. I took a deep breath. I needed to be strong now. The worry and apprehension on Ashton's face was enough to make me realise that I needed to get a hold of myself and calm down for him.

"I'm okay," I lied, willing my shaking voice not to betray me.

He backed away slowly; taking my hand and guiding me back over to the bed. As I sat down, I spotted his T-shirt in a pile on the floor, so I stooped to pick it up and pull it down over my head.

"Sir, are you still there?" Ashton asked, fiddling with the phone.

"I'm here," my father confirmed, his voice choked and strained.

I sniffed and wiped my face, forcing myself to be strong as I looked down at the phone, wanting answers. "So, what was in these letters? Does he know where I am?" I asked.

My father cleared his throat. "He knows what school you're at. For the last couple of months, the letters have been sent to the college," he said, sounding almost apologetic. "I'm sending four more guards over to your location, just to be on the safe side. They should be arriving within the hour. Agent Taylor, do you think you could organise them when they get there? Whatever you feel's best, I've already instructed them to that effect."

"Yes, sir, of course," Ashton confirmed in his business tone. He was already planning, I could tell by the look on his face.

"Okay, well if I hear anything else, I'll call straight away. If you need anything, call me anytime and Maddy will put you straight through," my dad stated.

"Yes, sir," Ashton replied.

"Annabelle, I'm sorry I didn't tell you, but honestly we thought that this was in your best interests," my dad said, sounding like he was asking for my approval.

In all honesty, it probably was the best thing at the start; I wouldn't have coped very well with that at all. But since Ashton, I could have been told. Maybe it would have helped me understand why he was always so strict and professional when we went out.

"Now isn't the time to start arguing over something that's done. I understand why you didn't tell me," I admitted. "I'll speak to you later, Dad," I mumbled, not wanting to speak anymore.

"Bye, Annabelle, Agent Taylor," he replied as he cut off the phone. I glanced over to the love of my life. He was worried sick, his beautiful face was pale and showed the picture of concern.

His arms encircled me, crushing me against him. When he moved towards me, the weight of his body meant I had nowhere to go but backwards onto the bed. His body covered mine, pressing me down into the mattress. "You don't need to worry, Baby Girl, I promise. I would die before I let him touch you again," he growled fiercely.

My heart stopped at his words. I could see the truth in his eyes. He wouldn't let Carter take me; he would fight for me to the death. And with that knowledge, my heart broke all over again. I knew what was coming. In my mind's eye I could already see it, Carter turning up, Ashton and him locked in some kind of death battle, Ashton being hurt or killed. Me, alone again, watching another person that I loved being ripped away from me.

I couldn't do it. I wouldn't allow him to be hurt. This time I had some control, this time I could prevent it, this time the boy I loved would live. I would never allow Carter to hurt Ashton, ever.

Forcing a fake smile, I tried desperately to think of a plan, an escape, something that would ensure that this time it all ended differently. Scenarios flicked through my head, us leaving, going into hiding, changing our names. But each one boiled down to the same thing – Carter would find us, and he would kill him in the slowest way possible. No, there was only one way I could ensure his safety.

"I'm going to go and have a shower before the new guards all come. I guess you need to go and talk to Dean and Peter and tell them what's happened," I muttered, trying not to let out the waves of emotion that were crashing over me show in my face or in my voice.

He sighed and dipped his head, capturing my lips in a kiss that was so sweet that it shattered my heart. I kissed him back, savouring every last second of it, knowing that it would be the last kiss I would ever have. I memorised the soft feel of his lips, the taste of his tongue, the smell of him, how the heat spread through my body making my heart throb. I memorised every single thing about it while my heart broke silently.

He pulled away and stroked my face softly. "Are you sure you're okay?" he asked, watching my face. I nodded, working hard to keep my face natural. I must have done a pretty decent job because he kissed me on the lips again quickly then pushed up off me and left the bedroom, looking like it almost pained him to walk away from me.

I sat up and put my head in my hands, thinking it through again. Was there any other option? Was there anything else I could do to protect him? Carter knew where we were. He wanted me back, and if he had seen any of the magazines or papers then he would already see all of the stuff about Ashton... and he would be murderously angry. The dream I had about Ashton's broken face and body flashed into my mind, and I whimpered. My eyes fluttered closed, holding on to the memory of that dream. I took a deep breath; I needed to draw on my inner strength now. It didn't matter how much it hurt me, I needed him safe. There was only one way to keep him safe, and that was to get him as far away from me as possible.

I couldn't live in a world where Ashton didn't exist. It hurt so much when Jack died, I couldn't go through all of that again. If anything happened to Ashton, my whole world would collapse. I *had* to keep him safe, even if the pain would be excruciating, I wouldn't allow Carter to hurt Ashton.

I swallowed my sob and picked up my cell phone before walking to the bathroom on wobbly legs. I scrolled through my contacts, finding the one I wanted as I closed the door behind me tightly and leant against it. Maddy answered immediately. "President Spencer's Office," she said politely.

"Hi, Maddy. Can I speak to my dad please?"

I heard her tapping on keys. "I'll just put you through, Annabelle," she stated as the hold music started. I took a few calming breaths, I needed to get this done without giving anything away.

"Annabelle, is everything okay?" my father asked worriedly.

Come on, Anna, you can do this! "Actually no, Dad." I took another deep breath. "I need you to do something for me, but I don't want you to question me. It's something that I need to have happen," I said, trying to stress the importance without giving anything away.

"Of course, Annabelle. What is it?"

I slumped down onto the bathroom floor, leaning my back against the door, gripping my free hand in my hair. "I need you to transfer Agent Taylor," I replied quickly.

His reaction was exactly what I thought it would be. "What? Transfer? I can't do that, Annabelle! He's there for your protection; he's the

431

best man for the job. With everything going on right now, you need him there," he said sternly.

I closed my eyes, trying to block out the pain that I was feeling inside. "Dad, I need this to happen. I don't ask you for much, do I? If you love me at all, you'll do this for me and not ask me anything else about it. Please, Dad, please?" I begged, my voice starting to break.

He was quiet for a couple of seconds. I couldn't breathe. I could feel my heart getting harder with each passing second; I was starting to push everything away again, just like I used to. I didn't care about my own life; Carter could do what the hell he wanted to me, as long as Ashton wasn't harmed.

"Annabelle, do you know what you're asking? You want me to transfer him even after I just told you that Carter knows where you are? This is that important to you?" he asked quietly.

Jeez, Ashton is the most important thing in the world. "Yes," I croaked.

"Has something happened? Has he done something wrong?" my dad inquired hesitantly.

I gasped. "No! He's done nothing wrong. He's an excellent agent, exemplary. I just need you to transfer him, please?" I said fiercely.

He sighed. "Do I get to know the reason?"

"No. Please trust me, please do this for me. Transfer him to wherever he wants to go. He wanted some Front Line thing in LA." I wiped the silent tear that fell down my cheek.

He was quiet again. "Okay, consider it done," he replied, his voice tender and worried.

Relief washed over me and my stomach unclenched. The fear loosened, and the muscles that I didn't even realise I had tensed, started to relax.

"Thank you, Dad. Thank you, thank you," I muttered.

"I'll call him and let him know," he stated sadly.

I gasped, panic stricken. "No, don't! You can't do that."

"What? You just said you-" he started, but I interrupted him.

"Dad, Ashton's not going to want to leave. If he finds out now, he's going to do everything in his power to stay. You can't tell him until he's ready to go. I think he's going to need to be escorted away," I admitted, biting the inside of my mouth hard enough to draw blood.

"But if he's that dead set against going, why is he being transferred?" he asked. I could hear the frustration in his tone.

"Because I *need* him transferred."

He sighed again. I could just imagine his defeated frown as he ran his hand over the back of his neck. "Okay," he finally agreed. "The four agents that are coming over should be there within about forty minutes. I'll call and have them escort him straight to the airport and wait until he's on the plane. I'll get Maddy to book his flight."

432

I smiled weakly. "Okay. Maybe you could call Dean Michaels and let him know what's going on, but tell him not to say anything to Ashton," I suggested.

"Yeah, I'll do that. So when the four guards get there, they'll take Agent Taylor to the airport and leave you with your two far guards," he clarified, checking I understood everything.

"Can I have Dean as my new near guard? He's the only one I wouldn't mind near me."

"That sounds like a good plan for the short term, but we might need to look at something else longer term. Maybe it's best if you come home for a while or something," he replied, sounding exasperated.

"I don't want to leave school," I replied quickly. "Can't we just see how this all goes for a while?"

"For the moment, but I'll keep a close eye on it. I already have people keeping tabs on what he's up to. If I get even one sniff that he's coming near Arizona, you're coming here to stay with us. Understood?"

"Understood," I confirmed. "Dad, one more thing before you go."

"What's that, Annabelle?" he asked curiously.

"Ashton's done an exceptional job here. I don't want you to think that just because I've requested this early transfer that this looks bad on him. He really deserves whatever recommendation you would have given him at the end of the eight months," I said sternly.

"Okay, Annabelle, don't worry, I'll take care of everything," he replied as he ended the call.

I let out the breath I didn't even realise I was holding. It was going to be hard enough to watch Ashton leave me, but I had a feeling I was going to have to *make* him go, and I would need all my strength for that. He was going to force me to lie right to his face; he was going to make me rip my own heart out when I explained it to him.

I refused to feel the pain that was trying to break into my heart; this pain was nothing to knowing he was hurt or dead. I couldn't change my mind, this needed to be done. I just needed to keep myself focussed and strong. This was the only way I had a chance at keeping him safe.

I closed my eyes and rested my head back on the door. "Please let me be strong enough to let him go," I whispered, before pushing myself up off the floor and climbing into the shower. As I cried helplessly in the spray, I couldn't get the thought of Ashton's broken, bloody face out of my head. My heart was breaking irrevocably. But that dream wouldn't come true. This time I would get to save the boy I loved.

Chapter Forty-Four

~ Ashton ~

As I walked out of the bedroom, I felt sick. I didn't want even an inch of space between us now that Carter was free. My hands clenched into fists. Half of me actually hoped he came after her so I would be able to rip his head off, but the other half knew that I needed to keep him as far away from my girl as possible.

When I stepped out of the front door, closing it tightly behind me, I beckoned Dean over. His face changed immediately when he saw mine, obviously catching on that something was wrong. "President Spencer just called. Carter Thomas has been released due to lack of evidence," I announced.

His mouth opened and closed a couple of times. "Released?" he said quietly.

I nodded. "They're sending over four new Agents from Washington. When they get here, we'll have a strategy meeting again, but I think we'll add an extra two for the day and night. One outside the building, one inside at night. Then during the day, I'll bring you slightly forward again so that you can act as second near guard. I'll then have the two extras take a fifty yard stance, one in front, and one behind," I frowned, trying to think everything else through.

Dean nodded in agreement, obviously pleased with my plan. "Do you think he'll come after her?"

A chill crept down my spine. I took a deep breath. "Honestly? Yeah I do." I would kill him before he touched her though. There was no way that sick, abusive, asshole was getting anywhere near my girl again. Dean nodded, his face angry. "Let me know when the four guards get here, the

President said within the hour," I instructed, checking my watch. It was now ten to eleven; I sighed and frowned, looking back at the door. "I'd better go back in. Anna's in the shower, I think she's freaking out. Her dad told her about the letters."

Dean winced. "Wow, shit, okay yeah, go be with her," he agreed, nodding over his shoulder to the door.

I turned and stalked back in, making my way to the bedroom; I could hear the water running, so I quickly slipped out of my jeans and pulled on fresh clothes, putting two extra gun clips in my pocket. I'd need to carry extra bullets from now on, just in case. When I was dressed, I headed to the kitchen and just stood there waiting for Anna. She was going to be freaking out about this, but she obviously wanted time on her own because she'd sent me to speak to Dean. I'd have to give her time and let her come to me. She knew I was here for her.

About forty minutes later she came out of the bedroom, wringing her hands nervously as she walked into the kitchen. She didn't look at me. I swallowed the lump in my throat, waiting for the outburst that I knew would come, and when it did, she would break my heart. I hated to see her cry, it was like physical pain.

"Hey, Baby Girl. You okay?" I asked quietly as she started making coffee.

She nodded. "Yeah fine," she replied nonchalantly. I rubbed my hand down her back tenderly, wanting to soothe her. Wordlessly, she shrugged off my hand. "You want a coffee, Ashton?" She sounded so cold that it sent a shiver down my spine. She hardly ever called me by my name.

I frowned. "Um, no thanks." She had her back to me, her shoulders were hunched, and her back was stiff. I moved close behind her and put my hands on her shoulders, massaging gently. She squirmed away from me. "Anna?" I whispered, frowning.

She just shook her head. "Just don't, okay," she said as she grabbed her cup and stormed out of the room into the lounge.

I stared after her in shock. She just needed some time, she'd come to me when she was ready for me to help her. She wasn't used to opening up to people so it would take a little time before she was ready to talk about it. I'd just have to try and be patient and not rush her into divulging her feelings.

My cell phone buzzed, so I answered it quickly. "Hey, Dean." I frowned, still watching the point where I last saw Anna.

"Hey, those four guards are here. We're at the door," he replied, at the same time that I heard him knock on the front door. I disconnected the call and walked out of the room, glancing into the lounge quickly.

"The four new guards are here. I might be planning for an hour or so, okay," I called through to Anna; I thought I saw her stiffen but I was too far away to be sure.

I made my way to the door and opened it to see Dean standing there looking at me strangely, with the four new guards behind him. "I'm sorry, Ashton. I don't know what's going on," Dean said as he stepped to the side.

The four other guards stepped forward in unison. "Agent Taylor, we have orders from the President to take you to the airport now," one of them said.

Panic surged through me; maybe they'd heard something new – was Carter on his way here?

I turned quickly. "Anna, grab your stuff, we're leaving!" I ordered.

The guards stepped forward again, looking at me apologetically. "No, Agent Taylor. We have orders to escort *you* to the airport, not Miss Spencer. You've been reassigned," the same guy stated. He held out an iPad, nodding down for me to take it.

I frowned, taking it from his hands and looking down at the official transfer request document that was signed and stamped by the President himself at the bottom. Front Line, LA office, immediate start.

My heart was crashing in my chest. "I don't understand. Why the hell would I be getting a transfer? I just spoke to the President like an hour ago!" I countered, confused.

"Ashton," I heard Anna say from behind me. I turned quickly, seeing her standing there, just watching me. "You've been transferred, because I asked for it," she explained, looking at me with her face stern and cold, showing no emotion whatsoever. My blood seemed to turn to ice in my veins. She'd asked for me to be transferred? I turned back to the guy and handed him the iPad before slamming the door in his face and turning to Anna.

"What the hell are you talking about?" I asked, stepping closer to her.

She stepped back, keeping the distance between us. "I'm sorry, but I can't have you here. You complicate things, you make everything harder for me, and I just can't cope with anything else. It's best for me if you just leave. You and I have been in this little protected bubble for the last couple of days, and I thought nothing could come along and burst it, but I was wrong. You and I just can't work, so it's best that it stops now. That way, I can just get on with things and learn how to deal with it on my own. I'm sorry, but you have to go." Her voice didn't waver once. I looked into her eyes, and my heart started to break, they were the cold, heartless eyes that she used to have when I first started my assignment.

I gulped, swallowing my panic. "What?"

"I have too much going on right now, I can't cope with having you here too and knowing that you think you're in love with me," she replied matter-of-factly, almost as if we were discussing the weather.

"That I *think* I'm in love with you? I don't think it, I *am* freaking in love with you!" I corrected, shaking my head incredulously.

She frowned. "Look, I have more important things to deal with than some agent trying to seduce me while I'm upset and vulnerable. It's best for me if you just leave so I can get on with it and deal with this all in my own way without you getting in the way all the time."

"What the?" I gasped. "You actually think that I preyed on your vulnerability so that I could seduce you?"

She ground her teeth and shook her head. "No, that's not what I meant, it came out wrong," she muttered.

"Then what?"

She huffed in frustration. "There are lots of things. Carter being out, the fact that I still love Jack, the way you lied to me all this time about Carter's letters and the reason you're assigned to me. I have so much going on in my head that it feels like it's going to explode, and most of them are because of you!"

Jack. I knew that Jack would come up at some point; for the last two days I had been waiting for her to freak out about the how close we'd gotten. "Anna, I know you love Jack and that'll never change, but Jack's not here anymore, I am. How the hell am I supposed to compete with a guy that's not here anymore?" I asked desperately. "Look, I don't need to complicate things for you. We'll work all of this stuff out together," I replied, stepping closer to her again. "As for the letters, I had no choice. It wasn't up to me."

She shook her head fiercely. "I just need to get back to basics, and I can't do that with you here. You have to leave." When she said it, she looked straight into my eyes. I could see she wasn't lying, her face betrayed nothing.

"You love me too though, I know you do," I said confidently, raising my chin challengingly.

Her eye twitched. "No," she whispered. "I care about you a lot, I really do, but it's not love. When you told me you loved me, I just said it back because I knew that's what you wanted to hear. But it's not true. Yes, I care about you, but my heart will always belong to Jack. I'm sorry. I was happy pretending otherwise, but now with this Carter stuff, I don't have the energy to keep up this act. I just don't have the mental strength to have you here. You'll get over it. A few cold beers and one night stands and you'll be right as rain again. You deserve better than me anyway."

It was like she'd reached into my chest, ripped out my heart and showed it to me. My blood ran cold. Her hard, resigned eyes never wavered as she spoke. "You're lying. I don't know why, but you are. You love me, I know you do!" I couldn't let her do this; I'd show her that she loved me. Before she had a chance to answer or react, I stepped forward, pressed my body to hers and kissed her. It took me a couple of seconds to realise that she wasn't kissing me back. I pulled back. Her eyes were still hard, her jaw tight.

"Finished?" she snapped angrily.

My mouth fell open in shock as she shoved me away from her. "Anna, don't," I whispered, now terrified because she looked so serious and

437

resigned. She really did want me to leave. "We'll work this out. If you're not ready for a relationship, then I'll wait. We can go back to just being friends. Just please don't send me away with Carter on the loose," I begged.

"This is what I'm talking about! You're not listening to me," she spat, waving her hand at me in example. "I have to do what's best for me now, and that's coping with all this shit the only way I know how. I don't need to be dealing with some emotionally draining love sick puppy too!"

I didn't believe her. Her words were harsh, hurtful and full of acid as she said them, but deep down, I knew that she loved me. This was about something else, something that I didn't understand and that she didn't want to explain to me. I decided to try another tactic.

"What about what's best for me? Have you considered me in any of this?" I shot back.

Anger crossed her face as she slapped me hard in the middle of my chest. "Considered you? Of course I fucking have, you stupid," she slapped my chest again, "annoying," slap, "frustrating," another slap, "son of a bitch!" With both hands she shoved me towards the door. "Just get the hell out. Go back to LA. Live your life, sleep with some girls, move on and forget the screwed up, little, rich girl that you fucked a few times!" She yanked open the front door while I stared at her, dumbstruck. My tactic had apparently blown up in my face and had just succeeded in making her angry on top of resigned.

"Anna..." I whispered, fighting for something I could say or do to make her reconsider. She needed me here.

She shook her head as she looked up at the four new agents and Dean, who were standing outside the door, probably hearing every word of what had just gone on. "Make sure he gets on his plane," she stated, pushing open the door before turning back to me. "I'll pack up your stuff and forward it on in a couple of days. Goodbye, Agent Taylor. Take care of yourself." She then proceeded to walk calmly into the bedroom, closing the door behind her, leaving me in the hallway with my heart in my throat.

My mouth hung open in shock. I hadn't even seen this coming. Everything was perfect before the news about Carter, and now she was trying to fool me into believing that she didn't love me and that I meant nothing to her. It hurt like hell.

Every muscle in my body was screaming for me to run after her and hold her. I couldn't leave her, not now. Carter would come for her eventually and she needed me to protect her. A hand clamped on my arm, I looked down to see it belonged to one of the new agents.

"Agent Taylor, my orders are to remove you by force if necessary. I'd much rather it not come to that," he warned.

I looked over at Dean, shocked. "What the hell just happened?" I asked, still confused at the turn of events. It didn't feel real. It felt like a nightmare was unfolding in front of me. *Maybe it is actually a nightmare, maybe I'm still sleeping...*

Dean shook his head. "I don't really know, Ashton. The President called me and said that Annabelle had requested a transfer and that I'm taking your position. I was told I wasn't allowed to tell you until the four guards arrived," he replied, looking just as baffled as me.

"But they can't transfer me, you need me here! She needs me here!" I cried desperately.

"Ashton, I said that to the President, but he said it was already done and that was the end of the discussion," Dean explained, shaking his head sadly.

"Damn it," I growled. "Anna!" I shouted, turning to go back into the apartment again. Another guard grabbed my other arm. I looked at him warningly. "You'd better take your fucking hands off me if you still want to be able to use them," I spat angrily. No one would keep me from my girl.

Dean stepped forward quickly. "Ashton, just go to LA, call her later once she's had time to think this all through. I'll talk to her, but for now you need to go along with your orders. If you go against a Presidential order, then you won't even get to come back here when she changes her mind again," he suggested, looking at me pleadingly. I squeezed my eyes shut. "Just go. I'll talk to her. You just do as you've been ordered," Dean persuaded.

I nodded, knowing he was right. LA was only an hour flight away from here, by the time I landed in LA, she would have cooled down and I'd fly back. It would be fine. A small part of me knew that it wouldn't, but all I had left was hope. Anna was my life. I couldn't be away from her, she was everything to me and she needed me to protect her.

I turned to Dean. "Take care of her until I get back then," I pleaded. "You know how important this girl is to me."

He nodded, smiling sadly as he patted my shoulder sympathetically. "Yeah, I do. Don't worry. I'll go talk to her right now. She may even change her mind before you get on the damn plane. You know what women are like, temperamental beasts, and Anna is the worst of them all, feisty little sucker her," he joked.

I didn't have the words to answer so I just stalked to the elevator, pressing the button. Two of the four new guards took my flanks, watching me cautiously as if waiting for me to sneak an attack on them or something.

Neither of them would talk to me on the way to the airport. Every time I asked anything, they just said they didn't know. Eventually, I stopped asking questions and rested my head on the window, feeling my heart break a little more with every mile they put between us. When we got to the airport, they booked me onto my plane. The timing was perfect; I only had to wait thirty minutes before boarding. I sat on my own with my head in my hands, praying that Dean was right and that he could talk some sense into her before I even boarded. Out of sheer desperation, I grabbed my phone and called her, it rang a couple of times before she rejected it. I squeezed my eyes shut and called her again.

Again, she rejected my call within a couple of rings. The third time it was turned off. Growling in frustration, I shoved my cell phone back into my pocket. My hurt was now turning into anger. She knew that I loved her; she knew that it would probably kill me being away from her and not knowing if she was safe or not, she would know that she was hurting me by doing this, but it was like she didn't care. She'd spitefully told me that she didn't love me, when we both knew that it wasn't true. The only thing I couldn't work out was why she was doing this.

When the speaker announced that my plane was ready to board, I called Dean. "Hey, what's going on? Did you talk to her? Has she changed her mind?" I asked as soon as he answered.

He sighed. "No, Ashton. I'm sorry, she doesn't want you here. I don't think she's going to change her mind today. She asked me to ask you to stop calling her," he said quietly.

I gripped my hand into my hair roughly. "Okay, thanks for trying. I'll give her a day to cool off and then maybe she'll talk to me. Watch her for me, don't let anything happen to her," I begged, trying not to imagine all the horrible things that could happen to her while I wasn't there to protect her.

"I will, Ashton. Don't worry, she'll be fine. Just give her some time to miss you, that's all it'll take," he reassured me.

I nodded knowing that, for the moment at least, it was hopeless. "Thanks."

When I disconnected the call, the two agents escorted me directly to my seat and even waited outside the door until it was closed and the plane had taxied out onto the runway. I closed my eyes, resting my head back against the seat as I prayed that Dean was right. I just needed to give her time to miss me; she would miss me, eventually. I'd just have to hope that the time apart from her wouldn't kill me before she changed her mind.

~ Anna ~

I couldn't look at him again; I couldn't watch him leave, it was too painful. Each step away from him actually hurt more than the one before. Eventually, my weary legs carried me into the bedroom. I'd barely managed to get the door closed behind me before my heart shattered into a thousand pieces. My legs finally gave out and I slumped to the floor, crying silently.

I felt sick; my whole body was shaking as I sobbed and sobbed. I knew I'd done the right thing; this really was the only way to keep him safe. But I just couldn't get the image of his pain out of my head. The way his face looked so sad, so rejected, I knew I'd never be able to erase that look from my memory. I'd never seen Ashton look scared before, and I never wanted to see that look there again for as long as I lived.

I heard my cruel lie repeating over and over in my head. *"I care about you a lot, I really do, but it's not love."* I kept picturing the exact moment that I broke his heart. How his eye twitched, his face dropped and his whole body seemed to slump when I said those words. All I had wanted to do was wrap my arms around him and hold him, explain to him that I loved him more than life itself, that I was doing this for his own good so he wouldn't get hurt. But I hadn't done any of those things; instead, I'd pretended Carter was standing there in front of me, remembering how much I hated him, just so I could convince Ashton that this was over. I needed him to believe me so that he'd be able to move on, be happy, and live his life.

I sobbed even harder when I thought about the fierce expression that crossed his face just before he kissed me, almost like he thought that one kiss would make everything better, or would change my mind. My lips still tingled from the intensity of it. Staying in control and not kissing him back was one of the hardest things I had ever had to do, but somehow I had managed to hold onto the memory of the dream that I had a few weeks ago. I pictured his broken face and his groan of pain, and that was the only thing that got me through what had just happened.

If I didn't love him so much, I would never have been able to cope with what I'd just done. In time, he would get over me and be back to his old self, his friends would help him through it, he would have his dream job, and in a couple of weeks he'd be right as rain. I, on the other hand, would feel this pain forever – but this was nothing compared to living with the knowledge that Ashton had been hurt or killed.

A few minutes later, there was a knock at the door. I stiffened. I couldn't let him see me like this. I wiped my face and took a deep breath. "What?" I huffed, trying to sound annoyed.

"Annabelle, can we talk?" Dean asked through the door. I pushed myself up and opened the door to see his sympathetic face. "Why did you do that if it's upsetting you this much?" he asked, clearly confused as his eyes raked over my face.

I shrugged, trying to pretend that I wasn't dying inside. "It needed to be done. I'm going to miss him, but I can't give him what he wants. He's in love with me, and I can't love him back. It's better if he's away from me so he can move on," I explained, lying through my teeth.

His eyes narrowed, clearly assessing me to see if there was some other hidden reason. "That's why you sent him away?"

I nodded. "I can't love him back; it wasn't fair to keep leading him on. I asked for him to be transferred so he could get on with his life instead of staying here with an emotionless wreck," I lied, swallowing my grief. "He complicates things with his feelings, and I can't be dealing with any more complications now."

He nodded slowly. "I can understand that, but you need him here to protect you, he's the best one for this job. What with all of this Carter stuff, we need him here to lead," he said, trying to convince me.

Wow, if only he knew that is the real reason I made him leave. "Dean, I'm sure you'll cope. Ashton's not the only guard in the world. I've requested you as my new near guard, I hope that's okay with you," I croaked, changing the subject.

"Yeah I was told, it's fine. But, Annabelle, you really should think about this," he pleaded, shaking his head in disapproval.

"Dean, it's done, he needs this. You must see how he feels about me, he needs a clean break. I'm sure he'll call you to try and get you to convince me to take him back, but that just won't happen, so just stay out of it and let him get over me. I don't want him to keep hurting and pining for me. I don't want him to know that I'm missing him or upset. He needs a clean break." I looked at him warningly, hoping that I made it clear and that he would help me by not interfering. I just prayed he wouldn't tell Ashton I was crying.

He frowned. "Okay, I understand, Annabelle," he admitted, nodding and looking at me fiercely.

"Great. Well, thanks. I'm gonna do some drawing." I stepped back and closed the bedroom door in his face, ending the conversation.

I went over to the bed and flopped down on my back, staring at the ceiling, focussing on my breathing to stay calm. I grabbed a photo of me and Ashton from the bedside unit and looked at his handsome, smiling face. This was harder than I thought. I knew it would hurt, but the thought of never seeing him again felt like someone was killing me slowly. I pushed up off the bed and grabbed a suitcase from the closet and started to pack up his stuff, crying silently the whole time.

When I was done, I called my father again. There was something else that would afford Ashton some more protection. "Dad, I think we need to put out the truth about Ashton being my guard and that we weren't actually together. It'll be better in the long run if people know the truth, rather than thinking we've just broken up," I suggested, grimacing. I knew it would hurt Ashton more, but at least it would keep him safer if Carter thought it was just an act. If Carter thought we were really together, he would hunt him down.

My dad's defeated sigh blew down the line. "Okay, Annabelle, whatever you think. I'll have someone draft a statement and have it released," he agreed quietly.

"Thanks for doing this for me," I mumbled gratefully.

"I don't suppose you'll tell me what this is about?"

"I'm sorry, I can't. But thank you for trusting me," I replied, willing myself not to cry anymore.

"Anytime, Annabelle," he answered, ending the call.

The next few days were awful. We were splashed all over the papers and magazines; everyone knew we weren't ever together and that Ashton was, in fact, a SWAT agent assigned to guard me. There were photos of him in the paper looking sad, his eyes cold and hurt, but he refused to comment on anything. Every day he tried to call me. I received about five texts a day, begging me to talk to him, telling me he loved me and that he always would. I didn't respond. Whenever he would call I would reject it or turn my phone off.

School was extremely difficult. The three day guards I now had followed me around closely, drawing more attention to me every second of the day. Rosie and the guys asked about Ashton and couldn't believe that he was a guard and nothing more. I changed back into the girl that didn't allow anyone to get close to her. I barely spoke to anyone and shied away from all contact with people, just like I used to. Every night I would read through the texts that Ashton had sent me, looking at the photo of him, and then cry myself to sleep. I'd never felt so lonely in my life.

Chapter Forty-Five

~ Ashton ~

By the time I got home from the airport, my head was pounding. I was so stressed and worried that I could barely walk in a straight line. All I could think about was if she was okay. What if Carter had come for her while I wasn't there?

I grabbed a cab and headed back to mine and Nate's apartment. When I stepped through the door, Nate twisted in his seat and a confused frown slipped onto his face. "Hey, Taylor! What the hell are you doing here?"

I sighed, not having the words to explain that my life felt like it was circling the drain at the moment.

"Good to see you, buddy!" he chirped as I flopped down onto the sofa next to him. "You bring that hot little girl of yours with you again?" He eyed the door, as if waiting for Anna to make an appearance.

I closed my eyes and rested my head back on the sofa. "It's over. She made me leave," I mumbled.

He seemed to choke on air. "What the actual fuck? You two broke up?" he gasped.

I shook my head. I could probably tell him the truth now. It was official that I was no longer her guard, I'd seen the transfer document, there was no staying undercover after this. "We were never really together. I was assigned to protect her; they wanted me undercover as her boyfriend. We were never a real couple," I admitted sadly.

He made a scoffing sound in the back of his throat. "Not together. What the hell are you talking about? I saw you two, you were all over each other. What do you mean you were undercover? I don't get it."

I rubbed my aching eyes with my fists, willing my headache to subside. "Officially, I was assigned as her near guard, her undercover boyfriend, but we got close. I fell in love with her. I thought she loved me too, but she just had me transferred away from her." Tiredness was trying to consume me, my words all seemed to jumble into one, but somehow he understood me.

"Transferred?"

I nodded in confirmation. "Yeah, I'm back in LA now." My voice sounded depressed even to my own ears.

"Why did she have you transferred? You do something wrong? Tell me you didn't cheat on her. If you did, I'm gonna have to kick your ass for being a fucking moron," he raised one eyebrow in question.

"I didn't cheat," I confirmed. "Everything was great, but then…" I swallowed, not wanting to divulge all of the Carter stuff. Actually, I didn't even think I had the mental strength to explain it all to him properly. "I'm going to bed. I can't talk about this now. I'll see you in the morning." I didn't wait for an answer as I pushed myself up and stalked towards my bedroom, slamming the door behind me.

I flopped down on my bed and pulled my phone out of my pocket, staring at it in frustration when I saw no missed calls or messages from her sitting there. She was killing me; the pain was unbearable. Suddenly an idea occurred to me and my thumb swished through my contacts quickly.

Maddy answered on the second ring. I closed my eyes. "Hi, ma'am, this is Agent Taylor. May I please speak to the President?" I asked hopefully.

She sighed. "Hi. Yes, absolutely. He's been expecting a call from you," she replied.

I groaned. He knew I'd call, which meant that he wasn't going to change his mind.

I was on hold for a few seconds before he spoke. "Agent Taylor, I know what you're going to say. I'm sorry, but this is what Annabelle has asked for, I can't go against her wishes," he stated, without even saying hello.

My lungs constricted. "I understand that, sir, but what with Carter being out now and the letters… Sir, he'll come after her, we both know it. It's not a matter of what she wants, it's a matter of keeping her safe," I countered, trying to reason with his protective parental instincts.

"I know, I know. I'm not happy with this either, but she specifically asked me for this, she said she needed it to happen. I don't suppose you can shed any light on the situation for me? Annabelle refused to give me a reason," he requested hopefully.

I sighed. I didn't even understand the reason myself, but I couldn't tell him about our relationship and that I 'complicated things' according to her with my love sick puppy act. I refused to make things harder for her on purpose. She wouldn't want her parents to know how close we had gotten, she was an extremely private person, and I respected that about her.

"Not if she doesn't want me to, sir, I'm sorry. But please reconsider. I'm the best one to protect her. Please let me keep her safe," I begged.

"I'm sorry, son. Your new assignment should be what you want. If it's not, then let me know and I'll arrange something else. I've put a glowing recommendation on your file. I'm glad you called me because I wanted to personally thank you for what you did for Annabelle. I've honestly not seen her this happy in years. I'm just sorry it had to be cut short."

He wasn't going to change his mind, this was it, my last chance and he wasn't even close to helping me. I nodded. "Me too." I swallowed the lump in my throat. "If you need anyone to help with Anna's safety at any time, please let me know," I offered.

"Will do, son," he replied as he disconnected the call.

The next few days were the worst of my life. On top of the painful, gaping hole that now resided where my heart used to be, the White House had put out a public statement stating that I was nothing more than Anna's guard and that the relationship was fake. As soon as the statement was released, reporters were hounding me for interviews everywhere I went, taking photos and asking questions. I refused to answer any, and after about a week it died down slightly.

I could barely sleep, but when I did, I had nightmares about her calling for help and I couldn't reach her or couldn't find her. Each time I would wake up in a cold sweat and roll over to cuddle her, only to have my heart break all over again when I remembered she wasn't there.

The only good thing going on in my life was my job. I had my dream job: Front Line. The Captain was extremely pleased to have me, and was majorly impressed with my letter from the President. I fitted straight into the team, and the job was everything I always thought it would be and more. But each day was like my own private nightmare. All I wanted to do was talk to her, hold her and keep her safe.

As the days dragged into weeks, it got worse and worse. I hardly wanted to get out of bed. Every night it would take me hours to fall asleep and I would have awful nightmares about her, then I would wake every single morning thinking she was there, only to remember and have to start all over again. My life was a steaming pile of shit. I didn't want to go to work or even see my friends. Everything was just too much effort.

What made it worse was the date that approached. Anna's birthday and the four year anniversary of Jack being murdered. She was going to be in pieces, I knew it, and I wasn't there to help her or stop her from attempting to take her life, like she had done for the last two years.

While I waited for the phone to connect, I stared down at the FedEx box on my bed that I'd just finished wrapping. The address on the front was to

Anna, care of the White House PO Box address that was for personal mail to the President. My heart sank. I wasn't even sure she would open it, but I had to try.

When Maddy answered the call, I ran my hand through my hair. "Hi, ma'am, it's Agent Taylor. Do you think it would be possible to speak to the President?" I asked glumly, flopping back and closing my eyes.

The click of her keyboard told me she was checking his schedule. "He has a couple of minutes before his next meeting, I'll buzz you through."

"Agent Taylor, you wanted to speak to me?" President Spencer asked politely when he came on the line a moment later.

"Yes, sir. Thank you for taking my call, I'm sure you're busy," I frowned up at the ceiling. I hadn't spoken to him since the day I was reassigned, and I was surprised by how much resentment I felt towards him because he'd sent me away from her.

"That's okay, son. What can I do for you?"

I ran my hand through my hair. "Well, I have a birthday gift for Anna, and I wondered if I would be able to send it over to you. I guessed that she's going to be spending her school break there with you." My frown turned into a scowl.

"Yes, she is. Of course you can send it here, Agent Taylor. I'll make sure she gets it," he replied kindly.

Now for the hard bit, that I wasn't sure how to word. "Thank you, sir. One more thing. I just wanted to check that Anna won't be left alone for her birthday. I'm worried that she'll…" I stumbled over my words and took a deep breath. "I guess what I'm trying to say is that the day is going to be hard for her. She promised me she won't do that again this year, but I'm still worried," I admitted. I hadn't been able to get the thought of her killing herself from my head. She'd promised me she wouldn't, but did that still count, considering I wasn't there anymore?

He sighed. "I'm worried too. We're taking every precaution, and I have given her guards strict orders not to let her out of their sight for a moment. Annabelle's stronger now, I don't think she'll try that again," he answered, sounding like he was trying to convince himself at the same time as me.

I nodded. "Yes, sir. Thank you," I mumbled gratefully. His reassurances did help a little; I trusted that he would do everything in his power to keep her safe. "Can I ask how Anna is? I've tried calling her, but she won't even speak to me."

He sighed deeply. "She's been here for three days now already, and she seems to be coping alright. She's a little quiet, but she always is around us," he answered. There was a moment of awkward silence where he seemed to be choosing his words. "Look, I know you're concerned about her and I appreciate that, but if she doesn't want to speak to you, then maybe you should just stop trying to contact her," he suggested.

I gritted my teeth. He was right; everyone had said the same thing – that I should forget her and move on because she wasn't going to change her mind. But I just couldn't. It wasn't possible for me to move on while there was still that small element of hope in my mind. When she'd told me she didn't love me, I didn't believe her. Deep down, I knew she had feelings for me, deep rooted feelings that she was obviously terrified of and needed space and time to work out. This Carter stuff just made her panic and the first defence mechanism for her was to revert back to what she knew – the cold, hard Anna. At least, that's what I told myself. In reality, there was just no getting over this girl, so hope was all I had.

"I'm sorry, I shouldn't have called you," I muttered.

"I don't mind you calling. It's nice that you care about my daughter. How about I ask her to call you? I can't promise anything, of course; Annabelle has always been incredibly strong minded."

I smiled. Strong minded was an understatement when applied to that girl. "Thank you."

"By the way, how's the job going? I've heard some good things about you here, you know," he questioned, probably to change the subject.

I smiled sadly. "It's going good, thank you. It's everything I thought it would be," I admitted, but the thing was, it just wasn't what I wanted anymore.

"That's great. With all the things I've been hearing about you, you'll be running the place soon," he chuckled.

I smiled at his compliment. "Not quite yet, I don't think they're ready for my style of leadership quite yet," I joked.

"I'll bet. I'd better go. Good to speak to you again, Agent Taylor."

"Good to speak to you again too, sir," I replied, disconnecting the call.

A knock sounded on my door, and moments later, Nate stuck his head in without waiting for me to answer. "Alright? Want to go play a couple of games of air hockey?" he asked, smiling sympathetically.

Nate had been great for the last couple of weeks. I'd told him everything, glossing over the whole Carter stuff with very minor details. He really didn't understand how I felt about Anna at all, but he was trying to. He stayed in with me if I didn't want to go out, was understanding and sympathetic when I needed to talk about her, and gave me space if I asked for it. He truly was the best friend a guy could ask for. I nodded, standing up and picking up the FedEx package I would mail on the way.

~ Anna ~

Two weeks after Ashton left, it was school break. Before all of this happened, Ashton and I had been talking through options for the vacation

– the one that seemed to be the winner was asking my parents if I could go to LA with him. So the fact that I was at the White House was now doubly hard for me. Dean and Peter both got the two weeks off, so they dropped me with my parents and then headed off in their separate directions to spend time with family.

My mom cooed how lovely it was to have me home and how much she'd missed me while she gave me a guided tour of the White House. I'd already been once before, on the day of my father's inauguration, but my mother seemed content to show me around again – probably to pass the time. She didn't once mention Carter or his disastrous retrial, or the fact that apparently my worst nightmare wanted me back again.

My bedroom was the blue one that I'd chosen on the first visit. As I stood at the window, looking out over the beautiful grounds at the back of the building, I couldn't even bring myself to smile a real smile. During the last two weeks, I'd become pretty adept at faking being alright though. People didn't realise how much pain I was feeling inside, which I was grateful for. I was pretty sure that Dean had an idea of my suffering, but thankfully he didn't mention Ashton anymore.

Staying here for two weeks meant I would spend my twentieth birthday here too. When I woke in the morning on March 12, I couldn't stop the silent tears that fell down my face. If there was ever a day that I regretted sending Ashton away, it was today. Memories of Jack and his death plagued me before I was even fully awake.

For the last two anniversaries, the sadness had consumed me. I'd gotten extremely intoxicated and I'd washed down a bottle of pills. This year would be different. I'd promised Ashton that I wouldn't ever do that again, and, to be honest, I didn't actually feel like that girl anymore. When I was in that dark, depressed state, I couldn't see any point in living; I couldn't see anything good in the world, but knowing that there was someone like Ashton out there just made the world a happier place for me. Yes, I was sad and lonely at the moment, but I just wasn't in that dark and depressed place anymore. I *knew* that there was a point to life. Sure, my heart hurt for Ashton, but I knew that he would be happy soon. I believed in what I was doing. If I didn't love him so much, I would've never been able to push him away and put myself through this.

My cell phone was buzzing happily on the side, vibrating loudly against the wood of my bedside unit. I ignored it, knowing it would be Ashton. He had been calling me every five minutes since seven o'clock so I'd switched my phone to silent. By the time I got out of the shower and dressed, the phone had finally stopped ringing. I picked it up, seeing twelve missed calls and eight new messages.

The calls were all from him in a series of five minute intervals. Five of the messages were from him too. The others were from Rosie, Serena and Monica, all of them wishing me happy birthday. I opened the messages from Ashton and took a deep breath before I read them:

1 - Happy Birthday! I hope you have a good day. Please call me, I really need to speak to you, today of all days. I love you x

2 - Anna, please don't do anything silly today, please? I love you.

3 - Please answer your phone. I just need to hear your voice and know that you're okay, please?

4 - Anna, you're making me crazy! I know today is hard for you but you promised me once you wouldn't do anything silly on your birthday. Please, Baby Girl, please?

5 - You're killing me, I swear. Please answer your damn phone! I miss you, I need you, I love you x

My hands were shaking. I felt sick. Knowing I couldn't put off contact with him today because of how worried he'd be, I sent him a quick reply promising that I wouldn't do anything silly and asking him to stop calling and leave me alone.

I forced myself to stop thinking about him. I knew he was hurting and that I was causing him pain, but it needed to be done and he would never have left if I'd just told him my reasons for wanting him transferred. He would have been confident he could have protected me, and himself, against Carter and his men, but he would have been wrong, and I couldn't take that chance with his life.

As I wandered through the exquisite hallways and made my way to the dining room for breakfast with my parents, I tried to ignore the guard that was following behind me, matching his step with mine.

I didn't really want to eat this morning, but my parents had insisted we convene in the morning to celebrate. They always had liked to make a fuss of my birthday – that never changed, even after I did.

As I sat down at the beautifully laid out table, my parents smiled warmly but managed to look concerned at the same time. "Happy birthday, Annabelle," they both said, almost in unison.

I faked a smile. "Thanks." To distract myself from the fact that they were watching me, I helped myself to some toast, spreading it liberally with marmalade. I wasn't hungry, but I needed to keep up the act for them otherwise I'd never get any peace today.

Suddenly, my mom jumped out of her chair and grabbed three presents off the floor, handing them to me. "For you."

"Thanks, you didn't need to get me anything." I set them on the table and picked up the top, beautifully wrapped, red box.

"Oh don't be silly, you're twenty today, no longer a teenager," my mom chirped, looking at me proudly.

I eagerly tore off the paper, finding a shoe box inside. On the side was printed the words 'Mary Shaun' – the designer who had made my dress and shoes for my father's party. I grinned as I lifted the lid to see a pair of electric blue shoes with a sparkly stiletto heel. They were absolutely beautiful. I gasped.

"Oh wow, these are gorgeous!" I gushed. They were almost as nice as the plum ones I'd claimed to have lost after the party.

"I thought you'd like them," my mom agreed, smiling at me knowingly.

I smiled gratefully. "Thank you, these are incredible."

"Open the others," she instructed, nodding at them.

I grabbed the next one and ripped it open to find a gorgeous gold watch. "Wow, this is beautiful, thank you."

I picked up the last one. It was wrapped in different paper than the other two. I smiled and ripped it open to reveal another shoe box. I smiled over at my parents who were watching me intently. When I lifted the lid, I'd expected another pair of gorgeous shoes; instead, my eyes landed on a perfectly dried white rose with a green ribbon tied around the stem, a bag of cola flavour fizzy candy, a small book called 'Graphic design and the meaning of colours and shapes', and a photo album. I frowned in confusion. This wasn't the type of thing my parents usually bought; usually it was all about the cost, thought didn't really come into the equation. I glanced over at my mom, seeing her sad smile and concerned eyes. That was when it dawned on me – this wasn't from them, it was from Ashton. I should have realised as soon as I saw the rose.

A lump had suddenly formed in my throat, and I tried my best to swallow around it. My hands shook as I picked up the photo album, flicking through to the first page. A photo of me, Ashton, and his friends in LA. My heart squeezed painfully. I thumbed through the rest quickly, seeing that every page was filled with photos of me laughing, me and Ashton together at school, at a bar, on vacation, or at my dad's party. In some we were joking around in the bed, holding it at arm's length, our faces filling the whole picture where we couldn't get it far enough away. I smiled and flicked to the last page, there was a birthday card there. I couldn't open it now, I could already feel tears prickling my eyes so I snapped it shut and put it back in the box.

"That was sent here a couple of days ago. He asked for me to give it to you on your birthday," my dad said, regarding me curiously.

I nodded. "Yeah, he's very thoughtful," I replied, trying not to let my emotions bubble over. The sweetness of Ashton came flooding back to me, almost making me burst into a fresh round of sobs, but I held it in somehow.

"He's been calling like crazy this morning. He wants to make sure you're okay, what with the day and everything. Why don't you give him a call?" Dad suggested, as if it was that easy.

"I already texted him this morning," I said casually. I couldn't talk about him anymore, my insides were squirming, my eyes stinging with tears. I decided to change the subject before I broke down in front of my parents. "I think I'll wear my new shoes today," I smiled at my mom, hoping she'd help me out a little. She did. As if knowing I couldn't cope with this heavy conversation, she started cooing about the shoes and other things that she had seen that I might like at the store. I just smiled and nodded along, grateful to be talking about something other than Ashton.

Once the breakfast was over, I headed up to my room and plopped down on the bed, pulling over the box from Ashton. I took out the dried rose and smiled as I put it on my bedside cabinet; it was perfectly dried and still beautiful. I laughed as I grabbed the fizzy candy; they were my favourites, he'd obviously remembered.

Lastly, I picked up the photo album, hesitantly looking through the pictures again, laughing at some of the funny ones where we were pulling faces or fooling around. I ran my finger over his handsome, smiling face. The pictures made me miss him even more, if that was possible. I moaned when I got to one of him kissing me and holding me tight. I would give anything for him to be here with me now.

When I got to the last page, I pulled out the card and took a deep breath before opening it. The front was fairly simple, it was a vase filled with white roses on a farmhouse kitchen table. I smiled, thinking about how long he must have been looking for the perfect card before he found this one. I opened it to see his messy writing inside; it wasn't just a happy birthday message, he'd written me a letter inside.

Anna,

I hope you have a really great birthday, you deserve to. I didn't know what to get you, I didn't know if you'd be allowed to go and do anything because of the whole guard situation, otherwise I would have bought you tickets for that show on Broadway that you wanted to go see, that's what I was planning on getting you before all this happened.

So instead of a bought gift, I've given you the next best thing. I've bundled all of my happiest memories into this album for you. These are the best things that ever happened to me and

452

every single one of them involved you. I know they didn't mean the same to you as they did me, but you looked so happy at the time.

Please give me another chance. We can just be friends, please? I really miss you, I hope you miss me too. Look at the album and remember how happy I could make you. Please, Baby Girl.

I know today is going to be really hard for you and I wish you would let me be there for you, but I guess I can understand why you won't. You once promised me you wouldn't do anything bad today, please, please, please keep that promise Baby Girl, please. Your life means so much to me and I can't bear the thought of you hurting yourself.

Anyway, I guess I'd better let you go and enjoy your birthday. I hope you're doing something fun.

Happy 20th birthday, Anna.

It doesn't matter to me how many miles you put between us, I still love you and I always will.

Ashton

xxx

P.s Nate and the guys wish you happy birthday too x

I read the letter three times; uncontrollable tears rolled down my face. My heart was aching, my whole being just screaming for him. I flopped back onto my bed and closed my eyes, hugging myself tightly. I could picture every single one of those memories without the photos, and they were the best things that had ever happened to me too.

The rest of the day passed as a blur. I hung out on my own a lot. My parents had arranged a 'special dinner' as they called it, but essentially it was just another dinner in the White House. They ate like this every night, as far as I could tell. After dinner, I went to my room and had a long bubble bath. I should have felt different somehow, but to me it just felt like any other day. Another day without Ashton.

When I finally crept into my bed, I glanced at my phone to see I had another text from Ashton. I sighed; he didn't seem to be getting over me at all. Maybe my idea of Nate and the boys helping him through wasn't going to work out the way I'd planned. Every message from him hurt worse than the last because they just reminded me that he wasn't here. The texts somehow made the time pass slower; the minutes seemed to drag between messages. My life blurred into one big, long, horrible, Ashton-less day that was broken up by messages I received from the love of my life.

I opened this new one to see that it was him asking me to text him again because he was worrying. The message had been sent while I was in the bath; it was almost eleven in the evening now. I opened up a new message and texted him back that I was fine and thanked him for the gift, just so he would relax.

After I sent it, I rolled over, trying to get comfortable. He didn't text me back, so I assumed maybe he was asleep, or working nights, or maybe even that he just didn't want to text me. The last thought hurt the worst.

Six agonising weeks had passed since I'd sent him away and, if anything, it only got worse. The dreams that I had every night were terrible. Every night I saw him die in front of me, and every night I would wake up screaming and sweating, with my heart trying to break out of my chest. Dean would look at me sympathetically, not knowing what to say or do. He was doing a good job of being near guard, living in the bedroom next door, but I preferred my own miserable company, so I hid in my bedroom most of the time, only coming out for school or meal times.

Ashton still called and texted me every day. He sent me a bunch of white roses every Friday morning with a little poem or limerick attached. He sent me music for my iPod, books, chocolates and stuffed animals. Every weekend I would get an emailed love letter, begging me to reconsider, telling me how lost he was without me.

I knew that he contacted Dean a lot too. Thankfully, I'd made a deal with Dean: he wouldn't tell Ashton how much I missed him, and in return, I would behave and do everything he asked me to without question.

I was so incredibly tired every day. Once I'd had the nightmare of Ashton being killed, I refused to go back to sleep, so I had on average about four hours sleep a night. I went to the gym twice a day and threw myself back into my old training method of exercise until I dropped. I wanted to be able to protect myself if Carter did come after me. It was my hope that if he did, that this time I'd be able to kill him. Then I'd be free to beg Ashton to forgive me for pushing him away and ask him to give me another chance.

What with all the exercise I did and the fighting training I'd received, I thought I would be prepared for the day he would come for me again. Unfortunately, I was wrong.

Chapter Forty-Six

I was yanked from my sleep by a loud bang in the hallway outside our apartment. My heart leapt into my chest as Dean ran into my room and over to my bed. His hands closed around my upper arms so tightly that I was sure to have finger-shaped bruises there in a few hours. I squealed as he pulled me from the bed, shoving me against the wall. My mouth popped open, shocked at the abrupt wake up and the force he was using. Wordlessly, he grabbed the heavy reading chair from the corner of my room and dragged it over to me, placing it in front of me as he grabbed my hand and made us both duck down behind it.

"Dean, what's-"

"Be quiet!" he interjected. My eyes widened as he pulled out his cell phone, frantically dialling someone. "Shit," he hissed, before he tried another number. This one must have connected as he spoke words that sent a mortified chill down my spine. "Someone's here. Get in here, now!"

Someone's here...

That was when I heard gunshots. I screamed and quickly clamped a hand over my mouth. Dean dialled his phone again, his eyes and gun both trained on the door to my bedroom. "It's Agent Michaels. The jewel's in trouble, send more people, now!" he growled as he snapped the phone shut quickly.

I couldn't breathe. Silent tears were falling down my face as Dean positioned himself between me and the door, with his gun pointed there ready. I heard more shots and then the bedroom door swung open quickly, slamming against the wall. Dean let off a couple of shots and the intruder immediately jumped back against the door frame, out of sight.

My breathing was coming out in pants as panic made my head swim. I tried my hardest to count my heartbeats so that I didn't have a panic attack. I needed to remain in control in case we needed to run or get out quickly.

"Put your gun down!" the guy ordered from outside the door. I whimpered, and Dean shushed me again. "Put your gun down, and you won't get hurt," the guy tried again. A cold trickle seemed to run down my back. I recognised that voice, I couldn't remember the guy's name, but he had dark hair. He worked for Carter. "We have one of your agents. We don't want to hurt him, but we will if we don't get what we want. All we want is Anna," he continued.

My blood ran cold in my veins. *One of our agents? Oh God, please let us get out of this, please!*

Hesitantly, Peter stepped into the doorway, looking terrified, his hands up in an 'I surrender' fashion. I immediately saw the reason for the pose. There was a gun to his head. His eyes found us immediately, his jaw tightened, and he seemed to be holding a silent conversation with Dean. I had no idea what the intense look on his face was; all I could see was panic and fear. The dark-haired guy stepped close behind him, using Peter's body as a shield as they both stepped into the room. The gun pressed harder into Peter's head, making him wince.

"Come on out, Anna," the guy sang, his tone amused. "You don't want him to get hurt now, do you?"

I didn't know what to do. I was always told to stay behind the agent, keep quiet, don't answer, stay small and alert and do as I was told. But that was Peter standing there. He was a friend of mine, and they had a gun to his head…

I whimpered, knowing that I couldn't do as I was always told. I shifted and Dean clamped his hand around my wrist, holding me behind him tightly. "Please don't hurt them, please!" I begged.

"Shh!" Dean ordered again.

The guy laughed quietly, sending a shiver down my spine as I recognised the laugh too, I definitely knew this guy. "I'm going to give you to the count of three to step away, Anna, or this one dies," he instructed. I groaned, not knowing what to do. Dean's grip tightened on my arm; it looked like he was trying to find a shot that wouldn't hit Peter.

"One," the guy called.

I shook my head. "Please don't," I begged. My heart was hammering in my chest.

"Two."

I couldn't let him hurt Peter, not because of me. Another person didn't deserve to get hurt or killed because of me, I'd already gotten Jack killed, I couldn't take another innocent life. I shoved off Dean's hold and jumped out from behind him, holding my hands high. "Don't hurt him, I'm here!" I cried desperately.

"No, Annabelle!" Dean shouted as he lunged for me again.

I saw the guy behind Peter smile as two others stepped through the doorway. I watched, seemingly in slow motion, as one raised a gun, pointing it in the direction of Dean. I realised too late what I'd done. I'd taken away

456

his only leverage; with me out in the open, there was no reason for them to be lenient on him. The sound of the first gunshot echoed in my ears, it seemed to reverberate around the room, making my ears ring. I didn't want to turn and look, but I couldn't stop myself. I turned just in time to see Dean's body slam back against the wall; the shot had hit him right in the face, leaving almost nothing recognisable behind. His blood stained the wall in an arc-shaped streak as his body slumped to the floor.

I heard screaming, and some part of my mind vaguely registered that it was me doing it, but I couldn't stop. I fell to my knees and gripped my hands in my hair as I sobbed. Something moved near me, a kind of scuffle, I glanced up just in time for the second gunshot to go off. I whimpered and flinched as my heart broke. Peter's eyes met mine for a second before he crumpled to the floor, clutching at his stomach as he groaned.

"I'm sorry. I'm so sorry," I whispered, my body hitching with sobs. He made a strangled gurgling sound in response. His pain-filled, frightened eyes locked on mine. Before I could reach out and help him, a shadow fell over us both and another gunshot rang out, followed by another and another. Each time a bullet hit him, Peter's body jerked slightly; by the time the fourth shot came, he didn't even flinch.

"Well hello, Anna. Long time no see."

I registered the voice, but I couldn't respond. I was so scared that I couldn't move. My muscles seemed to be made of rock. I couldn't take my eyes off Peter's body. He was dead because of me, and so was Dean. This was entirely my fault. Maybe if I hadn't stepped away then they would still be alive. I thanked God silently that Ashton wasn't here; I couldn't see him get hurt. I knew I had made the right choice sending him away.

A hand closed over my elbow, hauling me to my feet. I swayed, my legs almost not supporting my weight. The only thing that kept me upright was the vice-like grip on my arm. I looked up from Peter's dead lifeless body, to see Jimmy, one of Carter's men. I remembered him from Miami. Jimmy didn't like the way that Carter treated me and would always try to help me when he could, which wasn't very often.

"Hi, Anna," he said quietly, looking at me almost apologetically.

"Hi, Jimmy," I choked out. Internally, I desperately fought for control of my emotions. If I had to do this on my own then I needed to snap out of this. I'd grieve later, but right now I needed to focus on trying to get out of here. I took a few deep, calming breaths.

Jimmy smiled sadly and dragged me out into the lounge. I swiped at my face quickly, wiping away the tears, trying to stay strong. "Watch her while I get her some clothes," Jimmy instructed as he left me in the lounge. I looked around desperately, expecting to see Carter, but he wasn't there. Instead, there were eight of his men. I knew all of their faces but only a couple of names. These guys weren't like Jimmy, they were mean and heartless.

"Well, well, well, haven't you grown up nice," one of them purred. His eyes raked over me slowly, and my skin crawled. I wrapped my arms around myself, wishing I'd put on more than boy shorts and a tank top to sleep in last night.

One of the other guys quickly stepped forwards and punched him in the jaw. "Don't look at her like that! If Carter saw that, you'd be dead," he growled angrily.

I swallowed the bile that started to rise in my throat at the mention of Carter. "Are you going to kill me?" I asked, almost pleading for it.

The same guy that had thrown the punch smiled and shook his head. "No. Carter sent us to collect his wife," he answered, smirking at me nastily.

"Is he here?" I asked, wringing my shaking hands.

The guy shook his head. "No, he wanted to be, but they're keeping pretty close tabs on him. He sent us here instead. He'll be along later, don't worry."

I groaned and dropped my eyes to the floor; I didn't look up as Jimmy shoved a pair of jeans and a black top in my hands. "Get dressed. We need to leave," he ordered.

I nodded at the guys all standing there watching me. "You really want me to change here, in front of everyone?" I asked sarcastically.

"Don't worry, sweetheart, I'm sure you don't have anything we haven't seen before," one guy mocked, sneering at me, looking like he was already taking my pyjamas off with his eyes.

I smiled sweetly. "Okay, it's your funeral, I guess. When Carter finds out you all watched me undress he's not going to be best pleased. If that's what you want…" I shrugged and reached down to grab the bottom of my tank top, starting to pull it up.

A collective gasp filled the room. "No, wait! You can get dressed in the bathroom," a blond guy said quickly; his name was Lukas if I remembered correctly.

I smiled and followed him to the bathroom that was off the hall. There was a small window in this bathroom that led to the hallway at the front. I smiled and locked the door behind me, shrugging out of my clothes and putting the jeans and T-shirt on as quickly as possible. Once dressed, I boosted up on the sink and quietly pried the window open. I stuck my head out and saw there was no one there, so I boosted myself up and over, dropping down to the floor silently in my bare feet.

"Very clever," Lukas stated from the front door, making me scream as I jumped about a mile into the air. He tossed a pair of sneakers at me. "Better put those on too, don't want you to cut your feet," he said sarcastically.

I frowned and pulled them on. There had to be something else; if there weren't so many of them then I could have fought them. One of their guns would give me a chance, but would I actually be able to shoot someone like Ashton had taught me? I didn't know the answer. Shooting a human being was miles apart from shooting a paper target.

The blond guy grabbed my arm and pulled me out of the building. My emotions got the better of me again, the tears started to flow when I saw the first body of the new agents that had been sent to protect me. They were all lying, broken and still bleeding, on the way out of the building.

"Are they all dead?" I whispered to Lukas.

He nodded in confirmation. "Yeah, you had a lot of guards, but then I guess you are the first daughter now. It's a shame that one who was posing as your boyfriend wasn't here. Carter didn't like his hands on you, even if it was all a fake," he said, shrugging casually.

I closed my eyes, thinking of Ashton, allowing myself to be led along. "He wasn't my boyfriend. We had to act like that. My father made us. He was just a bodyguard," I lied desperately.

He chuckled darkly. "Oh, Carter knows that, if he didn't know that then that asshole would be dead already," he stated, watching me intently.

I didn't say anything as he led us to a black car at the front of the building and held the door open for me. I felt sick as I climbed in the car.

We drove for about an hour or so through the back streets until we came to a derelict-looking building. I looked around but didn't recognise the place at all. The sun was coming up just as we pulled into the underground parking lot. As we parked up, I closed my eyes. *Please God, let me get through this,* I prayed silently.

Jimmy opened my door for me, motioning for me to get out. "Come on, Anna."

I climbed out and looked around quickly. There were only four of them now; this was definitely worth a try. I knew that they wouldn't be expecting me to be any trouble, so their underestimation of me would work to my advantage. I punched Jimmy in the stomach, and as he bent over in pain, I kicked the other guy in the groin, hard, making him grunt and fall to the floor in agony. I turned and readied myself as saw another guy approaching, but Jimmy had righted himself and wrapped his arms around me from behind, grabbing my arms and pinning them down. I struggled and thrashed, but I couldn't get free, so I gave up. I wasn't getting out of here just yet.

"That was fucking stupid, Anna. Just calm down or you'll get yourself hurt!" Jimmy growled warningly in my ear. I sighed and nodded as he opened a fire door and started leading me up the stairs.

"Where are we? What is this place?" I asked, desperately looking around. It looked like an old factory or something; there were sewing machines, desks and tables all over the place. A thick layer of dust and dirt covered everything in sight, proving that this place hadn't been used for a while. Crude graffiti stained the walls, most of the windows were boarded up and the plaster on the walls was peeling and cracked. I had no hope of a caretaker or someone stopping by to check on the building and just so happen to rescue me; this place hadn't been used in years by the look of it.

My gaze immediately landed on a phone as I was led past one of the desks. *If I can just get to one of those phones! But who should I call, and what should I say? I don't even know where I am!*

Jimmy was still holding my arms tightly as he guided me through the different levels and doors of the maze-like place. With each passing step, my hope of ever getting out of here faded a little more. I probably just needed to accept the fact that this was my fate and that I wasn't going to be able to escape his men, there were too many of them. Jimmy shoved me roughly through another door and into a room that looked like some kind of disused office. I glanced around quickly, taking in my surroundings. There was one window, one door and no phone. It was hopeless. The door slammed shut behind me and I jumped at the click of the lock. Not ready to give up yet, I turned and hammered on the door. "Jimmy, please let me out, please!" I begged unashamedly as tears flowed freely down my cheeks.

"Carter will be here tonight, Anna. Just chill out for a few hours, okay? You hungry? I could get you some food," he offered from the other side of the door.

"I'm not hungry. Please let me go. You know what he's going to do to me. Please?" I slumped down to the floor, crying hopelessly.

"I'm sorry, Anna, really I am. But I can't let you go, he'll kill me," he replied.

I nodded. I knew he would. Jimmy was always one of the nice ones. Occasionally he would sneak me food and drink or some painkillers when Carter would starve or beat me. Carter didn't know, of course, Jimmy would have been dead a long time ago for even talking to me.

"It's okay, Jimmy." I wiped my tears on the back of my hand. I wouldn't cry anymore, crying was pointless, crying was weakness, and I refused to be weak. I wrapped my arms around myself and thought of Ashton. I could see his beautiful green eyes, and how angry his face would look if he was here right now. I closed my eyes and leant my head against the wall, praying that somehow I would get out of here before the inevitable happened. I would actually rather die than go back to living like a caged animal with Carter again.

Chapter Forty-Seven

~ Ashton ~

Exhaustion didn't quite cover what I felt as I sat on the edge of my bed. I'd just been to work for sixteen hours straight, and my body was hurting like hell. I flopped onto my back and glanced over at the clock; it was only eight in the evening. Unable to resist, I picked up my cell phone and texted Anna, the same as I did every day.

'I had a hard day at work today. I really would love to talk to you. Please call me. I love you, always x'

I sent it and closed my eyes, not even bothering to get undressed, and fell to sleep immediately.

I woke just after nine in the morning to my cell phone ringing on the bed next to me. I grabbed it quick and answered it, hoping it was Anna. "Agent Taylor," I croaked, my voice thick with sleep.

"Ashton, it's Officer Weston."

I frowned. "Yes, sir?" I replied, sitting up quickly. He never called me; I wasn't assigned to him anymore.

"Ashton, I've just heard something, and I thought you should know," he sounded remarkably stressed and I felt my body tense up. "Miss Spencer's been taken, her guards are dead. They think it's Carter Thomas."

My tired brain immediately registered what he'd said. Anna. Anna was in trouble. "WHAT? WHEN?" I cried, jumping out of the bed, stripping out of my uniform and grabbing the first clean clothes that I saw, throwing them on.

461

"Just a couple of hours ago. One of the agents managed to call through to the White House for backup, but by the time they got extra staff there, everyone was dead and she was gone," he said sadly.

Anger made my teeth ache as I clenched my jaw. I was angry at Carter, angry at myself for not being there, and I was also angry at Anna for sending me away in the first place. I should have been there, I could have stopped this. Out of frustration, I kicked my chest of drawers, taking my anger out on that. When that didn't help, I grabbed it and pulled it over, spilling everything over to the floor, making a loud crash as the mirror broke and my possessions scattered all over my floor.

"Do they know where she is?" I asked.

He sighed. "No, they have no idea. They don't think she got on a plane, they've been monitoring the airports, but she could be anywhere by now," he replied.

My heart was in my throat, my hands shaking with rage. If he touched one hair on her beautiful head, I would rip him to pieces! "I need to go, sir," I stated, not even waiting for an answer.

I disconnected the call and dialled Anna's number. It answered immediately. "Who's this?" a man's voice asked.

I felt the snarl try to rip itself out of my mouth. "Who the fuck is this and what are you doing with Anna's phone?" I growled as I threw a change of clothes into a bag along with my guns, ammo, knives and my other tactical gear.

"This is Agent Richards," the voice replied hesitantly.

"This is Agent Taylor. Why do you have Anna's phone?" I asked, trying to control my breathing; all I wanted to do was smash everything, and that wouldn't help at all.

"Miss Spencer didn't take her cell phone; it's here in the apartment."

I closed my eyes and groaned. They couldn't even track her through her cell signal. Why hadn't I ever thought about getting a tracking device on her body or something? I could have suggested it to her dad, I'm sure he could have commissioned something small enough to attach to the back of an earring or necklace.

I ended the call, pressing the phone to my forehead, thinking. Officer Weston was right, they could be anywhere by now, with Carter's money and contacts they could be on a boat, helicopter or private plane, on their way to goodness knows where. He even suggested in one of his letters that they go somewhere else for a fresh start when he got out of jail. How was I going to find her if I had no idea where to look?

I groaned and threw my bag onto the bed angrily. I felt useless; there was nothing I could do from here on my own. I would just have to fly to Arizona and wait in her apartment with the other agents; I would make her dad reinstate me as her guard so I could devote my time to finding her. I wouldn't give up, not even if I had to look for a lifetime.

If only I could find someone who knew Carter's whereabouts, or at the very least, someone who worked for him so that I could force them to tell me where she was. An idea suddenly hit me, I wasn't sure if it would work, but it was sure as hell worth a try. I held my breath as I dialled the one person who I knew would have a chance at finding her. He was a lying, cheating scumbag, and I hadn't seen him for five years. I'd met him when I was going through a bad stage in my teens and had fallen in with the wrong crowd. He was a low level criminal, but he had a lot of contacts. He used to make it his business to know everything about everyone. I'd looked up to him for a time when I was a young and impressionable seventeen year old, until I realised that wasn't the person that I wanted to be. That was when I decided to get my life on track and make something of myself, before it was too late. He was one of the reasons that I decided to train to be a police officer. If anyone would have an idea of how to get to Carter Thomas, it would be Julian Simms.

It rang for a long time. I was just about to give up hope when he answered. "This had better be fucking important! Do you know what time it is?" he growled sleepily. Julian didn't run the same type of schedule that normal people did; this was probably middle of the night for him.

"Julian, I'm sorry to call you so early. It's Ashton Taylor," I said, letting it sink in.

There was silence on the line, obviously he was trying to place the name; it had been a long time. "Ashton? Shit, man, I haven't heard from you in years! I heard you went over to the dark side," he joked.

I smiled weakly. "Sorry, but I haven't got time for pleasantries. I need you to do something for me, it's important. You owe me, remember? Well, I need to collect the favour," I said sternly.

He coughed a barking, hacking cough that was caused by too many cigarettes and too many drugs. "Yeah, what do you need?" he asked.

I need to you help me save my girl from a sick son of a bitch. "I need you to find someone for me. Or, at the very least, someone who works for someone," I answered, trying to keep the desperation out of my voice.

"Who?"

"Carter Thomas."

He gasped. "I can't help you, I'm sorry." His voice was gruff, he actually sounded a little scared.

"Julian, you fucking owe me, you know you do! I saved your life. Just get me anyone, anyone that works for him so I can get the information myself if you can't find Thomas," I growled, the frustration leaking into my voice now. I grabbed my bag and headed out of my apartment and downstairs, immediately hailing a cab heading to the airport.

"You don't want to find him, Ashton. Seriously, whatever you want him for, it's not important enough to find him for it," he replied, sounding terrified.

463

I snorted at that comment. "It's important enough, trust me. Find him and call me back. I'm serious; I'm calling in my favour." I hung up and closed my eyes as the cab sped me to the airport. I called ahead and booked the first flight they had, but I still had to wait almost two hours. At least I would be there with the other agents, so if they got any leads I would be able to go with them, if Julian came up with nothing.

I couldn't settle down. I was pacing back and forth, trying to think of any other way I could find her before he hurt her. I'd promised her that he'd never hurt her again – but what if he already had? Had I already broken my promise to her? The pain of thinking about it was torture. My whole body was tight with stress. The helpless, useless feeling was killing me slowly. My Baby Girl was in danger and there was nothing I could do about it.

Just as I was about to board my plane, my phone rang. It was Julian. "Tell me good news, man," I begged as I answered it.

"Ashton, are you sure you want to do this?" he checked.

"Just give me the fucking information, I'm about to board a plane," I snapped angrily.

He sighed. "Okay, well, I couldn't find out much about his whereabouts, but a friend of a friend has just been hired by him. He was bragging in a bar the other day that he'd been hired by Carter Thomas to retrieve something important. Apparently they've been hauled up in Arizona for the last few weeks, looking for something, but they couldn't find it. Apparently they were stationed in some abandoned factory on Western Ambrose," he said.

Arizona. Looking for something. Holy shit, this is it! Western Ambrose, I repeated it over and over in my head, committing it to memory. "Okay, what's the guy's name?" I asked curiously. I needed to find this guy, talk to him, find out anything and see if this 'thing' they were looking for was Anna. If it was, then maybe I could find out where they were planning on taking her. I just prayed that he would still be at this factory. I just needed to find the guy, get the information, and then I could pass it on to the relevant people.

"Justin Morrison. Asshole apparently, real nasty piece of work. He told the whole bar about him and Carter Thomas being like best pals apparently. Maybe you could get Carter's location from him," Julian suggested hesitantly.

"Thanks. I gotta go get my plane. If I need anything else I'll call you, okay," I muttered, disconnecting the call, not giving him the chance to say no.

I didn't call the White House; they wouldn't exactly approve of the way I was going to get Carter Thomas's whereabouts out of this guy who worked for him, breach of human rights and all that shit. Once I had more information, I would call them so we could move on Carter and get my girl back.

I called my new captain and told him I wasn't coming in for the next few days, and that I had an emergency I needed to get sorted out. As I expected, he was less than happy about it, but there wasn't much else I could do, and I didn't care anyway. Nothing else was important apart from Anna.

By the time the plane landed, I felt sick. It was almost three in the afternoon, so she'd been missing for hours now. He could have done anything to her. I got the first cab I could to Western Ambrose and had the cabbie drive me the length of the street.

"Do you know of an old abandoned factory along this road?" I asked the driver, holding him out an extra twenty.

He pocketed it and smiled gratefully. "Well, there are two; one's an office building really, the other one used to be a sewing factory years ago," he replied, raising his eyebrows curiously. I made him drive back down the road and point them out to me before I got out and headed across the street to get a better vantage point. I needed to make the sweep as quick as possible.

I quickly called Julian again. "Hey, man, did you say it was definitely an abandoned factory and not an abandoned office building?" I asked curiously. I didn't want to go into the wrong building and scare off this Justin Morrison guy. I needed him alive so I could beat the information out of him as to where Anna might be.

"Yeah, that's what my friend said," he confirmed. "Ashton, do you need some help?" he asked, sounding like he was hoping I would say no. I didn't think he would want to go against Carter Thomas at all, but I knew he would if I asked him to. A favour was classed as a debt to people like Julian; he would repay it to the best of his ability. I'd saved his life once when we were younger; he still owed me for that.

"Not at the moment, but thanks. I gotta go." I disconnected the call and pushed my cell back into my pocket before checking my ankle holster and pushing my other gun down the back of my jeans, covering it with my T-shirt. Next, I slipped my knife into my belt and pushed four extra clips into my pocket before casually walking over to the building, pretending to walk past.

I stopped to tie my shoe outside the door, sitting on the steps and looked around; no one was there so I slipped in. The fact that the door was unlocked made my heart leap, I was sure I was in the right place. This guy Morrison had to be here somewhere, I just prayed he knew where she was.

As soon as I was off the street, I pulled my gun from the waistband of my jeans and slipped an extra clip there instead in case I needed to reload quickly. I made my way through the building, keeping my back to the wall, checking each room for signs of him.

Suddenly, I heard the sound of a walkie-talkie up ahead, so I froze. My eyes narrowed. Why the hell would someone have a walkie-talkie?

Without hesitation, I slipped round the corner and put my gun to the back of the guy's head.

"What's your name?" I asked angrily.

He stood there, shocked. "Elliot."

Elliot? I frowned. So where was this Justin Morrison guy then? Maybe there was more than one of them assigned here to find this 'something important'. "Turn around," I ordered, pushing the gun harder into the back of his head as a warning. As he slowly turned to face me, I eyed the rest of the room. He was alone. "Where is Carter Thomas?" I asked, watching his face for signs that would give him away.

"Who the hell are you?" His voice was tight. He knew him.

"Where is Annabelle Spencer?" I asked, pressing the gun to his forehead. He flinched. He definitely knew.

He didn't answer, but his eyes flicked over my shoulder. I spun around to see a guy with a gun advancing on me from behind. I dropped to my knees and shot the guy coming in behind me just as he shot where my chest was a second ago.

I pulled my knife from the waistband of my jeans and grabbed the guy named Elliot, slamming him against the wall, pressing my knife against his throat. "Where is she?" I growled angrily.

He didn't answer, but his walkie-talkie started going crazy.

"Elliot? Tannor? What the hell's going on? Were those gunshots?" the walkie-talkie crackled.

"I don't know, secure her upstairs, I'll go check it out," another guy answered on the line.

Secure her upstairs. Holy shit, she's here? Anna's here in this building? Happiness tried to bubble up inside, but I pushed it down. I still had a long way to go and I needed to focus.

"Where is she? Which room?" I asked, grabbing his walkie-talkie from his belt and clipping it on mine instead.

"Fuck you!" he spat.

I pushed the blade of my knife harder against his throat, watching as a thin line of red appeared. "No, fuck you! You're going to tell me, or you're going to bleed to death," I growled angrily.

He sneered at me; he wasn't going to tell me. I pulled away slightly; I would just knock him out for now, just to take him out of the equation, I didn't want to waste time tying him up or anything. If Anna was in this building, then I needed to hurry. Obviously they knew I was here because they'd heard the gunshots, so I had no time to waste. When I moved, Elliot went for his gun. Before he could grab it, I reacted instinctively, slashing the blade across his throat, cutting deep. He clutched at his throat as he slumped to the floor, gasping for breath as he bled out. I didn't bother to wait until he was dead; I turned and made my way out of the room. She was upstairs somewhere, but this freaking place was enormous.

466

I knew I should call for backup, but I didn't have time. If they knew I was here then they could move her and then I'd lose her again. I couldn't take that chance.

I walked up a flight of stairs slowly, keeping my eyes and ears peeled for any signs of life. I saw movement ahead and spotted a guy crouched at the top of the stairs. He hadn't seen me yet, so I moved across the hall, hiding against a doorway to gain a better angle. I closed one eye and shot him straight in the head, suddenly wishing I had a silencer on my gun so that they wouldn't hear where I was.

Shifting my bag over my shoulder, I made my way quickly up to the next flight of stairs. If there were guys here then I needed to follow them to lead me to Anna. Another guy turned and leant out of the doorway, firing off a few rounds at me.

I pressed back around the corner, letting him shoot off a couple of shots as I grabbed my extra clip from my pocket. When his shots paused, I leant around the corner, shooting off a couple of rounds before changing my clip quickly but dropping the dead one on the floor on purpose. "Shit," I mumbled loud enough for him to hear. My plan worked. He stepped out of his little hiding place, obviously thinking I was having trouble reloading and that he could take advantage of it. As soon as he stepped out of this cover, I shot him twice, going for the kill shot. I didn't care about any of these guys; they were a threat to Anna so they needed to die.

Okay, Taylor, keep going. Four down, probably loads more to go!

As I pressed on up the hallway, Elliot's walkie-talkie crackled to life on my belt. "I don't know where they are, there must be more than one guy. Elliot and Tanner are dead, and I've heard a lot more shots since then."

I smiled; I could definitely use that to my advantage if they thought there was more than one of me.

I stopped when I heard whispering around the corner. Pressing myself against the wall, I reached into my shoulder bag and pulled out the little mirror I'd brought from my SWAT kit. I positioned it so I could look around the corner to see who was there. There were two guys talking in whispers, looking around desperately; one of them was running his hand through his hair nervously. Both were armed, but from the way their guns were hanging loosely at their sides, I knew that they had no idea how close to me they were. I shifted and dropped to one knee as I rounded the corner, shooting them both dead instantly.

I was on the move again. Further up the hall there was a large, expansive room. My eyes widened as I peeked around the corner, checking it was empty. *Shit, this isn't going to be an easy room to cross!* There were desks everywhere, giving so many places for people to hide. I frowned and looked at the door on the opposite side, knowing I needed to get to the stairs on the other side. This side of the building was now clear, so she had to be somewhere over there. *How the hell am I going to cross this room on my own?*

There was no possible way I could cover all of my hotspots and my back would be exposed. But there was no other choice.

I reloaded my gun and stepped tentatively into the room. Silently, I berated myself for not calling for backup. I knew I didn't have time to wait for them, but I should have at least sent someone a message to let them know where I was. I still would have had to move in on my own, but at least they would be aware of her whereabouts if I'd sent that message. If I died right now, they would have no idea. Clearly I had let my emotions get the better of me. I made a mental note to send a message to one of the agents as soon as I made it across the room.

There was a rustle of movement to my right. I flicked around too late, and a guy smashed my gun out of my hand, breaking one of my fingers at the same time. Before I knew it, there was movement from all sides; I knew I needed to move quickly.

I lunged forward and punched one of them in the throat; I gripped his hair and smashed his face into my knee, knocking him unconscious. Before he even hit the floor, another guy stepped out, pointing a gun at me. I grabbed my knife from my waistband and threw it into his chest. I turned to my right, readying myself as another one stepped forward. I knew that move would leave my back exposed, but I had no choice. I punched him in the face, gripped the back of his head and crashed it against one of the desks, just as another guy came from behind and hit me on the back of the head with something hard, knocking me out cold. I didn't even have time to feel it before I was unconscious.

Chapter Forty-Eight

~ Anna ~

I had no idea how long I had been slumped on the floor – it felt like days, but it was probably only a few hours. I sat there motionless as Jimmy came back, carrying a pre-packed sandwich and bottle of water, putting them next to the unopened one he'd brought me in earlier.

He looked at me apologetically. "I'm sorry, Anna, I am, but I had to. I don't have a choice," he explained, frowning. I nodded and turned away from him. I couldn't look at him because I knew I would cry again, and I needed to be strong now.

"I need the bathroom," I muttered, defeated.

"Okay, come on then." He took my arm, holding me tightly as he pulled me to my feet.

As soon as we stepped foot outside of the room I was being held captive in, I elbowed him in the face and ran as fast as I could. I had no idea where I was going as I stumbled along, opening doors at random, hoping to find fire escape or maybe a weapon I could use or something. As I rounded a corner, I ran smack into a beefy guy who wrapped his arms around me. I looked up into Mark's sneering face. My heart sped up as my mouth popped open in shock. Mark featured in my nightmares a lot of the time. He was Carter's right-hand man and second in charge. He was probably the one that had been running the organisation while Carter was locked up.

I struggled and thrashed, but he was holding my arms too tightly for me to get away. A muscle in his jaw twitched as he looked down at me distastefully. One of his hands wrapped around my arm with bruising force as he whipped back his other hand and slapped me hard across the face. His grip on my arm was the only thing from keeping me from flying to the ground. My whole face exploded in pain and little lights danced in front of my eyes, making me feel dizzy and disorientated.

"Stop struggling or I'll have to tie you up, and that would be uncomfortable. Carter said we needed to keep you comfortable," he spat, sneering at me angrily. He'd never understood Carter's fascination with me; he'd always looked at me like I was a piece of trash – but only when Carter wasn't there, he wouldn't dare do it in front of him.

A tear escaped, and I fought to keep them away as I stopped my useless efforts to escape. The best I could hope for now was death, but I knew that wouldn't be happening anytime soon. Maybe if I could piss Carter off enough, he'd kill me. Maybe he'd even kill me by accident, beating me for letting Ashton kiss and touch me. Mark led me to the bathroom and stood there watching while I went, which was humiliating to say the least. When I was done, he pushed me roughly towards Jimmy, so I tripped and fell into his arms. Jimmy looked annoyed as he put me back in the room and was wiping at his split lip with the sleeve of his shirt.

"Please let me go," I begged, falling to my knees in front of him, gripping his jeans. "I'll do anything you want." I hated myself for it, but I would do anything not to have to go through what I went through last time.

"Just a couple more hours and then he'll be here," he replied emotionless, pulling his leg out of my grasp and turning for the door. He slammed it shut behind him, making it rattle on its hinges from the force of it. Clearly, with that one little attempt to escape, I'd just lost all hope of Jimmy being nice to me and trying to help me like he used to. I slumped down to the floor and rolled to my side, curling into a ball, waiting for my nightmare to begin all over again.

After what seemed like forever, but could have been five minutes, I heard shouting from outside the door, followed quickly by gunshots. My head snapped up as my mouth dropped open in shock. *Gunshots. Oh my God, the police have come for me! Oh thank you, thank you!*

I jumped up and moved away from the door as I heard more shouting. Apparently someone was in the building; they were talking heatedly about repositioning or something.

I smiled hopefully. *Please, come on, please!* More gunshots. I pressed against the wall, waiting and waiting. My eyes were focussed on the door expectantly. Any second now, a couple of secret service agents would burst through. I chewed on my lip excitedly. I'd never complain about having guards again.

Nothing happened for ages. I was starting to lose hope because I couldn't hear anymore shooting. Had it been a mistake? Had they searched the building but not been able to find me? Had they left? Or maybe Carter's men had won and had killed yet more agents, more people could be dead because of me. Suddenly, the door burst open. I looked up, startled, seeing

470

two of Carter's men dragging someone into the room. The guy was clearly unconscious and his feet dragged on the floor.

My heart stopped as I took in who it was they were dragging. *No! Oh God, please no!*

I ran over as they dropped his lifeless body into a heap on the floor. "Call an ambulance! Jimmy, call someone! No, Ashton! Jimmy, help him please?" I begged, the tears flowing again now.

"He's not dead, Anna. They had to knock him out. He killed seven guys. He's gonna wish he was dead by the time Carter gets here," Jimmy replied, shaking his head grimly and walking out of the room.

I ran to the door. "Jimmy, please! Help him, please!" I screamed, banging on the door until my fists hurt. I ran back to an unconscious Ashton. Blood covered his face, his hands were red and bruised and a gash on the back of his head was slowly leaking blood onto the floor. I pressed my shirt on it to stop the bleeding; it didn't look too bad, but he probably needed stitches. A sick sense of foreboding and history repeating itself washed over me. I closed my eyes, horrified.

This was just like in my dream. The broken, bloodied face that I never wanted to see was now cradled in my lap.

"Ashton, please wake up, please," I begged, wiping some of the blood from his beautiful face. This was exactly the thing I couldn't have happen! I couldn't watch someone else that I loved die right in front of me because of me. "You stupid, stupid, adorable boy! Please wake up, please." I cradled his head on my lap, rocking him gently as my heart broke all over again.

After a while he opened his eyes slowly, groaning, looking around groggily. My heart sped up. "Ashton, are you okay? Oh God, what the hell are you doing here? Why did you come?" I cried, bending and kissing every inch of his face.

He seemed confused for a split second before understanding shot across his face. He immediately jumped up, wincing as he did so, and pulled me to my feet. He pushed me against the wall, pressing his back against my chest, protecting me whilst he patted his pockets.

"Stop it! There's no one here," I croaked, gripping his hand. He turned to face me. I could see the pain in his eyes, but he was trying to keep it from me. I lifted his shirt, and I could see ugly, purple marks all over his stomach, making bile rise in my throat.

"Anna, are you okay? Baby Girl, please say you're okay," he begged, pulling me to him and wrapping his arms around me tightly.

I closed my eyes as his smell filled my lungs. The familiar scent that was purely Ashton Taylor and no one else. I loved and missed that smell so much. "I'm okay. But why the hell did you come here? Ashton, I can't see this, I can't! This is the only thing I can't cope with. I sent you away so this wouldn't happen! Why did you do this to me?" I sobbed. My legs wobbled and finally gave way, so I slumped down against the wall, pulling my knees up to my chest and hugging them tightly. Carter was going to come in and have him beaten to death in front of me, and there would be nothing I could do about it but see it every time I closed my eyes.

Ashton slid down the wall next to me, trying to hide his grimace of pain. "I couldn't leave you, Anna, I had to try. I'm so sorry I couldn't protect you," he muttered, gripping his hair roughly. I could see he was trying not to cry, and it broke my heart; he never even got sad, let alone cried.

I moved and wrapped my arms around him tightly. "Please don't. Everything's going to be fine, we just need to think of a plan," I lied, knowing it was hopeless. I jumped up and ran to the door. "Jimmy, please! Talk to me please?" I begged, kicking the door in frustration.

"Anna, just settle down. Carter's just called, he's not too far away now, it won't be too much longer," he answered.

"Jimmy, you know who my father is, I could get a pardon for you. I'll tell him all the things you used to do for me. Or, I have money, I could give you money, please," I begged, pressing my forehead against the door.

"Anna, I can't, I'm sorry."

"Just get my bodyguard out of here then. He'll give you money. Please just sneak him out and say he escaped, please?" I screamed desperately. I needed Ashton out of here before Carter arrived, I couldn't bear to think of the alternative.

"Shh! He's here, Anna," Jimmy hissed, and I heard him walk away from the door.

Before I even had a chance to register what Jimmy had said, Ashton grabbed me and pushed me against the wall, pressing against me, hard. "Just stay behind me. Everything's going to be okay," he stated, obviously trying to reassure me with words, but I knew him to well, he had no hope in his voice at all.

"No, it won't. I'm just going to pray that he kills you quickly," I muttered hopelessly as the door opened.

Chapter Forty-Nine

The man who haunted my dreams walked into the room. I whimpered and pressed into Ashton's back, trying to disappear. My eyes raked over him, seeing that he looked exactly the same as I remembered him, although he had a few grey flecks in his brown hair now. Mark, Jimmy, and two other guys walked into the room behind him. I hated the fact that Mark was here. I had seen him torture people for hours before he killed them; he was going to torture Ashton, I just knew it. A sob rose in my throat, but I swallowed it back down. I couldn't cry, crying was weakness to Carter.

"Well, this is the guy, is it? The one who killed seven of my men?" Carter asked, sneering at Ashton. The sound of his voice made me whimper and clutch Ashton's shirt for dear life. It was just as I remembered and still made my blood turn cold in my veins and a shiver run down my spine.

Mark nodded in confirmation. "Yeah, I found some SWAT credentials on him. Agent Ashton Taylor, but then, we already knew his name," he stated, holding out Ashton's wallet to Carter.

Carter cocked his head to the side, his eyes raking over Ashton slowly from head to toe. "Agent Taylor. Well, I guess that saves me some time, now I don't have to come and look for you in LA. But why are you here all alone? I thought you'd been reassigned," Carter asked, raising one eyebrow curiously.

My breathing hitched as my eyes widened. They knew Ashton lived in LA and had planned on moving on him? Please let me get him out of here! "He's my bodyguard, Carter," I said, quickly stepping out from behind Ashton. Before I could get more than a step away from him, Ashton grabbed my wrist and jerked me back behind him.

"Stay behind me!" he ordered harshly.

I saw Carter nod, and almost immediately Mark punched Ashton in the stomach, making him double over with pain. I screamed, but he still didn't let go of me, he held me behind him protectively.

I can't watch this again, I just can't. I pushed Ashton, making him lose his balance and fall to the floor. I ripped my wrist from his hold and punched Mark as hard as I could in the face, looking at him challengingly. *Come on, asshole, hit me back! Come on, do it!* He spat blood onto the floor and whipped back his hand, slapping me hard across the face. My eyes rolled in their sockets as pain exploded in my head, making my eyes water.

In an instant there was a gun to Mark's head. "You touch her again and I swear, not only will I kill you, but I will kill your whole family," Carter growled menacingly at him.

And here was my chance. "Kill him, Carter. Please, baby, he really hurt me," I pouted, holding my face. *Please kill him; I can't have Mark hurt Ashton! Please.*

"You want me to kill him? Are you getting sadistic, Princess?" Carter asked, looking me over for the first time since he entered the room.

"That's not the first time he's hit me today." I raised my chin, pouting and trying to look wounded.

A look of hatred went across his face and his eyes flashed with rage. The shot rang out loud in the room. Blood splashed across my face. Mark slumped to the floor, dead. I watched, emotionless. All I could think of was: at least Mark won't be able to torture Ashton now.

"Come here, Princess," Carter instructed, smiling at me warmly. Without hesitation, I stepped over Mark's dead body, but Ashton was back on his feet. He grabbed me, throwing me behind him protectively, slamming me against the wall.

"You don't fucking touch her!" he spat at Carter, looking so angry that I was slightly surprised that Carter wasn't dead already from the force of the hatred coming from Ashton.

Carter's jaw tensed, his eyes locked on Ashton's in some kind of battle of the stares. "I appreciate you looking after my wife for me while I was away, Agent, but I'm back now, I can take care of her," he replied calmly.

Ashton's body tensed against mine. "Wife… but…"

When he looked back at me with wide, shocked eyes, silently asking if that was true, I pressed my lips into a thin line and nodded in confirmation. I couldn't deny it while Carter was there. I couldn't explain that I didn't want it, that it was forced upon me, that it repulsed me to the very core. Ashton's jaw tightened as his eyes shone with sympathy.

"Yes, wife," Carter confirmed harshly. His gaze flicked to me, his eyes hard and warning. I knew that look, and it was always one I didn't dare ignore. "Come here, Princess," he repeated.

I went to move, but Ashton wouldn't let go of me. Carter raised his gun, aiming it directly at Ashton's face. My world stopped spinning. This was it, he was going to die. He was going to be murdered right in front of me. I loved him so much that I would die for him; actually, I loved him so much I would *live* for him. Death was easy compared to Carter. If Ashton died it was going to kill me inside, and that would be worse than death. I couldn't go through that, not again. I loved Ashton so much, more than anything and everything. He was my life, he was my soul mate. I couldn't allow this to happen.

"Please don't, Carter, for me. Please, baby, I'm begging you, please." I tried desperately not to cry as I struggled against Ashton's hold. His gaze flicked to me, a little shocked expression on his face. He was begging me with his eyes to stay with him, to stay behind him. I shook my head. "Carter, please. I'll do anything you want, anything. Just don't hurt him. I can't see any other people die because of me, please?" Ashton still wouldn't let go of my wrist, so I elbowed him in the ribs where he had the bruises. He grunted in pain. It hurt my insides to know that I had caused him pain, but it worked to my advantage, just like I thought. His hold loosened for a fraction of a second and I scooted away just out of his reach, towards Carter.

"No, Anna!" he screamed, trying to grab me, but I was too quick.

Four guns all pointed in his face, making him stop in his tracks. He was looking at me, pleading with me to go back to him, but I couldn't. I needed to try; I needed to make him safe if I could. I put my hand on Carter's gun and pushed it away so it wasn't pointing at Ashton anymore.

"Please don't hurt him, baby," I pleaded, looking right into his brown eyes. I pushed away all my fear and hatred. I didn't care what he did to me, but Ashton had to live. I stepped forward slowly towards Carter. "Please," I whispered as I got right in front of him. I ran my hands up his chest, making him shiver. Lust crossed his face and I fought with every nerve in my body not to flinch. "Please don't hurt him."

He sighed deeply. "Tell me why not then, Princess," he suggested, lowering his gun and trailing his fingers across my face.

Oh shit, what the hell can I say? "I've seen too many agents be killed because of me today. Plus, I… I know his girlfriend. I like her. She really loves him, Carter, he's everything to her. He's all she has in the world. He's all she lives for. Please don't hurt him. She needs him," I begged, putting my arms around his neck. He looked at Ashton. I didn't move, I couldn't look back at him, I knew what I'd see: shock, love, horror and hurt. Carter regarded Ashton with indecision clear across his face. I could see how much he wanted to kill him for putting his hands on me, but he also didn't want to do it because I was begging him. He always had liked to try and give me everything that I asked for. "For me? Don't take him away from her. Just let him go home. I'm here now, we're together. No one else needs to die because of me." I smiled – at least, I *hoped* I was smiling, it felt more like a grimace. Carter rolled his eyes, and his face softened. My heart took off in a sprint knowing that he'd conceded.

Carter dipped his head slowly, and I held my breath, knowing what was coming. When his lips pressed against mine, I whimpered and fought the urge to recoil and gag. His arms snaked around my waist, crushing me against him. He moaned in the back of his throat and finally pulled away, his eyes shining with excitement.

"I've missed you, Princess," he purred, kissing down my neck. I swallowed my sobs and squeezed my eyes shut. I heard Ashton groan.

"I've missed you too, Carter," I mumbled.

My scalp suddenly burned as Carter gripped the back of my hair roughly, pulling my head back so I had to look up at him. "Don't mumble, Princess, you know I don't like that," he growled, pulling hard on my hair, making me grit my teeth against the pain that was shooting through my scalp.

"I've missed you too, Carter," I repeated, louder this time.

"Good girl." He smiled before setting a soft kiss on my cheek.

"Keep your fucking hands off her!" Ashton growled, trying to step forward as he reached for me.

One of the men that had entered with Carter smashed his gun into the side of Ashton's face, hard, sending him to the floor with blood pouring from his mouth. Carter ignored him. I glared at Ashton, begging him silently to be quiet. He shook his head at me as he spat a mouthful of blood onto the floor. I didn't dare move. I needed him to be safe, I would do whatever it took, but he needed to help me by being quiet. Carter was going to let him go, and that was all I needed.

"Princess," Carter murmured, running his hands down my body, squeezing my ass as he moaned in the back of his throat. "You are so fucking hot. I hope you got plenty of sleep last night because I've missed you so much, I don't think you'll be getting any tonight, Mrs Thomas," he purred lustfully. Vomit rose in my throat as a cold shudder trickled down my spine. Carter didn't seem to notice my reaction though as he used the sleeve of his expensive white shirt to wipe the side of my face. "So beautiful," he whispered, smiling at me proudly.

Behind me, I could hear Ashton pushing himself up. Carter's eyes flicked over my shoulder and he cocked his head to the side. "Right then, what shall we do about him?" he pondered, nodding at Ashton.

"I thought you were going to let him go," I mumbled. Had I not convinced him enough? Had I not made my case strongly enough? Knowing I needed to do everything in my power, I stepped closer to Carter and gripped my hand around the back of his head, guiding his mouth to mine as I went up onto tiptoes. He responded immediately, kissing me fiercely, taking control. The kiss was just like I remembered, rough and demanding.

Finally, he pulled away and put his forehead to mine. His brown eyes danced with excitement and joy. "Fucking hell, Princess, I forgot how much I loved you." He smiled, running his hands through my hair. "Tell me you love me," he ordered.

"I love you," I replied, instantly. It was a natural response to the order, although every single syllable left me feeling dirty and used.

476

He sighed contentedly, his hand cupping the side of my face, caressing it gently with his thumb. He nodded and pulled away, a playful smile on his face. "Okay, here's what we'll do; we'll play Russian roulette. We'll each do a shot, the three of us, and if he's still alive then he can go free," he offered, grinning happily.

I started to shake, I hated this game. This game was the reason that guns terrified me.

Wait, is he actually going to give me a gun? If he gives me a gun, I'm going to kill him with it! I felt the smile tugging at the corners of my mouth, and I fought to keep my composure so that he wouldn't know what I was thinking. I nodded eagerly, and he smiled at me curiously.

"Are you over your gun phobia now, Princess?" he asked.

I shook my head in response. "No. Guns still scare the hell out of me, but I really want him to go free. I'll do anything. I'll take his shot as well as mine," I offered, holding my hand out for the gun.

"No, you fucking will not, Anna!" Ashton cried, stepping forward. One of the other men shoved him against the wall, punching him repeatedly in the stomach and chest. The sound of Ashton in pain would haunt me forever.

"Stop it! Please, stop it!" I screamed, clinging to Carter's shirt, almost shaking him in desperation.

Carter laughed quietly. "Richard, stop, we have a game to play," he chirped excitedly. The guy stopped hitting him and stepped back.

Ashton pushed himself painfully back to his feet. "Anna, don't," he begged, barely able to talk. I turned away from his face. I couldn't look at him anymore; he was breaking my heart. He'd only just fixed it and now he was breaking it again. Worse this time, nothing could ever fix me; I would never get over him because he was everything that was good in my world.

I watched Carter take out all of the bullets and put one back in; the whole time a grin was stretched across his face. "Now, I don't think I want to give a SWAT Agent a gun so I'll pull yours for you," he said to Ashton, who actually didn't look frightened, just extremely pissed off and murderously angry.

I couldn't allow that to happen, I couldn't take the chance of the bullet being in the chamber when the gun went off. "No! Point it at me, I'll take his one too," I insisted. A lone tear rolled down my cheek as I reached for Carter's hand, trying to pull the gun in my direction.

Carter scoffed. "Princess, that's not how the game is played, you know that, you've played before," he stated sternly, raising his gun to Ashton, whilst holding me back with his other hand. Panic surged through me and I grabbed for his arm again. He shifted and rewarded me with another slap to my already sore face. I yelped and slammed against the wall, putting my hands out for balance to stop me from falling to the floor.

"I'm going to kill you!" Ashton growled through his teeth. "I swear to God, I'm going to rip you to fucking shreds with my bare hands."

Carter chose to ignore him and didn't respond. The gun was pointed directly at Ashton's face. "Carter! At least aim for his leg or something! Please, I don't want anyone else to die today. Please?" I begged.

My heart was in my throat as Carter's finger squeezed the trigger. I flinched, waiting for the loud bang, waiting for the sound of Ashton's agonising cry of pain as the bullet ripped through his flesh, waiting for the sound of his body hitting the floor.

But nothing happened. It just clicked.

Unable to hold my nerve anymore, I turned to the side and vomited violently. Carter laughed wickedly, gripping my arm and pulling me to my feet while I continued to dry heave. "Nope, not over your gun phobia. You threw up last time we played too, you remember that? Best night of my life," he cooed, looking right into my eyes. I was barely able to stop myself from punching him in the face; I just needed to get Ashton out first. "You remember that night, right?" he repeated, slipping his hand down to my ass and pulling my body flush against his. I nodded and closed my eyes, willing myself not to remember the night that he first forced himself on me and took my innocence. My whole body was shaking, my breathing was coming in gasps, and my heart was beating too fast. I closed my eyes, fighting for control of my emotions so that I didn't switch off and go into meltdown – that wouldn't help Ashton survive.

When I opened my eyes, I saw that Carter was looking at me, clearly amused. He wiped my mouth roughly, laughing before bending and planting a kiss on the corner of my mouth. "Your turn now, Princess," he instructed, waggling his eyebrows at me. He turned the gun in his hand so he held out the handle to me. I looked at it hesitantly, unsure if I would be able to do what I had planned. I took a deep breath before raising a shaky hand and taking the gun from his grasp. "That's a good girl. All you need to do is pull the trigger." He smiled and pushed the gun so it was pointing under my chin. I closed my eyes, taking a couple of deep breaths. When I opened them, I looked straight at Ashton. I nodded, hoping that he would get ready and know what I was planning.

I took one last deep breath before I whipped my arm down, aiming at Carter's chest and pulled the trigger again and again, counting them as they went through the chamber. Ashton had one click, and this was probably only a six shooter gun.

Click

Click

Click

Click.

Okay, it's the next one! I braced myself for the slight recoil of the gun. I pulled the trigger again.

Click

Nothing happened. I pulled again and again, still nothing. Ashton groaned. *What? No! Why didn't it go off?*

Carter burst out laughing and took the gun out of my trembling hand. "As if I would give you a loaded gun, Princess. You'd probably shoot your beautiful face off, then where would I be? Widowed at twenty-eight," he said, pulling me to him. "But I am pretty pissed off that you just tried to shoot me," he growled, pulling my hair back and slamming me into the wall.

Oh shit, this is it, Anna, fight or die.

I heard a gunshot go off. A real one this time, loud and horrifying. I heard a groan of pain, I snapped my head around quickly to see what had happened, and my world collapsed in on itself. Ashton was falling to the floor, blood seeping across the shoulder of his shirt. I screamed hysterically. He was dead. Ashton, the love of my life, my soul mate, the only thing I cared about, was dead.

Desperation and horror washed over me as Carter threw me to the floor. I wanted to stay there and curl into a ball and die, but I couldn't. Carter wouldn't let me die. I would have to live, knowing that Ashton was dead because of me, and I couldn't do that.

Either Carter was going to die or I was. I wouldn't live without Ashton. I pushed myself up off the floor and punched Carter hard in the face, catching him off-guard and sending him stumbling backwards. My foot shot out and landed a kick right in the middle of his chest which made him fall to his knees. While he groaned in pain, I took the advantage, grabbing the back of his hair and slamming his face into my knee with as much force as I could manage. I heard his nose snap and I smiled, throwing him to the floor, smiling as he writhed in agony. I kicked him in the groin and stomach, bringing my foot back again to kick him in the face, but he grabbed my foot, pulling hard so I fell onto my back, knocking the wind out of me.

"Shit," I gasped as I saw him getting to his feet.

I could vaguely hear sounds of a scuffle, a chair or table breaking, but all I could focus on was Carter. He was going to kill me, I could see it on his face, there was no going back this time; this was it. I rolled to my side, pushing myself up to all fours. As he went to kick me in the face, I put my hands up to shield myself and pushed his leg to the side, making him lose his balance slightly, allowing me time to get to my feet.

I smirked at his shocked expression; I'd never once tried to fight him back, well, not like this anyway. My meagre sixteen year old attempts at fighting him were pathetic because back then I'd known nothing, unlike now. "Yeah, I had lessons. I wanted to be able to kill you if I ever saw you again," I explained, shrugging.

I was actually enjoying this. My back was hurting like hell, but I ignored it as he came for me again, almost growling with rage. His hand shot out towards my hair, so I whipped my head out of the way and kicked him in the stomach. Stepping forward, I grabbed hold of his shirt, throwing my knee up as hard as I could into his stomach twice before he grabbed me and slammed me into the wall.

He pulled his arm back and I saw a flash of silver before pain like nothing I had ever felt in my life blasted through my stomach. It felt like a burning hot poker had been shoved into me. I grunted, gasping for breath as he pulled his arm back, sliding the knife back from my flesh before driving it back into my stomach again.

Using all of my might, I shoved him away from me, seeing the serrated edged flick knife he had in his hand. My blood dripped from the blade, landing in patters at his feet. I sucked in a ragged breath, leaning against the wall for support as my hand fumbled at my stomach, feeling my wet, soggy T-shirt.

I could taste the blood in my mouth and my whole body seemed like it now weighed a thousand pounds. My breathing was laboured as my lungs constricted because of the pain that was consuming me, crushing me, drowning me.

"Princess? I… Oh God, what have I done?" Carter gasped, stepping forward, his eyes wide and frantic. "Shit. I need to get you some help. You'll be fine, you'll be fine," he muttered, reaching down and pressing his hands over the wounds he'd inflicted, trying to staunch the blood flow. "I'm sorry, but you shouldn't have pushed me. You made me do this!" he ranted, shaking his head angrily. I wasn't sure if he was angry at himself for stabbing me, or angry at me because I'd 'made' him do it.

"I hate you, you sick son of a bitch. I never loved you. Just let me die!" I hissed, shoving his hands away from me with as much strength as I could manage.

He recoiled, his mouth popping open in shock. Clearly, in his sick, twisted, little mind, we loved each other and were the perfect couple. He didn't understand that he murdered my boyfriend, kidnapped me, raped me, beat me, starved me, and shattered my soul. He only saw what he wanted to see.

The pain in my stomach was blinding me. I was exhausted. I couldn't stand anymore; my legs wouldn't support my weight. I could barely breathe through the pain and the grief of seeing Ashton die. I slumped to the floor. Death was coming too slowly; I wanted it over with already. I knew just how to make Carter angry enough to end me quickly.

"That agent that everyone thinks was just undercover and an act, well, he wasn't. I love him. I'll always love him. You should just kill me now because I'll never stop fighting you, I'll never give in. I'll never conform. I'll never feel anything for you but hatred!" I spat.

"You ungrateful little bitch! Mark kept trying to tell me that it didn't look like a cover, but I refused to believe it," he growled. He stepped forward and I saw the resigned expression wash over his face as he finally realised that I would never be what he wanted me to be, we would never have what he wanted us to have.

"I hate you, you piece of shit!" I shouted, sneering at him. "Just kill me already!"

His eyes flashed with menace at my disrespect and he staggered forward, his lips pressed into a thin line as he twirled the knife in his hand. I fought a smile, knowing that death was coming for me now. For the last six and a half months that I'd known Ashton, I'd learned to live again. For those six and a half months, I didn't want to die. But he was gone now, and so was my reason for being.

I closed my eyes and thought of Ashton. His eyes, and the way his hair felt when I ran my fingers through it. I thought of the way he held me at night, his laugh, his smile, and the amused way he would look at me when I was behaving like a bitch to him. I remembered the way he kissed me, his taste, the way his smell made me feel, and how his voice sounded when he said he loved me. I smiled at the thoughts, and was thankful that the nightmare that I called a life was finally over.

A loud bang erupted out of nowhere. A gunshot, then another, and another, and another.

I waited for the pain, but it never came. My eyes fluttered open, seeing Carter's wide eyes. He coughed and blood gurgled out of his mouth. He slumped down onto his knees in front of me, and another shot filled the room. My breath caught in my throat as he fell, face first onto the floor, with a heavy thump.

He's dead? But he can't be dead; he was going to kill me! I looked up to see Ashton leaning against the wall, holding a gun out in front of him. His face was murderously angry. He was covered in blood and dirt, his T-shirt was ripped, and his body slightly hunched on one side as if he was nursing it. He looked like a hot freaking badass.

I couldn't speak. Confusion made my brain fuzzy. He was dead. I heard the shot. I saw him fall. He definitely died.

He pushed off the wall, leaving a trail of blood smeared there and limped over to me, practically falling down to my side. He looked like hell. His face was broken and swollen, there was blood everywhere and his white T-shirt was now almost entirely red, from where it was soaked with blood. His hands were swollen and grazed and he could barely breathe, but he was the most beautiful thing I had ever seen in my life.

My heart took off in overdrive. *He's alive? He didn't die? Or am I dead too? Maybe this is heaven…*

"You okay, Baby Girl?" he asked, taking my face in his battered hands.

"I… I… You… Ashton, you died. I heard it. You got shot, I saw you," I choked out.

"I'm okay, I promise. What about you?" he asked, touching my stomach worriedly.

I winced, gritting my teeth against the pain. He moved forward and wrapped his arms around me, holding me tightly. I wrapped my tired arms around him, noticing how he flinched as I touched him.

"Are you okay, Ashton?" I asked, touching his blood-soaked shirt. I pushed him away and moved the soggy, wet material away from his bicep, making him suck in a breath through the pain. I gagged as I saw the bullet wound on his upper arm, just before it met his shoulder. Blood was trickling out of it, running down his arm and dripping slowly from his fingers. I squirmed on the spot, thinking how painful it must be to have been shot. "Ashton, shit! We need to get you some help!" I cried, trying to get up. Pain coursed through my stomach and I screamed and slumped back to the floor in agony. It was so bad that I leant over and threw up again.

"Shh, stay still, Baby Girl. I'm okay, I promise. The bullet went straight through, no permanent damage done. I'll be fine," he assured me, kissing my forehead. "Don't move," he ordered, crawling over to Carter and searching through his pockets for something. He pulled back after a few seconds with a cell phone.

"This is Agent Taylor. I have the jewel. She's hurt, you need to send an ambulance, now! 4232 Western Ambrose. No, the threat has been neutralised. No, he's dead. They're all dead. Just get the medics here now!" he ordered.

They're all dead? How can they all be dead? I glanced over and saw five bodies on the floor in the room. Carter, Mark, the guy called Richard, Jimmy and the other guy that I didn't really know. Ashton had killed all three of them while I was fighting Carter? He got shot and still managed to kill three people? I smiled weakly because he was so skilled at his job. The pain in my lower body was starting to fade now, and I was grateful for that. The cold, hard floor made my teeth chatter, and my eyelids were getting heavier and heavier by the second. I decided just to sleep for a little while, just until the medics came, then that way I'd be able to stay with Ashton at the hospital when he had to stay there for his treatment.

"No Anna! Stay awake. I need you to talk to me," Ashton gasped, shaking my head.

"I'm tired," I whined, not opening my eyes.

"No! You need to stay awake, Anna. It's extremely important. Can you do that for me, Baby Girl? Can you stay awake for me?" he asked desperately.

I nodded. Of course I could. "I'd do anything for you, Ashton," I promised, forcing my eyes open to look at his broken face.

He smiled weakly. "I know you would, Baby Girl, I know." His arms slid under me, pulling me into his lap as he groaned in pain from his injuries. I hissed through my teeth as the pain doubled in my stomach and back. I forced my arms up around his neck so I could hug him back, but they were so damn heavy. "Stay awake, Anna," he rasped in my ear.

"You're so damn sexy, Ashton." I smiled weakly; even his painful voice was a turn-on.

He laughed at that statement. "So are you, Anna, so are you." He kissed my lips lightly. I moaned when I felt his soft lips on mine; I'd missed his kisses and his affection so much in the last seven weeks. I kissed him back with as much force as I could manage. He felt like home, like a safe, warm home, and I loved him so much.

When I opened my eyes from the kiss, it was so bright that I had to squint. I looked around, wanting to turn the light off, but I realised we were outside. I looked back at him as he sat down on the steps outside the building, resting his head against the wall, holding me tightly on his lap. He looked like he was in excruciating pain, his face deathly pale.

"How did we get outside?" I breathed, barely more than a whisper.

He smiled weakly, rubbing his hands over my face tenderly. "I carried you, Baby Girl. We just need to wait for the medics; it won't be long now. Just stay awake for me, okay?" he whispered, kissing my lips again. I was so tired that it was almost impossible to keep my eyes open, but I just couldn't look away from his face. I could barely respond to his kiss, even though I felt like it would kill me not to.

I pulled my mouth away from his, making him whimper, but I needed to tell him something, I needed to say it, he needed to know. "I love you, Ashton."

He grinned, his pained eyes shining with excitement and love. "I love you too, Anna." He pressed his lips to mine again in one of the sweetest, most tender kisses that I had ever felt in my life. With that one kiss, he showed me exactly how much he loved me, how much he cared for me and how much he had missed me. That one kiss was so special that it actually brought tears to my eyes because it was so beautiful.

I heard sirens in the distance, but all I could think of was the fact that everything was over and that we could be together. His kiss took away the pain in my lower abdomen.

"Agent Taylor, I need to take her," I heard someone say.

I squeezed my arms tighter around his neck. "No, I want to stay with you, please?" I begged, burying my face into his neck.

"It's okay, Baby Girl, I'll come with you. I won't ever leave you again, I promise. You're not getting rid of me that easily." He kissed my forehead and loosened my death grip that I had on his neck; he probably didn't even realise I was using all of my strength.

"Has she been shot?" I heard the same guy ask.

"No, stabbed. There's just so much blood and she says she's tired," Ashton answered, sounding incredibly worried.

I was moved onto a bed and the guy was looking at me, shining something into my eyes. "I'm fine," I assured him. "Help him, please, he was shot, please help him," I begged, trying to push his arms off me so he would help Ashton. The silly boy was worried more about me when he was the one that was shot; it was ridiculous.

The medic nodded. "We'll help him, ma'am, but right now I need to look at you."

I was vaguely aware of moving. I had a feeling I was in an ambulance. I could hear someone talking to Ashton, so I focussed on what he was saying. Was he finally getting treatment?

"I need to assess your injuries."

"I'm fine, honestly, I'll get checked out at the hospital," Ashton answered dismissively. I groaned and tried to sit up to tell him to just get looked at, but the medic pushed me back down again.

Another voice joined the conversation now too. "Agent Taylor, what happened?"

"There're twelve dead inside. Seven on the lower floors and five in a room on the top floor, on the east side I think, I lost my bearings a little. Carter Thomas is dead," Ashton growled, his voice sounded extremely exasperated, like he didn't want to be having this conversation right now.

Twelve dead? He'd killed twelve guys? Wow, my man is seriously good at his job!

"You went in without backup?" the guy asked, sounding shocked.

I turned my head, looking towards the back of the ambulance, trying to see Ashton. I just wanted to keep my eyes on him; I didn't want him too far away from me yet. I winced as an IV was inserted into my skin.

Ashton was frowning at a guy in a secret service suit, his eyes angry and annoyed. "Yes. Look, I need to go with her to the hospital with her. I'll answer anything you want there," Ashton snapped in reply. I heard him groan as he climbed into the ambulance behind me. I smiled weakly and closed my eyes. I could sleep now the ambulance was here, just for a couple of minutes. "No, Anna!" Ashton cried, grabbing my hand and squeezing it tightly.

I turned my head to look at him and smiled. He was just so perfect. "You know, even looking like you do now, you're still the hottest damn guy in the world," I mumbled.

He laughed quietly. "Thanks, Baby Girl, and you're still the most beautiful thing I've ever seen in my life, but you need to stay awake for me. Talk to me, help me keep my mind off my pain," he replied. I saw him look up at the medic; I flicked my eyes to him just in time to see him shake his head. Ashton's face fell and he dropped to his knees by the side of my head. "Please, Baby Girl, don't leave me. Don't you dare fall asleep, I need you," he croaked. Tears were falling down his face, washing some of the blood away.

"Don't cry, Pretty Boy, you're supposed to be a tough guy," I teased.

"Right, a tough guy, I forgot." He smiled, but it showed no happiness, only pain and worry. "Anna, please, I love you, I need you. Please be okay," he begged, kissing my forehead and smoothing my hair away from my face. I could feel tingles everywhere he touched, and my heart started to speed.

"I'll be alright, Ashton. Don't keep worrying about me. Ask him to look at you, you're hurt more than I am, tell him you got shot," I mumbled. *Why isn't the silly boy getting any treatment?*

He just smiled his heart-stopping smile at me. "Will you marry me, Anna?" he asked, looking into my eyes.

I looked up at him, shocked. Happiness made my heart start to race in my chest, which was pretty embarrassing with the monitor that I was attached to. I looked into his pleading eyes and smiled. I could see my whole future there, everything I wanted. Me and him – together forever. Maybe we'd have the little girl from that dream that I'd once had. Carter was dead so I was free now, I could marry Ashton. I wanted to be his wife more than anything in the world.

"I guess you're not too pretty for me now, huh?" I joked, raising my hand and wiping his blood and tears from his face, leaving a clean patch on his cheek.

He laughed and grinned. "I guess I'm not," he whispered, kissing my forehead lovingly.

I smiled happily. "Then I guess I can marry you," I agreed, gripping my hand into his hair and pulling him down for a kiss. I closed my eyes and kissed him with everything that I had, but when I tried to open my eyes again, I couldn't – they were just too heavy. I heard him shouting for me, screaming my name, panicked. I tried my hardest to answer, but I just needed to sleep now. I'd talk to him later. I felt my body relax as I finally gave into the blackness that I just couldn't fight anymore.

Chapter Fifty

~ Ashton ~

Panic. I didn't know what to do. The long, incessant beep of the heart monitor made my blood run cold. "Anna?" A sob rose in my throat. Her face was so still, her eyes closed. Her hand fell back to the bed with a soft thump. "Anna!" I cried, shaking her desperately. I jumped up and grabbed the medic roughly. "Do something! Don't just fucking stand there!" I screamed at him, shoving him towards her. I stepped back to give him room as my world crashed down around me. I gripped hold of my hair as he started trying to resuscitate her.

She'd lost too much blood; she was going to die. I was going to lose her, the love of my life, my perfect angel. I was losing her, and there was nothing I could do about it. The shrill, unbroken tone from the heart monitor was incredibly loud in the small space; the sound of it literally driving me insane as I just stood there barely able to breathe. She was killing me. She was literally ripping my heart out. This must be what it felt like to die.

The medic looked up at me with hopeless eyes as if trying to tell me that what he was doing was going to make no difference. I shook my head. I refused to allow him to give up. "You get her back or, so help me, I will throw you out of this fucking ambulance while it's still moving!" I growled angrily.

The medic jumped a little at my words and turned back to her, working her chest and squeezing air into her lungs. I watched with wide eyes, not knowing what to do, what to say or what to feel. I watched her face, willing her to take a breath, willing her heart not to give up on her, willing her to come back to me. I was more scared than I had ever been in my life.

After what felt like the longest time of my life, the medic moved back, looking a little shocked. "She has a pulse," he said breathlessly. They were the four most beautiful words in the English language. "It's weak, but it's there," he said, shaking his head. He looked a little scared of me, but I didn't care about that.

"Thank you, thank you, thank you!" I chanted over and over as we pulled into the hospital. As doctors ran out of the doors to meet us, I hung back, trying not to get in their way as I followed wearily behind them. All of my energy was gone. Now that the adrenaline from the fight was gone, I could finally feel the pain. It was burning through my chest and shoulder and my arm felt like it was made of concrete. Bolts of pain shot through my whole body every time I moved. One of the agents had followed behind the ambulance, so he slung my arm around his shoulder, helping me walk in, which I was grateful for. My legs felt like they would give out at any minute.

I followed her through the hallways but was told I wasn't allowed in the treatment room with her, so I slumped into a chair outside. I put my head in my hands, praying with my mind, body and soul for her to be alright. If we could just get through this, I could make her my wife and take care of her forever. I'd make her the happiest girl in the world, she deserved that.

"Let's go get you looked at," the agent suggested, nodding down the hallway and the emergency check in desk.

I shook my head. "I'm not leaving her."

"You'll just be down the hall," he encouraged, looking at me like I was stupid.

"Are you not fucking listening to me? I said I'm not leaving her!" I shouted, making him shrink back from the anger in my voice. He sat back down and didn't speak again. The pain in my upper body was excruciating, but I just didn't care, it didn't matter, the pain was insignificant when compared to the pain that I felt in my heart.

After about ten or fifteen minutes, I heard a commotion down the hallway. I looked up to see Anna's mother and father almost running towards me, surrounded by six secret service agents. They both looked grim so obviously they'd heard. I stood respectfully as they got to me.

"Agent Taylor, what the hell happened?" President Spencer cried as he gripped my hand tightly.

I gulped. "I followed a lead that turned out to be right. Carter was there, he stabbed her and she got banged up pretty badly. She's losing too much blood, I don't know if they can stop it," I rambled, all my words slurring into one where I spoke too quickly. My heart was breaking as I said the words out loud.

"Where is she now?"

"Treatment room. They've been in there for ten minutes working on her." I eyed the heavy-looking wooden door, watching for signs of news, but there was nothing.

"I was told Carter was killed, is that correct?" President Spencer inquired.

I nodded weakly. "Yeah, he's dead. She's safe now."

He seemed to breathe a sigh of relief as he nodded. "What were you doing there? You aren't assigned to her anymore. Why were you even there?"

I smiled weakly. "Sir, I love your daughter. I couldn't very well stand back and do nothing." I shrugged, immediately wishing I hadn't because the pain tripled. "I'm just sorry that I couldn't protect her. I couldn't even stop her being hurt. I'm so sorry," I croaked, looking down at the floor. I bowed my head. He could do what he wanted to me, it didn't matter anymore; all I cared about was in that room, fighting for her life. I was probably going to be in trouble for getting emotionally involved with my charge, but I couldn't care less.

"You mean, you and my daughter are really together?" he asked quietly, running a hand over the back of his neck.

I nodded. "Yes, sir. I love your daughter more than anything in the world. None of that matters though if she doesn't make it!" My legs gave out, and I slumped into the chair, putting my head in my hands as I squeezed my eyes shut.

Melissa scooted up next to me, wrapping her arm around my shoulder. "She'll make it. Annabelle is one of the strongest people I've ever met. She'll make it," she cooed.

I bit my lip, not believing a word of it. Anna was going to die, deep down I knew it, and there was nothing anyone could do about it. While we were all sitting there in silence, the door to Anna's room flew open and she was wheeled out on a gurney and rushed up the hall with four medical staff running along at her side. I gasped and jumped to my feet. "Where are they taking her?" I cried, shaking my head.

As I went to follow after her, a doctor stopped in front of us and held up his hands, smiling sadly. "Annabelle's had extensive blood loss. The knife didn't penetrate cleanly and has caused a lot of internal damage. The team are prepping her for surgery right now because she has some internal bleeding."

My heart sank at his words. Melissa burst into sobs next to me, and President Spencer stepped forward, confidently asking the question that I didn't dare ask because I wasn't sure I could handle the answer. "Will she be alright?"

The doctor's face was unreadable – probably from years of practice. "Honestly, it's touch-and-go at the moment, Mr President. She's lost so much blood that the surgery is going to be extremely dangerous, but we can't *not* do it. By all accounts, we almost lost her in the ambulance, but luckily she has a strong heart and the medic was able to resuscitate." He nodded behind him where Anna had been wheeled up the hallway. "I'd better go and scrub up, I'm assisting. As soon as there is any news, someone will be out to you. Please just wait here." Without another word he turned and dashed up the hallway. Wordlessly, we all sat back down, just waiting.

"Agent Taylor, have you had treatment? You look like death warmed up," President Spencer observed a few minutes later.

"I'm fine. I want to wait for Anna." My whole body hurt, but I wasn't leaving her again.

The agent that I'd walked in here with stepped forward, looking at the President. "He's refusing to leave here, sir. I've tried to get him to have some treatment but he won't."

President Spencer sucked in a breath through his teeth. "Go get a doctor, tell them to come now, they're needed," he ordered one of the agents.

I shook my head. "I'm fine, I just need to be here for Anna," I protested. They would have to drag me kicking and screaming away from here, there was no way I was walking away from her room of my own accord. He didn't say anything in response.

The doctor arrived a few minutes later. President Spencer nodded to me. "My daughter's boyfriend needs some treatment please, Doctor," he requested. My head snapped up to him at the words. Did that mean he was giving me permission to date his daughter? He wasn't going to have me shipped off to Antarctica or something?

"Okay, well, let's get you to a treatment room," the doctor suggested, holding out his arm to help me up.

I frowned. "I'm fine; I'm not going anywhere until I know she's okay." I flinched away from his hand.

"Doctor, please treat him here," the President stated.

"But we don't treat in the hallway," the doctor replied, frowning.

"Treat him here," President Spencer repeated sternly. The doctor hesitated for a few seconds, then nodded and walked off to fetch supplies.

I looked at President Spencer gratefully. "Thank you, sir."

He nodded. "That's okay, son. You really should go and get looked at properly, but for now, they can just check you over," he replied, nodding.

The doctor came back with a nurse and a little cart full of medical supplies; they pulled a chair slightly off to the side and motioned for me to come over. "Take your shirt off," he instructed, helping me to pull it over my head. I heard Melissa gasp behind me, and I grimaced apologetically, thinking of what I must look like.

"Sorry," I mumbled.

"You got shot?" the doctor asked, shaking his head. "I can't treat this here, I need to do x-rays and make sure everything's out. You could have shrapnel in there."

489

I sighed because this guy just didn't seem to want to give up. "Look, Doctor, it's all out, it didn't hit anything major I can tell. I also have a broken rib or two. Please just patch me up so I can go back to worrying about my girl. I'll get some proper treatment later," I snapped, frowning.

He sighed but nodded and started to clean my wounds. I needed stitches in the back of my head, and butterfly stitches across the bridge of my nose. "Okay, that's all I can do for now, do you have any cuts or anything on your legs?" he asked. I shook my head, I was pretty sure I had some bruises but no cuts. "But you're covered in blood," he protested, looking at my jeans.

"That's not mine," I answered quietly. That was Anna's blood from when I'd carried her out of the building.

He nodded apologetically. "Right, well, I'll order a chest x-ray and a scan for your bullet wound when you're ready."

"Thanks. You might want to go for a hand x-ray too, I think I've broken a couple of fingers," I admitted sheepishly.

"Right okay, a hand x-ray too then." He smiled weakly, scribbling on a pad.

The nurse handed me two pain killers so I swallowed them gratefully before moving to sit down outside Anna's room again. I didn't bother putting my shirt back on considering it was still wet with blood. I could see Anna's parents staring at my two week old tattoo on my chest, but they didn't say anything.

Melissa turned to the side. "Agent Franks, do you think you could get Ashton some clothes to change into?" she asked, smiling politely. He nodded and walked off, coming back a couple of minutes later with a surgical scrub set. I laughed humourlessly and quickly went to the bathrooms to change, washing my face at the same time. I was going to have wicked black eyes tomorrow – no wonder Anna thought I wasn't a pretty boy anymore. I smiled for a split second before my heart broke again at the thought of her saying she'd marry me. I wanted to be her husband more than anything; I'd never let her down or hurt her. I sighed and went back to the chairs outside her room.

After about two hours of working on her, the same doctor came back down the hall. He didn't look as tense as he had done earlier, and a spark of hope ignited inside me. My heart was beating erratically in my chest as I looked at him; waiting for them to say that words that would either make everything fine, or kill me. I felt like I was going to pass out.

The doctor came over to us, still in his scrubs. "Mr President, Mrs Spencer, your daughter has suffered immense bleeding, but we've managed to stop it at the source now. We had to remove part of her spleen, but she can cope without it. We've put her into an enforced coma to limit the damage and to give the site time to heal because we don't want to have to go in again, that would be too risky. The operation was a success, and we're very hopeful that she should make a full recovery, providing there are no post-operative complications," he said, smiling.

I breathed a sigh of relief and closed my eyes; she was going to be okay. I couldn't speak, I didn't know what to say, this man had just saved her life and mine.

Melissa burst into happy tears and President Spencer put his arm around her, smiling. "Thank you, Doctor, can we go in and see her?" he asked, rubbing his wife's back.

"We're just going to have her transferred to a different room, after that you can go in to see her for a few minutes. She'll be in the enforced coma for twenty-four hours to be on the safe side, and then we'll bring her out of it slowly tomorrow. It'll just give her body a chance to catch up," he replied, smiling and turning to walk off.

"Doctor?" I called, stepping forward; he turned back to me and smiled. I held out my hand and he shook it. "Thank you. Thank you so much," I said gratefully, feeling my heart start to slow down to a normal rhythm again. She was going to be fine; everything was going to be fine.

He smiled sadly. "You're welcome."

We sat and waited for a few more minutes while they cleaned her from surgery and then moved her to a private room in one of the wards. When we were allowed, the three of us, followed by the six secret service agents, followed the nurse to her room. As we entered, I stood back and let her parents approach the bed; he was still the President after all, not that it mattered either way, at the moment he just looked like a concerned father. They cooed and fussed around her bed, Melissa straightening the sheets and pillows, obviously not knowing what else to do.

Then President Spencer took hold of Melissa's hand. "Let's give Agent Taylor some privacy and go get a coffee or something," he suggested. She nodded and they started walking towards the door. As he walked past me, he patted me on the shoulder affectionately, making me swell with pride. I ignored the pain that blasted in my shoulder and neck. *I guess he really is okay with the idea of me and Anna dating. Either that or he's lulling me into a false sense of security so that he can plot an assassination without me being aware.* I smiled at my random thought.

Once they left the room, I walked to Anna's side and sat on the edge of her bed, just looking at her. She was covered in red blotches and bruises on her face and neck. I smiled sadly and traced my fingers across her face; it was red and puffy from where he had hit her. She had a large lump on her forehead where he'd slammed her against the wall.

"Hi, Baby Girl. You scared me for a while there. Don't ever do that to me again, you hear me?" I whispered, taking her hand and kissing it gently. "I love you, Anna. I love you so much, and I nearly lost you." My body started to calm down; now that I was near her, I wasn't as worried about her.

491

I sat there, just looking at her beautiful, bruised face until her parents came back in. I sniffed and moved to get off the bed to give them the space, but President Spencer shook his head. "No, it's fine, you stay there," he instructed, pulling over two chairs for him and his wife to sit in.

"Thank you, sir." I nodded gratefully.

"Do you really love my daughter?" he asked suddenly.

I smiled. "More than anything," I confirmed, rubbing my thumb over the back of her hand.

"And she loves you?" he inquired.

I nodded. "Yes, sir, she does," I said confidently. I would never doubt that after what she was willing to do for me, to go with Carter just to save my life. To sacrifice herself, her whole life, just to save me.

"Okay, well then I guess you should be calling me Tom," he suggested, smiling slyly. I looked over at him a little confused. "If you're going to be dating my daughter, then you should be able to call me Tom," he explained, shrugging.

"Actually, I was hoping to be marrying your daughter, I asked her in the ambulance and she said yes." I frowned as soon as I said it, knowing I'd just screwed up. I probably shouldn't have just announced it like that.

His eyes widened. "You want to get married?"

"Um, yes, sir. Though Anna's probably going to give me hell for coming out with it like that," I winced, thinking of the scolding she would give me for blurting it out to her parents, and while she was in a coma to top it off. *Great job, Ashton.*

He laughed. "That's okay, Agent Taylor, we knew you were serious about her when you refused to get treatment after getting shot. But I'm sure you're right, Annabelle's probably going to kick your ass," he teased, grinning and looking at his daughter lovingly. "Can I ask now though, why did she ask me to transfer you? Did you two have a fight or something?"

I sighed and shook my head. "We didn't have a fight. I think it was Anna's stupid way of protecting me. I couldn't understand it at first, but today she was so upset when I got there. She kept saying she couldn't watch it again. I think this is deep rooted issues from Jack, and she didn't want history to repeat itself." I looked down at her peaceful face. I knew it would have destroyed her to see me murdered just like Jack, and I'd almost put her through that.

The President sighed and shook his head, rubbing at his temples. "That sounds like Annabelle."

I nodded and shifted my weight on the bed, wincing because it felt like someone kicked me in the side. My whole body was aching now; I could barely think of anything else but the pain.

Melissa put her hand on my knee, squeezing affectionately. "Ashton, go and get your treatment now. She's not going to wake up; they've drugged her so she can't. You need to make yourself strong for her," she suggested, looking at me kindly.

492

I sighed. I knew she was right, but I didn't want to leave Anna, I didn't want her out of my sight. "Yeah, I guess," I nodded, and bent to kiss Anna's forehead. "I love you, Baby Girl. I won't be long," I whispered in her ear, before pushing myself up and forcing myself to walk out of the room.

It took over an hour for all of the necessary treatment. I had x-rays to check there was no remaining shrapnel in my arm, and a splint for my two broken fingers, some strapping for my three broken ribs, and some more painkillers. They changed the dressing on my gunshot wound and added some more permanent stitches once they'd confirmed there were no foreign bodies inside. Once I was done, I walked back into Anna's room and dragged another chair next to her bed so I could hold her hand.

I sat watching the rise and fall of her chest until one of the agents came in with a report pad. I sighed and looked regretfully at Anna. I didn't want to leave her, but they wanted my statement.

"You can do it here if you want, Agent Taylor," President Spencer offered, waving the agent in and pointing to a chair.

I smiled at him gratefully and went running through my statement. Everything that I saw heard or did from the point of hearing she was taken, to carrying her to the door. The only thing I left out was about her being married; she hadn't told anyone for almost four years, so she obviously didn't want it to be common knowledge.

When I'd finished, the President was staring at me in shock. "You took out twelve hostiles on your own?" he asked with wide eyes.

"Actually, eleven. Carter shot one himself," I corrected.

He shook his head, looking at me in awe. "You truly are a gifted agent. Annabelle was lucky to have you watching out for her, and the agency is darned lucky to have such a fine agent working for them," he stated. I smiled gratefully; the President of the United States had just given me a huge compliment.

"Thank you, sir."

"Tom," he corrected.

"Right sorry, sir, I forgot. I mean… Tom," I answered, stumbling over his name. It just doesn't roll off the tongue for someone like me, who had been taught for four years to respect authority, to call the President by his first name.

He laughed and shook his head, patting my knee. "You'll get used to it eventually."

"I hope so. I plan to be around a long time," I replied. "Well, as long as she'll have me for," I added, smiling and looking at her beautiful face.

"You're so good for her. From the moment you two met, we were all shocked at what she was like with you. You were holding hands and making her laugh and smile. It was so strange to see her smile after so long being

493

heartbroken. Thank you. I owe you a debt of gratitude," President Spencer said, smiling warmly at me.

"Sir," I started, then stopped and grinned sheepishly, "sorry, I mean, Tom. You don't owe me anything. I love your daughter. If anything, I should be thanking you for choosing me to guard her; otherwise I might not have met her." I bent my head and kissed the back of her hand, stroking my fingertips up her arm, just waiting for the time when she'd open her beautiful, brown eyes and my world would suddenly fall back into place again.

Chapter Fifty-One

That night was easily the most uncomfortable and pain-filled night I had ever spent. Every muscle in my body hurt, and I couldn't sit in the same position for more than ten minutes at a time. Thankfully, her father had insisted that I be allowed to stay with her – he told the doctors that it was guard duty, but everyone knew that it wasn't, so at least I got to sit in the chair in her room and hold her hand all night long. I had barely been able to take my eyes off her for more than a few minutes at a time. Bruises covered her arms, face, neck, shoulders, and I daren't even think about what her stomach and chest looked like, but she was still the most perfect thing I had ever seen in my life.

It was past four in the afternoon when they started to reduce the sedative that was in the IV so that she would start to wake. Her parents and I were all sat around the bed in silence, just waiting. Finally, her eyelids fluttered, and my heart leapt into my throat. President Spencer leant over and pressed the call button on the wall to alert the doctors of Anna's awakening.

"Anna?" I whispered.

She made a small groan and turned her head towards me. "Mmm, hi," she croaked, her voice raspy and sore-sounding.

Unable to resist, I bent over her and planted a soft kiss on the egg-shaped bump she had on her forehead. "Hi, Baby Girl. Are you feeling okay?"

"I have a stomach-ache," she moaned, moving her hand to her stomach.

I quickly grabbed her hand, stopping her from touching her stomach in case she hurt herself. "That's okay. They can give you something for it," I assured her.

"Who can?" Finally, her eyes fluttered open. "Holy shit, Ashton! What the hell happened to your face?" she cried, looking at me horrified. I winced, she was right, I did look a mess.

I placed my hand on Anna's shoulder, holding her in place as she tried to sit up. "Take it easy, Anna, I'm fine. Just stay lying down please, you'll hurt yourself," I instructed. Panic rose in my chest as I thought about her stitches breaking. The door opened and the doctor came in. I looked at them worriedly. "I don't think she remembers anything," I said, running my hand through my hair.

"Remember what? Ashton? What's happening? What happened to your face?" Anna cried, ignoring everyone else in the room and holding her hand out for me.

I sighed. "Anna, Carter found you, do you remember?" I asked, gripping her hand tightly.

She gasped and closed her eyes. "Oh God," she groaned, shaking her head as she obviously remembered. "Dean. Peter. They were all killed, they were all killed," she whispered.

I sat on the edge of her bed and bent over her so my face was only inches from hers. "I know, Baby Girl. But it's over now. I nearly lost you. Don't ever do that to me again, you hear me?" I rasped, dipping my head and capturing her lips in a soft kiss. She whimpered against my lips and her hand lifted, tangling into the back of my hair, holding my mouth to hers when I went to pull back. The kiss wasn't exactly the chaste, sweet kiss that I had intended it to be in front of her parents.

When the kiss broke, she winced and hesitantly touched my cheek. "Are you alright? You were shot! And your face."

"I'm alright. Stop worrying about me," I scolded, shaking my head disapprovingly.

"I can't. I never will," she answered, smiling at me tenderly.

The doctor cleared her throat to make her presence known. "Hi, Anna, how are you feeling?" she asked softly, taking hold of Anna's wrist and checking her pulse. I moved off the bed but Anna gripped my hand tightly as if she was frightened to let go.

"I'm fine. My stomach hurts, and my face is a bit sore," she told the doctor, her worried eyes still locked on me. "Did you have someone look at you, Ashton?"

I nodded in confirmation.

"Well, are you alright?" she queried.

"Anna, I'll talk to you in a bit, okay? Just let the doctor look at you, Baby Girl," I pleaded. She sighed and finally turned her head to look at the doctor.

"We had to operate to stop the bleeding. Your spleen was damaged too, so we had to remove part of it. You lost a lot of blood. It was touch-and-go for a bit, but the surgery went very well. You need to rest now, no sudden movements, just try to relax and let your body recover," the doctor explained, examining her stomach. Anna's eyes widened at the news, almost as if she hadn't realised she was that hurt. The doctor scribbled some notes on her chart. "Well, if you need me, I'll be doing my rounds. I'll get someone to come and give you something for the pain. If you get tired, Anna, sleep. And absolutely no getting out of bed," she instructed before heading out of the room.

Anna's parents cooed over her for a bit, hugging her carefully. Anna didn't let go of my hand the whole time, it was as if she was scared to in case I would run away or something. There was not much chance of that happening though, I wasn't going anywhere.

"Well, I think we should let you two have some time on your own. We'll come back after dinner to see you again, honey," Melissa said, kissing her daughter's cheek. President Spencer kissed her and shook my hand as he left the room.

Once we were on our own Anna turned to me and her eyes filled with tears. "Come lie with me," she whispered, trying to shift over for me but not really getting anywhere. I climbed on the bed, being careful not to show her that it hurt me to move, she didn't need to know that. I lay down next to her, and we looked into each other's eyes for a while before she spoke. "Are you really okay?" she asked, trailing her fingers over my face.

I nodded. "Yeah, Baby Girl. I have a couple of broken ribs and fingers, but other than that I'm fine." None of that mattered though while I was looking into her eyes.

She groaned. "Stop being such a badass, Ashton! You were shot for goodness' sake, don't pretend like it doesn't hurt," she scolded, rolling her eyes at me.

I smiled, trying not to laugh at her little outburst; I honestly did love it when she was all feisty like that. "Alright, alright, it hurts, is that what you want to hear?" I confirmed. "But I don't care as long as you're safe and here with me."

She smiled weakly. "You're so damn sweet, Pretty Boy," she whispered.

A tear slid down her face and I sighed, wiping it away gently. "Please don't cry. Everything's okay now, nothing's going to hurt you ever again."

"I don't know how to thank you," she muttered, finally losing control of her emotions and burying her face into my chest, sobbing.

I scoffed, stroking the back of her head. "Why on earth would you feel the need to thank me? Not only was it my job as your guard, it's also my job as the guy who's hopelessly in love with you."

She gripped my shirt tightly as if I was going to run away. "You were so brave. You saved me." Her body trembled so I held her tightly against me, waiting for her tears to subside. I didn't need her gratitude, but I wasn't going to say no to the hugs! "All those guards were killed. I can't think what their families are going through. Oh God," she mumbled, crying harder. My heart hurt because of how sad she was, and there was nothing I could do about it. She pulled back; her bloodshot watery eyes met mine. "Does it make me a horrible person that, deep down, I'm glad it was them and not you?" she croaked.

I sighed and shook my head slowly. "No, it doesn't," I assured her. I felt exactly the same. Of course, no one wanted anyone to die, but there would always be relief that it was someone else and not the one you loved. That was human nature. "Please don't start trying to take the blame for their deaths. Carter Thomas and his men did this, not you." I gritted my teeth when I said his name. The anger hadn't subsided an inch, even though he was already gone.

She sniffed, wiping her face on the back of her hand. "There was no warning, there were so many of them. If you were there, you would have been killed too," she muttered, clutching my shirt tightly. "I know I hurt you by sending you away, but I promise I was doing it for your own good. I didn't want you to get hurt. The only reason I made you leave was because I love you so much. I'm sorry. Please forgive me," she begged.

I cupped her face in my broken hands. "I understand why you did it, but you shouldn't have sent me away from you. We should have worked through it together." Her chin trembled as I spoke and her hand covered the back of mine on her cheek. "You don't need my forgiveness though. Everything worked out in the end; however we got there." I bent and kissed her lips. "But you don't ever send me away again, understand? Because I won't go. You're stuck with me now."

A smile twitched at the corner of her mouth as she nodded. "I won't."

"I love you, Annabelle Spencer." I stroked the side of her face, wishing I could make the marks fade.

"And I love you, Ashton Taylor," she whispered. I could see the love shining in her eyes, and hear the truth in her words. I just prayed that her feelings for me never diminished, because mine never would. She smiled and wriggled closer to me, wincing as she moved. I wrapped my arms gently around her and sighed happily. I wanted to ask her to marry me again, but I resisted the urge. I would do it properly this time, with a ring and a romantic setting. The last proposal wasn't exactly romantic – covered in blood in the back of an ambulance. I'd need to call Nate and get him to courier something over to me before I could do it though.

The knowledge that this girl was mine to keep made my heart soar in my chest. These last seven weeks had been the worst in my life without her, but having her in my arms again made up for all of that instantly. As long as I got to hold her in my arms every day, I would be the happiest guy in the world.

~ Anna ~

I ached all over. Even breathing hurt and the medication they were pumping me full of barely touched the pain. I felt as if I'd fought ten rounds in a boxing match. My stomach was hurting like I'd been trampled by a herd of elephants.

Ashton actually looked worse than I felt. His face was a mess. He had two black eyes, a cut with butterfly stitches over the bridge of his nose, a split lip and a swollen jaw. He smiled and leant in, planting a small kiss on my forehead. My heart stuttered in my chest, easily identifiable because I was still strapped up to the heart monitor, so a cocky, little smirk twitched at the corner of his lips. I didn't even feel ashamed or embarrassed by my body's reaction to his kisses.

A dreamy, contented sigh slipped out as my eyes met his. I could see how much he loved me by the tender way he was looking at me, and that knowledge made my insides squirm with happiness. How had I gotten so lucky to have someone like Ashton fall in love with me? He wanted to marry me. Well, he had asked me to in the ambulance, but he hadn't said anything about it again so maybe he was regretting the rash decision. If he was, I didn't even care, as long as he still wanted to be with me.

But I'd almost lost him. He could have died so easily in that room and I would have never gotten the chance to tell him how much he meant to me and how he'd changed my life. I would never be able to thank him enough for what he did for me. He'd refused to give up on me the whole time that I pushed him away.

"Ashton," I whispered, "I missed you so much these last few weeks."

"I've missed you too." He smiled his heart breaking smile and my insides melted.

My hand hesitantly caught the bottom of his T-shirt, easing it up slowly. I needed to see the damage that had been caused; I needed to see for myself that he was alright.

He chuckled wickedly. "Easy there, tiger. I don't think either of us will be able to do that much physical exercise this soon. Sex will have to wait a few days," he joked.

I laughed and nodded, deciding to play along. "Hmm, I guess you're right," I agreed. "But if you feel up for it, let me know," I added, smiling suggestively at him.

"I'm pretty sure you could get me up for it, Baby Girl," he teased, winking at me slyly.

I grinned, loving how he could make me feel better in an instant. My hand tugged on the T-shirt again, pulling it up so the bottom of his stomach was exposed.

"What are you actually doing, Anna?" he asked, putting his hand on top of mine.

I blew out a big breath, looking down at the small patch of exposed skin on his stomach. I could see the beginning of a bruise there that led up under the material; I knew this would be bad. "I need to see how badly you're hurt. I'm imagining all sorts of things," I muttered. "I just need to see for myself that you're okay, like you keep claiming." I wouldn't be able to rest easy without seeing it for myself. He frowned, seeming a little hesitant as his hand held mine still, not letting me remove his shirt. "Ashton Taylor, let me see," I ordered, moving his hand away, being careful of his broken fingers.

He sighed dramatically and rolled his eyes again. I lifted his T-shirt up. Every inch of his stomach and sides that wasn't covered in bandages and strapping was black and blue with bruises and little cuts. I gulped and swallowed my sob. This must be hurting him like crazy. I felt sick.

"I'm so sorry." I was trying desperately not to cry again.

His finger hooked under my chin, tilting my head up gently so that I had to look at him. "You don't need to apologise. I'm fine, I promise. It probably looks worse than it is, and anyway, I would die for you, so I got off pretty lightly." He smiled his sexy smile and wiped the tears from my face, looking at me pleadingly. I smiled weakly and pressed my lips to his gently, silently conveying through that kiss how much I loved him and appreciated him. Love and passion washed over my body, making my skin break out in goosebumps. He broke the kiss and smiled down at me sheepishly. "I have something to show you. I'm not actually sure how you're going to react to it." He actually looked a little nervous as he tongued his split lip.

I raised a questioning eyebrow. "Something, like what?"

"I got a tattoo," he stated.

I gasped, shocked by the revelation. Ashton Taylor didn't strike me as the tattoo-bearing type. "You did? Seriously? Where?" I was actually strangely excited about it. I wasn't actually a huge tattoo fan, but one on him would probably be sexy on a whole other level.

He pointed to his chest. "Right here, above my heart," he answered, looking at me intently.

"Can I see?"

He sucked in a breath through his teeth and then nodded uncomfortably. "I hope you like it. It just kind of belonged there, so I had it done a couple of weeks ago," he mumbled nervously. I nodded and looked at him expectantly. He sighed and gripped the bottom of his T-shirt in his broken hands, pulling it up to his throat. I gasped immediately at the sight of his damaged body. I forgot what I was supposed to be looking at for a few seconds, and then my eyes stopped on it. He had a tattoo on his chest, directly over his heart. An exquisite white rose in full bloom with one word underneath it written in beautiful, black script:

Annabelle

"You had my name tattooed over your heart?" I asked, shocked.

500

He nodded. "Yeah, that's where you belong."

I reached out and traced the letters with one finger. It was stunning. The artist had done an incredible job. The white of the rose and the black of my name contrasted shockingly well, and the whole thing placed against his tanned skin just made my whole body tingle. It was the sexiest thing I had ever seen. "But we weren't together when you had this done. I told you I didn't love you," I murmured.

He shrugged. "It didn't matter what you said, I loved you. I will always love you, nothing will ever change that." He took hold of my hand that was on his tattoo and pressed my palm over his heart. "That right there belongs to you, forever."

Happiness swelled inside me because of the sweet words that were coming out of his mouth. I bit on my lip as I looked at it again. A wave of desire for his body pulsed through me. "I love it," I whispered, looking at it in awe. My eyes flicked back up to his face, seeing a breathtaking smile. "It's so freaking hot, Ashton. I'm not kidding. If you hadn't just been shot and I hadn't just had surgery, I'd so be jumping you right now," I purred.

His body seemed to stiffen at my words. "I can take a rain-check on that, right? Like I can cash that jumping in as soon as we're better?"

I grinned, chuckling at the hopefulness in his voice. "Hell to the yes," I replied.

He cupped my face in his hands. "God, I love you, woman." He kissed my forehead.

"Woman? That had better be a joke," I scolded, laughing.

He laughed and ran his fingers through my hair, down my neck and over my shoulders before gripping my waist and pressing himself closer to me carefully. My whole being was just a mass of feelings, a big jumble of something I couldn't even describe because each individual emotion, feeling, and thought, was all tangled together into a big ball of passion. I longed to kiss every square inch of his chest, every bruise, every little cut or mark, to try and kiss the pain away, but my movement was limited.

Instead, we just lay there facing each other. We didn't speak, there was nothing to say and we both felt the same. After about ten minutes of just enjoying the closeness, he cleared his throat. "Can I talk to you about something?" he asked, looking slightly uncomfortable.

I nodded, raising an eyebrow curiously. "Yeah, sure."

"I don't want to upset you," he whispered, brushing his hand across my cheekbone.

I smiled at his sensitivity. "You won't upset me. What's wrong?"

He was absentmindedly drawing little patterns on the skin at the back of my neck. He closed his eyes for a couple of seconds, seeming to choose his words carefully. "You married him? Carter," he asked finally.

I drew in a shaky breath. *Okay, I wasn't expecting that!* "Not by choice," I whispered, praying that he wouldn't think badly of me. I didn't want to marry him, I didn't want anything.

He nodded sadly. "I know that, Baby Girl. I just wondered why you didn't tell me."

I winced. "I didn't tell anybody," I admitted.

"Nobody? You didn't tell your parents? All this time?" he asked, sounding a little shocked.

I shook my head. "No, I was ashamed; I didn't want anyone to know."

He kissed my nose gently. "You don't need to be ashamed. You never need to be ashamed because none of it was your fault," he said tenderly.

I smiled; he always knew just what to say to make me feel better. "I know. I guess it doesn't matter now," I shrugged, meaning the fact that he was dead and we weren't married anymore.

He was quiet for a little while. "How did you even get married at sixteen?" he asked curiously.

I sighed at the memory. "He took me to Vegas; we went through a drive-through chapel so I didn't have to speak to anyone. He used my fake ID that Jack had got me that said I was twenty-one," I explained, grimacing. I didn't want to think about it, or that fact that Carter couldn't wait until we got back to his house to consummate the marriage so he'd pulled over to rape me by the side of an old road in the back of the car.

"Vegas? When was that?" he asked, stroking my hair away from my face.

"September 16th, 2008." I bit my lip; that date was engrained in my memory.

He winced. "You'd been with him for six months."

"I'm sorry I didn't tell you, Ashton." I really was sorry, although I wished in a way that he had never found out; I could see this was hurting him.

"It's okay. I understand, honestly I do. I'm so sorry that all of this happened to you. I won't let anything bad happen to you again, I promise."

I smiled at his understanding, wondering again why on earth an incredible boy like him would want someone like me, who had so much baggage that I could barely carry it all. "The only thing that could hurt me now, Ashton, is you. I've given you the power to kill me and you don't even know it."

He laughed and laced his fingers through mine. "Then I guess you'll always be safe because I will never hurt you, not ever," he promised as he kissed me tenderly, making everything feel better in my world. He was so careful, always so gentle that it made my heart ache with love for him. I smiled and buried my head in his chest and felt a happy tear fall down my face. The reality that it really was over finally sank in, and I felt my tired muscles relax into his embrace. Everything was going to be fine from now on. Ashton loved me. The player had my name tattooed on his chest. He wanted me forever.

"I love you, Anna," he murmured into my hair.

"I love you more, Ashton."

I wrapped my arms around him and smiled against his neck, breathing him in. *Now* I was home. Lying in Ashton's arms was how I wanted to spend every waking hour for the rest of my life.

Chapter Fifty-Two

After a week of lying around in a hospital bed and being scolded by Ashton for overdoing it every hour of every day, I was finally discharged. The best thing about being discharged, as far as I could see, was that Ashton would finally get to sleep in a bed. He'd spent the week sleeping at my bedside in an uncomfortable chair because he didn't want to leave me. The silly boy was suffering for his chivalry too because every morning, I watched as he stretched his bunched muscles and winced. He'd refused to share the hospital bed with me because he was frightened he'd roll on me and tear my stitches. I was looking forward to tonight as he could finally sleep in a bed and relax. That wasn't happening at our apartment though; instead, we'd travelled to stay with my parents in Washington for a week at their request. Ashton had called his captain and had been signed off work for an extra week before he was expected to return to light duties, so the timing for being pampered by White House staff had worked out perfectly.

At dinnertime on our first night at the White House, I dressed in a plain, black T-shirt and baggy sweatpants. I'd become accustomed to wearing loose pants for the last week because I didn't want a pair of jeans to rub on my stomach and make me sore again. Ashton, on the other hand, looked incredibly handsome in a pair of perfectly faded denim jeans and a dark green shirt.

He held his hand out to me at the door; I gripped it tightly, loving the feel of his skin on mine. "I feel a little underdressed tonight. You look so damn hot, and I look like a bag lady," I admitted, scowling down at myself.

He sighed and hooked his finger under my chin, tilting my head up. "You're the most beautiful thing I've ever seen in my life," he promised, looking straight into my eyes. I smiled gratefully and, somehow, he managed to make all of my insecurities fade with that one intense look. His head dipped and his lips pressed against mine tenderly for a second before he took my hand and led me out of the room and down the hallway towards the dining room.

Instead of going in though, he stopped outside and looked down at me. He seemed a little nervous as he kicked his toes on the floor almost shyly. "Want to come for a walk with me before dinner?"

I frowned, confused. He'd been the one to agree to us eating with my parents tonight at eight o'clock, so why was he now suggesting a walk beforehand when he knew that would make us late? He never liked to be late, especially not if it meant keeping my dad waiting – he seemed to be making it his life's mission to gain my dad's approval.

"Um… sure, I guess," I agreed hesitantly. "Is something wrong?"

"It's a nice night, that's all. Just figured we could get some fresh air." He shook his head in answer, but he still looked like something was troubling him. His eyes were tighter than usual, his hand was gripping mine just slightly too tight to be natural. As he gave my hand a little tug and made me start walking again, I frowned at his back, letting him lead me along. Something was wrong. All day today he'd been a little distant and had kept walking out of the room to make phone calls. I'd put it down to the fact that we were travelling and so he was making arrangements with my guards and stuff. But was it more than that?

As we got to the side door, one of the staff opened the door and nodded in greeting. The cool air hit me in the face as we walked out of the house and down the steps. By day, the White House grounds were stunning, but by night they were spectacular. Little lights marked the edge of the path and illuminated the bushes and plants from underneath. The smell of the flowers was beautiful, almost as if it was artificial. Ashton walked along the path for a way before stepping over the little chain that lined the edge of it. He turned back to make sure I crossed it alright too. As he smiled, the stress on his face was easy to see. My insides clenched, wondering what on earth this was going to be about. I prayed with every bone in my body that he wasn't bringing me out here to break up with me.

"Is everything okay?" I asked, really anxious now.

"Of course," he replied immediately.

I swallowed the lump in my throat and looked in the direction that we seemed to be heading. "So, where are we going?"

He chuckled, squeezing my hand gently. "Damn, you hate surprises so much," he teased, shaking his head at me. *Surprises? What does that mean?* He sighed. "We're not having dinner with your parents tonight," he said quietly as we stopped next to a huge hedge.

I recoiled, shocked. He was the one who had agreed to it, he had even said how much he was looking forward to it.

His nervous smile widened as he stepped backwards, pulling me along with him around the corner of the hedge. My breathing faltered when I saw what he'd done. There was a picnic set up next to the large fountain that I knew was in the centre of the grounds. Little gas lanterns illuminated the scene, casting romantic shadows everywhere. I'd seen the fountain from my window last time I'd been here but had never bothered to venture out to it. It was incredible. Little cherubs and angels were all carved out of marble in the centre, and the water was lit from underneath, making it glow a pale blue.

Around the edges of the fountain stood bunches of a dozen white roses, probably about ten of them in total. There were rose petals scattered over the blanket and grass and it was a clear night, so all the stars were out. Everything was just perfect and incredibly romantic. Tears welled in my eyes because Ashton had gone to so much trouble, just for me.

"Ashton, this is beautiful! You expecting someone?" I joked, wiping the tear that fell from my eye.

He laughed and nodded towards the blanket that had cartons of food all laid out in the middle. "Sit down then, Baby Girl," he instructed as he picked up a couple of plastic glasses and poured some juice out for us.

"What's the occasion?" I asked, looking around at all the food that was here. Everything was my favourite: chicken; quiche; pasta; chocolate fudge cake; strawberries; peanut M&Ms; marshmallows and every other weird thing I liked.

He smiled. "No occasion, I just wanted to do something nice for you."

There was still something up with him, his body was still tense so it couldn't have just been the secret of the picnic that was troubling him. "But something's wrong, I can tell. Can you just please tell me? You're making me nervous." I bit my lip, silently pleading with my eyes for him just to blurt it out and get it over with.

He sighed deeply, shaking his head. "Damn it, woman, I wanted to wait until after we'd eaten," he scolded playfully.

I gulped, having no idea what he was talking about as he stood up and held his hand down to me. Hesitantly, I put my hand in his and pushed myself up awkwardly, wincing at the tug in my stomach as the wound protested against the movement.

When he shoved his hand in his pocket and then got down on one knee, my breath caught in my throat. The reason for his nervousness now hit me full force. It wasn't something bad, he wasn't going to break up with me and he hadn't been transferred to some random place and didn't want me to come. No, Ashton Taylor was about to propose to me again.

A little squeal left my lips as my free hand flew to my mouth, grinning behind my hand as he took a deep breath, clearly still nervous, and produced a little, black, leather ring box. He shifted awkwardly on his knee, obviously hurting himself because of his injuries, but it didn't show on his face as he looked up at me. I could see the love and tenderness in his eyes, and my insides trembled with happiness at the sight of it.

"Annabelle Spencer, I fell in love with you the very second I saw you. I would do anything for you; I'm going to love you until the day I die.

Please will you make me the luckiest man in the world and marry me?" he asked, his voice sounding thick with emotion.

My eyes were blurry with happy tears as his words sank in. "Yes," I managed to choke out.

His shoulders relaxed as his smile grew wider and his eyes twinkled with happiness. His hand left mine and he popped open the ring box, exposing the most beautiful ring I had ever seen in my life. "This was my mom's engagement ring. It's the only thing I have of hers. I'd love for you to have it, but if you'd rather me buy you something new instead, then I totally understand."

His mother's ring? I whimpered because of how special it was. Not only did I love it because it was a symbol of his love for me, I also loved it because he was giving me something that obviously meant a lot to him because he'd lost his mother so young. My heart swelled in my chest as my emotion threatened to bubble over and leave me a blubbering wreck.

"I love it," I whispered. And I did. It was the most beautiful ring I had ever seen, classy, not overstated, just perfect and something I would have chosen for myself. It was white gold, with three diamonds set into it – one bigger one in the centre and a smaller one either side.

"You do, honestly?"

I nodded, chewing on my lip, grinning down at him as I offered my shaky left hand to him. "It's perfect. I'd love to wear it. Thank you."

He grinned as he plucked the ring from the box before sliding it onto my finger. As he got to his feet again, he took my face in his hands and brushed my tears away with his thumbs. "Thank you, Baby Girl. I promise that I'll do everything in my power to make you happy every day of your life," he whispered against my lips just before he kissed me, stealing my breath and making my heart speed up uncontrollably.

I gulped. I just couldn't speak. So much happiness was swelling inside me that I could barely cope with it all. It was too much. "I love you, Ashton Taylor," I whispered, looking into his beautiful green eyes.

"And I love you, Annabelle Spencer." He pulled me closer so that my body was pressed against his gently, as he ran his hands down my back with his forehead still pressed to mine. "I can't believe you couldn't wait though," he said suddenly, shaking his head and laughing.

A blush heated my cheeks as I smiled apologetically. "You looked nervous; I thought it was something bad."

He sighed. "Don't assume the worst all the time. The worst is over. There are only good times for us now," he said tenderly.

I smiled at his beautiful words. "Get that from a how to propose to a girl book?" I teased.

He nodded, smiling. "Yeah, you know I like those *how to* books," he joked.

He pulled away and sat down, spreading his legs and patting the ground for me to sit between them. I sat obediently, leaning against him carefully because he was still covered in bruises. When his lips touched the back of my neck, I felt a little shiver of desire tickle down my spine.

I sighed contentedly and looked down at the ring that was now mine, tracing my thumb over the stones. "This ring is so beautiful," I gushed. I'd never owned anything so special.

His arms wrapped around me so gently, it was as if he thought I was made of glass. "Are you sure you wouldn't rather me buy you something new? I have money saved," he stated.

I shook my head adamantly and twisted so I could see him. "It means so much to me that you've given me your mom's ring. Honestly, I feel so special."

He grinned and kissed the tip of my nose. "You are special." I chuckled and sat back down, reaching for two plates before scooping up a few M&Ms. "You do know that I won't ever be able to give you everything you want, and I'll never have the kind of money that your parents have, but I promise I'll give you everything I can. I just hope it's enough to make you happy," he said quietly, sounding a little sad about it.

I turned to look at him and frowned. "You really think I care how much money you earn, or where we live, or what car we drive?" I asked. I was a little disappointed that he would think that of me.

"No, Baby Girl, I know you don't. I just wish I could give you everything in the world," he explained, his voice apologetic.

Now he was just being silly. "Ashton, all that stuff is nothing without this." I pointed to his heart. "I don't want anything else from you, apart from you to love me and be happy. I would live in a cardboard box with you, blissfully happy. It'd be a bit of a pain in the butt when it rained, but I'd do it," I joked, trying to lighten his mood. It worked, he laughed.

"Right, I guess soggy cardboard walls wouldn't be too good."

I smiled, leaning in closer to him. "But I'd love that box if you came home to me safely every night. That's the *only* thing I need from you," I said honestly.

"Well then, that I can do," he replied, smiling now.

I nodded, satisfied that he was happy, and then turned my attention back to the food that was laid out before me. "So, I guess I'll be needing to find a new school soon," I said casually, as I popped a couple of grapes into my mouth.

"A new school? Why's that?" he asked, sounding confused.

"Well, I'm not staying at ASU if you're in LA." I frowned, horrified at the thought.

"LA? Where did that come from?"

"Well, you'll go back to LA once your sick leave finishes. I figured you'd ask me to come…" I swallowed awkwardly as panic gripped my chest at the thought of being without him. Was he expecting us to have a long distance relationship until my schooling was finished? I couldn't do that. "Oh God, you do want me to come, right?"

508

He scoffed and stroked the side of my face soothingly. "Anna, calm down! Jeez, I can almost hear your heart speeding up," he scolded. "I'm not going to LA; I've asked your father to find me a position that's closer to you. He's found me a great placement in Arizona so I'll still get to live with you while you're at school, just like I always planned."

He was staying with me? But what about his friends? His dream job? "Ashton, no! I'll come to LA with you. Your friends are there, you've been living your dream job; I can't take that away from you. I can't ask you to give up your life for me," I argued desperately.

He smiled. "*You're* my life, Baby Girl, and there's no way I'm giving you up," he smiled at me wickedly.

My heart melted into a puddle. He truly was incredible. "But I have nothing tying me to ASU," I countered, trying not to think of the friends I'd made, or the year I was almost through this time, or the way that people treated me like I was a normal person even though my father was the President. I didn't care about any of that; I just wanted him to be happy.

"Anna, it's done. I want to stay with you and I want you to finish your course with people that have been good friends with you since before your father's election," he said seriously.

"You really are the sweetest, most thoughtful, romantic, special boy in the world." I looked at him in awe. I had never met anyone like him in my life, and I was honestly the luckiest girl alive to have him love me like he did.

He laughed. "Boy? Baby, I'm all man," he corrected, faking hurt.

Jeez, don't I know it! Damn badass! "Oh no, you'll always be my Pretty Boy," I teased.

"Oh yeah? Even when I'm old, wrinkly and grey?" he asked, raising an eyebrow.

"Oh yeah. You'll always be pretty to me," I promised, stroking his bruised face lovingly, tracing the lines and bruises carefully before pressing my lips against his. He kissed me back with so much love and passion that if I had been standing, it would have knocked me clean off my feet. I closed my eyes, and all I could think about was how this boy was mine, how he wanted to be with me forever and how he was my perfect other half.

For ages, we just lay on the blanket that was sprinkled with rose petals, looking at the stars, holding hands. Nothing needed to be said. Everything was perfect and incredible, and I knew that with Ashton at my side, it always would be.

Epilogue

~ Ashton ~

Anna had been named sole beneficiary of Carter Thomas' will. He left everything to her – his cars, houses, money, and shares. Of course, the police knew that it was all obtained through illegal means, so they petitioned the courts to impound it. However, to be able to confiscate the money, they had to prove, beyond a reasonable doubt, that the money had been obtained by breaking the law. The trouble was that Carter was incredibly proficient at covering his tracks.

It took over three years for them to build their case and prove the money had been made through illegal businesses. Just over a half of it was confiscated by the state; the rest had been laundered again and again to make it appear clean even though everyone knew that it wasn't. Anna was, therefore, issued just over twenty-nine million dollars of Carter's money.

Anna being Anna, hadn't wanted anything to do with him, even after death. So she gave two million dollars to each of the agents' families that died whilst guarding her, and two million to Jack's family. Then she gave just over ten million dollars to AWC, a charity called Abused Women and Children that helped victims of domestic violence. Her final icing on the cake? She gave five million dollars to a cat charity because Carter had a real hatred for cats. She said he would be turning in his grave, and had actually laughed when she signed the bank transfer order.

Lots of other changes had happened in the five years since Carter's death. The biggest change: we were now married. Just like I had promised her, I'd taken her back to the Maldives. Our wedding had been held in secret, on the beach, with just very close family and friends in attendance.

That was the proudest day of my life, the day I got to change the only thing that I didn't love about her – her surname.

Some things remained the same though. The press still loved us. Annaton fever still gripped the nation but, knowing there was nothing we could do about it, we just got on with our lives and tried not to focus on it too much. President Spencer remained in office; he'd been re-elected and had another three years left to serve his country.

Anna had finished school, so we moved to Los Angeles. For the last two and a half years, she'd been working for a large graphic design company, and she loved her job. My career had also taken a slightly different path. I was now heading up a brand new specialist department that was kind of a first base for terrorist attacks. Testing potential locations for weak points and running through possible attack strategies was a small part of my new job. That was what I'd been doing nearly all day today – scouting a couple of locations for a presidential seminar that was due to take place in a few months.

I was in desperate need of a coffee as I climbed the stairs and walked into my outer office. Immediately, Raine, my secretary, jumped out of her seat and ran towards me, looking slightly panicked.

"Ashton, where have you been? I've been trying to get hold of you for hours! Your cell phone's off," she scolded, following me as I carried on walking to my office at the end of the room. I really needed to sit down.

"I was scouting locations, Raine, you knew that." I laughed and pulled my cell phone out of my pocket, looking at the blank screen. "Battery must be dead. What's up anyway?" I asked, throwing my cell onto my desk and pulling out the charger.

"It's time! You need to go there right now!" she cried excitedly.

My heart stopped and my mouth popped open in shock. "Now? Right now?" I shouted, frantically searching my desk for my keys. I felt sick. This was too early. It shouldn't be for another two weeks. "Where are my damn keys?" I shouted, practically pushing everything off my desk in a bid to find them quicker.

Raine laughed and grabbed my wrist. "They're in your hand, silly! Just go," she ordered. "And make sure you call me." She was practically jumping on the spot with excitement.

"I will, and thanks!" I cried, as I sprinted at full speed back through the office, ignoring all of the stares. I jumped to the side just as someone stepped out of their office, narrowly avoiding taking them out because I was running so fast. "Sorry!" I shouted over my shoulder.

I couldn't help the nervous excitement that was building inside, but the thing I felt most was worry. What if something went wrong? What the hell would I do? As soon as I was at my car, I jumped in and threw it into drive, pulling out and snapping on my seatbelt as I drove through the parking lot. I plugged my cell phone in to charge for a few minutes while I drove. Thankfully, there weren't many other cars on the road, so I made it there in record time. The blue lights that I'd put on top of my car probably helped with cutting through traffic.

As soon as I was in the hospital parking lot, I pulled into the first available space and ran for the building, praying I wasn't too late. In the foyer, I pressed the call button for the elevator, but it was stopped on seven. "Come on, come on!" I chanted, practically bouncing on the spot and I tapped the button again and again. The elevator wasn't moving, so I decided to go for the stairs instead. I took them three at a time and got to the fifth floor, grinning excitedly as I spotted the 'Maternity' sign over the door.

I burst in and squirted some sanitizer on my hands as I ran to the desk. "Hi, where's Annabelle Taylor?" I asked the lady sitting there.

She smiled kindly. "Room three." She pointed down the hall so I turned and ran off.

As I got to the door, I took a couple of deep breaths. I needed to be calm. Being all super excited and scared shitless wouldn't help Anna. When my heart had returned to a normal pace again, I pushed the door open and peeked in. She was sitting up in the bed, chatting to Rick, her near guard. Her head snapped round to look at me as I walked in, her face lighting up. She looked incredibly beautiful as always, even in a hospital gown.

"Hey, you! I was wondering if you were going to show up," she teased, grinning.

"I wouldn't miss this for the world," I chirped, heading over and sitting on the side of her bed, putting my hands on her swollen tummy, rubbing it in small circles.

"I'll leave you to it now that Ashton's here. I'll just be outside," Rick announced, standing up and heading to the door.

Anna smiled and nodded. "Thanks for staying with me."

He grinned. "Of course." Rick had been guarding Anna for the last four years. When we were together, I was sufficient as her near guard, but when I was working, Rick took over. He was actually a great guy, and we were all friends outside of work too.

Once we were alone, I turned back to my wife. "You okay?" I asked, looking to see if she was in pain or anything. She seemed like she was okay though.

She smiled. "Yep, it doesn't hurt between contractions, so I'm good right now." I grinned and moved up the bed so I could kiss her softly. Her brown eyes were burning into mine making me feel slightly weightless. "You ready to be a daddy, Agent Taylor?" she whispered against my lips.

"Hell yeah I am," I admitted.

We'd been trying for this baby for the last two and a half years, practically as soon as she left college, and finally she'd fallen pregnant. Because of Anna's injuries to her stomach, and scarring from her miscarriage when she was with Carter, we'd had to try a lot harder to conceive than most couples, but we'd finally gotten there.

"The baby's eager to get out of there," she said, rubbing her stomach, smiling.

"Yeah, you know why he wants to get out of there?" I asked, raising one eyebrow.

"Why does *she* want to get out of there?" she replied, smirking at me. This was a running joke, Anna was convinced that it was a girl, and I was convinced it was a boy. In all honesty, neither of us cared as long as it was healthy.

"Because *he* knows I was going to finish painting the nursery this weekend, so he's trying to be awkward like his momma," I teased, settling onto the bed next to her, taking her hand.

"Maybe *she* wants to see you so she can… OUCH, SHIT!" she gasped, clamping her jaw together and squeezing my hand tightly.

I looked at her helplessly; I had no idea what to do to help. "Shh, it's okay, Baby Girl. It'll be over in a bit," I soothed as I rubbed her stomach lightly. *Oh God, please let everything be okay, don't let me lose either of them, please!*

"Shit. Ashton, go tell them I need drugs!" she hissed, looking at me pleadingly.

"Okay, let go of my hand then and I'll go sort it out," I replied, trying to pry her hand off mine, but she just held it tighter.

"Don't leave me!" she cried, breathing in pants. I nodded and slammed my hand down on the call button, and a minute later a doctor came in, just as the contraction was easing off. Anna slowly started to relax and sat back, looking pale and sweaty.

"Bad one?" the doctor asked, smiling kindly at her.

Anna nodded and pressed her face into my chest, catching her breath. I stroked her hair. I'd wanted this baby so much, but seeing her in pain kind of made me wish that we hadn't done this at all.

"Okay, well let's do another exam and see how you're getting on," the doctor suggested, coming over to the side of the bed and lifting the sheet. After a minute the doctor pulled back and smiled, throwing her gloves in the trash. "You're doing so great, Anna. You're almost nine centimetres. Just keep doing what you're doing." She patted her leg and smiled.

I looked at my wife proudly, she really was incredible, and I loved her more than anything. Suddenly, Anna leant forward and grabbed my hand, hissing through her teeth again as another contraction took hold. *Wow, that was fast. It had been less than two minutes!* "The baby's impatient to meet its parents," the doctor joked, rubbing Anna's leg as she squeezed the life out of my hand.

"Ouch… shit! Ashton, you better not want any more kids after this because I'm not doing this again!" Anna shouted loudly, squeezing her eyes shut.

"Okay, Baby Girl, one's perfect. I always only wanted one baby anyway," I joked, trying to make her feel better. "You're doing so great,

Anna, so great." I stroked her hair with my free hand and kissed her sweaty forehead.

"I need the gas! Get me the damn gas!" she screamed, pointing at it. I winced and jumped up, grabbing it. *Holy shit, in labour Anna is feisty!*

After three of the longest and most painful hours of my life, she was finally ready to push. Well, what was meant by 'finally ready' was that she had been pushing for almost half an hour, and they could finally see some progress. She had her legs up in stirrups with a sheet draped over so we couldn't see what was going down there. I stayed up near her head, having the bones in my hand slowly crushed where she was squeezing so hard. Anna was sucking on the gas and air like it was going out of fashion. She was a little woozy and kept saying things that made me laugh. It was kind of like she was slightly drunk or high.

"Okay, Anna, here comes another contraction. I need you to push real hard for me when I say, but not until I tell you," the doctor instructed, peeking over the sheet and smiling encouragingly.

Anna shook her head fiercely as tears rolled down her cheeks. "I can't. I can't do it anymore. Please just get her out!" she wailed. She grabbed my shirt and pulled me down so our faces were inches apart. "This is your damn fault, Ashton! Do you have any idea how much this freaking hurts?" she growled through clenched teeth. Her hand wound around the back of my head so I couldn't pull away.

"My fault?" I asked, confused and honestly a little scared of her. It looked like she was trying to kill me with her eyes.

She gasped and nodded. "For getting me pregnant! Oh God, I need to push RIGHT NOW!" she screamed. Her hand fisted into the back of my hair, making me grit my teeth as my scalp started to burn. I wanted to ask her to let go, but I couldn't exactly complain while she was pushing a little person out of her, my guess is I was getting off pretty lightly with a little hair pulling.

After a huge push and a lot of screaming, she narrowed her eyes at me. "If you think you're getting in my pants again after this, you've got another thing coming!" She shoved the gas tube back into her mouth and sucked on it hard, whilst glaring at me as if I was the one hurting her.

I grinned. I loved it when she was like this. I knew I shouldn't like it, but the bitchy side of Anna was kind of a turn-on for some reason. I loved that my girl had some fight in her and wouldn't take any crap. "Who said I want in your pants again anyway?" I joked.

She burst out laughing then immediately stopped and gasped. "Not again, not yet. I need a break!" she moaned, sucking on the gas as the little contraction monitor on the side started scribbling on the paper like crazy.

"Okay, one last push, Anna. Come on, you can do it," the doctor instructed.

I grabbed her hand and made sure she couldn't grip my hair again as she took a deep breath and pushed, squeezing her eyes shut. Her whole torso rose off the bed from the effort.

"Come on, Baby Girl, you can do it. Come on, push, Anna," I encouraged. After what seemed like forever, she let out a piercing scream and then slumped back down on the bed, panting for breath.

"You did it, Anna. It's a little boy," the doctor announced.

I heard a baby cry and I felt my heart stop. *Holy shit, I'm a dad!* I couldn't breathe. We had a baby. I looked back at Anna to see that she was smiling at me tenderly, her eyes glistening with tears. A sense of gratitude washed over me, making my whole body tingle. She'd made me a dad. This was honestly the best day of my life; the way Anna was looking at me made my heart ache.

"You were right," she laughed quietly.

I bent my head and kissed her on the lips. Her hand went to the back of my head, holding my mouth to hers for a couple of seconds. When I pulled away, I grinned. I was happier than I had ever been in my life. I had the most incredible girl, and now we had a little baby boy.

"Thank you," I said gratefully.

"You're welcome, Pretty Boy," she laughed. I pulled back, and she looked at the doctor, who was wrapping the baby up in a blanket. "Is he alright?" Anna asked worriedly, moving up on the bed.

"He's perfect. Ten fingers and ten toes," the doctor replied, walking over with a little bundle in her arms. She held him out to Anna, who took him immediately, looking down at him.

"Oh God, he's so beautiful," she murmured, pulling the blanket back to get a better look. A tear rolled down her face as she looked at him lovingly. I moved forward and leant over the bed so I could see. She shifted the baby in her arms, tilting him towards me. He was amazing, a perfect, little, scrunched up, dirty-looking baby with a mass of brown hair. His eyes were closed, and he was crying quietly as Anna rocked him gently. He looked just like his momma – incredible, and the most beautiful thing in the world.

"He looks just like you, Anna." I hesitantly reached out a hand to touch him. As my fingertip touched his face, I felt my heart speed up. He was so soft. His skin was flawless and creamy-looking, even though he was covered in mess and blood. "Hi, little guy. I'm your daddy."

"Want to hold him?" Anna asked smiling, still crying happy tears.

Oh crap, I have no idea how to do that. "Um, yeah okay," I nodded, looking down at him. How was I supposed to take him? What was I supposed to do if he cried?

Anna laughed quietly. "Stop stressing, Ashton. Hold your arm out and I'll pass him to you."

I sat on the edge of her bed and cradled my arms, wincing and feeling sick with worry. She shifted him in her hands and placed him so his head was in the crook of my arm. I tensed my back and stayed completely still. He weighed hardly anything at all.

"Relax, Ashton." Anna laughed and rubbed her hand on my leg reassuringly. The little baby in my arms was so special that I felt emotion bubbling up inside me. I was lost for words. I couldn't take my eyes from him as his eyes fluttered open and then closed again. "My two boys," Anna breathed.

I smiled and looked away from the perfect bundle in my arms, to his perfect momma. "I love you, Anna, so much," I promised.

She smiled at me tenderly as she stroked the baby's face with the back of one finger. "I love you too. I'm so sorry I shouted at you," she said, looking at me apologetically.

I laughed and shook my head. "Would you slap me if I told you it was kind of a turn-on?" I asked, grinning.

"If you weren't holding my son right now, then hell yeah, I'd slap you," she answered, shaking her head disapprovingly but laughing at the same time. "Seriously though, he was *so* worth all of that pain. So if you want to make babies with me again anytime soon, I'm up for that."

I laughed. "I'm always up for that, you know me."

"I know, pervert. Maybe after I've had some sleep," she joked. "So, what should we call him?" She settled back against the pillows, her hand still stroking his cheek.

I looked down at the little baby in my arms. A name sprang to mind instantly. "How about Cameron?"

"That was your dad's name," she said quietly. I nodded, looking up at her to see if she liked it. We hadn't discussed names much; just a couple that we both agreed on, like Will and Kaden, but he didn't look like either of those. "Cameron Ashton Taylor," she cooed as a wide smile crept onto her lips. "I love it. It's perfect." She bent her head and kissed his forehead softly.

"Ashton?" I repeated. We hadn't talked about a middle name.

She nodded. "Well yeah, he needs to have his daddy's name, silly."

After we'd both had plenty of cuddles, the doctor took him back, weighing him, checking him over and cleaning him up a little. Once he was decked out in a tiny, little white baby grow, he was placed back into his proud mommy's arms. My heart ached at the sight of them together. I couldn't keep the ecstatic grin off my face.

"I'd better get some photos and make the announcement," I suggested, pulling out my cell phone. Anna chuckled, adjusting my son so that I could get a few good pictures. After sending them to Nate, Rosie and Anna's parents, I settled down onto the bed next to her, still in slight disbelief that I was now a father.

"Your mom's gonna be so mad that she's not going to be first one through the door to visit," I stated, shaking my head and imagining the panic on Melissa's face when she heard the news that her only child had given birth to her first grandchild. They were currently in England so Tom and Melissa would have to wait a couple of days before they could meet the new Taylor family addition. She wouldn't be happy about that at all. She was ridiculously eager to be a grandmother.

"I know. She'll freak. She'd already ordered me to cross my legs before she went," Anna chuckled. "Nate will be psyched that he gets to be the first to meet him though." She stroked her finger across Cameron's cheek, smiling down at him. "Are you going to ask him today about being Godfather?"

"Yeah," I nodded. Nate was going to flip out when I asked him; he'd been on countdown to Anna's due date too, just like I was. He was already referring to himself as 'Cool Uncle Nate'. Anna and I had talked about Godparents before the baby was born and were planning on asking Nate and Rosie because they were our closest friends. We lived in LA so we saw Nate all the time; he practically lived round our place. Rosie lived a couple of hours drive away, but we still kept in contact and saw her whenever we could. She and Anna spoke on the phone for hours on end at least once a week. On the up side, Rosie was moving to LA soon too for a new job, so that would make seeing her even easier. Anna couldn't wait to see more of her best friend.

I sighed contentedly and wrapped my arms around the love of my life, dipping my head and planting a soft, lingering kiss on her temple. "I love you, baby momma," I whispered, holding her tightly. She smiled and pressed her face into my chest. My cheeks were starting to hurt where I hadn't stopped smiling. I'd known her for a total of five and a half years now, yet she still managed to take my breath away everyday. I hoped I never took her for granted because I was the luckiest guy in the world to have her love me like she did. Every day I thanked my lucky stars that I'd met her and that I had the chance to make her happy again.

Sounds of cooing came from Cameron's direction, so I looked down at him, cradled protectively in her arms. I was awed by him and his tiny frame. It was hard to believe that this little boy was something that mine and Anna's love had made. He was less than an hour old, yet I loved him so very much already. I knew I would give my life for him in an instant, the same as I would for Anna.

Reaching out, I picked up his little hand, just marvelling over his tiny fingernails. "Thanks for keeping up your end of the bargain and not hurting your mom too much when you came out. I promise to keep up my end of the bargain and be the best dad in the world," I murmured quietly. Anna chuckled, chewing on her bottom lip. I smiled at her before bending and kissing the tips of Cameron's fingers. "It's you, me, and your momma now. Us Taylor boys have to watch out for your momma. She's just incredible, and you are one lucky little baby to have her."

When I looked up to Anna, I saw that she had tears in her eyes. I sighed and shook my head in disbelief. After all this time, I still had no idea how I managed to get a girl like her to fall in love with me. Nothing had ever felt so precious to me. My little family. I stroked her hair away from her face before bending in and pressing my lips to hers softly. This girl and this baby were my world, and the only things I needed out of life. I just hoped I could somehow make them as happy as they both made me.

COMING SOON

Did you enjoy meeting Ashton's best friend, Nate Peters, in Nothing Left to Lose? Would you like to hear more from him?

ENJOYING THE CHASE
(A companion novel of Nothing Left to Lose)

Nate Peters is living the playboy life. He has great friends, a great job, no responsibilities, no girlfriend, and he loves it. Nate, being incredibly skilled with a pick-up line, has never failed to get a girl in his life… until one day he meets Rosie York. Rosie is completely uninterested in him. Being unable to stand a dented ego, Nate makes it his mission to win her over. Not used to putting in much effort, Nate is surprisingly enjoying the chase of this off-limits little brunette. Maybe he has finally met his match… But Rosie has a few surprises of her own which will make it remarkably more difficult for him to get close to her.

A Romance / Humour that will make you laugh, cry and scream in frustration.
Coming Spring 2014

6635362R00305

Made in the USA
San Bernardino, CA
13 December 2013